MW00932612

The Burden of Cane

Also by C. H. Lawler

The Saints of Lost Things

The Memory of Time

Living Among the Dead

What Passes for Wisdom

The Burden of Cane

A novel

C. H. Lawler

Walrus Books

Chartres Street

New Orleans, La.

Ego sum vitiulisque marinis

This is a work of fiction. Names, characters, places, and incidents are either the product of the author's imagination or are used fictitiously, and any resemblance to actual persons, living or dead, businesses, companies, events, or locales is entirely coincidental. Any and all resemblances to persons living or dead are purely coincidental.

Copyright 2021 C. H. Lawler

All rights reserved.

ISBN #9798710722732

For our parents, who did the best they could with little or no prior experience.

"Avarice, pride, and envy are the three sparks that have made a bonfire out of hearts."

-Dante Alighieri, *The Divine Comedy, Canto Six*

December 1915

On the train from Southampton to London

The air in the train car is filled with winter coughs and the smell of wet woolen clothing as the muffled rhythm of rails and crossties rattles monotonously below, pop-clack-pop, pop-clack-pop, pop-clack-pop. The whistle moans ahead, the sound of wind moving over the mouth of a glass bottle.

Near the rear of the car, a woman sits with her gloved hands in her lap. She is an Englishwoman returning from Louisiana, in America. Some of the passengers recognize her as someone famous, someone whose picture has appeared in the *London Times*, but they are too polite, too English, to say anything. Instead, they read and knit and nap and check their watches. When they return home, they will tell their friends and families that they rode the train from Southampton with the noted spiritualist and medium Gladys Osborne Leonard, consultant to famous mourners like Sir Arthur Conan Doyle and Sir Oliver Lodge. But for now, they sit quietly and pretend she is like any other passenger.

Across the aisle from her is an old man with an eyepatch surrounded by skin pushed up into the smallest ridges and whorls of scar. She glances across the aisle at him and then at her gloved hands and her lap and then out the opposite window, where she watches his reflection in it. He is easily twice her age with gray hair streaked with what must have been his boyhood color, sandy brown. He sits straight up, and she can tell that he was once a soldier in his youth like some of the younger men on the train. But that is not how he lost his eye. Rather, he was in some sort of industrial accident. An explosion, she thinks.

His reflection sees her and she pretends to be craning her head to see something out of the window on his side of the train. He looks to her, but she has looked away and out the window on her side. His reflection looks away, and she studies him again.

She is also quite aware that the man with the eyepatch has a strong connection to the recently widowed woman in America who hired her to contact her deceased husband. The Englishwoman spent several weeks in Louisiana speaking to those who knew the dead man, but she was unable to help the widow, who was greatly disappointed. But this man—this man sitting across the aisle from her on the train from Southampton to London—he and the widow in Louisiana were linked somehow. She isn't sure of the connection. They were involved romantically, perhaps, or perhaps only carnally. She can tell that it was a powerful attraction between them, however. She is quite sure of that.

They make eye contact occasionally and smile in the dim heat that radiates from the stove as it tries to drive away the English winter. He looks back to his reflection in the window. The English countryside whirs by, gray trees rising in feathered spikes out of snowy patches of ground. To the gentle jostling of the train, one passenger murmurs to another that he heard in Southampton that more snow is expected. And the train shivers on its tracks and the engine up ahead moans hoarsely. Shadows of dim winter light pass over everything.

There are quite a number of soldiers on the train, English soldiers returning from France, young men who smoke and chat and look out at the English January. The woman knows they are thinking about the ones who remain in France, both the ones who might return later and the ones who will never return. Crutches lean against windows in some of the seats. The soldiers all look blankly out the windows except for one with bandages over his eyes who faces straight ahead. He boarded in Southampton from the Royal Victoria Hospital, his hands on the shoulders of the man in front of him until the porter helped him into his seat. His seatmate lights a cigarette and puts it to his blinded companion's mouth. He puffs it once before his friend takes it back and takes a puff, and they share it back and forth until the conductor tells them *smoking only in the smoking car,* and *sorry, lads.* The sighted soldier cracks the window with a rush and tosses out the smoking butt, and the window thumps closed. And the train clacks and pops in the newfound silence.

The Englishwoman looks to the old man with the eyepatch and back to the blinded soldier, from the half-blind to the totally blind. She wonders if the boy with the bandaged eyes will regain his sight, and if he doesn't, will he remember what the faces of his parents look like. Does he have parents? she wonders. She looks out the window again where the reflections of the passengers ride some other train, a dim, parallel reflection, a ghost train. The train mutters beneath them and gently shakes them. Across the aisle, the man with the eyepatch closes his eye into a nap with his head resting on the cold glass of the window. The Englishwoman can study him more closely now.

On the floor at his feet, there is a dog curled up. The dog sleeps contentedly in a ring with its muzzle on its paws, even though dogs are not allowed in the passenger cars of English trains. Whenever the man coughs or clears his throat, the dog opens his eyes and lifts his head and then closes them and sets his head down again.

Now, sitting next to the old man with the eyepatch is another man, dressed in century-old clothes, a swallowtail coat and a beaver pelt hat. They look enough alike to be brothers, but she knows that they are father and son. Certainly they are, she thinks.

No one else can see the dog and the man in the beaver pelt hat. Even if the old man with the eyepatch were to wake up and look at the seat next to him or down at his feet, he would not be able to see them. The man in the swallowtail coat and the beaver pelt hat and the dog do not cast reflections in the windows. But the Englishwoman knows that they cannot and that only she can see them.

She wants to tell the old man with the eyepatch of the presence of the dog and the man, but she decides it is not her place to wake him up from his nap, and so she keeps her white-gloved hands in her lap and looks out the window at the English fields, still sleeping under winter snow. The old man's father looks to the Englishwoman with a pleading face, then strokes the dog's back and then fades away into the stale air of the train car.

After the man in old clothes departs, his son shifts in his sleep like any other old man might. He wriggles his nose to some dreamy annoyance, but the scar around the patch stays still, thick and rigid like rubber. The remainder of his face is slack, somewhere between peaceful and exhausted.

The woman looks at the man's hands, they are big and rough. He is the kind of man who has done hard work. She noticed them on the passage from America to Southampton, looking up from her book surreptitiously to study him, knowing his connection with the woman in Louisiana. The man kept the company of an Irish priest for most of the voyage, the one who disembarked at Queenstown. She senses that the old man is American and not English, though she has not heard him speak.

The conductor slides open the door at the front of the car, and the outside sounds of train and track and crossties fall through the door in an avalanche of sound until he closes it behind him. He calls out the next stop, *Basingstoke, five miles hence.* The old man emerges from the beginning of his winter nap to the touch of the woman's hand on his shoulder.

"Pardon me sir, but that's your stop, isn't it? Basingstoke?"

He shrugs off the first dusty layers of sleep and looks around.

"Yes. Yes," he says in the accent of the American south as he rubs his remaining eye, and he wonders how this woman, this stranger, knew where he was going.

Father Michael Connelly

If he told me the name he was traveling under, I do not remember it. I only knew him for those few days on ship. It was in the time of the First World War, on the *S. S. Olympic* bound from America for Southampton in England. We had just made a stop in Halifax to board Canadian soldiers and were setting out across the Atlantic to Southampton, with a stop in Queenstown where I was to disembark to visit my mother in Cork, which I did. It was the winter of 1915-1916, and I was worried for her safety in those troubled times for Ireland and for Europe. Everyone on board was worried, whether they said it aloud or not.

He was an old man, in his seventies, I am guessing, which is my age now. He was somewhat taller than average, with gray hair, much like his eyes, or, I should say, like his right eye, as the left one was covered with a patch, having been lost in an accident. I assumed that he had lost it at the same time he acquired the rugged scars on that side of his face, where his hairline was unnaturally high and the skin rolled into a swirl of fine pink scars.

I was taking a stroll on the deck, bundled up against the North Atlantic cold, watching the escort of American military ships that plowed the cold waters, raising jagged flashes in the winter sunlight a quarter mile off our flank. There was a lingering tension in the air, as the *Titanic* had been sunk a few years before, and the *Lusitania* just six months. There were hushed conversations about war, as if German U-boats far below in the deep water might hear our whispers. Several people were out on the deck at the railing despite the weather, no doubt quietly and anxiously looking for periscopes and icebergs.

On that day as cold as iron, he seemed less bothered by the weather or U-boats and stood staring out at the ocean. He pulled something out of the pocket of his woolen great coat, pondered it for a moment, and then tossed it into the Atlantic. It plunked into the passing water and disappeared into the depths. He looked up to the heavens and then out to the horizon. I caught myself staring and then he caught me. I admit I was curious as to what he had thrown into the sea, and so I got up and went to the railing just a few yards away from him. He looked at me and then remarked, more to the horizon than anything else, "Her eyes were as blue as that."

"Pardon, sir?" I asked.

"Her eyes were as blue as that, as the sea out there," he said, and he fell silent again. The wind buffeted us, and I pulled my hat down against it.

The quiet begged that I fill it, so I said, "Well, she must have been a very beautiful woman, then."

"Yes," he said, "that she was, but just as dangerous as she was beautiful. And there was the problem. How often do danger and beauty keep company."

A gust of icy wind surged again, and we drew our coats around us. He looked from the ocean, as blue as a beautiful woman's eyes, and to me, an Irish priest less than half his age.

"In seminary we were taught that sin isn't ugly," I said, "but rather, beautiful, for how else would men find it appealing?"

The man turned from the sea and looked at me. He was like something exquisite but flawed, like the masterpiece of a sculptor who upon completing it finds a fatal crack in the marble and must decide if the entire work should be patched in some way, or thrown on the heap with the chips and shards.

"I see that you are a man of God. Catholic, I suppose?" he asked.

"Yes," I said. "Returning to Ireland to see my mother in Cork."

"That is very commendable. I've heard that it is the desire of every Irish mother to have a son enter the priesthood. She must be very proud of you. I've always thought it must be a great blessing to be the son of a proud mother."

I said, "Yes, and it is true, then, but Ma is proud of all her sons, like all mothers."

"Not all of them" the man snorted quietly, and he looked out to the sea again. "I was raised Episcopalian myself," he said, "though I seldom attend anymore, only the funerals of friends, almost all of them old like me. Tell me, sir, do you truly believe in forgiveness?"

"I believe that God hears the confessions of the contrite, the penitent, and that redemption has been won through Christ's suffering," I said.

He puffed on his cigar and muttered, "Christ came to change our sinful natures and we killed him for it."

"But he could not be killed and he rose again—"

"—and so now we simply ignore his teachings. He might as well have stayed dead—"

The man looked out to the sea again and smiled, a small, desperate thing, a sardonic smile that quickly fled from his face and its scar and its gray eye. "Forgive me, Father, that was harsh and uncalled for."

I said nothing, knowing that such talk, though sacrilegious, frequently comes from a place of great pain and suffering. The smoke from the convoy of ships billowed gray and black into the blue sky, the smell of burning coal lingering in the salt air amid the murmur of great engines. I lingered on the railing just down from him. I thought he might walk away, but when he turned from the railing, he said, "Come, let us adjourn to the saloon and talk, Father. I suppose I should call you Father?"

"You can call me Father, or Michael, if you'd rather," I said.

"Well, Father. The German Navy has U-boats in these waters, and the crossing is risky. Let me tell you these things, these events of my life, in case we find ourselves subject to a fate similar to that of the *Lusitania*. I have much to say and no one to tell it to. Would you hear the confession of a lapsed Episcopalian like myself? Might we adjourn inside? Perhaps the steward will bring us coffee, or tea, if you'd rather. And maybe a Catholic priest like yourself will grant an infidel like me absolution."

He held the door to the ship's main saloon, and I went in to sit and hear his confession, though truly I did not want to hear it. It was still early, and across the saloon seated at a table by herself was a woman whom I recognized as the spiritualist and medium, Mrs. Gladys Osborne Leonard. There had been hushed talk that she was onboard, the woman who knew the king and could speak to the dead and had been hired by a wealthy widow in Louisiana to contact her recently departed husband. As the man and I sat down, she looked up from her book and gazed at us, but it seemed more at the man than at me. When the steward had taken our coats, I looked up and she was reading again.

And as soon as we were seated, I became quite sure that the object he had thrown in the Atlantic was a revolver.

Editor Lucien Braud

St. Matthew Parish Compass

Mrs. Gladys Osborne Leonard, the English spiritualist and medium to famous Britons Sir Arthur Conan Doyle and Sir Oliver Lodge, will arrive in Donaldsonville this week for a stay at Mount Teague Plantation in St. Matthew Parish. We hope that Mrs. Leonard will enjoy her stay 'down the bayou.'

In December of that year, 1915, I ran this notice in the society section, written by yours truly under the *nom de plume* 'Merry Chatsworth.' We rarely had visitors from outside the state, and never from outside the country and certainly never from England. It was like a visit from the King of England himself. All wondered how Miss Eva could have arranged something like that, for certainly a visit from someone like Mrs. Leonard came with a hefty fee, especially considering the hazards of transatlantic travel during wartime and the dire straits that Mount Teague was under at that time. Indeed, the great house was falling into disrepair, shutters askew, flower beds untended, outbuildings sprouting weeds at their bases. She was delinquent on her taxes again, but I deferred to past experience and to her widowhood, and so I didn't publish her name among the other debtors to the state that November. She was certainly among them, however.

The Burden of Cane

A carriage was sent for her, to the train station in Donaldsonville. Miss Eva said that she wanted Mrs. Leonard to have the 'authentic experience' and that a good old-fashioned open air carriage ride would be in keeping with that. Of course, everyone in St. Matthew knew that all the automobiles had been sold to keep Mount Teague from sinking. But no one said anything about it. Miss Eva could twist the truth and then ruin you with the result.

The day was anything but conducive for such an outing, however. The sky rained as cold as nails, managing to soak our visitor despite the umbrella given to her, a feeble maneuver against the elements. In true British fashion, she tried to make the most of it, waving off the apologies of the driver sent with the carriage. Miss Eva herself had opted to skip the inclement weather and remain at Mount Teague waiting for her guest.

Several men, more curious than civic-minded or chivalrous, followed the carriage on horseback in oil-cloth slickers as Mrs. Leonard hunkered down under the umbrella, tilting it against the winds that picked up the sheets of rain and hurled them in her direction. I was not there, but it was the talk of the servants (down to just a handful and all of them paid on credit) that the reception at Mount Teague was warm enough. Miss Eva received her visitor in as elegant a style as could be managed.

Mrs. Leonard was greeted with a request, a demand, almost, to hold the séance right away, but she told Miss Eva that rather than proceed in such haste, as Miss Eva wished, she would need several days to interview her and whoever else knew 'the departed.' Miss Eva balked at this, but the Englishwoman cut her off immediately asking her, "Do you want this done quickly or do you want this done correctly, madam?"

Miss Eva answered, "Yes, yes, as you will."

Mrs. Leonard spent several days interviewing those who knew the deceased, including his widow, Miss Eva. There was something about the Englishwoman that compelled honesty. Her eyes were dark, and her gaze was frank. Only after several days of preliminary interviews was the séance held and attended by myself and several others.

When it was completed, Mrs. Leonard departed much more quietly, and there was talk that a couple in a mule-drawn wagon picked her up on the road to Napoleonville, carrying her baggage as night fell, and gave her a ride to the train station in Donaldsonville. They said she was quiet and would not speak of her stay at Mount Teague, but they merely thought it was the way of the English. It was certainly a contrast to the way she had been welcomed to St. Matthew Parish, like a heroine possessing a sacred key. In the end, she was turned out like a stray who had darted in through a crack in the door.

Part I

Eva

Please do come in, come in out of this horrid weather. The rain here in Louisiana this time of year can be just as cold and unpleasant as it is in England, but spring is never long in coming. Why, in a month or two, the trees will bloom bright green and soon after that the azaleas will begin to bud. Until then, I apologize for what must have been a chilly carriage ride under an umbrella. Our chauffeur was let go when the last of the automobiles was sold, and the bonnet of our remaining carriage is ripped, and we can't get anyone to repair it. But I certainly do appreciate you coming from England, across the Atlantic in these treacherous and uncertain times. And in this appalling Louisiana rain! Your fee shall reflect it, of course. If you can help me.

And so I welcome you to St. Matthew Parish and Mount Teague, Mrs. Leonard. May I call you Gladys?

Oh, well, then. As you please, Mrs. Leonard.

You very likely couldn't see it well in the rain and the dark and from under an umbrella, but this is sugarcane country, and this summer it will be leafy green and chest-high. It has been grown here for the better part of a century, a source of prosperity and empire.

Ruthie, please take Mrs. Leonard's things to the guest room upstairs, the one with the Italian marble mantel, the white mantle, not the green. And start a fire for her. I'm sure she'll want to get out of these wet clothes.

Yes, that is a portrait of my husband, my *late* husband, in his captain's uniform. It was done by some anonymous French itinerant painter who was passing through New Orleans some forty years ago. It has captured his vitality and youth, and in it he still has most of his hair and his teeth. He was once a handsome enough man, but he departed too soon, as most do. We were married thirty-five years. It is still hard to believe he is gone. And so suddenly. He left me with so many unanswered questions.

What kind of question is that? Yes, certainly I grieve! I just don't show it like most women might. It is still a bit of a shock to me.

That empty space on the wall next to his portrait is the spot where my portrait once hung. It was painted in London, as a matter of fact, by Mr.

Sargent. Yes, John Singer Sargent. The very one. My late husband and I were in the habit of summering in Europe during more prosperous times, and I agreed to sit for him. My portrait hung there for many years, but, unfortunately, it has left Mount Teague. I would dearly love to have it back so that my husband and I might be together again, though only on the wall here in the central hallway of our home.

My husband departed this world suddenly and with a certain knowledge which he did not pass along to me, and it is imperative that I find this thing out. And so I have sent for you, knowing that you are recognized as the best in the world. Yes, only the best at Mount Teague. That has always been our motto here. The finest china, the finest carriages and then automobiles, the finest drapes and linens, pillows and mattresses. Only the best. And of course, the best spiritual medium in the world. Oh, you're welcome, Mrs. Leonard. Money has never been an object for us, and with your help, it will continue to be a secondary concern. It is of the utmost importance, therefore, that you contact my husband, or all of that shall come to an end.

Another medium, a Mrs. Piper from Boston, came in the fall, but she proved to be nothing but a sham, and I learned nothing from her. Twenty dollars frittered away just like that, and for no useful information whatsoever! Perhaps it was because I wasn't completely forthcoming with her, or perhaps she truly was a fraud. I suppose one gets what one pays for, and that is why you are here. Certainly, the expense of bringing you here should be worth it. I trust that we will soon be in contact with my dear late husband, as I have something very important that I must ask him.

Shall we begin?

Forgive me. Yes, certainly. I suppose you would want to dry out before we begin our interview. Very well, when you are ready. Perhaps in the morning when you are rested and dried out.

Ruthie? Ruthie! Take Mrs. Leonard to her room. Never mind tea. Bring me a toddy to calm my nerves.

Ruthie

Come with me, ma'am. Watch your step on them stairs. Miss Eva ain't paid the light bill and we got to use them old kerosene lamps again. I got you a fire set in the fireplace up yonder your room, ma'am. As soon as you gets yourself ready for bed, I take your things and set them up to dry on a line up next the fire.

This your room. Many a guest done stayed here in my days with this family! Almost fitty years! Now how can that be! We host some fine parties and goins' on, yes ma'am. I seen all of 'em. Show have.

I got you a screen there the corner what you can undress behind it. Hand me them wet clothes when you take 'em off.

Now I know Miss Eva show anxious to get started, but you sleep long as you needs to. I have breffast in the morning when I hear you stirrin'. I know England a long ways off and you must be tired comin' that long way. Yes ma'am. Here you go, now.

We got a pan of grits on the stove down the kitchen. You want me to get you some? Ma'am? Grits is ground up corn. All right, you say if you change your mind, now. Let me take that dress from you.

Ma'am?

Well, it's a sin to speak ill of the dead, yes ma'am, but that Marse Sam, he was show somethin'. Yes, Lawd.

Here, I take that slip, too. It soaked through. You want me draw you a bath? I put some that lilac water in there like Miss Eva like, and she show like her baths, yes ma'am. All right. You change your mind, you just let Ruthie know. Let me hand you your dry thangs. Here, I turn my head.

Yes ma'am, Marse Sam was married four times. The first wife died havin' a baby. I never did know her. She 'fore my time. The second wife run off and leff Marse Sam and he had Judge Anderson, ol' Judge Anderson, God grant him peace, he give him a divorce cause Marse Sam never could find her. I never did know her too good, 'cause I's just a girl then.

Hand me them draws, ma'am, and I put 'em on the line here front this fire. Here you go a hand towel on this washstand.

Well, the third Mrs. Teague, Miss Alice, I knew her right well, and she was an angel, show. She died when that ballroom caught fire. Used to be right out that window yonda. Marse Sam was show broke up over that, and didn't none of us think he was ever gone marry again. Yes ma'am, that's right. Miss Alice the one play the piana, show did. Now how you know that?

Here, ma'am, here your nightgown. I got your covers turned down for you. Here you go. You sleep tight as we say here 'merica. I hear you stir in the mornin' then I start you some breffast down the kitchen. Sleep long as you wants and don't give Miss Eva no mind.

Jack

Well, then, Father. That blue sea out there, dark and deep and cold. And when the weather is up, dangerous. So much like her.

Now that I am leaving my home country for good, I may speak of these things. For one thing, the name on the ship's manifest is not my real name. But I have had to change my name before, and I have many secrets. We accumulate them, we men and women, the things we do not wish to be known by others. But they gnaw. They gnaw. And so as an old man I must turn them out if I am to ever get any peace.

At seventy-two, I am no longer the sandy-haired youth I once was. Even though I grew up among agriculture, in Mississippi, in cotton country, I have always had a boyish fascination with the mechanical, windmills and cotton gins and steam engines, steamboats, circles of slats that pushed water and men and cargo, flywheels, cog-toothed gears, pulleys, forces amplified and diminished by men and science. The glowing heat of the blacksmith's forge and the shaping of metal with the blows of a hammer and the sudden quenching of the heat into a plume of steam from the water basin. Tall wagons of cotton pulled by mules, burdens made exponentially easier to pull by working them in tandem and in teams. I have retained that fascination and it has been the refuge of that boy whom I once was and whom I carry protected inside me as a precious other-self.

My first memory is of my brother, his face peering down at me from behind the mosquito netting around my bed, a narrow four-poster. His vague face behind that veil, watching me. I couldn't have been more than four or so. Perhaps that was the beginning of the unmerited worship I developed for him, which is the way for most younger and older brothers. With time, he became everything I wanted to be. At first. Later, he became everything I wanted to avoid being.

It is written in the Bible that no man can serve two masters. It may also be true that it is just as difficult for a boy to adore equally both parents or for a parent to adore equally his or her children. It was certainly the case for my parents and for my brother and me. I was the favorite of our father, and my brother was the favorite of our mother. In church, my parents would sit together, and I would sit on my father's side, and my brother would sit on my mother's. Nothing was ever said of it, to be sure, but it was the state of things. It was much like the story of Esau and Jacob.

My father was an easy going man who enjoyed a toddy in the evenings and listened to me and my boyish musings about how things worked. I once made a slingshot out of an old rubber belt that could launch a persimmon across a hundred rows of cotton. My brother and I measured it, and our father tousled my hair at my cleverness when we demonstrated it for him. He said nothing about my brother, from whom I could feel disappointment emanating, the aura of the passed-over and overlooked.

My father was a man with an obscure past. He had scars on his back and shoulders and arms. When I asked him about the scars, he said that he got them from a fall from a horse-apple tree and that his mother had had to pluck thorns from him for the better part of a day. I could easily imagine my father and the face he might have made as my grandmother, whom I had never met, plucked thorn after miserable thorn from his back.

He also had HT written in a raised, pink scar across the base of his left thumb. He said that it signified that he was a member of a society called the Jovial Knights of Jocularity but that he had taken an oath not to speak of its workings. He said he could only tell me that HT stood for their motto, Honor and Truth.

In the firelight over his toddy-glass of *Old Monongahela Rye Whiskey*, he would tell us stories of river pirates, of the Murrell gang and the Alston brothers and Tower Rock and Cave-in-Rock in Illinois. And we were amazed how he could know so much about such things and still be a quiet and peaceable man. Then in the quiet sphere of yellow-brown light, our father would drain the last drops of his toddy which glowed like amber against the flames, and he would bid us goodnight with the parting admonition for us to aspire to be good men.

The Burden of Cane

In those younger years, my brother and I played roughly, though he was older by four years and would best me time and again, pinning me when we wrestled, pushing me under when we swam, outrunning me when we raced. He would hide from me and lose me in the woods, forcing my father to come and look for me, his lantern and those of our servants floating through the tree trunks and mist to find me where I sat shivering on a log. Despite this, or rather, because of it, I wanted to be everywhere my brother went, so great was my idolatry for him. Our father would lightly scold him, knowing that it was the way of brothers to joust. But Mother would take up for my brother, saying that I had badgered him into it in some way and that I had deserved it to a large degree.

For years, I thought it was just how brothers got along, having no more experience with being a sibling than anyone else does. But I would look to the examples of our servants and our field hands, how siblings cared for each other, older ones looking after the younger ones. It began to occur to me that my brother was the exception rather than the rule. I started to see that my brother took glee in hatefulness, knowing that Mother would excuse him and somehow, someway turn the blame on me. Yet, I grew up in awe of him, in that reverence that younger brothers have for their older brothers.

During harvest one year, when my brother and I sat in a large wagon of picked cotton, he took my hat and cast it into the gin and said, "Look, there! Your hat is going to be in a bale now!" I cried and cried, for it was my favorite hat, given to me by my father, made out of beaver pelts like his.

Once, my brother and I were in the top of a sweetgum tree, surrounded in its curtains of summer leaves. I told him that one day I would make a machine that someone could fly in. It was something I had been thinking on for some time, watching the hawks glide over our fields.

"Fly! Ha!" he said derisively. "You'll no more fly than a pig, Jack!"

I said I would too, he would see. One day he would see me, up in the air in my machine, gliding like a bird and that I would figure it out. And I called him a name, a cruel name I don't remember, but it was the cruelest I could think of, and he threw me out of the tree and I plummeted like Icarus through a rush of leaves and limbs and I hit the ground.

The doctor was sent for and set my wrist to the pain I felt and the howls that I made but didn't hear, despite a dram of my father's *Old Monongahela* I had been given with a generous dollop of honey. I told neither my mother nor my father that my brother had thrown me out of that tree. My brother, of course, never owned up to it. He only smirked and said that I must have lost my footing.

As he neared manhood, it became more and more apparent that my brother had a head built for scheming and subterfuge. How well it has served him in getting ahead in this life. In time, he became everything I wanted to avoid being.

Every June when the crop was laid-by, that is, allowed to grow with little tending, I took pleasure in picking blackberries and fishing with our hands. Certainly, they were our slaves, we owned them and they did as our parents and the overseer said, but I was only a boy then and it never occurred to me that they might prefer a life somewhere else doing what they pleased. They were kind to me, and all these years later I wonder if they truly liked me and my company, or were they kind because it was expected of them and they had no say so in the matter. If I had known the true cruelty of it, of families separated in the commerce of human beings, I would have been ashamed then.

We would gather great buckets of blackberries, the older ones admonishing me, 'look out yonda for Mr. No-shoulders, now' and 'whew, child, Ima make us a cobbler, show."

We were taking our pails of blackberries up to the house when I saw my brother disappear into the woods, alone. I followed him there, and, from behind a tree, I saw him produce himself from his trousers and begin fondling himself. I was not yet at the age to understand this private pageant, having not received nature's summons on these matters. But I watched him as he twitched and panted. When he was finished and catching his breath, I silently crept back to the house with my pail of blackberries. I did not follow him after that. Save once, on his invitation.

It was several years later, as we grew closer to becoming men. My brother was a fop whose fine dress and frippery won over our mother, who prized the outer appearance of things to a high degree. He was not at all accomplished when it came to scholastic pursuits. Indeed, I have always wondered if our mother completed his application and accompanied him to his interview at the

University in Oxford. Not once do I remember him reading a book in our boyhood as I did, but I read enough for both of us.

One night after supper, he took me out to the Quarters. He swung open the door of a cabin unannounced, quickly enough to surprise the inhabitant, a young negro woman who had just put her baby down and was reading the Bible by candlelight. The small light pushed hopelessly at the darkness in the cabin. She turned her face up to us with a look of sudden surprise. My brother grabbed the Bible from her and said, "You know you darkeys ain't supposed to be reading, don't you?"

"Yas-suh," she muttered to her empty hands.

He flung the worn book out the open door into the night where it landed with a wet, distant splash. Without needing to say what he was there for, he began unbuttoning his shirt. Her dejected eyes kept to the floor as she undid the sash around her waist. My brother unshouldered his suspenders and lowered his trousers. Her baby stirred in the simple cradle next to her bed, and she paused from her disrobing to shush it and resumed her undressing. Her dress fell in a puddle around her feet at the base of her body, which was lithe and brown. My brother grabbed her breast roughly and kissed her neck, and she sat down on her bed like a man visiting with the preacher before a trip to the gallows. He put his mouth to her breast and pushed her back onto the plain straw mattress.

I looked away and to the crib where her baby slept serenely knowing nothing of violence or lust. I looked away, but I could not keep my ears from hearing the huffing and grunting of my brother. After a time, the rustling of the mattress and the thumping of the bedstead stopped. My brother rose and dressed. The woman rose also, but remained naked.

She looked at me and what she said wandered from her mouth bleakly, "You take a turn, suh?"

"No. No," I muttered.

My brother was slipping his suspenders back over his shoulders. He straightened his hair and adjusted his shirt in the smoky depths of a chipped mirror. "Go ahead, Jack. Take yourself a turn."

He said it as if the poor woman were a ride on a whirligig or a horse. I shook my head. I felt an immense sadness, a guilt. I knew little of the process, but I knew this was wrong, an abomination, that we were robbing her of her self-respect, and only because we could and she could say nothing against it.

We left the half-dressed woman rocking her baby, who had awoken to my brother's activity and was crying. The night was cool, my brother's cold breath fogged out into the air.

"What's the matter, brother? Don't care for women?" he said lightheartedly as he stepped over a puddle. The Bible had landed in it. It took no more than a glance to see that it was ruined.

"No," I mumbled. "Not—not tonight." I meant to say 'nor any other night,' but I knew to admit it would be to invite his derision and accusations that I was a Sodomite preferring the company of men. So I said nothing else in the way of an explanation. I just wanted to leave and never come back.

But I did come back. I came back several days later with a new Bible, leather-bound, purchased from a bookstore in Memphis, the nicest they had. I placed it on the front porch while the woman was out picking our cotton, with the baby wrapped to her breast in a sling made out of cloth.

As we grew older and my brother saw the attachment that I enjoyed with our father, my brother began saying belittling things about him, that he had been a river pirate himself and that was why he knew so much about the Alston Brothers and the Murrell Gang and Cave-in-Rock on the river in Illinois. That there was no organization called the Jovial Knights of Jocularity, that it was all a pretense to cover a dishonorable past. It was calculated to bother me, and it did. I was incensed, and we began wrestling in the barn and I pinned him and bloodied his nose. The memory of my fist covered with his blood and recoiled by my ear for another blow I carry with me yet.

It was the first time I had bested him, and so I taunted him and called him all the cruel names I could think of. The web of my hand between the thumb and forefinger pressed under his chin and into his neck. He cried and begged that I let him up. Finally, I rose and extended my hand, thinking he might clasp my shoulder at this moment when he might see me as an equal and be proud of me somehow. But when he gained his feet, he pushed me down, and as I turned and swept the hay dust from my eyes, I saw him wielding the hayfork.

I rolled quickly, narrowly escaping the tines as they buried into the ground beside me. I ran from the barn and to the house. I kept from my brother that afternoon and from then on, staying in the safety of my father's study, accompanying him on rides into the fields, or staying in the companionship of our servants in their sundry duties. From that moment in the barn, I would not be alone with my brother. It was as if he had suddenly become ten times as powerful as any man I knew. Our mother said that I had pestered him into it and that certainly he only meant to scare me. I did not tell my father of it, as the source of the scuffle had been something my brother had said about him.

Our mother, of course, took my brother's side and punished me with silence. She refused to look at me or talk to me. When I spoke to her, she would not answer, pretending she didn't hear me. It was unbearable and finally broke me to tears and coerced me into a feeble apology to my brother in the presence of my mother and our house servants.

The next week, my brother left for the university in Oxford. Within a few months, fortune and chance smiled upon him, and he left the university and Mississippi for an opportunity that had fallen into his lap, financed by money borrowed from our father. In a sheriff's sale in Louisiana, he had bought the sugar plantation from the estate of a man whose name was Savoy or something like that. This man Savoy and his family had all died of yellow fever within a space of two weeks of each other, leaving no heirs.

I suppose it is not only the meek that inherit the earth. So also do the proud and the conniving, no matter how ignorant they may be. And so, my brother, the sugarcane planter, the owner of ten thousand acres, a veteran of the late war like me, though a man who had our mother's favor simply because he wasn't captured during it like I had been. He was set on the path to become great, his name among the men who would become the giants who would trample me later. Of course, at that young age, I could not foresee the disaster that would befall me.

I have told myself all my life that it is better to be a simple man and retain one's dignity than to be a great man and lose it. Perhaps this is sour grapes, the consolation prize of those left behind. My brother left, and within a few months, through luck and cleverness, he began a life of ease and privilege. He rose in society and married the first of four wives. Good men are fortunate enough to marry women like their mother. Of course, the same is true for bad men.

Jack

When my brother left for Oxford and then Louisiana, someone new fell into the void. My new friend was a boy named Neely, one of our slaves and a year or two younger than me. It never occurred to me that his job was to be my playmate. He never affected that it was a burden to him, though I suppose he couldn't have.

In the winter when the crop was picked, we hunted together and camped in the cold under bright stars by icy streams. I brought plenty of blankets from our great house, enough for him and for me, though I wonder if my mother would rather him shiver than to know that a black boy was being kept warm under them.

We developed a signal to each other, a peculiar clicking like the chirp of a cricket. We used it if we ever got separated, trailing a deer or a rabbit, and we were always able to find each other. Oh, I couldn't make it now, Father, my lips are too old. But it could blend into the sound of the wilderness while still sounding bright and cheerful enough for us to recognize it.

We talked under the stars, and I wished this boy could be my brother, rather than the one God had given me. In the spring, our idyll was done until the next winter, when the cotton had been planted and picked. Still, I would follow him down the row as his brown hands darted in and out of the leaves, securing the feathery white from the bolls and deftly placing it in the sack. It would drag behind him like the tail of an insect as we would talk excitedly of what we would hunt and how we would prepare it over an open fire, deep in the woods. He told me the stories that were murmured by the old people in the firelight of the slave quarters, of talking animals and good and evil spirits.

When he had told me a story, I would tell him mine, though mine were from books that I had read. As we waded through the sea of cotton, white-specked green leaves, I told him that one day I would fly, and he said that he would be there when I landed and be the first to shake my hand and tell everyone that he was my friend from boyhood and that I had said I would do this very thing, even back then. He would tell everyone there that I said that I would fly one day.

He never said that he hated having to work like that, dragging a cotton sack down a row, cutting his hands on the sharp bolls of our cotton, living in a shack riddled with cracks and holes that the winter wind always found and entered through. He never mentioned that he had seen friends and family sold or whipped or both. He could have, though, and I would not have had an answer for him.

I asked my father if Neely might be my valet. It was not uncommon then, for young men to take a favorite and make him his personal servant. It would mean Neely might become even more of a brother to me. He would sleep on a pallet in my room. He would wear nicer clothes. He would eat better. He could quit the cotton fields and accompany me on trips to Memphis and we would see things together. We would talk in the nights under the breezes that seeped from underneath the curtains and the stars and the insect sounds outside the windows. He would become, in fact, my brother. My father agreed, over my mother's objections, and Neely became my valet.

Neely and I studied the works of science. I taught him to read, late at night in our room under the dim light of a candle. His face would look to mine and then to the page, and he would haltingly recite the words to me, and then sentences. We traced our letters on a slate, or on papers that we would burn in the fire, lest there be evidence that I was teaching and he was learning, something that was considered both immoral and illegal. My father seemed pleased that I had a companion and would ask us what we were after as we headed to the river with our poles over our shoulder. When we returned, he would examine our catches and compliment us and say that Aunt Rosalie would surely know what to do with those 'flappers' as he referred to them.

The two years after my brother left were the best two years of my childhood.

My mother, however, kept my brother's presence felt, reading letters which were certainly written in the fine hand of his wife, my sister-in-law. Mother said that he was clearly making a name for himself and I could do the same, she said, 'if I would learn to keep better company.' She said this with a voice raised to the kitchen, where Neely was eating with the kitchen girl and her mother, Aunt Rosalie, also considered the 'kitchen girl,' despite her age.

My father knew better than to openly confront my mother and would only snort quietly as he put his fork to his mouth. Still, I think it pained him that my brother and I were at odds. No, I am sure of it.

It was sometime later that I was summoned to my father's bedside. He had developed a cough and been losing weight so that his skin hung from his large frame and he slept much of the time. He was dying, the doctor said. So I went to my father's room to see him one last time. His beaver-pelt hat and swallowtail coat hung from the bedposts in the dim light.

"Jack, my son," my father said in a voice that was little above a whisper, a pale shade of the raspy boom that it once was, "Whenever it is possible, choose what is honorable over what is profitable. It will be the account of your time on earth." Then he looked away from me and to the firelight dancing on the ceiling and he added, "I wish I had done so. But soon I will have to render an account to God for a misspent youth filled with dissipation." His face was lacking his characteristic smile, and the neutral expression it wore seemed tragic by comparison.

It became clear to me that although we had fought over it and I had licked him for it, my brother had been right. There was no benevolent and fraternal organization called the Jovial Knights of Jocularity and the scars on my father's back weren't from a fall from a horse-apple tree and the HT at the base of his thumb didn't stand for Honor and Truth.

Then my father looked again to me, amber-faced in the darkness, said, "Please tell me that you and your brother will remain on friendly terms. Promise me that you will do this."

I gulped back tears and nodded that I would, though I had no idea how I could make such a unilateral bargain. Father took my hands in his, and I could feel the raised pink of HT on the base of his left thumb. And I hated my brother for the knowledge he had given me.

HT was the mark of a man caught as a Horse Thief.

Father died soon after, and, to my knowledge, the money borrowed by my brother was never repaid to the estate. In fact, a portion of my father's estate was sold so that we could bury him. Our neighbors and our slaves gathered around the rectangular pit dug in the Mississippi earth. Everyone took a handful of it and tossed it on the coffin when it had found the bottom. Neely was there with his hat over his heart, right next to me.

My brother did not come home for the funeral. My mother did not take it as a slight and said that my brother was a busy man who was making something of himself. She said it not only with an air of great reverence, but also with an air that said that I myself would never 'make something' of myself.

As my boyhood fell away like an evening shadow, I came to a decision that I thought would make me a great man, the kind of man that a mother might admire and might give honor to a dead father. Events at the time in our country's history would call many a man to greatness. To both greatness and to tragic ends.

Well, Father, I suppose a man my age should be turning in for the night. Shall we meet for breakfast?

Jack

Good morning, Father. I trust you slept well. I think the birds will abandon us by day's end, we will be too far out for them.

Ah, yes, the birds. When I was a boy, I dreamed of flying with them, that I could build a machine like the Wright brothers and soar with them. But now those Ohio boys have done it, and many others after them. It has taken us barely a decade to put guns and bombs on them and turn them against each other. Such is human nature, I suppose.

Steward, sir, could you bring me a coffee and a tea for his holiness? Thank you.

Well, then. I was telling you of the change in my life, then, wasn't I?

I was determined to gain Mother's favor and at the same time learn more about science and the natural world. I came upon a way that I might do both simultaneously and, in the process, 'make something of myself.'

Our neighbors in Tunica County were connected in some way to our Congressman, the Honorable Lucius Lamar, through the Masons, I believe, and I was able to obtain an interview with the Hon. Mr. Lamar when he returned from Washington on break. We met at his law office in Oxford. He was a man with a head of hair he wore over his collar in the back with a widow's peak in front. His wooly, wispy beard came almost to his tie, a small, black bow that seemed even smaller set against his barrel chest and gut. He had the look of an animal that might push its way down into a hole, a face that a burrowing rabbit might see as an intruder into its den. He ushered me into his office and showed me to a chair in front of a potbellied stove which he fed a stick of wood from time to time.

He asked me my business, in a way that was both kindly and annoyed. Did I want to study the law? he asked. No, I said, I was more interested in the mechanical world, the world of cotton gins and bridges and locomotives. I said that I meant to make an engineer and that I had come to see if he could write me a recommendation for the military academy in West Point where I might meet those aims. I didn't tell him that part of my errand was to achieve something to make my mother proud. Perhaps he already knew it.

"Well," he said as he raised his eyebrows, as if he wasn't aware that he could grant such requests. "Tell me," he asked, "if Mississippi were to subtract herself from the United States, would you follow her?"

It was becoming the question of the day, as talk of secession was beginning to simmer but had yet to come to a boil. My mind worked quickly as I thought of the answer he wanted and which would serve me best. He reached a poker through the door in the belly of the stove, fiddled with the fire a moment as he waited, and then leaned back in his chair. His expression asked his question again, for him.

I folded and unfolded my hands, and then I told him that my hope was that I could remain a citizen of the United States, but that first and foremost, I was a Mississippian.

Somewhere in the dense underbrush of his beard-and-mustache, his lips pursed into a smile as his chin rose and his head tilted back a little, a gesture of approval. The fire in the stove hissed on finding a hidden droplet of moisture in the stick of wood. He turned to his desk and pulled a sheet of paper from a slot. His pen dipped into the inkwell on his desk and he said, "Well, then, you seem a quick sort of boy and I feel that I can recommend you with no reservation whatsoever."

I returned to Tunica County with news of my appointment to West Point, dreaming of the hero's welcome I would receive there. I gave the reins of my horse to our stableman and vaulted up the steps and into the parlor where Mother was dipping a needle in and out of an embroidery hoop. I handed her the letter, but she did not take it. Instead she nodded to the side table where

The Burden of Cane

I placed it. Breathlessly, I picked it up and read it, the announcement of the first great turn in my life's path.

And my mother's first words were not, "My, what a fine son you are!" or, "You have made me very proud this day!"

She said, rather, "Who will see to the planting of our crop?"

I was crestfallen, to say the least. I felt as if I had been doused with cold water. My proud offering had been pronounced worthless.

"Why, Mr. Hartwick would, as he has always done," I said. Mr. Hartwick was our overseer.

"I would rather you were here to manage with Mr. Hartwick."

It was all we said of it. That spring, I rode the fields as Mr. Hartwick supervised the hands in sowing our cotton. I rode the fields as Mr. Hartwick supervised the hoeing of it. I rode the fields with Mr. Hartwick as he supervised the chopping and weeding of it. That June, before the harvest, when I would have the chance to ride with Mr. Hartwick as he supervised the hands in the picking of it, I packed a satchel and a valise and I had Mr. Hartwick take me to the landing for the steamer upriver. I did not tell Mother good-bye.

Neely rode with us to the landing in Tunica. He helped me with my bags, and we shook hands just before I ascended the gangplank to the steamer waiting for me at the edge of the broad blue-brown water of the Mississippi. But he did not smile. I tried to, but I couldn't. I felt that I had used him for his friendship, his gentle companionship, and now I was abandoning him for something bigger and better, a grand and gaudy scheme to secure a mother's pride.

The steamer pulled away and he became smaller in the distance, still perched upon the buckboard of the carriage, he and the brown mare, two beasts of burden with their heads sagging. I did not think of Neely or the fact that he would be returned to the fields. But that is what happened.

Eva

Good morning, Gladys. Yes, of course, of course. Pardon me, *Mrs. Leonard*. I trust that you are rested and dry. Shall we begin our efforts to contact my husband?

Yes. Very well. I understand, you must gather information first. If you insist that this is the way of these things, then yes, I will wait, but, I admit, I won't like it.

Let me set Ruthie to seeing to your breakfast. You prefer tea, I presume? If it's not a bother, I'll begin telling you what you would like to know while you eat.

Now that I am a widow, I can speak of these things, things that I could not say when my husband was alive. I will be frank with you and tell you all so that you might use your talents to their fullest. You have my word that what I am about to tell you is the truth, though I tell it in strictest confidence.

We all have secrets, then, don't we? Private matters discussed with no one else? Private indulgences, worries? I am certainly no different. There are things that no one else knows about me. For one thing, I was born in a cave. Yes, that is the truth of it, a cave set in a hillside. But I have bigger, more salacious secrets than that. The people of this place don't know it and shall never know it, but I am a woman with a rather scandalous past. Were it known, it would ruin my social standing and influence.

In private, we are all victims of our own natures. You and I and all of us may refute them and rail against them when we see them portrayed in others, but our natures are still our natures and largely unchangeable. None of us may necessarily like them, but they are as undeniable as cold in the winter, heat in the summer, and gravity all year round.

Here is another secret: even though I am now twice the size of my girlish former self, my hair would be scribbled with gray if I didn't dye it with coffee grinds, a trick borrowed from the Creoles up in the city. Certainly, however, I am still the envy of every woman in St. Matthew. Perhaps it is my eyes, still an intense blue capable of mesmerizing any man if he isn't careful. Now that I am a solitary woman again, I shall have to try it. But there is something else as well. In addition to these luminous eyes, I have been given the gift of exquisite instincts.

The Burden of Cane

We Teagues are among the finest of the fine families here in St. Matthew, our name among the loftiest boughs of society. Any man or woman ambitious for social status here must first come to me. Matters of society and class are largely what those at the top or perceived to be at the top dictate. Whether it is America or England, Turkey or Timbuktu, people will worship what they are told to worship and fawn over what is selected for them to fawn over. Merit, true merit, has little to say in the matter. And so yet I reign over social matters here in St. Matthew and so shall I always. People are as faithful as dogs when it comes to the order of society and the expectations of it. As faithful as dogs, Mrs. Leonard. Human nature is insurmountable, and contented ignorance is a feathered bed.

And so again I remind you, if I am to tell you the truth, and I am, for so much depends upon it, that I must ask you to keep the things I am about to tell you in the strictest confidence.

Ruthie? Ruthie! Bring me a Gin Rickey. What do you mean, we don't have any limes? Use a lemon, then. Bring it and then leave Mrs. Leonard and me to ourselves. That will be all.

We have much to talk about, you and I. Where shall I start? What?

Yes, Mrs. Leonard, that is correct. I was born in a cave. It was in Vicksburg, in Mississippi, in June of 1863 in the midst of the late war. The city was under siege, encircled by an enemy who made war on the army and the citizenry alike. Devils, all of them.

I can imagine that hot summer night when I was born, explosions from shells lighting the sky over the river, momentarily giving glimpses of the gunboats that hurled them into the bank and us cave-dwellers, the sounds of my shrieking mother dulled by the explosions as she endured the bewildering cruelty of nature, nine months after enjoying its gift of rapture. She was attended by old Aunt Hattie, the only one of my grandparents' servants to follow us to Vicksburg, the rest having stayed behind across the river in Louisiana to enjoy the protection of the Union Army and the free rations they dispensed.

I was what was then called a 'natural' child, born of a woman, a girl, really, who was unmarried. My mother was a woman prone to sexual irregularities. This is something I have never told anyone, not my children, and certainly not my husband. But it isn't the worst thing they could know of me, not by any stretch. But I will get to that if you bear with me.

Of course, I have no more memory of my birth than anyone else does, and I tell you this from equal parts my imagination and the recounting of it by my Granny, who told it as a cautionary tale against an enjoyment that she did not fully explain, as I was only ten when she told me. I thought at the time that any enjoyment, even saltwater taffy and penny candy, could lead to a painful consequence.

My memory of my mother is only vague, though my Granny's tales of her and my imagination have always colored her like me, dark-haired and blue-eyed. My mother was a poor, tormented young woman troubled with voices and urges and then the laudanum and brandy the doctors used to silence them. I have only vague memories of her then, of a woman with hair as dark as the breast of a blackbird and eyes as blue as an autumn sky. And skin like cream, just like mine. The memory of her was just alive enough to fire a spark of recognition when I briefly saw her later in life.

I never knew my father, and I am fairly certain that my mother only knew him a short time, a few days, and perhaps as short as an hour in some back alley or barn loft tryst. I often wonder, who was he, my father? A soldier? A Jew peddler? A Vicksburg banker or cotton broker, an otherwise contented husband who was momentarily bored and who had strayed into the arms of a pretty girl with a wild mind and intensely black hair and blue eyes equally intense? Whoever it was will remain a mystery to me, as my mother was committed to the state asylum in Jackson just as my memory began. My grandparents seldom spoke of her and never spoke of who my father might have been. They likely had no idea.

When I was four or five, she was sent away by her parents, my grandparents, to Jackson, that great warehouse of invalids and oddities, where she could be cared for. I didn't think that I would see her again, and perhaps I didn't, though I will never be sure of it.

My grandparents were not tender people, and I can't remember them displaying so much as an ounce of affection to each other or to me. My Pappy always wore a suit of black broadcloth in the winter and a suit of white linen in the summer, his change in wardrobe as dependable as the greening of leaves in the spring and their browning in the fall, as predictable as the tilting of the earth on its axis.

When the war was over and my mother had been sent away, my grandparents and I returned to their place McCarron Hall to find the servants living in its rooms. My grandparents never spoke of it, but I read an article years later in the *Times-Picayune* about a Mr. McCarron and his return to his cotton plantation in Carroll Parish at the close of the late war to find it filled with 'wooly-heads,' who would not allow him or his wife or their granddaughter (me) to enter. There had been great bickering over who should live in which room, including, it was said, one which ended in a knifing. My grandfather was up in years and in no shape to contest the new inhabitants who felt that they had earned it, and perhaps they had. I was three or four and had no opinion of it then, and have very little memory of it now, only the look of consternation on my grandfather's face, a look that comes from unsatisfied rage. My Pappy surveyed it one last time, the fortress he had erected now inhabited by its very builders and sustainers. The article said that Mr. McCarron and his wife and granddaughter left without gaining admittance to their former home and their whereabouts were unknown. I, of course, and now you, know that we arrived in Shreveport to begin a new life.

Set it right there, Ruthie.

Are you sure you don't want a libation, Mrs. Leonard?

Very well, that will be all for now, Ruthie. Now go and leave us to ourselves.

Now about my grandparents. They were both thrifty and devout, whether by nature or by circumstance. Both believed that God never made mere suggestions. Theirs was a God who had smote Sodom and Gomorrah with pillars of fire and might do so again to other places and with less cause. They also believed that if you prayed on something and there was no audible response, then God was in agreement.

I was not so much the oddity one might suppose, a parentless child, raised by grandparents or aunts and uncles. The war had seen to that, and Shreveport was filled with fatherless and motherless boys and girls like me. And so the days before I turned ten were much like those of other children. I was enrolled in the Travis Street school, where I was an average student, uninspired for the most part. My recollection of my childhood is that we moved around the city quite a bit, and with each move the wagon loaded with our possessions was emptier, though I always carried my doll and parasol with me. At last, we settled into lodgings in the boardinghouse of a Mrs. Marshall at the corner of Texas and McNeill, the final move before I moved into the house on Commerce Street when I was ten.

My grandfather was not a man accustomed to work. He had been a cotton planter who always had others do it. Now that it was left for him to do, he struggled, chafing at orders put upon him by men he saw as his inferiors. I believe that he was let go for it at least once, though I can't be sure, as I was only a child. I only remembered he worked here, and then there, and then another place. At last he found work in Buckelew's hardware store, pushing a broom while the local war hero, a Mr. Lockett, held court telling stories by the potbelly stove.

For my grandfather, there was a right way and a wrong way when it came to the work and moral comportment of others. In thinking, there were proper thoughts and there were improper thoughts, there was acceptable reading material and unacceptable. In religion, there was heathenism and there was the Presbyterian church and a broad gulf between the two. He was a dour man with a pointed nose and a pointed chin with a tuft of a white beard upon it, such that he had the appearance of a goat. It did not help matters that his Christian name was Billy.

If I were to describe my grandmother, it would be some sort of bird, one with large eyes and a small beak of a nose. She wore the large bonnet of the earlier part of that century, the round brim of it framing her face, a face that scowled like a saint bearing a painful trial. My granny's bonnet was either a halo or a crown of thorns, depending on her mood, though it varied little, going between very little joy and completely joyless. Of course, it has never deterred me in my pursuit of pleasure. She worked in a shop as a seamstress to fashionable ladies, and though my grandparents were teetotalers, Granny took an occasional dose of *Bradfield's Female Regulator*. She maintained it was for her *vim, vigor, and acuity*, which is what the label said it was for, as well as *loss of the marital impulse*. They were neither kind nor unkind to me, and, all these years later, the best I can say of them is that they were dutiful and sincere in their obligations to me. There was certainly no joy for them in it, raising a bastard granddaughter.

My grandparents only had two books that I remember. One, of course, was the Bible, fancifully embossed letters in gold and inside on the front page the dates of births, deaths, and marriages. The other book was a copy of Milton's *Pilgrims Progress*. Most of the time Pappy read the papers, the ones he agreed with, and Granny knitted or did embroidery.

On Sundays, we went to the church that God Himself attended, the Presbyterian church, attending the services with the other Presbyterians complete with dinner on the grounds and the clucking of the women at the state of the women in the boardinghouses for young ladies on Commerce Street on the riverfront. I would see these women on the front porch and it seemed to me as though the girls were having the time of their lives, like an exclusive club where a girl might wear fancy clothes and rouged cheeks. Little did I know that one day—

Why look at the time! I must prepare for church. Before I leave you here for a while, let me again tell you the plain truth of it, Mrs. Leonard. Mount Teague is heavily mortgaged.

You are my foremost hope, and so I mention this to you frankly. Despite my financial reverses, I have always been an exalted member of society in St. Matthew Parish, the elite of the elite. Those whom I accept are accepted. Those whom I shun, are shunned. Cotillion, Garden Club, and, of course, the Krewe of Jupitre, all are under my influence. Parties hosted here are coveted invitations. What I say socially is implicitly the last word. I can ruin a woman's reputation through gossip and innuendo, or easier yet, indifference, and in so doing, ruin her husband's reputation. It has been my life's work.

And so I am off for church. We will talk again on my return.

Eva

You ask me how church was, and since you are in the business of knowing the truth I will say it was as tiresome as always. We sit there and pretend to listen on Sundays, singing the same old dry songs and mumbling the same old prayers to no one in particular, and then we get up and go about what we were going to do anyway. Truthfully, I have never viewed church as anything more than a social occasion, a chance to wear one's finery and see and be seen. Of course, it is also a fine time to engage in gossip, whispered across the back of a pew or into an ear on the church steps afterward. A cruel truth, yes, but a truth nonetheless, pews full of peacocks and penguins just as anxious for glory, status, and mammon as anyone outside of it. Perhaps they should place a treasure chest or a golden calf on the altar. That is what most worship, the revered and much sought after dollar. I do not judge them, I am merely honest about it. It is well that no one has seen the face of God, for we might put his image on our currency.

I hope you won't think ill of me for getting out of this mourning attire for the afternoon. Come speak to me while I change. I'll stay behind the changing screen if bare skin is a bother to you.

Tell me, Mrs. Leonard, what is the prescribed length for mourning in England? I'll be happy to quit this costume of black silk and widow's lace in favor of bolder colors and dresses cut for flirtation, and it cannot be too soon. Then, if you can't help me, I may well have to seek my fortunes with another husband, but it will have to be a man drawn to a woman with an ample figure, especially around the middle. Perhaps a much younger man who is well-endowed, both financially and physically. I suppose it is never too early to begin planning for such things.

Hand me that dress there on the settee, would you? Thank you, madame.

Yes, that is my ballgown on the dressmaker's dummy. The seamstress from Donaldsonville is letting it out and putting in some gussets. Ordinarily, I would simply purchase a new one, but money is tight and my credit, tighter. Not as tight as my ballgown, however.

Carnival, under the name Mardi Gras, is observed here as it is in every Catholic place, though one does not have to do be Catholic to do so. The Krewe of Jupitre has been celebrated here since the late war. There is a ball and a procession. I am the Queen of Jupitre, and my late husband was always its King. Soon my son will be installed as the next King of Jupitre now that his father has passed.

Ruthie! I know you're listening in the next room. Remind me to have the king's tunic taken in before then. Ruthie?

Oh, never mind.

The Burden of Cane

If you can help me contact my husband, Mrs. Leonard, and get me an answer to my question, perhaps I shall simply have a new ballgown made. Only the best at Mount Teague.

Would you hand me that comb on the dressing table, Mrs. Leonard? Don't look so put off—it was a simple request, really.

This is my oldest possession, a hair comb made of imitation pearl. It was given to me by my first gentleman admirer the summer I turned ten. He was a boy named Willie, the son of the saddlemaker Mr. Bissinger, who had a shop on Texas Street in Shreveport just down from the rooms we rented from Mrs. Marshall.

Willie was a boy with hair as fine as cotton, so fair as to be just a shade or two from white. He wore it to his eyebrows where it grew despite his mother's constant trimming. This boy and I were enamored with each other in the sweet way of boys and girls of that age, aware of a certain attraction but with no idea how to go about it or even get started toward it.

His father was known in town and throughout the surrounding villages as an exceptional craftsman, one who didn't need to advertise like the other saddlermakers in town, the ones down on Levee Street. His quality spoke for itself through the mouths of satisfied customers. My Pappy scoffed at this, saying that the best saddle a man ever rode in was not a great deal better than the worst. Nevertheless, I was drawn to Willie because he took up for me against the teasing of the other children, especially the girls who commented on my secondhand dresses, some of them the girls recognized as having been their own.

Would you loosen my corset, Mrs. Leonard? I can barely catch a breath. Wretched things. I have mixed feeling about them going out of style. I might spill out everywhere, but on the other hand, at least it will be more comfortable.

Well, then.

This young gentleman, perhaps a year older than I, would put his arm around me as I sobbed in response to their barbs, telling me that they were just jealous cause I was 'a real purty gal,' quite a bit 'purtier' than they were, and they couldn't stand the thought of it.

I suppose it was true. I had the looks of my mother. I was certain about this. I was also certain that she had managed to inherit every bit of

45

handsomeness that each of my grandparents had to offer her. Whenever I asked my Granny about my mother, she would only say that my mother was a woman of 'loose morals' who 'had a weakness for a certain enjoyment' and was troubled by it, and that she had gone to a place to live among other troubled people. Whenever she was feeling more charitable, my grandmother would say that my mother was a very beautiful woman with blue eyes and black hair and fair skin like me and that those things were a gift from God and only that, and we shouldn't become conceited on account of it because conceit was the snare of the devil, or one of them, at least.

As I waited for more information about her, a silence would descend upon the little parlor in our apartment above the dry goods shop on Texas Street. No more information on my mother would be forthcoming, and so I wondered about my mother and her weakness for certain things, which, as a girl, I thought was an enjoyment of sweets and maybe a tendency to daydream during church. I never asked about my father because when I did, my grandparents said that God was our father and for me, in my case, that would have to be information enough.

If, for my grandparents, the divine goal of life was heaven and a favorable audience with God, then the earthly goal was the accumulation of wealth. They did not speak of lawyers and judges and bankers and merchants without the description 'rich' or 'well-off' before them. These were the men who sat in the coveted front pews and whose wives and children wore different clothes each Sunday. We might all sing the same hymns and pray the same prayers, but it was understood that God could hear them more clearly and easily. Rather than bemoan this separation of the favored and the ordinary and our inclusion in the latter, my grandparents were resigned to the belief that it was the natural order of things. They might have regarded Darwin as a godless heretic, but they unknowingly agreed with his doctrine of survival of the fittest, as least in social matters.

I was teased incessantly by the girls of the wealthier families about my clothes and elderly parents, even though I would raise a blubbering shout that they were my grandparents. I would add that my real parents were dead, but it did not diminish their taunts but, rather, emboldened them more. One of the girls, a rat-faced girl named Gwendolyn Mosey, would enjoy iced lemonade on her front porch in the summers. She and her friends would make sure to rattle their glasses as I passed, taunting me with the tinkle of the ice in them, as we could not afford ice. Granny said that when you're hot and thirsty, water without ice was suitable and sufficient for its purpose. She made it sound like iced beverages were an indulgence of the wicked, whereas the righteous made do with simpler things, including lukewarm water.

Perhaps worse than Gwendolyn Mosey was her friend Polly Calhoun, a girl with a round face with an upturned nose in the middle of it like a Pekingese dog. She would launch cruel taunts directed to the air but always theatrically loud so that I would hear them. She and Gwendolyn Mosey would speak of the fine things they ate and the fine things they might wear and the fine places they would travel to during fever season. Then they would say in an off-hand manner as if they had not seen me, 'Oh, hello, Eva.' Then another of this group would say, 'is that a new dress? It looks so much like your others,' and they would all cackle. After school, it was the same business, cutting remarks that left invisible wounds and an ache as I held back tears and shouts.

This is when Willie would step in, redirecting me to his father's saddlery where I would compose myself on a bench inside while we watched his father pull and push rawhide stitches to gather sheets of leather. His father had the same cottony hair and red face as his oldest son and seemed to enjoy our society, always telling him, "Ah, I see, Villy, you gots a friend vit you." All the while his needle dipped in and out of the leather as his eyes watched his hands make it go. At noon, he took a beer with his lunch, and I waited for the damning bolt of lightning to strike him, but there was none, and when his glass was empty, the big blonde German Mr. Bissinger nonchalantly wiped his mouth with his sleeve and went back to work.

We grew closer that spring and fall, at first barely aware that we were members of different sexes. Then we began holding hands and exchanging innocent pecks. Once, driven by some primitive curiosity, we compared our anatomy behind the Methodist church, astonished how differently we could be made under our clothes. It was the first time I saw a penis, but it was certainly not the last. Nothing came of this innocent inspection, no touching, only a brief glance. We had no sense or desire for passion, no idea how, nor, for that matter, why. It was simply a shared secret born of inquisitiveness.

He gave me this faux-pearl comb, and Granny asked me where I had gotten it. When I told her it was from Willie, the saddler's son, she tut-tutted.

Granny discouraged our friendship because of his 'commonness,' even though we ourselves could easily and rightfully be described thusly. The other issue was that he was a Catholic, a thing that in my grandparents' view was tantamount to satanic. My grandparents believed that there was a ladder than ran from hell up to heaven, and the Pope and the devil were on adjacent rungs at the bottom. Granny never said which of the two was lower.

I have always kept this comb as a memento, wondering what my grandparents feared most, that I would become the wife of a saddlemaker or a Catholic. As it turned out, they had nothing to fear, as I became neither.

Shall we go down to the sitting room, then?

Eva

Ruthie? Ruthie! Where is my cigarette case? The one with the red and black oriental garden scene on it?

Yes, Mrs. Leonard, another one of my secrets. I might as well tell you all of them. I picked up the habit long ago. As time went on, I encouraged my young son to pick it up so that I could blame the butts and smoke on him. My husband never knew. Would you care for one?

Very well. They're right there if you change your mind.

Yes, smoking is one of my secrets, but not the worst of them, by far.

So good to get out of my Sunday clothes, shapeless, black mourning clothes at that. Not to mention that corset. You should have seen the stares in the pews today. Maybe the old biddies are worried about their husbands. They see me as extravagant, even by their profligate standards. Well, so be it. There is more than a shred of truth to it. I have enjoyed nice things, good food, clothes made from all over the world and travel to those places, shoes enough for an entire army of centipedes. I have gone to London and had my portrait done by Mr. Sargent. It once hung on the wall next to my husband's, there in the central hallway.

Pardon the smoke. Are you sure you don't want one?

I was telling you about my childhood, wasn't I?

The Burden of Cane

Despite the teasing of the girls of the more prosperous families, I grew into the kind of girl who grown men and women would stop and admire for my raven hair and blue eyes. *Oh, now, but ain't she a picture!* One might say. *Pretty as an apple or a peach!* Another might say. Granny would thank them and then remind me to thank them also and then whisper into my ear not to be too proud, as pride was a sin and perhaps the worst of all. I, of course, have sampled many sins in my life and have found pride a run-of-the-mill sort of sin and perhaps the easiest to indulge in, though the hardest to abandon.

I grew thusly, becoming lovelier with each day, though my loveliness did nothing to diminish the taunts of the prosperous, popular girls. Rather, they were both sharper and more frequent. I know enough of human nature now to recognize that it came from the threat of being outshone.

The summer that I was ten, the fever sprang upon us, not suddenly, but slowly like the patient squeeze of an anaconda, a little at a time. Before long, our little household fell ill, but at first it was just my grandparents. I knew Pappy was sick when he slept in on the Sabbath. It was heretofore his custom to rise early on Sundays and study the scripture, sometimes reading it aloud in a wiry voice, particularly the passages in which damnation is meted out. Granny would lay out my Sunday clothes, looking carefully for little tears and painstakingly repairing them through thick lenses, her gnarled hands pushing the needle, pulling the thread, those old, yellow teeth nipping the filament in place of scissors.

But on this day, with the sounds of church bells and carriages saturating the thick air of a late summer morning, I found that my grandparents had slept in. I was certainly happy that we might skip church. It was a thing we seldom did, like a snow day for school, a chance for true leisure, for playing with dolls and reading and naps. When the noontime bells rang after church, the signal for the churches to disgorge its inhabitants so that everyone might forget what they had just heard for an hour and go and do as they pleased, I crept into my grandparents' bedroom. Granny was holding an enamel basin for Pappy, who was still in his drawers and vomiting into the basin. He wretched and heaved and made little sign that he was troubled by me seeing him do it.

Granny did not look much better. After she had vomited a coffee-grind looking slag into the basin with Pappy's, she knelt on the side of the bed and put her cheek to the comforter and said, "Eva, run and fetch the doctor on Milam." And then she added, "Put on some clothes."

"My Sunday clothes?" I asked.

"Any clothes," she murmured. Her face was close to the bedpost, so close that it looked like she was addressing it. Her eyes weren't focused on anything. "Don't go in your dressing-gown," she added in a murmur, for I was the kind of child who just might do something like that. I dressed hastily, at last putting my pearl comb in my hair.

I ran to his house on Milam, our doctor whose name I forget now, but the servant girl said that he was at church, and I remembered that he was Presbyterian like us, and in fact I could go even now, all these years later and sit in his very pew if you asked me. She said that I might try the doctor on Crockett Street. I was not ill whatsoever at the moment and took my time, as a ten year old might, happy to be out on a lark by myself, looking in shop windows, climbing a tree on the courthouse lawn. I had dressed myself, and I was enjoying being garishly mismatched, going up Edwards Street, down Market, up Cotton Street. I forgot what street the doctor lived on and then I remembered it was Crockett but I forgot what the doctor's name was. I was, as I say, just barely ten at the time.

A nice dressed couple was returning from church, and I asked them where the doctor lived and they took me into their carriage. They asked me if someone was sick. Yes ma'am, I said, my Pappy and my Granny, and the lady made the sign of the cross. I thought they might be Catholic and that it was nice of her to be concerned and that perhaps Catholics weren't as evil as Pappy said they were. They even waited in front of the doctor's house while I went and knocked on the door. His housekeeper, a red-headed Irishwoman named Bridget answered, and the doctor came downstairs and gathered his bag. He went and spoke with the Catholic couple who had given me the ride and dismissed him and then he and I walked together to our rooms on Texas Street above Phelps Brothers.

Granny and Pappy were still abed, and the doctor examined them, looking under eyelids and at nailbeds. Then he examined me, doing the same, asking if I had been sick, and I said that I felt just fine, there swinging my legs in the chair by their bed. The doctor said that some of the town was beginning to get sick, or "fall ill," as I remember him putting it.

He left but returned later that day. I had napped all day, waking with regret that I had squandered a free day with only napping. The doctor returned that evening and the three of us, Granny, Pappy and me, were put in a carriage and taken to the house in which I would grow into a woman.

Jack

The last boat of well-wishers pulled away from the landing to return downriver to New York City, and we were marched up the bluff to the plain above the Hudson. Some boys had been accompanied by proud parents and fought back tears upon being separated from them. I had not. When we gained the top of the cliff and stood at the gates of West Point, we looked down at the boats departing and leaving us behind. One of the upperclassmen smirked and told us, "Say goodbye, boys. The Corps is your family now."

We were assembled in the parade ground and addressed by Superintendent Delafield, who gave a speech on tradition and duty and honor and courage. He spoke reverently of the history of West Point and the 3 D's of old General Sylvanus Thayer: Discipline, Decision, and Devotion to duty and country. When he was done, he stepped away from the balcony from whence he had spoken, and then the upperclassmen descended upon us like wolves. They began yelling at us, right in our faces and ears, and we sprinted in the June heat to collect our uniforms. In the open air of the parade grounds, we hastily put them on, fingers fumbling for buttons as we looked one to the other trying to figure out how our uniforms were supposed to be worn. With more shouting, we assembled again, and the upperclassmen berated us for how sloppily we had dressed ourselves.

There were four classes at the military academy at West Point. What are called seniors everywhere else are called First Class there, or 'Firsties.' A year behind them in seniority are the Second Class, or 'Cows.' Then, the Third Class, or 'Yearlings,' and then what we were, Fourth Class, or 'Plebes.' We were also called 'animals' and 'things,' 'reptiles' and 'beasts.'

We plebes camped in the parade grounds that summer, drilling and being addressed while standing at attention as gnats alighted and gnawed on us and flies buzzed at our ears. We stood still and endured them rather than take a demerit for moving. We were drilled in marksmanship and horsemanship, though some boys, those from the cities, had never ridden a horse nor shot a rifle.

At the close of summer, the tents were struck, and we were given room assignments. My roommate was a boy from South Carolina who played the cornet in the band. He was a slight boy with brown hair and freckles who accrued demerits so rapidly and was dismissed so quickly that I can't remember his name, only his face. The end came when he snuck out after Taps and, in a bout of drunkenness, gave most of his buttons to a barmaid down at Benny Haven's Tavern in town. He returned just before morning parade and was found half-buttonless, and that was the occasion of his final demerit. He was dismissed and sent home to South Carolina, and the Corps of Cadets was without a cornet player and I was without a roommate. The poor boy had been too jolly and fun-loving for military life, and so he didn't last long. The weather hadn't even turned cold yet.

The summer had been mild compared to Mississippi and barely noticed in the whirlwind of barked orders and the stamping of marching feet as drills were executed. Likewise, after we had moved into our quarters, the vivid splendor of multicolored autumn leaves slipped by, and before anyone knew it, winter came. The leaves fell, and then snow fell, more snow at one time than I had ever seen, and still we were summoned with the bugle's reveille call before the eastern sky paled, and we arose and went about our duties, uniforms straight, quarters tidy with bunks neatly made, the crunch of marching cadets, to classes, to drill, to the Call to Quarters, to the bugle's taps in the evening.

We were taught history and French and mathematics—pure, sweet, sensible mathematics, glorious in its fairness, a pleasure in its directness. A problem could be worked forward and then backward, symmetrical in its certitude, as true now as it had ever been and would always be. Mathematics was like a truth spoken directly from the mouth of God. Sine, cosine, tangent, velocity, mass, acceleration. The trajectory of an artillery projectile like a boy launching persimmons over rows of cotton with a rubber belt. We waited for the day we would be taught its application in war, but it was only when we were upperclassmen that we would be taught tactics and strategy, fortifications and artillery, drilled in the poetry of combat.

The Burden of Cane

Reveille sounded every morning at five, though in the winter we were given an extra hour to six. After time to shine ourselves and our weapons and to study our lessons for the day's recitations, our quarters were inspected. Then we were marched to the dining hall to our places. We stood at attention until we were told to sit with a loud ringing voice shouting, *Take Seats!* Then with a great scraping of chair legs on the floor, we took them and sat erect and recited in unison the same communal prayer over the same communal food. Then we paused in the odd silence until the order was given to eat. Our young appetites released the deafening scrape of utensils on pewter plates, of mouths chewing and gulping. When we were done, we all rose on the order to rise and marched erect on the order to march to our classrooms where we gave recitations. At one in the afternoon we were marched back to the dining hall and repeated the process before our afternoon classes and recitations, and then parade, supper, inspection again, Call to Quarters. We moved between each like cogs in a wheel or the gears sliding effortlessly in a machine. We were being made into both men and machines, engines that could recite pledges and formulas. On Sundays, we were marched to chapel where we again sat erect and prayed simultaneous prayers that we would be examples of Christ and follow His teachings and that we would also be given the courage and power to smite our enemies.

The ways of the academy on the plains were hard but fair, in accordance with the making of great men. If a plebe were to fail, he was called 'found' as in, '*found out.*' We had one professor who, on seeing one of us taking the wrong path in our recitations, would click his tongue tsk-tsk and mutter, '*facilis descensus averno,*' a quote from the Roman poet Virgil, "easy is the decent into hell." In order not to be 'found,' we studied, or 'boned,' by the gas lamplight. When called upon in class, a cadet rose and went to the blackboard where he would state the problem by announcing, "Sir! I am required to deduce a rule for extracting the nth root of polynomials," or "Sir! I am required to discuss the four forms of the quadratic equation," or , "Sir! I am required to conjugate the French verb *avoir*, meaning *to have.*" We were taught French, because Napoleon was French, and his military skill was still considered the pinnacle. I patiently bore all these, waiting for my third and fourth year, when engineering would be taught.

I was too busy to be lonely, too busy to miss home and Neely, too busy to consider how I had betrayed him. But I thought of him on nights when the bugle played taps to summon us to bed and the lone voice shouted the order, *Lights Out!* I thought of him sleeping in a cabin with cracks and holes in the walls after a day of picking cotton in the once nice but now weather-worn clothes of a young southern gentleman's valet. I wonder if he cursed me as his hands braved the sharp edges of bolls in the quick and never-ending search for the soft spheres of cotton. He certainly could have. I would have if our places had been reversed.

In the winter when the icy wind plowed down the Hudson and across the Plain, I sat and wrote letters home, hoping that Mother would send one saying that she was proud of me. But when she did write, which wasn't often, her letters were filled with news of my brother and the fortune he was making and the fine house he was living in and the number of servants and field hands he owned. He and his wife, a woman whom I had not seen since their wedding a number of years before, had had another daughter. Mother said that they still held out hope for a son but that God was the supreme judge in such matters and that His will would be done and not ours. She would close those infrequent letters reminding me to mind my manners and dress warmly and remember to write my brother. She hinted that he was becoming fabulously wealthy, mentioning the fine things that he was enjoying and the number of people he owned. I could not bring myself to do it, however, and he never once wrote me, though I did not expect him to.

As much as I wanted to, I never sent letters to Neely, lest it be found out he could read them. Gradually, I forgot him altogether, other than as a dim light in the darkness of the memory of my former life in Mississippi. Every time that small speck of remembrance complained to me like a pebble in my shoe, I threw myself harder into my studies.

At West Point, we took an oath to uphold the Honor Code, which demanded that we were not to lie, cheat, or steal, or to tolerate those who do. I have tried to adhere to it as my guiding principle, though there have been many times when I have failed. My main trouble has been in identifying those who lie, cheat, and steal and then tolerating them.

I was no longer as lonely as I was. Just as the upperclassman had said that day, the Corps of Cadets had become my family. But like many families, it would be torn in two by passions. A schism was developing among the country and among the Corps of Cadets, sliding in as stealthily as the serpent into the Garden of Eden. Discipline, Decision, and Devotion to duty and country, yes, but duty to which country?

Jack

Good morning, Father.

You missed it this morning. The Canadian soldiers on the ship across the way and the ones on our ship serenaded each other over the waves with jaunty drinking tunes. I'm assuming they stumbled upon an early morning after a night of revelry down about ship. Poor boys. I wonder if they truly know what awaits them in France. We certainly had no realistic idea of what awaited us in Virginia. So much like the new plebes that arrived at West Point in June of that year, 1860.

They stepped off the boats at the landing on the Hudson fresh and eager and proud with heads full of honorable notions and hearts already beginning to long for home. After bidding their families farewell, they were set in rows and columns and listened to the speech by Superintendent Delafield, the same one I had listened to while standing at attention the June before. When it was concluded with the solemn pronouncement of the 3 D's, Discipline, Decision, and Devotion to duty and country, we set upon them.

We appeared in their faces as billed caps and snarling mouths. Our sighs of relief at no longer being pledges ourselves came out of us as shrill shouts delivered right into the ears of the new plebes. Some might have yelled at them out of sadistic pleasure, but I did it more out of a sense of duty, a need to warn them, *Buck up! Buck up, Cadet, lest you be found!* Whenever their bewildered eyes cut to look at us we bellowed, *Don't look to me! Look to your duty, Cadet! Eyes forward!*

Then they were sent scuttling out of formation to get uniform pieces which they hurriedly put on as the rest of us harangued them, blistering them with questions designed to expose the weak and the self-doubting. I wouldn't say I enjoyed it, Father, I would only say that I felt it my duty to protect the honor of the Academy. They were raw boys to be hammered into the shape of great men. We were merely the cold, iron striking plates.

They were drilled that summer like we had been drilled, until they were like us, unflinching at attention to the bite of gnats and flies, marching in precision like a human centipede, the feet of each cadet moving rigidly through the litany of commands, like the orderly shuffle of a deck of cards, a finely regulated stampede, rows and columns breaking and reforming to the serious lilt of martial music. Each note and step in perfect unison, starting and stopping together with irrefutable exactness.

I was now a yearling, having not only survived my plebe year but excelled in it. In that year, I had accrued only two demerits, one for a tarnished button and another for being 'found' in my inability to parse the French verb *savoir*, to know. Of course, I had neglected my boning for French in favor of Mathematics. Two demerits was not a record for fewest, but it was certainly an admirable showing, and my name was mentioned among those who might lead a brigade my senior year and earn a commission in the Corps of Engineers after graduation. I was top five in all fields of study, Mathematics, Physics, Geology, Astronomy, as well as horsemanship and marksmanship. I was serious about my duty and lacking any source of temptation since the departure of my roommate, the carousing cornet player from South Carolina, though it meant that I was frequently left out when parties were put together to go into town to Benny Haven's tavern. The other cadets took to calling me 'Friendless Jack,' but it didn't matter to me. I was there to earn high marks and the pride of my mother. We had only two days off that year, Christmas Day and New Year's Day, but as each ended with the Call to Quarters, I was quickly back at my studies, and especially Mathematics, so fascinating in its fairness and certainty.

Things began to change in November. Lincoln was elected president, and talk began to revolve around the impending rift between north and south. Small cliques were formed among northern boys and southern boys. There were some fistfights, and demerits and guard duty, and at least one expulsion. I largely stayed clear of them. I was only interested in my studies. But tension like the buzz of electric current hung in the air and sparked like a lightning flash in April of the following year when Fort Sumter in South Carolina was fired upon and states began 'subtracting' themselves one by one, as the honorable Lucius Lamar had put it. I had returned home by then.

We were mere boys, and we readily succumbed to the flimsy excuses for war which were given us. Afflicted with this national madness, I made good my promise to the Honorable Mr. Lamar. I returned to Mother Mississippi and threw my fate in with hers.

On hearing word that I would be resigning my position and heading home, Professor Bartlett asked to see me. He was a wild-haired professor of geology—among other things—with a beard that hid under his chin. He said that he had heard that I was considering leaving the academy, as hostilities between North and South seemed all but a foregone conclusion. I stood at attention even when offered a seat. He asked me if the rumors were true, but I responded, "Sir, the cadet declines to answer the question." He seemed disgusted with me, disappointed in me, massaging his forehead and looking down at the inkwell and pen on his desk. Next to them was a specimen of cobalt, one of the 'lustrous ores,' as he called them. It was a mesmerizing blue, as hypnotically blue as the eyes of a beautiful girl.

He rose in the silence to feed a lump of coal or two into the fire and poke them with the iron. I remained at attention. Outside the window, the gray sky threatened snow. At last I was dismissed with an admonition, "Beware the folly that approacheth, Cadet. Beware. It shall be more easily started than finished. *Facilis descensus averno,* young man, *facilis descensus.*"

The Hudson was icy down at the wharf, the leafless trees bristled up gray on the bluffs above the river, up from the snow-patched ground. I took one last look up onto the bluff, the building looming above it into the gray sky. It was a mistake and I knew it, but I could not avoid committing it. I gathered my things and got on board for the trip downriver to the train station.

The trip home took three days. I watched out the window as the countryside slept its winter sleep, dreaming of sunshine and warmth and green, unaware that there would also be smoke and sweat and blood. At home, I was greeted warmly enough by Mother whom I'm sure was delighted to see me in the gray uniform of a cadet, though she could not or would not say it. I told her that if there was to be a fight to preserve our way of life, then I was going to fight it.

That spring, in the wake of the firing upon Fort Sumter, the Honorable Lucius Lamar, representative to Congress from Mississippi, came to Tunica and gave a rousing speech under the eaves of the courthouse in favor of retribution and might, and the churchgoing and teetotaling men and women of Tunica began to align themselves to the tribe rather than the truth and to swear a bloody oath of allegiance to it. There was no room for dissent and those who spoke against the tribe were labeled as one of 'them,' that anonymous plurality that sought to undercut the peaceful way of life they had lived for so long. Deep within me, I had the notion that it was wrong, but I was young and of insufficient stature to speak out. Thus, I fell in with the tribe in its fight against the truth, the truth being that no man should be able to own another.

As a West Point man, even though just a few years removed from being a boy, I was seen as a desirable commodity and found myself a sought after man. I joined a Mississippi infantry regiment that was forming, and because I had been at the academy, I was elected one of my company's two lieutenants.

And so I traded in my West Point gray for Confederate gray. The uniform had been hand-sewn by the adoring ladies of Tunica County. I put it on in my old room. The bedstead with its veil of mosquito netting drawn around the posts seemed small, the bed of a child, the boy I had been. My playthings and books were in an old chest at the foot of it. That boy was gone now, no different than if he had died and was buried. He no longer existed. Instead, I, the man, was there in his place.

When I emerged from my room, my mother looked at me, and it was the moment when she seemed to have been most proud of me, the zenith of her affection for me. I felt I had made something of myself, that I was a man in full. I was tall, proud-chested. I was a noble warrior on her behalf. I was her defender. I felt that in her eyes I had eclipsed my brother.

That is, until later that day when a telegram came from my brother in Louisiana that he had been made captain in the Home Guard there. Our mother made great mention of it, implying that I was but a lieutenant in an ordinary infantry regiment, that I was the sole of the army's boot and my brother was the feather in its cap. And so I assumed my role of second-born and second-fiddle.

The Burden of Cane

We Tunica boys assembled in a field opposite the courthouse. Prayers were prayed, invoking a righteous and angry God to assist us in our errand. Songs which were both bellicose and jaunty were played by the handful of musicians in our company. They sounded much like you would expect from farm boys and store clerks who had been given secondhand musical instruments and told to make a go of it, blaring and belching horns and tubas that seemed to wander off in different directions with the war cry of the only two songs they knew, "Dixie" and "The Bonnie Blue Flag." They seemed to know most of them, at least. They would soon be absorbed into the regimental band when we arrived at our encampment. Then, to the cheers and fluttering handkerchiefs and the escort of sprinting boys much too young to go, we marched away from Tunica. For some young warriors, it was their last look at home, though they did not know it and could not fully appreciate it if they had known it.

The army had a particular aroma, the smell of the unwashed, the unwiped, the unbrushed, men who were largely undereducated and overpromised and with time would be underfed and underclothed and generally underequipped. Those men were not assembled for their betterment. They and we, their officers, had all fallen under the same national madness and were ready to be used for its purpose. Men go to war to prove themselves as men or to win the affection of a parent or a sweetheart or to gain standing in the eyes of other men. Some go to satisfy a simple lust for adventure. All others are conscripted. It both appalls and fascinates me how people can blindly pledge allegiance to a czar, a king, an emperor, a president. But politics has always been the process of promising the right things to the right people and convincing them that you are sincere about it. You might as well forget horseracing, Father. Politics, and only politics, is the true sport of kings. A poor man has never been elected so much as dog catcher. Persuade the people that you hate the same things that they hate and the people will bow down and pray to you like you are the Eucharist spouting the gospel. I am not saying that I am in favor of it, nor am I saying that there is a better way. I am only saying that it is a fact. We are pack animals, though most, at the core, are more interested in what the pack can do for them and not vice versa. I suppose that wolves are more altruistic that humans.

I had come home to win Mother's adulations, or at the very least, a little weak praise. I received neither, other than a brief glow of something close to pride. Before I marched away I did, however, rescue Neely from the fields.

It was planting season, and he was out in the endless rows with a hoe and a sack of cottonseed. He still wore the nice clothes of a young southern gentleman's valet, though they had been tattered by almost two years of hard work in harsh cottonfield weather. He was chopping the crusty soil and scattering seed, one of many doing the same monotonous chore which would lead to another monotonous chore in the fall. I dismounted and tied my horse to an oak limb at the end of the row, along with the chestnut mare I had brought for him. He looked up, and he didn't address me as Jack anymore.

"Sir?" he asked.

"I need you to come with me," I said.

He looked up to Mr. Hartwick and wiped the early spring sweat off his brow with his forearm. Mr. Hartwick, our overseer, stood his horse among the bare rows with his hands on the horn of his saddle.

"Mr. Hartwick, sir, I need this man to come with me," I announced, the authority of West Point having found its way into my voice. And I added, "the state of Mississippi needs it to be so." Mr. Hartwick nodded, and Neely followed me down the row, still clutching the hoe. At the end of the row, I told him he could put it down, and he leaned it against an oak tree and shrugged off the sack of buttery-smelling cottonseed that had been hanging around his neck and shoulder. There was a button missing from his livery, and I had the odd thought that he could receive a demerit for it. I gave him the reins of his horse, and we each mounted. As we trotted away, he asked me, "Where we going, you don't mind me asking?"

"Virginia," I said.

Professor Bartlett would indeed be proven right. It was easier started than—*listen, Father—do you hear it?*

The Canadian soldiers are singing again. A song about a girl with eyes as blue as violets.

Jack

Too cold and windy to be out on the deck today, Father. Best we stay inside. I believe I was telling you of Neely and me, and the rest or our regiment, headed off to Virginia, wasn't I?

When we got to the house, I gave Neely some of my old clothes, gray trousers, white shirt with suspenders and a black jacket. It wasn't a uniform, but it was more suitable for traveling and being part of the army.

Mother was in her parlor writing a letter. I didn't tell her goodbye, but I did leave her a note telling her that I was off to war in Virginia and that I should be back in time to assist Mr. Hartwick in overseeing the cotton picking and that I was bringing Neely with me as my valet. I explained that in the army it was customary for officers to bring personal servants with them. I underlined *officers*.

In Memphis, we boarded a train, and we rode for two days and two nights, east to where the trouble was, though we thought there would be little of it. Most were certain that the Yankees would see our numbers and our courage and elan, our precise and orderly marching and hear the manly shouts of our cheers, and they would be troubled. After a few days or weeks of bluffing, they would back down and we would come home victorious with scarcely a shot fired. We were certain of it.

Springtime in the South flashed past us, flowers blooming madly in every happy color. Neely had never ridden on a train before, and he put his head out the open window and said, "Jack, this here must be what it gone be like when you fly. Wind pullin' at you." I smiled because I thought it was possible, any good thing was possible in those days, indeed, not only possible but quite likely. Neely and I watched together with our faces at the window, the wind buffeting us and our confident smiles, our faces and skin and hair so different. We were off to camp in the woods for the summer, just two boys off on a lark.

In places of any size, more newly-minted soldiers boarded the train to the strains of hastily assembled bands, and the townspeople gave us lemonade and sugar biscuits. Night fell and the sun rose, and our procession continued east stopping at other towns to fill our train with high-spirited adventurers. We detrained somewhere in Virginia and began marching to our camp. The men sang the merry songs of men marching off to kill other men, but without the particulars of how this was to be accomplished, with no verses about gaping, festering wounds or bloody dysentery or men shot as deserters. Brass bands and bass drums hoarsely boomed out songs along country roads that before had only heard fiddle and banjo. People turned out along those dusty thoroughfares as we passed by, women and children who gave us drinks of water and cold milk, and old men who gave draughts of whiskey from jugs. They were auspicious times.

That first night we were in Virginia, Neely and I made camp with the rest of our regiment. It was a cool, late spring night with crickets chanting in the trees at the edge of our field. This sound was soon supplanted by the chorus of snoring and coughing and low singing. After an hour or two of trying to ignore these sounds as they rumbled in the dark, I asked Neely with a chuckle, "how you feel about spending a summer listening to that?"

You see, Father, we only thought we would be away for a few months at the longest. 'Back in time for the harvest,' was the saying. Neely said nothing, and I assumed he was already sleeping soundly. I turned on my cot and fell asleep to the night murmur of the encampment.

I woke to discover that Neely had left in the night. At first I was worried that he had been captured somehow. Though it was implausible, I wanted to believe this rather than the more likely possibility that he had left on his own will, that he had had a small sip of freedom, and now he wanted a deep draught of it.

I could have sent out an alarm over an escaped slave, but I didn't, not until several days later when I knew he had had a good head start and when our captain questioned where my valet had headed off to. I told him that Neely had returned to Mississippi, that he had seen me off, which had been his intention, and that he was missing his mama.

"Hope he's got a pass, otherwise he might get picked up and sold."

Picked up and sold. It was then that I wish I had written him one. I could have, couldn't I? I thought. And he could have asked me, and I would have done it. Now I was afraid that he would be captured and sold and that I might never see him again. I was a young man then, far from home and suddenly alone. I missed him more than I thought I would, possibly to the degree that he missed me when I left for West Point. On those long nights looking up at stars and night-clouds, I realized that my dear ones were not my indifferent mother, but our slaves, those people we owned and whose continued bondage I had come half a continent to defend. I wondered how they were fairing back home, if they would be liberated by Federal troops, and if they were, would they run off like Neely. But those thoughts were dismissed then. This scrap would only last a little while, and we would, of course, be victorious, and I would see them all next autumn. I was sure of it. We were all sure of it. Home in time for the harvest.

We broke camp and moved again, but my eyes couldn't help searching the passing fields for Neely, perhaps emerging from the woods with the prize of a rabbit and the news that he had gone to fetch us some meat other than the boiled beef we ate. But the fields and tree-lines were empty of him. And so I let him go, in my mind. And I wished him well, a life of freedom of movement and association. Like anyone would wish for a friend.

The other lieutenant in our company became my companion on the march. His name was Homer Prentiss, and I will admit that of the two of us, he was the favorite of our company. He was about my age and had freckles on his forearms and face and neck, the mark of a boy who had spent a great deal of time outdoors, a farm boy as opposed to a clerk in a dry goods store or a law office. I never knew much about his past, his upbringing, his schooling, any of that. He could read and had a grasp of mathematics and the sciences. He was a decent sort of boy, a sincerely polite boy with a head of auburn hair that shined on marches when we sweated under the midday sun. He had a quiet humility that was as much a part of his makeup as his honest brown eyes.

He was popular because he would not eat until all of his men had scooped their tin cups into the big iron pot set out by the cooks. Only then would he do it and not before. He never rode among the men, perched above these common soldiers, but walked his horse among them. The men knew it and loved him for it. He never said it, but it was clear that he believed that the best men lead by example, just as most men learn by example. His horse was an old nag with a simple saddle, not the fancy sort of saddle I had, fashioned by an expensive craftsman in Memphis with my initials, *AJT*, embossed into the leather. His was made by some local tanner with rawhide stitching and simple construction. His company was quiet and easy as we walked among the aroma of horses and unwashed men and Virginia earth.

Though I received few letters from home, he never received any, and I always assumed he didn't have family. So he and I would pass time, talking about things. Once, when we spotted a reconnaissance balloon overhead, Homer asked me, without looking away from the stick he was whittling, "Do you think man'll ever fly? Without a balloon, I mean?"

"Maybe," I said.

His knife pulled up a thin shaving of white wood. It curled away from the gray bark and fell to the ground with the others. Homer reached down and tossed them all into the campfire.

"Would you fly, if you could?" he asked.

"Yeah, I believe I would," I said, but I didn't add that it had been a dream of mine for as long as I could remember. "Would you?"

"Naw," he said, tossing the stick into the campfire, "I'm scared of heights."

I looked up into the blue Virginia summer sky and watched the birds circle in the air, higher even than the balloon. I had the habit of watching the sky. By day, the clouds and the birds and the way the wind moved the tops of trees and the smoke from our campfires, by night, the moon and stars and the constellations, Orion, the Big Dipper, Cassiopeia. This was in the early days of the war, when everything had the same sense as a prolonged hunting trip or a surveying expedition, the enemy only spoken of in vague terms.

The seriousness of the whole affair turned on a single event. Before we even caught sight of the enemy, it fell to Homer and me to complete an unpleasant task. A man in our company had had second thoughts about the whole thing and had quietly slipped off, intending to head back to Mississippi. This man was a few years older than the other simple privates and also older than Homer and me, and maybe he was just wise enough to see that this wasn't going to be the simple school picnic in the country like it had been advertised to us. He had a wife and children and a farm, and the call of them was too strong and he slipped away like Neely had but was caught.

The trial for desertion took all of fifteen minutes. The colonel of our regiment presided with several of the other higher-up officers. The man could offer no account for himself, and there was no exoneration. The sentence was passed down not only to him, but to Homer and me, as we were the ones to carry it out.

I would like to say that I would have taken his place, this family man whose only crime was yearning for his own fields and hearth, but I did not. Instead, he was tied to a hickory tree and a blindfold was put on him. He breathed heavily, whimpering staccato breaths as he waited for the percussion and the thud. I asked him for his last words, as the regulations called for, though this was the first of this sort of business that I had been involved with. He could get out only these three words before he fell into a shuddering sob: *tell my wife—*

The drums rolled and there was a staggered cracking of the guns and a plume of gray-white powder spent in the cause of liberty. The homesick father and husband slumped between the trunk and his bindings, staring into the eternal darkness of his blindfold. Another detail of men was charged with putting him in the box made for the occasion, and he was fed to the earth. I wrote his widow a letter, one surely to be read to his children by a hearth with a vacant chair. I imagined an older son, perhaps no more than twelve, elevated into the role of man of the house, his true childhood now only a brief passage in his life.

And in the letter, I violated the Honor Code of West Point. I lied and said that this husband and father had died a brave man defending his hearth and fields. It was at that moment, even before we had heard the first shot of enemy fire, that I realized that this entire thing was a bad bargain. The whole business was changed for me and maybe for all of us. We could see the seriousness of the matter. This was not a game, not a turkey shoot, and certainly not a school picnic in the country. But I was in for a penny and in for a pound. All of us were.

Eva

The nap I took that day was like no other nap I had ever had, profound and intense, as if everything and everyone, Pappy, Granny, and I, all of us, were underwater. It was the end of a long, hot summer, and dark clouds boiled up into the sky. It might have rained that day, but for that matter it might have snowed or hailed and I would have been oblivious to it. I vaguely remembered the ride down Texas Street and the big blue-gray clouds that drew heat and moisture from the earth and held them high above our heads. The wagon we were in rocked us as we lay in its bed. That we were all lying down together was in itself odd. It was a strict rule in our household that everyone kept to their own bed and that children didn't lie down with adults.

The wagon stopped rocking and creaking, and I was carried up some stairs, the first of many times I would be taken up those stairs. I was laid in a bed with my grandparents on either side, probably on the faulty assumption that our little family was one of warmth and affection and that we would be comforted by being together. The window was open to the river, but there were no sounds of men shouting and snapping whips or mules braying and hawing or steam engines chugging and horns blasting. There were only the sounds in the house, sounds of coughing and retching and heaving and quick footsteps on the stairs outside our room, and the tinkle of the bell on the front door announcing that someone else had been brought in.

It was certainly ironic that such a God-fearing man as my Pappy should have his small household deposited there. Perhaps by luck the next carriage would have taken us to a more acceptable location, a private home or a church. Better the Grand Opera House or the Methodist Church, or, for that matter, the pews of the Catholic Church or the Jew Temple. Anywhere other than Miss McCune's 'boardinghouse' for young ladies. My grandparents would have been horrified if they had known we had been taken there of all possible places. I have often wondered how my life might have turned out if we had been driven somewhere else. But it is no matter now. Fate had dealt the cards evenly, the indifferent spin of a roulette wheel, and my grandparents were in no shape or position to protest. I suspect they were too sick to even know where we had ended up.

That September 1873, certain places were being established as houses of aide, and we had been taken into the home and business of Miss Annie McCune, a woman of notorious fame in Shreveport at the time, as she is to this day. She was young, and petite and pretty enough, though now I understand she has more than tripled in size. Ha! I have only doubled!

The girls of the house had been promoted by necessity to nurses, and they came and went in my watery vision carrying towels and water pitchers and basins. Pappy always harrumphed and Granny clicked her tongue when the house on Commerce Street was discussed. They said that Miss McCune ran a 'house of sin,' but they never expounded on what that sin was. At that age, I thought the transgressions of the inhabitants were merely gaiety and cheerfulness. Now we found ourselves unwitting inmates of that house, and in my delirium I thought that the girls were painted as gaily as clowns, quite as if one were caught in an opium dream at the circus. The doctor came and went, peering at me and Pappy and Granny with a look of concern as he pinched our wrists and glanced at his watch and lifted our eyelids and pursed his lips. For all of it, I didn't care a fig.

Pappy was sleeping soundly and still, without snoring, which was very odd, for he was quite a beast when it came to his snoring. It occurred to me later that he was dead then or nearly so. But no sooner had I noticed him than I slept again. The garishly dressed women of the place continued to attend to us, hurrying around with basins and cloths. All commerce with gentlemen was ended during that time of sickness. I slept like Lazarus in the grave, waking to see these fascinating creatures, angel-women painted like carousel ponies. Night fell and then it was sunny again, terribly hot and still, and then night fell again with its cloying heat. I had preposterous dreams, full of absurdities, of clowns riding carousels and talking horses and my Pappy and Granny laughing and dancing.

I awoke to the feel of soil scattered on my face, the sprinkle of it like earthy rain. I must have moved, swatted at my face, or brought my arm up or something, because a man sweaty-black threw down his shovel and ran down into the pit where I was and exclaimed, "this'n here still alive, boss!" I was handed up one man to another and smelled the tang of perspiring bodies leaked into clothes. I was escorted out of the hole in the earth, past a man and woman whom I dimly recognized as Mr. Bissinger the saddlemaker and his wife, both of them sad-faced and wet-cheeked looking down into the crater. I was thrown over a shoulder and when I looked back into the burial pit, there among the bodies was a head of blonde hair as fine as cotton and the color of blanched wheat. I thought, 'that doll down there looks like Willie. Who made a doll to look like him, and exactly his size?'

A check on the other bodies in the pit was performed, including those of Willie and my grandparents. They were judged to be thoroughly departed, and the earth was laid upon them and I was taken back up among those who were yet living. With no place else to go and still quite sick, I was returned to

Commerce Street in the plush black seat of a carriage through a quiet city still under quarantine. The sawmill across Commerce Street by the bank of the river was silent, the church bells were silent, the levee was silent. That summer and fall, 1873, Shreveport lost almost a fourth of its inhabitants and resembled a ghost town, peaceful and macabre.

I was put back to bed and promptly fell asleep again. Another child was brought into the bed with me but then was gone. Again I slept, and in a day or two or a week, I woke and asked for my grandparents. The girl who had been giving me spoonfuls of brandy sent for Miss McCune, who came in and sat on my bed and took my hand. Hers was fine and soft.

"Your grandparents are no longer among the living," she said. She said it as many people did then, not as an apology or a condolence, but as a sad and solid fact, much in the way of 'People die and people live, and the survivors get on with the business of living.'

Then she asked me, "Do you have other family?"

I shook my head no.

She looked out the window at the Red River, mud-scented and cinnamon-colored. Twin smokestacks of a boat drifted by. Traffic was beginning to move again now that the fever was moving on. She directed her words to the window.

"I suppose we should take you to an asylum."

She meant an orphanage, but I thought she meant an asylum such as my mother was in, one with shrieking and babbling half-naked people covered in their own filth. Gwendolyn Mosey had heard a rumor, well-founded, that my mother was in one and had been all too willing to gleefully paint a very vivid picture for me. After she'd told me, I had held my tears until I got home.

"No, don't make me go," I said to Miss McCune. "I'd rather stay here with you."

Miss McCune turned from the window and looked at me.

"Do you know what goes on here, dearie?" she asked.

"You entertain people who are lonely," I said innocently.

She looked down to her rings as her fingers toyed with the pearl pendant that rested on the smooth skin of her upper chest. The house was so quiet that day, though I didn't appreciate it then, not until I experienced it in one of its more vigorous moods with laughter and giggling and the tinkling notes of the piano downstairs and the wheeze of bed springs behind closed doors.

"All right," she said. "But no one lives for free, not in this house, this town, or this world. You'll have to pull your weight." And so began my days on Commerce Street.

When I was strong enough, we rode in her carriage, as nice as any in Shreveport, and we stopped in front of our old rooms above Phelps Brothers on Texas Street. I was still weak, and the stairs were like an ascent up Everest. As Miss McCune stood at the door, I floated through the emptiness.

Relics of our former life were everywhere. Pappy's Bible and *Pilgrims Progress*, his dark wool suit and his white linen one. He had been buried in his nightshirt, I suppose. Granny's knitting, her simple frock and bonnet, her stove and skillet and teakettle, three plates, three cups, three spoons. Their bed, my cot, my clothes, my doll and her parasol. I took the doll and my parasol, and I left everything else.

On the way back to Commerce Street, we stopped at Hearne's and Miss McCune had me fitted for nice clothes, including a new dress for every day of the week. It was in a back room behind a curtain, a room that I never knew existed. The merchants of town all liked doing business with Miss McCune, it was lucrative, but it also carried an element of shame, hence, the curtained-off back room that few knew about. I had lost weight, and Miss Annie knew this. A few days later, when the first of the new dresses arrived, I found that my new clothes hung on me in anticipation of the return of my weight. Within a month, the clothes fit perfectly. Miss McCune was always quite savvy when it came to the future and a girl's figure.

She employed a cook named Minnie, which was a misnomer, because Minnie had a frame so immense that it obscured the stove in the kitchen. Miss McCune made it clear from the start that I was to obey Minnie and give her whatever assistance she asked for. My grandparents would have turned over in the grave they shared with so many of Shreveport's townspeople if they had known they had died in a brothel, and they would have given another turn if they knew that their granddaughter was taking orders from a member of the darker race.

One of my jobs was to run to the henhouse and gather eggs whenever Minnie told me to. The chickens nested in brown and white lumps with their heads on their chests. There was a snow white one that looked like my Granny, and so I called her Granny. She was ill-tempered and would jab her beak at me when I tried to lift her to retrieve her egg. I held her away from my face, sure that she would peck an eye if given the chance. I wasn't raised with them, or at least, not raised to have to deal with them. Vile creatures.

Miss McCune also had a hired man, a light-skinned negro named Foster. He chopped wood and cared for her horse and carriage, and on those late nights, he escorted drunken patrons to a nearby saloon. It was better to be arrested for drunkenness there than at the brothel. It was a clear rule: no one ever died or was arrested at Miss McCune's. Patrons were quietly taken elsewhere for those sorts of things.

I may have battled the chickens over their eggs, but my main job was to carry water and empty the chamber pots, as these were the days before indoor plumbing. When commerce resumed on Commerce Street, I changed sheets dozens of times a night. A laundryman came every morning to fetch the dirty ones in a specially fitted black carriage with *Excelsior Laundry* written in fancy gold letters on the side. At that point I still didn't know what the girls in this house did for a living, but in time I would find out of the secret purpose of flesh and the strange new language of ecstasy like trumpets blown by the lungs of angels. New bedsheets waited in every cabinet and chifforobe in that house, stacks and stacks of sheets, thick and soft and of high quality that came in the delivery wagon of the Excelsior Laundry. One of my jobs was to take them when they were delivered and stow them away in the places where they were kept. I also brought up the laundered clothing of the girls, the fine dresses with flounces and ruffles in taffeta and velvet, and frilly, silky, lacy stockings and drawers and sheer gowns.

Every night I made beds one after the other and well into the night, unsure what the girls and the gentlemen were doing to get the sheets in such tangles. Maybe, I thought, they were having pillow fights or tickle fights or jumping on the bed. If I didn't move fast enough in getting the rooms ready, the girls would clap their hands and scold me to hurry while their gentleman callers would look away. After the rumpus inside, the door would open to the gentleman straightening his jacket and the girl fixing her hair, I would scurry inside to collect the messy sheets and bring them downstairs to a bin at the back door, a bin as big as a bale of cotton that waited the Excelsior man's arrival the next morning.

Most men came in through the front door with the tinkle of the bell, but there was a class of men whom Miss McCune and the girls called 'side door men.' They were the same nicely dressed men I would see on the plank sidewalks of Texas Street, cotton brokers and bankers and merchants. They were men who sat in the foremost pews of the churches and at least one of them was a minister. None of them, neither front-door nor side-door men, ever brought their wives with them, nor did women of any age come for the music and refreshments in the downstairs parlor. I thought this unfair. Women would have enjoyed the comfortable couches and chairs and the piano music as much as men would. Naiveté, Mrs. Leonard, the bread-and-butter of youth.

Miss McCune was fair and generous with me when it came to money, and if I got up early enough, I might spend an hour or two in the shops before reporting back to Commerce Street for an afternoon and night of changing beds and filling pitchers and basins. I walked proudly down Texas Street on those mornings, painted and dressed like a doll by the girls of the house, a pet to them, though still not understanding the shame and derision and admiration the town had for them.

One Saturday morning I was standing in front of Mr. Bissinger's saddlery shop, thinking of the times that Willie and I sat and watched his father stitch leather pieces together. It was empty now, for as soon as the quarantine was lifted, Mr. Bissinger and his family had departed to somewhere out west, and I never saw them again. It occurred to me then, only ten, that the people in our lives are as temporary as guests for tea, keeping company with us for a short time, an hour, a year, or fifty years. Then each of us parts ways with the other. Even our health flees from us. It is only our wealth that remains faithful to us to the end. If we are faithful to it. Of course, that is why you are here, Mrs. Leonard, to help me reunite with it.

That morning as I looked through the window at the empty workshop, I was approached by Polly Calhoun and Gwendolyn Mosey. They seemed hesitant to say anything at first. Perhaps they thought that I had left town or, better yet, that I had died and was buried in the mound of Yellow Fever victims and that I was my own ghost. The Mosey family had left town, sneaking past the quarantine set up by the army, and removed to Monroe. They were too late, however and had brought the sickness with them and been ostracized by the townspeople there. They had all survived and returned to Shreveport as if nothing had happened.

They asked me why I wasn't in school on Travis Street or living in the apartment on Texas. I replied that I was living in a house out in the country with a rich uncle and being taught by a private tutor and that I was asked not to associate with inferior girls any longer. I turned and drummed away on the wooden planks, leaving them speechless.

The truth was, Miss McCune had one of her older girls, Alma, tutor me in my studies. I say older, but she was only in her early twenties at most. She had brown hair and eyes, and she smoked, holding the cigarette in the fingers of one hand while she pointed out flaws in my studies, the fuming cigarette indicating where I had failed to carry the one in my addition or that the rule was *i* before *e* except after *c* in my spelling. If I did well with my assignments, she would nonchalantly give me a cigarette, and we would smoke them together, even though I was ten. Alma was vague about where she was from, vague about what she wanted from life, vague about what occurred upstairs. When I asked her, she tilted her head back and blew smoke up to the ceiling and laughed. Then she put her hand to my cheek and gave me a look that was equal parts sadness, irony, and compassion. But she wouldn't say anything, no matter how many times I asked. But I would find out soon enough about the other tasks a girl might take up in a boardinghouse for young women.

Jack

Good afternoon, Michael. I had to ask the ship's doctor for something for seasickness. It worked pretty well, but I'm afraid it provoked a long nap that was only broken when I smelled cigarette smoke and overheard some of the Canadian soldiers through the porthole of my berth. They said they heard that after stops in Queenstown and Southampton they'll disembark in France. LaHavre, I believe they said. I'm sure they'll arrive wide-eyed at the grand adventure before them, something to tell their grandchildren about if they live through it. From LaHavre, they'll board trains and go to Paris where more than a few will drink wine and flirt with French girls. Some will fall in love, and some, I'm sure, will just visit the brothels. A few might go to the Louvre or the Luxembourg Gardens or the Tuileries. Then they'll all be put on rail cars again and head to the front where they'll discover the real reason and purpose for their being there. How soon before they meet the enemy, I wonder? I certainly remember my first encounter. No soldier ever forgets it, the feeling that something in the very center of you is threatened, an instinct that all living things share.

I can scarcely believe that it's been over fifty years that we were marched forward and set to wait on our adversary. We stood there in a line, a string of faces set on shoulders of different heights and widths. There were no smiles on those faces, no laughing, no joking, no songs from those lips now tightly closed as ears strained and eyes searched for what could be in the Virginia woods waiting for them.

And then we saw them, blue and brass within the backdrop of green. I lifted my field glasses to my eyes and I could see the same expressions on their faces that I saw on my own men. I could see a few of their boys mumbling something, certainly prayers or maybe sick, sad jokes. I put my field glasses back in their case, lest I become attached to those men over there. Boys, rather. Let me call them what they were, Father. They were boys. Just like our boys. All of them sold an idea and hurried to it by the pressure of their peers, a force like something geologic about to become volcanic.

No sooner had I looked up than a voice shouted small in the distance and the first shots popped and smoke rose into the air like a steam engine sputtering to life. Our captain gave the order to fire and I repeated it like a parrot and a sound erupted, that sound, like being inside a cloud during a thunderstorm. And then the smoky breath of an angry god. And then the order to advance with the roll of the drums.

There is a sound of men running toward battle, a clatter of the things they are carrying, the brush of their pants legs, the quickening of their breathing from equal parts fear and exertion, their footfalls battering the ground, the whisk of the earth pushed up by their shoes. Voices are hushed, though some murmur and some whine in fear like the complaint of a dog, all these small sounds becoming part of the same voice, the voice of impending violence.

Then the violence is there, the cracking of rifles and the smell of burned powder, and the whiz of hot hail, falling sideways, at them and at us, at everything living and dead. Bullets ripping at the air and the leaves. The grunts of those hit, some dying before they could begin the serious work of begging for water or their mamas or for death to hurry. Men are picked up, some are sent to the rear to be fixed. Surgeons hurry, their aprons splotched with the blood of farm boys who wouldn't be home in time for the harvest. Some are dead and some will die. And then their lieutenant must write a letter home for them which is just what I did, time and time again.

Pardon my macabre thoughts, Father. Perhaps I was dreaming of this after my sedative for sea sickness, but these Canadian boys have no idea, no sense of what they face, nor did most of the ones who sent them. People have an intrinsic ingratitude, complaining though they have plenty to eat and a warm place to sleep and people who love them, while they have no appreciation of the hells which they've been spared. But I have seen them. I have seen perhaps the worst of them.

After that first battle, having driven off the enemy, we sat around our campfires and tried to inure ourselves to the moans of the suffering in the dark and tried to understand the losses, to convince ourselves that the missing ones had only slipped off home. Otherwise the injury was too great to bear.

That first battle was a victory. There were others that were losses. Our ranks thinned but were replenished by others from home. A year passed and there were more battles and rain and cold and heat and then more battles. I wrote letter after letter home, to the point that during spare time, I composed a letter that was merely a form letter where a name could be placed. I kept at least ten of these letters ready to have the name filled in when it was needed.

I myself rarely received a letter from home, and when I did, my mother spent two sentences asking how I was and imploring me to do my duty for Mississippi and our country. Her words hinted that I might not remember to do it if I wasn't reminded to. The rest of her letter was a glowing report that my brother had been promoted to major in the Home Guard and that his health was good and that he had managed to get a crop in and that his wife had had another child, another girl. There were several things that his daughters had said that she found endearing and she spent several paragraphs recounting the things they did and said. Then there was more about the splendor of my brother's estate and that she was able to visit and with God's help would do so again if the bloodthirsty Yankees could be held off. I wrote her and told her that there was talk of a captaincy for me, perhaps just a few months away, if our own captain were to fall in battle or be promoted. In the few letters I received, she never acknowledged it, and I stopped mentioning it altogether.

I did, however, receive a few letters from my niece, Jenny, my brother's oldest. She was perhaps seven or so, just old enough to write. They were sweet missives written in the hand of a child, large, looping characters filled with kind sentiment and misspellings. She was learning to play the 'vilin.' Her mother was going to have a new 'babby' and her daddy wanted it to be a boy. Her mother was teaching her to 'emberodery.' In short, her letters were what you would expect, wonderfully disjointed with a new subject discussed in each sentence. At the bottom of each was a short line from my sister-in-law telling me that she was praying for my health and safety. She seemed to be a nice person, though I never really knew her. I found out later that she died in childbirth, and I believe it was with the next child, her third girl. I wrote them back and then they wrote me again and so forth until my military career ended two years later in Pennsylvania.

Would you like some coffee or tea, Father?

Pardon me, Mr. Steward, would you kindly bring a coffee for me and tea for this young man I call Father?

But about the army and battle. There are two things that men who are about to face death do, Father. They pray and they joke. Some do both. Some of our boys were simple and some were educated, though most were simple. Simple men who would never have much, let alone own other men to do their work for them. As the drums rolled and rifles clicked and officers shouted orders, some prayed, some recited scripture. A favorite was the 91st Psalm, *"he that dwelleth in the secret place of the most High shall abide under the shadow of the Almighty. I will say of the Lord, He is my refuge and my fortress: my God, in him I will trust."*

Others favored the 144th, *"Blessed be the Lord my strength which teacheth my hands to war, and my fingers to fight, my goodness, and my fortress; my high tower, and my deliverer; my shield, and he in whom I trust; who subdueth my people under me."* Still others recited quietly through trembling lips Psalm 18, *"The Lord is my rock, and my fortress, and my deliverer."*

Those who didn't pray often made jokes to keep a light heart. They joked that they were headed over to trade Billy some tobacco for some coffee if they had any over there and did you want any if they did? Or that the fish weren't biting, so he thought he'd run an errand. They were wry jests at best and no one laughed. All eyes were on the line of blue across the way.

Then the woods would begin to rustle and stir, and rabbits, deer, and squirrels ran past us to the rear. It seemed as though every creature in God's creation was fleeing in a scampering stampede as if the flood were coming and they were late for the ark. The cracking and popping of gunshots filled the air with cheers and groans and shouting.

When it was all over, in what would seem somewhere between an eternity and a minute, one side found itself in the possession of the small plot of land, a small fraction of the earth's surface. Men were killed, and the wounded were sent to field hospitals where little could be done for them. Hospital tents were pitched over earth that would become muddy with blood. And then the quiet returned, and then boredom settled in again.

In those lulls, many men received mail, though Homer and I weren't among them. I certainly *sent* a great deal of mail, however. I wrote letters of condolence to families, without regard to the guiding compass of the Honor Code. All of the fallen had died as patriots to their country and its cause, that cause being that no one can tell us who we can own and what we can make them do. In those lulls between battles, some men died and some deserted. Gradually, they were replaced by younger men barely past boyhood and older men well into middle-age. It had long become clear to all of us that the war would not be over in a few months. Farms would be tended by women and children, and the heavy work would be done by old men, while the most able-bodied fought.

All the while, the army was followed by another army, one composed of camp followers, preachers and sutlers, loose women and gamblers. I sought the company of none of them. Rather, I read every scientific tract I could get my hands on and studied the sky.

Summer came again and we were marched north. The corn in the field was beginning to tassel, nudged by the summer breeze in the bright light of midday. We marched on until the faces we passed watched us with scowls and spit on the ground. We were in hostile territory.

During this time, our captain died, not leading a valiant charge or capturing enemy field pieces but by cholera, his life leaking out from his bowels while the regimental surgeons stood by with no answer. As he dwindled, I had the selfish thought that now I might be made captain and how pleased my mother would be to hear it.

While the captain was feeling the deadly weight of cholera, we received word that the enemy was on our flank. We were drawn up in line of battle listening for our adversaries. The silence was oppressive, a ruse that we all knew was hiding something. We had all heard it before, the shrieking quiet. I assembled our company in line of battle and was thinking that with a good showing, I might have the leg-up on Homer in the bid for captain.

A crow cawed off in the trees, and the quiet pushed around us again. Then there was a distant crack, no more sound than a limb breaking a quarter mile away. Gunshots began popping and cracking, and gray smoke lifted up into the trees across the way. The order to fire was given on our side, and blue-gray smoke lifted up over the fields like a thundercloud. Men were jamming ramrods down barrels and then peering down them at any possible targets. I was pacing behind them, up and down the ranks as volley after volley snapped. Homer was nowhere to be seen. I was hoping the colonel of our regiment was watching through his field glasses.

Men fell and men ran, and still I exhorted them to do their duty to God and Mississippi. I kept looking around for our other lieutenant, Homer Prentiss. At first I didn't see him and I assumed that he had run off also and I rejoiced that, if I survived the battle, I would surely get the captaincy. The smoke of thousands of guns obscured the sunlight and I worked to bolster our sagging lines.

And then I found Homer. He was slumped over a split-rail fence, his hat fallen on the ground on the other side and his auburn hair glossy from his sweat. Just then I heard them, the shouts of the men who were advancing toward us in a blue wave with the flag whose honor I had sworn to uphold, the American flag. Our lines managed to fire a volley and then the majority broke and ran, leaving me exhorting the remainder to stand fast. Bullets began to clip limbs above my head. Blue men swarmed from every direction, save one, to the rear and left. Our flank was turned and we were being routed. I was about to run myself when I heard a voice.

"You ain't gonna leave me, are you, Jack?"

It was Homer Prentiss. I had presumed him dead. It was the first time he had ever addressed me as anything other than "Lieutenant." He suddenly sounded like any other Mississippi farmer's boy, which he must have been, but since he never received any mail I had no idea. An odd thought that here was one letter that I wouldn't have to write as I had no idea who it would be to. It had always worried me a measure that he was alone in the world, an orphan in a universe that was indifferent to him, until he joined in with the great family of men that made up the Confederate Army.

I couldn't leave him behind, I couldn't let him be orphaned by the Confederate Army. I shouldered Homer Prentiss and ran for it. I could feel a certain wetness on my shoulder and back, and, as I ran with him, I wondered if I was feeling his blood or his sweat or his intestines. It was a fleeting thought, quickly covered over by the terror I felt. Bullets pocked the trees to my left and right and I was certain that one would pock me and I would fall with my burden and we would both slowly become mounds of flies and then flesh-tattered skeletons, the kind we had seen on year-old battlefields. A violent death was right behind me, its mangled claws pawing at my heels. I thought of the letter my mother would receive back home in Mississippi. She might weep a tear at finding that I had died in the service of my country. Perhaps she would have a tintype made in her mourning veil, the widow's lace obscuring her damp cheeks and sagging mouth, with my portrait in her lap and a handkerchief to her eyes.

I ran with Homer on my back until I found a secluded spot and laid him down, my back still warm and wet. I looked into his face, and his face looked out and away past me and into the sun and I knew he was gone.

I sat with him for a while as if I thought he might have some final words of wisdom for me or that we might discuss the flight of birds or balloons or our plans when this God-forsaken spectacle was over. But our days of easy conversation were over. And so I found a wooded place, peaceful and secluded, and I laid him in it with his hands fixed over his chest, as if he were plunging into the water of a favorite swimming hole. I read some words from the Testament about goodness and mercy following us all the days of our lives, words from the old Twenty-third Psalm. The wetness on my back was drying, and I took off my coat, for it was July and hot, even for Pennsylvania. I covered Lt. Homer Prentiss with my jacket. When I turned around, I saw them, and when I saw them, I heard the hammer-clicks of several guns at once.

My hands went up and then slowly down when they demanded that I hand over my Colt revolver. I did as they said. A man whom I remember as a pimple face plebe a year behind me at West Point came close to me and said, "Well, then."

He had grown a mustache, but he still looked young, and if I saw him today, both of us in our seventies, I would likely still see him as a boy.

"It pains me to see that you are a traitor to the United States, Jack," he said.

And it pained me because he was right, I *was* a traitor to the United States. I was marched away like one with my hands on the top of my head and made to sit in a circle with other prisoners. Some smoked, some stared at the ground, but none of us said anything as we sat there and pondered what they might do to us. Suddenly we didn't look like our country's patriots. We looked like agitators with wild eyes and hair, sweaty and dusty, with our captors watching us, contemplating what should be done with us, imprisoned, shot, or hanged. I sat there in the circle with Homer Prentiss' dry, rust-brown blood on my shirt under the careful watch of a handful of northern farm boys.

A party of men had come and taken Homer Prentiss away for burial. I had wondered how I might be awarded a captaincy and still retain my friendship with him. In the space of a summer afternoon I had lost both.

Jack

We were marched off to the margin of the battlefield to a farmhouse with the bitter knowledge that our army had retreated south without us. The setting sun drew out our shadows and the night drowned them, and we lay like wide-eyed scarecrows in the barnyard of the house. The sounds of the wounded were distant, almost like the mewling of a litter of kittens. In the amber shadows I counted among our group of prisoners three Tunica County men:

Bibb, Tyner, and Sandifer. Their silhouettes were outlined in the campfires that our orange-faced captors sat around, watching us without blinking.

"Sir," Bibb whispered, "What you spose they gonna do with us? Reckon we'll get exchanged?"

"Shhh," I hissed in the firelight, "You ought not call me sir any longer. Y'all might get exchanged, but if they find out I'm an officer, they might just hang me. Better call me Jack from now on."

I had left my officer's tunic covering Homer Prentiss. Now I was in shirtsleeves and suspenders, nothing to signify that I was anything more than an enlisted man. When one of the Yankee soldiers guarding us asked, "Any among you an officer?" I kept my mouth shut.

But being hanged was only a small part of it. The bigger issue was the promise I had made to the people of Tunica County and myself that I would watch over their sons and husbands. If the Yankees found out I was an officer, they would, at the very least, separate these three from me, and I couldn't abandon them. I had led them into trouble, now I had to lead them out somehow. Staying with them is what Homer Prentiss would have done.

At daybreak, after a night of unsatisfying sleep, our eyes blinking in the darkness, we were formed up and marched through a hot, dusty summer day that only got hotter and dustier as the sun rose higher. We moved like despondent men with hungry families who had just been let go from a job. They shuffled us off to some unknown destination taunting us all the while, derisively referring to us as our heroes Jeff Davis, General Lee, Beauregard, and so forth. They also called us cruder names which I will not repeat, Father, as they nudged us along with the butts of rifles and the threatening points of bayonets. We could not so much raise our heads, let alone our fists. Men who had led singalongs of jaunty tunes of how we would hang Abe Lincoln from a sour apple tree were now forced to wonder if the same thing might be tried on us. At one point along the march, a voice within our ranks whimpered, petulantly asking if we were to be hanged. No one answered, and we all swore at the man under our breath for having asked the question in the first place. The silence contained only the sound of our feet on the dry road, and one of our guards simply growled, "Don't drag your feet, Stonewall Jackson. You're kicking up too much dust."

The Burden of Cane

After several days, we were marched through the streets of Baltimore past the silent stares of the townspeople to Fort McHenry and crowded within the casements next to Baltimore Harbor, our conversation burbling off the red brick ramparts over the possibility of cleaning up and being fed and then exchanged. We were more and more certain that it was just a matter of time. Within a few days, several hundred more men arrived, and the noise amplified. News of the recent battle was painted in cheerful enough colors, although those of us who had been there knew we had been routed and retreated in disgrace. Our biggest hope was to be repatriated south.

In a week or two we were placed on steamers and taken out into Chesapeake Bay. The wind whipped our scraggly hair and beards and we smiled against it. A sense of hope told us that now we would be taken across the way to Virginia and exchanged for northern prisoners. We were going home, certainly we were. Under escort of several Union gunships, we turned into the broad Potomac but stayed to the eastern shore. But instead of freedom on the Virginia side of the river, we were taken to Point Lookout, Maryland, a lonely outpost on a peninsula in Chesapeake Bay, an acute triangle with water on two sides and the Union Army on the other.

The Stars and Stripes whipped and lapped lazily in the summer sky. We looked up at it, the flag of our former country now the flag of our sworn enemies and captors. At the wharf, we were nudged forward onto the landing with rifle butts and bayonets and cursing and then marched in loose order through a grove of pine trees. The four of us Tunica County men stuck together with our hands on each other's shoulders. We were stripped and inspected, then we dressed again and were issued a moldy old Sibley tent. At first it was ample for the four of us, so that we could cluster together on one side and so avoid the holes that poured rainwater that boiled up off the bay. We found a layer of clay under the sand and mud, and we made bricks in the sun and then a simple chimney of the bricks. We were determined to make it a home, though we all assumed that it wouldn't be for long.

But the days began to slip into weeks and the weeks into months. At first, when the weather was hot, I stayed in the shade, reading whatever I could get my hands on, usually a newspaper or from a tract, the Psalms and part of the New Testament, the Acts of the Apostles. When I had read everything several times, I watched the ships pass up and down the bay. Every now and then, a stingy breeze would blow only to vanish after only a few seconds of relief from the smell of sweat and urine and filth. Within a month, the breeze turned on us and began carrying the stench of the latrines perched over the water. The winds that swept off the bay conspired with high tides to flood the whole of the prison, and we woke with water in our tents and wet blankets, so we took cracker boxes to make a floor for the parts of our tent where we slept.

Soon, a second inundation came—more prisoners flooding into the camp. The few short avenues of tents grew in length and number with each reverse of our armies as more and more captured men were packed into the space. Our tent of four took on eight, then twelve, and then fifteen, mostly Alabama and Georgia men. The forty or so acres of prison now held hundreds of tents and thousands of men.

The food may have been passable, but the wells inside the stockade were poor, and diarrhea and other fluxes ran through the camp faster than gossip. On rainy days, the foul ditches between tents overflowed, and the fifteen of us jammed into a corner of our tent like rats and filled our tin cups and bowls with the rainwater that poured through the hole in the roof. At night, guards would roam the yard with revolvers and shoot into tents if they heard noise, so we kept as quiet as a graveyard. In the almost two years I was confined to Point Lookout, I didn't see a single smile or hear a single laugh. The place had all the levity and good cheer of a funeral as the lighthouse on the very end of the point glowed over the trees and the hospital buildings, projecting their shadows onto the roofs of our tents.

Some of the imprisoned couldn't bear the thoughts of family and untended fields and the freedom that shimmered in the distance across the bay. During the time we were granted to go through the three stockade portals to bathe in the bay, these men would begin swimming and simply not stop, even as the shots raised plumes of water around them and gunboats patrolled the bay.

The other, less honorable, way to leave Point Lookout was to go and see the provost marshal to take the oath of allegiance to the United States and be released. No man ever announced he was going to do it. He simply had a word with the Yankee officer of the day and walked through the gates. He never looked at the rest of us, and when he had departed, no one was allowed to speak his name again. It was understood that the man taking the oath would never have any social standing when he returned home, whether it be Texas, Virginia, or anywhere in between.

Like any other army encampment, there was reveille every morning, taps every night, inspection of our quarters on Sundays, and a crushing boredom that filled every minute in between. We lounged under the sun or in our tents or in their doorways or in their shade. Those who had anything printed read, whether it be portions of a Bible or a penny novel or a month old newspaper. More than a few gambled, and after breakfast and a period of cleaning the camp while our quarters were inspected, the men passed the rest of the day gambling for crackers, the currency of prison life. They played card games like chuck-a-luck, vantoon, seven-up, faro. They raced lice from the center of a hot tin dish. They bet each other if the next ship plying the bay would be heading in or out to sea, or if it would be a sailing ship or a steamship. All the while on the stockade ramparts, boy soldiers with new rifles paced and spat and looked out over the bay to see what we were looking at and then gave us a scowl that said we shouldn't be wasting our time with the notion of freedom. I tried not to concern myself with such unrealistic things and spent my time looking up into the colossal blue Chesapeake sky filled with squawking, chattering gulls and wispy clouds, both gulls and clouds floating high over the bay and the camp.

As the days shortened, the boredom was condensed. It became too cold to do anything but sit inside around the small fireplaces that could only be lit a few hours every other day due to lack of firewood. To make matters worse, there was bickering over the boxes of eatables sent by families, and those who were receiving them were now prohibited from it.

The earth revealed and obscured the moon, and the moon pushed and pulled the tides which found their way through the walls of the stockade to flood the prison. The nights turned colder and colder, and one morning we woke to a layer of silver frost on the ground and the lines of tents in the stockade. That was just the beginning of a hard winter. On a particularly cold night, I dreamed that I was chasing the jacket I left in Pennsylvania. I ran behind it as it flailed its armless sleeves and floated through fog over hills and through vast moonlit fields. At last, it turned and Homer Prentiss was wearing it. His expressionless face looked at me and his pale hands grabbed my shoulders and shook me rapidly. I awoke to find that I was only shaking from the cold.

Men began dying in the night at greater numbers, but I did everything in my power to see that my three men from Tunica held up. Out of necessity, the men of our tent began sleeping pressed together like a den of mice, none of us in any position to criticize the odor and grime that clung to each one of us. Snow fell, and the tides invaded and froze a layer of water beneath us and then receded back into the bay. I saved a little of my rations for my Tunica men and listened to them speak of the ones they left behind.

We could send and receive mail, and, once we were settled in our lodgings, as it were, I wrote letters home for my three, as Tyner and Sandifer could not read or write and Bibb, only a little. Letters from a prisoner were to follow strict rules. A single page, and any intimation of poor treatment would be stricken from the letter. Stationery and stamps could be bought from sutlers, as much a parasite to armies as lice, at a ten-fold markup. There was no dickering for a better deal. Take it or leave it. And so I told the Tyner, Sandifer, and Bibb families that their soldiers were holding up well, as they were brave men, and that we were being treated fairly. We were being given enough to eat, though the bread was so hard you couldn't scour a plate with it. I read the letters aloud to my three before sending them so that they might hear the good report furnished to their kinfolk. I myself did not write any letters home to Mother with the shameful news that I had been captured.

My three received letters from home, poorly spelled and with whimsical grammar but all filled with heartbreaking sentiment of empty chairs at sparsely set tables, fallow fields picked clean by moving armies, and lonely beds at night. My Tunica men listened silently as I read these lonesome missives from home, and, from their faces I could tell that these simple farmsteads were heaven to them. I began to wish that I had such a place, small children to come and hug my legs after a day of hard work, a table set with food prepared by loving hands, and a bed to warm with a soft-skinned angel.

Spring arrived on the bay and the camp swelled even further as the Confederate Army suffered reverse after reverse. Every new contingent of prisoners told stories of scant rations and desertions. Tyner began receiving letters from home with news that there was no one to sow the new crop. He had had all he could take and was homesick and hungry. By this time, of course, everyone among the living was homesick, but none more so than Tyner. He wept as he confided in me that he had two small children, two little girls at home in Mississippi, and he wanted to take the oath of allegiance and go home and that he might get home in time to put his corn in the ground. I told him I understood and that I would tell the others that he had escaped by floating across the bay in a barrel.

He quietly took leave of us while Bibb napped and Sandifer played chuck-a-luck, and the next day I whispered that Tyner had done exactly as we had agreed upon. All summer Bibb and Sandifer made Tyner the hero of every tale, a simple Mississippi private who could barely swim but who had managed to outwit the whole Union Army with simple determination and a barrel. It mattered little to Bibb and Sandifer that men were shot weekly trying to escape. To them, Tyner had made it, and they would hear all about it from Tyner himself when they were reunited on a front porch in Tunica County. I kept my lie, my violation of the Honor Code, to myself and let the two have their hope.

About this time the complexion of our guards changed. The New England men were sent off into battle with their r-less accents, and colored troops were set over us. These new guards took great delight at having authority over us men down in the pen. Their eagerness to use their guns caused us to be especially quiet at night lest we get a shot fired into our tents.

"Hey Reb, how you like to hear from this here gun Mr. Lincoln done gimme? Bottom rail on top now, ain't that right, Marse?"

On top of this outrage, when the weather first started to warm again, in April, our rations were cut, it was said in retaliation for conditions in southern prisons, though the rumor was that the camp commandant, Gen. Marston, was pocketing the unspent funds. By June, coffee was forbidden us, though our guards drank it atop the stockade walls in full view of us, lifting their cups in a toast to those of us who had none. And, on the Fourth of July, we were forced to stand outside of our tents, face the flag, and put our hands over our hearts and sing the Star Spangled Banner. In August, the sutlers were banished, those men with their stovepipe hats and frock coats and pushcarts loaded with overpriced goods that most could only covet. We were still fed twice a day, but the rations per man were reduced to three ounces of pork or beef or a thin bean soup. The food was routinely poor and to this day I will not eat soup if I can help it.

With food becoming scarce, we dined on rumors, which were plentiful. Rumors that gunboats had broken the blockade and were coming to free us, or the one that a division of our calvary had sacked Washington and was coming down the peninsula to free us. But the rumors were less nourishing than the weak soup they fed us. Eventually we laughed dryly at them, and then over time we could only give them a weak chuckle and then nothing. As summer slipped into autumn again, we became exactly what we were, a vast field of aimless men with nil chances of going home anytime soon. Wagons came to fetch the ones who had died still with a small spark of hope and those who had simply given up.

Having listened all summer to the heroic tale of Private Tyner's escape, on the last warm day of 1864, Bibb swam out into the bay in an attempt to copy the feat of Tyner. He began swimming, lured by the wavering image of the opposite shore. Guards shouted and shots cracked and sprays of water launched upward all around him. Yet on he swam as we watched him go, our hands shielding our eyes from the early autumn glare.

Bibb washed up two days later. He hadn't been hit once. He had simply tired and drowned.

Now, Bibb and Sandifer were not only good friends and neighbors, but also cousins who had been raised as brothers. After Bibb's bloated, crab-adorned body returned to Point Lookout, Sandifer sank into a depression, and the short days crushed him, body and spirit. Our rations were cut again, it was said in an attempt to get us to take the Oath. The prospect of another winter loomed over us like death itself. We were all weak, though Sandifer was especially so. At last, I traded my scant rations for a little brandy for Sandifer, but he only took a few sips and refused the rest. I knew I couldn't keep him alive much longer. Our rations were insufficient, and the coldest of winter was still ahead of us.

Then one evening I heard the clicking noise from my youth, the one that Neely and I used to make in the woods at night when we got separated, like the chirp of a cricket. I looked up into the sun but I couldn't make out who it was. I put my hands to my eyes and looked again at the figure with the gun standing guard over us. The light of the sunset glowed around the silhouette. Whoever it was wore sergeant stripes.

"Jack," the shadow hissed, "Jack? That you?"

"Yes," I croaked. "Neely?"

He didn't say yes or no, but only, "Come round here this side when the moon set. But don't cross that dead line yonder."

When the moon had cleared the tree line, I returned looking around in worry that I might get shot. Again his shadow was outlined against the light, and he made the cricket chirp. He turned and looked up and down the ramparts, then his shadow pointed to an area where there were no other prisoners and motioned that I go there. It was a low area that flooded frequently and was deserted because it still had ankle-deep water. I moved down to the place and looked back up to him. He looked to the other guards again and threw down a small sack tied with a string. I turned my back to the other prisoners as my shaking hands opened the strings. In it was a chunk of cornbread, still warm. I began eating. Halfway through it, I looked up, wanting to thank him, but he had moved down the parapet. I saved a little less than half and took it back to Sandifer. He was lying on his back with his fingers feeling his forehead and looking at the hole in the tent, all he ever did anymore. I gave him the warm cornbread. He only took a bite and would eat no more, so I finished it.

Neely's gifts continued. A generous hunk of salt meat. A small loaf of bread. Hoecakes like our slaves used to make in the field. A canteen too hot to handle except with the hem of my shirt. When I turned my back to the rest of the stockade and unscrewed the top, the delicious, brown-roasted aroma of coffee rose out. I was near tears as I looked up wanting to thank Neely without getting him in trouble.

Once he threw me an apple, the biggest, sweetest, fattest apple I have ever tasted. He touched the bill of his cap and looked out over the field of aimless men, who had barely looked up from the patches of ground they stared upon or their games of vantoon and faro. I held the apple close to my stomach and took it to my tent. I pulled off a chunk and gave it to Sandifer who took it with his dry lips. He chewed it slowly and held it in his mouth before a feeble swallow. I offered him another chunk, but he refused it, so I huddled under my blanket and ate all of it save the stem and seeds. Though I always saved a little more than half for Sandifer, he refused to eat or drink more than a dainty bite or a reluctant sip.

The days compressed us and the nights froze us. The ground crunched under our feet and the holes in our shoes registered small, ragged circles of cold on the bare skin of our soles. Neely and the other guards had fine blue cloaks to wear over their uniforms, and their breath steamed into the cold as they walked the parapet with the long points of rifle-shadows.

On the first cold night, after a day cold enough for us to hold our arms around ourselves, he clicked again. I looked up to the parapet like a dog awaiting a treat. Then an object obscured the yellow paleness of the moon and floated down. I looked both ways quickly and then pulled the object away from the dead line. I knew at once by the scent that it was the quilt made back home by the loving brown hands of Aunt Rosalie. Neely's voice then said, "Get on way from that line yonder, Reb." But he tipped his soldier's cap and made the cricket noise. I couldn't make it back, not with tearful eyes and dry lips.

"Gettin' transferred out," he hissed as loudly as he could and still keep it a whisper. "Guess this goodbye for sure. Lord keep you, Jack."

He walked down the parapet of the stockade and I looked up and watched him go. We never dared speak, but I'm convinced that Neely saved my life that winter. He would have saved Sandifer, too, had Sandifer not given up.

In the morning there were new black faces, delighted to have dominion over us, their former masters. They would say things like, "Look like Jeff Davis catchin' hell, now Marse" and their favorite, "Bottom rail on top now, ain't that right?"

I felt that if I could just hold on to spring, that I could save Sandifer. On those cold nights, I held him close to me under the quilt. He stayed in the tent all day and stopped eating altogether and said next to nothing. I awoke one morning to find his skin cold and his chest still. I picked up his body and when someone else offered to help me carry him, I refused. These were the wages for my sin and a promise unkept. I laid Sandifer out lovingly on the wagon near one of the gates and they took him to the burying ground up the peninsula. Then I went to the provost and took the oath.

I was taken across the Potomac and set free, and, unlike Lot's wife, I did not look back. It was April 1865. My twenty months at Point Lookout seemed twice as long as the decade I would spend on the railroad.

Well, there is the bell for dinner, Father. If we are served soup, you are certainly welcome to mine.

Jack

They released me on the Virginia shore, without a mount or a railroad ticket or a fare-thee-well, indeed, without shoes, and I was left to find my way home. I wandered west amid the desolation, a man plodding through a landscape that had been bled dry of men, men who had tried to make this place a new country only to have it remain part of the United States. Lonely women were everywhere, doing the tasks that men had once done, plowing fields and splitting firewood and only pausing to watch with pleading eyes as I wandered alone.

I found him stuck in a blackberry patch. He was a nondescript little rust-brown cur with white markings including the shape of a bowtie or a bone or an hourglass on his forehead. I didn't know where he had come from, only that he was like me, all alone. I covered my arm with my knapsack and reached in to get him, ignoring the thorns. Then I fed him a little and petted him a little, and that night he stayed close to me and we enjoyed the firelight. In the morning, he followed me. I looked into the yards of the farmhouses that we passed and watched the pup to see if he showed any signs of recognition of any of them. But he was uninterested, and I knew I had gotten myself a dog.

A dog does not care who you are, as long as you are kind to him, as long as you can share a meal with him, as long as you will take a long walk with him, or take shelter from the rain with him. He does not care if you are rich or poor or loved or hated by other men, he does not make you feel ashamed, nor does he care if you feel the shame of others. Dogs are pure love, and nothing else. And so the dog became my friend, and I, his.

We wandered together in the blossoming spring, the dog I named Pinch trotting at my heels and then riding perched in my knapsack when he tired. In a town in North Carolina, we found out the war was over. A few days later, in South Carolina, news spread that Lincoln had been shot, the thing we had hoped for so long. Then, in the next town, there was news that Jefferson Davis had been captured in Georgia. The newspaper said that he had been dressed as a woman. I refused to care about it. Old Jeff Davis and his hot-headed cronies had made a bad bargain for all of us.

After several long weeks of walking through the aftermath of that bad bargain, I arrived hungry, dirty, and shoeless to the house where I was raised, with Pinch riding high in my knapsack. When I got to the door, I wasn't sure if I should knock or not, but before I could decide, it opened and there was the kind, round face of Aunt Rosalie.

"Hep you, sir?" she asked suspiciously, but just as she did, her face rose like the sun and she said, "Lawd Jesus, it's Marse Jack! Back home from Virginny an' the Ermy!"

Suddenly I began crying, crying and thinking about the quilt that her brown hands had sewn, the lifesaving cover that had kept me warm against the brutal Chesapeake winter. I sobbed like a baby and she took me in an embrace and I sobbed harder and she shushed me and murmured to me, "Welcome home, boy, you's home now."

I'm sure I smelled atrocious, but the only mention of it she made was "Let Aunt Rosalie draw you a baff." I stood there a stranger in my own home as she hurried with buckets of hot water and towels and soap. When the bath was ready, she left me to it, saying only, "We gone have to feed you, Lil' Jack. You right near a skell-ton."

I soaked in the tub, my first bath in a proper tub in four years. The smell of a Sunday roast told me what day it was, the smell of beef and carrots and onions and love finding me. When I stopped crying again, I rose and shaved two years of beard from my face, watching the sandy hair fall like cobwebs. All my old clothes I pulled from my chifforobe swallowed my gaunt frame, and my shoes felt strange on my feet. I straightened my wet hair in the mirror and then my collar, and then I waited on the front porch.

By and by, the revolving spokes of a carriage's wheels flashed between the trees on the lane. Mother's valet George helped her down, and she paused at the foot of the steps to the porch when she saw me. I thought I might be hailed as a hero, albeit one whose cause had failed.

"Andrew," she said, for she never called me Jack, short for my middle name Jackson, like just about everyone else did. "I assumed you were dead." She didn't seem pleased or displeased by my survival nor did she ask about my health. "Where have you been?" she asked.

"Prison," I said. It was an unfortunate choice of words, for when they came out of my mouth, I regretted them. It sounded as if it had been no more than a stint in the Tunica County Jail for public drunkenness or stealing chickens.

"That is shameful," she said, but then she added, "Unfortunate, rather."

I didn't tell her that I had gotten out of that prison by taking the Oath of Allegiance to the United States. She would have thrown me out—I'm sure of it.

Aunt Rosalie announced with a little bell that dinner was ready. It took great effort for me to eat civilly, to put down my fork between bites, to blot my mouth with my napkin, to avoid making snorting noises, to make polite conversation. I asked about the men of Tunica County I knew, and in particular Mr. Tyner, but she had but little news of them, as they were far below our caste.

"Andrew, am I expected to keep up with every poor farmer in Tunica County?" she said, and I didn't ask again.

What we did talk about was what my mother couldn't stop talking about, the impending visit of my brother. I endured her continued hymn of unending praise for him and his accomplishments in Louisiana. Listening was all I could do, as I had nothing to match it. Mother said that he had 'made something of himself' and in such a way to imply that I had not.

I was given my old room, the one I had occupied with my brother when we were boys and then by myself when he left for college in Oxford and then for Louisiana. It was all too small for me, the bed small, the chair small, everything small. I had outgrown the house. I had outgrown my childhood, as people do and should do. I chafed at it. But I had no place else to go.

When my health returned, I rode our land and looked into getting our crop along. I had had plenty of time to think of things, including the building of an efficient new cotton gin that we could use to gin our neighbors' cotton as well as our own, which would save them money and provide an income for us. It was completed within two weeks and worked splendidly.

Just after the new gin was completed, my brother returned home for his much anticipated visit. He arrived on the landing from his first class berth aboard a first class steamboat, wearing fine clothes with a trunk of more fine clothes brought to the house. We rode in Mother's carriage as he told tale after tale of his fine house in Louisiana and his thousands of acres of sugarcane. Later, over dinner, our mother's eyes sparkled as my brother told story after story in which others called him 'Captain' and 'Massa.'

I smiled the called-for smile but inside my belly, anger blew the fire of envy like a forge of coals and I used the red hot hatred to imagine beating his head into a thousand horrid shapes. He said that his second wife had either run off or had had to be committed to an asylum for 'irregularities of personality,' the story changing according to which toddy he was on. After post dinner cordials, our mother retired to bed, and my brother proposed a little trip out to the quarters for 'horizontal refreshments.' I declined, and he went out there without me. He returned promptly and, I assume, unrefreshed after finding that his favorites had left when the Union Army had arrived in Tunica County.

When he departed several days later, Mother fluttered her handkerchief and used it to blot her eyes. The gangplank was taken up, and the steamboat pushed away from the bank. My brother stood at the rail and waved briefly before lighting one of the fine cigars he boasted he could afford. He puffed like Satan himself would and threw the match into the river. When the boat was off a distance, the slapping paddlewheel disappearing around a bend in the river, Mother turned to me with a look that said, *well, I suppose I am left with you, then.*

That evening over dinner, I told her that our cotton gin was the talk of the county clear up to Memphis and that it would generate a nice income in the fall at ginning time.

She replied only, "that's nice" between dainty bites.

At last I had enough, and Mother and I argued. This may sound like a shouting spectacle full of fists slammed on tables and smashed dishes, Father, but it was not. Rather, it was a jousting match with blows traded between bites and sips of the supper we were eating over a linen table cloth on fine china and silverware. I reminded her of my position as an officer and veteran of the

Confederate Army. Her prosecution of the charges against me was unwavering.

"Valiant men do not get themselves captured and spend the remainder of the war as the guest of the enemy," Mother said, and then she looked at Pinch who was curled up on the other side of the screen door, "And they do not return with mongrels."

She made it sound as if Point Lookout had been some sort of seaside resort where the Yankees had fed us champagne and oysters and entertained us with theatricals, not the reality of cold, hard winds coming off Chesapeake Bay with threadbare blankets and lice and typhoid, all presided over by guards, both negro and white, but mostly negro, all of them full of pent up animosity and just barely old enough to be considered men, armed with rifles and itching to use them 'just to see' what it would be like to kill a man. I wonder if Neely ever had to persuade a fellow guard from collecting the bounty from my head. It was the common belief that the guards were given bonuses for each prisoner they killed and some said it was ten dollars and some said it was as little as two dollars.

"The real hero is your brother who has made something of himself," Mother said.

Hear me when I say this, Father. Envy is not green, it is colorless and odorless. If it did have a color, it would be black or gray, and if it had an odor, it would be both foul and sweet, sulphurous and fragrant. But from that day it followed me, did Envy, it followed me like a vapor to every obscure corner of the world to which I fled. That black cloud, tinged gray-green, stagnant and sweet. I was under its spell. It was my master. Envy.

In the wake of our argument, Mother left for Louisiana to go see her golden idol. While she was away, I thought I should go and visit Tyner at his place in the eastern part of the county not far from the Coldwater River. I saddled up Chester, a dappled white gelding with a gray-black mane, and Pinch trotted along at his heels.

I had to stop and ask directions several times, and after many a twist and turn, I found the Tyner place. It was far from the paradise Tyner had described, nor was it squalid, though it seemed to be teetering on squalor. The house sat in the middle of a handful of cleared acres, mostly corn that was only knee-high while the rest of the county's corn was waist-high or better. In the middle of it was the Tyner house. The gray vertical planks were unpainted, the windows without glass panes with limp burlap curtains hanging and waiting for a summer breeze. The front porch sagged a little, and the chimney listed the slightest bit off plumb. Chickens strutted and pecked and muttered through the yard. Pinch sniffed after them until a rooster chased him across the yard in a broad sweeping arc.

A woman was working a patch of garden around the side. She looked up from under her straw hat and then back toward the rear of the house and then to me again.

"Help you, sir?" she asked from under the brim of her hat. We introduced ourselves.

"I'm here to see Mr. Tyner. We were in the war together," I said as I approached. Pinch followed, though he kept an eye out for the rooster.

She leaned on the hoe and put a finger across her lips as she looked to the back of the house again. Then she removed her hat and wiped her forehead with her forearm.

"He's sleeping out back," she said, pointing off in that direction. "In a tent in that pine grove yonder. Sleeps out there most nights. Some nights he comes in."

She was a pretty woman who would have been even prettier under better circumstances. Her figure was lean and athletic like women had in those days from long hours of doing the work of the men who had gone off to war. Her hair was a dull gold, and the faintest touch of brown wove in and out of the long braid that fell over her shoulder from under the straw hat. Her eyes were brownish green, hazel, I believe they call it, though they were tinged red and her lids were swollen and her eyelashes were matted together, and I wondered if she had been crying. She seemed like the kind of woman who would never cry in front of others. Regardless, I could easily imagine her on the day that she became Mrs. Tyner, with a bouquet of wildflowers in her hands and a wreath of them in her hair. We walked around the side of the house, and I saw the tent which was actually an old bedsheet hanging over a rope tied between two trees.

"I just put the girls down for a nap. We were up all night with him," she said in little more than a whisper. "We sleep when he finally sleeps."

I found him dead to the world in a tent with a revolver and an empty pint of whiskey next to him. I studied his face, looking for the man who had confided in me that he was ready to take the oath but was afraid that dishonor would find him if it were found out.

"Don't wake him up," I said quietly, though, in truth, I didn't think we could have woken him if we wanted to just then.

"Oh, don't worry. I ain't a-fixin' to," Mrs. Tyner said. "Ain't pretty."

I went down on one knee and carefully took the revolver from his limp hand. His hair and beard were long and likely had not been cut since before his capture and confinement to Point Lookout. I offered the gun to Mrs. Tyner.

"You keep it," she whispered. "He was either gonna kill us or himself with it. He gets real mad and waves the thing around and points it at us and then hisself and then he sits down and cries."

Pinch's nose bounced in the air as he sniffed the sleeping man. Tyner's snoring broke with a smack, and Pinch retreated a few steps until the snoring resumed. We tiptoed away from Tyner and his tent and the empty whiskey bottle half hidden by his tangled beard.

We went back through the side yard and then through the front door of the simple cabin. She opened the door and Pinch slipped through in front of us, then she closed it quietly behind us, careful not to wake the sleeper in the tent around back. In the corner of the room was an old bedstead with two tousles of blonde hair and mouths open in exhausted sleep. She looked at them with the anguish of a worried parent struggling to keep her children safe and said, "It's like he went off to war and some other man come back in his place."

It was obvious how precarious their situation was. A keg of gunpowder was sleeping under a blanket in a grove of pine trees behind their house, and no one knew how long the fuse was. Just a stray whisper or a misunderstood look and it could go off and up.

"I believe it might be best if you take the girls and go away for a while."

This, of course, was no revelation to her.

"I have a sister in Missouri," she said without a pause, as if she had been considering it for some time. "They're Union, but good people all the same."

"It's a dangerous trip for a woman alone with two children," I said. I wasn't proposing that I would take them, but apparently that's how she took it.

"Would you 'company us, sir?'"

I had worked myself into a corner. As I thought upon it, Pinch stretched up from the floor and put his paws on the bed and sniffed the two sleeping girls. Then he leaped and curled up next to them with his tail curled under his nose and his eyes on me.

There was no reason I couldn't take them. The cotton was laid by and wouldn't need my attention for a while. Mother had gone for an extended visit to Louisiana. And I had almost as much reason to leave as Mrs. Tyner and her girls did.

"Gather the things you want to bring," I said.

She sat on the side of the bed and leaned over to wake her girls touching their hair with a mother's gentle caress. They woke scratching their heads and rubbing their eyes, and then they instinctively hugged their mama. Pinch got up from beside them and stood on the bed and wagged his tail. They smiled and stroked his head. He vaulted down and yipped once, and I grabbed his snout and shushed him.

"You girls get your things," she murmured. "We're gonna go visit Aunt Mary and Uncle Thomas in Missouri." She said it as if it were a trip down the lane, not the three week trek across two states it would be. They slid out of bed and knelt and rubbed and scratched Pinch. When they did, I saw that both of the girls had bruises on their arms and legs. She pulled the quilt off the bed. "This is Mr. Jack," she said with a corner of the quilt tucked under her chin as she folded it, "He's gonna take us."

Mrs. Tyner quietly gathered the things she held most dear. The folded quilt, the family Bible, a cooking pot, all her clothes and the girls' clothes. She put them all into the pot. I put the three of them up on my horse, Mrs. Tyner in the back and the two girls in the front, the young mother's arms around her children. I noticed more bruises on their arms and legs. I walked them down the lane, and we turned the corner on the simple shack. I took the pot with their belongings in one hand and led my horse with the other. Pinch scampered at my heels.

I kept looking over my shoulder, waiting for Tyner to come running and firing the revolver, shouting, "That's my wife! Those are my girls!" But he was fast asleep in the pine grove. And we had his revolver.

After a couple of miles of awkward silence, Mrs. Tyner asked from astride Chester, "Kind sir, would you like to ride for a while?"

"It's no issue," I said, looking back one more time for Mr. Tyner. "I marched many a mile with the army. Used to it."

"Have you been to call on Mr. Bibb and his cousin Mr. Sandifer?" she asked. "Mr. Tyner says they come and visit him purty regular though I ain't seen 'em."

"No ma'am," I said, but I didn't tell her they were dead. What I did say was, "Well, once Mr. Tyner gets himself straight, they'll be better days for y'all."

But I knew that would be impossible, and I believe Mrs. Tyner knew it, too. It was clear enough that although Mr. Tyner might have left Point Lookout prison, Point Lookout prison would never leave him.

Back at our big house, I went looking for Aunt Rosalie to tell her goodbye and to tell her that I was taking the wife and daughters of one of my soldiers to Missouri to her sister's house, but Aunt Rosalie had taken advantage of Mother's absence to do a little visiting herself. So I gathered things for our trip. The girls seemed even more ragged sitting on the settee in Mother's parlor. Their eyes, the same hazel color and shape as their mother's, cast about the house as if it were a full size dollhouse and the last word in opulence compared to their humble dwelling. As I went from room to room, the girls followed me, gazing in amazement at the drapes and rugs and upholstered furniture and windows with glass panes.

"Mr. Jack, is this your house?" the older girl asked. I spoke a truth that I had not considered yet.

"No, little Miss, it's my mama's house," I said.

They followed me up the stairs with hands sliding up the polished banisters and around the newel posts. They looked in the rooms upstairs as I went in mine.

"Is this your room, Mr. Jack?" they asked.

"Used to be," I said. "When I was a boy."

I found my old knapsack and put my things in it. I took one last look around the house to make sure I hadn't overlooked something that might be useful to us on our journey. The Tyner girls may have seen wealth and splendor in every room, but I only saw my brother's smirking face and smug body language. I put the revolver in the knapsack and closed the latch.

I gathered a side of bacon and a ham from the smokehouse and a couple of our hens and a sack of cornmeal. I thought of leaving a note for Mother telling her where I would be, but I didn't see the point, so I left without saying goodbye to anyone. I thought I'd be back in a month or so, when the Tyners were safely in Missouri.

I loaded the chickens and the side of bacon and the ham and the cornmeal into a wagon along with several more quilts, and I hitched Chester to the wagon. Pinch vaulted into the back with the girls, who gathered under the quilts and giggled as Pinch nosed under there with them.

"First time they've laughed in a long time," Mrs. Tyner said, and she almost smiled. We pulled away down the road.

And so I left Tunica County and the house I grew up in without saying goodbye to Aunt Rosalie or anyone else, certainly not to my mother as she was off fawning over my brother in his palace in Louisiana. Over my shoulder set above the green corduroy that would be speckled white by summer's end was the small pinpoint of the home in which I grew up. I watched it over my shoulder one last time, thinking it might reach out to me, call for me. But it sat smugly in the afternoon light facing the levee and the river.

I meant to be gone for just a matter of a month or so and be home well in time for the picking of our cotton. Instead, it would be thirty years before I returned, and then, as a man with a different name and missing an eye. We crossed the river on the Tunica Ferry. The girls never once asked why their daddy wasn't going with us.

Jack

The landing on the Arkansas side of the Mississippi was concealed in deep evening shadows that reached out toward us on the surface of the river as we approached. The small spot of a steamboat coming upriver appeared on the horizon well downriver. The girls watched it silently as Pinch sat between them and enjoyed their petting. By the time it was close enough that we could see its paddlewheel and the froth of river water it churned up, we had made the far bank. The wooden gate of the ferry swung open, and Chester clattered over the wooden landing and pulled us into Arkansas and the falling light.

Up the road a mile or two, we made camp when it became too dark to see. Fireflies floated in the clearing and the girls caught them in cupped hands and showed them to me before they let the glowing specks wander into the gray sky of a summer dusk. We had a hasty meal of ham and bread and turned in without a fire. Mrs. Tyner and the girls slept in the back of the wagon, and Pinch and I slept under it on one of the quilts.

I woke in the morning to the smell of woodsmoke and bacon and hoecakes. She had made a fire and was humming to herself as she went about the beginning of her day, a day which would be largely devoted to taking care of others. I thought this might be what the blessing of married life was like, enduring struggles with a strong partner at your side, looking out for your children. It became as much of a pipedream to me as flying someday. Maybe one day I would find such a woman and we could make a life together. For now, I hoped that the Tyners would be able to find the life they had lost.

We were off after breakfast, the girls singing little songs they made up and changed. After a sunny morning, clouds rolled in from the west and a light rain became a dense downpour. We decided to stop for the night, so I put an oilcloth tarpaulin over the bed of the wagon. Mrs. Tyner and the girls slept under it that night with Pinch while I slept under a tree. She offered for me to come and join them, but I declined. I had no more desire for sleeping in a tent than I did for eating soup. I had had enough of both in Maryland.

By morning the weather had cleared, though the road was muddy and we found ourselves stuck several times. Mrs. Tyner vaulted down to help me as Chester struggled, his hooves stomping circles into the mud as he strained against the traces and the wagon. I took a rope and tied it to a tree and then used a limb to twist the rope shorter and pull the wagon free, a trick I had thought of as a West Point cadet and used in the army.

After several days, the flat cotton fields gave way to rocky hills and the streams changed from muddy to clear. We stopped and camped at the edge of an open field full of summer flowers to give Chester a day of rest. The girls ran and held hands and giggled and made flower wreaths for their hair and for their mother's hair. Chester pulled at the grass of the meadow, shaking his mane against the quick peck of insects before leaning in to pull another clump as Pinch nosed through the tall grass, the tip of his tail just above it as he followed a scent.

The girls and I lay on our backs and watched the summer clouds drift across the sky and the birds drift under them when Mrs. Tyner's figure appeared towering over us. She sat next to us in the grass and nestled into her skirts, and I rose to a sitting position. Worry was leaving her face and her posture, and it was impossible not to notice that she was a pretty woman, particularly when she smiled which was more and more often. Her freckled cheekbones and cheeks were filling out. Her girls made a wreath for her hair, and she looked at it and put it on her head but then took it off after a while and held it in her lap. That night after supper, she and the girls lay in the bed of the wagon under the stars and I sat on the buckboard and pointed out the constellations above us.

The next day we were on our way again. We made steady progress for another week and then stopped at a clear-running stream for another day of rest. The weather had gotten warm, Mrs. Tyner and her girls bathed in it while I respectfully stayed with Chester and the wagon. I heard Pinch barking in excitement and the girls ran up from the creek, naked and laughing. Mrs. Tyner came chasing after them, her hastily put-on dress clinging to her body and the subtle brown in her golden hair shimmering to near-copper. Her eyes seemed more green than brown, more vibrant, her face relaxing into what was surely her former beauty. I caught myself laughing, a thing I seldom did anymore and Mrs. Tyner said, "Mr. Jack, will you help me round up these rascals?"

I ran after them with a quilt and scooped them up as they wiggled and twisted. There was laughter, that angel song, laughter. The girls dressed, and then we ate the blackberries we had picked that morning and I told them the story of how I found Pinch in a thicket of blackberry bushes.

Over the next few days, I caught Mrs. Tyner smiling at me as I read to the girls or listened to their stories or clapped along with their little songs. I read to them from the Bible, all the Old Testament stories of Jonah and the whale, Joshua blowing down the walls of Jericho with his trumpet, Samson's strength and Delilah's beauty. Their mother gave me a sidelong glance and a smile as the girls fell asleep slumped into my sides in the orange glow of the fire.

Once on the road again, Mrs. Tyner began sitting on the buckboard next to me. She tucked her hands under her thighs at first, but gradually the one closest to me began to rest itself on the buckboard between us, asking to be held. I kept my hands on the reins and my eyes down the road past Chester's swaying white flanks and swishing charcoal gray tail.

On the next rainy night, she again offered for me to sleep under the tarpaulin with them, and I might have considered it, but she was still a married woman, no matter if it was to a shell of a man. I declined as politely as I could. I was seeing how a life with a loving family would be, something to desire. In my mind I began taking inventory of the daughters of our neighbors in Tunica County. They were all pretty, some beautiful, but they all had a demure prissiness that bordered on haughtiness, which I did not find appealing in the least. I thought I might like a woman with whom I could laugh with and struggle with and overcome obstacles with, in other words, a partner. Someone much like Mrs. Tyner, only not already married.

Then one night I was sitting against a tree watching the fire as she put the girls to bed in the wagon. I could hear her humming lullabies to them and Pinch, who enjoyed curling up with them, and I smiled at her songs' simple sweetness, their tenderness. The clearing was quiet except for the crackle of the fire and the night noises off in the darkness. Then silently her head appeared above the side of the wagon, and she paused to look down and make sure her girls were asleep. She cautiously stepped over the buckboard and out of the wagon.

She straightened her nightdress and came to me in the firelight. Her hair was down. She made comments on what a nice night it was and how nice the stars looked and wasn't the moon nice up there. I said, yes it was and was pointing out Cassiopeia to her in the northern sky when she opened her nightdress and bared her breasts. They seemed to have been reduced in fullness by hardship and deprivation, and I couldn't help but to imagine her worriedly breastfeeding her girls with them. She approached in the dance of the flames and put her hand to my cheek. She looked at me, a sublime look, a beckoning look. She closed her eyes and put her lips to mine, but I withdrew.

"But you're the wife of another man," I murmured.

It was as if she hadn't considered this. She wrapped her nightdress around herself and turned away, suddenly ashamed of her overture. She addressed the darkness at the edge of our camp.

"You're a handsome man, Jack. One day you'll lose your heart to someone and you'll lose it completely." She paused to sniffle and wipe tears out of her eyes and embrace herself. "I apologize, sir. A woman gets lonely. My husband is a broken man in just about every way a man can be broken."

She shook her head to herself and stepped up onto the buckboard and over it into the back of the wagon with the girls without saying goodnight. I remained watching the firelight dance on the branches and the smoke wander into the heavens where dwelled Cassiopeia, the beautiful and arrogantly vain queen of the Greek myth.

Mrs. Tyner said very little for the rest of the journey. She never addressed me as Jack again.

"Have you had enough to eat, sir?" and "Shall we stop in another hour, sir?" and "How much further down the road is West Plains, sir?" When I tried to help her with the dishes, she said, "I can manage on my own, sir."

The rest, as Shakespeare said, was silence. Since she continued to cook, I insisted on helping her with the dishes afterwards. We endured the silent buzzing tension, side by side with our sleeves rolled up. Once, when the girls said, "Mr. Jack, I wish you could be our daddy," Mrs. Tyner snapped, "You girls done got a daddy."

We moved north through Arkansas and into Missouri. Virtually every town of any size had been raided by both Confederate and Union guerillas. The fields and woods gave way to the blackened bones of burned farmhouses and barns. At night when we stopped to camp, Mrs. Tyner would turn in early with the girls, leaving Pinch and me to watch the campfire and the night sky.

Two weeks later we arrived at St. Joseph on the Missouri River and her sister's house, a house with a small library and a parlor and a piano. Her sister was the reverse image of Mrs. Tyner, clean and well-fed. Mrs. Tyner's brother-in-law Mr. Belcher was a somewhat learned man who I believe was postmaster for St. Joseph or a telegraph operator, or something like that. He had a prominent forehead and wore round spectacles and took the newspaper. He was a man who was as dour and pious as his wife was prim. They were an older couple with no children, or none who I ever saw or were spoken of.

To say we were welcomed into their home would be something of an overstatement. We were tolerated in it, not with a spirit of good cheer but some other emotion, something like pity. I introduced myself and when I did there was a subtle look on their faces as if they were inwardly sniffing for the scent of impropriety on the situation of an unmarried man escorting a married woman for three weeks alone in the wilderness.

We had arrived on a Saturday, and despite our fatigue, we were expected to attend church with the Belchers the next day, which we did after no small amount of cleaning ourselves and the girls. Mrs. Tyner and I sat on the pew with the girls between us, all of us still thoroughly exhausted and fighting our fatigue through the lengthy sermon. On the steps afterward, the congregation filed past us newcomers, complimenting Mrs. Tyner and me on our beautiful family and telling me that my girls looked just like my wife. No one corrected them, for to say that I was a man unrelated to them would have been to set tongues wagging.

Over Sunday dinner, Mr. Belcher said that the new railroad to the Pacific was the talk up and down the Missouri and that men were coming through St. Joseph daily on their way to Omaha looking to work on it. It would be an industrial marvel, Belcher exclaimed, the longest railroad in the world! The envy of every country! Months of hard travel to San Francisco would be reduced to a comfortable week, filled with good meals and contented sleep and the carefree panorama of plains and mountains. *Harper's Weekly* had an article about the Pacific Railroad being built which echoed Mr. Belcher's assertions.

It sounded much more interesting to me than cotton, and, as you can imagine, Father, home and my brother's shadow had but little appeal for me. I thought I might go and work the summer on the railroad and return in time for picking season in Tunica County. It was becoming clear to me that I was a complication for Mrs. Tyner and a potential source of gossip for the town, not to mention a continued source of temptation for her and perhaps for me as well. If I stayed, we might give in to the attraction, and she would be whispered about as the woman who had left her husband and taken up with another man. And I would be whispered about as being that man. I thought it best that I leave as soon as Chester and I were rested.

Pinch was having his own troubles. The Belchers had a wolf-like dog, some sort of half-feral breed which tormented him. At various times during the day, a sudden flurry of yelps erupted from the yard announcing that the Belchers' dog had pinned Pinch and I would rush out to find the beast wild-eyed with Pinch's head or neck in his jowls. I nudged the dog with my foot, and he loosened his jaws and raised his hackles at me showing me the entire length of his teeth. Pinch promptly ran under the house where the Belchers' wolf-dog couldn't reach him.

The Belchers for their part had welcomed Mrs. Tyner and her girls, but I wondered if their compassion would last when it went from being the *emotion* compassion to the *decision* compassion. I wondered if the Tyners would be pitied and pitied and pitied until there was nothing left of them. The Tyner girls were already beginning to change from the free spirits of our journey to the rigid forms of town girls.

Mr. Belcher kept speaking of the railroad. Perhaps he was simply fascinated with it like many were then, or perhaps the potential shame of our situation made him suggest it to me as a place I should go, but for whatever reason, the railroad sounded more and more appealing. I announced that I was leaving, and Mrs. Tyner feigned indifference, though there was a slight fall in her cheeks when I told her. I hugged and kissed the girls and made them promise that they would be kind and good and help their mama and their aunt and uncle and that I would always keep a place in my heart just for them. They pressed their little heads into my waist and then stooped and hugged Pinch. As I was about to climb into the saddle, I offered Mrs. Tyner her husband's revolver.

"Keep it, sir," she said. "There's talk of all sorts of low characters workin' on the railroad up yonder in Nebraska. Injuns too. We're safe here. We don't need it no more."

Being safe is not the same thing as being happy, but I supposed for now safe would have to do. I kept the revolver, although I had made a vow in Point Lookout that if I survived, I would never take the life of another human being. I left the wagon and the chickens as appreciation for the Belcher's kindness, a kind of dowery for Mrs. Tyner and her girls.

Pinch jumped up behind me onto Chester's flanks, the dog's new trick, and we turned away to the road that followed the river north to Council Bluff and Omaha, the gateway to the Nebraska Territory. I planned to spend a few months working on the railroad, aiming to gain a break from my brother's shadow and spend a summer of fresh air and hard work on the plains. I ended up spending fourteen years. And I encountered my brother's shadow, this time a shade blacker than before.

I never saw any of the Tyners again. But I always kept the revolver with me, though I renewed my vow never to use it to kill another man.

Part II

Eva

With the first fresh breaths of autumn, the fever left us, and gentlemen began to show up again, though I wasn't sure what for. They came alone at first and then in small handfuls, but as the weather and the threat of illness cooled, more and more arrived. The piano player made his return and the gaiety of my new situation made up for the droll austerity of all those years with my grandparents in our succession of cobbled-out households. Why, madame, I do believe I heard more laughter in one night than I had in all my years before. Downstairs, there was good food and music, and upstairs there was shrieking hilarity, though at the time I thought someone had told an especially funny joke. Springs squeaked, and I thought that the gentlemen were much too old to be jumping on beds. I supposed that their wives had forbidden it at home. I was quite naïve back then, Mrs. Leonard. A babe in the woods!

It might have been called a boardinghouse for ladies, but I viewed them as girls like myself, though older and with figures. The men who called on them were simply well-meaning gentlemen who came to enjoy refreshments and the piano in the parlor and then adjourn upstairs for a game of cards (gin-rummy, I thought) and perhaps look through picture books with the girls. These gentlemen callers, as we were all instructed to call them, would bring bonbons and bouquets, part of the great masquerade of securing the girls' affection, even though it was a certainty, provided the fee was paid to Miss McCune. They would come with carnations in their lapels and take off their hats, and the girls would take them, sometimes tossing them from one to another in a ritual of flirtation until one girl would take it and she and her escort would join hands and ascend the stairs. And go to a room to play cards and look through picture-books, you see. It was perhaps a year before I began to understand the true nature of the ritual, that it was akin to the act that dogs and horses and other animals performed so shamelessly in the streets.

I was in the room of a girl called Mae-I—as in *may I?*—when it finally dawned on me. I had just made the bed and had laid down my armload of rumpled sheets to pause and try on her jewelry. I must have lost track of time as I admired my reflection in the mirror, lifting my hair off my neck and turning my head this way and that. I have always had a penchant for shiny things, Mrs. Leonard.

Well, there were footsteps in the hall, and I pushed the dirty sheets under the bed and hid behind the chifforobe just as Mae-I and her gentleman turned the knob. I bit my lip and stifled a giggle as she and the man kissed. My eyes blinked as she broke the kiss and touched his nose and smiled playfully. She turned and lifted the hair at the base of her neck and he unfastened her dress. And I'm sure my jaw went slack as clothes were shed and flesh became engorged and the old wrestling match-ballet was enacted right in front of my wide eyes.

I began to compare my plain, featureless girl's body to that of the women in the house, and I longed for the changes which would make me like them. But my body was an unremarkable thing then, as thin as a sprig of hay. With time, of course, the changes appeared. It seemed that my figure was growing each night, reinventing itself, and I woke each morning with a new fullness like something out of a fairytale and I, the princess. I strode and pranced before the looking glass, watching side-eyed the lovely, loping bounce of my breasts and the emerging tangle of black beneath my navel. There were places on my body that were a pleasure to touch, and I began touching them.

I also began hiding in the rooms to observe the act, hearing my name called in the hallway beyond the closed door whenever a room was ready have the bedsheets changed. But I was fascinated by it, the nakedness, the breathlessness, the heaving, the straining. Now I knew it. The act was what the men were paying for, not playing cards or looking through picture books. I began to wonder what it might be like, to fall onto a bed in the embrace of a man and be taken, to feel the rigid strain of another's flesh.

On Sunday mornings, Miss McCune paid the girls. Alma would always take her pay with a cigarette in her mouth and stash it in the cup of her corset. I couldn't tell how much it was, but I was certain that it was plenty enough to buy anything a girl might want, with enough left over for ice cream and lemonade. In the way of girls of that age, I wanted to be a woman like them. At last, I broached the subject with Miss McCune.

It was in the afternoon before the evening rush. She was directing her hired man, Foster, in removing a rug from one of the parlors downstairs. An overserved patron had gotten sick on it and ruined it. I waited at the periphery for Miss McCune and Foster to conclude their business. When he left with it rolled up and on his shoulder, she and I sat down on the settee.

She seemed to have known that this day would come. She asked me how old I was. Fourteen, I said. She asked if I had been with a man before, and I said that I had not. She asked if I had seen the 'love-act' as she called it, and I confessed that I had been in a room when I found myself surprised and I had hidden behind a chifforobe. I didn't confess to having purposefully hidden and watched dozens of times afterward.

It never occurred to me that Miss McCune might have been keeping me in anticipation of this day, but I am quite convinced, now that I am educated in the way of human nature and flesh, that she knew it would come to this all along. It was to be just a matter of time, and she had waited me out.

Miss McCune said that if I was going to change my function in the house, then I should change my name as well. Girls were encouraged to change their names lest they show up in the newspaper as being arrested for lewdness, a thing which was possible but in reality rarely happened. These assigned names were encouraged to allude to the female sexual apparatus and the enjoyment of it, Fanny, Kitty, Ophelia, and so forth. I suggested the names Polly Calhoun or Gwendolyn Mosey as my *nom d'amour*, but she said that those were too plain, and I smiled when she added, *for a beautiful girl like you.* I was given the name Lottie Blue and a date was set for my 'debut.'

He was a prominent man and paid a high price for deflowering me. There was no parlor auction for it as there were then and still are in other houses. Everything was kept private and discreet, and it was treated as a special occasion. There were no other customers in the house that night. I had my hair done up with flowers and was dressed in a gown of white tulle. Little imagination was required to admire the nature of my body.

As he ascended the stairs with me, Alma stopped him on the landing and whispered in my ear, "When he puts it in the first time you smile, you hear me? Smile. Close your eyes and smile. I don't care how much it hurts." Then she put her palm to my cheek and patted it gently and kissed the other cheek.

He placed me on the edge of the bed and gently shut the door, looking back at me with a thin smile in the amber lamplight. He undressed me and admired me, and then he undressed himself. And then we did it, or, I should say, *he* did it. His blurry shadow moved on the ceiling and the walls. It seemed to go on forever. He pretended to be caring, but in the end, there was a subtle tinge of violence to it, as there frequently is. Afterwards, he dressed himself as I sat naked on the side of the bed looking at my lap and my hands. He folded my tulle gown unevenly and placed it next to me, and I covered myself with it, clutching it over my body. I had never felt so naked. Then he gently put a hand to my temple and kissed my forehead, and he left, straightening his tie and collar. I saw many men after that, but I can't say that I ever saw him again. I suppose he took the last of my childhood with him.

Alma came and sat on the side of the bed next to me and put her arm around me. I put my head on her shoulder, but I didn't cry. None of the girls asked me what it was like. They already knew. A robe was put over me and we all went downstairs. Finger sandwiches and lemonade were served, and one of them played a tune on the piano, frequently missing notes and singing woefully out of key.

What's that, Mrs. Leonard? Oh, no need to be sorry for me, ma'am. Pity is a useless commodity. We all become like we are for one reason or another, and there's no use moaning about it. I will not say if I regret it, such thinking is a fruitless annoyance. We all must do what we must do, and that is all I will say on the matter. I refuse to dwell on it. What's done is done.

Yes. Well, then.

For some, those subject to the vulgar judgments of obscure people, it would have been a shameful time. For people like me, those with puny consciences and a limited sense of dishonor, the time spent in Miss McCune's house wasn't all that bad. Of course it mattered little to me—I didn't care a fig what people thought. I was making money doing something I enjoyed most of the time and was able to endure the rest of it. It was an education of a sort. If there is one thing I learned from the business of pleasure, it is this: We are made male and female out of flesh and blood and subject to the desires of flesh and blood. Why, the very population of the earth is living testimony to the popularity of that naked ritual, sex! Everyone one of us is the result of another person's—*at least one other person's*—moment of ecstasy, and there can be no denying it.

They came from the woods and cotton fields, cattle drovers and stevedores and deckhands and railroad men, store clerks, brokers, judges, carpenters, liverymen. All came with money in their pockets and a feral itch that had to be scratched. All departed with less money and no itch. Miss McCune was fond of saying that men not only wanted their bodies stroked, but their egos as well. And so every new patron, no matter how well or ill-equipped, when showing himself for the first time was greeted with a gasp behind fingers and a 'oh my, I hope I can accommodate you, sir.'

Then, we endured the boorish manners and clumsy advances of the stevedores and the country ogres and the flea-bitten scarecrows in soiled homespun. Some were lighthearted and playful, and others were grimly committed to their task as if they were paying a debt or solving a problem. I had no issue with any of them. We were all simply following the dictates of our natures. I enjoyed the feeling of making money, and they enjoyed the feeling of spending it.

So much so that I was always the first to volunteer to go on overnight trips on the train to Marshall and Dallas with the upper-crust, side-door men, where I was signed into the hotel register as the young wife of my gentleman friend, or outings in the country, where after a picnic lunch, I myself was dessert, on a blanket upon the grass under the green boughs of the trees. These things paid extra, and they paid well.

A traveling photographer once called on the house and asked if he might take some pictures of us. Some of the girls demurred, afraid that the photographs might fall into the hands of someone they knew, but I and a couple of others readily accepted. We were the girls with no family, and his price was generous. And so we posed for him, together and separately, in whatever state of dress or undress he desired, in whatever act he desired, though not without a firm negotiation for the more risqué poses.

A book existed then which served as a directory to the girls of the house, with little rhymes and sayings composed by Miss McCune. It had a blue cover and was distributed to gentleman stepping off the landing on the river and the trains at the station. In it were descriptions of us, things such as 'with a boy, she's never coy' and 'I dance with my left leg and then my right, and between the two I make my living.' One of the girls had a little ditty persuading gentleman callers to come and visit her 'berry patch.' My entry was a short poem which read 'sometimes haughty, always naughty, on Commerce Street, ask for Lottie.' It is well that I had been persuaded to change my name. Many in town might have remembered me as ten-year old Eva McCarron, though my body had grown up with little resemblance to that child, other than the blue eyes. Some of the local men made the connection, however, which only added to my allure.

The men and boys came and quenched themselves at our fountains, following more or less the primitive sequence of touching, kissing, caressing, then the great 'rupture, rapture, and relaxation.' If there was a downstairs parlor of eager gentleman callers or if a girl found herself just plain bored or tired or raw, we said those breathless things into their ears and touched those secret places to bring the thing to a swift conclusion, followed by the sighs and coos of admiration to make him come back with his next paycheck.

Some of the men would murmur and weep afterward, telling stories of indifferent wives and loveless marriages and unenjoyed advances. I, for my part, would absently stroke their backs and whisper, 'there-there' and 'well, Miss Lottie certainly enjoys you,' all the while thinking about the fine things for sale in the shop windows on Texas Street. Such affirmations for the men usually meant a generous tip.

I would perform any act you or they could imagine, Mrs. Leonard, alone or with others, and some you could not imagine and I will not describe for you, as it would likely offend your sensibilities, madame. I will only say that no request was too obscene, as long as I was paid and paid well. In fact, whenever a man would blushingly confess his hidden desires for a certain act, no matter how outlandish, I would lightly bite my lip and murmur, "Well, sir, I have always dreamed of being pleased in that manner." And the men believed it because they wanted to believe it. Whether alone or with others, there was practically nothing I wouldn't indulge a man as long as it meant feathering the nest of money in my hatbox.

I have always taken great pleasure in accumulating money, Mrs. Leonard, though, especially in recent years, I have also taken great pleasure in spending it. I found that I could play upon the sympathies and egos and desires of my gentlemen callers and have them make purchases for me. I could simply coo and blush and toy with his buttons and say, "*I have a special item set aside at Mr. Jacobs' on Milam—*" here I would whisper in his ear— "*I think you would like to see me in it.*" Or, to another, "*I have a lovely little thing in the backroom of Hearne's behind the counter—"* then, with a light touch of a finger to his nose, *"—buy it for me and I'll wear it for you in private. Only for you."*

Only for you was a thing I told all the men, and they invariably did as I directed. It got so that I was able to put most of my own money to savings, as anything extra I wanted I could cajole out of my admirers. When Miss McCune paid us on Sunday mornings, I put it all in my hatbox.

There were generally half a dozen or so of us girls working in the house at any one time. I remember some of their names, some of their faces, some both. If a man were to ask about our past, we told him an embellished variation of the same sympathy-evoking story, that we were poor girls who had been the victims of scheming family members, especially siblings (better yet if they were step siblings), an abusive father, an indifferent mother (better yet, deceased), etc., difficult situations that led us to do the things we did.

Nell Jester was the only one who used her real name unless she was lying to us also. She and I once fought like a couple of tabbies over a stray tomcat when I thought she had been snooping in my hatbox. I understand that Nell has her own house now back in Shreveport and that the old institute of love-for-sale is now legal and practiced openly. I am sure it is as popular as ever.

There was a girl named Ophelia, a dim-witted girl who had as much mental wherewithal in her head as a milliner's dummy and who never spelled her name the same way twice. When it came to the love act, however, she was both prodigy and maestro and quite popular on account of it. Fanny was a girl more thoughtful than the rest of us, good and cheerful enough but not clever, though certainly not a feather-head like Ophelia. Both Ophelia and Fanny had been at most partially raised, as the saying was then. Kitty, a small-breasted girl with auburn hair who seldom spoke but was frequently heard behind closed doors. Hermine, a girl from Arkansas whose real name was Sally and who pretended to be French and spoke with a ridiculously exaggerated accent, though it always fooled the amorous young men who were well-played by her. *Oui, oui, what-evaire monsieur would a-like.*

And Alma, sweet Alma. Almost too sweet for that line of work. So much of what I learned about the business of pleasure I learned from her. She was the oldest of us and guided us in wearing the most fashionable clothes. She instructed us in the theatrics of love, the ballet of passion. Most men were rather quick about it, the act, but for a patron whose exertions had grown tiresome and who would not finish and be done with it, Alma told us that a girl was best served by the pantomime of her own climax, animal sounds through an open mouth and squinted eyes, fingers digging into the skin of a bare back, a quiver of the hips, the clinching of a leg-embrace. If those things failed, the touch of fingers or a tongue in certain places. Time was money then, as it still is.

One of our lighter pastimes, late in the night after the house was cleared, was to imitate the exertions of our gentlemen callers to the howls of each other's laughter between sips of the cheap beer or whiskey the house served. We laughed, doing dances for each other and comically using our whole bodies to portray the rise and fall of that noble but unruly organ. Then it was off to actually *sleep* in our beds after a long night of working in them.

There were other girls, girls who came and went. They came out of a sense of curiosity or necessity or both. Some found religion and left, some found the bottle and left, and some simply found themselves too old and left.

So it was for Alma, dear Alma, who had been like a mother to us. She was always the oldest of the house, biding her time waiting in the parlor as the men came and passed her over in favor of us younger girls. She couldn't have been twenty-five. After yet another night of sitting on the tufted settee waiting to be chosen, she rose the next morning and packed her suitcase. She was dressed as plainly as I ever saw her. Her face was unpainted and her hair was simply done. She looked like a tropical bird that had been plucked of its colorful feathers, as unremarkable as any other woman. She could have easily passed for a pastor's wife.

"I'm too old for this kind of work, Lottie. You see it. You see how their eyes pass over me to you younger girls, to you, to Fanny, to Ophelia. I'm a passed-over thing, yesterday's special. As stale as last week's newspaper." She turned with her suitcase at her knee and I watched her go down Commerce Street to the steamboat landing. One or two of the other girls joined me on the front porch. No one called out after her. We knew it was her business and that she was right in it.

I thought for a moment about going with her, but where she was headed surely meant poverty and I was not about to return to the shabby dress and rented rooms of my grandparents. I had money and the things it could buy. I had dreams of owning my own house, bawdy or not, and filling it with nice things. Alma left, and we girls on the porch smoked and watched her go. And I have not seen her since. I've always wondered if Alma was her real name. She was fond of saying that it means 'soul' in Spanish.

There were others who also left having had their curiosity satisfied or out of a sense of shame. But I ask you, then, Mrs. Leonard, what is that, *shame?* The falling-short of some self-imposed ideal? Some fluty, flowery unobtainable? I will say only this: get ahead as far and as fast as you can and may the devil take the hindmost. See this fine house? Well, now that my husband has passed, I am its sole possessor and mistress—unless, of course, the bank takes it. These countless acres? I am their queen. All because of my maxim, Get Ahead. Get ahead, as far and as fast as you can.

Of course, eventually, I left also. It was after a woman old enough to be my mother and with eyes as blue as mine appeared at the door of Commerce Street.

Jack

I saddled up Chester and left the Tyners with their relatives the Belchers and rode up the Missouri River. Pinch trotted alongside, nosing through the grass along the riverbank, pausing to sniff and then ambling to catch up. Steamboats rode low in the current, the fountain cascade of their paddlewheels urging them and their heavy loads upriver, decks burdened with immense stacks of iron rails and lumber and locomotives secured with ropes and wires and heavy chains. In Council Bluffs, we crossed on the ferry into Omaha where more steamboats were unloading rails and ties and mules and wagons, so much like the depot of a military expedition. The town of Omaha was tumbling forward on its way to becoming the city of Omaha, as awkwardly as a teenage boy rapidly outgrowing clothes. Great hills of newly arrived material for the building of a railroad lined the riverbank. The streets smelled of fresh-cut lumber and the dust of newly laid brick and tobacco smoke and bacon frying.

In front of the offices of a Mr. Hoxie, the hiring manager of the railroad, a line of men stood around waiting. I tied Chester to a hitching post and stood with them. In a few minutes, a man in shirtsleeves and suspenders came out, and men who had been smoking threw down their cigarettes and stamped them. The man announced, *any of you what is veterans, step forward.* Most of us did, but it made no difference. Everyone was hired.

Some waited for the next train to take them to the end of the rails, then just forty miles out, a tiny fraction of the eighteen hundred that it would reach. But I was anxious to get started. Pinch vaulted up onto Chester's dappled flanks, and we rode along the Platte River, which was said to be a mile wide and a foot deep. After a morning's ride, we found the construction camp, the tip of the spear that was being thrust into the heart of the wilderness.

The grade had been completed beyond the end of the rails, off into the distance that only a man with field glasses could see, and beyond that, surveyors were plotting more of the railroad's course along the Platte. Telegraph poles marched alongside the rails, trailing into a spool of wire on a wagon at the end of the tracks. These were the days of wagon trains, and off in the distance one would pass every few hours heading west. It took six months to get to California then. When we were finished, if it were found possible, it would take less than a week.

We were put in the charge of an Irishman from Kilkenny, a veteran of the Union Army who still wore his blue jacket with sergeant stripes on the sleeves. He gave us hasty, almost breathless instructions on the laying of rails, and then with no more direction than that, we began our work. The Irishman shouted harangue after harangue, some of the foulest cursing I have ever heard. He swore at our mothers and questioned our parentage, our willingness to work, our very worth as men.

"Work like heaven's ahead o' ye and hell's behind!" or "You bastards are about as effective as a fart in a whirlwind!" he yelled, his face as lumpy and red as a new potato. The abuse continued as he marched alongside us, until we reached the correct spot and lowered the rail into place with his command, "*Down!*"

Somehow, it was all great fun.

We were worked hard and fed well. Rails and spikes and fishplates were brought up and dropped on either side of the track to be carried forward as the railroad grew like Jack's beanstalk, only horizontally instead of vertically. Miles upon miles of rolling prairie and swaying grass were invaded by mile upon mile of wagons bearing supplies in the wake of the slender line of twin rails stretching into the west, rails that were an exact four feet, eight and a half inches apart. For mile upon mile upon mile. The locomotives of the supply trains puffed patiently at the end of the track as it followed the grade that followed the surveyors who were probing the wilderness. Mile upon mile of it.

We lugged the heavy rails over the crossties, fishplates were placed, the gaugers measured the distance, and then the spikers hammered them into the wood, three blows per spike, never any more or they would receive a foul blast of Irish cursing. Then it was repeated. Ties, plates, rails, gauge, spikes. Over and over, gobbling up the graded distance until *'Time!'* was called at noon and then again as night fell. There was not a complainer nor a fat man among us. Nor was there a wasted minute.

At breakfast, dinner, and supper we ate at long benches in a box car which was referred to as the dining car, simple, plentiful food—bread, potatoes, and meat courtesy of the herd of cattle that was marched along with us. At night we slept in a dormitory car, a common box car divided up into berths. Pinch slept with me in mine, curled up in a rust-brown ring under our blanket. On nights when it was hot, I carried him up to the roof where we slept under the stars. Then, in the morning, I started down the ladder while he stood wagging his tail at the top. I grabbed him and backed down the ladder to breakfast and the new workday and the battle with the distance.

In the beginning our pay was steady, and I was careful not to spend any of it in the tents that followed our flanks, the tents with the drone of wheezing fiddles and roaring laughter and gunshots. Men worked and gambled and drank and whored and came and went, and, though the Arapaho and the Sioux and the Cheyenne were a danger to us as we crossed their lands, the even bigger danger to the men was each other. Some became drunk and genial, some became drunk and agitated, and some shot and others were shot, frequently after card games.

I myself went from a dependable man to an indispensable man, a man of first rank, earning the respect of the men on my crew and the praise of my superiors. Others might choose to drink and gamble in their spare time, but I preferred to study the sky, brilliant blue and cloud-streaked in the daytime and midnight blue and star-speckled at night, and breathe the smell of the grass brought to me on the prairie breeze. When the autumn winds began to sweep down the plains from Canada, Pinch and I huddled around our potbellied stove, and I read aloud to him from the Bible. He would rest his muzzle on his paws and pretend to understand, much the same way as people do. He would paw at things for me to read him. For some reason, he seemed to especially love the Psalms. Then his eyes would close, and he would emit a muffled bark and chase things in his sleep. I suppose I was something of an oddity, the man who read the Bible to his dog, but there were plenty of odd men and women in the west in those days. On foggy mornings when the vastness of the prairie was only an idea, he would come bounding out of the mist with a grin and I would scratch his neck and caress his flank.

Our one day of rest was Sunday. While a fair number of the men nursed hangovers or went to prayer meeting or both, Pinch and I rode Chester over the plains among the buffalo and the streams lined by cottonwood trees. The sky is bigger out there on the plains, expansive and colossal blue. I would tie Chester up to one of the cottonwoods, and he would clip the grass and Pinch would lay his head on my chest and we would gaze up into it, watching hawks soar in the cloudless blue. I imagined soaring with them with wings outstretched, rising and falling and rising again. Somewhere cotton was growing, but it didn't concern me. We stayed reclining in the prairie grass, reading the Psalms and napping until the shadows of the cottonwoods stretched across the prairie, and only then did we return to our camp.

Sometime in late October, when the first snow fell as white as cotton, I realized that I had stayed longer than I had intended, much longer. No one back home knew where I was. There were many times I thought to write my mother explaining my absence, but the longer I was away, the more impossible it became, as I thought of how displeased Mother must have been at having to deal with our overseer and our cotton herself. I could only imagine the level of her disgust with me. And so I let it go and continued my anonymous life.

Winter fell upon us in icy waves blowing cold rain and then snow. As a Mississippi boy, I had never seen so much snow, not even in Virginia. Work came to a standstill as we couldn't shovel it fast enough to grade the ground and lay rails over it. I volunteered to stay at the end of the rails and arranged for firewood for the stove, food for Pinch and me, and fodder for Chester, and I read all winter.

Spring returned and began to drop hints of summer. In May, our Irish foreman from Kilkenny was shot in a drunken squabble and two days were lost to his wake, another drunken affair. I was chosen to replace him as foreman. With my promotion, I received a portion of a boxcar converted into my quarters with a potbellied stove and a warm bunk with a buffalo skin rug for Pinch and a small bookshelf and a calendar from my employer, Crédit Mobilier, the contractor building the railroad for the Union Pacific.

Mentally, I understood my work and the work of the men above and below me, and physically I was able to do all of it, though I also knew the right words to inspire those in my charge to take up their tasks gladly. The music of our industry captivated me, the ring of hammers, the thud of crossties as they hit the graded ground, the clink of iron spikes and the clang of steel rails and the cursing and shouting and singing in half a dozen languages. Men who were veterans of the opposing armies would break into scuffles, and several times I had to fire Tyner's revolver in the air and remind the men that the war was over, it had been in all the papers, and that we were building a railroad here. Then I would tell them that they were about as effective as a fart in a whirlwind and to start working like heaven was in front of them and hell was behind them. The men gave up their quarrel as if awakened from a sleep walk and took up their rails again.

We bridged the Loup River at Columbus and by July we were in Grand Island, by August, Kearney, and by October, we had reached the 100th Meridian, where another roundhouse and machine shop were built. Finally, we crossed the North Platte and passed the town named after it. Two to three miles a day.

Rail by rail, end to end, we moved west along the Platte through the hunting grounds of the people who had been there centuries before us. They watched us from afar, puzzled by the strange ways of the white man, who built a metal road for an iron horse that puffed smoke like a pipe. They seemed baffled by our penchant for misplaced industry. At first they were all the same to me, but with time, I learned them all, the Pawnee and further in the distance, the Sioux and the Arapaho and the Cheyenne. The rails continued across their hunting grounds scattering and separating the herds of buffalo.

There were four construction trains and a train with a blacksmith shop, a saddler's shop, a feed car, carpenter's shop, and a sitting and dining room for us foremen in the car where our quarters were. There was a storekeeper, a draftsman, a telegrapher, a kitchen and a cook, and a car full of engineers. There was also a doctor who set bones and stitched cuts, treated gunshot wounds and snakebites and social diseases. And sometimes he had to pull arrows from men.

Jack

It snowed half a foot the night I lost Chester, one of the first snows of the year. I had gone forward with the surveyors to see where we were headed and to see if I might like that sort of work, and we had camped in tents at the end of the grade. Chester trailed from the stake he was tethered to and nosed under the falling snow for the last of the autumn grass. Pinch and I retired to our tent, and I read in the light of a lantern until the fire in the stove burned down and then we turned in.

I woke to Pinch's barking in the night. The fire in the stove had long since burned down, so I struck a match and checked my watch. It was four in the morning. I put my head out of the flap of my tent. The men in the other tents were all still sleeping. I looked to see that Chester had come free from his tether. Then, in the glow of the moon on the snow, I saw the fleeting shadow of Chester being ridden off by someone. I grabbed the revolver, forgetting my vow never to kill another human being, and I pulled on my boots and coat and ran after him into the night.

I ran until I tired, pausing with my hands on my knees to catch my breath. I straightened and kept following the tracks. The sun came up and everything was brilliant-white and cold. I spent half the morning following them, ignoring the work that I had left behind. Rage consumed me. I had been stolen from, violated. I followed the tracks for several miles with my breath steaming into the cold air and Pinch bounding through the snow next to me.

At last I found a smudge in the snow about a dozen feet in width. Next to it was the horse thief, a Sioux brave who couldn't have been more than fifteen. He wore a simple hat of black fur, from a beaver, I suppose, and a cape made from buffalo hide that was flecked with snow. It was obvious what had happened. Chester had rolled over him and run off, and the young man was hurt, clutching his leg.

That was only one of his problems. His other problem was my rage, which was red-hot. He looked up to me as I leveled the revolver and pulled back the hammer. His eyes pleaded to me as I aimed the barrel between them. The moment lasted a small eternity, until I remembered my vow and let the hammer off slowly. He said something to me in Sioux and then touched his chest and pointed to me and repeated it in awkward English.

"Brother."

I repeated it, "Brother," and I left him in the snow. When Pinch and I made the next small rise in the snow-covered prairie, I looked back to see that his party had returned for him and was pulling him up onto a horse. Even from that distance, I could tell it was Chester by his charcoal tail and mane. What Indian name would he have from now on, I wondered?

I turned back and disappeared from their sight down the other side of the rise, and we followed my tracks back to our campsite. I was sorry I had taken off after him. It was foolhardy. I might have been killed or frozen to death, and I might be let go for missing a morning of work. When I neared the end of the tracks, both my own and those of the railroad, I found it swarming with blue-coated soldiers. In the midst of them were the rest of the surveying crew laid out in a row in the blood-covered snow. They had been filled with arrows and scalped, right in the middle of breakfast. If I hadn't gone after the young horse thief, I would have been among them. And I thought of the English word of the horse thief. *Brother.*

Jack

I was taken back down the line and ushered into the private car of the Casement brothers. The U. S. Cavalry general Phillip St. George Cooke was there with them, and they all stood up as I entered. We sat down together, and they asked me my name and what had happened. I gave them a full report of the incident as they pursed lips and knitted eyebrows and looked at their hands and out the window. I ended by respectfully asking to be relieved of further surveying duty. They asked me my name again and about my background. When they found out that I had spent two years at West Point and that I was well-read and had a more than basic knowledge of science, I was transferred to work under a man named Hezekiah Bissell who managed the building of bridges and tunnels.

Bissell reported directly to the Casement brothers who reported to the vice superintendent of construction Samuel Reed, who reported to the man himself, the superintendent of construction Grenville Dodge, who either reported to or pretended to report to the vice president of the Union Pacific Doc Durant. Above him was Mr. Ames, but Durant didn't pretend to report to anyone. Durant's stealth and crookedness were whispered about by the common foot-soldiers in the war against the western distance. It was said that even though Durant's outfit Crédit Mobilier might miss our paydays, the stockholders never missed a dividend. But that would come out later, one stockholder in particular.

New surveyors were sent for and arrived. They were given an armed escort and moved forward, and we continued to advance behind them. Up ahead we would need cuts, fills, bridges and tunnels. Things like cold and heat and rain and Indians and distance and mountains and ravines were no match for us, nor was the North Platte River, and we bridged it. The grading and the ballast and the crossties continued west, topped with rails four feet eight and a half inches apart and a train at the end patiently puffing with more crossties and rails. We pressed westward, one length of rail after another, chasing the sunset toward the spot where it fell into the mountains at the end of each day. Behind us, towns erupted out of the empty plains along the thin double line dotted with station houses, roundhouses, and machine shops, hotels, livery stables, and, occasionally, a church.

At the new town of North Platte, a contingent of wagons began to follow us to quench thirsts and satisfy appetites with all the amusements lonely men might have a taste for. There was a barber and a laundry and a saloon and women who populated 'amusement tents.' They were the same sort of camp followers that trails any army, barkeepers, card sharps, and hucksters, troops of lewd women engaged in the vilest sort of sexual commerce. One house reportedly contained a midget, but I never went to see for myself. In short, the cars held the pursuits of unprincipled men, men of a different stripe than me. There were places where a man could get a bath and a shave and a meal and an hour's worth of a woman's company, and from those planked façades the women would call to me, "Won't you come and see me, Jack? For you, it won't cost nothin'."

I would always wave them off with a smile. I wanted more than an hour's romp with a woman. I wanted a lifetime with a good and faithful mate. But out west, good women were few then. Most of them were already taken, and the rest were for sale by the hour. Neither suited me.

The signs in those shanty towns might have said, 'no dogs or Irishmen allowed,' but in reality, anyone who drew a paycheck and was willing to spend it was allowed. 'Hell-on-wheels' as it was called followed us like fleas follow a dog. The saloonkeepers kept us flush in drunken men, and drunken men kept us flush in murders. Men might get shot outright in broad daylight or they might just disappear after going out for a drink and a hand of cards after dinner. The Sioux and the Cheyenne were a danger to them but nowhere near the threat that the men were to each other.

The men, many of them Irish like you, Father, filled the nights with shouting and laughter. If something was said or done that had offended someone, that man would come at the insulting party with a cigar on his lips and pounding a shillelagh in his palm. The *Frontier Index*, a newspaper that was printed on a hand-press that was taken from town to town, carried a section called, 'List of Those Shot Last Night.'

Nevertheless, when morning broke, everyone reported to breakfast and then work, ignoring sour stomachs, bulging head, and bruised faces. There were men who never seemed to fall asleep sober nor wake up without a hangover. They rose early and worked all day, spitting and swearing but never stopping work to do it.

The tracks reached a town called Julesburg, and the shanty and canvas saloons, gambling houses, and brothels were set up again as if picked up by a giant hand and set there. In the fall of 1867, after a period of bawdy calamity and near-calamity, it was all moved again and a town called Cheyenne was founded as Julesburg's hell-on-wheels became Cheyenne's hell-on-wheels. Everything was unloaded from the train, tables for faro, keno, and chuck-a-luck, crates of whiskey, beds, mattresses, mirrors, chests of frilly underthings, billiard tables, a chandelier, and the printing press for the *Frontier Index*. Everything was taken down from the flat cars and moved into the tents and glorified shanty watering holes with names like the *Keystone* and the *Palace* and the *Headquarters Saloon.*

Every new town along the tracks fancied itself the new Paris, the Athens of the West, the ascendant New York. When the feverish building of the railroad moved on and away, the saloons and dance halls and brothels were plucked up and moved with the men and the railroad, and most of those hopeful places withered into smudges in the prairie. Cheyenne and Laramie and Evanston survived. Benton and Bear River and countless others did not and were reduced to a few gray boards that would fall to the parched earth. Trains would never again stop there, and their locomotives would plow past the smeared blemishes of red dirt without so much as a whistle-shout to the dust and sagebrush, and their passengers wouldn't give a glance up from their newspapers and coffee as the cars rumbled by. But no one knew that then, and the *Frontier Index* talked them up like they were the next and greatest pinnacle of civilization. I suspect that Mr. Freeman, the editor of the *Index*, had bought lots to re-sell.

In April 1868, we reached Laramie, and hell-on-wheels was unpacked and set up there, too. That summer was hot and waterless, so we built a $10,000 windmill, said to be easily the largest in the world, to pump water for the town and the engines that passed through it. It was my first experience with drilling into the earth but certainly not my last.

Beyond Laramie, whirlwinds of dust painted everything the same reddish orange of the desert, men, mules, ties, rails, dogs, but it was no deterrent. The rails followed the ties and the ties followed the grade and the grade followed the surveyors into the hazy cloud. The town of Benton sprang up there, possibly the nearest representation of Sodom and Gomorrah as any place I have ever seen. West of there was nothing green except for the few things that were painted green, but the dust of the place soon covered everything with a fine brown powder. The countryside looked like an Arabian desert or hell with all the fires put out. Nevertheless, we graded it, bridged its fireless ravines, and laid track over it. An orderly pair of double rails had split the chaos. Word of our coming preceded us to every obscure mining camp and outpost, and we entered them like Christ entering Jerusalem. That November 1868, we moved into the ramshackle town of Bear River City, which we all called Beartown. Of course, hell-on-wheels and the *Frontier Index* came right on our heels. When we were done, hell-on-wheels moved on with us. The *Frontier Index* did not.

Editor Freeman and his newspaper incensed the majority of his readers with stories deriding President Grant in Washington and the lawlessness of the men in Beartown. They burned the tent that housed the *Frontier Index*, smashed the printing press and scattered the type in the main street, and Editor Freemen rode off on a mule. The men laughed that he had saved his life *and* his ass. Just like that, there was no one left to tell the men what to think anymore. They would just have to figure it out on their own. The riot was the beginning of the end for Beartown, and with time it went the way of the *Frontier Index,* though not as quickly.

The railroad moved west to Evanston leaving only empty whiskey bottles and untended graves. But like a racehorse that senses the finish line, we continued working. The objective was Humboldt Wells in Nevada. Both the Union Pacific and the Central Pacific wanted to take all of Utah and the lucrative commerce with the Mormons there. It was still January, and the frozen ground rejected our picks and shovels, so we blasted it out with black powder and nitroglycerin. We were instructed to lay track over the frozen grade, but I knew that when the ground thawed the grade would sink and the rails would sag into puddles. But time and distance were money, and we built it quick so that Doc Durant and the stockholders of Crédit Mobilier would get paid for the mileage by Congress. Later someone would come back and build it right. It wasn't the last time I would be pressured into shoddy work. Years later, I would pay dearly for it.

From the other direction our rivals, the Central Pacific and their workers imported from China, were making excellent time through Nevada and beating us to some uncertain point in the desert. The way they were spoken of, we thought the Chinese all eight feet tall with broad backs and big hands, but when we finally saw them at the connection point in Utah, we were surprised to find most of them no taller and just as slight of frame as schoolboys. They only worked like they were eight feet tall.

Doc Durant contracted with Brigham Young down in Salt Lake City, and Mormon boys were brought up to speed us along in our race with the eastward approaching Chinese of the Central Pacific. The Mormons neither drank nor swore nor gambled, but they were unyielding when it came to the sabbath, and they worked as hard as any Irishman, German, or Czech. Regardless, God-fearing Mormons or not, hell-on-wheels followed, and in the Utah Territory the town of Corrine sprang up, a gentile town which advertised itself as the 'Chicago of the Rocky Mountains,' a gross overstatement. The town became a bur under Brigham Young's saddle. An editorial in the gentile newspaper the *Corinne Reporter* said that the only difference between polygamy and prostitution was that polygamy involved multiple women and one man and prostitution involved multiple men and one woman. Brigham Young got the last say when he suffocated the town by building a railroad from Salt Lake to Idaho through Ogden rather than Corinne, effectively bypassing it.

Because Congress was paying both railroads for miles graded, our grades approached and then passed each other for miles, passing parallel to each other but going in opposite directions, redundantly cutting the same ridges and bridging the same ravines. Sometimes the grades even crossed each other. I suppose that when you're being paid by the mile, being finished is no reason to stop. President Grant finally forced an agreement for the two railroads to meet at a place called Promontory Summit.

The graders and track layers were no longer needed and were let go, and that great army of male appetites melted away like an April snow. Hell-on-wheels no longer had anyone to cater to, and most of the polished mahogany bars, brass beds, looking glasses, and gaming tables were sold at a loss. The town of Promontory had only respectable businesses left, for the most part.

A ceremony was planned, and Doc Durant himself traveled westward from New York to be at Promontory to hammer ceremonial spikes, *if his soft hands could hold a hammer*, the men murmured in chuckling whispers. His train was delayed just short of Evanston when an armed mob of unpaid Union Pacific workers hijacked his rail car and chained it to the rails until they were paid. He wired the money and was released. While everyone waited, not sure of what was going on, General Casement sent up an excursion train complete with good food and champagne to greet Governor Stanford and the rest of the Central Pacific dignitaries.

At last, Doc Durant's train arrived. There was music from bands and speeches, a Mormon bishop, and a photographer Mr. Savage to take our picture. A special crosstie of polished laurel wood was brought in from California, and Mr. Strobridge of the Central Pacific and Mr. Reed of the

Union Pacific dropped it into place. A preacher from Massachusetts gave a two minute prayer that was about a minute and a half too long and filled with 'thou's' and 'thy's.'

It was obvious to everyone that if either of the two men, Stanford or Durant, had ever operated so much as a broom, it had been a long time since they did it. Someone had had the foresight to drill holes in the laurel tie so that the officiants might have an easier time of pounding in the ceremonial spikes. Doc Durant placed the two golden spikes into the holes and was expected to give a speech, but he didn't look well after a night of either celebration or calming his nerves as a result of his detainment in Evanston. General Dodge ended up giving the speech. An argument ensued between Governor Stanford and Doc Durant on who should hammer in the last spike. Finally Governor Stanford was given the ceremonial maul made of silver. He swung and missed. Maybe he was just nervous, which is a more forgivable sin than being soft.

The spikes were driven in for Stanford and Durant by someone else, like every other spike on the two thousand mile railroad, and the great panting locomotives inched toward each other like two race horses in their paddocks at the end of a derby. Bottles of champagne were crashed against them as if they were new ships, and we climbed up on them. Mr. Savage took our picture, that famous picture of us gathered on the Central Pacific's *Jupiter* and our *No. 119*. I climbed up on *No. 119*, holding Pinch under my arm, though in the picture he was hidden by the man in front of us.

When the flash faded and Mr. Savage emerged from under the black photographer's hood, we gave a great shout with hands in the air. We had gone and done it, built the longest railroad in the world. The United States was now linked north and south, east and west. Congress had given us ten years to do it, and we had done it in four. For Americans, it was nothing less than brilliant. For the Indian, it was nothing less than disastrous. Now settlers would pour in at a rate that would make Noah's flood look like a spring shower. But on that day, May 10, 1869, we shouted and cheered and the bands played and dignitaries gave speeches few could hear and most were grateful not to. At last, General Casement motioned for me. He was a short man, five-foot-nothing, was the joke, and I had to look down on him.

"Take this list of stockholders to the telegraph office and send them messages that we've done it," he said. His hair and suit were wet and sweet-smelling from champagne. I took the list and was walking to the telegraph office looking at it when I came across my brother's name among the names of the lesser stockholders. It was then I began to suspect something sinister and sour about my employer, Crédit Mobilier.

The whole sordid story would come to light several years later, a tale of a fifty million dollar railroad built for a hundred million dollars with nine million of the surplus used to bribe members of Congress for votes favorable to the Union Pacific, which, as it turned out, owned the shell company Crédit Mobilier. Charges were levied against Durant and Ames but no one I knew ever served any time for it, and the lesser stockholders like my brother in Louisiana slipped through the net with all the smaller fish and faded away richer and untarnished.

I had given four prime years of my life to Doc Durant's railroad. Men had been overheated by the cruel sun, frozen by the snow, rained upon, snake-bit, pierced by the wind and by arrows, shot by each other, crushed by rock, fallen from bridges, and drowned. There were times when pay was slow coming from our employer, Crédit Mobilier, but apparently there was never a time that stockholders failed to receive a dividend on time, and a handsome one. My brother had been among them.

Eva

Ruthie? Ruthie! Come make us a fire! This instant! Our guest and I are getting a chill.

Now, that's better. Ruthie takes some prodding sometimes. Empty-headed girl, though I must admit, loyal to a fault. Everyone else has run off to the city or the north. Would you care for a splash of rum in your tea, Mrs. Leonard?

I believe I told you that I never knew my father, and, in fact, I wouldn't know him if I saw him on the street. I'm not so sure about my mother.

It was a late winter afternoon much like this one, and the light was much like it is now, bright but fading quickly into an early sunset. The church bells were ringing five o'clock as we sat around the parlor in our drawers and smoked, though some of us girls had already begun to get dressed in preparation for getting undressed over and over again. We listened to the bells sound off, one church to the other, carriage and wagon wheels clattering away through the streets. As we thoughtfully pulled on our cigarettes, there was a knock at the door, the hard, hasty rap of the insistent. At first we thought it was a gentleman caller, either young or old but certainly too early, and certainly beset by the feral itch and anxious to have it scratched.

Foster opened the door in the middle of the knocking, and the cold air rushed in as she appeared in the door frame. Her hair was black and streaked with the first strands of gray, and even from the door, she smelled like liquor. As soon as the door opened sufficiently, she pushed her away in.

"Lemme speak to the madame of this whorehouse!" she bellowed.

Here, she made a misstep, Mrs. Leonard. No one ever called Miss McCune's place a whorehouse. The term, though accurate, was also indelicate. It was more gingerly referred to as a boardinghouse for ladies or a house of pleasure or an amusement parlor, rather. Before Foster could return her to the outside and the cold, she was in our parlor raising her raspy voice, a voice gained through years of cigarettes and strong drink and shouting.

"Lemme speak the madame!" She said again, adjusting her cleavage and palming her breasts into place. Her skin was better called a hide, but the patches that had evaded the sun were as creamy as mine. And she had eyes identical to mine, though they were bloodshot red around the deep blue. And hair as dark as a blackbird's breast, like mine, though gray-streaked. Miss McCune came hurrying into the parlor in her petticoats with her auburn hair half done up.

"What is the disturbance here?" she asked with the pressured speech of someone who is in a hurry but trying to be civil. She saw the woman and said, "Can I be of assistance to you ma'am?"

"I'm lookin' to make some money. Can't a girl make some money?" she slurred, and then she released a wet belch and wiped her mouth with the back of her hand.

Miss McCune politely declined to point out that this woman's day of being a girl had long since vanished. She only said, "I'm sorry ma'am, but there are no opportunities available in the house at the moment." She said it as if it were she were operating any other place of employment, a millinery or a laundry.

"Ain't I good enough?" she slurred. Then she announced in a voice that could easily have been heard on Commerce Street, "I can out-fuck any you gals!"

Pardon my language, Mrs. Leonard, but you wanted the unvarnished truth and that is what she said exactly. We girls snickered and smirked at her appearance and her raw manners.

She approached me with the sour aroma of spent alcohol and wasted youth, and she looked at me. Her face was like something long-forgotten but suddenly remembered, like an image seen in a flash of lightning at night, a face peering down into a crib, fingers gingerly pulling back the folds of a baby blanket. Hers was a face with eyes as blue as mine. I stopped my snickering as I realized that this is both where I had come from and where I might end up. She put her hand out to touch my cheek, but I recoiled.

"Say," she said, "I had a baby once. In Vicksburg, during the war, but my folks had me put away. She woulda looked just like you. I've always wondered what she woulda looked like when she grew up. I have." There was a sudden tenderness that was difficult to witness and painful to endure. She seemed on the verge of drunken sobbing.

"That can't be," I stammered as I felt the eyes of the girls on me. "My mama—my mama died. I don't know you. I've never met you."

"She'd be about your age," the woman said as she put her fingers to my face again. I turned my cheek away but I kept my eyes on her. Struggling to make light of it, I pulled on my cigarette and let out a mouthful of smoke to the side. It had burned down to the end and I could feel the heat on my fingertips, so I put it out in my coffee cup. But her blue eyes—our blue eyes—bore into me and accused me.

"It's impossible, ma'am," I said callously, though my hand was shaking, "My mother is dead...in a train accident..." my mind whirled and landed on any plausibility, "...a steamboat accident."

The craziness in her eyes seemed to have burned down into blue ashes, set in a body withering like a finished blossom, over and done with and decaying from white to beige, no longer sweet scented, but rather sour like spent alcohol and dust. She became agitated at my denial, and Miss McCune had the police come and arrest her for disturbing the peace. She resisted at first, but they rapped at her legs once or twice, and she winced as they pulled her away and down the street, holding their breath as they did it.

When the woman was gone, Miss McCune only looked to me and said, "Anyone you know, Lottie?"

"Just some old hag," I said and I looked out the window. It was dark enough for me to see my reflection in the night. "Just some old drunken hag."

"Certainly," Miss McCune said, though I'm sure she didn't believe me for one single second. I didn't believe myself either.

But the truth is irrefutable, Mrs. Leonard. Life might not be fair, but it is nothing if not honest. The gentleman callers found the older girls—and what I mean is, older than twenty or so—stale and unappetizing, as uninteresting as last week's newspaper. I could see myself as one of them, a washed-out has-been bawdy girl, tossed upon the scrap-pile of spent passions. Like Alma or like my mother, if that was who the woman was. You yourself are still in the flower of spring, Mrs. Leonard, but let me tell you a dreadful truth. Youth lasts but an hour. This is a fact, though you and I and all of us bemoan its certainty, old age is as inevitable as sunset. It was becoming as clear as gin to me that my days as a budding flower of youth were numbered.

I became worried that the woman would return when she had served her sentence for disturbing the peace, which in those days in Shreveport was seven days. My hatbox had slowly accumulated a nice sum but not quite enough for me to make a break from this dead-end life. I wanted to travel, to dress nicely rather than theatrically, to enjoy fine meals and nice linens, not boardinghouse fare and sheets changed six times a night. I said nothing of this to Miss McCune. To her I was still enthusiastic Miss Lottie, 'sometimes haughty, always naughty,' one of her top performers. But certainly she knew as I did that eventually that season of life is over and other, younger girls rise to the top and the old are tossed upon the refuse pile of what once was.

It was January 1880, when one naturally begins to think ahead to what the new decade might bring. I was certain that by 1890 I would be, at best, running my own house, and at worst, a passed-over girl who sat in the parlor while gentleman callers ascended the stairs-to-heaven with other, younger girls. I was still the main reason so many came to the 'boardinghouse for ladies' on

Commerce Street, but I knew it would not always be so. I braced myself for the return of the blue-eyed woman when she was released from jail.

Now, in those days, among my regular customers was a prominent and wealthy gentleman, a side-door man due to his position in town and the fact that he was some sort of potentate with the Baptist church. He was much older, a possum-headed man who visited at least once a week, always carrying flowers or chocolates, or a box containing a fancy, fussy thing that I whispered I would wear for him while doing certain lurid acts.

He was admitted that evening, through the secluded entrance of the side-door where Foster took his hat and coat. I met him on the stairs in my gossamer frilliness, my hand caressing my inner thigh as I moaned, "I've been waiting for you, Mr. Standproud, oh, please come up, please do." You see, Mrs. Leonard, we girls had secret, comical nicknames for our callers, unknown to them. There was a man with luxurious, simply ape-like body hair whom we called Mr. Wooly, and another, Mr. Thimblepecker, for reasons which should be obvious to most anyone with knowledge of the male anatomy. Of course, the men knew nothing of their nicknames.

So, anyway, I took this man, this so-called Mr. Standproud, upstairs and shut the door behind us. Well, as luck would have it, soon after his moment, he fell on top of me, and I giggled as I was taught to do. I felt more of his weight than before. I waited, examining the room with my eyes. His trousers and suspenders on the chair by the washstand. The clock on the bedside. The framed lithograph of the goddess Aphrodite on the wall. I spoke his name, which I remember well but I will not recount to you.

"Well, sir," I said, "you certainly were inspiring."

Nothing. I checked the clock again. He had not moved in ten minutes. Then fifteen. Then twenty.

I managed to wriggle out from under him. He remained in place, his face and chest pressed into the sheets and mattress, so tightly that I was afraid he couldn't breathe. Then it occurred to me that he might no longer have any need for breathing. I wrapped a sheet around myself and pushed my hair out of my face. The sounds of the house were far away for me, separated by thin walls, the muted sounds of the piano and conversation and laughing downstairs, and the moans of rapture and the wheezing bedsprings upstairs. Mr. Standproud did not move one inch. I put my hand to his pale sagging buttocks and pinched them playfully and he did not stir in the slightest. I slapped them and they did not redden. I rolled him over and his stare was blank. At last I took the bedside mirror and held it to his gaping mouth. The mirror remained clear and fogless.

A girl must recognize her chances if she is to get ahead in this world. This is a truth which is both hard and simple. The fates had handed me a boon. I had no choice but to take it.

Clutching and then tying the sheet around myself, my shaking hands looked through his trousers and found his money-purse. In it was more than enough to give a girl a new start, especially a pretty girl with a good head on her shoulders. I put most of it in my hatbox, but I was careful to leave him a little to avoid suspicion. Then I arranged myself, took a deep breath, and I shrieked.

Miss McCune and Foster clattered up the stairway. They knocked briefly and I opened it in mid-knock.

"Mr. Standproud!" I cried, using his nickname, and I put my hand to my mouth and paced and pretended to sob. Soon a couple of the girls appeared in the doorway, and one of their paramours, who was quickly ushered away and back into the room from whence he had come.

The hired man Foster and Miss McCune dressed Mr. Standproud with some difficulty, as he was beginning to stiffen again, though this time all of his body and not just a certain part of it. The hired man Foster and Miss McCune cleared the parlor, and then Mr. Standproud was carried downstairs and through the side-door whence he had come and loaded into Miss McCune's brougham. He was taken to the nearest church and placed on the front kneeler, slouching over the rail in front of the altar.

The next day the *Shreveport Times* carried the announcement of his passing. The article said that he must have known that the end was eminent and so he went to the nearest house of worship, even though it was the Catholic church and he had been a lifelong Baptist and a deacon.

Over the next few nights, I found that I had lost my will for that type of work. I told men that I preferred to be on top or to sit on their laps in a chair, something which the house referred to as 'riding the pony,' though secretly I was terrified of being crushed again by a dying customer. I guarded my hatbox jealously, finally transferring the money to a rolled up petticoat placed under an overturned chamber pot.

My mother, if that's who the woman was, would most certainly return to find me when her sentence for disturbing the peace was fulfilled. It seemed as good a time as any to leave the house. I had seen the older girls' charms fade away as they were pushed aside in favor of us younger girls. Alma had been sent off because of it and my time would come in a year or two. I decided then and there that I would learn etiquette at the table and in my dealings among others, even if I had to gather it from books. I would no longer rouge my cheeks and nipples. I would wear drawers all the time. I would wash my face. I would dress myself as a refined lady suitable for polite society. I would read all the popular magazines and books and speak proper English. I would learn which fork to use and how much face powder was enough and how much was too much. I would cultivate elegance. In short, I would become a lady. At long last, I would become a respectable lady. And I would marry a man of consequence.

I bought a ticket to a most suitable marketplace for rich husbands, New Orleans, and I would find one, even if it meant taking someone else's. I left Shreveport perched on the bank of the Red River. The last thing I saw of the place was the cupola of the Ziegler Mansion reaching erectly up into the sky. It would be years before I would return. It would be so much different and so much the same.

As it turned out, I didn't have to take the husband of another. I found one who was in need of a wife, though he didn't know it at the time.

Jack

After the golden spike, I moved on from the Union Pacific, sensing that Crédit Mobilier was too crooked an outfit for the type of man I aspired to be. Pinch and I stayed in Utah for a time, as I initially thought Utah might be a good place to look for a wife. The Mormon girls were pretty and sweet and industrious, but they were also forbidden by both their parents and their church leaders for a gentile like me, unless I wanted to join the Mormon church which I wasn't prepared to do. There were no real opportunities for advancement for a gentile, either, so I left Utah altogether.

Denver had been jilted by the Union Pacific when the line was surveyed to the north through Cheyenne, and there was a common belief that Denver's days were numbered and that Cheyenne would outshine it. Perhaps that would have happened, were it not that Denver had gold and the promise of more gold in the mountains. The city fathers of Denver were determined to get even with Cheyenne by building their own railroad to the Pacific.

In those days, there was a man named Palmer who had started up an outfit called the Denver & Rio Grande Railroad. The slogan of the D&RG was, 'Through the mountains, not around them,' a not-so-subtle dig at the Union Pacific. Railroad work was what I knew, and so I signed on with Palmer and the D&RG building a railroad through the mountains. It was a narrow gauge track with rails three feet apart, more nimble and economical for the mountain terrain. The pace of cutting the grade was tediously slow through the canyons and gorges, so much slower than the frenetic pace of the Union Pacific on the plains, and Pinch and I spent many long months and then years in the mountains. In the end-of-the-track shanty towns, I had a somewhat comfortable bunk where Pinch could stay with me, and we would sleep around the glowing hiss of the stove in a bunkhouse full of men who snored and farted in their sleep and occasionally muttered a half-formed word in English, German, Czech, or Chinese before rolling over.

In the winters when the snow in the mountains became too deep, work came to a standstill, and I came down into the railroad towns where I might look for a girl who would make a suitable mate. I found that I had no idea at all how to go about it, and so I became a wallflower, reading *Scientific American* and *Van Nostrand's Eclectic Engineering Journal* by the fire with Pinch curled up in a rust colored ring at my feet. I had become a shy man, not a recluse, not a hermit, but simply someone who enjoyed a quiet life of books and tinkering. Bachelorhood, quiet, unadorned bachelorhood, was beginning to suit me.

Though I was well into my thirties, my physique and complexion benefited from the clean air and sunshine. In those towns where I wintered, the gaily painted girls in the windows of the houses of assignation called out to me asking when I might come and pay them a call. As always, I politely declined. I could never take a reformed bawdy girl and make a wife out of her.

I continued to hold out hope for a woman I could build a life with, but there were still fewer women than men in the west and even fewer ones suitable for marriage.

Several times Mr. Palmer offered to move me into Denver to an office, but I declined, saying that I preferred the outdoors and that Pinch would never do in the city. I enjoyed the beauty, the roar of the rivers through the gorges, the sunlight through the trees, the perfect quiet of morning snow and the sharp bright stars at night. I especially loved looking out from the mountains east over the plains and imagining soaring above them in flight, much like I used to daydream as a boy.

Time passed by. Every so often, I thought of writing Mother, telling her that I was all right and making a small something out of myself. But I had no riches, no mansion in Denver or anywhere else, only a strong body and the love of a dog, two things that would never serve as a favorable comparison when it came to my brother. Certainly, any letter from her would simply be a litany of my brother's opulent life, how much money he had made, how many acres he owned, the rich and famous people he had met and befriended. He would always be her golden idol. I knew this, and there was no need for me to hear it again.

In 1873, a financial panic raced across the country, fueled in part by the Crédit Mobilier scandal coming to light, and I hoped that my brother had suffered a debilitating financial catastrophe. Indeed, it became my habit, my guilty pleasure to search out any of the southern newspapers and scan them for his name among the notices for bankruptcy and indictment. Yes, Father, a mean-spirited notion that shamed me when I paused to reflect upon it. His name never appeared, and I figured he had evaded either bankruptcy or the publicity of it.

After the Panic, the nation began to revive itself, and the steady heartbeat of its economy recovered and Colorado began thriving and then booming. There was talk of statehood for the Territory, and it happened. Then there was talk of Denver becoming the state capital, and then that happened. Denver prospered as farmers harvested golden wheat in the plains to the east and miners harvested golden ore in the mountains to the west. With every trip into town, Pinch and I found new and prettier streets with new and prettier houses on them.

But trouble came again as it does when men and opportunity for money collide. We were vying with our rivals, the Atchison, Topeka, & Santa Fe for the same passes and canyons to build our railroads through. The A. T. & S. F. hired Bat Masterson and other roughs to come in and guard what they felt was their right-of-way. The work camps were beginning to resemble army camps with drill and stacks of rifles.

Mr. Palmer knew that I was an army veteran, and an officer at that, and he asked if I would lead a group to confront the A. T. & S. F. men. I had had enough squabbling and violence, so I sat in his carpeted office in Denver and told him I had taken a vow never to kill another human being, and I aimed to stick to it. He said that he had been raised a Quaker and understood but that he had been pressed to ask me as he was losing men daily to the gold fields in the mountains.

I had no stomach for it any longer. I couldn't kill again, nor did I want to let my employer down, so I decided to leave the Denver & Rio Grande altogether and take Pinch and head down out of the mountains. Ten years was enough time on the railroad, especially when I had only planned on spending a summer.

Mr. Palmer gave me a ten dollar gold piece and a watch for my years of service, and I had some money saved. I bought a secondhand wagon and a mule, and a small forge and other tools. I had sketches of windmills and bridges and cotton gins and wheat threshers and old issues of *Scientific American* and *Van Nostrand's Eclectic Engineering Magazine*. I thought I might make a go of their design and manufacture. I packed up my things, including the revolver I had only fired a few times in the air, and I left. Pinch trotted away with me. We departed Denver and followed the South Platte out onto the plains. Behind us loomed the black shadows of the snow-capped mountains like a perpetual bank of purple thunderclouds.

We passed places where the Big Tent Saloon had been raised and taken down and the places where the process had been repeated. Places where girls in corsets and stockings had called for us to come spend some time and a bit of our pay with them. Places where men had gambled and won, places where men had gambled and lost. Places where they had fought one another, shot another. Places where they had vomited up their paychecks, wiped their mouths on the back of leather gloves, and got up to go work and wait for another paycheck. The camp, the men, even their ghosts, all was gone. Only their unmarked graves and the red boulders and the sagebrush and the rusty dirt remained. And the big sky, always the big sky. It raced the broad, flat earth to the horizon in every direction.

We creaked and trundled down the wagon road that had worn ruts into the ground beside the tracks. Pinch slept a great deal at my feet or on the buckboard next to me, though now he could no longer jump up onto it. Storms blew through and put the wind in our ears, and then it would rain, and Pinch would sleep under the buckboard while I huddled under an oilcloth slicker. When the sun was hot, dragonflies flew random paths around the ears of the mule and the poles and wires of the telegraph, landing and taking off to dart along the tops of the grass. The evening shadows of man, mule, wagon, and dog stretched out before us on the road east. It was late summer, and rattlesnakes were on the move, so we slept in the wagon at night.

We plodded east into the sunrise each morning, ate and rested under the shade of the wagon at noon, and watched the stars like we did when he was a pup, my back against the prairie grass and his muzzle on my chest watching the constellations in the sky. The sound of the wind coming across the prairie would be broken from time to time by a diminutive horn blast in the distance which would rise into a shrieking moan, and then the ground would tremble and the rush of the cars would crescendo. The trains would pass us, initially in a blur. Inside the cars people read and chatted and supped and looked out the windows. Some waved at me, and I waved back. Then the shadow would pass over us and we would be in sun again, and the train would decrescendo into the distance leaving only a popping of crossties and then the rush of the wind through the tops of the prairie grass again. And the slow rattle and squeak of our wheels as they dipped and rose in the ruts of the wagon road.

We wandered east past the ruins of towns that had vanished and through the industrious chatter of towns that were flourishing, neither recognizable as their former selves. We went from one place to the next, places with neat-planked sidewalks and courthouses where lawyers and judges and the first-rate men of those villages practiced their mischief, and other towns, tin-roofed, mud-streeted hamlets that were ugly and lonely, wheezing and gasping in their poverty, towns that would not live to see the next century.

The prairie grass had given way to wheat and corn where I remembered herds of buffalo ten years before. We were somewhere between North Platte and Kearney, and I tried to remember the place as it had been, before it was plowed and planted in corn, but I couldn't. It was as if those days of grade, ties, and rails had not existed at all, and God himself had made this farmland at the same time he created Eden. The corn opened into a clearing with a farmhouse. Behind the house, a man was trying to raise a barn by himself. He had a gin pole and a system of pulleys to help hoist the long boards up onto the ridge beam, but it was hopelessly inadequate for him to guide them into place and virtually impossible for him to nail them in. A boy of no more than ten dressed in denim overalls like the rest of the children followed below on the ground looking up at this father.

We approached the farmhouse, and the fair-haired children of that fair-haired man crowded around Pinch and patted him and stroked him, and his graying muzzle broke into a reluctant, panting smile. The man looked down and jumped from board to board to the ground. He took off his gloves, and we shook hands. Our hands were big and firm, our fingers could barely reach around the other's palm. The shake was one of silent mutual admiration between two men who used their hands often and for heavy work.

When he introduced himself as Karl Fohlmann, I heard the slightest of accents. As we talked, his wife came out of the farmhouse to greet me with several children around her, one in her arms and one obviously still inside her but perhaps not for too much longer. Fohlmann and his wife and children were all blonde, but she was so blonde as to be almost silver, like cornsilk. If she spoke English, I never heard her say more than a scattering of halting, well-practiced words of it. To her husband and children, I only heard her speak German, or I presume it was German. Together, they had filled their fields with corn and their house with children, both topped with silky yellow-white.

Their happy industry was apparent. Dark green fronds of cornstalks drank the Nebraska sunshine and rain and stretched far off into the distance, and a milking cow clipped grass with several beef cows as a calf reached under her to take her udders. A pen of pigs rolled and grunted in the mud of their pen, and cotton-headed children ran and played in the yard.

None of them were really old enough to help their father with the barn he was building, nor could his wife, being well-on in her state. One hand rested on her soon-to-be-born child and the other on her hip as she listened to us talk. I suppose in the isolation of the prairie any new human voice is like music, even if it's in a foreign tongue. The children leaned in and patted and stroked Pinch and coaxed him into chasing them.

Fohlmann didn't ask me to help him and likely would never have asked, he was too proud. He did ask if I would stay for dinner, and I said only if I could help him for my board. He was in no position to decline. The boy led the wagon into the shade of the lone tree in the yard, an old cottonwood, and unhitched the mule and put him out in the pasture with the cows.

The work of raising the barn under the summer sky was suddenly made entirely possible with two of us working, the effort reduced by half and more than a half. We raised the remaining sections by mid-afternoon and had rafters up by the end of the day. Fohlmann's oldest boy followed him around with the sweet idolatry that a boy has for his father, much like I had had for mine. Fohlmann was patient with the boy, who rapped away with his hammer, hitting wood or his own thumb half the time. When he managed to hit the nails, they would often bend and twist. When the boy finally tapped one in start to finish, Fohlmann smiled and said quietly, "That was a good one, Jacob," and then he gave the boy another.

I thought of my father and his easy way with me, and the way he always entertained my childish imagination and my dreams to fly one day. He not only sincerely listened to my fanciful notions, but he always spoke of them as if they were very likely. I felt a nearness to him that day, as I have from time to time in my life. As the sun sank to the west and the Swede and his son went in to wash for dinner, I tarried for a moment to watch the sun sink into the west. Again, I daydreamed about what it would be like to fly, bursting through the cloudless sky, watching the landscape below me change like a kaleidoscope with each turn of my head. My eyes scanned the corn and the tree lines and back. I was brought back to reality when the breeze shifted and carried the scent of the pigpen and the slap of my brother's words, "Jack, you'll no more fly than a pig." I went down and washed for dinner.

The children crowded around the table with Fohlmann and his wife at the head of it, all with heads of diaphanous hair, like spun pale yellow gold, like the tassels of corn, like the children of angels. The boys all wore the same denim overalls, and the girls variations of the same flour sack dresses. A summer breeze pushed the scent of the lilacs through the window, and they colored the air with their fragrance. They bowed their cottony heads and Fohlmann gave the Lutheran blessing in German and then in English. Then plates were set in motion.

Dinner conversation was doubled as everything said was translated from German to English and then from English to German. Mrs. Fohlmann watched my words as I spoke them and then turned to her husband as they were translated, nodding her head when she finally understood. I suppose I did the same thing as she talked.

When we were done eating, without so much as a nod, the children got up and cleared the table. It was so different from my childhood. We had house servants—people we owned—who cleared our table and did our dishes at the conclusion of our meals. Then my brother and I would be excused to go and study. I always went straight to my books, though my brother found excuses to avoid anything scholarly. I was deeply suspicious that he never read at all.

After the Fohlmann's dishes were cleaned, dried, and put away, Fohlmann's wife—Rachel, I believe her name was, Father— Rachel took a tin plate of scraps out to Pinch who wagged his tail like a willow in the wind. The oldest girl brought her father his pipe, and he read to the children in English from Grimm's fairy tales. Then their mother read to them from a book with the title, *Heilige Bibel,* written on it in elaborate, pointed gothic letters, and from the cadence of her reading and the names, I knew it was the story of Noah and the flood.

When the children filed up to bed in longjohns and nightgowns, Fohlmann poured two glasses of cider for us and made a toast, "In this world, my friend, there are only those who fix things and those who break things. Here's to those who fix." We clinked our glasses, the only two vessels they owned that weren't made out of wood or tin.

We talked for a while on the porch to the summer night sizzle of insects in the corn. He said that he had come from Germany to seek his fortune in America but had enlisted with the army when the war came. When the war was over, the call of the west seized him, and he bought a quarter section from the Union Pacific and found a good woman to make his wife. I said that I had fought, too, but on the opposite side. It made me wonder if we had ever sent bullets over each other's heads.

He said his brother was in the Confederate army and lived in New Orleans doing foundry work. It had been Fohlmann's greatest fear that he would somehow face his brother in battle and have to kill him or disobey orders and not kill him, but luckily it never happened. Killing my brother in battle would not have bothered me, Father. If I am to be honest about it, I have imagined it more than once. When Fohlmann asked me if I had siblings—here his accent betrayed him and he said, 'bruddas und sistas'—I only said, 'yes, a brother, but we were never close.' It would have been impolite to tell my host that I hated my brother more than anyone or anything.

Fohlmann said he missed his brother terribly and that one day he would visit him in New Orleans. "New Orleans is the place, sir," Fohlmann said, "All that goes out from here to market goes through there. Oh, yah, some might go out through Chicago, but New Orleans is the stopcock at the rivers' end, the place that controls the commerce."

It was a common belief in the west that New Orleans was a place of supreme opportunity. Crates of things made their way on the decks of steamboats, and then flatcars and boxcars, all the crates and barrels with *Ship via New Orleans* stamped on them. There were foundries and machine shops and iron works being set up in New Orleans. I began to think on it. Perhaps I could find a suitable mate in New Orleans. Beautiful girls were plentiful there, if you believed the railroad songs sung to the cadence of picks on rocks and mauls on spikes.

When our cider was gone and a second glass was gone, Rachel prepared their divan, one of their nicest pieces of furniture, for me to sleep on. Then she opened the door and Pinch rushed in and curled up on the quilt at my feet. And the profound silence of the prairie night curled up around the house.

The moon was full, and the pale yellow light flooded the farmyard and the bones of the barn going up and the sodhouse-turned-smokehouse. Pinch had gotten up and gone to the window. He was watching something in the moonlight. I rose and opened the door, and Pinch and I sat on the porch. The edge of the corn seemed to part, and shadows disappeared into deeper shadows. I thought it might be my imagination, maybe the pork was slow in digesting. Just then, out over the fields, the eastbound Union Pacific headed in from Cheyenne and California came by in a rush. It disappeared into the night leaving silent stalks of moonlit corn. Pinch and I went in the house and went back to sleep. Upstairs, in their room across from where all their children slept, I could hear Fohlmann and his wife practicing their attempts for even more children. I put my pillow over my ears.

After breakfast the next morning we roofed the barn. Down below, his wife watched us from the lilacs she had planted. Her eyebrows and eyelashes were a feathery blonde, so pale as to seem almost translucent. She had a hand to her brow and a hand to her midsection. I asked Fohlmann what they would do when her time came.

"Nearest doctor's in Lexington," he said, and he rapped his hammer and moved down to the next rafter.

"Who'll deliver the baby?" I asked.

"Me," he said as he pulled a nail from his pouch. "Like the others," he added, and he hammered the nail in with three sharp blows and moved down to the next rafter.

"What if there's trouble?"

"Any trouble is between us and God."

After a morning of work, we slaughtered one of the inhabitants of the pigpen, a thing I had learned how to do in the army and not as a boy, as we had had slaves who did that sort of thing for us. Fohlmann deftly went about it as his children watched the hard and fascinating truth of how animals become our food. His oldest, the boy Jacob, helped his father, who gave him simple tasks and quietly praised and corrected his son with their completion.

The chops were brought in the house and Rachel prepared them, while the rest of the pig was reserved for some sort of sausage and salted and taken to the smokehouse. Jacob was given the hams, and Pinch trotted at his heels lending moral support and hoping for a misstep. The meat was too heavy for the boy, so I wiped my bloody hands on my apron and went with him to help him hang the meat on hooks in the smoky air of the smokehouse. When the hams and bacon were hanged, Pinch was rewarded by Fohlmann with one of the bones. Pinch draped a paw over his prize as his old, yellowed teeth gnawed carefully at it all afternoon.

We washed and the Lutheran prayer was given in German and then English, again, perhaps for my sake, and we ate amid the orbit of plates and dishes passed around and the clatter of forks, knives, and spoons. There was corn on the cob, creamed corn, corn pudding, corn bread and some German-style dish, though it too was made with corn. There was also something that involved pickled cabbage and onions. It was all first rate cuisine for people who had put a day and a half of hard work into a single day. We ate heartily and wordlessly until Rachel said something and looked at me with the object of having her husband relay what she had said.

"She says she has a sister in the old country. She wishes she were here to meet you," he said. His wife said something else.

"She says you would make a good brother-in-law," he said.

I nodded and told her, "Thank you."

She smiled and closed her eyes and opened them to summon the response, "You a vill-comb."

The children giggled at their mother's English, and she smiled and everyone laughed saying, "You a-vill-comb, you a-vill-comb," to more laughter.

There was a strange kind of beauty to their marriage. They cherished each other's strengths, and though their faults were surely known to each other, they were held as mere trifles. Their children were growing up in the protection of that strength. I began to see it as the supreme blessing that it is, the love of a good mate.

That night, Fohlmann and his wife and their children had given over to sleep, but I was awakened by a dream. I had been having a series of dreams, most of them centering around my father. Some were comforting, some vaguely troubling, but all of them were strange. I woke from one of them in which my father had banished Fohlmann and his wife from their farm which somehow in my dream was synonymous with the Garden of Eden and Doc Durant was the serpent, though he looked like my brother.

I rose and took my quilt, and Pinch and I went out on the porch to look at the moon and stars and listen for the train to pass off in the distance. It was another nice night with a full glowing moon and the sound of chirping crickets. The sky was silver-gray over the dark outline of the corn. I was almost asleep again when Pinch nosed out from under the quilt and sat on the edge of the porch tilting his head this way and that as he watched the edge of the yard. His claws clicked on the porch, and he vaulted down the steps. His moonlit shadow disappeared and then reappeared at the edge of the corn, pausing to stand still and listen to the night. He returned with a light, muffled thump of paws on the steps and the porch, and he nosed back under the quilt with me. The ivory moon held its breath in the gray sky.

The next day as Fohlmann and I worked, Pinch returned to sniff the edge of the corn. Grassy clods of horse manure appeared scattered at points in the yard. Fohlmann and I examined them with the toes of our boots and with sticks. He looked at me, and, without a word, he went in to attend to something in the house. Later that day I saw that he had put a shotgun and a rifle by the window of the parlor. I picked them up and took a closer look. He had loaded them.

We said nothing of it as we worked that day. In the afternoon, I repaired some things he needed fixed, his plow, Rachel's sewing machine. I went up on the windmill to grease the wheel with some bacon fat. It had been a dry spring, and the Almanac said that the dry spell might prolong itself into a drought. I climbed to the top of the windmill with a tin cup of bacon grease to look at its workings.

I fixed the windmill, the simple matter of a stuck gear needing a little lubricant. I pulled down on one of the blades and, after an initial creak, the rest of them followed as the wind pushed them into a circular blur.

I took a moment to feel the wind push my hair. The enchantment song began again and I imagined myself flying as the blur of blades caught the wind in front of me. Pinch was down below, a small rusty brown blur looking up at me. I put my arms out and thought again of how marvelous it would be to be free of the earth, flying, cleaving the rising air, the air lifting me like a mother lifts her baby from its crib and then lovingly setting me down to earth again. Birds flew in the distance, merrily rising and falling. I closed my eyes and imagined doing the same.

I opened them when I heard Pinch whining down below. Something was moving in the corn, a ripple in the pattern of stalks. Feathers and the tips of spears and rifles appeared among the green leaves and golden tassels. I hastily climbed down the ladder, shouting to the children to get in the house quickly. Their mother came out and grabbed a child and I grabbed another, only pausing to shout into the barn to Fohlmann that we had trouble coming through the corn. He came out of the barn wiping dirt off his hands. We all piled into the house, and he barred the door and sent his wife into the bedroom with a rifle and the children. I took the revolver from my knapsack and filled the chambers with bullets. If I were going to break my agreement with God, I would break it in the defense of this family.

The feathers appeared over the tops of the spent tassels of the corn. They came out on horseback, single file, and then spread out in each direction to encircle the house. There were perhaps a dozen of them. One of them came so close so as to peer into the window. I clinched the revolver and pulled the hammer back and waited. He withdrew, and I scanned the yard.

Just then I saw Pinch wander out from under the house grinning and wagging his tail. He approached one of the horses, and the dog and the horse touched noses. It was then that I recognized Chester and his rider. The Sioux warrior was no longer the boy I came within the flex of a finger of killing. He had grown into firm manhood and wore a hat made of beaver pelts with long hair about the same color that hung down over his shoulders. Dried, cupped scalps were tethered by their hair around his waist. There was at least one of every color, including one with long blonde hair, and I wondered it was General Custer's.

The Sioux warrior looked at Pinch with a stoic expression that bordered on amusement. Pinch stretched his paws up onto Chester's flanks, and the Indian reached down and scratched the dog's ears. I set down my revolver and called across the farmyard, "Brother."

I unbarred the door as Fohlmann protested, "What are you doing, man?" In a leap of faith, I stepped out with my hands up and out. "Brother," I said again from across the porch.

He looked up from Pinch and with a slight smile replied, "Brother."

Then he whistled and yipped, and the rest of his war party came from their circle around the house and joined him in front of it.

"Mr. Fohlmann," I called out over my shoulder. "Have one of the children bring out that plate of leftover cornbread. Trust me on this."

The oldest girl, Frieda, I believe she was called, came with the cornbread wrapped in a kitchen towel. She was on the verge of tears, but I knew that this gift must be brought by someone who the Sioux would see as the least threatening. I took it from her and said, "Now there's a good girl. Now go back in the house."

Beaver Pelt—that's what I've always called him, as I never knew his name or knew how to ask him his name—took a piece of cornbread and gave half to me and a little to Pinch. The rest of the party shared the cornbread, though none of them smiled. When we were done, he took an arrow from his quiver and snapped it. I had heard of the custom. We were to put the broken arrow over our door as a sign not to be harmed.

Then Beaver Pelt whistled and yipped again, and his party formed up in single file and disappeared one by one into the corn. He was the last one of them in the yard of the farmhouse. He turned his horse and gazed at me for a moment. I didn't know if the Fohlmanns still had their guns trained on Beaver Pelt and me or not. At that moment, it seemed as though the house, the barn, the cottonwood tree, none of it existed. Pinch stretched his front legs up onto Chester, or whatever he was called now. Beaver Pelt traced his brown finger over the outline of the hourglass on Pinch's forehead, and he looked at me and said again, "Brother." He didn't seem to be calling me brother this time. It was the second and last time I saw the Sioux horse-thief, but in that moment it seemed as though I had known him all my life. He turned completely and rode into the corn, the beaver pelt hat swimming over the leaves and tassels and disappearing into the bursting, divergent rays of the setting sun.

Inside the house, the children were crying. Fohlmann stared at the floor with his head in his hands. His wife rocked and shushed their five year old, cradling the child's head in her neck. No one dared look out the windows for fear that the Sioux had returned.

Night fell without supper. No one had had the desire to cook nor consume food. I slept soundly that night and dreamed about my father, who in the dream could speak Sioux though I understood it as English. He said, "Promise me you will do this." The rest of the dream was spent rambling from one situation to another trying to remember what I had promised to do. Nevertheless, it was satisfying sleep.

The Fohlmann family, on the other hand, could not sleep. Every cricket in the corn was the signal of one Sioux warrior to another, every feather of every bird on every swaying branch was the approach of all of them. The children woke crying from nightmares, interrupting the small parcels of sleep their parents had managed to carve out from the long nights. Painted faces and braids peered at them when they closed their eyes.

The days were little better. The apple tree saplings Fohlmann had ordered arrived at the station in Cozad, and we undertook to plant them. Our labors were constantly interrupted by Fohlmann's checking the north and west, the direction from whence the Sioux party had come. We planted several dozen, but then he lost his will to plant the rest and they leaned against the barn, their roots enclosed in burlap. I tried to reassure them that the broken arrow was a symbol that would safeguard them, and I made a great show of nailing it over their door. Fohlmann tried to believe me but in his heart he couldn't.

There was no more work for me to do. Everything had been built, repaired, or sharpened. I offered to plant the rest of the apple trees, but Fohlmann said that wouldn't be necessary. All that was left was to wait for the corn to be harvested, but it still lacked a few weeks before it was to be brought in. No amount of suggesting or coaxing could set Fohlmann back to his tasks, which I gladly would have helped him with. His Eden had been poisoned.

With nothing left for me to do, I announced that I would be going. Pinch enjoyed one last round of petting from the Fohlmann children before he and I were sent on our way with a basket lunch of bacon and cornbread. I shook the reins, and mule and wagon, man and dog trundled out from under the shade of the farmyard's ancient cottonwood tree. The Fohlmanns gathered together on the porch and waved, looking oddly like shipwreck survivors crowded in a lifeboat. They no longer seemed at home, they didn't seem to fit any longer. High above the farmhouse, the prairie wind pushed the blades of the windmill into a perfect blurry circle, pulling water from the ground to nourish this man and his tow-headed family. I felt a pang of guilt, but I left them there. No one can rescue another man's dream. A man has to do that himself.

Several years later when I was back through western Nebraska, Pinch and I stopped in to pay a call on the Fohlmanns. I was hoping that Rachel Fohlmann had persuaded her sister to come over from the Old Country, and, if she were anything like her sister Rachel, I might decide to court her, if I could figure out how to go about it.

The fields were fallow, and the house and the outbuildings were empty, including the barn Fohlmann and I had raised. The nascent orchards were stunted and choked with weeds, the saplings Fohlmann had neglected to plant were gray, skeletal sticks with tattered burlap around their withered roots. The windmill creaked in slow revolutions, and the cottonwood tree in the empty farmyard threw down its shade for no one. Above the doorway the broken arrow safeguarded a vacant house.

A man at the neighboring farm said, "them Germans, or Swedes, I believe they was, left soon after their baby was born and took the whole gallery of them cotton-headed young-uns back east to one of the cities, Pittsburgh or Cincinnati. Or maybe it was Minneapolis. Left their crop in the field is what they done." He shook his head in disbelief of how a man would not reap what he had sown. "They done quit the prairie," he said as his eyes trained across the vast field to the abandoned Fohlmann Place.

I knew what had happened. For the Fohlmann's, every rustling feather in the corn would always belong to a Sioux war party and not a thrush or a magpie. The green fronds of the corn were the tips of spears and rifles, and the tassels and cornsilk were the manes of Sioux horses. There was no way they could bear it.

I have often thought of that German farmer and his handsome, healthy family and what became of them. Sometimes I wonder about Rachel Fohlmann's sister in the old country and if she married and decided to stay put. And now that the *Lusitania* has been torpedoed by a U-boat and we are on the brink of war with Germany, do the Fohlmanns fear coming under suspicion? Have they stopped speaking their native language? Are they worried that they might be caught with a book written in German, the one entitled *Heilige Bibel?*

Jack

Pinch and I headed east along the line carved out by the Union Pacific and the farms that sprouted along it in green corn and gold wheat. We passed places I recognized, places where I clearly recalled men staggering in late and drunk, arms braced around each other's shoulders, shirts open and untucked, singing, "The Wild Irish Rover," and "Whiskey in the Jar," out to the prairie night. Any buildings left behind by the work crews were only a collection of gray planks hanging on rusting nails trying to support slant roofs and failing. The prairie wind whistled through holes and gaps in them, and the earth, which was now domesticated and called Nebraska, slowly devoured them. Saloons, boxcars, tents, men, all gone. The only thing left was the railroad they had built.

There were few covered wagons creaking across the plains anymore. The travelers who had them were mostly people who had more time than money. They rolled across the prairie, usually with a woman under a bonnet on the buckboard next to her husband and a scrawny milking cow tethered to the back of the wagon, which was often full of children, and the quiet clang of household goods. For everyone else, the six month odyssey behind the shifting flanks of oxen was now a mere two days, and you could have coffee service from a sterling silver pot. If you could afford it.

Further east along the Union Pacific line, farms were becoming numerous enough that in some places you might be able to see one farmhouse from another, though it would be a speck far in the distance. Towns were building opera houses, schools, train stations, all out of handsome red brick and limestone, the mark of permanency. Near Kearney, we came upon a crew replacing the cottonwood crossties we had been given with more sound hardwood ties brought in by the railroad itself. We had been told to build it quickly, and now the crews were building it right. Overhead, the telegraph wires chattered in dashes and dots relaying a conversation between parties a thousand miles apart. What were they singing up there in electrical this-or-that language? What futures were being discussed? What plans were being hatched?

Almost as fast as the telegraph, word had gotten out up and down the Platte River and the Union Pacific line that I could fix things, and customers would be waiting at the next farmhouse or village. We became known as 'The-Tinker-and-His-Dog' and then, as we became even more widely known, "Jack-and-Pinch," The people of those prairie hamlets might say, "You oughta get Jack-and-Pinch to come and take a look at the thing next time they're through here," or "Jack-and-Pinch could sure get you a water well and a cistern. And a windmill what to pump it out with, too. Real reasonable and first-rate work. Oh, yah."

I replaced blades on plows, disks on harrows, slats on windmills, treadles on sewing machines, tines on threshers. I dug wells, fixed water tanks, coopered cisterns, sharpened knives and axes and plow points. I helped build houses and barns, all in the shadow of the whistle of passing trains bringing in more and more settlers headed out to plow and irrigate the land and build more houses and barns. I took what payment the farmers and townspeople could spare, room, board, a little change. I wasn't getting rich, far from it, but I was staying lean, muscular, strong. I felt like old age would never find me. But of course, Father, with time it has. So it is for all of us. And so it found Pinch, sooner than anyone who loves a dog wants to believe.

Before, as I worked, I would see Pinch's white-tipped tail cruise among the tops of wheat or prairie grass and then emerge with the limp, furry gray lump of a rabbit in his jowls. Now he would frequently return with nothing. In the evenings, we camped in the fields or in the barns or spare parlors of farmhouses. Pinch would give a contented half-yawn and push his nose under my quilt and nest into my side.

He and I crossed and recrossed Nebraska through summers and snows. The geese flew north and south and north again, the leaves changed, corn and wheat were sowed and reaped and sowed again. Babies born in the farmhouses grew to be children, and children grew to be young men and women who courted each other. The days had gone by like minutes, months like hours, years like months until fourteen years had gone by like a fortnight. A summer of working out west had turned into more than a decade. Where does time go, Father? Where can it hide? A whole decade, the 1870s, slid away somewhere, evaporating as Pinch and I wandered through it as if it were a fog bank on a cool night.

I was well into my thirties then and as fit as I had ever been. The cold western air and sunshine were only enhancing my stamina and virility. Pinch, however, continued to age in that accelerated pace of dogs, with a graying muzzle and an intermittent limp. Things in the mist no longer warranted a trip outside for him to investigate, only a brief muffled bark or a growl and a return to sleep. He chased things in his sleep, a sudden sideways scurry of his feet and a muted '*burf!*' as he pursued those dream-creatures, like when he used to chase prairie dogs, running from hole to hole and frantically pawing the dirt at each entrance. Now he would wake himself with his movements and look up to me blinking as if to say, "There were so many of them, Jack. I almost had us one." Then he would yawn and fall back on his side, blinking at the fire, and I imagined that he was frustrated that they had gotten away and that he was wishing he could summon the dream back to finish them off.

He was a friend to me when no one else was. He was more than a friend. He was my family. But the sad truth is that we outlive our dogs. I couldn't imagine life without him. He had become like a child's threadbare stuffed animal, much-beloved but beginning to fall apart. Even under a blanket he shivered. I knew I couldn't keep him in the cold climate anymore. I needed to take him somewhere warmer so we could have a little more time together, just a little more time.

The men of Nebraska and the United States had lined up to vote that year, and Garfield had been elected. I had caught snippets of the stump speeches in the towns I passed through, the transcripts published in their newspapers, which I read aloud to Pinch. I read the new president's inaugural address to him also, my dog's eyes blinking at the strange, fancy language. Another winter was approaching, announcing itself with each cool whispered breath from the north. I looked up into the sky where the sun was adjusting its path south, and birds were following it on the first chilly draughts of winter. Pinch shivered on the buckboard next to me where I had set him. I didn't think he would survive another northern winter. So like the Fohlmanns, we quit the prairie too.

My plan was to move quickly to the east and take the southbound from Chicago to New Orleans. Fohlmann had spoken of New Orleans as the hub of the universe, though I don't think he had ever been there. I knew that it was warmer there and rarely snowed. The songs sung on the railroad to the cadence of picks and shovels extolled the beauty and grace of the *pretty girls in New Or-Leans, as fair and regal as the queens.* I resolved to go and take Pinch there. I was a hard worker and a quick study. Certainly I would be able to find employment in "New Or-Leans."

My only worry was how to get Pinch on the train in Chicago. I thought of how we might do it. Dogs were only allowed if you were a first class passenger, something I couldn't afford. I thought of getting a basket and putting Pinch in it under blankets as if he were a baby. If I failed, perhaps we could stow away on a boxcar. Otherwise, we would be stuck in the infamously brutal Chicago winter.

We pressed eastward toward that dilemma, through the cornfields and wheatfields for the last time, through crossroads that had become hamlets, hamlets that had become villages, villages that had become towns, and towns that had become cities. Among the places flourishing along the Union Pacific line was Omaha. Of all the settlements, it was perhaps the most unrecognizable. Gone were many of the wooden buildings and the muddy main street. There were churches with soft ringing bell towers and a theater where productions were staged most nights of the week and with two matinees on Sunday by troupes of actors from Chicago and New York. Dress shops and millineries had replaced the saloons and gambling dens. Only the banks and brothels had survived the success, though both were now housed in respectable brick and mortar buildings with glass windows and curtains.

The Missouri River at Omaha had been bridged, and we crossed easily into Council Bluffs and Iowa. Pinch could no longer walk alongside the wagon for any appreciable distance and could no longer vault up and into the bed of it, so I lifted him up and in like a sack of flour, and we nestled in under the stars on clear nights and under an oilcloth tarpaulin on rainy ones. In the morning, I would lift him out so we could relieve ourselves. He sniffed the earth and the grass and the wind, his canine nose taking inventory of the scents and the memories they held. His old eyes were becoming gray and cloudy, and they ran with the secretions hardening at the corners. The days were shortening and so I hung a lantern and we traveled through the night as the north wind blew across our path. We crossed Iowa in a week, and then the Mississippi River at Davenport on the Government Bridge, a two-tiered marvel with rails on the second level and a path for pedestrians and carriages on the bottom.

The weather toyed with us like a cat with a flailing mouse. Sleet turned to snow flurries as we crossed into Illinois, and then they vanished but left the cold air as their warning. At last we reached Chicago. The brick and stone buildings rose toward the clouds that squatted down on the city, and a cold wind was blowing off the lake serrating the water into whitecaps like teeth. Traffic was still brisk, and as I began navigating the streets, making way for carriages and wagons and pedestrians bundled against the cold, it began snowing again, cold flecks swirling around buildings. I pulled over and wrapped Pinch in a blanket.

I didn't have time to sell the wagon and the mule, so I gave them to the Poor Handmaids of Jesus who ran the Angel Guardian Orphanage. The nuns pressed their palms together and bowed and looked up to the gray sky and genuflected. They offered me money from the drawstring purses at their waists, but I declined. I ran my fingers over the flanks of the mule I had never named, and Pinch nuzzled him. Then I turned away carrying Pinch, my body hunching over him to shield him from the cold wind.

The train station was a lovely building rendered in some fine architectural style. In the crowds disembarking, a big man in a wool coat and a bowler hat was moving from gentleman to gentleman and offering cards. He wasn't approaching any of the women travelers, only single men. We made eye contact, a mistake on my part, and he immediately approached me as if he knew me and had business with me, saying with a raised finger, "Sir! Sir!" His right eye was lazy and drifted off as he addressed me, and it seemed as though it was looking on its own for the next gentleman to accost.

He offered me one of the cards. On the front written in elegant, embossed font, was an address on Custom House Place, and, on the reverse side, a drawing of a girl in her underwear and a short poem advertising the charms and talents of the girls in the house with the boast in quotation marks, "*Most Favored Sporting House in Chicago.*" He said to make sure that I mentioned his name, Mr. Buckley, as he got a commission on every gentleman he referred to the house. I studied it for a moment and gave it back to Mr. Buckley, telling him that I did not partake in that sort of thing. He followed his wandering eye and faded away into the crowd looking for his next mark.

I consulted the timetable and found the ticket window for the train to New Orleans. The bespectacled clerk behind the iron bars told me that the next train south to New Orleans was the following morning. He looked down through the grate and pointedly told me that dogs were not allowed on the Chicago, St. Louis, & New Orleans, except in first class. I wished then that I had taken something from the Poor Handmaids for the mule and the wagon but I couldn't go asking for it now.

C. H. Lawler

Seeing no way out of Chicago that night, nor, perhaps, the next morning, I took a moment to think by a bulletin board with notices for traveler services. I pulled a flier from it and went to the rooming house advertised. It was only four blocks, but the frigid wind made it seem like four miles. I entered the place which had surely seen better days and still smelled faintly like smoke from the great fire almost ten years before. On the lobby wall, a framed handbill read: *Fireproof! Survived the Great Fire, October 8, 1871!* It certainly couldn't boast of being cold-proof or damp-proof. The man behind the desk said that it would be a dollar and a half, but when he saw Pinch at my feet he scowled, "Dogs is extra."

I gathered up Pinch and my bags and went behind a building looking for any warm place where we might spend the night. The corner of something protruding from a snowdrift caught my eye, and I pushed away the snow and found some discarded crates I pulled one after the other, shaking snow off them and comparing their sizes to the shivering dog at my feet, his rusty fur collecting snowflakes. At last I found one that had carried fine china to a dry goods store called Schlesinger & Mayer's. The lid was not far away, and I brushed the snow away from it, too. I took Aunt Rosalie's tattered quilt out of my knapsack and put Pinch in it and wrapped him up and put the lid on the crate. I could see his gray whiskered muzzle through a hole in it.

At another boardinghouse, I was able to take a room for the night, and I took Pinch up in his fine china crate. When he was fast asleep and chasing prairie dogs in his dreams, I left him and went out into the cold to make myself acceptable to my future traveling companions, if I were allowed to travel at all. I found Fields & Leiter's beyond my means, and so I bought a three dollar, second-hand suit from a discount store on Randolph. Cast-off, discount clothes would have to do. The man tried to sell me a greatcoat, but I couldn't afford it and didn't think I'd need it in New Orleans. On my way back to our room, I spent a quarter on a bath and a shave and bought us a little meat, cheese, and bread. That night, as we had every night for fifteen years, Pinch and I slept under the warmth of Aunt Rosalie's quilt as snow fell outside our window.

The next morning, men were shoveling it off the sidewalk. Through a hole in the crate I lugged down State Street, I could see Pinch's sniffing black nose surrounded by the quilt. It was cold, and I was wishing I had taken the clerk's advice on the greatcoat. I was grateful to enter the train station and escape the beating wind.

A different man was on duty at the ticket window, and he commented on the crate of Schlesinger & Mayer china I had, "Someone shall have a very fine Christmas!" he said with a smile.

"Mother loves fine china," I said, a truth that in the context was a lie. Mother would never be pleased with the contents of the crate. He stamped my ticket while humming "Silent Night." I presented it to the conductor, and he took it without a word. Just like that, we boarded the southbound. In our second-class berth, I pulled the thick curtain closed and set Pinch up in the bunk, covering him with blankets and the quilt.

With Pinch settled in, I moved forward to the passenger car and sat down, aware of how my frame made the most of my second-hand suit. A whistle blew and steam boiled from the locomotive and everyone in the car smiled with the motion. Outside the train window, Chicago slid past us as more snow began to pile up on the roofs and around the footings of its buildings, and trails of vapor and smoke struggled to push their way upward through the heavy, cold air. People held hats and bonnets down on their heads and snatched greatcoats around themselves, staggering forward against the icy wind coming off the lake. They disappeared into the distance as the conductor fed coal into the stove of our railcar and the stove fed us its heat.

On the seat directly in front of me, a woman slept with her head nestled onto the shoulder of her husband. The woman shifted, and her husband kissed the top of her head. She looked up to him and smiled and closed her eyes again as she nestled her head into his shoulder. I leaned into the window without a head to lean on my shoulder. I thought of the merits of a wife, a kind smile, a cheerful laugh, a breast as soft as a pillow upon which to lay my head, lips for the quick peck of a kiss at the start and close of every day. And at night, the naked rapture of the marital mystery. A mate seemed a fine thing to have, the finest of all things, someone to value above all others. Someone to sit beside in front of the fire awaiting honorable old age, perhaps with our children gathered around us.

The warm car of our train rumbled through the cold, and the snow turned to sleet, which turned to a dense rain. The woman on the seat slept with her head on her husband's shoulder. I wondered how one might go about wooing a beautiful girl from New Orleans or anywhere else. Was French necessary? Should I review my Napoleonic French, taught to me at West Point almost twenty years before? Would it serve? If only there were a formula for it, a set of instructions, an article in *Scientific American*. At last I drifted into sleep as we rattled over the work of unknown men who had graded and tied and railed all of it in all sorts of weather, each backbreaking section, a day's work raced over in a matter of minutes. I could almost hear their singing and shouting and cursing and spitting within the sounds of the train.

I woke to see that new passengers had taken the seat across from me, a young lady and her mother. The girl, perhaps twenty, perhaps a little older, had brown eyes and chestnut ringlets and a light scatter of freckles over her cheeks. Her burgundy dress had horizontal pleats all the way down to her fashionable boots. The pleats reminded me of ripples across the surface of a lake, and, when our eyes met, I told her so. Her freckle-spangled cheeks rose and her lips broke wide over perfect teeth. I found her very attractive. Her kid gloves braced herself on the seat in front of her as she and the rest of us swayed with the motion of the railcar.

As we began talking, I tried to remember my West Point manners buried under years of almost exclusively male company, from incarceration at Point Lookout through employment on the railroad. I'm afraid I prattled on about locomotives until she asked me if I was a Garfield man and if I was pleased he had been elected. I said I had no preference in the matter. She said that her father was vice president of a brewery in St. Louis and a Garfield man through and through because he had served under him in the late war. I said that I was in the late war, though on the losing side. She took that as an opportunity to ask me about my time in the war, expecting to hear about dashing charges into clouds of gun smoke, the sanitized version of the war taught to schoolchildren. Instead, I babbled about men ripped asunder and bodies found days later, and wounds and sickness and writing home to bereaved families. Her attentive smile faded, but she gamely changed the subject and asked to hear tales of the plains, of buffalo and gaily painted, noble savages, and I blurted out the tale of a Sioux horse thief and bloody snow and scalpless men. Our conversation faltered and fell between us.

She was too polite to get up and walk off. Rather, she gradually drifted away. I retired to my berth. While Pinch slept on my quilt, I tried to read but instead wallowed in the embarrassment gained by my clumsiness. The girls in the east were different from the girls out west. I resolved not to be so forthcoming next time. No one wanted or needed the details. Perhaps they would like to hear about bridges and tunnels. They might like to hear of noble savages on horseback, but not bloody snow and scalpless bodies filled with arrows. At breakfast the next day, I saw the girl and her mother disembark in St. Louis without so much as a glance or a goodbye.

After a solitary breakfast, I returned to my berth to find Pinch missing. I patted the quilt and turned over the bedsheets, but he wasn't there. There was a commotion in the aisle outside my curtain and when I looked outside it, I found one of the younger conductors hurrying toward the back of the train carrying something.

It was Pinch. He had gotten up and wandered off while I was at breakfast. The man stomped with the march of the righteous as my old friend looked over his shoulder at me with the bewildered gaze of an old dog.

"Where are you going with him?" I asked, following him.

"No dogs on the train!" he said, "Unless approved by the supervising conductor. Do you have a note?"

I didn't have a note, so I said, "Give him to me and we'll get off here."

"We're not slowing down the train," he said with the air of new authority, "Not for those who violate the rules."

Whether or not he meant to do it or was just bluffing to teach me a lesson, I was appalled that he would even consider throwing an old dog off a moving train. I was about to grab the young man by his collar and show him how things were settled on the old railroad when I felt a hand on my shoulder. A voice behind me said, "Could it be? Well, if isn't me old friend Pinch."

I turned to the voice, an accent from old Ireland like yours, Father. He gently pushed past me, this man in the crisp navy blue suit of a railroad conductor. He moved forward and cradled Pinch's rust-brown neck and scratched his gray chin and traced the white mark on his forehead. "I knew 'twas him the moment I saw the hourglass on the old feller's head." The conductor looked at me and said, "I recognized him 'fore I recognized you, Jack."

Ten years had passed since I had worked with Jimmy Mulligan building the Union Pacific. He had gained some weight, and it pressed into his waistcoat which had the chain of a pocket-watch trailing into it. The red hair I remembered had gray streaks in it and his beard was gone, traded in for a drooping moustache.

"You look just the same, Jack," he said, "But I see you have an old man with you now." He turned to the young conductor and motioned to take Pinch, and the young man handed Pinch over to Mulligan.

"But he soiled the aisle—" the young conductor protested.

"Well, go and clean it up, you *eejit*. Then later, when you're done, you and I will have ourselves a talk about hospitality, duty, and perhaps your future with the Chicago, St. Louis, & New Or-Leans."

The young conductor departed and left Mulligan and me.

"How've you been, Jack?" he asked as he lay Pinch on the bunk, and we sat on either side of him stroking his fur. We began reminiscing of our time on the UP, and, to hear us talking, that era seemed prehistoric and we had roamed it with the dinosaurs. We spoke of who we had seen and not seen, who was living and who had died and who had simply faded away. We laughed about the time Mike York and Billy McCarthy got drunk and fought naked in the muddy main street of Julesburg and the vile language of our foreman from Kilkenny, "and may God rest his soul," Mulligan said as he took off his conductor's hat, held it over his heart, and put it back on his head.

Pinch leaned into his leg, and Mulligan gave the white hourglass one more scratch before pulling out a notepad that shared the pocket with his watch. The pencil looked as tiny as a toothpick in the hand that used to wield a maul.

"Here, I'll write a note for me old friend," he said, and then he wrote slowly, carefully, clumsily, "*DOG O.K. FOR TRAVEL. J. S. MULLIGAN.*" He folded the note over and ripped it from the pad and gave it to me, and reached down and scratched Pinch's head and neck again.

"I see you have a little crate to keep him in. Let me suggest to you then, Jack, to keep him in it. Just in case."

I asked Mulligan if he still played his fiddle, and he said yes and that next time I found myself in Chicago to look him up and perhaps he would play it for me and we could have ourselves a 'wee dram,' and that Mrs. Mulligan would be glad to meet me. He scratched Pinch under his old snout one last time and said with that exhalation of angels, an Irish sigh, "Ah, but is there anything rarer or more honest than the love of a dog, I ask ye then?"

He rose and went forward up the aisle to the window. He looked out it, checking his watch again and waiting. A landmark whizzed past us, and he closed the brass cover. He came back to me and gave me his rugged hand and said, "God be with you, then, Jack." Then he tucked the watch into the pocket of his waistcoat and walked up the aisle calling, "*Pass-engers-ladies-gent-le-men-children, all what is departin' for Dyers-burg, we'll be at the station in eleven minutes!*"

A family with a little girl began gathering their bags. The girl clutched her doll under her arm and reached out with her hand for Mulligan's big hand, and he took that little doll-like hand in his big mitt of a hand and escorted the girl and her parents onto the platform in Dyersburg when the train had stopped. Clearly, he loved what he did. I knew for a fact that it beat what he used to do. The family safely on the platform, he bounded back aboard and went forward. As he walked away, a man who no longer dropped ties in place or slammed spikes into them with three smart blows, I knew our chance meeting had been a blessing. He disappeared up the aisle and into the first-class car. I thought I might see him again, but I suppose he was consumed by his duties up there.

Pinch lay on the aisle with his belly pressed into the floorboards of the car, fascinated and comforted by the strange rumble they made. While he ate his breakfast scraps, I lined his crate with Aunt Rosalie's quilt and picked him up when he was finished eating and put him inside. He curled up in a ring and went to sleep.

I read that morning as the gray-brown corduroy of winter cottonfields raced by. As I was returning from the dining car with some scraps for Pinch, the conductor announced *All for Grenada! Grenada, Mississippi!* I paused to look out the window at the coming and going of people. There on the platform I saw another face from my past, one I thought I would never see again.

Jack

At first I didn't recognize him. The last time I had seen him, he was on the parapet of Point Lookout dressed in Union Army blue with sergeant stripes on the sleeves. Now he wore a smart gray wool suit with a starched white shirt and a top hat. I let the window down to the dismay of the other passengers in the car as cold air rushed in, and I made the cricket noise of our youth. Several on the platform turned their heads, but only one recognized the sound, but he didn't see the source and was kept moving along by the conductor. The group of Negro passengers were quickly ushered into a car near the back of the train.

I hurried back to one of the rear-most cars, and there among the overalls and homemade dresses was the man in the nice suit with a carnation in his lapel. He was no longer the skinny colored boy of my youth, and the weight suited him. His manner and dress were those of a gentleman, and his beard had the first few strands of white on it. He had just taken off his hat and sat down with the evening edition of the *Memphis Commercial Appeal*. He looked up from his newspaper to me, and the expression on his face was like that of a man peering into a dusty pane of window glass. He asked himself a question aloud.

"Jack?"

He folded the paper and stood, and we clasped in an embrace of hands until we fell into an embrace of chests. The train began moving, and we lurched with the movement. He took up his hat and newspaper and invited me to sit.

I had not seen Neely since he was up on the parapet, and I had not talked to him in more than a whisper since we had moved with the army that day in Virginia. My impulse was to thank him then for saving my life at Point Lookout, but I didn't think I could do it without openly weeping in front of the strangers in the car with us, so I kept my gratitude to myself. I asked him where he was going, halfway hoping he was traveling to New Orleans like me. He said he was returning from a funeral 'back home' in Tunica, headed home to Tougaloo, just shy of Jackson.

"Whose funeral?" I asked.

"Old Aunt Rosalie, God bless her," he replied.

The urge to sob returned, stronger than before, but I suppressed it again.

"I wish I had known," I managed to say.

"She was a mother to all of us. Those hands prepared many a meal and sewed many a quilt and garment."

I nodded against the lump in my throat.

"Where have you been, Jack?" he asked with a degree of tenderness and wonder.

"I've been out west, working."

"I went by the big house looking for you. I don't think your mama remembered who I was. When I asked about you, she said she hadn't talked to you in years and had given you up."

"I think she gave me up long before I left," I said.

"She always favored your brother," Neely said. He could always see the truth in things even though he wasn't always at liberty to speak it. He said my mother didn't go to Aunt Rosalie's funeral, the woman who had kept her house and fed her family for decades. The reason was my brother was in for a visit.

"Your brother has a limp now. He makes a point of telling people it's a war wound. Word is he has a new wife, too, but that she and your mama don't get along. I suppose two women can't love the same man." Neely smiled wryly at the old joke. "Your new sister-in-law stayed behind in Louisiana. Folks who've seen her say she's quite a bit younger than your brother and uncommonly pretty and uncommonly headstrong."

Neely asked me if I had found a mate, and I told him no, that I moved around so much that it would be hard to ask a woman to adopt such a lifestyle. Now that I was headed to New Orleans to settle down to a job in a foundry or a machine shop, I was hoping to find a mate there. He said that he hoped I did, that he was married and what a treasure it was to have a good woman to enjoy life's blessings and endure life's hardships.

Our conversation became less constrained as our shadows raced over the sleeping gray cottonfields next to the tracks. We spoke of rabbit stew cooked over a campfire and the tug of fish on the line and the big buck we had seen through the clearings in the woods but that neither one of us had ever got a clean shot on. We spoke of people we had known and their habits and tics and things they had said. We spoke of the mule that wouldn't let anyone on his back and how as boys we had to find out for ourselves. We spoke of my dreams of flying and Neely said that if anyone could figure out how it would be me and he still believed I would. The train stopped at towns as their names were called, Winona, McGee, Kosciusko, Canton. White people and colored people, sharecroppers, laborers, preachers, judges, washerwomen, got on and got off, and still Neely and I talked, and I realized that Neely had been responsible, or at least present, for most of the happy moments of my boyhood. We talked so that I forgot that I was the only white man in the colored car and that I had Pinch's dinner scraps in my pocket.

The sun was setting, and the shadow of the train grew tall over the woods and fields on the east side of the tracks. The conductor called, *Tougaloo, four minutes!* and I rose and Neely rose. We shook hands as the eyes of the other passengers looked in admiration at the colored man in the suit with the carnation on his lapel. Neely wished me a Merry Christmas and told me to take care and come and see them sometime.

"Jack," he said as we parted over one last handclasp, "I'm not sorry I slipped away that night. It was the most frightening thing I've ever done. It was also the most important. I'm only sorry I couldn't tell you. I know you wouldn't have turned me in. I was only afraid you'd have gotten in trouble for letting me to go."

"You did the right thing," I said. "I admire you for it."

And I meant it. My boyhood friend had become a man the night he ran away from the country that claimed I owned him. He was at a loss for words and busied himself with his valise and his newspaper, though when he turned away, he wiped his eye with the side of his hand. When he had everything, he set it down for a second and gave me his calling card. "Come and see us sometime, if you're ever in Tougaloo."

I looked at the card,

Prof. Neely Moses

Mathematics & Science

Tugaloo University

Tugaloo, Miss.

We no longer shared a last name. He had changed his to Moses, after the Old Testament slave who had become a leader of his people. I put the card in my pocket and watched him as he stepped off the train with an almost military bearing, upright and steady with the newspaper under his arm. His wife was at the station waiting for him. She wore a dress with a long dark skirt and a white blouse with an ornate front and a high collar. Her eyes were long-lashed, and she had her hair swept up. She greeted him with a kiss, and he stooped and hugged his children and pointed to me and I waved. And then the train gave a gentle jolt and we slid away from each other. I watched him recede, and the admiring brown faces watched him recede also.

They couldn't help but admire him, nor could I. His suit was nicer than the one I was wearing, and he was going back to a home with a wife and children and a job, a *profession*, a purpose he was passionate about. His voice was sonorous and even, the voice of a lecturer and a teacher. He was what any man of any color should aspire to be, honorable and learned and dignified. A man of merit, a man worthy of another man's admiration and praise.

Because he was educated, he was my equal. And because he was my equal, I knew there would be those who hated him. He was no longer the class of man that illiterate and ignorant white men could feel better than. And so, despite his merits, he rode in the rear car.

I took Pinch's meal to him, a generous slice of railroad bacon and a hardboiled egg. I thought he might greet me with a wagging tail thumping in anticipation of food, but I had to wake him. His nose sought the air for what I had brought for him. He gingerly put his mouth around the bacon but then downed it in several gulps. The egg vibrated on the floor to the rumble of the train, and he steadied it with his paw. When he finished his bacon, not long, he dispatched the egg, shell and all, with a cheerful crunch. I scratched his soft forehead. His appetite had given me hope. In reality, it was the last nourishment he was able to take.

Jack

We made New Orleans early the next morning. The young conductor appeared cheerful and reformed after his talk with Mulligan, and he was pointedly helpful with Pinch, even offering to carry him off the train in New Orleans, as opposed to his inclination to throw him off it in Tennessee. On the platform, I arranged Pinch's quilt in the crate and placed him in it. I put on the lid, peering in to check on him, then I slung on my knapsack, put my satchel of tools on the crate and lifted them all. The sum total of my life, carried next to my body like a turtle.

The city of New Orleans bustled before me. I had been to Memphis as a boy and young man many times, but never to New Orleans, and it was an exotic place even then. Hearing it spoken of and sung about on the railroad had only amplified its stature. In reality, it was a frantic place. Whistles from the river and from the rails shrieked and moaned. In the daytime it was filled with scurrying people and hurrying wagons and carriages of all types. At night, it was filled with shouting, cursing, breaking glass, gunshots, and fighting of the kind I hadn't seen since the days of the celebrated York-McCarthy bout in Julesburg. I knew it was no place for an old dog.

Perhaps in the nicer parts of town, shop windows and porches were decorated with red ribbons and greenery and wishes for a Merry Christmas, but in the Irish Channel, where I had landed, gangs of slouching men and boys gathered at street corners, their eyes on my knapsack and my satchel and my crate and the bodies of passing women, some of whom pulled their garments about themselves and some of whom lingered to enjoy the stares. It was as if hell-on-wheels had settled down and made itself a city.

As I walked down the cobblestone streets, dogs approached, sniffing me and the crate and growling low warnings and nipping at my legs. None of them were friendly. All of them were city-bred and fearful of new dogs and men and aggressive in their expression of it.

To make matters worse, it was still winter and still cold, even in New Orleans. I realized that if I stayed and worked in the city, Pinch would have to stay locked up in the rented room I took. I knew Pinch only had a few weeks left at most. He was tottering and slow, limping and gray-muzzled. I wanted him to have a more rural place for his last days, a rented house with a sun-dappled yard to lie in and sniff its sunlight and shadows and relieve himself in.

After a night in a rented room and a dog who slept in a china crate and a lumpy mattress and rickety nightstand with a revolver on it, I decided it was best that we quit the city. New Orleans was a hard place for a man new to town, and no place at all for an old dog. The *Times-Picayune* advertised a position at Keefe & Bodley's foundry in a place called Houma, fifty miles to the south. For Pinch, I would go to the end of the earth if I had to, and Houma certainly sounded as if it were on the way. I telegraphed down to this place Houma, which I at first pronounce How-ma until corrected by the telegraph operator. I received a reply to travel down to Hoe-ma for an interview. BRING OWN TOOLS, the telegram said.

The Burden of Cane

The next-to-back page of the *Times-Picayune* held an advertisement for a steamboat that ran service there via a place called Donaldsonville on the river and then down a tributary called Bayou Lafourche. That evening, we left New Orleans like Lot and his wife leaving the babel of Sodom and Gomorrah. On the packet, we watched the river unfold before us and the city recede behind us. The river came alive, swirls and lines on the surface, birds wading along the shore, turtles on logs projecting from the bank into the water. A warm wind from the south caressed us, lifting Pinch's ears as he blinked into it.

At Donaldsonville, our packet developed boiler trouble, and we were disembarked there with the captain's apologies. The steward said that with a brisk walk, I could reach Houma in a day, just make sure I kept to the bank of the bayou. The weather was pleasant, and so we started off. I lifted Pinch and the quilt from the crate and left it, carrying Pinch in the crook of my arm, my satchel of tools in the other, and the knapsack on my back.

It was all too noticeable that Pinch was fading. He trembled when I stopped and set him down, and he could no longer bear his own weight. When I tried to pick him up again, he yelped in pain. Then he raised his old gray snout and looked at me, and his tired, cloudy eyes asked me, *why am I like this now, Jack? What has happened to me?*

I could no longer extend his suffering. I realized it was selfish of me to ask him to prolong his misery just so I wouldn't be alone. In a little town called Paincourtville, I stopped and bought him some meat, a choice cut, and he gummed it and looked up to me. I stroked his flank and his muzzle and the hourglass mark on his head. Fighting my tears, I pulled the revolver out of my tattered valise. I knew it was time, and it broke my heart. It broke my heart to endure it, and it broke my heart to have to relieve it. I put it to his ear and pulled back the hammer.

But in the end, I couldn't do it. Instead, I slowly let the hammer off, and I cried. We went to sleep together that night in the dance of the firelight, amber-faced in the glow of it, listening to the crackle and shift of the wood divided by the flames into orange and yellow squares. His old chest rose and fell under my hand, and in the morning I awoke to find it still.

It was my intention to leave him under an oak, as if peacefully sleeping under it. But after I had read a few lines from the Psalms, I saw a buzzard circling in the sky above the limbs, and I knew there would soon be more. I could not bear to think of my boy becoming their supper. So I began digging with a stick and then my hands and his dish, frantically trying to protect him from their deprivations, as well as the appetites of other creatures who might come for him on a moonless night, attracted by the scent of his flesh. I dug deep in the earth so that he would not be disturbed from his rest, my faithful companion.

When the grave was deep enough, I wrapped him lovingly in Aunt Rosalie's quilt and lowered him into the earth, pausing to weep violently. I tried to read some fitting words, something more from the Psalms, but my eyes would not see the page and my mouth would not form the words and my throat would not allow the air for them anyway. Then I gently packed the earth down with my bare hands, as if putting a child to bed, telling him and myself and God, we shall meet again, surely we shall meet again.

I slept that night by the grave, without a fire, for I could not bear the thought of a firelight without him in it. The next morning, I rose and left, resisting the urge to look back upon it. But I left the tin dish that the Confederate Army had issued me nailed to the tree with his collar I had made from braided telegraph wire. I'm not certain, but I believe it might have been Christmas Day, 1880.

Pinch

I curl up under the table as my master Jack talks with the man in the black suit with the white collar, the man he calls 'Father' though the man is much too young to have sired him. We dogs follow, and forever, in flesh and then in spirit, because a dog's faithfulness doesn't end with his time on earth. It extends forever, until the hereafter and beyond. Men believe they are the pinnacle of God's creation and the perfect representation of His image. In that they are mistaken. In truth, we dogs are. But because we have the loving hearts and temperaments of the Supreme Master, we dogs let men believe whatever they wish. We are angels, that is all and nothing less, too good, too divine for human form while on this earth.

I have been with my master Jack since he found me in a blackberry patch almost fifty years ago, partly in body, mostly in spirit, which is the way of dogs when they love someone. He was wearing tattered gray clothes the day he found me. I was separated from my littermates and napping, exhausted after having tried to fight my way out of the briars. He reached among the thorns and pulled me out and I yelped and he made shushing noises and stroked my fur. It felt good, to be stroked did, and I gave him my belly, and he gave me a piece of bread and salty meat and he had some himself. The man got up and I followed him hoping for more bread and meat and stroking. I forgot all about my mother and my littermates under the porch of the farmhouse. It was well, for she had denied us her teats now that we could eat the scraps set out for us.

The man Jack and I stopped again and he ate and I ate and I wanted to play with my littermates but I remembered that they were back at the farmhouse where we were born, and so I brought the man a stick and we tugged on it and he threw it and I brought it back and teased him with it. Darkness seeped into the day and he made a fire and we lay down in the light of it and he scratched the fur of my back and side and head and he said, 'Well, I was looking for a friend just now but I guess you'll do in a pinch,' And that is the name I answered to the rest of my life on earth, Pinch.

The plains was a wonderland of smells for a dog's nose, the traces of a multitude of prairie creatures, pheasants, buffalo, jackrabbits, antelope. And the painted men like the one who stole the horse and who we chased through the snow and who my master decided not to kill.

During those years, my master the man called Jack would whimper and howl in his sleep, and I would creep over to him and curl up next to him, pushing my body and head into his. I myself have always slept soundly, having a good, pure heart which leads to a clean conscience.

It was in old dog age when I awoke from a dream in which my littermates and I were chasing possums. In the dream there were hundreds of them, and great was our pleasure in chasing them. I had almost caught one, a fine, fat, sharp-faced, white-haired fellow when I awoke to the feeling of my master the man called Jack, stroking my belly and ears.

What is it, Jack? I asked with my eyes as I smacked and blinked. He tried to smile but his eyes were red. He put the gun to my ear and I felt it waver and he withdrew it. Then he put down the gun and put his paws in his head-fur and wept. He was weeping for me and the sad state I had slipped into. He wanted to release me from my suffering but he could not do it. And so later that night, as he rested, troubled (for a dog can always tell these things), I departed into this place, like becoming a reflection. The next morning he found me. It was only then, after he had wrapped me in our quilt and the dirt fell on my lifeless fur and muscle and bone that I realized this to be true:

The soul of a dog may not leave this world until so does the soul of its master. The bond is too great to be so easily broken. And so I have followed unseen at his heels, patiently waiting for him to join me here.

Part III

Eva

This is not the first time I've adopted the black attire of mourning, Mrs. Leonard. The first time was when I left Shreveport thirty-five years ago, the winter of 1880. Of course, I wasn't mourning anyone, not even the so-called Mr. Standproud, who had departed the earth on the front kneeler of Holy Trinity Catholic Church if the *Shreveport Times* was to be believed. My plan was to use a covering of black lace as a ruse to safeguard my identity from the prying eyes of any former patrons on my way down to New Orleans and then quit that costume on my arrival, which is exactly what I did.

I bought a second hand mourning dress of black taffeta and lace from a shop on Texas Street. It was much too large for my lithe frame, though I believe that these days it would fit me much better and perhaps rather snugly. I also purchased a book called *Good Manners for Young Ladies, The Ladies' Book of Etiquette, and Manual of Politeness, A Complete Handbook for the Use of the Lady in Polite Society*, by one Florence Hartley. Perhaps you are familiar with it, madame.

My last purchase in Shreveport was a berth on a steamboat to New Orleans. Miss Hartley suggested that if I were to pass a night upon a steamboat, I should secure a stateroom, as I would enjoy the luxury of being alone, able to retire and rise without witnesses and that it would fully compensate for the extra charge. It would be important for the steward to escort me to it, lest I be seen as 'vulgar' and 'ill-bred,' the worst things that could become of a young lady according to Miss Hartley.

On the levee in Shreveport, the agent behind the iron bars took my money and pushed my ticket under the grate of the window and said, 'Sorry for your loss, ma'am.'

"What did I lose?" I replied before I remembered my role. Recovering quickly, I nodded and sorrowfully thanked him for his kind sentiments, which is what Miss Hartley's book said I must do.

In my stateroom on the steamboat, social status became my catechism, advancement was my prayer, and *The Ladies Etiquette Book* was my Bible. I studied it and then went up to the salon, where behind my lace curtain I observed the refined ladies and their families, how they ate and talked and carried themselves. One stood out in particular, a statuesque lady with a husband whom I knew quite intimately down to the raised mole on his backside and the *Oh my!* he exclaimed at the height of his ecstasy. I couldn't remember his name, if I ever knew it. We girls generally referred to him as Mr. Mole-bottom, though never to his face, of course.

A flash of blue must have seeped through the black lace of my veil, and I enjoyed the glances of the men, several of whom came to offer their condolences and make an attempt at conversation. I sent them away as politely as I could, afraid that any prolonged encounter might have aroused their suspicions that I might have once aroused their passions. 'I appreciate your kindness, sir,' was all I said as I made the show of blotting the nonexistent tears behind my thin lace curtain.

For the most part, I kept to my stateroom, studying Miss Hartley's guide and reading the New Orleans papers, memorizing the society pages. Carnival would be approaching on my arrival, and I meant to secure my admittance to the balls and soirees where I might find a suitable husband, well-endowed financially, and with any luck, physically. The advertisements for dresses and corsets and so forth all had drawings of women in the latest hairstyles, and I now forsook my ponytails and braids which had given me a youthful air and took up a more involved coiffure, experimenting in the looking glass as outside the engines chugged and the paddlewheel slapped the water on our way downriver.

Let the hair be always smooth and becomingly arranged, Miss Hartley's book urged. *When traveling, avoid carefully any article of dress that is glaring or conspicuous, above all, never wear jewelry (unless it be your watch) or flowers; they are both in excessively bad taste.* Here, I slipped off my bracelet, a trinket affectionately given to me by one of my gentleman callers.

In Baton Rouge, Mr. and Mrs. Mole-bottom departed, and I seemed to remember that he had some connection to the university there. I was relieved to bid them a silent farewell, as I recognized none of the remaining passengers as patrons. However, I kept my visage concealed as we resumed our voyage downriver.

I disembarked in New Orleans where I had the porter procure me a hack, and I took a room at the St. Charles. The bellman opened the door and asked me if I required anything else, and then left me with it. After so many years, it seemed odd that a gentleman shouldn't join me in the enjoyment of the room. Just as he left, I called to him, telling him at what hour I would be dining, as Miss Hartley said I should. When I was finally alone, I quit my mourning clothes and donned a walking dress with a cape and bonnet.

At six o'clock, I was escorted by the waiter to my table and dined alone, no bustle of bawdy, smoking women eating bread and cheese and drinking cheap beer in their drawers. Instead, I ate slowly, mindfully, politely and with good posture. I practiced with the butter-knife, salt-spoon, and sugar-tongs, more advice from the tiresome Miss Hartley. I turned in after another evening of studying her guide and woke with it buried under the covers. I took it up again over morning coffee in bed, served in fine hotel china amid linens that had not been changed six times the night before. I found my place marked with a small sheet of hotel stationary with the imprint of the hotel's columned façade.

Dark silk in winter, and thin material in summer, Miss Hartley cajoled, *make the most suitable dresses for evening, and the reception of the chance-guests ladies in society may usually expect. At breakfast let her wear a close, morning dress, and never, even at supper, appear alone at the table with bare arms or neck.* And, of course, no bare back, breasts, buttocks, or thighs, Mrs. Leonard. I made a note of it.

I dressed suitably and studied it again over breakfast and planned my trip to Madame Olympe on Canal Street, the foremost dressmaker of her day and a woman of superior taste, according to her advertisement in the *Times-Picayune.* To conserve cash, I planned to buy the rest of my wardrobe at Godchaux' and Levois & Heirs. I also had calling cards printed, Eva McCarron, McCarron Hall, Madison Parish, Louisiana. To expedite them, I gave the clerk a tip and a shy glance, and he said they would be ready within the hour.

At Mme. Olympe's on Canal Street, I was greeted by the proprietress who wore a tape measure around her neck and draped over her ample bosom. She brushed away a stray strand of hair impossibly black for her age, no doubt dyed with coffee-grounds which was the way of the French women of the city then and now. She seemed mildly annoyed or rushed or both. Carnival season was fast approaching, and in the back were seamstresses pushing and pulling needles and working the treadles of sewing machines, arranged in rows much like a group of convicts working oars on a galley.

I produced my calling card, worrying as I handed it over that the ink might not be dry. She took it and gave it back to me. I told her that I had just emerged from mourning and had inherited a 'tidy sum,' and I was looking to have some dresses made including a pair of ballgowns. At this, her demeanor improved immediately and I understood without it being said that she, like I, was a follower of the golden calf. She said that she had on hand a bolt of royal blue silk just in from Paris and that it would suit my eyes perfectly and that she had shown it to no one. She waved away her shop girl, taking me to a fitting room and circling my waist and breast and buttocks with her tape measure and calling out the measurements in French to her girl, who wrote them down. Mme. Olympe pronounced me to have a fine figure, or 'fig-yare,' as she said it. I refrained from cupping and jiggling myself, and only thanked her and smiled. I'm sure Miss Hartley would be proud.

As we emerged from the fitting room, Mme. Olympe gushing over what my appearance would be in the blue silk ballgown, a woman came in attended by her colored girl. When Mme. Olympe saw the woman remove her gloves and give them to her servant, she quickly piled the blue silk and the sheet with my measurements into my arms and turned her attention to the woman, like a dog dropping a small bone when presented with a larger, meatier one.

"Bonjour, Madame Howcott!" she exclaimed with great pleasure. To me, Mme. Olympe said dismissively, "my girl will see to you now."

The name rang a bell, and I remembered her from the society pages as Mrs. Edith Howcott, one of the pinions of society and a war widow. Here was my chance, the first rung on the ladder, a small hole in the garden wall to squeeze through. The moment was mine and I seized it.

"Oh, you are Mrs. Howcott!" I remarked, "My late father always spoke so highly of your late husband. They were in the war together. Why, I believe he was there when your husband fell in battle."

This had a wonderful effect. I introduced myself for the first time in years, correctly, as Eva McCarron, and we chatted for a few moments. While Mme. Olympe waited for a few moments, anxious to tempt her customer with finery, Mrs. Howcott asked that I might pay a call, as she had a son who was of marriable age who could benefit from the society of a beautiful young woman like me. I blushed and told her I would be by that afternoon if that suited her. Time was of the essence, Mrs. Leonard. I knew that at the present rate of expenditures, my hatbox wouldn't hold out forever.

That afternoon Mrs. Howcott and I had tea as I struggled to remember Miss Hartley's dictums and manage the sugar tongs and my grammar at the same time. In fumbling a cube which landed on the carpet, I apologized with the excuse that I was new to town and had just come out of mourning. As I reached for it, the servant girl stooped and got it and put it in her apron.

Mrs. Howcott had a son she called Alexander, never Al or Alex, who was the effeminate version of his warrior father in the portrait above the mantle. The three of us sipped tea as his mother tried to draw him into the conversation of his late father and my fictitious one and the glory of the Howcott and McCarron names and the regrettable outcome of the late war. He only commented once or twice, both times remarking that he hoped the azaleas would bloom soon and that the camellia blossoms were certainly lovely and that he preferred the pink ones to the white and red.

It soon became apparent to me that this son she had set aside for me was an impossible case, a skinny pansy of a boy with full, womanly lips and a wan look on his face. Every shy glance and subtle flirtation as allowed by Miss Hartley fell to the floor between us. There was nothing at all manly about him, and I suspected he was a fancy-pants and possibly a sodomite, or prone to being one. There was no chance of a match, though Mrs. Howcott vainly tried to make one. It was hopeless, though at the end of our visit she insisted that he escort me back to my hotel. We rode silently under the oaks of St. Charles as the horses trotted and the driver ticked-ticked to them and the opulent houses receded past us. At last he assisted me out of the carriage, taking my hand in his, which was cotton-soft and silk-smooth. He did not ask to call on me again but only wished me a good day and a pleasant stay in New Orleans. I could see at once that he would not be in play. While the money was the main thing, I had no intention of giving up physical pleasure and this milquetoast showed no sign of delivering it.

Once in my room, I consulted with Miss Hartley who gave me the following advice:

The Burden of Cane

Immediately upon returning home, compose a note of thanks to your hostess with an expression of your gratitude for having spent time in her company. Within the next week, you should call upon her, if it is the first party you have attended at her house. If she is an intimate friend, the call should be made within a fortnight.

I composed a note full of flowery gratitude and in return was asked to dinner. Again, Alexander and I endured his mother's futile matchmaking over as sumptuous a meal as I had ever consumed. A servant in fine livery with white gloves and skin so dark that he was a mere shadow in the gaslight carved servings from an immense beef shank while another ladled soup into fine china bowls. Mrs. Howcott, Alexander, and I ate together, he as blank as ever while his mother used the conversation to fan the spark which had no chance of becoming even the slightest flame. He was again asked by his mother to accompany me back to my rooms, and again he politely bid me good night without the slightest caress or look of desire. I believe he had no more appetite for female flesh than a lamppost.

Mrs. Howcott and her limp-wristed son were only my portal. With good looks and aggressive flirtation, it was easier than you might suppose for a girl to gain access to society in New Orleans. I continued to pose as the recently orphaned daughter of a wealthy cotton planter, now alone in the world with a small fortune which was at first whispered of, but which grew with each hushed telling behind waving fans in the parlors of St. Charles Avenue. The rest of my story I kept purposefully obscure, though I spent money, even in smaller purchases, in a showy manner. My hatbox, however, was growing empty.

From Mrs. Howcott, I pressed my circle outward, first by courting aging women with motherly instincts, playing upon their inclinations to have something to pity and nurture and advocate. Through them, I was invited to all manner of social occasions. The names from the society columns came alive for me as I worked at securing a foothold in the realm of persons of consequence. The Howards, the Isaacsons, the Nashes, the Morrises, members of the Pickwick and Boston Clubs and their wives, the mayor of New Orleans, Mr. Patton, and congressmen home on recess from the capitol. It helped that carnival season of 1880 was approaching, a time of merriment and extreme. Guards were lowered, inhibitions surrendered, which made navigating those levels of society much easier and the prey less elusive.

As my social opportunities expanded, I found it necessary to purchase a third sumptuous ballgown from Mme. Olympe on Canal, an investment from the till of my hatbox. I could now see the bottom of it in places. Each soiree and tea and dinner became a stepping stone for more soirees, teas, and dinners. These clever blue eyes and the instructions of Miss Harley worked their magic, and soon I found the need to purchase a fourth gown on credit and a pair of walking dresses with matching bonnets and kid gloves for visits to parlors, invitations extended from prior social events.

From one parlor to another and with each soiree my circle of acquaintances grew, I cultivated the art of conversation, however tiresome it might have been. I collected stories of one person, relayed them to another, corroborated or dispelled. The more hushed the tone they were told, the closer I listened. I took these stories and fixed them, twisted them a little, never too much, to my liking and my purpose, and then passed them along at the opportune times. Within a few weeks, my new identity as the recently orphaned daughter of a cotton planter, left modestly well-off was secured, and it was time to ascend ever higher.

At last I found myself in an opulent parlor casting glances and smiles in a room full of distinguished guests in gowns and tuxedos. It was in one of the fine homes off St. Charles, a lavish place full of sparkling chandeliers and flickering gaslights and leafy palms, busts of Greeks and Romans on pedestals and portraits of past kings and queens of carnival on the walls, all looking down on us mortals and the mahogany furniture and Persian carpets and the steady boil of conversation and polite laughter that filled the drawing rooms and parlors. The musicians released sedate music into the amber light, so different from the bawdy music played by our colored piano player on Commerce Street. Men in tuxedoes and women in spectacular gowns sipped from glasses of glittering liquid. I smiled and nodded, clinging to the importance of maintaining a cheerful deportment *'whilst avoiding being seen as ill-bred and vulgar.'* I listened attentively to discussions of politics and horseracing and carnival, attentively, that is, in appearance. Though I kept my eyes on the speaker, I would glance around occasionally to scan the room. Once or twice I closed my eyes to recall Miss Hartley's words:

Never interrupt anyone who is speaking. It is very ill-bred. If you see that a person to whom you wish to speak is being addressed by another person, never speak until she has heard and replied; until her conversation with that person is finished. No truly polite lady ever breaks in upon a conversation or interrupts another speaker. It was in a section entitled, *How to Behave and How to Amuse.* I already knew how to amuse. It was the behaving that I would have to learn.

I was holding my plaster-of-Paris smile trying to keep my eyes from rolling back into my head when I saw him there, much like a lioness spots the weakest member of a herd and devotes her energy to bringing him down. He was thin armed and bandy legged, with an overfed gut that pushed out against his cummerbund. His hair was graying from a color that had once been the color of sand with a hairline that was in full retreat and halfway to the rear. His beard held even more gray hair and there was a hint of a scar within it. There was something about him that exuded wealth, perhaps his finely fitted evening clothes, perhaps the set of his jaw, but I could tell from my dealings with the wealthy side-door men that this fellow had treasure laid up.

I cast a glance to him, but he didn't see it. I was about to try again when I was fetched by my hostess, Mrs. Wheelock, *the* Mrs. Wheelock, wife of the king of Rex a few years prior, and ushered into a room where there were several young men my age. Before I left the room, I made eye contact with my quarry and gave him a sly smile and pushed out a blush and softly bit my lower lip for his amusement. I knew his look. He had gotten his first sniff of the bait.

In the adjacent room where Mrs. Wheelock had led me, I found a trio of three young men, men who were handsome enough, I grant you, but nowhere near old enough to be of any means, young men who were still under the auspices of wealthy fathers, still too young to have established themselves. They were strapping young men in evening clothes but still a tad self-conscious in their unaccustomed finery. These young bucks were not what I was after. These fellows had been the theme of my life so far, so I was not taken in by this display of virility and pent-up youth. Instead, my thoughts were in the adjacent room and the old, limping lion who had taken up my scent. I was after the old and the infirm, and, of course, rich.

I endured the boastful conversation of this trio, each trying to out-posture the other for my approval and affections. Little did they know that just a few months earlier it could have been purchased by the hour with their pocket change. I was wondering if any of them ever attended the various sporting houses there in town or if any of them had even been with a woman at all when, out of the corner of my eye, I spotted the old lion. He had caught the colorless, odorless scent of attraction and was following it.

I excused myself from the trio and turned to go for the stairs. At the top, I cast down a careless glance and let my fingers toy with the banister. Down below, he watched his foot on the first step of the stairs. I ducked into a room with a mirror which happened to be placed facing the doorway. His steps patiently trudged up each tread. I paused until I heard him make the landing and then I began fixing my cleavage in the mirror. He appeared in the dim depths of the mirror and I ignored his wide-eyed stare as I innocently, inadvertently, surreptitiously straightened my décolletage, giving him a brief, immodest glimpse of blushing pink half-circle before pulling up the low neckline with a jiggle and a bounce. I tilted my head and brushed back a few strands of hair from my face, all the while pretending that I didn't see him.

There were cheers down in the front parlor, and the old lion turned when someone called, 'Sam! Sam Teague! Your old friend Mr. Howard is here!'

So the old lion's name was Sam Teague, I told myself.

I decided then that I would become the tamer of this lion whose mane was halfway between turning gray and turning loose, and whose mouth had lost a number of teeth, it was said from a bout with cholera almost ten years before.

Once again in the parlor I was set upon by the cloying young men who did their best to seem interesting. At last, I was able to work free from the tiresome conversations. I cast glances back to my prey, this Sam Teague, and he could not help to break from his conversation in midsentence. One of the women in his circle looked over to me, and I saw her mouth form the words, *'well-off.'* I smiled a blushing smile, part of the ruse and part of it congratulations at having passed myself off correctly.

The older matriarch of a woman took this old lion, whom I now knew was Sam Teague, from the knot of conversation and escorted him toward me where I waited at the base of the stairs. We were introduced and began talking, the older woman dripping in pearls and diamonds, driving toward the subject of yet other balls and parties and soirees, which she pronounced affectedly, 'swore-raaays.' I pretended to be a friendly listener until, mercifully, our host was called away to attend to a matter and left the old lion and me to ourselves at the base of the stairs.

"My, but your eyes are the deepest blue, Miss—" he said as he took my hand and I forced out a blush and batted my eyes. They had worked their magic again. They had once, over time, gotten me a small fortune. Now they would fetch me a large one and with no time to spare.

"—McCarron," I said, "Eva McCarron."

I smiled and blushed and pulled in my lips and twinkled my eyes—all maneuvers that I had been taught on Commerce Street, now that I think of it. At the end of the evening, I whispered to him that I had taken rooms at the St. Charles and that I should like to lunch with him the following day at Antoine's if he could secure a table and that I hoped it was not too expensive. Here I was throwing down the challenge. He said that of course securing a table and paying for the meal was not a problem for a man of his situation. I knew then for certain that I had found my mark, a man with both money and a pride in having it.

The next day we met and I ordered practically half of everything on the menu, taking only a bite of each dish. This man Teague did not balk at my wastefulness and caprice. He had passed another test. It was time for me to make another step.

I leaned into him under the dim murmur of conversation in the main dining room and whispered, "Sir, allow me to say that I am drawn to you in a way which I do not understand." This, of course, was part of the old Commerce Street nonsense, the kind of talk that was reserved for the side-door men, though I doubt that any of them ever truly believed us.

He had the hook well-in then, and I could not have gotten rid of him if I had tried. I put my hand on his, moving a dish of trout meuniere to do so. He had the vacant look of the vanquished. He paid the bill after scarcely looking at it, and we departed to the St. Charles.

In the lobby, he hinted at coming upstairs, but I only looked away, allowing him to take my hand and kiss the cotton of my glove. I ascended the stairs, knowing that now he would do anything I wanted. It was only a matter of timing. At the bottom of the marble staircase he had the empty look of something wild having become domesticated.

Eva

Are rubber water bottles also used in England, Mrs. Leonard? For relief from the pain of the monthly malady? A simple rubber water bottle was the key to finally landing my husband.

We met again at another party hosted by yet another New Orleans well-to-do. There was a scandal that year that the Krewe of Momus had dressed as women, and conversation buzzed around it. Some thought it an outrage, though most thought it all in good fun.

I arrived just a little late and gave the called-for apology to my host, as Miss Hartley directed. Mr. Teague was in the front parlor speaking with another gentleman, his friend Mr. Howard. Mr. Teague's eyes caught mine, and I purposefully ignored him and proceeded to the servant who took my coat and placed it with those of the other guests. I tarried a moment in the hallway by the stairs, and when I saw Mr. Howard leave the sitting room with an empty glass, I went into the room.

"The others are in the parlor," Mr. Teague frowned, perhaps feeling overlooked.

"I didn't come to see them," I blushed, perhaps a bit theatrically, though he was too spellbound to give any notice to it. "I came to see you, Mr. Teague."

I gave a furtive glance to the parlor, and I took his hand. They were singing in there, some sentimental ballad from the late war about waving handkerchiefs and sad farewells. I put my hand to his doughy waist and raised up on my toes and put my other hand to his bearded cheek. I closed my eyes and put my lips to his. His mouth tasted like any of the mouths on Commerce Street, like bourbon and cigars, but I kissed him on it, fully and with closed eyes, opening them at the conclusion of our kiss to flood him with their blueness. His gray eyes were completely stunned, but when he recovered his senses, he tried to kiss me again. I only smiled and went into the parlor singing along with the other guests in there the ballad, "Because She Wore a Yellow Ribbon." I didn't give him an opportunity for another kiss that night. Instead, I let him simmer.

He called on me at the Saint Charles the next day and took me to Spanish Fort to hear the orchestra and see the fireworks. The day after that, he took me to the races and let me pick the horses capriciously on their names or the colors of their silks and did not flinch when we (or *he*, I suppose) lost big. It further underscored the fact that he was my man.

On each carriage ride, he began brushing a bosom or thigh. To a certain point, I allowed it, but if the hand lingered, I nonchalantly replaced it somewhere less intimate, a forearm, usually. I began to wonder if he would tire of being delayed in this manner, so when his hand would linger on an inner thigh or a breast, I would close my eyes and sigh, and let it caress me a moment more before replacing it with a shaky hand in a show of crumbling resolve. I didn't want him to lose heart in his efforts.

It was Mardi Gras night when I finally sprang the trap. We were in a private box above St. Charles watching the Comus parade pass by below us. The theme was the Aztec peoples or some-such, but the streets were alive with color and sound and the flames of capering darkeys. Mr. Teague and I sat together under a blanket, and he stroked my inner thigh causing me to become distracted with the passing spectacle. As the last of the parade passed, all those in our box adjourned to a ball held by our host. He and I had danced but one loping quadrille before he proudly proclaimed that his war-wound, which he seemed to both endure and cherish, prevented him from further dancing. But I knew what he had in mind, and it was not dancing. Not vertically, at least. We left early without bidding our host goodnight, a breach of Miss Hartley's dictums, and he escorted me back to my rooms at the St. Charles. This time I asked if he would come up.

Upstairs, I closed the door behind us and lowered the lamp. In the dim light, he smiled, which for Mr. Teague always came across as a sneer, and the scar on his cheek writhed under his beard. Outside the window on the street below, revelers sang and shouted, and their faint noise hung in the silence between us. He approached and began undressing me. I looked down and away as a show of innocence, but also to avoid his stale breath. His hands undid the rows of buttons down to the small of my back and lifted my ballgown off my shoulders. Then my chemise, then my corset, then my petticoats, then my drawers.

I demurely wrapped a forearm over my breasts and put a hand over my nether regions. I trembled, a little theatrically, I admit, but he took no notice. He was mesmerized by my skin, ivory and pink, and my blue eyes and hair as black as onyx. His fingertips reached out to me as if he expected to be burned but nonetheless couldn't help himself. I shivered when he touched me, but not out of pleasure. It was February, and his hands were cold. He got down on a knee, and I felt the brush of his beard on my navel. He rolled down my stockings, and I stepped out of them, biting my lower lip and forcing out an innocent blush. It was the practiced art of making the thousandth time being undressed by a man seem like the first time.

"I have never been with a man," I murmured, a colossal lie, of course. Then I repeated the tired old line, *but I am drawn to you in a way which I do not understand.* This was also a lie: I completely and thoroughly knew it was his money I found attractive. He said that he would be gentle, as it was my first time. I bit my knuckle and nodded and turned away as if I might cry, though in reality it was to keep from falling into a long, roaring bout of laughter. He picked me up and limped to the bed.

He was a vigorous lover, as if his physical exertions were trying to make up for a lack of rigidity. He rutted himself into a sweat, and still he rutted on like a man desperately trying to push a rope, though his rope was not my concern, only his purse. I moaned and cooed, but what I really wanted to do was shout, "When will you ever finish and be done with it, sir! No need to be all day about it!" At last he succeeded in gaining entry, but then the act was hurried and found a quick end, like the sudden eruption of a pimple-faced Texas cattle drover.

Afterward, we made small talk as I traced a finger over his chest and hip, where there was a scar from his war wound.

"This sugar farm of yours," I purred, "I should like to see it sometime."

He became genuinely incensed.

"Farm! Farm! Why, it's a plantation! Largest in the parish, is all! One of the three largest in the whole state!"

"All the more that I should see it!" I laughed. "Don't you think I should see it? Perhaps we could take a ride around it."

He declined by changing the subject, and I'm sure it was to keep the wagging tongues of St. Matthew Parish from enjoying the story of a single man of the highest social rank taking a mistress into his house. Instead, he retained an apartment in the city for me and furnished it lavishly, as he could not have me in his house and taint his honor in the eyes of St. Matthew Parish.

The Burden of Cane

Before long, my account with Madame Olympe was paid in full and my credit there was extended on the word of Mr. Teague. I also had accounts at all the shops, millinery, dresses, bonnets, everything a girl could want, paid for by this man, this sugar planter. It was good, it was comfortable, luxurious, even, but it wasn't sure. I needed the commitment. I needed a ring and a license. Otherwise, I could be easily dispensed with. I waited for a proposal, keeping in mind the adage about the cow and her free milk, but there was none forthcoming.

This arrangement lasted through the spring and into the summer. His bedroom abilities were barely so-so, and, as you know, Mrs. Leonard, I may rightfully regard myself as a judge in these matters. But that was not my concern. I was not so much a lover for him as I was a trophy, this older man with thin hair who had acquired this young, exquisite, raven-haired, blue eyed creature, displayed under a parasol at the races at the fairgrounds and at spring balls and dinner parties. It was much like an old crow bandying about with a shiny object in its beak, a decoration like bunting on the Fourth of July.

That summer, as the city of New Orleans cleared out for fever season, he brought me with him to White Sulphur Springs in the mountains, his usual summering spot. I posed as his niece, and in public at least, we eschewed any open affection, other than that which would be expected from an uncle. It was delightful enough in the cool of the mountains, away from fever and the discomfort of hot, wet air. I thought I might receive a proposal there, but our time in the mountains came to an end, and we returned to Louisiana where I was dropped off like a used plaything at the apartment in New Orleans. He would come and visit at first, but as the cutting and grinding season came on, his visits were less and less frequent. I began to feel marginal. And so I thought of a plan, a scene in the script that would bring me to the middle of the stage.

I put a small rubber plaster in my drawers, inflated with water to give the appearance of the early stages of expectancy. When he returned to the city for a brief visit and a romp in the sheets, I rejected his advances, telling him that I was with child and that it most certainly was his.

He said he would deny it. I burst into tears thinking that he would relent and assume his responsibility, but that was not the way of my husband. He said that there was no way to prove it, and so I told him that it had to be his, that I had never been with anyone else, and how could he be so cruel to insinuate that I had?

He puffed his cigar, and I believe he was about to dismiss me, so I said, rather childishly, "Very well, I shall have my baby alone and name him Samuel Teague Junior and raise him by myself and he will be a great man and be in the papers and achieve a fortune and perhaps be a senator or some other man of great importance."

Of course, there was no question of it being a boy or a girl. In fact, it wasn't a baby at all. Indeed, at this stage of my pregnancy it was only a rubber plaster lodged in my drawers. He asked how I knew what it would be and I told him that an old gypsy woman had passed her hands over my body and she could tell, and that she had never failed before. He pursed his lips and puffed his cigar.

We were married by Judge Anderson in his chambers. On the carriage ride home from the courthouse, as Mr. Teague dozed, I removed the rubber bottle from my drawers and flung it into Bayou Lafourche where it landed with a splash. It had served its purpose and achieved its aim. He woke with the sound and asked me, "What was that?"

"A fish must have just splashed in the water," I said nonchalantly looking up the road.

"Hmp," he grunted. "In the winter?"

I gave him a placating smile. When we arrived here at Mount Teague, my first ever visit, he hung up his hat and coat in the hall and said to the servants, rather unceremoniously, "Here is the new Mrs. Teague," and he went to his study to smoke a cigar.

I was alone with my husband and his people, the upper crust of the Sugared-Royalty. Rather than be intimidated by them, I resolved to rise among them and then above them. And I have done it, in no small part to that favorite tool of intriguers and schemers, gossip. If performed correctly, gossip opens doors on some and closes them on others. If my husband had any issue with this tactic, he never spoke of it. I became quite sure that he was complicit, as it brought about the continued rise of his own social star. Perhaps I am a schemer, but I am convinced that my husband never saw me as one.

It took longer than it should have for Mr. Teague and me to loathe each other, perhaps a week, perhaps less. For one thing, he snored like a sawmill and passed noisy wind in his sleep that was simply horrendous, like a plague that God did not have the heart to inflict upon Egypt, lest He be seen as cruel rather than just. With time, I adjourned to a separate chamber to sleep. I claimed that I had lost the baby and that I needed the rest. With this revelation, he was not sympathetic, nor compassionate, but something more like angry or disappointed, as when an investment fails.

Our separate sleeping arrangement was well, for his sexual powers were becoming rarer with each passing week. They either left him before he was completed or sometimes never showed at all. Perhaps it was the cholera or perhaps he had no desire for me, as his loathing for me would not allow it. I myself felt as though I had been sold a lame horse. But he kept me for my beauty, an ornament, a decoration for Mount Teague, and I kept him because he could afford me.

Besides ornamentation, there was another task that I was expected to fulfill. I was to read to him, as he said his eyes would tire or his vision was dulled or he had misplaced his glasses. This was well before I learned of his illiteracy. I quickly tired of reading to him. The Latin Book of Quotations was the worst.

"You might have an interest in this, but I don't," I complained, "Give me a good penny-novel any day, not this Latin jibber-jabber." He looked at me as if I had slapped him.

I was also expected to read the newspapers to him. This blustering buffoon of a man I now called my husband was simply infatuated with politics. He and his cronies were terrified that those elected would take from them their rights or their money or both, or that they would fail in their bid to wrest the rights and money from the opposition.

You see, Mrs. Leonard, my husband was a devotee of wealth long before I met him, a horse fancier and a pillar of St. Matthew well before I arrived, and believe me, I did nothing to reform him. Though he was also pompous and a loafer by nature, he pulled many years in the yoke I had put upon him, though he never knew it. I fancy that he would have been glad to do it, had he known. I was an ornament to him, polished to a shine, radiantly prepared, admired for my beauty in those exquisite dresses and ballgowns, the whispered-about pinnacle of society here in St. Matthew. As I still am, Mrs. Leonard, as I still am, despite my increase in size. They will never be quite on my level and my heart goes out to them for that. Surely it does. Young bodies may enlarge and sag, but clever blue eyes never fade.

We had been married several weeks when the grinding of our cane into sugar was completed, largely managed by our overseer, Mr. Landry, who endured my husband's anxious attention to the matter. The day after Christmas my husband departed to the city to spend the New Year with the Howards and the Burkes and his other associates and their wives. Mr. Garfield had been elected president, and my husband and his cronies were greatly agitated. To avoid going with him, I feigned illness, much as I had done with my grandparents in Shreveport when an unwanted event, usually church or a chore, reared its head. I didn't care for his friend Mr. Howard who would sometimes smirk at me, and once I thought he addressed me as Lottie. This may have been the voice of my scruples, my puny, tinny-voiced conscience.

I was happy that my husband was absent and I could sleep until noon or after. Having a husband whose conjugal abilities were depleted was becoming dreadfully dull. But that would be no issue for me. I have always found other outlets for my amorous inclinations. After all, a girl used to a diet of love retains an appetite of her own.. Let us leave it at that.

Jack

Some men would have folded completely, some would have shaken their fist at the Creator. Some, perhaps, would have looked deep within themselves, searching for some touchstone of grace and strength. I chose none of those. I wandered forward and stopped in the next little town, a place called Napoleonville. And I bought whiskey.

I had never been one to drink to excess, but I did then, trying to dull that unbearable pain. My heart was empty, my soul vacant and yawning, and so I filled them with whiskey. I poured glass after glass of it down myself into the hollow space shaped like a dog's love. I drank to dull the pain, and I stayed drunk and missed my interview with the Keefe & Bodley Foundry in Houma.

Several days—or weeks, perhaps, I had lost track of time completely—I paid the last of my money to send a telegram to Houma apologizing for my delay.   A message was returned.   POSITION FILLED MORE DEPENDABLE MAN.

The words stung me because they were true. *More dependable man.*

I wandered, feeling utterly alone. I passed simple farmhouses where children shouted in French to their dogs, who seemed to bark back to them in French. Clothes were being washed outdoors in big iron kettles and hung on lines, and it occurred to me that it must have been Monday. The fields were being cleared of cane and from time to time I would pause to let tall shaggy wagons pulled by mules pass, each step straining the harnesses and traces that attached them to their burdens.

I had tarried out west much too long, and the sun would soon be setting on my youth. I was without work and without money, so I thought I might do some traveling and fixing things like I had done in Nebraska. Perhaps it was time to begin seriously looking for a mate. I had no more thought it than a carriage appeared on the road.

Part IV

C. H. Lawler

Ruthie

Yes ma'am, Miz-riz Lennid, I speak with you if it help you have a word with Marse Sam, if you don't mind I keep workin' while we visit. Just don't tell Miss Eva what I say, just say it show help you get a hold a Marse Sam over yonder in heaven or wherever else he be at. It's a sin to speak ill of the dead, yes ma'am, so I ain't gone say nothin' on Marse Sam, no ma'am I ain't.

Pass me that rollin' pin by that cupboard?

Miss Eva show upset 'bout Marse Sam passin'. Some peoples don't show they pain and Miss Eva one a them peoples. She huff and she puff up and growl, yes ma'am, but she can't help how she is no more can anybody else.

It must be thirty, forty years Miss Eva come to live in this house. We didn't know nothin' about it, one day she just showed up with Marse Sam. Marse Sam didn't seem too happy about it, neither, he just say 'this here Miss Eva, she the new Miz-riz Teague,' and he give me his hat and coat to put away and he went onna his study an' have hisseff a toddy and a cigar.

It didn't take long 'fore anybody with any sense could see how she play one woman off on another, or a man against his wife, or one man against another, and she clever as a rat how she do that.

Let me git them shortbreads out the oven, ma'am, 'fore they burn up.

Yes ma'am, but Miss Eva could show tell a story.

Let me set these here on that table yonda so's they can cool.

Hear that? Chime a that clock that man come fix that year. I's a girl back then, jus' old enough to be in charge a the house by myself.

Ma'am?

Well, yes ma'am, but let's keep our voices low-low, quiet as a mouse. If you wants the trufe, Miz-riz Lennid, it ain't no secret that Miss Eva pass a gentleman through this house from time to time when Marse Sam away. All us what work for Marse Sam and Miss Eva knows it and we knows we ain' spose to say nothin', no ma'am.

First one of them gentlemens come through here when Marse Sam and Miss Eva ain't been married a month. He that man what fixed that clock you

194

hear down yonda in the hall. Now that clock-fixer, I tell you what, ma'am, he was show one good-lookin' man.

Miss Eva say, 'Ruthie, this here my brother, now go draw him a baff and set him up out the guesthouse. And don't say nothin' to Marse Sam cause he don't like my brother no ways,' and she say, 'And y'all better keep y'all black moufs shut.' And we keep 'em shut, too.

Well, just about everybody could see that weren't Miss Eva's brother, lessen they had different mamas or daddies. They didn't look nothin' alike. Didn't none of us servants say a thing to Marse Sam 'cause we 'fraid of Miss Eva on account she clever as a rat how she play folks off on each other and mean as a snake just like them French folk say. So I ain't never said nothin' 'bout it to nobody, 'cept just now when I told you, ma'am.

Well, yonda come Miss Eva. Yes ma'am, you's welcome. Remember I ain't told you nothin'.

Jack

A carriage passed and then stopped ahead of me. I moved slowly toward it carrying my knapsack and my satchel. The driver was a Negro man who kept looking forward over the traces and the swish of the horse's tail, as if disinterested or maybe even embarrassed. As I approached, a voice in the shadows of the carriage said, "Good afternoon."

"Good afternoon," I said as I peered into it. The soft, sweet smell of lilac water scented the relative darkness of the carriage. My eyes adjusted and I saw her eyes, radiant blue, the color of the ocean out there, Father.

"Are you a tinker?" she asked with a smile.

"Ma'am?" I replied, pulling up my knapsack, worn and patched over and over from my army days and my railroad days and my wandering days.

"I have a clock that's broken. Do you think you might fix it?"

"I can repair most anything," I said. "What's wrong with it?"

"It only tells the correct time twice a day," she said, and she broke into a light laugh at the old joke about broken clocks. I must have grinned, for she added, "Allow me to say that you have a very handsome smile, sir."

195

She invited me to climb into her carriage, and I did it, though I was ashamed of my appearance before her in that small, elegant space. It was a warm day for winter, the very reason for my being in Louisiana in the first place, and I was self-conscious of the odor I emitted. She made no mention of it and instead gave me a kid-gloved hand.

"Eva McCarron," she said, and she withdrew her fingers across mine. That small gesture, the light, lingering friction of her touch was nothing less than exhilarating. I had never been so close to so much beauty. My breath seemed confused as to which way was out of my body, and I muttered a feeble half-introduction in the glowing presence of this masterpiece of a woman.

"Jack—" my shyness mumbled.

"Well, Jack," she said, "Tell me how a handsome man like you finds himself on the Bayou Road in St. Matthew."

I swallowed and stammered, and then I began to tell her about the war and the west. She listened attentively with those blue eyes as I babbled on about working on the railroad and being present at the driving of the golden spike in Utah and having my picture struck with the dignitaries in the desert. She was easy to talk to, and we chatted as we rode to her house. And what a house it was.

When we got down from the carriage, I saw her in the bright winter light. She was the most beautiful woman I have ever seen. She was as pretty as an angel, in a dress of blue velvet that made her eyes seem blue velvet as well. She was not merely pretty, she was beautiful, absurdly beautiful, like a color advertisement for a tonic made for rosy cheeks and luxuriant hair and a blaring-white smile.

I fell in love with her the first time I saw her. Oh, certainly I had seen many beautiful women earlier in my life, the adoring wives and daughters at military balls and in the homes where we were billeted during the war, even on the road home when loneliness had made ladies call to me as I passed. Even the west had its pretty women, mostly in the frontier town bawdy houses and the hell-on-wheels dance halls, but I had avoided those places. Now it occurred to me that I had saved myself from such debasement, waiting for such an angelic creature as this raven-haired, sky-eyed creature, this exquisite Eva.

The walls in the central hallway were bare so that they could be repapered. The paintings and portraits were stacked together like cards, facing the wall to protect their faces. The outermost of the stack had an inscription obscured by dust but the part I could read was in French. My curiosity urged me to lean the painting from against the stack and look at it, but politeness prevented me from it. I have often thought of how differently my life would have turned out if I had seen that portrait. I would have known then, and perhaps I would have been able to make a better decision. But perhaps it would have made no difference. She had me in a trance.

Midway down the hall was the clock in question, a tall case clock, we call them grandfather's clocks now in America. Parts were scattered on the floor around it.

"There is the clock, sir," she said as she held her hands before her and looked at the clock as if it were in an art gallery.

I unshouldered my knapsack and opened my satchel as I studied the mechanism in the case, pendulum-sprocket-pulley-gear. My eyes made inventory of how they might work together and then my fingers arranged the parts on the floor in an order and then rearranged them into a better order. As I studied the clock and its pieces, I could almost feel her eyes on me, studying me. One by one, I assembled them and my tools nudged them into place.

"A man from Donaldsonville tried to repair it, but, as you can see, he only made a mess of it. I'm afraid he was a bit of a simpleton, a man who could not complete his duties." And then she murmured, "I so admire a man who can complete his duties."

Within an hour I was polishing the brass pendulum and setting it in motion. It swayed in even, balanced meter, and the second hand ticked away toward eternity. I set the time by the pocket watch given me by Mr. Palmer and the Denver & Rio Grande Railroad. The pendulum paused for a moment as I set the hands and then let it resume coasting back and forth. This young lady Eva seemed mesmerized by it.

"Ma'am? Ma'am?" I asked her. "Anything else?"

"Oh—oh—yes," she stammered, emerging from whatever private reverie had taken her. "Quite a number of things, actually."

She asked if I might stay a few days as she was sure she could find other tasks for me. I waited for someone else to emerge from another part of the house or to come home to it, a father or a mother or both, or an aunt, an uncle, a sibling, someone. But in the house, there seemed to be only a handful of servants and this exquisite young lady. I asked her about her family, and she said that her mother had died of scrofula and her father was away with her stepmother, who hated her, and the two of them frequently attended balls in the city leaving her alone like Cinderella.

"I might like to attend balls," she said with a sly pout.

I was doubting the propriety of staying in the house of this man alone with his daughter. I told her that I could find a place in Napoleonville to stay and return in the morning, but Eva said that she got frightened sometimes staying by herself and that it would be a comfort to her. She said that there was a guesthouse in the back, and wouldn't I stay, Jack? Hearing her say my name set off some electrical something inside me and her blue eyes told me to say yes and I did.

She had her house girl draw me a bath, and then I was given a fine suit taken from her father's armoire. Her father's pants were a little large in the waist for me and hung on me from the suspenders. The house-girl, whose name was Ruby or something like that, prepared us a dinner, which I struggled to eat slowly and civilly. My appetite had finally returned after its absence when Pinch died.

Eva asked about my family, and I said that my father was long-since dead, but that I had a mother and brother though I didn't keep up with them. I spared her the details of a mother who held her older son as an idol while largely discounting or belittling the younger one. Instead I told the story of going off to West Point, and I wonder if she believed that the raggedly dressed man who had been walking down the road earlier in the day had ever worn the crisp gray uniform of a military man. But she listened with wide blue eyes at the stories of the war and of the west as if she had been waiting all her life to hear them.

After we finished eating and had lingered for quite a while over dessert, the girl—Ruthie, that was her name, Ruthie—cleared the table, and Eva went and got one of her father's cigars and asked if I might like a snifter of brandy to go with it, but I declined, still queasy at the thought of any spirit after my drinking binge the week prior. The pain I had tried to drown still lingered in a dull drone. I still expected to look down and see Pinch, and it took a moment each time to realize he was truly gone.

The Burden of Cane

She showed me to the guesthouse, a small outbuilding which was part guestroom and part icehouse, hence the name, the Ice Parlor. I turned in that night in a comfortable bed with sumptuous sheets. Through the window, the big house glowed, and I watched the coming and going of the servant Ruthie as she put the house and her mistress to bed. Ruthie closed the curtains in one room and went to the next to attend to something there. When she left, Eva opened the curtains again and looked out across to the guesthouse. She began undressing, her backlit silhouette turning to give a brief shadowy glimpse of the geometry of her body. She nonchalantly lingered before the window behind the squares of glass, her fingers tracing the curves of her body. I didn't look away. It was an impossibility. At last she turned down the lantern and fell into darkness, but she inhabited my dreams that night.

The next morning I rose to find Ruthie in the kitchen. She fed me as if I were a king, saying that Miss Eva generally kept to bed till noon or after. I told Ruthie that if there was nothing left for me to do, then I suppose I should be on my way. I went to gather my things.

As I was packing my knapsack, Eva appeared in her nightdress at the door of the Ice Parlor. Her hair had been hastily arranged, and she kept brushing it back from her face. Her eyes were sleepy under long black lashes.

"Where are you going so soon?" she asked. "I have other things I need you to do."

Her nightdress was thin and I could easily see all the things I saw in the dim lantern light the night before. In fact, thirty-five years later, I still see them.

"The girl said you were asleep and I didn't want to disturb you," I said as I paused in my packing.

"You could have come in and disturbed me," she whispered with a thin smile.

I felt like I was falling, like my knees would give out and I would fall forever.

"Come," she said, and she took my hand in her hers. It was creamy-soft. Her bare feet picked across the frosty ground as she led me to the big house. There was no sign of Ruthie. Eva took me into her chamber. The bed was unmade, a jumbled tornado of sheets. She sat me in a chair and went behind a screen. "Sit and talk to me while I dress," she said.

It was highly improper, but I was powerless to do anything but what she said. There was a dressing mirror arranged at the corner of the screen, and I could see her movement, and if I leaned a little, I could see everything. She was naked behind the screen and in the mirror, and I caught myself leaning to get a good look. She caught me, too, and gave a clever smirk before pulling on her corset and skirts.

When she was dressed, she had me sharpen knives that didn't need sharpening and shoe horses that didn't need shoeing and repair things that didn't need repairing. She sat under a parasol and watched me sharpen and shoe and repair. Nothing much was said, she simply kept her eyes on me, smiling at me when I glanced at her between my labors. From time to time, she would pick up my tools and ask, "What is this one called? What does it do?" Then she would blush and fan herself and purr, "I do so admire how you use your tools, sir." I thanked her, oblivious then to any hidden meaning she might have intended. At one point she reached into my knapsack and pulled out the revolver. She pointed it off into the distant cane fields, looking down the barrel aiming at nothing in particular. I held out my hand for it.

"Have you ever killed anyone with it?" she asked as she handed it back to me. "Out west, I mean."

"No. In fact, I've only fired it in the air a couple of times. It was given to me by someone."

She seemed a little disappointed that I hadn't killed anyone with it. As I put the revolver back in my knapsack, I thought of Mrs. Tyner and her girls. What was their lot now, I wondered?

After an early dinner, again prepared by Ruthie, who disappeared soon after the kitchen was cleared, Eva asked me to climb the ladder to the top of the water tower to view the sunset with her. We listened to the wind and watched the bare fields below us. I told her, boasting to her like a schoolboy, that when I was out west building the railroad (I had made it seem as though I had built it rather than just worked on it) I had seen herds of buffalo and Indian camps and the rails push into the wilderness and the mountains. Though there was a warm south wind that promised rain, she complained that she was cold and stood next to me. "You can put your arm around me if you like," she smiled with a face turned up to me, "to keep me warm."

I did it, and the feeling of pulling her next to me, my hand on her lithe waist, was like the jagged electrical discharge of the telegraph carrying a strange and wonderful announcement. She turned to me in the blaring sunset light and pulled a black strand of windblown hair from her face. She raised onto her toes and pressed her lips to mine and then scampered down the ladder to the ground giggling. For some reason I chased her.

I looked for her but couldn't find her, so I retired to the guesthouse, the Ice Parlor. I was aching for her, but I resolved to forget the press of her body into mine, the press of her lips into mine. I lit a lamp and read an old copy of *Scientific American.* I told myself over and over that it was wrong to take advantage of a man's daughter, particularly in his absence, and I would banish any thought of it if I had to read all night.

A storm was pushing in, the wind picking up and pushing the clouds under the moon. The first few cold, hesitant drops of rain began falling. I was about to turn in to see if sleep would help me forget when she appeared at door in her nightgown, murmuring in a bewildered tone, "I am drawn to you in a way which I do not understand. Come, Jack, let us celebrate our bodies."

Any questions about the impropriety of bedding a man's daughter in his own house while he was away evaporated into lust before things like a proposal of marriage or even permission to court her could ever be considered. They vanished into the atmosphere occupied by this ivory-skinned, raven-haired, blue-eyed Eva as I fell into romantic thoughtlessness. I was completely unburdened by reason and principle, and we shed our clothes and partook in sexual communion. The serpent beguiled me, Father, and I did eat.

She was an angel fallen from heaven into my midst. Eyes as blue as the ocean out there and skin as soft as the ring of far-away church bells. She seemed to know the things I would like, the things that would thrill me, and she enthralled me time and time again. She guided me through love acts I could never have imagined, lurid things surely first contrived during the sinful days of Ancient Rome. And, though they are things that I am too ashamed to recount to you, a man of the cloth, they all seemed so natural. I have never been able to forget them, even now, over thirty years later.

She touched me, and she seemed to put her hand over the envy of my brother and trace her fingertips over my resentment for him. Her blue eyes looked into mine and saw the bitterness there and then she closed them and threw her head back in ecstasy. We had no sooner completed one love act, lying naked, side-by-side, smiling and holding hands than we began another.

Afterward, when we could love no more, we lay and watched the lightning flash and we counted off the seconds-as-miles before the thunder. I said that I would always hear the sound of artillery in thunder, for the rest of my life. She toyed her finger over my chest and kissed me there. She listened as I spoke of small things, of how an old man on our place in Mississippi would talk about the 'man a-workin' upstairs' when the weather was like this.

She asked if I was religious, and I said that after being in battle you were either completely religious or not at all religious and that I was one of the few who was somewhere in between. She surprised me by saying that she thought that religion was a tool to keep people stupid and afraid. I told her that questioning the faith of another is like taking their blanket because you're not cold and that I had seen many a poor country boy-turned-soldier shiver to death under the thin blanket of his faith.

"Perhaps so," she said. "But if anything, I worship the golden calf, and, if the truth be told, and so do most other people." She said that she found it odd that people think God always sides with them and, for that, she had always had but little use for religion, though she goes to services each Sunday. "Where else would I wear my best dresses?" she laughed. At the time, I wondered if she meant it as a joke or not.

For the next few days, we lay together either exhausted or in the process of exhausting ourselves, talking afterwards the small talk of lovers washed up on the bank after a trip through the rapids. At night when she fell asleep, I listened to her, feeling her inhale and exhale.

Here was something that my brother couldn't take from me, a sweet well-spring of constant and lifelong satisfaction. I easily fell into a state somewhere between simple preoccupation and a pernicious obsession, a mad, sacred reverence, an insane reckoning for this creature who I was sure was an angel. I resolved that I would ask Eva's father for her hand in marriage when he returned from the city. My heart and everything else about me were suddenly, strangely, completely afire. I didn't know that those flames were the outermost rings of hell.

Eva

Mr. Teague left just after Christmas to spend a few days ringing in the new year with his friends the Howards and the Burkes. I was supposed to go but feigned illness, because honestly, Mrs. Leonard, I had tired of him and needed a respite from his boorishness. He boarded after a thin peck of a kiss from me, much thinner than one would expect for newlyweds, and I left before the train even departed the station.

Having seen Mr. Teague off for the city, I returned home from Donaldsonville down the Bayou Road. It was a winter day, mild and bright. On the road ahead, I saw a man with a knapsack on his back, carrying a satchel. He was lean and muscular, his skin set in healthy tones, like a more virile version of my bloated, pasty husband. Even from down the road, this traveler was as fine a specimen of manhood as I had seen in a very long time. I will again be frank with you, Mrs. Leonard, that after months with only Mr. Teague's puny abilities, I was so thirsty for the love act and its excitement and fulfillment that I was like a man in the desert is for water or a young, barely pubertal Texas cattle drover come to town on payday or a schoolboy who has just noticed that schoolgirls have bosoms. I knew I had to have him, if only for a little while.

I introduced myself as Eva McCarron. I still wasn't used to Teague, but when I realized my error, I left it at that. For the tasks I had in mind for him, there was no need for him to know my new name, nor was there any need for me to know more than his first name, Jack, so that I might shout it in the throes of passion as I dug my fingernails into his back. I asked him if he would come and look at the clock in our hallway. He said he would but that he would walk along side of the carriage, as he was dusty and dirty. I insisted that he ride—dusty and dirty have always been something of an aphrodisiac for me.

Well, it took him less than an hour to repair the jumbled mess the man in Donaldsonville had left. He asked if there were any other tasks for him. I could think of several rather private duties he could perform for me, but he seemed the straight-laced sort, and I didn't want to scare him off. I knew his type; he would take finesse.

I told him that my father and stepmother were away in the city attending a ball and welcoming the new year with friends there. I proceeded to paint the old Commerce Street vignette of an evil stepmother and the poor little stepdaughter forgotten in the new wife's shadow, and that I was left in this great big house and that I was scared to be alone and won't you stay here with me, Jack? At first he declined, but when I said he could stay across the way in the guesthouse, he relented.

I told Ruthie that this man Jack was my brother and to draw him a bath and to fetch him one of Mr. Teague's suits from his armoire full of suits. Then after dinner, she might leave us to ourselves so that we may get caught up on old times telling stories of our childhood. Of course, she and the rest of the servants bought that lie without hesitation. Simpletons.

We chatted over dinner about his life and my pretend one. All the while, I tried to entice him with amorous innuendo. He was apparently too much of a gentleman and too disciplined to succumb. He retired to the guesthouse and to his own bed, which I was simply aching to share with him. That night through the curtains, I offered him furtive glimpses of my naked body, but he was too timid or too honorable to come back to the big house and take the bait. But as you know, Mrs. Leonard, I am nothing if not persistent, and I vowed to continue my efforts the next day.

I woke midmorning and rose, which was still much earlier than my practice. Ruthie said that "clock-fixin' man" was about to leave. I chastised her for not telling me and then hurried out to the guesthouse without so much as putting on a dressing gown or shoes. I caught him packing up his things and convinced him to stay.

After a day of dreaming up aimless tasks for him, I invited him to watch the sunset with me from atop the water tower. We watched the birds soar in the winter air, and he talked of his dream of flying one day. I feigned a chill and asked him to draw near, and when he did, I kissed him and ran down the ladder, and at last he chased me. But he was more disciplined than I supposed, perhaps from his military training, and he retired to his quarters again. I was as on fire for him as I had ever been for a man, or, at least, not in a very long time. I decided to lay myself bare, and quite literally, Mrs. Leonard.

I came to him where he was reading in the guesthouse, and I told this fellow, this repairer of clocks, the same old hocus pocus about feeling drawn to him in a way I didn't understand and had never felt before or some such foolishness. And he fell like Samson for Delilah.

I looked up to him in the winter moonlight and I kissed him. He didn't kiss me back at first, but his hands began kneading my soft skin and then he began kissing me, and we fell into a most passionate state like something rolling downhill and gaining speed with each revolution. I climbed on top of him lifting my arms to the ceiling as I shed my nightdress. In the dim winter light, the moon was in his eyes and his eyes were on the breasts which I had just bared for him and my bare flesh was on his and my hair fell like a black curtain over our faces and lips. I took his rough palms and put them on my soft breasts and held them there with my delicate hands.

He was even more of a specimen without clothes than I had imagined, and believe me, madame, I had spent most of the last two days imagining it. The purpose of the act was as clear as it had ever been to me and I found myself racing, racing, racing for something. And I found it. I found it several times, in fact. It was and is a rare thing that I didn't have to pantomime my ecstasy, but, in this case it was so, quite powerful and with several tempestuous aftershocks.

We lay panting in the aftermath. A storm was pushing in and the moon vanished and the night became darker. I was about to get up and go inside the house, when the first crack of thunder rattled the wooden bones of the ice parlor, which was our guest house in those days. Soon after the thunder, the rain began to pour down, and so I decided I would stay there rather than get wet. Wetter, rather.

He murmured that for each second of delay after a lightning flash before the crash of thunder, it meant the strike was a mile away. We lay and counted them, and he stroked my back and I nuzzled into his chest, and if I were the kind of girl who succumbed to tender moments like that then certainly I would have. But you are surely aware now, ma'am, that is not at all my nature.

I had never spent an entire night with a man other than my husband, at least not for free. I admit to enjoying the closeness of it, the warmth of a shared bed on a winter morning, the feel of taut muscles and rugged flesh against my smooth, bare skin. It would certainly be something to get used to, and perhaps I would have if that exquisite body endowed with a generous and talented manhood hadn't belonged to a pauper of a man.

We spent several days enjoying rather frequent and *vigorous* sexual congress. We wore ourselves out, but what did we care? Words became unnecessary, as our bodies spoke for us, casting us again and again into that sweet, breathless delirium.

The old year fled and the new year came, and the peasants of St. Matthew celebrated it by firing guns into the air. I awoke in the night to find him at the window running his fingers through his hair. He asked if we had a dog, as he thought he had heard a dog barking. No, I said, and he confided in me that the sound of great amounts of gunfire still made him nervous. I pulled back the sheets and bade him return to bed.

He looked into my eyes, and he seemed to see the girl who had been teased on Texas Street for wearing the same old clothes every day and the woman who had had her innocence sold from her to the highest bidder that afternoon on Commerce Street in Shreveport. He saw the only part of me that was vulnerable and afraid, the part I have always repressed and hidden away in a dark cabinet inside myself. Oddly, the comfort of that gaze made me uncomfortable. My dalliance with him was becoming more than a mere transaction. This could be something big and life-changing.

I knew we had come to a crossroads. I could remain the wealthy wife of one of the biggest planters in the South or I could take up with this traveling tinker. I was coming to my senses at last and recognizing the look on his face for what it was, the vacant gaze of the spellbound and adoring. It was something that Miss McCune warned us against, as it could lead to more than the wanted amount of attention. My husband might return at any moment, and I would be thrown out and lose everything I had gained, all for this penniless, wandering tinker.

Oh, certainly I had a natural and profound affinity for him, but, of course, in the great course I had plotted for my life, that was worth nothing if he was worth nothing. My husband, the one who was worth a great deal, would not stay gone much longer. It was time to act, and, unfortunately, there was no painless way to do it. I went to my room and dressed formally. When I emerged, he greeted me and said that I looked exceptionally beautiful.

I curtly thanked him and added, "The time has come for us to bid adieu."

"Adieu?" he asked.

"I must ask you to leave now," I said.

He looked at me as if I were speaking in a foreign tongue.

"I was thinking of asking your father—"

"—my father would never give you consent to be so much as in the same room with me."

Yes, Mrs. Leonard, it was cruel, but the cruelty of it couldn't be avoided. People have always had a tendency to ruin things, and especially ruin other people. And in that I suppose I am no different than anyone else.

I told him that we had had our fun, but, in the end he was far below my station in life. A girl like me! Marrying a traveling tinker! A fixer of clocks and cotton gins! A common man like him, though handsome, and I must admit, gifted in that manly manner, and as you now know, I can certainly be considered a knowledgeable judge of those things.

In truth, he was everything that my husband might have once been, and I briefly contemplated leaving with him for love's sake. But in the end, and, in the beginning, too, really, I had come too far to sacrifice all I had gained for this tinkerer, this repairer of clocks, no matter how gifted he might be as a man, for, as a lover he was—he was very *pleasing*, if you understand me. The money was too good, and so I had no choice but to reject him. But as he left down the lane of oaks, I did a thing I rarely do. I cried.

And that, Mrs. Leonard, is the story of my passing infatuation with the traveling tinker who once fixed the clock in the central hallway there. Let us draw the curtain over that scene, shall we?

Why yes, you are correct, madame, it was not to be the end of my intercourse with him, social or otherwise. How did you know? Oh yes, of course, you are a clairvoyant. Here, do try some of Ruthie's shortbread.

Pinch

We stayed in a little house away from the big house where the woman lived with her mate, though of course no one could see me, not even Jack who had loved me more than anything else in the world. She appeared at the doorway and said in so many words that she was in heat and needed to mate with Jack. That is not what she said, but that is what was on her heart. We dogs know these things. She came in with bare feet though it was cold to those

who could still feel things like cold. I sniffed at her bare ankles as Jack let her in.

She pushed him back on the bed and they shed their clothing. She bared her teats to him and he pawed them and they kissed and licked and they mounted and humped for a very long time. I shouted and screamed and barked but he couldn't hear me. *Bad! Bad! Bad! Bad! Bad!* I barked. *Careful! Careful! Careful! Beware! Beware, beware, beware!* All in the barks that he could have recognized as we had spent my whole life together and he loved me more than anything. But he couldn't hear me, and even if he could have, and even if I had been flesh-and-fur, he would not have cared. Perhaps he would have said, *go lay down, Pinch, go lay down and get some sleep,* like he did when I barked at things in the night when we lived in the place with great fields of grass and buffalo.

I put my paws on the edge of the bed and twisted my head this way and that, then I jumped on the bed, without a sound nor pawprints on the sheets. I circled the bed with steps lighter than the air. I whined seeking consolation as he moaned and she shouted his name. They only paused a little while and then they began again. And I jumped from the bed and curled up on the floor with my head on my paws, a frustrated shadow in a pool of moonlight.

Jack

I was thinking of how I would approach her father when he returned from the city when I realized that she had gotten up and was in the house. I rose and dressed and went in to find her. The house girl was busy in the kitchen, scrubbing a pot in the sink and humming a tune to herself, and she didn't notice me as I passed through.

Eva was nowhere to be found in the great house, but the door to her chamber was closed. I knocked on the door, and she emerged dressed in a dark colored day dress. It was odd, for she hadn't gotten fully dressed in several days, and at first, I thought that she had come up with yet another way to please me. I told her that she looked beautiful, but she was rather cold in taking the compliment. I wasn't prepared for what she said next.

The Burden of Cane

"It is time for us to bid each other adieu," she said flatly.

"What—what do you mean?" I asked.

"I must ask you to leave, now. I'm sorry, sir, but it just cannot be," she said. "We are from different worlds, you and I. My father would never consent for us to be so much as in the same room together." She almost seemed amused at the preposterous notion that I would consider myself to be on her level, her station.

There was nothing I could say. I had no idea how to deal with a resolute woman. Perhaps no one does. I went out to the guesthouse and packed my satchel and my knapsack and the revolver, and then I went back through the central hallway of the house. She was in the sitting room looking out the window over the bare fields.

"I won't forget you," I paused to say through the doorway to the back of her dress and the carefully brushed black gleam of her hair.

"That is your choice, sir," she said without looking away from the window.

And so I departed, feeling like Adam must have felt on his banishment from Eden. The gray clouds in the north promised more cold rain. On that January day, my footsteps scuffed the frozen ground and my breath steamed into the dense air. I reached the end of the lane of oaks and turned onto the Bayou Road with the taste of her still in my mouth, remembering the words of Mrs. Tyner as she tearfully clutched her clothes over her rejected nakedness: *One day you'll lose your heart to someone and you'll lose it completely.* I'm afraid she was correct. Her words had been both a prophecy and a curse.

A thought came to me, a glimmer of desperate hope. It grew like a flame and then a fire and then a bonfire. I would convert my knowledge of science into position. I would ascend, by God, I would ascend. I would return in a nice suit, well-made and well-fitted, and in a carriage that matched the gentleman I would be. I would reenter her life with the splendor of a comet and she would be awestruck. And not only would she be, but also her father and her stepmother and all the servants. The other fine people of St. Matthew would cluck and crow in their parlors and their pews over the fine luck of this girl Eva McCarron and her family.

Then I would ask Mr. McCarron for his permission to court his daughter and then, in due time, I would ask his permission to marry her. And it would

209

be a certainty that he would be pleased—no, *elated*—to give it to me and he would slap me on the back and eagerly say *yes, of course, son*, and we would have cigars and port to honor the occasion.

I resolved that one day I would triumphantly return to the paradise at the end of the lane of oaks. As I thought of this grand quest, this singular purpose, I was no longer shuffling down a winter road, slinking away in dispirited retreat. I was marching toward victory. I would just have to figure out how to achieve it. As I approached the sleepy town of Napoleonville and its smoking chimneys and barking dogs, I realized that I had never told her my last name. Perhaps we had been too busy. Nevertheless, she would come to know it, and when I had won her hand, she would come to wear it. My heart gladdened at the certainty of it, and I began to whistle a jaunty tune into the chilly air as I walked.

At West Point we cadets had a professor who was fond of the Latin saying *Facilis Descensus*, 'easy is the descent.' It was part of a quote from Virgil's Aeneid, *Facilis Descensus Averno*, easy is the descent into hell, while the ascent up and out is difficult indeed. The professor would click his tongue and mutter the quote when a cadet was having trouble with the line of questions during a recitation, his fingers sweating the chalk dust into a sticky white paste as he fell deeper and deeper into failure, in danger of being 'found,' as it was said. *Facilis descensus*, Cadet, *Facilus Descensus*.

Having gotten into that carriage on the Bayou Road, I found the old Latin warning to be true.

Facilus descensus Averno.

Easy is the descent into hell.

If only I had known that McCarron was merely her maiden name.

Eva

My husband returned the afternoon that the tinker left, laughing about something his friend Howard had said about the widow Howcott's effeminate son. We greeted each other with a quick, dry kiss. A handshake would have carried more passion and affection. After almost a week of an erotic free-for-all that would have exhausted a Roman emperor, dullness had returned to Mount Teague.

Over the next few weeks, I began to notice that something had changed. My monthly malady went missing and I couldn't find it anywhere. At first I was elated that I had been spared it. Then the truth dawned on me. This was no case of a rubber water bottle concealed inside one's drawers. I was with child. There was a swimmer inside me, underwater in a lightless sea within my body.

This simply wouldn't do! Carnival season was fast approaching and I had a number of fine new ball gowns I was anxious to wear and an account with Madame Olympe on Canal Street in the city for more if I chose. An expanding torso would have ruined all that. I considered going into the city where there were people who could end situations like mine with potions and procedures, but with a busy schedule of soirees and the important business of sleeping in before and after them, time slipped by and I decided against ending it. I was stuck with it, whatever it was that had taken residence inside my body. I would have to risk it ruining my beautiful figure for a season.

With that decision made, I went and spent the night in the bed of my husband. When he awoke, I told him, 'well weren't you the tiger last night!' I'm sure he was confused at what had gotten into me, other than him. Oh, the things we let ourselves believe, especially when we know they can't be true.

As the cane grew lushly in the fields, so did my body. My breasts and hips filled out and my skin glowed, my cheeks took up an even rosier blush. I welcomed the respite from the monthly malady and pretended it would all end as easily as it had started. I began to think of the child in the way that a girl dreams of a new doll. The baby would be compliant to my desires for sleep and would itself sleep in its crib when I had tired of it and wanted to do other things. It would rise at noon with me, both of us having gotten all the sleep we required.

My body grew to a point of voluptuousness and past it. The novelty of it faded, and it became tiresome. In the August heat, I had no desire for anything and lay around in the Ice Parlor completely naked or nearly so. My body had overdone it when it came to the pleasant swelling and now it was an encumbrance. By September, it began to rumble like a volcano and I thought the time had come. But after a few hours of squeezing, my womb gave up and went back to sleep, leaving me to endure the increasingly annoying antics of its occupant.

After the hottest summer I could ever remember, labor came. The first few dozen contractions were mere trifles that provoked lighthearted exclamations. Those were nothing. Next came the real attention-getters, then my water broke and flooded the bed. I shrieked at Ruthie to change the damp linens, and then I shrieked at the pain that increased with each squeeze of my body against itself.

I began to doubt the necessity of propagating one's self, one's bloodline. It now seemed to me to be the pinnacle of human conceit. The very idea! I thought. I secretly wished that the father of this baby would feel a tenth of the pain that twisted me, trying to disgorge this interloper free from my body, this creature that was now trying to vacate it in a most insistent and traumatic way. Then the pain trebled, and I wished the father, the perpetrator of this crime, to feel all of it and half as much as interest. I spoke the wish aloud, and then I growled it and then I shouted it. And I am almost certain that I heard laughter and the clink of glasses downstairs in the gentlemen's parlor where my husband had gathered with his friends to wait and celebrate.

At last, my body broke open and the horrid thing wrenched its way out of me and came squalling out into the world. I relaxed as if circling in an eddy. Dr. McKnight's voice announced downstairs that it was a boy, and there were shouts of congratulations in the gentlemen's parlor and the clink of glasses.

The sheets were damp again, and when I touched them I held up a red palm. My heart raced weakly and the scene in the bedroom spiraled shut. The murky faces of my grandparents and Willie Bissinger whirled and faded away, and I saw the pit in the ground behind the Methodist Church in Shreveport, and at last Mr. Standproud appeared and said in the hollow echo of his forgotten voice, "I've been waiting for you, Lottie, do come up, do."

I woke up several days later. The summer heat had gone and the windows were closed against the first cool autumn breeze. Dr. McKnight said that I came very close to dying.

Mr. Teague was deliriously happy to have a male heir to the Mount Teague throne, as he had been resigned that it would be another girl. His girls from his first marriage were grown into womanhood or nearly so, though I believe the youngest spent her time at boarding school and then with Mr. Teague's mother in Mississippi. None of the girls seemed to have any fondness or attachment to their father, and he seldom spoke of them, and I've never seen my stepdaughters nor have I cared to see them. Likewise, I have never cared for my mother-in-law, just as I'm sure my new daughter-in-law will never care for me. I say so be it. A kingdom only needs one queen, and I am she.

Of course, my husband named his son Samuel Teague Jr. I had neither choice nor preference in the matter. He was not an appealing looking child, not at all. In fact, he looked something like a rat. He soiled and wet himself as babies do and bawled nonstop when he was given to me. I soon found that being a parent takes a large degree of selflessness. As you might imagine, Mrs. Leonard, I have never been cut out for it. I made Ruthie get up with him and took to sleeping in the Ice Parlor. This was not only for the rest, but, I admit, the erotic nostalgia my mind wandered through as I thought of the tinker Jack.

Yes, Mrs. Leonard, certainly you may talk to Junior if it helps you contact my husband, but I'm sure I don't have to remind you to repeat nothing of what I've told you. He should be returning this afternoon from his in-laws in Mississippi. He usually goes straight to his late father's study.

Junior Teague

Yes, ma'am.

Do have a seat. I thank you for coming all the way from England in the winter and during wartime at that. Mother is beside herself with grief, and she thinks that if she could have one last word with Daddy it would help her. She says she has to ask him something but she won't say what it is.

I just got in this afternoon from Mississippi—I dropped off the new Mrs. Teague at her parents' place. She's early in the family way and her stomach's a little unsettled. I thought she might rest better there where her own mama can look after her. My Mama's never been cut out for that kind of thing. Just her nature—

Yes ma'am, about the day Daddy died.

Well, my wife and my son and I were in New Orleans about to leave for a trip to Cuba when we got word that Daddy had been killed out in the fields. Of course, we came back home right away. As you can see, the great man's desk is exactly as he left it that day. Invoices, reports, newspapers from New

Orleans, Houston, Memphis, and the *Compass* from right here in St. Matthew Parish, all of them open to the business pages, lists of commodities and trading, with his eyeglasses still resting where he had placed them when he took his last trip out into the fields. He ran this place with an iron glove, and now it'll be my turn. I hope I'm up to it. A place like Mount Teague gets in your blood just like the soil of it gets under your fingernails. I've been looking over these ledgers, and for the life of me, I don't know where all the money's gone. But it'll be up to me to get it all sorted out and running smoothly again. Frankly, though, right now it's a mess.

I have no doubt I'll be able to do it, for I come from good stock. From my father, Sam Sr., I've received the gift of grit and the thirst for scholarly advancement. Just look at all the books on those shelves, some of them in Latin. One can certainly see how important knowledge and the pursuit of it was to him. Of course, from my mother, I have the gift of honesty—brutal honesty, at times—

—Yes, I can take you out to where we laid Daddy to rest. He has a magnificent tomb out near the Twelve Arpent Canal. I hired the finest sculptor in New Orleans, a Mr. Carriere, to see to the crypt, truly a grand monument to the man who built this empire. Made out of a red stone called porphyrian marble imported from Italy. Yes ma'am, let me get my coat.

Ruthie, if Mama wakes up from her nap, tell her that I'm taking our guest out to see Daddy's tomb.

Yes ma'am, Mrs. Leonard, as a matter of fact, there is something I want you to ask Daddy if you can contact him. Something I myself would dearly like to know.

Jack

I left the big house and the lane of oaks that day and turned onto the Bayou Road with my face set into the north wind. I had nothing more than my knapsack, a revolver I would probably never fire again, a satchel of worn tools, and the clothes on my back. She hadn't paid me for fixing the clock or anything else, but it made no difference to me, for I would return. I would return in fine clothes with money in my pockets. I would return having molded myself into a respectable suitor so that I would win over the beautiful Eva McCarron of St. Matthew Parish and her father Mr. McCarron and her stepmother Mrs. McCarron and whomever else I must. No sooner than the big house was at my back did I vow to return when I had made something of myself, something proper and highly desirable.

I drifted into Mississippi watching the flight of geese, admiring their effortless transit north. In each town, I gleaned the local newspapers and sifted through the notices on general store bulletin boards, looking for jobs repairing things, and the bigger and more complex the tasks, the better. Certainly, I sharpened a lot of knives and scissors and plow points—I needed the money—but it was the big jobs, cotton gins and steam engines and sawmills, that I was seeking. The south was still trying to get to its feet after being pummeled in the war, and even a decade and a half later, there was still much to be fixed. Antiquated machinery had wheezed along for years, quickly patched and hastily rigged. Now everything needed to be repaired and updated correctly, and I was going to do it.

And I did do it. In Butler County, Alabama, I repaired a cotton gin that was deemed beyond hope and then set the owners up with a new steam engine to drive it. In gratitude, the leading citizens there held a dinner for me with toast after toast rising in the amber gaslight, despite the fact that they wore their finery and I wore a simple work shirt and dungarees. The heart of Butler County, the cotton gin, was beating proudly again.

The gin's owner, a short man with side whiskers and a protuberant belly, raised his glass and the men and women seated around the table raised their glasses, and the man gave a heartfelt speech saying that for small places like Butler County, I was an agent for overcoming disaster and a 'hero striking a sure blow against adverse fortune, a simple and enduring heroism more important to them and their daily lives than any battle fought a thousand miles away.' I could only blush under his praise.

One of the faces around the table, a man with a jacket with a beaver pelt lapel, reminded me so much of my father that it made me pause with my glass in the air as everyone else tipped theirs back. The man nodded to me and I to him, and we sipped and nodded to each other again. He smiled at me, the same face that had beamed at me as a child when I launched persimmons over cotton rows with an old rubber belt from a cotton gin. One of the other gentlemen at the table asked me something and when I looked back, the man I had toasted had taken his leave, leaving an empty chair and an empty glass. No one else at the table seemed to know much about him.

The people of Butler County recommended me without reservation to a similar gin in a neighboring county. I fixed it in less than two days, better than it had been before the war, much better. Its gears moved effortlessly, almost noiselessly, whirring and spinning out clouds of white cotton and bins of seeds. Hats and hurrahs sailed into the air, and the men slapped me on the back. I gathered my tools and my burgeoning reputation and moved along. Just like in Nebraska the decade before, word of my skill proceeded me, and at each new town a committee of men met me with entreaties to come and see about their sawmill or their combine or, that vital organ of each community, the cotton gin.

But a name that was a professional success wouldn't be enough for Eva McCarron. I would have to rise socially as well. So I scanned the newspapers for announcements of reunions of army veterans, and I began attending them to cultivate friendships with influential men. Their wives and daughters stirred the air with fans and talked in whispers behind them, their faces emerging from the hidden conversations with coy smiles and batting eyes. But theirs were not the coy smiles and batting eyes I was interested in. Those were in Louisiana.

Hand over hand, rung over rung, I ascended the social ladder. I bought new work clothes and new tools and a new suit. I bought new books and read the latest scientific and industrial journals. I invested in whatever I thought would better my station in life, which in turn would bring me the love and admiration of the girl with the black hair, porcelain skin, and blue eyes, the lovely Eva McCarron of St. Matthew Parish, Louisiana.

Scientific knowledge was advancing then at a rate never seen before and Industry, capital I, Industry, was in the ascendancy, even in the sleepy, agricultural South. Old inventions were being refined while new inventions were being developed almost daily. Thomas Edison had invented the phonograph and the light bulb, George Westinghouse the railroad airbrake, Alexander Bell the telephone. There was talk that someday, perhaps in our lifetimes, men would mount engines on wings and fly.

A group of men had discovered that the Alabama hills held the perfect ingredients for the production of iron—iron ore, coal, and limestone—and a new acquaintance of mine from the old army introduced me to that champion of iron manufacturing, Colonel James Sloss. I secured an interview and bought a train ticket to Birmingham and a new suit crafted by the finest tailor in Montgomery. I was gratified to find that Colonel Sloss had already heard of me, as had the Woodward Brothers who owned the other foundry in Birmingham. The brothers rushed over an offer, and Colonel Sloss quickly countered it, and I went to work for him making iron at his works, a place called the City Furnaces.

I had found my purpose. Old knowledge gained at West Point was returning as disciplined as geese returning home with the change of season. My talent had been ignited, and it moved along like a chemical reaction, like the combustion in a piston pulling and pushing the great sweeping arms of machinery. At the City Furnaces in Birmingham, I worked under the English engineer, Mr. Harry Hargreaves, who himself had been taught by the famous Thomas Whitwell of that country. The new bee hive coke ovens were the latest thing then, and I had already read all about them and soon we had them in Birmingham.

In 1882, we the men of City Furnaces produced twenty-thousand tons of pig-iron. Yes, Father, twenty-*thousand*. The following year, at the Southern Exposition in Louisville, City Furnaces of Birmingham, Alabama, a newcomer, was awarded the bronze medal for iron production. Soon our iron was being shipped to places all over the country. My star rose with each new addition to the foundry, with each new blast furnace and boiler, with every new ton of Sloss iron. And with each wreath of laurels placed on my head, my only thought was how proud Eva McCarron would be.

Colonel Sloss had acquaintances then living abroad, one in Brazil and one in Puerto Rico, both having fled the Confederacy at its demise for fear of the noose. Both were growing sugarcane and both needed a sugar mill to process it. Iron and sugar may seem dissimilar to you, Father, but in actuality, both are hot liquids which are refined to solids, one black and one white. And both processes involve intense temperature and pressure and carry an inherent danger because of it.

I was sent for by these men and oversaw the completion of their works, with excellent results. Soon, I was approached by planters all over the western hemisphere, men who needed the new, efficient sugar mills that I designed and built. My reputation was without peer, my name much sought after. Colonel Sloss was good to me and gave me great credit and freedom to work as I chose. After a trip to Santo Domingo to set up a sugar mill there, he greeted me back home in Birmingham with a hearty handshake and a bonus and news that a Mr. Franklin Morehead had come to solicit our appearance at an exposition in New Orleans commemorating the hundred year anniversary of the invention of the cotton gin. *The World's Industrial and Cotton Centennial Exposition*, as it was called, was to run the first six months of 1885. Mr. Morehead had come singing our praises, and especially *my* praises.

My star was ascending to a new zenith every day. I had a nice home and a housekeeper and a carriage and cabinets of nice suits and leatherbound books. Good food was served at my table by a good cook. There was talk of partnership, both professionally and personally, and I was welcomed in the Sloss pew on Sundays where the lovely niece of Colonel Sloss, Fanny Sloss, was steered toward me. Soon we made a couple that was the envy of Jefferson County. My name began to appear in the society columns with hers. Colonel Sloss was happy. His niece Fanny was happy. Everyone was happy.

I should have been happy. I had everything a man could want except for a nagging vision, white-hot in my memory, a pebble in my otherwise comfortable and stylish shoes, a piercing, jabbing memory of raven hair, porcelain-white skin, and pink flesh. And blue eyes, always those blue eyes, as blue as violets. Compared to that vision, Fanny Sloss, pretty, sweet, congenial Fanny, was merely the consolation prize, the girl who would always be second-place. That, of course, was something I could never speak out loud, though a voice inside repeated it constantly.

I struggled to convince myself that the blue-eyed woman in the big house in Louisiana was an apparition, a phantasm, a wisp of steam on a night long ago. Years had passed, and I assured myself that Eva McCarron had been paired by her wealthy father with a suitable mate, the son of some other planter or a cotton broker or a banker in New Orleans. My life was in Birmingham now, and so I resolved to quit that fleeting pipe dream, that blue-eyed Eva, the goddess of deception, the patroness of mirages. She was becoming as remote as Greece and Rome.

It would not stay that way.

Eva

And so I settled into the business of being Mrs. Teague. I took photographs on the arm of my husband, and other photographs seated with Sam Junior on my lap, smiles, smiles, smiles, always smiles, pasteboard smiles until the flash evaporated and the smiles faded. I played the role of virtuous wife and doting mother, though frankly, Mrs. Leonard, neither one suited me particularly well. And for that deficiency, I did not and still do not give a fig. There, you wanted the truth, and now you have it.

Sam Junior had sandy brown hair like his father and cried more than any baby born since the birth of Cain. Oh, the noise! Squalling, squalling, squalling! Shouting, shouting, shouting! Red-faced, shrieking! He grew into a toddler who couldn't seem to keep his finger from probing his nose, and he asked question after question after question. I told him to go ask his father.

What in blazes did I do to deserve that torture? The house a wreck, so that extra servants had to be hired to keep it straightened, for I certainly wasn't going to do it! It was no better years later when his sister was born. Every day the act of having propagated myself seemed a fool's errand, even though they stayed largely in the care of their nursemaids. I vowed that I would send them both away when they came of sufficient age, to boarding school or wherever else I must, and that is just what I did. By hook or by crook.

Would you care for tea, Mrs. Leonard?

Ruthie! Tea! Now!

Well, Mr. Teague was the perennial King of Jupitre, the local carnival association, with a ball for the upper crust and a parade for the troglodytes. Because my husband was the king, naturally, I should be its queen, which meant a flowing, sequined, fur-lined cape with a matching gown and jeweled scepter crafted by the finest jeweler in New Orleans. Our wealth grew out of the black earth into green-leafed stalks, which were ground and boiled into white sugar, which, of course, was turned into gold for us. We were among the best of All-the-Best-People. There was only one thing lacking, and that, naturally, was to be the *very* best of All-the-Best-People. In that, there was only one other family that outshone us in St. Matthew, our neighbors, the Parrises.

Of course, they flaunted it—we would've done the same thing in their shoes. They built a carriage house for their fine new brougham with gleaming brass lantern holders and tufted velvet seats and a fringed top and white-spoked wheels, pulled by a team of magnificent white draft horses with plumes of feathery white hair at their hooves and manes that drifted over their immense necks, tended by exquisitely liveried servants. That was their everyday arrangement. There was also an even fancier 'Sunday brougham' for the purpose of conveying them to church to thank God for the riches he had bestowed on them and withheld from others.

Their parties and balls were the pinnacle, each new passing fad acquired and conspicuously displayed no matter how far the distance and expense required to get it, champagne fountains, jeweled party favors, cufflinks for men, brooches for women. The ballgowns of Mrs. Parris were exquisite creations, not from the Canal Street shop of Madame Olympe, but from the House of Worth in New York. Her jewelry outshone mine, as did her children, always dressed and indulged in the latest, so that we also felt we must do the same for Sam Jr. It was an affront, a challenge to our social supremacy, our place as the *very best* of All-the-Best-People.

All this largely because of their sugarhouse, built by a local man named Buquoi. It was twice as big as ours and efficient enough to grind their cane more quickly than ours and get it to market first. The entire arrangement, this fancy sugarhouse, put us in the Parrises' shadow. We produced more sugar than they did, but refining it was the problem. By the time we got ours to market, the price had dropped sufficiently to the point that the Parrises had made substantially more than we had. We knew we must eclipse them somehow, and that *somehow* would involve an up-to-date sugarhouse. At last my husband and I could agree on something.

We produced more sugar because we had an advantage. There was an old coot named Barbagree who could predict the weather with great reliability, and we had a French-speaking overseer named Landry who was the only person with whom Barbagree would agree to talk. We could time our harvests with great precision, waiting to give the signal until the last moment and maximizing the sugar yield, but it meant nothing if we couldn't grind it and get it to market in advance of the Parrises. Our second place showing to the Parrises was the problem my husband and I shared. There was another problem during this time, and it was mine alone.

During these years, I developed a nagging suspicion that my husband's friend and business partner Mr. Howard knew of my past. I felt uneasy around him, and his blank countenance only made me more suspicious that he had some idea of who I had been. He would ask probing questions, which prompted me to speak of my poor departed parents and excuse myself to another room where my husband and Mr. Howard would find me red-faced with a handkerchief full of crocodile tears. The outbursts were certainly enough to convince my husband, but he was a dullard when compared to Mr. Howard. I became more and more convinced that my husband's friend knew the most salacious parts about my past.

He began referring to me as 'Lottie,' trying to get a reaction from me. He never got one, but Mr. Teague certainly did. In private, I harangued my husband, telling him that his friend was comparing me to a prostitute I had once heard of who plied her avocation in Shreveport. I insisted that he confront Mr. Howard for his disparaging remarks, but my husband, ever the coward, said, "Oh, Charlie has been a friend of mine for years. Lottie is a fine name, and I'm sure he's only giving you a lighthearted nickname. It's all out of affection for you, my dear!" He, of course, had no intention of confronting our so-called friend, that spineless bastard, my husband. Yes, of course, Mrs. Leonard. *God rest him,* of course, *God rest him.*

As we were dancing a waltz at the Planters' Ball that year to celebrate the beginning of the growing season, Mr. Howard recited the full rhyme in a low voice just above the music, "Sometimes haughty, always naughty, on Commerce Street, ask for Lottie." And he did so looking straight at me and without a smile. I matched his gaze as the waltz came to an end with polite clapping from the other dancers. As the quartet launched into a quadrille, Mr. Howard smiled and adjourned to the porch. I followed him out onto it, jerking him around by his shoulder.

"What did you mean by that, sir?" I demanded.

He grinned and lit a cigar and blew out a gust of smoke. Inside, the music and the dancers whirled, and I could feel their motion on the porch under my feet. He blew out another puff of smoke and looked at his cigar and said,

"What do think your husband would do if he knew?" He looked out into the night and added, "Lottie."

So he did know. This called for a change of tactics. I offered him the gift of my body, but he only nudged me away and snorted. He mentioned a sum, and an exorbitant one, not just a king's ransom but a kingdom's ransom. I said there was no way I could come up with that amount, but he said, well, then there is no way I can keep hold on this information.

"Think on it," he said, throwing his cigar into the azaleas. "Flora and I are going to our house in New York for the summer. Think on it all summer, if you please, but in the fall when I return you can either buy out my half-interest in our secret, or I can give it to your husband for free."

He stepped away from the porch railing and made a big show of planting a kiss on the back of my glove as he added, "Lottie."

I was so angry that I swatted at him, but he ducked, and I knocked over a planter. The crash of it caused the music and laughter and conversation inside to stop momentarily.

I knew something had to be done, or I would be exposed. Mr. Teague would divorce me out of disgrace, the money would be gone, the social standing would evaporate, and I would be an ordinary woman, with no talent, save one, and I was becoming too old to use it. I thought of sending a girl from New Orleans to visit Mr. Howard and at the same time sending a note to Mrs. Howard telling her to come at once, that her husband was *in extremis* with another woman. I was sleepless and became even more short-tempered than usual. In early May, Mr. Howard and his family left to spend the summer in New York, and I was left to ponder my next move.

Well then, as it happened, on the last day of May that year, 1885, a great tragedy befell Mr. Howard at his summer house in New York. The carriage in which he was riding developed some sort of mechanical trouble, and he was thrown from it and broke his neck. What horrid luck!

I will say, Mrs. Leonard, that the now dearly departed Mr. Howard was well-known to have an affinity for fast horses which he conducted rather recklessly, whether saddled or in front of a carriage. And, I do not feel the slightest remorse that I sent him the gift of that horse and carriage. I will say also that sometimes carriages develop trouble in the axle, and wear may abruptly appear and defects might be suddenly and tragically exposed.

The Burden of Cane

What sort of a question is that, ma'am? You are the clairvoyant. You should know. Let us conclude, then, that I knew that I could finally trust Mr. Howard to keep his half-interest in our secret forever. If Mr. Teague had known the true events of what had happened, perhaps he would have been elated, as he got to keep his money *and* his wife. But he was none the wiser and died without knowledge of any of it. Of that, I am quite convinced.

When he received the telegram of Mr. Howard's untimely passing, Mr. Teague immediately made plans for the two of us to go to New York and fetch his friend's carcass and bring it back to New Orleans for internment at the cemetery in Metairie. We left Sam Junior in the care of his nursemaids and departed St. Matthew wearing mourning attire, and, although I wore the black taffeta and silk of a grieving friend, I also wore frilly, lacy red drawers under it in secret celebration.

We crossed the ferry from Algiers, and at the train station in New Orleans, I saw an advertisement for a great exhibition that was being held. Indeed, talk along the platforms was of nothing else, and it was set to close the next day. I had wanted to see it for months but when one is in the habit of sleeping until noon or after, such opportunities are frequently lost. I was at once taken with the idea of attending, and so I told my husband that I had second thoughts about leaving Sam Junior behind with his nursemaids. He seemed perplexed at my sudden display of maternal instinct. Nevertheless, he departed for New York without me.

To gain entrance on that day, the final day, I put myself in the company of the Director-General of the exposition, my husband's lottery crony Mr. Burke, who was then also state treasurer and the editor of the *Times-Democrat*. I'm sure he was pleased to be accompanied by a beautiful woman and show her around the exhibits. He agreed at once to escort me.

We were greeted inside the Main Hall by an immense portrait of President Arthur and then strolled the promenades touring its exhibits, thirty-three acres under one roof, *the largest building in the world,* Mr. Burke crowed. In its halls, the throngs never lacked for music as bands and a grand organ played constantly.

He boasted that he had solicited exhibits from countries all over the western hemisphere and all the states. There was a pavilion from Mexico with a big brass band, and that new curiosity, Electricity, was on display, with thousands of electric lights and an electric streetcar, all thought at that time to be a passing fad, a flash in the pan. To get to the exhibit, one could take the train or an omnibus. "Why, you could even take a special steamer the short distance upriver!" Mr. Burke rattled. It was, I admit, all very impressive.

Mr. Burke asked me if I might like to go and tour the exhibits at the Woman's Department and that Julia Ward Howe was set to speak and present a gift of over a thousand books to the Art Union Library. I told him that Mr. Teague and I were looking into a new sugarhouse and would like to see an exhibit of something along those lines. You see, Mrs. Leonard, the problem of Mr. Howard had been solved, and now I thought I might look into solving the matter of the Parrises.

"Well, ma'am, if you and Sam are thinking of expanding your sugar production with an efficient and modern sugar mill, then I have just the man for you!" Mr. Burke said. "Some mention him as the new Hargreaves or Whitwell, of the same rank and stripe as Edison. Trained at West Point—until the late unpleasantness—and then an officer in the Confederate Army! A true genius of industry! He's rapidly gaining a name for himself in the manufacture of sugar mills—"

"—where might I find this genius of industry?" I asked Mr. Burke.

"Why, he's at the Alabama pavilion. Do let me introduce you to him! I'd be delighted!"

In the main building was the Alabama banner with exhibits of timber and coal and stone and three large, well-appointed reception rooms done up nicely with damask curtains and Arabian rugs and polished wood arches in a sort of Moorish style. As I rounded the immense chunks of rock on display, I saw that genius of industry, that designer of blast furnaces and sugar mills. To say that I remembered the traveling tinker would be an understatement. Indeed, I remembered him, and often, on afternoons alone behind a shut door.

He was talking with a group of men and their wives about a large outcropping of reddish brown iron ore, and when he saw me, he stopped in midsentence. In fact, it was so abrupt, the people with whom he was conversing looked up to me as well. It goes without saying that he remembered *me* at once.

Jack

Though I could see she was a very beautiful woman, I didn't recognize her at first. She came down the path opposite me where I was explaining the manufacture of iron to a small group of men and ladies gathered around a large deposit of Alabama iron ore, part of our exhibit. Between the woman and me were several ten-ton blocks of coal and limestone. When she rounded the last immense block of coal, my first thought was that the woman's hair was just as black. And then I saw her eyes, as blue as a gas flame.

I saw her, and it started all over again, like falling through a thin layer of leaves into the trap of a pit dug in the ground. I remembered instantly the thing I had fought so long and successfully to forget, that porcelain skin, as fair as cream, those blue eyes. When I would shut my eyes in sleep, I would see them as radiant blue in the darkness behind my lids.

She was in the company of the Director-General of the Exposition, Mr. Burke, who was also the Secretary of the Treasury for the state of Louisiana and the owner and editor of the *Times-Democrat,* if I'm not mistaken. The moment yawned a great silence between us as our gaze in each other's faces said everything. Mr. Burke was about to introduce us, but before he could, she spoke.

"I believe we have met before, have we not?" she said, presenting me her gloved hand. I took it and bowed slightly and said, "Yes, I believe we have. Eva, am I correct?"

"Yes," she replied in what was almost a giggle. "You remembered!" Though I'm sure that she could tell from my face that I had not forgotten in the first place, not for a moment. She asked Mr. Burke to leave us to discuss a few private matters. Mr. Burke seemed perplexed, like her company had been taken from him, but he excused himself to attend to a matter with the president of Honduras in their exhibition area.

We were left to ourselves. She stood balancing her hand on the large stony, chunk of phallic Alabama iron ore shipped in for the fair. She looked from her hand on the tip of the oblong rock pointing skyward and then back to me.

"Mr. Burke tells me that you are just the man to build a sugarhouse. And we are in the market for one. As big as you could build us."

"How big would that be?" I asked, both relieved and disappointed that our conversation was merely about business.

"We have almost ten thousand acres now," she said, "I'm sure a man of your abilities can readily calculate the yield in barrels. A man of your...*station*...in life. Mr. Burke tells me you are quite handy," she murmured as she watched her finger reach and barely touch my lapel, "but I already knew that."

Her eyes looked me up and down with the rapt appraisal of someone finding something unexpectedly pleasing. I stammered and cleared my throat and finally managed to tell her that I was impressed with her knowledge of her family's operation.

"You, sir, have certainly become a man of means," she murmured as she put her fingers to the lapel of my suit and began toying with it. "I find that so appealing in a man," she mumbled to the gray flannel. She looked up again, and it was as if everything else in the big exhibit house stopped, the discussions silent, the music from the pavilions faded away. And then those eyes, as blue as the sea ice out there. My heart was racing like a cornered animal under the shadow of the predator. I tried to breathe, I tried to swallow, I tried to think, I tried not to think.

"I have a proposition for you, Jack," she cooed, the leather of her kid-glove touching my ear and then my lips. She looked around and then put her lips to my ear and whispered, "Come with me, Jack, come, and let us speak of it in private. Come—" She put her lips to mine and I tasted them, as sweet as windfall apples. "—are you taking a room in town?" she asked in a breathless sigh as she withdrew her lips from mine.

I murmured a feeble *yes* with the last wisp of air from my body which was vibrating for her. My will trembled and wavered. And then, as if summoned by a trumpet blast, it rallied. My lines held, and at last she retreated. It was my turn to decline, and in a sudden burst of extreme mental strength, I did it.

"I am afraid I'm already engaged. For the summer. I have a commitment to my employer, Colonel—"

"—certainly you'll drop those things and come and help us. Help *me*," she clarified.

"I'm sorry, ma'am, I regret that my schedule won't allow."

Her demeanor changed, subtly at first. She seemed to be fighting pent-up rage. She wasn't used to being denied.

"Very well, then," she said, and she turned on her heels and left. And at last, I took a breath.

She left petulantly disappointed, almost irate. Perhaps the neutral cordiality I tried to project came across to her as coldness. I had not meant to be cold to her. That was not it. I was in danger of falling again and struggling to maintain my balance.

The next day, the World Industrial & Cotton Centennial closed its doors, and the ten-ton monoliths of stone and coal were packed up and returned to Alabama. The chunk of iron ore she had fondled remained behind and today is nestled into one of the fairways in the golf course they built on the site of the exposition after it closed. To see it is to have one more reason to remember her.

I left her behind in Louisiana, but I did not leave the thought of her behind. She had stowed away in my imagination. I thought of her as I sat in the pew next to Colonel Sloss' niece. I thought of her over dinner at the club. I thought of her during the engagement party. I thought of her until I resolved not to think of her, and then I thought of her again. I hoped there would be a formula for forgetting her, an equation to disprove the intriguing hypothesis presented by the curves of her body. There was none, and her spell persisted. I, who had always foregone the distractions of Benny Haven's tavern at West Point and the bawdy girls of hell-on-wheels and the brothels of Denver and Cheyenne for the loving discipline of scholarly pursuits and the hope for a meaningful union with a congenial mate. Now I could think of nothing else other than blue eyes, ivory skin, raven-black hair, and pink flesh. I would shut my eyes and I would see hers, blue as violets. A snapping of Colonel Sloss' fingers and the gentle jostle of my shoulders brought me back to Alabama.

"Yes, Jack, you have my permission to marry her."

"Who, sir?"

"Oh, Jack, you are love-struck! My niece, Fanny! Of course you have my permission to marry her!"

And so the date was set for October of that year, 1885. Announcements were sent, and Fanny's picture in an organdy dress with a matching parasol appeared in the newspapers in Alabama and in those as far away as Nashville and Atlanta. I would have had a happy, tranquil life. If only Eva McCarron hadn't been as persistent as she was beautiful.

Eva

At the time of our first meeting, I had only known his first name, though I had known it well, as I had moaned it in pleasure and shouted it in ecstasy. Now, having heard his last name, I thought it nothing more than an interesting coincidence. It was clear that he had certainly become desirable, having acquired the things he was formerly deficient in, namely, wealth and status. This man was clearly the best at what he did, which was exactly what we needed done. *Only the best at Mount Teague* was the saying, and so why shouldn't he be the one to build our sugarhouse?

I made an overture for him to come and do it, but he declined saying that his employer in Birmingham had a summer filled with projects for him. They were enlarging their works, and it was necessary for him to be there. He had no time to spare for a sugar mill in Louisiana, and so he gave me his regrets.

Can you believe it, Mrs. Leonard? He turned me down! Even after rigorous flirting! He had no idea that he had deprived himself the private spectacle of my lacy red undergarments. If he had seen them or simply known of their presence under my dress and over the contours of my body, we would have had our sugarhouse that summer, I am convinced of it. Perhaps I should have given him a glimpse.

I returned to Mount Teague crestfallen, and when my husband returned from getting Mr. Howard set up in his new abode in the Metairie Cemetery, we had no choice but to go and ask old Buquoi to build our sugarhouse. Buquoi said he would be personally agreeable, but his contract with the Parrises forbade him from working with other planters in the state of Louisiana. He could have worked in any other state or country, but his reputation didn't carry sufficient weight to be solicited from outside the state, or, for that matter, abroad. So he was locked up as the Parrises' man, and we were locked up having them grind our cane. *After* they had ground theirs, of course. Still stewing from this, we departed for White Sulphur Springs in July, which was our summering place back in those days. We left our cane growing in the field knowing that the Parrises would beat us to the best price.

The first summer that Mr. Teague took me to the mountains, the summer before we were married, I went as his niece. No one had questioned it then, having taken it for the truth. When I began returning as his wife, the whispers began. Those who summered there regularly wondered if he had married his niece or if we had come as two unmarried lovers on our first trip, both shameful circumstances. More well-off men would have been excused on either count, but we found that our wealth among the summer inhabitants in the mountains was now commonplace.

Whispers and disapproving glances had increased each summer, until we were excluded from the private parties attended only by the select in sequestered parlors of the hotel. Few wanted to be associated with a man and his wife who had formerly posed as uncle and niece. We were relegated to the sphere of the run-of-the-mill wealthy. I began to feel like the girl Gwendolyn Mosey and Polly Calhoun had taunted for wearing old clothes.

I was having tea in one of those ordinary parlors with two women and their husbands while Mr. Teague was out shooting clay pigeons. The two couples were textile people from the Carolinas. The husbands were keen on business and especially the business of adding onto their mills. Talk always gravitated back to throbbing shuttles and whirling spindles and units produced. We three women listened politely. My ears picked up when they began talking of expanding their works.

"There's a man down in Florida or Puerto Rico somewhere who hired an engineer out of Alabama, Birmingham I believe it is," one of the men said. "Worked for this feller named Sloss. Well, this engineer set him up with an A-1 sugarhouse that outproduced the competition and made the man a millionaire—"

"—I know the one you're talking about," the other man interjected, "That's right, works for Colonel Sloss making iron, but he's done some work with the sugar industry. Cotton, too! A real wizard! A genius! The whole crop can be refined and ready for market within two weeks! Capacity is no problem. Can't remember his name, Tate or Smead or something like that. I bet he's just as good with looms and could sure set you up down in Spartanburg."

Well, Mrs. Leonard, I remembered that wizard. In fact, I knew what he looked like naked and the faces and sounds he made when he was approaching ecstasy. And I knew where he was and that I—we, rather—had to have him. Mount Teague would benefit from his professional services and I might benefit from his physical ones. I would find this fellow. I would make him make those faces and sounds and I would secure him for me—for us, rather—so that Mount Teague might become extraordinary. It wasn't enough to be among All-the-Best people. It was essential that we be the *very best* of All-the-Best people.

My husband wouldn't have to know how this man was retained, as long as we had the world's finest, most efficient sugarhouse. Our sugar would promptly find its way into barrels and to market, ahead of the Parrises, and the money would roll in, falling down like green autumn leaves at our feet. It would be the talk of the state of Louisiana, the country, even, and the envy of St. Matthew Parish. After all, the saying was, *only the best at Mount Teague.* The very best. And our substantial wealth would command admittance to whichever parlor at whichever resort we might choose.

I would lure him from Birmingham to St. Matthew Parish with all the tools at my disposal, and this time I would succeed. Once in St. Matthew, however, it would have to be all business, but by then I would have him under contract. However, if he would be willing to overlook my position as wife-to-a-boor, brief trysts could be arranged in Mr. Teague's absence.

I rose and took my leave of the textile people of the Carolinas. We were not long for the society of these weavers with their ordinary wealth. Our cane was growing back home in St. Matthew Parish. Time was of the essence. I would return home immediately, and on the way, I would stop to pay a visit to my tinker-turned-sugarhouse genius. This time he would say yes. I would make him say it, *yes, yes, a thousand times yes.* He would arch his back and shout it to the headboard and the wall, *yes Eva, yes, I'll do it! For you I'll do it!*

I told Mr. Teague that I had had enough of White Sulphur Springs and that I was leaving. I would rather the stifling heat and threat of fever than the stares down lifted noses of those people in their forbidden parlors. The true stars of society were in places off-limits to us, and I could abide it no longer. He offered to leave with me, and for a moment I was afraid he would, but I convinced him to stay by telling him there would be a high-stakes horse race the next week, that some men in the saloon had been discussing it but that word wasn't out yet. And so he stayed.

I took the train out of the mountains, and though I rarely get nervous, Mrs. Leonard, I was as breathless as a school girl on my errand. I got off the train in Birmingham, where I took a room and dressed for my quarry, from the skin outward— undergarments, petticoats, corset, dress—everything carefully chosen for the ballet of seduction. Once freshened up, I took the trolley down to the City Furnaces and presented myself to the offices. The employer of our engineer, this Colonel Sloss, asked who I was.

I said that I was Jack's cousin from Jackson, come to see him to tell him that Grandma had died. Colonel Sloss' suspicions turned to condolences, and he personally ushered me to one of the enormous sheds out back, and I began thinking that our sugarhouse should be just as big or bigger when it rose over the cane fields. Men moved like demons within its darkness, wielding iron rods with buckets on their ends and other strange instruments in their toil. Just then, in the background, a huge vat of molten orange iron tipped forward into a mold, and liquid fire poured out.

He was quite a picture, sweaty with sandy brown hair matted to his forehead, shirtsleeves rolled up and giving a hint at the powerful forearms of a man who had once pounded spikes into rails. He paused, looking dumbstruck at the vision I must have presented as molten iron found the molds and raised a massive plume of rushing amber steam. Colonel Sloss stepped forward and, in a very fatherly way, gave his condolences which Jack didn't understand until his employer left and I explained the ruse. Jack's will broke much more easily than I had imagined, and we left under the cover of the story of a dearly departed grandmother that we shared.

In the room I had taken, we certainly didn't behave like cousins. I filled his eyes with delight as I unwrapped myself, a sensuous feast, each layer of my clothing a different flavor until at last I was in the vanilla. And he devoured me, madame, without so much as a spoon. Of course, he had his own utensil, if you understand me.

Afterwards, we lay together exhausted with the soft press of my breasts into his chest. I raised onto an elbow and looked down into him and he up into me, and I asked him once more to come and build our sugarhouse. He asked if he might speak to my father about my hand in marriage, and I smiled and nodded and kissed him, and he agreed. Oh, you may think it a bit cunning, Mrs. Leonard, but lots of fine and well-meaning people have been betrayed with a kiss.

We gathered our things at once and bought tickets on the train south. I rode with my head on his shoulder, and I forgot about Gwendolyn Mosey and Polly Calhoun. I forgot about my husband and Sam Junior. I thought that perhaps we could forget about Mount Teague and just keep riding, out west to California. He could work out there, and I could open a shop, a dress shop or a millinery, and we could love in its back room during the day and we could have a comfortable house to love in at night. I thought I might leave Sam for this man, perhaps after the sugarhouse was done or perhaps before. Or perhaps not at all. If Jack were willing, we could make an arrangement for us to fulfill our physical needs that were being unmet by my husband.

I went back to sleep with my head on his shoulder and my hand inside his thigh under his sketch of our sugarhouse entitled *McCarron Sugar Works*. I wondered how I would tell my husband if, by chance, the sugarhouse wasn't complete and Jack was still around when he returned from the mountains. Certainly, he would have to find out sometime, in one manner or another. Unless Jack and I simply ran away together. Perhaps I was falling in love, that most pernicious of emotions. So I shut my mind to it, lest it devour me.

Jack

She appeared in the doorway of the furnace where I was looking over a blueprint of the planned expansion. Her parasol was over her shoulder and she twirled it in the September heat. It was hot, and even hotter in the furnace room. My sleeves were rolled up, and my shirt was stuck to me and my suspenders were drenched.

Colonel Sloss came with her and put his hand on my shoulder and said gravely, "Sorry for your loss, son. I know we're in the middle of an expansion, but Mr. Hargreaves will take it from here while you go to Jackson and arrange things. Take as much time as you need, Jack." With that, he returned to his office. I had no idea what he was talking about.

Eva looked at him leaving and then turned to me. "I told him our grandma died," she laughed quietly.

It was such an audacious lie that I asked her, "Why did you say that?"

Her smile fell and she looked at me with piercing sincerity and said, "So I could be with you." Her fingers trailed over the lower edge of her bodice and around her inner thigh. "I have thought of you and nothing else all summer," she whispered. "I should like to be alone with you, Jack."

Just hearing her speak my name was like a trumpet blast from the lips of an angel. The flames from the furnace were icy compared to my body and my soul. The emotion I struggled all summer to sequester suddenly crashed from its cage. It did not matter what she wanted. I would do it. I would do it gladly. I would do it without thinking of the consequences. I would do it ten-fold. I could do nothing else. Without changing out of my sweat-drenched shirt, without so much as rolling down my sleeves, we returned to her hotel room. And there I fell again, and I fell recklessly.

Afterward, we lay naked, and she traced her finger over my ear and my cheek.

"Come and build our sugarhouse. I hear that you are the best, and if you are half as good as you are with my body, then I suppose you are."

She kissed me, chest, cheek, chin, lips, and my convictions, my ideals melted like molten iron and then evaporated into steam. I rose and we dressed, pausing to kiss to the point that we might undress again. Finally, we walked to my house, avoiding any public token of being lovers, as I was still a man engaged to the niece of one of Birmingham's leading citizens. But I could feel the current arcing between us, Eva and me, invisible and silent.

She waited demurely in my drawing room, looking about the walls at the art I had begun collecting. I assembled some clothes and packed them in my knapsack I had kept out of habit and nostalgia, a reminder of where I had come from. I placed the revolver I would never fire among my clothes, but I had to leave most of my books and suits. I told my housekeeper that I would return, though privately I didn't know when or even if, nor did I care. I had no concern left for anything or anyone other than raven-haired Eva.

On the platform in Birmingham I took one last look at the life I had made with skill and determination. At the conductor's last call for New Orleans, she took me by the hand and we boarded together. The smokestacks of the Sloss Furnaces slid away.

She rested her head on my shoulder and looked out the window. I watched her reflection in the window, and I thought of the train ride from Chicago and the girl from St. Louis with the chestnut ringlets. Eva was so much prettier and with an excellent head on her shoulders. Here was a girl who had come all the way to Birmingham from Louisiana, by herself, to solicit a bid for a sugarhouse on behalf of her father. Certainly, she would make an excellent mate, and I could easily imagine the two of us having a contented life, a partnership, surrounded by children like the Fohlmanns on the prairie. I vowed that I would change Eva's last name as soon as I had spoken with her father and gained his approval. *Mr. McCarron, sir,* I would say—

The conductor called for Meridian, and she nestled closer and slid her hand on the inside of my thigh under my sketch pad as passengers filed past us unaware. The train pulled forward again, shifting us into each other and into our seats and moving her hand into me. And I could no longer think of her father with her hand where it was. She gave me a playful squeeze and a lingering touch before withdrawing her hand. My chest rose and fell as I tried to gather my fleeing breath. At last, I did.

She slept as I sketched the plans for the McCarron works in my sketchpad. The project centered around three twenty-eight foot boilers for the purpose of rendering the cane juice into sugar. It was to be the largest of its kind in the state and a match for any other sugarhouse in the south, on par with any in the world.

I giddily sketched out the specifications of the sugarhouse, this new monolith to rise above the fields of cane that would be cut and passed through it, according to the parameters of acreage and assuring a maximum yield of sugar per acre from the hot, sweet juice of the cane. I woke Eva to show her the plans, and she looked at them with her head on my shoulder, her fine, creamy-skinned finger tracing the lines to the boilers and the smokestacks I had drawn. As she did, I realized that the bid for it all was less than was reasonable, ridiculously less. But I was drunken with her, and reason had no business with me nor I with it.

In New Orleans, I sent a telegram to Colonel Sloss with my resignation from City Furnaces and a hastily composed letter to his young niece Fanny, releasing her with a puny explanation about incompatibility. I'm sure both had repercussions as subtle as a blast of dynamite.

I had violated the Honor Code and allowed Colonel Sloss to believe the lie that Eva had told him, that she had come to tell me our grandmother had died so that we might go and mourn her together. Colonel Sloss, who had been so kind to me. The betrayal of a man who took me in when I was nothing, who welcomed me at his table, who felt highly enough of me to offer the hand of his beloved niece in marriage, who treated me with nothing but kindness, the betrayal of this man and his goodwill is among my most supreme regrets.

And his niece, poor, dear, Fanny Sloss. She was a lovely girl, but in our entire courtship there had never been so much as a spark of the erotic or romantic, never once a sensuous kiss or a fleeting touch of a bosom. Our rare kisses were short, thin pecks, our caresses carrying little more substance than handshakes between business partners. I have no doubt that she was fond of me and I of her, but our arrangement had more to do with what was sensible. She would have made a fine mate, a faithful companion with whom to navigate life's revolutions. We could have had a comfortable and cozy marriage. But my heart was tormented by the pink and ivory thoughts of Eva's nakedness, the tactile pleasures of tense nipples and a coarse black triangle which would not leave me be.

Dear Fanny, my poor, true betrothed, outfitted in a dress of white organdy with a matching parasol, a beauty in the engagement photographs that had been published in the Mobile and Birmingham and Montgomery newspapers, the future wife of one of the preeminent engineers in the new south. She was so beautiful, so innocent, so trusting. She would have made a wonderful mate. And she did make one, though with someone else.

Instead, I threw my lot in with this woman Eva, that blue-eyed sorrow, that siren on the rocks. I still knew so little about her, her family, her parents. I only knew that my body craved hers and that my conscience was no match for that craving. In the final round of that long wrestling match, lust had pinned good sense, and desire had slapped the mat to signal its victory.

I arrived at the great house in St. Matthew Parish having made good on my vow to become a man of means. On the front porch, I took her hand in mine, and we exchanged a deep kiss before opening the door. She said we would have the house to ourselves for several weeks, and I was aching for her and frankly only concerned about the next few minutes when we would fall upon each other.

The wallpaper in the central hallway had long since been replaced and the framed lithographs and paintings were up again. One in particular demanded my attention, a portrait of a man in a Confederate uniform now prominently displayed in the center of the long hall. The subject of it stung me like a whip.

"Excuse me," I asked Eva, pointing to the portrait. "How do you know this man?"

At about that time, the man himself appeared in the doorway of his study. She was obviously not expecting him to be home, and she hastily refastened the topmost buttons of her dress.

"Sam, darling, this is the engineer for our new sugarhouse, his name is also Teague. Perhaps you two are distant cousins—"

"I know who this is," the man said, and then he added, without a handshake, "Hello, Brother."

Part V

Eva

Well after a time of pawing and scratching and rolling around, the cat finally gets out of the bag, doesn't he, Mrs. Leonard? Say what you will about my late husband. He may have been illiterate in those days, but he always had a sense when something was being done behind his back.

I had intended to get back to Louisiana well before his return and ensconce my engineer into the guesthouse and with any luck the sugarhouse would be complete by my husband's return home in a month or so. By then, I would have dismissed my lover again, though with each day I was becoming more and more attached to him, and I was as wild for him as I have ever been for a man. He would have been difficult to abandon. Perhaps we could have made some other special arrangement. Or simply run off together.

I grant you that perhaps I should have suspected it, but Teague is a common enough name here in America, not like Smith or Jones, but still common enough, especially in the South. It had never occurred to me that they were anything more than distant cousins, if that, and certainly not brothers. They always seemed so different to me, complete opposites, in fact, but now that they were in the same room, I could easily see that they were closely related, though they looked more like father and son than brothers. They had the same gray eyes, and their hair was the same color, though my husband's hair was thinning and his body sagging and pale. It was if Jack was the good-looking, kinder, smarter version of Sam and certainly more gifted in the sexual manner than my husband had likely ever been. Nevertheless, it was nothing new for me. I had entertained several pairs of brothers in my past, including a regular pair who always came to Commerce Street at the same time.

They stood there eyeing each other. It was perfectly awkward, even for a girl like me, raised in a brothel and used to awkward situations. But there it was, Mrs. Leonard, and there was no way around it. My lover and my husband had met. I had been given no time to come clean to this reformed fixer of clocks, and we were quite fortunate that he and I hadn't been in the act of ripping off our clothes to engage in the sexual rite, right there in the central hallway. I had certainly imagined that setting for our initial tryst, right on the floor under the clock. In fact, I had sent a telegram to Sam Jr.'s nursemaid instructing her to take the boy to his grandmother's in Mississippi. Of course, I did not add that it was so that my lover Jack and I might enjoy a nice long love-banquet, beginning right there in the central hallway.

As it turned out, the nursemaid never got the message, and both Sam Sr. and Sam Jr. were still in the house. Junior came squalling and running down the stairs, '*Mama, Mama, Mama!*' like this, with his hands in the air. I suddenly felt a migraine coming on, and I retreated to my bedroom and told the servants to see to him. Perhaps, while I slept, it would all just go away.

Jack

We stood and stared at each other.

My brother was no longer the good-looking icon of Tunica County, nor the stalwart chap in the portrait on the wall. He had not aged well at all. What hair was remaining was graying with only a little of the sandy-brown I remembered from our youth. He had a rounded paunch that his trousers struggled to deal with. His hair was thinning and he was missing several teeth, both said to be from a bout with cholera several years prior, right after his third wife had died in a housefire. He didn't look four years older than me, he looked forty years older.

"Well, Brother, so you are the new draftsman and engineer for our sugarhouse. Eva's told me of you. But not everything. Certainly not your name."

Eva looked at me with a look like that of an animal caught in a trap, a look of both resignation and defiance. He pulled her to him and made to kiss her on the lips, but she manipulated her frown into a weak smile and gave him her cheek. He seemed to know the degree to which I desired her, but he could not see how ashamed I was at having bedded her. For Eva's part, her weak smile became a smirk.

The sounds of a servant struggling with a child came from upstairs, and I saw that not only did she have a husband, but she also had a son. Her sudden change was dizzying. The coy girl with the parasol in the furnace shed and the creamy nakedness draped over mine and her hand on my inner thigh on the

241

train had vanished. Now I found myself in the central hallway with her husband, my brother. I felt disoriented, that sense we had in battle that the enemy had turned your flank and was waiting in the silence of the fog for the right moment to spring upon you.

The child had the look of the Teagues, gray eyes and sandy hair. He came red-faced and squalling, dressed in a sailor suit like little Lord Fauntleroy. When he saw me he stopped crying long enough to wipe a trail of snot from his upper lip.

"This is my son, Samuel Teague, Jr.," my brother said, unconcerned by the boy's exorbitant display of emotion and mucus. "This is your Uncle Jack, your Daddy's little brother."

The boy brought his sleeve up and wiped his face with it, and then he ran squalling again to Eva with his arms up, '*Mama, Mama, Mama!*'

Eva disappeared with the sudden onset of a migraine, and a servant picked up the boy and took him upstairs. His crying trailed off to a murmur and then nothing, and in the quiet I heard the Negro lullaby that had soothed him.

My brother and I adjourned to his study, the throne-room, the Mount Olympus of what I now knew wasn't the McCarron Plantation, but Mount Teague Plantation. There were shelves filled with books, and I wondered if he had ever read any of them. I sat in one of the chairs across from his desk. It was placed deliberately at a lower level than his, to give him prominence over any interview. I've heard the railroad barons and other tycoons of industry do the same. He offered me a cordial before dinner, but I declined, saying that I was not in the habit of taking strong drink while discussing business. I watched him enjoy his expensive whiskey—I knew it was expensive because he told me so. He smacked his lips in the process of savoring it. I said that it must be a far cry from the Old Monongahela brand that our father used to drink.

"Ha!" my brother said. "That old horse thief. Never had any sense of taste or refinement. Let him rot." My brother's cheeks billowed in a suppressed belch. I took a deep breath as my anger gripped the arms of the low chair in which I'd been relegated. My brother had their house-girl—Ruthie—bring me an iced tea, as late September had warmed again and brought the late afternoon heat with it.

"We make our own ice here," he bragged, dropping a jagged chunk into his tumbler of bourbon with a clink. I don't think he realized that most places of any size now did, but I didn't correct him on that. We held our glasses up to each other and exchanged nods but didn't touch them.

"So tell me your circumstances, Brother," he asked in a somewhat bored tone, as if finding out about me was a necessary but unenjoyable formality.

"I worked on the railroads mainly," I said, my eyes just above the level of his desk, "I was there when the golden spike was driven in the Utah territory—"

"—that's all well and fine," he interrupted, "but have you laid much aside money-wise? For a rainy day?"

I said that I owned a home in Birmingham, a nice one, though it was not nearly so grand as his, and that my travels brought about by my expertise made it so that I didn't stay there as much as I might like.

"What about your homelife? Is there a Mrs. Teague? *Another* Mrs. Teague?" he asked pointedly.

I said that I had a fiancée in Alabama. I should have told him that I had *had* a fiancée in Alabama. That would have been more correct.

"Well, I do hope she's as lovely as Mother," he said.

We made a toast to the three Mrs. Teagues. I asked about Mother, and he said that her health was declining. He didn't admonish me for not visiting her, and he didn't say if she ever inquired about me. Either she didn't ask about me or my brother wanted it to seem that way. Our conversation waned and gave way to the tick of the clock I had repaired when Eva had seduced me four years before. Finally, he asked me if I might read the newspaper to him as he had left both pairs of his reading glasses at White Sulphur Springs in the mountains where they summered. I read to him from the *Times-Democrat*, an article on cattle futures, and he pursed his lips as if kissing an invisible aunt on the cheek and pressed his fingers against each other like a spider on a mirror. Reading the newspaper to my brother was the last thing I wanted to do, but he had a strange way of mesmerizing others into compliance with his blustering and bullying. I was relieved when we were called to dinner with the tinkle of a little silver bell.

We rose, he from his elaborately carved chair, I from the depths of the low chair across the desk from him. We passed a mirror, and suddenly I saw that we didn't look like brothers at all. When he walked, it was with a limp which he explained over and over in two terse words, *war-wound*, and he had a scar on his face which he was also explained in two equally terse words, *sugar-*

kettle. He added something about saving a man from being scalded by a sugar kettle. I found that hard to believe. The limp from the war wound was more plausible.

We sat down to dinner at one end of a long mahogany table, and my brother gave a long, rambling prayer loosely based on the parable of the prodigal son, with aspersions cast that I was he. The prayer ended suddenly after a roundabout journey through several other parables and something about Moses in the bullrushes and the walls of Jericho, I seem to recall. My mind had wandered off when it was called back by a sudden, *Good-food-good-meat-good-God-food-let's-eat*.

Dinner was exquisite, an immense cut of beef well-prepared with accompaniments from the Mount Teague fields, dished out on our plates by the servant girl Ruthie. My brother sawed away as I can remember him doing, talking with his mouth full. Eva stayed upstairs wrangling with her migraine or her conscience, though likely the former as I doubted she possessed or was influenced by the latter.

We three Teague men shared a meal together, I with rigid West Point table manners, Sam Junior with the manners of a four year old, and Sam Sr. with manners somewhere in between. Sam Junior pushed and pulled at the food on his plate as the nursemaid tried to feed him. He slapped at her patient brown hands and grabbed the spoon out of them and threw it down and sulked.

I thought how our father might be pleased that we were sitting and sharing a meal together as men. Perhaps this would be the beginning of the reconciliation with my brother that my father had begged me for on his deathbed. I vowed that I would overcome the shame of what I had done, and I would build my brother his sugarhouse and I would do it at the ridiculous price I had quoted his wife in the throes of passion.

My brother held up his glass and looked at it and asked, "Well, Jack, are you still planning on flying one day?"

He said it congenially, as if he would like to see me do it and would be proud to see me do it, as if it would be a red-letter day in his life, a day on which he would point to the sky and say, "Look there, everyone, that's my little brother up there. Why, just look at him, flying like a bird!"

I smiled and said, "As a matter of fact, I was reading in *Scientific American*—"

"—har! You'll no more fly than a pig, Jack!" he exclaimed before shoveling in another oversize bite like it was coal and his mouth was the firebox of a locomotive. All the while, Samuel Teague, Jr., sat and pouted at his plate and hugged himself and pressed his lips and craned his head away when the nursemaid tried to feed him.

"Sam Teague Junior," my brother said in admiration as he motioned with the end of his fork at his progeny. My brother chewed vigorously, his jaws and lips slapping open and shut and then open again as he tossed in another mouthful.

"Maybe one day—" he swallowed noisily with a great up-and-down heave of his Adam's apple "— you'll have a son of your own with this Ferney gal." He said it with the air of having something I wanted but couldn't have.

"Fanny," I managed to say, and I felt deflated as I realized that Fanny was a person who was now in my past. What I had given up and how I had done it horrified me more each time I thought of it.

"Yes, Fanny," he said.

I said next to nothing after that. There was an apple pie after dinner and a cordial for my brother, a brandy which was old and rare and much sought after, for he again told me so. I had coffee instead. I bid my brother good night, and I retired to the guest quarters in the old Ice House, the scene of the love that I now saw for what it was, debauchery. The day had been shorter than the one before it, and that meant the time to cut and grind the cane was approaching.

That night, I saw Eva, whom I now knew wasn't Eva McCarron, but Eva Teague, part the curtains and look out across the way and close them again. In that brief glimpse, I saw that she was naked. She smiled, I cringed, and shame forced me to close my curtains. Over the course of the next few days, she would appear on the periphery while their overseer Mr. Landry and I were making important decisions regarding construction. She wanted my attention, but I had none to spare and no time to spare it, and I wouldn't have given her any, anyway. I had been lured into something forbidden, enticed with unholy pleasures. I wanted to leave in the middle of the night, but to quit now would be to cast suspicions on the true reason for my errand to Mount Teague, which frankly would have been to unwittingly cuckold my brother. The embarrassment of what I had done was a shadow over me, so I resolved to make amends and see the sugarhouse to completion and then leave and start over somewhere, somehow.

I rose early the morning after my arrival and sat down with Mr. Landry, and we set about finalizing the plans for the new sugarhouse. At once, I realized that the price I had quoted would be woefully inadequate, perhaps a little over half of what was needed. I believe Mr. Landry realized it, too. We kept looking at the plans, pointing our pencils at them as if trying to coax them into allowing something less expensive. Each time we were about to write down a change, we withdrew our pencils realizing that any change would save nothing. We pressed forward knowing from the start that it would be impossible to build it for the price I had agreed to.

We staked off the footprint of the main building and began erecting it out of immense cypress posts and beams rather than the iron ones I had planned. It was the first of many shortcuts that I was forced into. Hands who in a few weeks would be swinging knives and stacking cane and driving mules and wagons were, for the time being, swinging axes and pushing and pulling saws and hammering pegs. Soon, there were no more reasonable shortcuts, and I went to see my brother. I begged him to spend the money necessary.

"Brother, don't go trying to pick my pocket. Do it for the price quoted, and no more."

When the first gusts of cold air came in from the north, the pace quickened to that which Noah must have adopted when the first rains of the flood had begun to puddle the ground. I became worried that things were left undone, tenons unpegged, beams unsupported. The iron for the boilers that had been shipped to us from Pittsburgh—for I couldn't ask for it from Birmingham, that bridge had been burned—was the wrong gauge. A telegram there said they could send the proper thickness, but there would be a delay and a surcharge. The boilermakers threatened to walk off the job if we used the thinner gauge, but I managed to talk them out of it.

I reported this to my brother with the fact that there would be shipping charges in addition to the delays. He exploded. He again accused me of trying to 'pick his pocket' and that I was 'in cahoots' with the foundry. "Certainly it can be done for this bid!" he bellowed like a bull elephant. Of course, his opinion was unencumbered by any knowledge of engineering or physics.

Every blast of cold air from the north was a reminder that the sugarhouse was falling behind schedule. Cane grew in the fields, the chilly winds whispering taunts through the leaves, *hurry, hurry, hurry.* Work continued by torchlight into the night and under tarpaulins in the rain, and in the paltry hours that I slept, my dreams were haunted by themes of inadequacy, like the tragic and tortured Greek Sisyphus futilely struggling to push his rock uphill, only to have it roll back down.

I asked Landry how much time we had before the first frost, and he said that he knew a man who could predict things like that with great certainty. We left the rapping hammers and the arcs and rivets of iron being joined, and he took me out into the swamp where this sage lived. If I had time to slow down the pace even a little, it would help.

Pinch

Death doesn't take curiosity from a dog. If anything, it makes us more curious because in death we can go wherever we please. And so I wandered from room to room in the big house. My master Jack's littermate was in his room, the one with walls made out of books. He wasn't reading any of them. He was just sleeping in his chair. He made a great snore that moved the scar on his face up and down. It squirmed and writhed like it was a worm that was happy to be deep in his beard. I sniffed him and moved on. The stairs were right outside of his room, the one with so many books, and I vaulted up them.

The boy was playing in his room upstairs. If I were still flesh-and-fur, I would bark and entice him into play, but instead I sat on my haunches and watched him. He made towers by carefully stacking one block upon another, like Jack might do if he were a boy, but then the boy smashed them with a blow from his little paw. He left the blocks scattered over the floor and looked through a book with pictures and simple words, many times over, then he became bored with that and mounted his rocking horse.

I yawned and got up and went downstairs. The woman who Jack had lain with was in her bedroom sitting on her bed and looking in a mirror. I found it odd that she didn't share the same bed with my master Jack's littermate. She had a suitcase open on the bed with clothes in it, though she was neither putting clothes in it nor taking them out. Without a noise or even a rustle of the bedcovers, I jumped on the bed and looked into the mirror with her. She cast a reflection but I didn't. She looked sad. She looked as if she did not like to be sad or have others see that she was sad. She pushed the heel of her paw across her face to wipe tears from her eyes. I sniffed her paw to see why she was sad, but I couldn't tell. I wanted to know why she was sad. Such things are always important to dogs.

She rose, still pushing tears from her eyes with her paw. Blue is a color dogs cannot see in life, but when we are spirits we can see it and now the blue eyes that Jack always found so beautiful were red. She stopped pawing at her tears and they trailed down her face and she let them fall as she looked out the window.

Then I saw it. She was sad at something outside the window. I jumped from the bed and put my paws on the window ledge and I saw my master Jack walking across the field to the barn where there were horses. I left the crying woman called Eva and the house and I scampered after my master Jack and the man Landry. They had mounted horses and were riding down the road. I ran between the legs of the horses, in and out without fear. That is an advantage of being a spirit.

I ran without tiring, following my master Jack and the man Landry. They tied up their horses at the edge of a swamp, and when they got in the boat, I leaped silently and invisibly into it with them.

Jack

Mr. Landry, my brother's overseer, took me with him to see a man who he swore could predict the weather, particularly freezes. Maybe we had more time than I thought, and I desperately needed more time. If only I had had more time, then perhaps I wouldn't be wearing this eyepatch.

We started off on horseback, and, after an hour or so, we tied our horses to a tree at the edge of a cypress swamp and took a boat, one of those pirogues, another half an hour to a shack deep within the swamp. Everything was mirrored in the water, the reflections of the trees reaching down into the earth. Somewhere among the massive trunks, an alligator bellowed rhythmically like it was trying to clear its throat. Far below the brownish orange needles of the cypress canopy, an egret fished the shallow water with slow steps and a patient yellow eye. We poled by him as he stabbed the water and produced a fish, a beakful of thrashing shimmer that disappeared in three snatching gulps. Fall vines grew with blue and orange flowers up the trunks of trees, some incredibly large. Some of the cypresses surely must have been seedlings when Christ was alive. It was so peaceful, heavenly, even. Enough to make a man forget machinery and deadlines and rapidly growing sugarcane.

We pulled up to a shack where piles of gray moss sat in the small yard, with a wooden boat like ours, a pirogue, they're called there. Black and brown pelts were nailed onto the gray-planked sides of the house to dry. Mr. Landry introduced me to Mr. Barbagree, an old man with skin that seemed to be an average color of every human being everywhere, and with a long gray beard so much like the moss hanging from the limbs outside his dwelling-place. I offered him a gift of a sack of coffee and a pouch of tobacco, as Mr. Landry said they were two things he couldn't produce for himself here, down in the swamp. Mr. Barbagree seemed pleased with the gift and said, *merci, merci, mon fils.*

We sat and smoked and conversed, though the Napoleonic French taught to me at West Point would not meet with his patois. At one point, he oddly reached down and scratched the air at his feet. At last he told us that the first freeze of the year was little more than a week away. I thanked him, and rather than saying *de rien*, you're welcome, he seemed to be trying to warn me of something, though either he couldn't express it or I couldn't understand. Nor could Mr. Landry. Finally, Mr. Landry and I left, but not without Barbagree's worried look following us. As Landry and I poled back out of the swamp, *la cyprière*, the knobby black hide of an alligator floated in a wreath of white egret feathers on the surface of the black water.

Immediately on returning to Mount Teague, work was redoubled. Extra hands were hired. Thanksgiving was postponed until after grinding was done and a larger, more lavish celebration was promised. Time was short. And at last it was complete, or complete enough. Or so I prayed. Wagons of cane were already lined up a quarter mile as the boilers were lit and the wheels began to grind. I suppose I could have demanded my fee then and left. I assume that my brother and my sister-in-law would have paid me before the crop was in. Perhaps they wouldn't have. Perhaps they never would have.

But my conscience tethered me to the place as I held my breath and prayed that everything would hold. I prayed to the Lord Almighty, the God of Physics and Chemistry, Temperature and Pressure, to keep together the iron sheets and rivets, that though they might bulge and strain, by his grace, they would hold. I vowed that if he would grant me that, as soon as the boilers were extinguished and the crop was put to market, I would sigh in relief and chuckle at myself for my lack of faith in myself and God, and I would leave with my paltry fee and not come back, not richer but wiser.

It was not only my conscience that kept me there. I stayed there also because I had no job to return to, no loving fiancée. When this project was complete, I would sell my house in Birmingham and move north to a new future somewhere, to Pittsburgh or some other hub of industry. I would find a new position and a new mate. I had my good looks and an impeccable, enviable reputation. But I would have neither much longer. I stayed there planning a new life and hoping that the gauge of iron that the boilers were made of would be thick enough to withstand the temperature and pressure of sweet, boiling juice.

It wasn't.

Editor Lucien Braud

Yes ma'am, Mrs. Leonard, I have it right here. We keep this cabinet here with old issues, however yellowed and frayed they might be. Maybe one day someone will figure out how to photograph them instead. The archives of the *St. Matthew Compass* and the French version *La Boussole de St. Mathieu* go back all the way to the 1850s, before the war. Of course, now that the French language has been forbidden in schools, it's only a matter of time before *La Boussole de St. Mathieu* ceases publication for lack of readers.

Now, let's see. Eighteen eighty-three, eighty-four, eighty….five. Now. October…November…December…here it is. December 20, 1885.

Sugarhouse Explodes!

Loss of life, property
Overseer Landry calls it a total loss

The new sugarhouse at Mount Teague, which once promised to hold up the banner of progress and industry here in St. Matthew, gave way Thursday night during its inaugural grinding season. Local men who were in the army and heard the explosion say that it was comparable to anything they heard during the late war. In a matter of a few fateful seconds, the sugarhouse was reduced to charred timbers and twisted metal and is considered a complete loss.

The remains of men were found in trees, and flaming rafters were launched a quarter mile away. Four perished, two are unaccounted for, though an arm was found on the back step of a house across Bayou Lafourche. A mule's carcass was also found blasted to the other side of the Twelve Arpent Canal.

It is almost certain that the cause of the disaster was shoddy engineering and construction. Mr. Andrew Jackson 'Jack' Teague was the man in charge of its fabrication.

Mr. Sam insisted that I put that last bit in, and as you can see, as the article goes on, it is repeated several times that Jack Teague and no one else was

251

responsible for it. I suppose if you repeat a lie often enough, it becomes the truth, and more so if it's printed. It was against my journalistic instincts and ethics, for I didn't know if it were true or untrue, but I was a young reporter then, and I had been warned not to cross Mr. Sam and Miss Eva. And so I didn't, and in doing so, I helped ruin a man's name. And that I have always regretted.

Yes ma'am. Is there anything else I can do for you?

The overseer at Mount Teague was a man named Landry. Several years after the accident he moved on to St. James Parish. Yes ma'am, I'm sure he'd talk to you, but St. James is too far to walk from here. I'll have someone drive you over.

Oh, and Mrs. Leonard. Please keep this between us. Mr. Sam was someone who was either *canaille* or *coullion*, clever or foolish, you could never tell which one. But Miss Eva, now she was *canaille, tout canaille*. In fact, the saying in St. Matthew was and still is that Miss Eva is '*canaille comme rat, méchant comme serpent*.' Yes ma'am, 'clever as a rat and mean as a snake.' She can ruin you.

Yes ma'am, I have your word.

Adolphus Landry
Former overseer,
Mount Teague Plantation

No, madame, I don't mind meeting with you. Welcome to Little Ada. Yes, that's right, named after a child. Mr. Broussard named the place after his daughter. How'd you know that?

I hope the roads were passable. We just finished grinding here. Watch that puddle there. The cane wagons can make a mess in the mud, though it's mostly dried ruts now. Here, let me help you over. We just got the last of the sugar in and the crew is cleaning the mill for next year. We can take a little rest now, and we can talk, and talk freely. Now that he's dead.

Yes, madame, I was overseer the year the sugarhouse went up, though I've never spoken much about it. But now that Mr. Teague is dead, I believe

I might tell you. I trust you'll keep this between us, as Miss Eva still has considerable influence in this part of the world. The expression around here is that Miss Eva is *'canaille comme rat, méchant comme serpent.'* Yes, madame, 'clever as a rat and mean as a snake.' She wouldn't ruin *me*, she would go after Mrs. Landry and her reputation. My wife and her honor are the most precious things in the world to me. So let's keep this between us.

Yes, then. You're asking about the sugarhouse explosion. Well, it was thirty years ago, the 1885 grinding season. On her own, Mrs. Teague had gone up to Birmingham and engaged her brother-in-law, Jack Teague, to come and set us up with a new mill. Mr. Jack was an engineer and a fine one, the best in the world at the time when it came to any kind of mill or gin.

Well, as I say, I was overseer for the Teagues from about 1878 until I was fired by them in 1888, just after the close of grinding that year. We enjoyed some banner seasons in those days, all made possible by the impeccable timing of our harvest. We never failed to get the last of our cane cut just before the first ruinous freeze, whether it be early or late. The reason for that was this: I would meet with a man called Barbagree, and we would share a meal and talk about the weather, in French, as it was his only language, and I speak both French and English. It helps in directing the field hands. Most of them just speak French.

Monsieur Barbagree lived in an old shack back in an area everyone called *la cyprière de Barbagree*, Barbagree's cypress swamp. It was a place alive with wildlife, fish, birds, deer, bear. Flowers bloomed deep in the depths of it, trailing high on vines that rose up into the branches of the tupelos and cypresses. Some of the trees were big enough that you could have hollowed them out and lived inside. But Barbagree lived in a simple shack, one room with a potbelly stove. He was every color a man could be, an average of all skin tones. He had a gray beard like the Spanish moss that hung from the cypress branches, and so the name, Barbagree, barbe-gris. Yes, madame, *graybeard*. He collected the moss to sell to people to stuff furniture and mattresses and the like. He was a friendly enough man, if you approached him correctly, but he could also be reserved if he didn't like you or distrusted you.

He accepted me, for I would travel deep into the cyprière, by pirogue and then on the plank walkway to his hut, and I always brought something with me. A sack of coffee or a pouch of tobacco, something like that, madame.

We would sit and smoke and speak in French, often about the beauty of the cyprière, and the age of the trees and the spirits that lived in them.

During these visits he would warn me of freezes and droughts, and Miss Gladys—may I call you Miss Gladys?—he never failed. Not once. He would always deliver the advice at the close of our meeting, something like, *Garde la ça, temps froid*—that means 'watch out for that freeze'—before the next new moon, or plenty warm weather for two moons, or something like that.

Though he rarely took visitors, I brought Mr. Teague's brother Jack, then as I say, a crackerjack engineer from Alabama, down to see Monsieur Barbagree at Mr. Jack's insistence. We sat and visited, though Mr. Jack's French, the fancy French of Napoleon and Paris, didn't always mesh with Monsieur's, and I had to translate from time to time. Mr. Jack had brought Monsieur a little tobacco and coffee and we enjoyed that. It was a beautiful day, the cypresses rusting into fall colors, egrets roosting white in them, the water lazily pushing around the knobs of cypress knees. Mr. Jack had been accepted by Monsieur, who stroked his gray beard and recounted stories of the days when all the area was cyprière, not just those thousand acres around his dwelling-place. Mr. Jack listened in rapt attention, and I could see what he must have looked like as a boy, when he and Mr. Sam were growing up in Mississippi.

We rose at the conclusion of our visit, and Monsieur Barbagree's entire demeanor changed. It was clear that he liked Mr. Jack, but it was less clear what he wanted to tell him. It was a warning of some sort, but it was vague to us, and perhaps it was something that Barbagree himself couldn't understand enough to put into words. As he clasped hands with us in farewell, Barbagree said, "Be careful, you boys, be careful, against death and disaster."

I had an idea that this had something to do with the sugarhouse Mr. Jack was building, and, though we never spoke of it, I think Mr. Jack did too. I discussed it with my boss, Mr. Sam, that Mr. Barbagree warned us of a disaster and that maybe we should take a little extra care and time and have our cane ground by Mr. Parris' outfit one more year and then the new sugarhouse would be ready for the next year. Monsieur Barbagree was always right on everything, so I warned Mr. Sam. But Mr. Teague berated me, saying, "We're about to leap ahead of our competition. Now just whose side are you on here, Landry?" Those were his exact words, Miss Gladys.

And so construction continued on the new sugarhouse, under bright sun and drizzling autumn rain by day and by torchlight by night. What a giant it would have been! Bigger than anything in the western hemisphere, or the world, maybe. The *St. Matthew Compass* and the New Orleans papers declared that it was the biggest construction project since Noah's ark. The Louisiana Sugar Planters' Association sent a committee down to inspect this new colossus. They pronounced it a 'jewel in the crowns of Queen Agriculture and King Industry.' That may or may not have been a reference to Mr. Sam and Miss Eva, but that is certainly how they took it.

When it was completed, or completed enough, the ribbon was cut and grinding began. Wagons were lined down a great long way, full of sugarcane ready for the mill. It was already well into the season, and we knew time would be short, according to Barbagree. Well, as you've heard it ended in disaster. As it turned out, I narrowly avoided disaster myself.

I had gone up to the big house to ask Mr. Sam if we could knock off for the night, as the hands were becoming exhausted and I feared that they might make a mistake and injure themselves or others. Just as I made the porch, there was an explosion and a flash of yellow and orange into the night sky like judgment day, then the raining down of timbers and, I am almost certain, bodies of the men I had just come to intercede for.

The great sugarhouse, what was left of it, was aflame, lighting up the night sky. It was like a square skeleton in a bonfire. Posts and beams were cracking, slumping, falling. Mr. Jack was pulling himself along the ground and clutching the side of his face. I ran to him, but he threw off my hands and went in to pull a man out, and then another. I tried but it was just too hot. And then he realized it and we stopped and looked at it together.

In the firelight, I saw his eye, bulging and gray and surrounded by skin that was already sloughing. His clear eye was red as he sobbed and sobbed. I put my arm around him as we all stopped what we were doing, including the bucket brigade, all of whom stood holding their buckets uselessly in a line that stretched all the way to the bayou.

Mr. Sam turned his brother out immediately, and Mr. Jack was looked after in my home by my wife and the doctor whose fee I paid out of my own pocket. He convalesced slowly and hovered near death's door, and several times he begged death to come for him. I told my wife not to tell him that charges had been prepared against him. Not until he was well enough to take the news. But charges were filed, and when Mr. Jack was well enough, a trial was held.

I could have told Judge Anderson and the court everything, and I would have, but I was prohibited from testifying. Instead, the court found against Sam's brother, Mr. Jack Teague. It ruined the man, and, after he posted bail, no one ever saw him again. It was a travesty, *mais n'a pas du toupet*, that is, but nobody had the nerve, the guts, to speak against Mr. Sam and Miss Eva. It was widely known that they could ruin you, find things out about you and your family and twist it and spread it. Oui, madame, just like I said, *canaille comme rat, méchant comme serpent.*

Mr. Jack was held in the St. Matthew Parish jail but made bond and was never heard from again. When I went to visit Barbagree afterward, all he said to me was, "listen to me, boy, next time, listen to me."

I hear that Mount Teague is on hard times. Everyone I know is secretly happy about it, though I suppose it's an empty enjoyment, feeling happy at the misfortune of others, no matter how hateful they might be.

Yes, and thank you, Miss Gladys. Let me walk you to your automobile. It was nice of Mr. Braud to arrange a ride for you. He's a nice fellow, for a newspaper man, at least—

Ma'am? Yes, as a matter of fact we do have a telephone. Have the operator, Miss Faustina Templet, call me through the Vacherie exchange if you have anything else you'd like to discuss.

Eva

Good evening, Mrs. Leonard. You've certainly made a day of it, all the way to Vacherie and back! I trust your ride in the countryside was enjoyable now that the roads have dried sufficiently. We once had a fine set of automobiles here. One day I hope to acquire several more of them to replace the ones that we had to sell.

Yes, about my husband's brother.

Mr. Teague, my husband, watched me like a hawk as I in turn watched his brother, the handsome, virile, and now more accomplished Mr. Teague. I was sure that I had thrown my saddle over the wrong Mr. Teague, and so I decided that I would leave my husband. In fact, I packed a bag with some clothes and other necessaries and hid it under the bed. There was only one problem.

Apparently in addition to good looks and a firm body and a now-promising future, Jack was also a man afflicted with a surplus of scruples. That night, through the window across the way from the guesthouse, I offered Jack a glimpse of my body in hopes that he would come in, and we could slip away someplace for more than a glimpse. But he drew his curtains closed on me and my delights, and in the days that followed, he never gave me so much as a passing glance. Still, I had lured him before and I would lure him again, likely with a melodramatic tale told with theatrical tears of how I was mistreated by my husband and how I needed to be saved, a scenario that might appeal to Jack, as he had the noble impulses of a knight. It was clear to anyone how much they loathed one another, and I was confident I could sway Jack again.

My husband seized on the low offer for the sugarhouse that his brother had given me and pressed him on it, even though it couldn't be done for that. I myself might have interceded for Jack, had I felt up to it, but it seemed as though I had misplaced my monthly malady again, and all I could find in its place was a sick and contrary stomach.

On the night when the sugarhouse exploded and illuminated the night, I was confined to my bed under a pall of nausea. The smell of the smoke in the air and the shouts of the bucket brigades stretching down to the canal were enough to provoke new waves of retching. Jack had been absolutely right about the danger inherent in the design, but he had built it how my husband wanted it, cheaply and quickly.

Through the efforts of my husband and his coercion of Judge Anderson, Jack was charged with manslaughter and taken into custody. I thought of going to post his bail and so win back his favor. He would have been grateful, perhaps grateful enough that we could have run off together, but my queasy stomach wouldn't allow my going anywhere and to see him maimed wouldn't have helped matters. As it occurred, after Jack stood trial, he posted bail himself, then forfeited it and left, and was never heard from again. If ever I had a chance for true, honest love, madame, he was it. I am convinced of it.

My husband pronounced it good riddance from a man who had only brought us trouble, a man who delivered substandard work that resulted in the maiming and death of our workers. The newspapers—through my husband's insistence, I'm sure—pronounced Jack Teague a failure as a man and as an engineer. I can tell you candidly that as a lover and as a man who truly cared for me, I have never met his equal. Nevertheless, madame, when he forfeited his bail and fled, I had no choice but to stay with my husband. So I suppose everything works out for the best or, at least, second best.

My second child, a girl, was born the May following the trial, in 1886. Yes, that is quite a coincidence isn't it, Mrs. Leonard? Three months shy of a year after the visit of our engineer! My, my. Let me remind you that my husband's conjugal abilities were quite limited from the start of our marriage, and we kept to separate beds soon after our honeymoon, largely due to the wind emitting from his nose and his *arse*, as you say in England.

Well, madame, some there say it.

Regardless, when I again found myself with child, I fought through my nausea and snuck into his room, took off my clothes, and pulled up his nightshirt. When he woke, with me draped over him, I said something such as, 'I am quite satisfied this morning.' He of course had no recollection of it, but desperately wanted to believe in the myth of his own sexual prowess. He was like the king who slept through his own coronation.

The house servants named the new baby Missy, and I let them do it, as I had no interest in the matter. Junior, then five or so, hated his sister from the start. He was certainly a little tyrant, in the mold of my husband, I suppose. No one likes things taken away from them, toys, attention, limelight, and little Sam Jr. was no different. But it was a matter for the servants to deal with. They had but one rule: none of them were to lay a dark hand on a Teague child in anger.

That summer Mr. Landry and my husband worked on getting a mill together that was just big enough to grind our crop, but no builder within a hundred miles would work for us. We were left without a sugarhouse, and again, we were at the mercies of the Parrises.

As it happened, the following fall, we cut the cane early because of a freeze predicted by Mr. Landry through this old fool Barbagree who lived in the cypress sloughs called Barbagree's swamp. The last of our cane was in before everyone else woke to find that a hard freeze in the night had stopped everything green and sweet in its tracks. The sugarcane of the Parrises and everyone else thawed and rotted in their fields. We paid the Parrises pennies on the dollar to grind our cane, and they were glad to have the paltry income. Due to the shortage, our barrels of sugar brought top dollar. Now it was the Parrises who were over a barrel, namely a barrel of Mount Teague sugar. We made an offer to them for their mill, and they had no choice but to agree. And so now we had our mill.

It is time for my nap, Mrs. Leonard. We no longer have a telephone—I find them nothing but an intrusion, and so I banished them—but Mr. Aucoin in Napoleonville has one. He's just down from the courthouse. Why do you need a telephone, may I ask?

Yes, I suppose it's none of my business.

Adolphus Landry

Yes, Miss Faustina, this is Adolphus Landry. Sorry for the delay. I was out in the fields. Yes, I'll accept the charges.

Miss Gladys? Good to hear from you again, and so soon! Where are you calling from? Aucoin's store in Napoleonville? Oh yes, that's right. I've heard Miss Eva had the telephones at Mount Teague turned off. Or the telephone exchange turned them off. I guess that's the more correct way to put it.

Faustina, please get off the line. This conversation is private. *Merci, sha.*

Miss Gladys, can you hear me?

Well, as I say, madame, over the years it became clear to me that this man Barbagree could predict freezes and drought with absolute certainty. I don't know how he did it, but he was a genuine oracle on the subject. That next year, 1886, after the sugarhouse disaster, we had an unusually early freeze. I warned Mr. Sam that it would happen, and he grudgingly set me to cutting our crop. As it turned out, old Barbagree was exactly right. We had the earliest freeze anyone could remember. Everyone around us took a loss that year, with frozen cane in the field rotting as it thawed. But we came out sitting pretty with a banner crop.

With the payout, Mr. Sam and Miss Eva bought the Parris sugarhouse, and from then on they would grind the cane, and they made all the surrounding planters pay dearly. It made for some bad blood, or *mauvais sang*, as we say in French. And it didn't help that Miss Eva would flaunt it. New carriages, fine horses to pull them, the whole of Mount Teague redone by some big-name decorator from New York. Summering in Europe. The Teagues weren't people to hide the light of their wealth under a bushel, no ma'am.

The next year they went to Europe for the fever season, 1887, if my memory is correct. My family and I, like most ordinary people, 'stayed and prayed' that we wouldn't get sick. It was still a very real possibility then, before we knew the mosquito was responsible for it. Everyone with means would get away, and the Teagues now had the means to go to Europe for it.

Well, ma'am, that year, 1887, the Knights of Labor came in from someplace else and began stirring up the hands. Terrebonne, St. Mary, Lafourche, St. Martin, all the planters in the surrounding parishes were troubled by it. The hands wanted $1.25 a day, plus board, which was double what they were getting at the time. I was in a hard place. Pay up, or refuse them and risk having them walk off and us lose our crop.

I sent a telegram to Mr. Sam in London and received a reply that they had moved on to Paris. The reply from Paris said they had removed to Rome. Finally I was able to track them down in Venice. By that time, to keep the hands from walking off, I had given in to their demands. I had no other choice. It was perhaps the loneliest, most trying days I've ever known. I felt the weight of the world, or at least the part of it that was Mount Teague, on my shoulders.

The Teagues returned from Europe early and were exasperated to find I had given into the demands of the Mount Teague field hands and given them a raise to $1.25 a day. I had no choice, as they would have struck and the entire crop would have been lost. I was the one who was sold out for it, but I wasn't the only man the Teagues ever took advantage of, as I've told you.

I thought Mr. Sam and Miss Eva would turn out the hands *en masse*, but instead, they gave the hands an even better deal, which undercut the surrounding planters, who could not keep up with the offer, and some of the smaller planters failed and were bought out by the Teagues. In the deal, la cyprière de Barbagree was given over to them. Though the previous owners had allowed Monsieur to live there for as long as anyone could remember, the Teagues would eventually have it cut for the timber, and Barbagree faded away.

The deal the Teagues gave their hands turned out to be no deal at all, a deal that tied them tightly to the Mount Teague commissary. Their pay had been doubled, but the prices in the commissary were tripled. The hands had struck a bad bargain with the Teagues. And then, when the crop was in and off to market, January of that year, 1888, the Teagues fired me either for overstretching my boundaries or not stretching them far enough, they never gave me a clear reason. My family and I moved on, here to St. James Parish, to work for Mr. Broussard, a man who is both prosperous and fair to what he refers to as 'his families.' And I have not looked back, glad to endure any hardship rather than be involved in unclean business.

No ma'am, I did not attend Mr. Sam's funeral, as I had no respects to pay to such a man as him. I hate to say it, but that is the truth under God.

It's been a pleasure speaking with you again, ma'am. I hope the rest of your stay and your return home to England are likewise a pleasure. Yes ma'am, the courthouse is there in Napoleonville, right across Bayou Lafourche. You can see the cupola of it from a mile away. I'm sure Mr. Aucoin can point you the way.

Miss Gladys, before I hang up, let me say this. It was foolhardy what Mr. Sam did, trying to get cane out of that wet ground. I would have strongly advised him against it. It wasn't worth a man's life. If he had just waited. Yes ma'am. And ma'am, please keep what I have said between us. *Au revoir, madame.*

Jack

It was thirty years ago this month, the night the sugarhouse went up. I barely remembered it happening, just a sudden blare of yellow and orange and a monumental noise. I woke days later with a bandaged eye and a forehead that seared with pain. Word got out quickly, largely through the newspapers and most notably the St. Matthew Parish *Compass*, that I alone was responsible for its failure, through shoddy engineering and the use of inferior materials.

The name and reputation I had worked to advance and sustain were ruined, and thoroughly so.

A trial was held under the gavel of a Judge Anderson, a man who was a crony of my brother as every other man of substance in St. Matthew Parish was. He wore a black robe like a member of the devil's choir and stared around the courtroom and occasionally peppered the air in it with words like 'sustained' and 'go on' and 'overruled.' In between supporting the side of his head with his hand, he would make rolling gestures with it. He never made eye contact with me, nor I with him. But of course, I now only had one eye. The other was ruined and hidden under a bandage.

My brother testified that I had always been hasty, even as a boy, which was a lie, and that now that he knew the truth about me and my abilities, he would not hire me to build so much as a chicken coop. The lawyer for my brother, a walrus of a man from a prestigious Canal Street firm in New Orleans, painted a fictitious picture of me, that of a man quick to make a profit through shoddy design, materials, and workmanship. My own advocate, a young man just out of Tulane law school tried well enough. The two lawyers boxed verbally for a day and a half, each new argument by my brother's attorney finding its mark, each objection sustained, while each one on our part was overruled, until finally my attorney, the young Tulane man, began to sink to his knees as far as the argument was concerned, and I, and I alone, was found culpable for the sugarhouse disaster. And so Fate turned its thumbs down on me, and I was ruined.

But that was not all. Charges of manslaughter were brought against me, and there was talk of them being upgraded to murder. I wired instructions for my home in Birmingham to be sold, and with the last of my money I posted the exorbitant bail set by my brother's lapdog, Judge Anderson. The door slammed behind me, and I faded away into the night.

I left St. Matthew Parish a bitter, broken man, ruined monetarily and in character, as broken as it is possible for a man to be and still live. Colonel Sloss would not have taken me back and in fact, retired from the Sloss Furnace a short time after I left. The favored niece turned her affections elsewhere and married someone else within a year.

My name and my reputation were annihilated, my looks were destroyed, and so I departed to find a place to finish the destruction of what was left. I headed down the road, looking for a quiet place to do it. I had promised God that I wouldn't kill another man, but I had made no such pact about killing myself. As I walked, friendless and penniless, owner of only a shattered reputation, I desperately searched for the oak where I had buried Pinch. I found it, his dish nailed to its bark and his collar of braided telegraph wire hanging from it. My fingers traced the weave of the wire and the rusty tin where his faithful tongue had gratefully scoured any scrap I had for him. I scribbled a note and secured it to the collar. It read, "Please forgive me the scene you have come upon. I went in search of peace. Passerby, I beg you to bury me here next to my faithful companion."

I looked into the water to see what I had become, a man with a bandaged head, slipping over half of my face, like an Arabian knight with a fallen turban. The weightless moon floated in the sky beyond the shadows of limbs. Night had fallen, but I didn't bother to make a fire. In a few moments I would be insensible to its light and heat, and the cold and dark. I rose and went and sat on a log and took the revolver from my knapsack and put the cold steel barrel in my mouth. I began crying, weeping, so that the metal knocked against my teeth, the cold metal which would soon and suddenly heat up.

Pinch

I followed him along the road, though I was still a spirit he could not see. And, because I was a spirit, I could feel the pain emanating from him like heat, the despair like that of a dog driven from the pack and set to wandering.

He sat and he wept and shook and howled in despair and he read from the book aloud, *my soul is weary, even unto death*, and I put my paws on his knee but I was only a spirit and he could not feel them any more than he could hear my sympathetic whining. And so I sat close to him, frustrated that I could not give him solace.

He stopped to look into the water and I wondered if he would enter for a swim like we used to do when I was flesh and fur, but he only looked into it and put his hand to his head as his reflection did, touching the cloth there. He decided against a swim and went and sat on a log and pulled the gun from the sack. It was the same one that he had touched me with when he knew of my suffering at the end of my days but could not end me. He put the end of the gun in his mouth, and I curled up at his feet and waited for him to join me, as a spirit.

Judge Anderson

Ma'am, I speak to you from this place because you can hear me and what is more you can understand me. On moonless nights people say they see a light in the window of my chambers, that I am here poring over law books and searching the state statutes for answers. They are correct.

In almost forty years on the bench, I strove to be thoughtful and fair, and I was so.

Save once.

The facts of the case were clear. Sam Teague and his wife Eva had retained Sam's brother Andrew Jackson 'Jack' Teague to design and build a new sugarhouse, three times the size of their former one, and twice as big as that of the Parrises. There were rumors that shortcuts were taken for the sake of expediency, and midway through the first night of the grinding season, a boiler gave way, scalding to death several hands and maiming half a dozen others. In the subsequent fire, Jack Teague was himself seriously burned over his face and upper chest, pulled weeping from the wreckage after going in several times to rescue the men inside.

I excused Eva Teague from testifying, as she was early in the family way and unable to take the witness stand. At trial, Sam testified that he had fully relied on the expertise of his brother and could not be reasonably expected to shoulder any of the blame for the explosion and fire. Jack Teague, for his part a West Point trained engineer and student of a Mr. Hargreaves who in turn was a student of Thomas Whitwell of England, and a former employee of the famous Colonel James Sloss of Alabama, testified that he implored his brother that the materials employed in the construction were substandard and used for expediency and that he had recommended, nay, begged the use of thicker iron plating and additional rivets. Jack Teague was a compelling witness and all the evidence weighed on his side. He could not look up and had to be reminded several times to address the court clearly, his voice sometimes barely above a whisper.

But the outcome was decided at the outset, before any testimony was ever heard, by an envelope with money, addressed to me in the lovely hand of Eva Teague on the desk in my chambers. And so I listened to two days of testimony, or pretended to, my guilty eyes on the gavel as if I were on trial, while a man with bandages over half his face explained that he had argued against the use of inferior methods and materials but that his brother, Sam Teague, one of the wealthiest pillars of St. Matthew, had undercut him at every step, coercing him with the threat of dismissal and the ruin of his reputation, even though he pleaded with them that the machinery in their new sugarhouse would not withstand a single grinding season. And he was correct, it did not, and men were killed and maimed as a result. Those facts do not lie.

After two days of empty, inconsequential testimony, I found for the plaintiffs against Andrew Jackson 'Jack' Teague and exonerated Sam Teague. In doing so, I ruined a man's name and took his fortune and future away from him, this unfortunate man with a half-ruined face.

Then Sam Teague pushed for a criminal trial, and charges of manslaughter were entered. And even that was not good enough for him, and so the charges were upgraded to murder. Before that could happen, Jack Teague forfeited his bail and was never seen again.

The money in the envelope in my chambers went to build a beach cottage on Cheniere Caminada, a place that I had planned as a retreat for my family, for my children and their families, in the warm months as a respite from heat and fever. It was to be a lovely place, away from dockets and arguments, filled with children and grandchildren. I also hoped it would be a refuge from the gnawing regret of what I helped do to this innocent man, Jack Teague. But my howling conscience followed me, and it was never so.

The year after the beach cottage was built, 1888, my youngest grandson drowned there, and after that, it was associated with such painful memories that none of us could bear to go there again, lest we be beset by melancholy. It stood empty, the curtains twisting in sea breezes that curled in through broken window panes. Then, the hurricane of 1893 scattered it so that only the foundation was left. All that remained visible were brick pilings and a portion of the cistern. Brick pilings like the pillars of justice

I ask you, then, what sum is given? What is the worth of a man's soul? The splintered wooden remnants of a ruined beach cottage, scattered into the sand and dust like Judas' thirty pieces of silver? Let the auctioneer rattle the price.

Eva

Well, what was the talk in Napoleonville, Mrs. Leonard? I suppose it's a far cry from the sights of London. We've toured Europe several times, after we decided not to frequent White Sulphur Springs any longer, as we found the people there boors and we could afford better.

The grinding season after the sugarhouse disaster, we endured the embarrassment of having the Parrises grind our cane. They did it with the silent, smirking charity that one would expect of them. It was the following season, which was 1886, I believe, that our fortunes changed.

That was a banner year, thanks in large part to Mr. Landry's consultation with Monsieur Barbagree and our decision to cut our cane extremely early. We did so largely at night, our hands swinging their knives and stacking our sugarcane under lantern light and strict orders to avoid singing and extraneous conversation. In fact, we cut the innermost portion of the cane first, leaving a wall of cane to guard against the prying eyes of neighboring planters.

It wasn't two days after our cane was in that the deep south was struck by a hard and sudden freeze, the earliest on record. Our neighbors, including the Parrises, and especially the Parrises, they of the fine teams of white draft horses and carriages and outlandish soirees and beautiful ballgowns, took an almost fatal blow to their fortunes. There was a shortage of sugar that year, but we made out like bandits thanks to the scarcity filled only by Mount Teague sugar, '*sweetest-purest*,' as our boast has always been. And, no, madame, I do not feel any remorse for turning our backs on the Parrises after their charity towards us the year before.

Our fortunes had done an about-face, and so, the next year, 1887, we decided to tour Europe. Or, I decided it, as Mr. Teague did not 'give a good God-dam,' as he put it, about a collection of countries who didn't have the good sense to speak English, save England, where they spoke it all wrong. Those are his words, not mine, Mrs. Leonard.

The Burden of Cane

It was the first time we summered in Europe, rather than at the ocean or the mountains with the common uncommon people. It was what the finest families did and still do. The seaside and the mountains were never enough for my tastes. Yes, of course, it was more expensive, quite a bit more, but, although he balked at the cost, I reminded my husband time and again, only the best at Mount Teague! What good is good fortune if it can't be flaunted in the faces of others? Answer me that, madame.

My second child, Missy, was two years old, and I was looking forward to leaving the little heathen and her brother behind with my mother-in-law, that other Mrs. Teague. She would always look at Sam Jr. and Missy and say, "Why, this boy and his sister favor Sam's brother Jack!"

The old bitch. I've always wondered if she knew.

Once the children were settled in with Mrs. Teague—or her servants, really—we departed by train to New York and then went by steamer to Liverpool. The voyage over was a difficult one for Mr. Teague, as he was confined to our cabin with seasickness the first few days. This gave me the chance to engage in parlor games like charades and whist and dominoes, much like we girls did on Commerce Street back in the day, except that now we were fully clothed and there was no swearing at the loss of a hand or a well-played bluff. It was also a delight to adjourn outside for a smoke break by the ship's smokestacks.

We were three days out, and I was just returning from a cigarette smoked between the funnels of the ship when I was approached by a man named Dawkins or Hawkins or something like that. He had been watching me and I was sure he was taken in by my raven hair and blue eyes. Well, he had been served well and often by the bartenders and I could smell it on his breath.

"Pardon me, ma'am," he slurred, "but you remind me of a girl I once knew when I was a cattle drover bringing the herd in from Texas to Shreveport—" Here, he slurred Texas into Tesses and Shreveport into Shreepert. "Her name was Lottie and she worked in one of them bawdy houses on Commerce Street—"

Well, Mrs. Leonard, I slapped him so hard that conversation in the parlor stopped abruptly, leaving only the drone of the ship's engines as a distant backdrop.

"How dare you, sir! Impugn my honor!" I shouted through a face replete with horror.

His apologetic wife came to fetch him and put him to bed in their berth, this common cattle drover who had somehow made good for himself and married a woman who could overlook his social shortcomings. He came the next day with his hat in his hands, bearing a hungover apology, though he spent the rest of the voyage eyeing me suspiciously. I was happy when we quit the boat in Liverpool and he and his wife went a separate way. As he assisted his wife into the hack on the quay, his mannerisms brought back a memory from long ago, and I vaguely remembered that he had an interestingly shaped mark on his penis.

Mr. Teague pouted the first few days in England because the bacon looked funny and he could not get grits and the water tasted strangely and he could not understand the way people talked half the time. I tried to remind him that we were there to try new things, but he was like a schoolboy kept in from recess. Finally, I reminded him in an urgent, hushed tone that summering in Europe was what the finest families did, not only of the South but of the whole country.

After a few weeks in England and its splendid summer weather, not at all the raking heat like here, Mrs. Leonard, we crossed the Channel to France with a tour group, which included some fine old families of Boston and Newport. In Paris, we toured the Louvre, where a guide, some expert, gave a pitiless talk at length on what we would see and what we should look for. We attended the opera, and though I understood none of it, the costumes were pretty and the singing was first rate. My husband was completely out of his element.

"You ever see so many fiddlers?" Mr. Teague said, craning up in his seat and gawking down into the orchestra pit. He soon settled back into his seat and nodded off, sleeping through the entirety of it and then waking with a great smacking of his lips. As he slept, I took the opportunity to preen and exchange glances with several gentlemen in the audience, and I'm afraid I lost any awareness of the production. All the same, however, as it was in some foreign language, French or Latin or something, and I could have understood none of it.

We toured Italy, and my husband, ever the man of culture, said that he didn't see the grand appeal of the antiquities, that most of the statues were 'nose-less and pecker-less.' I silently agreed with him, though I must admit to finding Michelangelo's towering statue of David rather inspiring. His lean, muscular body reminded me so much of the traveling tinker who returned as the engineer who bungled our sugarhouse, my husband's brother. I found I had to go and find an outlet for this inspiration, no thanks to my husband. But that passing dalliance is of no consequence, Mrs. Leonard, and we shall speak no more of it.

Our tour continued, a parade of my husband's wrinkled up nose and pinched countenance to each new change in cuisine. We became immune to old churches and towers and sculpture and paintings and public squares and arches and columns. I had to keep reminding him that we would return to St. Matthew Parish with this feather of culture in our caps, something to expound upon at soirees and balls back home.

In Venice, Mr. Teague and I, admittedly easy marks with our nice clothes, were accosted by beggar after beggar who came with pleading eyes and one palm cupped in another. My husband would reluctantly hand over an Italian coin but not before holding it up to our guide and asking him 'how much is this'n worth?' and telling the beggar 'you should get a job.' To the quizzical look of the recipient, Mr. Teague said slower and louder, 'You. Should. Get. A. Job,' while making a variety of pantomimes such as digging with a shovel or swinging a cane knife. Then he would ask our tour guide to tell them that if they came to Louisiana he would give them all cane knives and plenty of sugarcane to hack with them. Our guide declined to relay my husband's offer of employment and instead conducted us to the Rialto Bridge, which Mr. Teague said was like any other bridge, except it was in Venice and that he could have one just like it, or even nicer, built over Bayou Lafourche.

How ironic that upon returning to our hotel that afternoon that we should receive an urgent telegram from our overseer Mr. Landry that our hands were threatening to walk off en masse if we did not accede to their demands of a dollar a day, almost twice what they were already making, not to mention room and board which we also provided from the goodness of our hearts and the depths of our pockets. We sent back a telegram directing him to fire those men and hire others. He replied in another telegram that it would be no different, that all of the surrounding parishes were under similar conditions.

In the end we told him to make do, and we would see to it when we returned. It was a needless bother on what was otherwise a fine trip.

We decided to cut our trip short at once, forgoing Spain and returning to the United States early. It was well. Our traveling group had become tiresome, shushing Mr. Teague whenever he made a comment, which was often, and then gathering in groups to look over their shoulders and whisper. We left without so much as a 'fare thee well.' May the devil take them all, snobs as they were.

When we arrived in St. Matthew almost two weeks later we found the hands in a state of surly agitation. What was more, Mr. Landry said that we had less than a month before the first freeze. Mr. Teague was beside himself.

"They will be the ruin of us!" he said, pacing his study in his limping manner and wringing his hands.

I was looking at the fine ballgowns and dresses and bonnets in a catalog for the House of Worth, calmly wetting a fingertip to turn each page.

"Fear not, husband," I said, "I have a plan."

We met with Mr. Landry, my husband chiding him for summoning us home early. Mr. Teague had missed the bullfights in Spain, a blood sport that would have been right up his alley. Mr. Landry apologized and apologized, hat in hand, feeling awful, I'm sure, at having had to do it. We did not fire him then. He was still of use to us. The hands may not have cared for us, but they loved Mr. Landry and would generally do whatever he said.

We sighed as if we had reluctantly given in to the exorbitant demands of an extortion plot and offered to raise the wages of the hands to $1.50 a day, the most in the parish. The other sugar planters struggled to keep up with this offer as their hands were siphoned off to Mount Teague. The only concession we asked from our hands was to let us pay them in scrip, to be used at the Mount Teague Commissary or, *La Commissaire*, as some of them put it. There was some wavering, but my husband, to his credit, told them that the inventory was in the process of being expanded and that they might buy any manner of exotic goods there. He crowed that it would be like an Arab bazaar, the likes of which we had just seen on our tour overseas.

Heavens no, we didn't go to Arabia, madame! It was an exaggeration. My husband always had a way with the spoken word, though as you will see, Mrs. Leonard, not the written word.

Well, this was the matter of it. They all agreed to our generous offer, and so a bargain was struck. Mr. Landry explained the deal in French and the harvest proceeded. It was another banner crop, well-timed with the help of the old coot Barbagree.

When it was in, processed into sugar and sold, we fired Mr. Landry for his poor management and lack of initiative. Then we quadrupled the prices in the commissary, which offered the same old cheap goods as before. Ha! New, exotic goods indeed! They all wished they had kept the deal they had—sixty cents a day, plus room and board. I suppose they should be thankful they weren't shot like the workers in Thibodaux that year.

The Parrises had given in to the pressure and offered a raise to their hands, one dollar a day in cash to be paid monthly rather than at the conclusion of the harvest. That was their mistake. They took a loss that year and handed over to us the deed to the vast tract of timber called the Barbagree swamp. January of that year, 1888, marked the high point of the wealth of Mount Teague. You, Mrs. Leonard, are here to help me regain it.

Would you care for tea? Or perhaps a toddy?

Part VI

Jack

Of course, Father, it is self-evident that I could not end myself. They had not robbed me blind, only half-blind. They had taken most of my life but not all of it.

Hope is a glimmer, a pinhole of light in the darkness, a lone, bright star in a night sky painted black with circumstance, a divine whisper from the silent depths of emptiness. Perhaps I saw that small speck of light and heard that murmur of a promise that things might be tolerable one day. It sounded so much like the whine of a faithful dog, sympathetic and pleading and low.

My shaking hand set down the gun and supported my bandaged head. On the ground next to me and on the trunk of the oak were the shells of cicadas, exoskeletons of their former inhabitants. I studied them for a moment. They had wrenched themselves away from what had bound them in and flown off with a new skin, leaving the old shell behind. A butterfly landed on my hand, blinking its wings and then scampering off high among the boughs. I looked up to the last of the sunlight piercing the foliage, streaming through the leaves like hope, as fragile and as captivating as the wings of a butterfly.

I took it as a sign. I placed the gun in my bag and shed my former self, the identity, the skin of Jack Teague, and moved on to another life. I made a fire to warm myself, and I placed the note for the passerby in it and watched its edges curl into singed brown. The man Jack Teague disappeared from the face of the earth that night, and that is well, for the newspapers picked up the story, and I was tried and convicted there, too, including the newspaper of my former champion Mr. Burke, the New Orleans *Times-Democrat*.

I slept and the next day I woke to a new morning. I wandered then, a man with half a face and no name. On the ferry crossing at Donaldsonville, there were stares and whispers behind hands. I heard murmured fragments of news of what had happened down in St. Matthew, but I couldn't tell any of them that it had not been completely my fault. I had been driven to hastiness, and I had only failed in confronting it. I watched the water plow under us and when the ferry made the opposite bank, I disembarked and I began walking. I had no money to my name and, in fact, no name, only a valise with a few tools and a knapsack with a spare change of clothes and a revolver. There was one place in the world where they might take me in, and I was headed there.

Spring was emerging. The days were pleasant but the nights were cold, and without a blanket, I put on all the clothes I had to keep warm. I had no money for food, and my stomach complained at its hollowness, but I kept walking. In a couple of days, my eye and my face hurt less, but sometimes in my sleep I would forget and scratch the eyebrow to find it wasn't there.

It was difficult, the adjustment to seeing the world through one eye. My bandages were soiled reddish brown, but I had no others to change them for. In towns where my infamy was unknown, no one met my gaze, the man with the blood-soiled head-wrap, some sort of wandering Bedouin plopped down in Mississippi. When I asked directions, usually from the most sympathetic looking person in town, they pointed down the road but looked to the ground away from me. Wagons and carriages might stop to see if I needed a ride, but on seeing me, there was a quick shake of reins and a *sorry, sir.*

I arrived on Neely's porch like a swimmer arriving on the shore after a shipwreck. His wife Lorena answered the door and called over her shoulder, "Neely." He appeared behind her in shirtsleeves and suspenders, holding a folded copy of the *Jackson Clarion Ledger.* He didn't say that he had read about what the unscrupulous Jack Teague had done in Louisiana, but I'm sure he had. News of the blast and the trial had been in all the papers. He only asked once what happened, and when I didn't answer, he didn't ask again. Instead, I cried, and he quickly ushered me into his study, past the curious looks of his children. He shut the door behind me and sat with me while I wept as bitterly as I ever have, heaving, shaking, almost as if I would split in two.

I woke in the slant of late afternoon light on the sofa in his study, peering at the books he had accumulated, this man who was once a boy whom I had taught to read under the dim light of a candle. There was a knock on the door and a quiet invitation for dinner from Neely. I had eaten little in the last few days, and my appetite returned like an avalanche. The smell of food lovingly prepared and about to be shared among people who loved each other, it spoke of hope. I was surrounded by this family of dark-skinned people, the wife and children of my childhood friend.

One of the younger ones asked me, 'Mr. Jack, what happened to your eye?' Their mama shushed them, and we bowed our heads, and Neely blessed the meal. But in my head, I cursed God. Forgive me, Father, but I did. I wanted to shout out to the sky, *I was a good man, a good enough man, and you did this to me! Why God? Why did you smite me?* But I knew the answer. I had given in to seductive folly and I knew it, and God certainly knew it. '*You lusted, Jack Teague, you sinned, and now you have your wages for it. Go and do not trouble Me again.*'

The children and parents spoke among the tinkling of utensils on plates and the requests for things to be passed. I heard nothing else and said nothing at all. I felt like an oddity, an ogre asked to dinner, a leper among the clean. After dinner, Neely and I sat on his porch. The screen door squeaked open, and Lorena brought us peach cobbler. We ate it without speaking and put our empty bowls on the railing. A mockingbird landed in the grass with a flare of white-striped wings, pecked the ground, and lifted up again as gracefully as it had descended. Neely watched it with a smile.

"Remember when we were boys that you said you would fly one day?" he asked.

"I suppose I said that. I never realized that I would end up crawling instead of flying."

He smiled to himself and shook his head in sympathy.

"Where to now, Jack?" he asked as his children clambered over a swing hanging from a tree limb in the front yard. It was evening, and the long pendulum-shadow of rope, seat, and rider swept across the front yard and back again.

"What am I fit for, Neely?" I asked. "Half a face? One eye?"

"But a good heart and a fine mind," he said. "You ever thought about teaching? You taught me to read, and you did it so well that now I teach others."

It had never occurred to me. As I thought upon it, a squabble erupted on the lawn around the swing. Neely shouted to his children, *give your brother a turn.* Fireflies were beginning to coast around the yard in the twilight, wavering pinpoints of golden light.

"Where does a man pursue such work?" I asked.

"I've got a friend at the Collegiate Academy down in Jackson. He gives us the used textbooks when the white children get new ones. The last time I saw him, he said they were looking for a mathematics professor."

I stayed that night in Neely's house with its occupants sleeping peacefully in the gray shadows. It occurred to me that if I were Negro and he were white, society would dictate that I would have to sleep in his barn or storeroom. Would I have the courage to put him up? Could I have matched his kindness to me?

My thoughts raced thusly; I could not cry anymore. I could only lust after retribution against my brother. I dreamed of a thousand gory ways I would do it, knives, shotguns, nooses. I mangled him, and I made it last. I burned his house with him in it. I had him drawn and quartered, hung, tortured. I thought of horrific vengeance in every possible permutation. Then I fell into sleep and dreamed it. I woke exhausted from my dreamy massacres.

Mornings brought breakfast and conversation, days brought more rest. I read a little. I ventured out for walks. I listened to Lorena sing to her children and practice reading with them. Once, Neely's youngest son, Alfred, asked me in a whisper why I wore a 'mask over my eye.' I whispered back that I used to be a pirate, but I had given up such work and was thinking about becoming a teacher. He lowered his brow and drew his lips together and nodded. It was as plausible explanation as any for a boy his age. After a week of loving care, of good food, of clean bandages and fresh sheets, of a new eyepatch, I rose in the morning, and Neely and I went to see Brother Roudebush at the Jackson Collegiate Academy.

Roudebush was a Presbyterian minister who had a doctorate in divinity and a wooly white moustache like a Fuller brush. He was also the head of the Academy on North Street in Jackson. I asked that Neely introduce me as Homer Prentiss. Lt. Prentiss no longer needed his name, lying in a nameless grave in Pennsylvania, and he never had any family that I knew of. The name Jack Teague was sullied past redemption. It seemed like a fair trade and one, of course, the original Homer Prentiss could not speak against. I was introduced thusly, the three of us shook hands, and then Neely was off to teach school at Tougaloo.

I told Dr. Roudebush that I was a West Point man, to have graduated in the class of '63, had it not been for the late unpleasantness. He studied my face, one clear eye and one patched-over eye, and he silently answered his question for himself about what had happened to the missing one. Certainly he assumed it was lost in the late war, and so I did not have to lie about its loss in a shameful accident. In those days, I was not alone in the business of lost limbs and organs. He said that he himself was a chaplain with the Confederate Army, and after a perfunctory interview, I was hired to teach mathematics and physics, though the physics would only be to a select few, high-performing students.

I found I had a talent for it, one that Neely had recognized when I had taught him to read clandestinely in our days growing up. I will admit, Father, that I was still a decent-looking man, though only on one side of my face. The other side was covered by the eyepatch and scar. Maybe this gave me an air of mystery and manliness, a man who had faced danger and lived, but who was too reluctant and too modest to tell of it. A beard would only grow so far, so I fashioned it in the style of the Van Dyke.

The Jackson Collegiate Academy was a coeducational endeavor, and I endured the admiring gazes of the boys and the dreamy stares of the girls. I ignored these, focusing on the noble, unwavering honesty of mathematics, much fairer than life, a discipline both certain and constant. The first day of every class I told them that knowledge never deserts us, and we should strive for it, as it will most certainly pay a turn in our lives.

The boys wanted to hear about the past, the war and how I lost my eye. I was vague about this. They also wanted to know about the future, the possibility of personal carriages propelled by steam engines and if man would ever fly. I told them yes to both, likely not in my lifetime but possibly in theirs. They asked again how I had lost my eye, all of them waiting for a retelling of some battlefield triumph or disaster, but I would tell them only that I had lost it quite by accident. In their eyes, my coyness seemed to magnify the heroic circumstances in which I had lost it.

The girls largely wanted to hear about the places I had been and if there was or had ever been a Mrs. Prentiss and whether I preferred light haired or dark haired girls and if I found brown eyes or green or blue most fetching. Of course, the troubles in my life were caused by blue eyes, but I declined to declare a favorite in the matter. Still, they crowded around me after classes, asking me trivial questions and hanging on my answers as if I had the meaning of life in my coat pocket.

Neither the boys nor the girls ever got the whole truth. The whole truth, which involved cruelty and deception, would have been hard for them to digest. Instead we talked about favorite Sunday dinners and whether I preferred cats or dogs. I received Valentines from the girls in February, and drawings of fanciful machines and such from the boys. All of the gifts I made over as if they were worthy of a museum, and I would have kept them if I had not left so abruptly.

Without meaning to, I had become a favorite, a man of regular habits who neither drank nor smoked, a teacher who could present a problem in just the sort of way that the student could see it and find its solution with little further prodding, as if they had discovered it for themselves and for all mankind, as if they had stumbled upon it accidently. My students, both boys and girls, began winning prizes in mathematics competitions, in trigonometry and geometry particularly, and their names and my name, Professor Homer Prentiss, were published in the newspapers as far away as Atlanta and New Orleans.

Brother Roudebush insisted on strict church attendance, and I went, though I felt like Job, stricken down by a capricious God for His amusement. I mouthed the words to the hymns and the prayers and then I left, taking a deep breath on the church steps like a man grabbing air after coming up from a hundred foot depth.

It was enough to have made the contented remainder of a life, and I resolved to live the balance of my years there. That was not to be. I should have seen it coming when a student asked me if I was related to the Prentisses up in Yazoo. No, I said, not that I was aware of. And then, on a rainy winter afternoon, I received a visit from one of them.

Eva

Our holdings were at an all-time high. We could have bought out St. Matthew Parish twice over, had it not been for my dimwitted husband, bless his heart and rest his soul. He committed an unfortunate error, and I could have just killed him for it, and perhaps I would have, had I taken out a sufficient life insurance policy on him. That year, 1888, was both the zenith of our prosperity and the beginning of a decline into hard times. My husband, bless his tiny heart, made a critical error then, one that threatened to put us in rags.

He was, at the time, a partner with the state lottery and had been so with Mr. Howard, now defunct after his rather unfortunate carriage accident. Another of his partners in the lottery, and a man of great importance, was Edward Burke, who was also the state treasurer and editor of the *Times-Democrat* in New Orleans. Unbeknownst to me, Mr. Burke had some state bonds that he sold my gullible husband in large quantities. Mr. Teague was quite proud of the 'investment' he had made and showed me his whimsical signature at the bottom of the purchase agreement, his crude initials, some sort of backward S and a T with a large upper stroke upon a short base. It occurred to me that my husband's inability to read had cost us.

Yes, that's correct, Mrs. Leonard. A well-kept secret. My husband, the great pillar of St. Matthew Parish, could not read so much as a syllable. How he made his way all these years without knowing how to read the printed word is a small mystery to me, though it may have something to do with his mastery of people through bullying and bluster. I knew of his illiteracy early on, just after we were married, and rather than be mortified by it, I used it to my advantage, hiding purchases great and small and becoming the *de facto* head of Mount Teague. But here, it had bitten me. He had gone out on a limb and bought into this useless tomfoolery proposed by our so-called friend Mr. Burke. These bonds he purchased were actually old state bonds that had already expired and hence were worthless, absolutely worthless. My husband's longtime associate had defrauded us.

Mr. Teague could not believe it, and, though he would never admit it, it was perhaps a low point in his life. I sat dumbfounded in the study as my husband looked out the window upon our fields. Neither of us said anything as the clock in the hall ticked and motes of dust floated in the afternoon sun. He was embarrassed, as well he should have been.

We looked into litigation, but by the time we found out, Mr. Burke had fled to Honduras. He chose the place well, as Honduras had no extradition treaties with the United States, and by 1889, when his chicanery was brought to light, Mr. Burke was safely ensconced in the capital, Tegucigalpa, where he lives yet in the Hotel Ritz. Then, just a few years later in 1893, I think it was, he took the whole lottery operation with him, depriving us of that source of additional income. But I suppose calling Mr. Burke unscrupulous and shameless would be a case of the pot calling the kettle black.

Well, Mrs. Leonard, I scolded my husband severely. He seemed not to understand that his friend Mr. Burke could take advantage of him. Simpleton. To make matters worse, we could no longer time our harvests, as Mr. Barbagree would not speak to us after we fired Mr. Landry. However, we owned the land under him and his moss-gathering enterprise, and he was our tenant, or potential tenant. We gave him an ultimatum, through an interpreter, that he would need to cooperate with us, or he would find that we expected rent to be forthcoming and that it could not be paid in gray moss. Again, he refused to see us.

My husband was in favor of turning him out and burning his shack, but I had another idea. Hoping to play on the old man's sympathy, I sent word that what I really needed him to do was to heal my husband, as he was afflicted with an obscure illness that kept him from reading the printed word. I begged him, beseeched him, groveled before him (through an emissary, of course—I would never stoop to that level in person) to heal my poor, stupid husband of whatever deficiency he had that kept him from reading. I didn't tell Barbagree that it was to keep my ignoramus from entering into another opportunity that might ruin us for good. This supplication did the trick, Mrs. Leonard. Monsieur Barbagree agreed to see us. Such are some people's sentiments. They feel it is their duty to heal the world of every malady.

Happily and hopefully, I summoned him to Mount Teague, but he sent our emissary back with a message that he would only meet us at his shack in the swamp. I sighed and rolled my eyes but agreed. I lured my husband by telling him that Barbagree would tell us when the next freeze was, but as he was the head of Mount Teague, the old man would only deal with him. Puffed up with this sense of importance, he agreed to go at once.

We were led through the shadows of the God-forsaken swamp to the shack of this character, this Barbagree who was either Indian or darkey or both or neither. He was outside attending to some nets when we came up. He did not speak English, so we had brought with us one of the hands who spoke

French, Mr. Templet. He, of course, was made to swear an oath not to reveal the secret of our dealings.

In French, Mr. Templet explained our errand to the old oddball, including that I wanted my husband cured, if possible, of any impediment that might keep him from learning to read and write. I certainly couldn't have him repeating his error of being duped and swindled. My husband had no idea that I had asked this, nor was he even certain that I was aware of his illiteracy.

The old man was at first unwilling to help us. He seemed to have changed his mind. I then had Mr. Templet explain to Mr. Barbagree that he was living rent free in our swamp and that, unless he agreed to help us, he would find the rent due at the beginning of each month. The old man sat on a stool and pulled through his moss, his beard seeming like just another strand of it. We were on the verge of leaving when, at last, he mumbled something into his hands and without the least bit of emotion, either. There was a warble of some bird and the grunt of some animal that broke the silence, and then the silence prevailed again. Our interpreter Mr. Templet asked the old man something, and the old man stood and wiped his hands on his dungarees and turned and repeated what he said.

"What did he say?" my husband asked.

"He said he knows when the first freeze will be."

Barbagree said something else. Mr. Templet hesitated. Then, with a sigh of resignation, he said, rather reluctantly, "He said that he also knows you can't read or write. He said he can give you the knowledge of both, but that he won't give them to you separately."

"This is outrageous! Certainly I can read and write!" Mr. Teague bellowed his lie into the cool air, and his voice echoed among the enormous cypress trunks and caused the wings of birds to flap away in the distance. "Tell him I can have him thrown out!"

The interpreter was silent. It appeared that Barbagree understood my husband's threat. He sat again and resumed stringing out his moss and appraising it. Then Barbagree spoke again to the moss and his hands and the ground. The interpreter cleared his throat.

"Get on your knees, he says," Mr. Templet said uneasily.

"What? Forget it!" my husband said.

But just then, the old man looked over his shoulder and rose. He walked up to my husband, and though at first Barbagree looked to be smaller, suddenly it was apparent that he was as tall as Mr. Teague, or taller. He looked right into my husband's face, and it was like a hypnotist's trick. My husband fell to his knees and bowed his head. The old man put his hands on my husband's head and began squeezing so hard that I thought it might crack my husband's skull. The brown fingers trembled with their exertion. All the while he incanted French.

My husband's hands reached up and tried to pry the old man's hands off his head, but Barbagree only gripped his head harder. The chant was prayer-like and became more intense, finally ending with a shout that seemed to echo off the trunk of every tree in the swamp. The old man threw my husband's head down like it was a melon that he was trying to smash into the black mud. Mr. Teague fell to the ground, with his dazed expression turned to the sky.

I told Barbagree, via Mr. Templet, that I supposed I should thank him if it came to pass that my husband should suddenly be able to read. I was still skeptical. The old cloudy-eyed gray-beard spoke and pointed to the sky. Mr. Templet's eyes were locked onto Barbagree's face as he relayed his message to me.

"Oh, he say it will come to pass. But he say it ain't him you should thank."

I looked up into the sky and back to Barbagree as I wondered who he was talking about.

The old man went back in his shack, and Mr. Templet and I collected my husband. He rode slumped in the boat like a sack of gray moss, babbling nonsense, his hand trailing in the water, and it was only with great effort that we were able to put him in the carriage. When we got back to Mount Teague, we put Mr. Teague to bed, where he slept for three days and nights, without speaking to anyone other than simple requests for water. Dr. McKnight was called for and gave a diagnosis of 'agitated fatigue' and prescribed brandy toddies and rest. After a week or so, Mr. Teague began to get around in the house in his nightshirt and dressing gown.

Well, our daughter Missy was about five years old at the time and learning her letters. She had a picture book with pink-cheeked children who appeared with the letters of the alphabet and things that began with the letter. A, apple, and so forth. Well, Mrs. Leonard, Mr. Teague picked up the book and traced his finger and said to her, "That letter is an A, isn't it?

"That's right, Daddy," she said.

He looked about himself with a bemused smile.

"It's an A! An A!" He hurriedly put his attention to the next page, where there was a picture of the little cherub-cheeked girl holding a ball.

"This is a B, isn't it?" he proclaimed, as if he had just discovered gold.

"That's right, Daddy, B is for ball," little Missy said kindly, as if talking to another five-year old. Her father took no notice.

The next pages followed, with pictures of cats and dogs and elephants and fans. My husband and his five year old tutor went over the alphabet, A to Z and back again. Within a week he knew half the alphabet, within another, the other half. By the next month, he was reading one syllable words. Father and daughter were each on par with the other, halting pronunciations of simple words traced by his thick finger and her little dainty one. When he had mastered that exercise, he spent whole days reading Sam Junior's speller. Within a few months, he was able to read the newspapers. And through the magic, the miracle of the old coot Barbagree, my husband became a prolific reader. With the enchantment of a boy under the covers figuring out the secret purpose of his manhood, my husband began reading voraciously, his new trick, his key to the universe and its riches. His writing was still infantile, but he could do it, though it was always printed and no better than any schoolboy dragging chalk across his slate. He could recognize the signature that he still had me sign for him.

But make no mistake, madame, I continued to hold his bad bargain with Mr. Burke against him. This was to keep me at the reins of Mount Teague. It was important that I keep him just doubtful enough of his abilities that he would defer to me in important financial matters.

Well then, Mrs. Leonard, the clock chimes in the hall. It is time for my afternoon nap before Altar Society.

Ruthie? Ruthie! See to getting the carriage ready for the trip into town. I have the Ladies' Altar Society Christmas social this afternoon.

Jack

As I say, Father, it was on a rainy winter afternoon. My class and I were discussing geometry, for I never 'taught' or 'instructed,' rather, we 'discussed' and 'discovered.' Brother Roudebush appeared at the door with a message that there was a man to see me. I asked him if it could wait until the break and he said no, it was a matter of importance and I should come then.

This man had been sent in a cold rain by a mother who would forever grieve, even to the point that she would send her son, her only remaining child, to Jackson from Yazoo in a steady Mississippi rain. He sprang to his feet as I entered the headmaster's office and introduced himself as Noel Prentiss, the son of Homer Prentiss.

That is, the real Homer Prentiss, the one that was buried at Gettysburg.

"You're Homer Prentiss?" he asked.

"I am," I said, though even after more than a year as Homer Prentiss, the lie was sour in my mouth.

"From Yazoo County?"

"No," I said. "I'm from—" My mind squirmed as a map whirled in my head like a globe. "—Georgia. I'm from Georgia."

"Oh," he said, and he paused a moment as he wrestled with his disappointment. "My name is Noel Prentiss. From Yazoo. My father was also named Homer Prentiss, though he never returned from the war. We've always held out hope that he might return, but we never heard from him. I came across your name in the *Clarion Ledger* and thought he might have returned. It was a forlorn hope."

He opened a case that held a metal framed tintype. And there he was, my friend from over twenty years before, in the uniform we wore, when we were as confident of a swift victory as we were of sunset. I was with him when we had the portraits made in a Memphis photographer's studio before we departed for Virginia. It was a good thing we had posed for them separately and not together. If the Prentiss family had seen us side by side in the same image, it would have been obvious that I had stolen this man's name.

My fingertips touched the image reverently. We had talked beside many a campfire under starry skies amid moonlit fields of snoring and coughing. We had smelled the burning gray of powder ignited in the air. We had sweated and shivered together, eaten out of the same dish. We had seen men rush forward as we yelled and they yelled. We had marched until we were footsore and then marched further.

I was there when the ball thudded into his body. I had heard him beg me not to leave him. I had carried him off, felt his blood on my back, and I had seen him taken off to be buried in an unmarked grave in Pennsylvania. And then, when my own name was ruined, I had taken the liberty of using his. I looked up to his son who eyes were fixed on me.

"I've—I've heard that there was another Homer Prentiss in the Army of Northern Virginia," I said. "But I never met him. I'm sorry—that I'm not the one you're looking for, I mean." And I was, I was sorry for this bereaved man still clutching at the wreckage of hope, and I was sorry that I so easily broke the Honor Code yet again by lying to him about his father.

The man Noel Prentiss, the only child of Homer Prentiss, left. He paused before ascending the step up into his wagon. The rain had slackened, he sighed and looked off a moment. Then he placed a foot on the step and ascended onto the buckboard and gathered the reins. He paused again, looking at his feet as his hope bled away and he thought of how he would tell his mother the war widow. Then he shook the reins, and the wagon rattled off down North Street.

I wonder if it was, and still is, discussed around the Prentiss family dinner table as dishes are passed that there was a man with the same exact name teaching down in Jackson. If after grace was said, there was, as a postscript, a supplication that their father and husband might appear one day like Rip Van Winkle returning after twenty years in the Catskills. If the dinner conversation continued with the orbit of dishes that the man named Homer Prentiss, the professor with the eyepatch was a nice enough feller but wasn't our beloved husband, brother, uncle, etc. If the conversation moved on to the weather and the meal and wasn't-that-a-first-rate-pie-mama-made, all the while everyone chewed on the mystery of the other man named Homer Prentiss, the professor down in Jackson.

As Noel Prentiss disappeared down the road, I wondered if my mother had the mate to his father's picture, the one that I myself had taken that day in Memphis, if it was placed lovingly on a lace doily on a hall table, or if it was hidden in a drawer someplace. Maybe she had thrown it out, now that the name Jack Teague was synonymous with shoddy workmanship.

I could not think upon it long. My past had come to visit me. It was as if it were pursuing me. I knew I had to leave, but I had to take the name Homer Prentiss with me. You see, Father, I had built a reputation under it, and I could not forsake it without starting over completely again.

I could not let it vanish. So I took it with me, and I vanished.

Jack

When I felt my position suddenly become tenuous, I began to look for somewhere else to go. As it happened, Brother Roudebush was at that time contemplating retirement to a farm in Madison County, and I took the opportunity to move along as well. He said that I would be a loss to the Academy, but that if I needed a recommendation, he could furnish one without reservation. He knew a man from his army days, an Episcopalian Bishop named Telfair Hodgson who was Vice Chancellor at Sewanee in the foothills of Tennessee.

Through a telegram to Rev. Hodgson, a meeting was arranged, and I arrived in Sewanee with a letter of introduction from Brother Roudebush and a suitcase with my belongings, a satchel of tools, and a knapsack with a revolver in it. I left a letter to my students to be read after my departure, imploring them to secure knowledge so that they might be able to support themselves and better the world. I told them they would always hold a special place in my heart and that I could not have asked for better students. I also left a drawer-full of Valentines and drawings. They were too numerous to bring with me. My departure was a quiet one, unrecorded by the newspapers.

I appeared in Sewanee and held an interview with Rev. Hodgson, a man with a luxurious coif like a tropical bird. We spoke of my past, and I filled in the blank spot with a tale of teaching school in California after the war, from whence I had appeared in Mississippi. Being a West Point man and a veteran of the Confederate Army was a ticket to anyplace then, and he hired me within the hour. The eyepatch spoke to my valor to the cause, and I did not dispute its silent witness.

I had only one request when I was hired to teach mathematics and physics. I told Rev. Hodgson and the headmaster, Mr. Weber, that I was an extremely private man and that I preferred not to have my name in the papers. It was a part of my humility as an emulator of Christ. And so, in the years that followed, with the winning of competitions by the boys of the Sewanee Grammar School, I was mentioned only as 'our able professor of mathematics.' My work continued in the instruction of these sons of the New South, anxious as they were to learn the arts of science and industry rather than the tired old ideas of agriculture.

I never heard again from the Prentisses of Yazoo, though I sent them a letter saying that I was a friend of Homer Prentiss—the real one—from the army and that he had fallen in battle at Gettysburg and that his men had loved him. I said that I had buried him in a peaceful spot and said a prayer before I was captured and that I was sorry for their loss and that he was a brave man and a good friend. I told them that I would have let them know sooner but I only recently knew of the existence of his family. I also sent a letter to the Veteran's bureau in Jackson testifying that I knew Homer Prentiss and that I was with him until his death and that he never deserted or failed to do his duty. I signed it Lt. Andrew J. Teague. I hoped it would be enough for his widow to draw a pension.

The boys of Sewanee were much like miniature West Pointers, military-style uniforms were worn, an honor code was enforced, young men were marched to chapel to sit erect and listen to stories of divine mercy and the flaming sword. A bugler played for vespers and lights out. The whole show was run by Episcopalians, several of them soldiers-turned-bishops. I felt right at home, and the years followed one after another.

It was the sport of the wives of the other professors to play matchmaker for me. Several women of various ages were tried, but my capacity for romance and courting had been used up by the black-haired woman with eyes as blue as violets, my brother's wife, my former lover. Rumors circulated that I had very little interest in the fairer sex, with an implication that I might prefer the company of gentlemen. Such was not the case. Still, I bore the good intentions of my colleagues' wives, and we enjoyed holidays and outings together, sing-alongs in the parlor, Christmas dinners, as well as the theatricals and choir performances and commencement ceremonies. I was content in the mountain air. In the fall term of 1892, Sewanee Grammar School welcomed a new pupil, one whom I remembered as a five year-old boy.

Junior Teague

Why, good afternoon, Mrs. Leonard. Yes, Miss Gladys, then. Where has Mama gone off to? She and her social clubs. Why, they're like a religion to her, never misses. She certainly enjoys the fellowship of the other high and well-born women of St. Matthew. Of course, she's always considered herself the highest and most well-born, and don't try to tell her otherwise!

No ma'am, I don't mind sitting down with you and telling you what I know, especially since you've come all the way from England, and during wartime at that. Mama sure would like to hear from Daddy one last time. It surprises me—she's never been at all sentimental. But, I suppose, they were married a long time, thirty-five years. She must miss him more than she lets on, and there is nothing she would like more than to speak with him again. For the life of me, I never realized the depth of their attachment. They always seemed so distant with each other. I never knew what lovebirds they were. Maybe because it happened so suddenly. Daddy being killed, I'm saying.

I apologize for the state of this place. This house is over sixty years old and shows its age. I have a mind to get after Mama to have Mount Teague refurbished, but I'm afraid she is just too bereaved right now to see to it. I can't imagine she would lack the money for it. I'm sure Daddy's left her well off.

She was once on the verge of razing the whole place and rebuilding in the Victorian style. She even had Daddy convinced of it. I arrived home from the war against Spain just in time to keep them from tearing the old house down and rebuilding it. I suppose I'll always have an attachment to this place. Home is that place you dream of when you aren't there, such as when I was at school in Tennessee and then off with the army.

Let's sit here on this settee in the central hallway. That's Daddy in the painting up there, when he was a younger man, during the war between the states. There used to be a bust of him on that pedestal there, but I haven't seen it for years. Never sure what happened to it. His health might not have been what it was, but, nevertheless, his death was still quite a shock to us. He still was able to assist in the management of Mount Teague, limping around as he did, supporting himself on a cane and giving everyone an earful on how he thought things should be handled.

Yes ma'am. All right, I'll tell you.

Well, this is what happened. My wife and my son and I were in New Orleans preparing to depart for a trip to Havana when we got the news. There had been talk of a hurricane, but everyone thought it would blow through with rain and wind and that would be it. We had no idea it would be as strong as it was. We decided to ride the thing out in our suite at the Hotel Monteleone. Well, the voyage was delayed, as the city was thrown back thirty years to the time without electricity. Funny how you get used to it. A bellhop came and knocked on our door and gave us the telegram from Mama. It said that Daddy had been killed. The new Mrs. Teague and I and our son returned at once to St. Matthew.

When we got home, we found Mama nervously looking through desk drawers and cabinets. She had every book in Daddy's study down and was thumbing through them, turning them spine up to see if anything might fall out. I asked her what she was looking for and she jumped a little and then said, "Oh, nothing, just doing a little cleaning now that your father has passed." I thought this was odd, as I can never remember her cleaning anything in my life. But I suppose everyone grieves in his own way.

Rev. Gladney performed a beautiful service, and we sent Daddy on to his eternal rest. Mama hired the best sculptor in New Orleans, a Mr. Carriere, to come down and do up a fine mausoleum for him and for the rest of us when our time comes. The turnout for his funeral was the largest ever recorded in St. Matthew Parish, even bigger than that for Judge Anderson, when he—well, when he did what he did. As the people filed past Daddy's coffin, many said they couldn't believe that the reign of the man, almost seventy years, was at an end.

The Burden of Cane

Daddy, or Marse Sam, as many of the old timers still called him, was certainly a force in my life. He shaped this place, Mount Teague, out of the swamps and grew it into the empire that it is now. He shaped me, too, and made me into the man I am today. In fact, of all the men I've met, he and one other have been most important in my formation as a man. Daddy was a—

Well, Miss Gladys, the other would be an instructor I had in my days at Sewanee, Professor Homer Prentiss. So, as I was saying—

Ma'am? Professor Prentiss was a professor of mathematics and physics at Sewanee.

No ma'am, if you'd rather, we can talk about Professor Prentiss.

So when I was eleven or so, Mama and Daddy sent me to Sewanee Grammar School in Tennessee to better myself as a scholar and a man. I was the youngest boy ever admitted in the history of Sewanee, up to that point, but Mama and Daddy felt I was ready and so I went.

There I met the man whom I must thank for shaping me into who I am today, Professor Homer Prentiss, instructor in mathematics and physics. He became as much a father to me as my own father, though much kinder, a gentle encourager who guided me through my course of study and prepared me for my days at the University of Mississippi.

Eleven years old is mighty young for a boy to find himself without the familiarity of family around him. So you can imagine how lost I felt when the train carrying Mama and Daddy departed from the depot in Sewanee without me on it. At first, I was put up in a room I shared with a boy from Nashville who was preoccupied with preparing for his studies and gave no heed to the crying I did at night when the lights were dimmed and I longed for home.

Classes started, all of us in the uniform of the school, like little soldiers. I stumbled along, bewildered, alone, and afraid in this new environment. It was everything I could do not to burst into tears. Then, in mathematics class, as roll was called, this man, Professor Prentiss, went down the list he was holding and looked up with the answer of each student. He paused on my name.

"Teague. Samuel Teague, Jr.?" he called out as he looked out to us.

"Here, sir," I responded, my voice a mere chirp compared to the other boys.

"Where are you from, Mr. Teague?"

You see, ma'am, we were all addressed as Mr. This and Mr. That, even me, though I was only eleven and wearing my uniform like a little toy soldier.

"Louisiana. St. Matthew Parish."

His eye paused on me. He only had one. The other he had lost somehow, and he wore a patch. Everyone assumed it was in the war, but no one ever asked.

"You wouldn't be Eva and Sam Teague's boy, would you?"

"Yes sir."

He didn't say how he knew them, and to this day, I still don't know, for he would never say. It seemed to take a little effort for him, but he continued down the roll, *Tucker, Westbrook, Williams,* so forth. After class, as we gathered up our things, he asked that I stay a moment. He inquired about the health of my parents, and I told him they were there at Sewanee the day before to drop me off but that they had headed right back home to prepare for the harvest and that we grew sugarcane. He asked how I was getting along.

I paused, and then I found that I could not hold back my tears any longer. The other boys had thankfully left the classroom, and he closed the door and had me sit on his desk. He sat next to me. My clothes, the uniform of a Sewanee cadet, were still brand new and uncomfortable without the softness that comes from repeated washing. He said he knew what it was like to feel alone in the world and that he had felt it too when he had gone to West Point before the late war. He said that I might come to his cottage anytime I like, the third one down from the headmaster's office. He gave me his handkerchief, embroidered with the initials HP at the corner.

I took his advice and began spending time with him. We discussed the classics, the works of Newton, Archimedes, Socrates, Descartes, Euclid. We read poetry, *Dante's Inferno,* and all the classics. We fished and hunted. He taught me to box. He told me stories of his days in the Confederate Army. He never said it, but I have always assumed that's how he lost his eye. It was the consensus among all of us boys. We attended the football and baseball games which were becoming the thing then, with banners that read *Sewanee's Right.* At Christmas, he gave me a set of handkerchiefs of my own with my initials, ST, at the corner like his.

My grades, my discipline, my very outlook on life changed from my dealings with Professor Homer Prentiss. His gentle way, his friendly discipline, shaped me, and for the better. It was no secret how much I idolized him. I've always wondered what became of him.

I wrote him letters during summer breaks, and he wrote me back, telling me to mind my studies and asking me what I was reading. When I returned to Sewanee in the fall, just before the yellowing of the leaves, I would find that he had read the same books. We would then discuss them over lemonade or iced tea.

About my third year or so at Sewanee, when I was fifteen, my Granny Teague died in Mississippi, and Professor Prentiss cried with me as if she had been his own mother. He even accompanied me on the train to her funeral. There, he respectfully stayed at the periphery of the funeral gathering. It was the last time I saw him, in the gray drizzle under an umbrella, dabbing his eye as Daddy and I paid our final respects. I asked Daddy where Mama was, and he said that she had stayed behind to see to my younger sister. That's what he said, but it was never a big secret, even to a child, that my mother and my grandmother never got along.

Daddy asked me who the man was over by those trees under the umbrella, and when I told him Professor Prentiss, he snorted, as he often did, and said, "Hardly!"

I turned to walk away from the new grave, a rectangular patch of grassless earth in the graveyard, when I heard Daddy spit a large spattering drop and I saw Professor Prentiss clinch his jaw and frown like a man who had been challenged. I looked to Daddy, who had the same expression, and when I looked over again, Professor Prentiss had departed. They were the two most important men in my life, and I had wanted to introduce them.

I was granted a leave of absence through the Christmas holidays to go home and be with family during the time of mourning, though what I really wanted was to return to school. Later that winter, Mama and Daddy saw me off at the station, both of them with a collegial handshake for me and an admonition to keep better company from now on. I returned to Sewanee to find that Professor Prentiss' picture, a framed photograph of him, with his eyepatch and sincere smile, had been removed from the line with the other instructors on the wall of the foyer of the chapel. No one would speak his name. It was as if he had never existed. I still don't know where he went or why. But I think of him often.

Yes, there's Mama coming down the stairs on her way to Altar Guild. You can always tell by the approaching scent of lilac water. Perhaps we can speak again later, Miss Gladys.

Eva

Well, son, I see you have met our houseguest, Mrs. Gladys Leonard. Don't make the mistake of asking to call her Miss Gladys as is our way here! She prefers Mrs. Leonard. Please leave us to ourselves, will you, son?

That Sam Jr. A decent head on his shoulders, not prone to foolish decisions like my late husband was. Junior graduated from Sewanee Grammar and then the high school, early and with honors, thank you! He was certainly a fine little scholar. One of his principle duties had been to practice his reading with his father, and so the boy grew up reading the newspapers to Mr. Teague, never suspecting that the reason for it was because his father couldn't read them himself.

But after the meeting with the old coot Barbagree, there was no need to keep Sam Junior at home. Junior was a rather thin-skinned boy who was afraid of bad weather and unfamiliar dogs and snakes and alligators, among other things. He has certainly come a long way from the boy who had spent the entirety of the hurricane of 1888 under his bed, howling at the limbs that scraped the windows and the rain that drummed against them and the steam-whistle of wind through the live oaks. His sister Missy slept through the whole thing, but of course, she was only two. My husband and I thought the storm a perfect diversion, but we had contented ourselves with a succession of libations that dulled the tempest for us.

It was and is the mark of a good family to educate their sons elsewhere, and so we sent him off to Sewanee, where the South's best families sent their boys. We were hoping the faculty in Tennessee might convert him from a snuffling crybaby to something resembling a man. It was in 1892, the same year that Judge Anderson quietly rapped his gavel for the last time, went to his chambers, and put a bullet through his head, still in his robes. Junior had only been eleven at the time, but we insisted that he was ready. The school was still hesitant, so we underscored our belief in his readiness with a sizable monetary donation.

He blossomed into a fine young man then, robust and intelligent. He thanked some Professor Nonesuch or Something-or-other for his development, never mind that Mr. Teague and I had been the ones to fund the whole endeavor. When war was declared with Spain, he enlisted immediately and was with President Roosevelt in his famous charge up San Juan Hill in Cuba. A splendid moment for a boy who had been afraid of his own shadow!

When he returned from the war, my husband insisted on sending him off to the University in Oxford. No. There is an Oxford in Mississippi also, madame. You English! Every time there's lightning, you all think that it's God taking a photograph of you. Why that look, Mrs. Leonard? Of course I jest, madame.

With Junior off at Sewanee and his sister in the care of the servants, Mr. Teague and I were free to move about at our pleasure. It was during this time that Mr. Teague and I fell into the habit of attending the prizefights at the Olympic Club in New Orleans, including the celebrated bout between Gentleman Jim Corbett and John L. Sullivan. It was considered inappropriate for a woman to attend them, but with the suitable amount of money in the proper hands, it could be arranged. Mr. Teague enjoyed the blood sport of it, cut and bruised faces and bloody knuckles, and I enjoyed the young athletic bodies and the spray of sweat that flew from their muscular physiques...

Well, yes, Mrs. Leonard. What were we discussing? Oh, yes, the prizefights in New Orleans in those years.

It was on a trip into the city to watch the fight between a young Jew from Shreveport named Morris Taylor and an Italian named Messina. There were thousands packed into the Olympic Club as the boxers threaded themselves through the ropes and began warming up by running in place and stabbing punches into the air. I was admiring them when Mr. Teague said, "Look there, Mrs. Teague. You aren't the only woman here."

And there working the corner for Morris Taylor, the "Hammering Hebrew," was a woman who seemed so very familiar to me.

"Well," I said, narrowing my eyes at the woman, trying to place her. As the bout progressed, I watched her, trying to remember where I had seen her before. From the start, Messina was too much for Taylor, who valiantly flailed against the Italian but whose head recoiled with blow after blow. Finally, it was all too much for the Jew from Shreveport, and his cornerman, or woman, actually, threw in the towel and Messina's hand was lifted up into the air as the winner. Mr. Teague was disappointed. He had put money on the Jew.

My husband was ready to leave right away, but we waited in the stands as the crowd thinned, and I watched the woman in the corner tend to her boxer, not like a trainer, but as a mother tends to a child. Gray streaks were appearing among the auburn of her hair. She turned from Morris Taylor and looked up into the stands. And our eyes met. She said something to her boxer, who was on a stool in his corner with his elbows on his knees and looking at the canvas. His sweat-soaked head nodded yes, and she turned and ascended into the stands to us, where I sat with my husband who was anxious to leave.

She made her way up to us, gathering her skirts away from her steps. Her ankles were rather fat and freckled, and her dress still had blood on its collar from her fighter and her administrations to him. As she approached I remembered her at once from her bright green eyes and freckled cheeks. It was the Irish woman who once brought dinner to us girls on Commerce Street. Bridget Fenerty. How long had it been? Fifteen, twenty years?

When I realized who it was, I felt a need to flee, and I poked Mr. Teague, who was occupying himself with reading the program bill. Though he could read now, it took all his energy and concentration. I told him we must be going, but it was too late. She was upon us and there was no getting away.

"Well, hello," she said cheerfully, "Lottie, isn't it?"

Mr. Teague looked up from the program, the cover of which had a lithograph of two bare-chested and bare-knuckled mustachioed boxers addressing each other with raised fists.

"I'm—I'm afraid you are mistaken, ma'am," I managed to say.

"So sorry, then, ma'am. Bridget Fenerty," she said as she offered her hand, which I took briefly and released. "You remind me of a girl I once knew in me youth. I suppose it's the blue eyes. Lovely they are."

"Mrs. Samuel Teague," I stammered weakly, forgetting to introduce my husband, whose attention had again descended fully into reading the program. Instead, I thanked her and told her we needed to be going.

As we departed up the stairs away from her, toward the exit, my husband asked me, "What is this Lottie business? Isn't that what Howard used to call you?"

"Pish posh!" I said. "Whoever this Lottie was, she must have been a striking beauty for her to be remembered so!"

At the top of the steps, I turned and looked down to the ring and the woman and the boxer she treated as a conquered son. She looked up from him to me, and she winked and put her finger across her lips. The gesture of a secret kept. As, I'm sure, you will keep these secrets, Mrs. Leonard.

Jack

He arrived in Sewanee the day before the fall term of 1892, two days after incoming students were told to report for orientation. His parents brushed off their tardiness, saying that they had had important tasks to attend to at home and that they were busy people and generous donors. Then they quickly departed without so much as a handshake or an embrace for their son, even though he was the youngest student ever admitted to Sewanee Grammar School. They only said things like, 'mind your studies and make us proud' and, when he seemed to be on the verge of tears, 'try to be a man about it.' Dear God, Father, he was only eleven years old.

Among the faculty, it was said that the young man sat on a bench at the station and sobbed for several hours after his parents left. Most said they could not conceive of such callousness nor fathom such isolation. Of course, Father, you are now aware that I could, for his parents had done much the same to me.

As I say, Samuel Teague, Jr., was the youngest student ever admitted into Sewanee Grammar School up until that time, in large part due to the financial insistence of his parents, Mr. and Mrs. Samuel Teague Sr. of St. Matthew Parish, Louisiana. He was a painfully shy boy, a boy who wore pink circles around his eyes from being kept indoors for long periods of time, a 'hothouse child' as they're sometimes called in America. He was a bright enough boy, but a boy who was in danger of being ruined by being told how brilliant and privileged and special he was. He was like a plant being asked to grow with an overabundance of manure but no sunlight.

I also knew that because of this he was at risk of being teased and quite possibly hazed. Mr. Twain said that 'children have but little charity for one another's defects,' and I was certain that this age-old force would be brought to bear on this boy. There was another defect to attend to. In addition to being thin-skinned and sensitive, it was not long before it was discovered that he was a sleepwalker, something I did as a boy.

A week into the fall term, he was discovered by the night-watchman halfway down the road to Monteagle. Breaking curfew was a dismissible offense, and he was about to be turned out for it, when I stepped forward for him. I vouched for him that he held much promise and was only struggling with his circumstances owing to his age, and I offered to let him stay on the sofa in the parlor of my cottage. So I took him under my wing. I put him up with me, at first to protect him from the upperclassmen, and then because we simply got on so well together. He never had any idea that he was my nephew and my father's grandson, and I felt that it might be an indirect way of me fulfilling the promise to my dying father of reconciling with my brother. I had been dreaming of my father again, and once when I woke, I thought I saw him sitting and looking out the window with his ever-present beaver pelt hat. But when I rubbed the sleep from my eyes, I saw it was only the mountain breeze pushing the curtain.

The following morning over breakfast, I asked Junior Teague about his grandfather and what he knew of him. My young housemate said that he had never met Grandpa Teague, as he had died long ago, but that his father implied that his father (*our* father) was an idiot who had lucked into marrying well. I gently told Junior that we should withhold judgment on those we haven't met and that his Grandpa Teague must have done something right to raise such a successful man as his father.

I asked Junior about his Granny Teague, and he said that her health was declining. It had been years since I had been home, and I would have liked to have seen her one more time, but I could not absorb another comparison to my brother, the successful planter in Louisiana. I asked Junior if he had any other family, aunts, uncles, cousins, and he said that he had an uncle whom his father called a swindler and a fly-by-night who was no better than his father. I switched the topic to something else, anything else, and never brought it up again.

I reminded myself that this boy had had no say in who his father was, and I saw to it that Junior applied himself. The first thing that had to go was his fear of failure. He had been raised to walk the tightrope of perfection. This would not do. Failure is inevitable, success comes from repeated correction and application from what is learned in failing. I gently encouraged him to reapply himself when he erred. Things he missed in his studies we redid until he mastered them, and he rose in rank.

Then there was the issue of this skinny, pale, twig of a boy. This boy needed sunshine and plenty of it. We went outdoors, we hiked in the mountains, we fished, we hunted. In time the pink circles under his eyes vanished. His color was healthy, his body took on muscle. He grew taller, his voice began to take on manly characteristics.

We also studied, boxed, wrestled, recited. We learned the stars at night. We invented, we studied the earth, the sky. We talked about the flight of birds and other winged creatures. He was enthralled that I had gone to West Point and had served in the late war. And he was curious about my missing eye and scars. He didn't seem to notice that my eye was the same nickel gray as his or that he and I could pass for father and son. I don't think he ever knew who I truly was. I, of course, knew right away that we were uncle and nephew.

In the summers, he reluctantly went home on break, then to the seaside to flee the fever. His absence from me made for long weeks. I spent the long, tedious vacuum without his company, fishing and hunting and reading without him, longing for him as a parent does for a child, I suppose. I felt a great pride in him, and I told him so. They were good years, and I had found a joy in his company. I believed it was true what was written in the Psalms: *weeping endureth for a night, but joy cometh in the morning.*

When he returned in the fall, I carefully avoided meeting his parents, even though he brought them around to see me. I even pulled down my picture in the foyer of the chapel and put it in my desk drawer, lest my brother and his wife see me and recognize me by my half-a-face. When they had returned to Louisiana and the semester was in progress, I put it back up again. When the headmaster asked about it, I brushed it off as a prank by the upperclassmen.

Each fall, I could see more of the man that Sam Jr. would become, or might become if his parents didn't ruin him with privilege and excess. If you want to ruin a boy, truly ruin him, tell him how wonderful he is, excuse his every fault, ask nothing of him, coddle him morally. He will wither, Father. Internally, he will wither.

Late one fall, Junior received a telegram that his Granny Teague had died in Mississippi. We wept over it together, as it brought me the pitiful feeling that I had not seen her in decades and the ruthless finality that I would never see her again. He wept because his mother, Eva, refused to attend her funeral, saying that they had never gotten along. I suppose that the saying is correct that two women can't love the same man. I resolved, however, to attend the services of my mother, his grandmother, for I pitied the young man and didn't want him to make the journey alone. I knew she would never be proud of me, much less tell me so. If not for Junior Teague, I would never have known that she had died.

On the train to Tunica, an older woman across from us remarked that 'my son' was the 'spitting image' of me. I was about to correct her and tell her that he was only my pupil and I his professor and that any resemblance was pure coincidence, but Junior's smile on that grim day held me to keep it at that. I only thanked her for her kind words.

I realized that I wouldn't be able to show my face in the church, not even half of it, and risk my brother recognizing me. So at the train station, I told Junior that I remembered a pressing matter, some undone something, and had to send an urgent telegram back to Sewanee. I told him that I would see him at the internment perhaps, and if not, then back at the train station. I walked with him the short distance from the station to the church, mindful to keep our umbrella low over my face. Then I left for the cemetery.

I wandered among the sleepers, remembering almost everyone with it, people who had moved on from this earth while I was away. I moved toward the corner where my mother's people were buried and with them my father. His stone read *John Malcom Teague, Gone from Sorrow*, with a hand pointing skyward. I silently asked that I might be relieved from my deathbed promise to him. I received only the caw of crows in the cedar trees at the edge of the graveyard.

The Burden of Cane

The hooves of carriages and the hearse rose in the distance as the funeral cortege approached, and I moved to the corner of the cemetery and pulled down the brim of my hat. The rain had stopped, but I kept my umbrella open and tilted forward. Perhaps I would be able to hear the preacher say the final words commending her body to the earth and her soul to heaven. I stood alone in a neglected corner of the cemetery where a grove of pine saplings had grown up over some untended graves. I looked at the tombstones in front of me, four uncared-for graves, all in a row. I stooped to scrape away the moss with my fingers, and I found a familiar name.

The Tyners. I worked away more of the moss and grime of the decades. They had all died on the same day in 1866. My mind easily put the scene together. A return from Omaha after the conclusion that she and her girls weren't cut out for city life and the northern winter and the cloying pity of her sister and her husband. The hopeful reunion after a period of estrangement, and the cautious anticipation of a new start together with a reformed and penitent husband and father. But something had gone horribly wrong and had ended here in some sudden and tragic way that I could only imagine. Those girls, those precious girls. Had they cried out for me to save them on that day it had happened, whatever it was? I moved on to the shelter of some cedar trees. It had begun to rain again, a slow, leaking patter.

Black umbrellas dotted the churchyard as the priest with a white stole draped over his shoulders held up a book and intoned the graveside rites, and then they lowered Mother into the earth. Across the cemetery from me, the gravediggers huddled under the thorns of a horseapple tree, planted to keep livestock out. The men smoked and waited for the mourners to drift away with the rain.

Eventually, as the rain slowly grew colder and more intense, only Sam and Junior were left. The gravediggers put out their cigarettes and approached the grave with their shovels. I positioned the umbrella, hoping it might cover all of my face. When I peeked from under it, my brother looked right at me. He scowled and turned his head and spat on my father's headstone. I fought my red-hot fury and hurriedly walked away, almost tripping over Mrs. Tyner's headstone. Had it not been for Junior, I would have rushed my brother and beaten him to a bloody death and left him there for the gravediggers to dispense with. I took my seething anger with me, though I glowed bright with it on such a dismal day. Junior ended up leaving with his father to return to Louisiana for a period of family mourning.

I returned to Sewanee alone, and when I arrived, a colleague met me at the train station with word that there were rumors, fueled by a telegram from the parents of the Teague boy, that my relationship with their son was indecent and that my conduct with him had been inappropriate, and beyond that, a violation of the laws of God and man. The scene made too much sense: an adoring pupil and an old bachelor professor who had a mysterious past and preferred to remain anonymous in the newspapers. What sort of unholy mischief had I left behind wherever I had come from? With a few deft brushstrokes, applied as whispers, I was painted guilty.

I quietly cleaned out my classroom and lodging and left in the middle of the night. And so I shed my identity like a skin, like a cicada molting its shell. Homer Prentiss, like Jack Teague, vanished from the face of the earth. The Psalm was proven only half true: Joy may have cometh in the morning, but weeping had returned again with the evening.

Eva

It was not long after our trip into the city that my husband, now a man of letters, at least compared to his former self, read the notice in the New Orleans newspapers that the Louisiana Lottery had been struck down. Mr. Teague was howling mad, pacing his study in limping strides between the window and the door with Mr. Burke's former newspaper, the *Times-Democrat* in his hand. His lips were pursed, and his face was red, save with the pale crescent of scar on his face which never reddened, no matter how mad he got.

The Louisiana Lottery, the 'Golden Octopus' as it was called because advertisements for it invaded every mailbox in the United States, was dead. And, along with it, the income it had generated for us. The final blow had come when President Harrison gave the postmaster the right to limit the lottery's use of the United States mail, and its charter expired in December of that year, 1893, I believe it was.

What was worse, our so-called friend Mr. Burke, now living in exile in Honduras, was attempting to resurrect it there as its sole proprietor. Mr.

The Burden of Cane

Burke, that son-of-a-bitch—*do pardon my language, Mrs. Leonard, but it is simply a fact*—that bastard tried to run the lottery from Honduras where he had fled after defrauding me and my husband and the state of Louisiana. But it soon folded there also and he had to make a living defrauding someone else in some other way. I have seldom prayed, Mrs. Leonard, but I did ask whatever deity might be on the throne up there to send down an ill-fate upon the head of Mr. Burke, and that I did not care which one, as long as it was slow and painful. Instead, Mr. Burke lives yet, and comfortably, in Tegucigalpa.

We, however, were rewarded with the financial Panic of 1893. The price of commodities hit rock bottom, and among them, the price of sugar. Our finances fell so that we were unable to summer in Europe in those years, nor could we even afford to go to the mountains at White Sulphur Springs. Rather, we spent the fever seasons with the common folk in Biloxi. Our financial reverses were the source of shouted discussion between Mr. Teague and me. We had many an argument over my spending, and I regretted my role in his expanding literacy. It would have been easier to have simply kept him an imbecile.

In 1894, short on money, we considered keeping Sam Junior home from Sewanee in order to conserve our finances. He cried and cried and sent letters to this Professor Prentiss he was so enamored with, until finally Mr. Teague relented and let him remain in school, but not before he had lashed our son with a belt and told him to be a man about it all, that hard times needed fortitude, not tears.

We still had fine things, and we wanted to keep them. There was only one recourse, and so we took it. Lumber was the thing then, and cypress was considered a desired commodity, and we were sitting on over a thousand acres of it. Of course, there was an old coot in a shack in the middle of it. But never mind him.

Some speculators from Pennsylvania came down and made us a handsome offer for the trees on it, some as 'old as Jerusalem' as one of them said. We drove a hard bargain with them and managed to bring them up on the price. They agreed and a deal was struck. A sawmill was set up, a great conglomeration of train tracks and steam engines and axes and saws. The day air was filled with the apple-sweet smell of cypress dust and the ripping shrieks and whines of great saws. The night air was filled with the sounds of our brawling workforce and the saloon and its piano and, occasionally, a gunshot. And then again in the morning the sounds of the saws dismantling *la cyprière* of Monsieur Barbagree.

It could not be helped. In the end, the whole of it was cut, right down to the old gray-bearded coot's shack in the center of it. It took the better part of a year and a half, but when it was all down and converted into board-feet and hauled away, we had made a pretty penny. The saloon, the laborers' cottages, their families, the train and its tracks, all of it was pulled up and hauled away leaving no trace. The only thing left in the sea of stumps was the old weathered shack in the middle of them. Barbagree himself moved on somewhere, though the superstitious of St. Matthew Parish said that he became a spirit that still wanders his stump-ridden fields. We decided to help him keep his feet dry in his wanderings, and so we had the whole of it drained, and then, in 1896, the stumps dynamited and burned, and it became another cane field, spirit or no spirit. Ha! We left his shack, at least, so his spirit could not complain about that.

Well, Mrs. Leonard, I suppose my carriage is ready for the Ladies' Altar Society social. Time for me to set a good example to those gilded hussies of how a woman of culture comports herself. Someone must do it for them.

Jack

When I left Sewanee in December of 1894, I also left behind the name Homer Prentiss. I was fifty-one years old and forced to start over again, without a name. I took a cheap flophouse room in New Orleans, with a new name as plain as I could come up with, John A. Jones. The A was for Andrew, the only vestige from my former names. I began a new life, and I was alone again in having to do it.

It was a cold winter, too. That Christmas, I'm sure the faculty and their wives celebrated the holidays with a lavish buffet at the home of the Vice Chancellor, as it did every year. A home warmed by fireplaces in every room and good wishes from the people gathered there, with toasts and songs and small gifts exchanged. If the name Homer Prentiss was mentioned, it was only in a whisper.

The Burden of Cane

I celebrated Christmas alone in my rented room in New Orleans. The only thing warm in my room was a fire inside of me like that in the center of the earth, a molten slurry deep under the surface like liquid sulfur that began to bubble, popping and hissing with each thought of my brother. I watched carriages in the city trundle merry occupants from ball to feast to ball, men and women wrapped up against the cold. My room was cold despite the thumping, hissing pipe meant to heat it. It mattered little to me. My rage kept me warm.

I resolved to confront my brother for stealing my life and name from me yet again. Through January of 1895, I plotted the confrontation that I would have with him. I relived the dreams of torture I would visit upon him. When my anger cooled a little, I would think I might get him alone and reason with him, scare him into sense, put my gun to his ear in the dark and tell him that I only wanted peace and if he didn't reform, I would return in the night and finish him. *Mark my words*, I would tell him in a low growl as I pulled back the hammer of the gun before I slowly released it.

But no, I thought, I wouldn't reason with my brother, no one could. He was too strong willed. I would pull the trigger and I would end him with a great flash of powder and a bang and a scattering of skull and blood, and I would take great delight in it. When my hatred for my brother returned, as it always did, it was hotter than ever each time. Eventually, my demons and angels deliberated to a verdict. In February, I packed my revolver and a change of clothes, and I bought a train ticket to Donaldsonville. I was going to end him and myself, for good. The world was unbearable with both of us in it.

On a cold, gray day with a wind that spooked ripples across the surface of the water, I took the ferry across the river to Algiers and the station there. I boarded the train, which beat a rhythm like a drumroll as we traveled through the lead-cold. In Donaldsonville, I checked into a hotel on Railroad Avenue. I had my last meal. I went to bed for the last time. I woke to my last morning on earth. I made my morning necessities for the last time. I dressed for the last time. Then, I loaded my revolver and put it in my coat pocket.

Outside my window, the daylight seemed brighter and denser than it had been the day before. Voices laughed and shrieked and dogs barked. I pulled back the curtain. Something magical happened that night, something that rarely occurs in south Louisiana. It had snowed. Children were wrapped up against it as they played with the adults, who were now also children again. I leaned into the window and pressed my cheek against the cold glass panes. The streets, the buildings, the carriages that had been left out, the train depot, all was draped in white, and everyone in Donaldsonville was out in it. Crude snowmen had been constructed, snowballs were hurled. The voices of the town echoed off buildings only to be absorbed by the cold white powder. It was the source of such joy, such merriment, such revelry in the power of nature, that I became caught up in it and as carefree as I had felt in months.

I was brought back to earth when I felt the pistol in my pocket and I remembered what I had come for. I decided I wouldn't end both of us, only my brother. He was the issue, not me. I deserved to live, he did not. I would kill him, and I would flee, leaving only footprints in the snow.

Rather than manage a carriage on icy roads, I rented a horse and rode down the bayou toward Mount Teague. The cypresses were clothed in white, and snow and ice skirted the edge of Bayou Lafourche. The breath of my horse and me steamed out as we jostled down the road. It was a pleasant ride, almost enough for me to forget my errand. In fact, I had to remind myself of what I was there for and what I was about to do.

I thought of the *cyprière* and the old man Barbagree and how quaint and cozy his shack must look in the snow. I felt the need to visit with him, to seek his counsel, to perhaps gain his blessing, even though my old West Point Napoleonic French would make it difficult. He might try to talk me out of it, or perhaps he would be in favor of it. But I had to visit him.

When I approached the road that branched away from the hand-painted sign, *La Cyprière de Barbagree* with an arrow under it, I took it. My horse's steps shuffled through the snow. There were no tracks and I wondered if he ever had any visitors and hoped he would be glad to receive me.

As I approached where the water's edge used to be, I found only snow, and an immense field of white mounds. Snow-covered stumps. Off in the distance, where alligators and herons and egrets used to live in balance was an old shack. It appeared even smaller exposed to the gray, pressing sky. My horse and I weaved through the white mounds to the dwelling. The snow was uniform and undisturbed. Pelts were still tacked up to the outside, though wearing small drifts of white. Wisps of gray moss were on the porch. I dismounted and knocked, but when I did, the door opened on its own.

The Burden of Cane

I quietly moved into the dwelling-place, one simple room with gray-planked walls. I called out quietly, *Monsieur? Monsieur?* The bedstead was neatly made, wood stacked by the stove, the rocking chair next to it. I sat down in it and looked out the window. The snow began falling again, a soft blur of white drifting onto the white hillocks of snow-covered stumps. I began rocking and looking through the window. It was the most peaceful I had been in years, perhaps, ever. It was like being rocked by a loved one, as if I were a child, a baby.

I woke to find that it had stopped snowing and that I was understandably cold. The light was beginning to fail, glowing out on the fields that had once been swamp. I wasn't ready to move on, so I set a fire in the belly of the stove. There was a small bit of newspaper, neatly folded over. I shoved it under the small teepee of kindling in the stove, and as I struck a match, an advertisement in it caught my eye.

A man named Captain Anthony F. Lucas was looking for a someone with mechanical inclinations and skills to join him for the purpose of mining salt. My match went out as I read, so I lit another and read on. He was drilling for salt and sulfur in a place called Petite Anse on the coast, a place that I believe is called Weeks Island now. I tore the advertisement from the newspaper and lit the rest. The yellow light advanced over and consumed a story about a man who had been hung for killing another man. The last word to disappear into blackened edges and then flame was *'revenge.'*

I remembered my horse, and I rose to go and see to him. When I did, the pistol fell from my pocket with a hard clunk on the floor. I placed it on the simple table where Barbagree and Mr. Templet and I had visited that day over coffee and I had received the warning about the sugarhouse. I could not hear the old gray-bearded man, I could only feel his words. I imagined him at the table, so clearly, leaning over a cup of coffee and saying, *Don't let him ruin you. Move on, mon fil, move on. Your life is worth more than this, my son.*

Outside, in the lee of the roof and protected from the snow, my horse had nosed his way under the snow-hillock and discovered a mound of Spanish moss and was happily eating it. I whisked away the snow on top of the curly gray, and he shook his neck in appreciation. I went back inside and sat by the cheerful glow and warmth of the fire, reading the clipping from the paper. I couldn't tell what paper it was from, or when the advertisement had been placed. I only knew that this yellowed scrap represented hope. On the back was a list of cotton prices and part of a railroad timetable. The first entry was the rail line that ran from New Orleans to New Iberia and Petite Anse. I folded up the paper and put it in my pocket.

When the fire had burned down, I rode back into Donaldsonville in the glow of the moonlit white landscape sleeping under a sky speckled with hopeful stars. I returned the horse to the stableman, whom I woke with a rap at his window. Inside, he too, was enjoying a fire. I apologized for my late hour, and he said that it was no issue and invited me in for a nightcap, which I accepted. Then I wished him a *bon soir*, and I adjourned to the hotel. I slept as deep as I have ever slept. And I dreamed of my father, a smiling face under a beaver pelt hat.

Junior

Has Mama left?

Yes, Miss Gladys, I thought we might speak again, if that's all right with you.

After a long winter of mourning in a house which, frankly, was devoid of joy even on the best of days, I returned to Sewanee that February 1895. I was anxious to see Professor Prentiss and resume the business of learning. There was snow on the ground, a thing only the old timers of St. Matthew had ever seen before. My sister Missy and I played in it while I waited for the train to take me back. We were making snowmen and throwing snowballs and so forth. I had seen snow in Tennessee at Sewanee, but she had never seen it before, as it happens so rarely here.

It occurred to me how much I was beginning to enjoy being an older brother. Before, I had only seen her as a pest. I was about fifteen, I guess, and she was nine or ten. The train approached the station, the cowcatcher pushing snow out of its way. I picked up my suitcase filled with several months' worth of clothes, and when I did, she hugged me around my midsection and pushed her head into my chest. It made me press my cheek into the top of her head, smelling the sweat provoked from our play in the snow. Perhaps any other family would have said, "I love you," or "take care of yourself." We were Teagues. We said nothing, though we did exchange a wave through the window of the train.

Our parents did not come to see me off, they never did. They had other affairs to attend to and had taken little notice of the snow. Missy and I had reasoned that Mama and Daddy had both grown up in places that saw snow, north Louisiana and north Mississippi, and the novelty of it had long since vanished. Besides, Daddy had contracted 'oil fever' and spent the day combing through the newspapers circling opportunities for investment. He was also annoyed that the snow had delayed the putting down of seed cane.

When I got back to Sewanee, I was shocked to find that Professor Prentiss had left suddenly and with no forwarding address. As I gathered my things out of his cottage to move to one of the dormitories, the Vice Chancellor and the bishop came and had me pause and sit in a chair, the one that Professor Prentiss sat in as we discussed matters long into the night. They asked me if there was anything I needed to talk about concerning Professor Prentiss. Their faces were pained, like when the news of a sudden death or a great disaster is related to someone who is completely unaware, painted with a sort of awkward sympathy.

"No," I said, "I just wanted to talk to him again" I asked them the circumstances of his leaving. They only said, "there, boy, it isn't necessary that you speak of things of that nature." His picture had been taken down from the line of faculty, and I was asked never to speak his name again. I wanted to send him a letter, but there was no address, and no trace of him in his cottage. He vanished, simply and succinctly. He disappeared as if the earth had swallowed him.

I contemplated returning home, as I was becoming lonely for my sister, though not especially so for my parents. But I knew exactly what my mentor Professor Prentiss would have me do, and I finished my studies at Sewanee and graduated in 1897, early and with honors. In my valedictory, I at last mentioned the name of Professor Homer Prentiss and paid tribute to him, which raised the eyebrows of the faculty. In the front row, my parents scowled. Between them sat my sister in a white dress and a bonnet to shield her against the June sun. Of the three of them, she alone showed pride in me, her face framed in admiration and white organdy.

I have always held out hope that one day I would receive a letter from my old teacher and that perhaps we would meet again and that he would be proud of my gains. But I never have. Is he still alive, Miss Gladys? What ever became of him, I wonder? If you could find that out, if he is among those in the great beyond, well, ma'am, at least that would be something.

The year after I graduated, the *Maine* was sunk in Havana harbor, and we all rushed off to war. I was a little underage, and I had to get Mama to sign for me to go. The country was all on fire for it, none more than we boys, and I contracted war fever like most of my peers. And so I went off to fight the Spanish. We sailed from New Orleans, all of us in our new uniforms, to Tampa, and there we waited to go to Cuba.

But within a few months, it was over, and we came home. Even though it was just a matter of months, when I returned, I found that Missy was taller and not as spindly as she was when I left. She giggled and preened, for she was beginning to notice boys. She had big blue eyes like our mother but sandy hair like me and my daddy. We were happy to see each other.

With war unexpectedly over, I went off to Oxford—yes ma'am, Mississippi. I had wanted to study the classics and perhaps pursue an academic life, like my idol, Professor Prentiss and maybe meet up with him at some academic meeting somewhere down the road. But my parents objected, saying that life in a classroom was no lifestyle for a Teague, and so I studied economics and commerce instead. All academic roads were meant to return back to Mount Teague and the running of it.

When I returned from school at the end of each term, Missy was closer and closer to womanhood. On break one summer, we took a long carriage ride among our family's cane fields, and she confided in me that she was in love with one of the field hands but she didn't want to tell Mama. I agreed that that it would be disastrous and to think wisely upon the matter and that it would be best to banish such thoughts. Then I left for school again. Missy, as usual, was the only member of my family to see me off. That was also the last time I saw her.

A few months later, she was diagnosed with leprosy and committed to Carville. The inmates there are encouraged to take on new names to save their families the shame of that diagnosis. Mama told me to say that Missy had gone to study in Europe and that she had married a baron and was residing there in a large estate. I couldn't remember her being sick from it and wondered how it had come up so suddenly. Mama said she noticed the signs of it and they took her to a doctor in New Orleans who confirmed that it was leprosy and that the best place for her and the Teague name was Carville. I went many times to the iron fence that surrounded it hoping to see her, but every time one of the Daughters of Charity in a big gull-winged bonnet shooed me away from the fence. Finally, I was brought to the front office and told not to return again.

I sent word to her at Carville that Daddy had died. I wonder if she ever got the message and if she had to grieve alone. She's never come home again, not even for holidays, and I'm afraid she has disappeared from my life just like Professor Prentiss. My mother's story about my sister marrying a baron and residing in a fancy estate was a lie, a face-saving lie. But she wasn't the only one to alter the truth. And so here is another lie, and this one is mine.

Miss Gladys, I suppose you've been told before that there is something about you that compels the truth. I feel that not only do I want to tell you everything, I need to tell you everything. Just as it happened, and skipping any pretense. And so, this is the part of which I am not proud. Please don't repeat it to anyone, not to Mama or anyone. I'll tell you, if it might help you contact Daddy.

I never did ride with Teddy Roosevelt up San Juan Hill. In fact, Miss Gladys, I never did leave Tampa. Instead, I drank rum and smoked cigars and paid for the company of the five-dollar girls down in the Spanish quarter. We debauched them, too. I paid for them to do things that my poor mother would blush upon if she knew that such lewd acts even existed. Things she could not even imagine, lascivious acts performed by bawdy women. At the brothels in Tampa, you could get a pretty fine girl to do about anything for five dollars and two of them to do it at the same time for twelve. I collected postcards of them that we boys in the barracks traded in card games. We drank, we gambled. We whored. We were young and bored, with army paychecks and time on our hands. It's not that we shirked our duty. We all wanted to go to Cuba and fight. It's just that the whole thing was over before any of us got a chance.

I knew my daddy would be disappointed, and so—so I told him that I had ridden with Teddy Roosevelt up San Juan Hill. To my knowledge, he never knew any different. It is perhaps the closest he ever came to expressing satisfaction in me. I told it to please him, to gain his favor. My mother overheard it and spread it, as it was a great credit to the Teague name. The lie soon traveled hard and recklessly fast, as lies do, especially when retold by my mother to her society friends. A lie repeated often enough becomes a fact. I could not call it back, and, honestly, I didn't want to, because it had put a glimmer of pride in my daddy's face.

I was sent back to finish college in Mississippi, though I would have been happy for Tulane or Baton Rouge, but Daddy insisted on the University of Mississippi. He had attended but had not finished, and so he wanted me to go and get my degree. He said that finally a Teague would graduate from there, and graduate I did, but instead of taking on a life of academia, I have seen to the day to day operation of Mount Teague, working alongside Daddy. But really, I have had to run it myself and let Daddy pretend he ran it. But no matter how much we've produced, we barely seem to make ends meet. I don't know where it all goes. But it hasn't been for lack of trying. I've tried to make him proud. I've tried to make them both proud.

You ask me what I want to ask Daddy and what I would like to hear him say.

Well—

Well, I—

Pardon me, ma'am. I apologize for this show of emotion—

I might like to hear him say— I'd like to hear him say—

—say that he was proud of me.

He never told me, not once in my life. How I should like to hear him say it, even if it is from the great beyond.

Yes ma'am. I, I guess I should be going now.

I have some things in the field I need to see to. It'll be time to put down seed cane soon.

Jack

Icicles dripped from the live oaks along the main street of New Iberia, and under their crystal branches, crude, tilting snowmen sweated in the warming air. Children played in the last of the snow, though about all that was left for them to gather up was in the shade of the trees. The hopeful force of Spring is something insistent and primal, and she can never be held back.

I asked around town, in French and in English, where I might find this Captain Lucas, and I was directed to a house a few doors down from the twin belfries of the Catholic church, St. Peter's, I believe it was. His wife answered the door, and I asked her if I might speak with her husband. She said he was drilling a well down at the actor Joseph Jefferson's place on Orange Island. She pointed me to the road that went off into the distance, and I took it as the church bells tolled the noonday hour.

Although the road down to Orange Island was surprisingly good, paved with oyster shells dredged up from the bay off to the south, it turned out to be a three hour trip on foot. As I walked, the warm breath of the Gulf wind bathed my face. The air had the tropical heaviness of Brazil or Puerto Rico, and after an hour or so, the snow had melted completely and spring was emerging like a butterfly from an icy chrysalis. Azalea buds were pink and red and white tipped, and bright green shoots of new leaves dotted branches. In pastures along the way, new calves stood next to their mothers, whose tails swished as they clipped the new grass.

I found the house with a sign that said *J. Jefferson* and under it *Rip Van Winkle*. Enormous live oaks twisted up from massive roots, and the breeze tugged at the moss hanging from their limbs like a child playfully pulling on a grandfather's beard. I ascended the deep front porch and knocked, and the housekeeper answered. She was a woman with a dark, round face and a black dress with a white apron. Inside the house I could see framed portraits of Joseph Jefferson in his various roles, most notably Rip Van Winkle, which he had played almost exclusively for forty years. Only an actor, or someone with a grandiose vision of himself, would have his portrait displayed so prominently in his own home. Of course, so did my brother. But who was I to cast stones at an actor, someone playing a part? I had created the fictitious role of John A. Jones for myself, and I would have to play it the rest of my life.

"Mr. Joe in Florida for the winter on account his jints," the woman said wiping her hands on her apron, "but that man Cap Lucas out drilling a mineral well what to help Mr. Joe's rheuma-tiz when he get back from down yonda."

"I'm here to see Capt. Lucas, ma'am," I said.

"Check with them mens in the barn. They ought know where he at."

Two men in the barn were pitching hay. They paused in a thin cloud of straw dust to say they didn't know, and sent me to see the gardener. The gardener, who was trimming camellia bushes, told me in a thick French accent that the last he knew, Capt. Lucas was a quarter mile away, beyond those trees out there. I walked out to them and past them, but there was still no sign of this Capt. Lucas. I was beginning to doubt if he really existed when I heard the sound of a steam engine chugging. I followed it to the edge of a field of sugarcane.

He was a man with Mediterranean features, bronzed skin even in the winter. He wore a beaver pelt hat over a head that was as even in dimensions as a cube. His eyes were dark and held a frank, thoughtful expression, and a full moustache encroached over his upper lip and the sides of his mouth. He was tending a steam engine that drove a flapping belt that pushed pipe into the earth. He was completely absorbed in his task and at first never took his eyes off the drill pipe, peering down it as if trying to see to the bottom of it deep under the ground. All the while, the steam engine huffed and grunted and the belt fluttered in its revolutions to and from the engine. Finally he looked up and pointed to his eye and said in some Mediterranean accent, "How you lost eye?"

"Accident," I said.

"Always is accident."

"John Jones," I said with an outstretched hand.

He took no notice of my hand or my name and didn't offer his. Instead, he busied himself with the business of drilling Mr. Jefferson's—Rip Van Winkle's—mineral well. The pipe slammed into the earth and retreated and slammed into it again. I thought maybe he hadn't heard me.

"Here to see about a job," I said over the metallic ring of the pipe and the loud putter of the engine. He kept looking from pipe to steam engine and back to pipe.

"Trained at West Point," I said.

He took off his beaver pelt hat and looked down the shaft with a squinted eye. What hair he had left was cropped close to his cubic head.

"Worked on the Pacific railroad," I said.

He moved to the steam engine and read a gauge. I was beginning to feel invisible.

"Drilled many a water well up on the plains," I yelled above the din of the pipe and the belt and the engine.

He looked up from the shaft, and a smile pushed up his thick moustache. "Oh! A driller! Why you no say so?"

He shut off the engine. The chugging stopped and the belt slapped to a halt, but for a moment the silence was still tainted with the lingering ring of noise. He motioned with his hand for me to follow him to his carriage, where he took his coat off the seat. He put it on, and we rode back into New Iberia.

Our dealings improved like the thawing winter. Suddenly he considered us birds of a feather. He talked nonstop of the riches under the earth, of gold and silver and copper, of sulfur and salt. Of oil and gas. For as long as I knew him, it was his favorite topic. Petroleum and its uses.

"Where is salt, is sulfur, and where is sulfur, is gas, is oil. And where is oil, is future. There is man in New York, man named Selden, has patent for a carriage he says 'road-engine.' No need for horse, no mule, no need for nothing."

Lucas' moustache was suddenly bristling with excitement. His upstretched finger stabbed up into the air as we swayed and lurched.

"Is man in Michigan, Ford, working on similar carriage what is called 'quadricycle.' Run on ethanol! One day such vehicles will be everywhere and they run on such things as kerosene. Gasoline, perhaps."

Lucas would gesture with the reins in his hands, sometimes so emphatically that the horse would get confused and slow down, only to pick up his pace when Lucas shook a snap into them again. I was just as fascinated to hear him talk as he was to tell me.

I was hired before we got back to New Iberia, where we dined at his house a few doors down from the church, the belfries of it outlined against the setting sun. And though I might have taken a job drilling into the earth, I always kept my eye, my only eye, gazing at the sky-blue sky above it, thinking that if it were possible to travel over the earth in a road-engine, then why not through the sky?

We worked all over, at places with French names, Belle Isle and Grand Côte and Anse la Butte, drilling water wells, salt wells, and sulfur wells. We used a cable-tool bit that frantically gouged out earth, like a dog digging for something he can only smell. In 1896, several hundred feet under the earth at Petite Anse, we found a vein of pure salt that extended down half a mile and possibly further, though that was as deep as we could go. In 1897 at Belle Isle, we bailed up salt particles from the drill shaft and dumped them onto the derrick floor, and they jumped around like popcorn, popping like fire crackers. Capt. Lucas said that it was because there was gas in them that was liberated when brought in contact with the air.

We kept a crew of anywhere from five to ten men, depending on who was drunk and who was sober and who was in jail or out. Sulfur and salt were not considered nearly as lucrative as gold, and we lost several of our hands the year that gold was discovered in the Yukon in Alaska and the siren call of it blared through the papers. News of the discovery even made it into the *St. Matthew Compass*, a copy of which I found on a bench of the Vermillion Parish Courthouse in Abbeville where I had gone to file a lease.

The *Compass* also carried a story about a young man from St. Matthew Parish named Samuel Teague Jr., who had graduated early from Sewanee in Tennessee and was valedictorian for the class of '97. I began subscribing to the newspaper. The next spring, April of 1898, the *Compass* reported that Samuel Teague Jr. was among those who had enlisted to go to war with Spain. Then, that summer, the *Compass* proudly related the news that Teague, Jr., had charged up San Juan Hill with Teddy Roosevelt. I was proud of the boy who was once as timid as a mouse, but I feared how all the adoration would affect him. Delicious, corrosive adoration, as addictive as opium. I considered sending him a letter, as Homer Prentiss, but I considered his parents and thought better of it, and Junior Teague was left to wrestle with the octopus of success by himself.

The drilling for water, salt, and sulfur continued. At the close of each day, despite being in my fifties, I would climb the derricks to watch the sun set into the western sky and I would say a prayer for Junior Teague. Perhaps it was more of a wish, that neither success nor failure would ruin him, for one can do it as easily and quickly as the other.

Pelicans and ducks flew in silhouette against the western sky, flickering black Vs against the cantaloupe orange of the setting sun. I still imagined being among them, watching the ground shrink beneath my wings and peeking over the horizon to the sun which could not escape my vision as I rose higher. Up on the derrick, I felt fifteen, not fifty. That is, until my brother's derisive words boiled up from my memory and into my consciousness:

Jack, you'll no more fly than a pig.

He had been right, and I hated him for it.

Eva

Well, if you must know, Mrs. Leonard, there was quite a bit of smirking today at Altar Guild. Let them smirk! Let them smirk just like Gwendolyn Mosey and Polly Calhoun once smirked. Smirk until their heads split in two! They are simply consumed by jealousy, and that is all. Perhaps they fear for their husbands now that I am available again for marriage.

Ruthie? Ruthie! Come and take my coat so that I may visit with our guest. This instant. And bring me a gin rickey!

On my way home from guild, I saw Junior in Napoleonville, Mrs. Leonard. He said that he was able to speak with you again when I left for Altar Guild. Did he tell you that he was with President Roosevelt during the charge up San Juan Hill? Perhaps not. He has a modesty that his father certainly never had. My husband, that great, spouting whale, loved to tell tales of his military days. He was up for a colonelcy at the end of the war. Unfortunately, the war ended before he could get it. Which reminds me, I must see if he had a Confederate pension that as a widow I might be entitled to.

Yes, I believe we were talking of my son.

Toward the close of the old century, Junior finished at Sewanee, and in his valedictory speech he tearfully gave credit to this Professor Purvis or some-such, not to his father or to me, saying that this strange case of a professor 'inspired him to a career of scholarship and learning.' A slap in our faces, we who had funded the whole enterprise! To make matters worse, our daughter Missy was now a teenager who was becoming incorrigible regarding her choice in company, spending far too much time with the local French jabberers than was good for her or the Teague name. The lure of them was such that we ended up sending her away for it. Our very social standing was at stake!

Would you like a cocktail? At Mount Teague, it's never too early, nor too late! Yes, tea, then.

Ruthie!

We were discussing the end of the last century, weren't we? Well, then. After the cutting and sale of *la cyprière de Barbagree*, we had enough money to sustain us for a while. Some would call it a rape of nature, Mrs. Leonard. I regard it as a heady business decision, and it lined our pockets nicely.

My husband, as I say, had developed the dangerous habit of reading everything he could get his hands on, all the newspapers, He had always had them delivered to the house, though the children and I read to him. Now that he could read them himself, he spent a great deal of time poring over them, circling things and keeping a journal, though still in primitive script, like the printing of a six year-old. Indeed, there were times when I would come across a scrap of paper thinking it was the work of our daughter Missy or Sam Junior, only to find that the subject was commodities and opportunities for investment.

It was in the late 1890s, and the newspapers carried news of the search for oil in Texas and Pennsylvania, and many a night I would leave him in his study as he searched the latest on the fields in places like Nacogdoches and Lufkin. His face would be inches away from what he was reading in the lamplight, hurriedly turning the page like a man in the desert drinking from a spring, as if getting closer to the printed page would give him a jump on the competition. Then, the next morning, I would find him at his study again. Sometimes I wondered if he had gone to bed at all. Not that I would have noticed.

Well, he had come across an advertisement in the *Times-Democrat* placed by a man named Joseph Cullinan in Corsicana, Texas. This Mr. Cullinan had found oil there and was looking for investors. He hinted that there may be as much as one hundred barrels a day waiting under the Texas dirt, not a fortune, but certainly a good return on one's investment. We bought in for a meager return, enough for us to summer in Europe again.

We continued on for several years dabbling here and there. Of course, everyone was certain there were vast riches under the earth, whether it be salt, sulfur, or oil, and my husband was smitten with the idea of it, like a gambler playing one more hand and certain it was the one to pay big. He put up a large amount of money in this speculation, against my wishes.

At the time, there was a man in Texas named Higgins who was certain there was oil and quite a bit of it in a place called Beaumont, and he persuaded Mr. Teague to invest a tidy sum in the venture. I was against it, thinking that perhaps it would be better to finance an expedition to the Yukon where gold had been found. I told my husband that he might drill holes in the earth all he wanted around there, but all he would ever find would be debt. The oilfield was a volatile place, both physically and financially. It was said that this Higgins fellow was missing an arm and that there was another man named Jones who was missing an eye, and I admonished my husband that he might find himself missing his money if he persisted in this gamble.

But I let my husband overrule me, a rare thing, and we invested with this man Higgins and his partners Lucas and Jones. With time, it proved to be nothing but a sinkhole that demanded more and more of our money, and Mr. Teague and I went personally to the Crosby Hotel in Beaumont to meet with these men and demand our investment back. We would let others lose their money there, and perhaps we would come in when it was safer.

Are you sure I can't interest you in a cocktail, madame? Very well, I myself will have another.

Jack

In 1899, Capt. Lucas and I answered an ad in a New York trade journal placed there by a man named Higgins in Texas. Oil had been discovered there in trifling amounts, in places like Corsicana and Nacogdoches, but nothing like it would become later. The consensus from drillers and geologists alike was that all that could be found had been found. Higgins thought otherwise.

We arrived late on a Saturday and met Mr. Higgins at the Crosby House Hotel in Beaumont, a sleepy little town that catered to the farmers and lumbermen of the area. He greeted us in shirtsleeves, putting his cigarette to his lips as he shook our hands with his single one and mumbled his introduction, "Pattillo Higgins." His empty left sleeve quietly announced that he had one arm, but he was too young to have served in the war. I thought he must have lost it in the cause of industry, like I had, and I wondered if he was thinking the same about my eye. We adjourned to the dining room for a drink, though Pattillo had coffee, saying that he no longer took strong drink. As we sat and were served, Capt. Lucas asked if there were other respondents to the ad, and Higgins said with Texan candor, "you're it."

"Well, then," Lucas smiled, pushing his moustache tightly up against his nose, "tell us of proposition."

When he saw that Lucas was willing to take him and his ideas seriously, Higgins became a bubbling font of conversation, launching into his life's story as if it were what we had come to hear, about how as a young man he had had a rowdy past and fallen under the spell of evil. He had drunk and gambled and fought. With some other boys, he had harassed a church of Negroes who were simply trying to worship God, and when the sheriff had come to drive them off by firing a warning shot above their heads, Pattillo Higgins had shot back and killed a deputy. The deputy had 'winged' him, Higgins said, and the wound got infected and he lost his arm. He was acquitted in the deputy's death, however, claiming self-defense. Then, at a revival meeting at the Opera House in Galveston, Pattillo Higgins had given his life over to Jesus. "I used to put my trust in pistols," he said, "now I put my trust in God and I feel much safer."

This one armed man worked in the lumber business and then, fascinated by geology, found a deposit of clay and began making bricks. His kiln was fired by wood, but the price of wood was high, so he investigated the use of oil to fire his bricks. He knew of a place south of town called Big Hill where he was convinced there was oil.

"You are sure there is oil in this place, 'Big Hill?'" Capt. Lucas asked.

"I'm right sure," Higgins said. "I done prayed on it."

Higgins met us at Big Hill the next afternoon after church. With him was his Sunday school class, a group of boys and girls in their early teens, dressed in their Sunday clothes, the boys in suspenders with jackets over their arms, the girls in flouncy dresses with their hair in ribbons and bows. They followed Higgins like he was their shepherd. One of them, a girl with big brown eyes, asked him, "Mr. Higgins, do that trick with the match."

"Yes sir," one of the boys seconded, "the match trick!"

A smiling Pattillo Higgins walked up to the hill, looked back to his flock, and poked a stick in the ground. A foul smell like rotten eggs bubbled up and out, and several of the girls giggled and put their palms over their noses. Then Higgins deftly struck a match on the box with his lone hand and flicked it over the hole. A flaming jet erupted in a brief rush. The girls squealed and clapped, and the boys shouted and laughed. Capt. Lucas looked down at the spot where the flame had erupted and said to Higgins, "I believe you may be right."

"Respectfully, Captain sir, I know I'm right." Higgins smiled. "I done prayed on it, you see."

They shook hands, and Capt. Lucas agreed to return and start drilling in June after we had satisfied our commitments in Louisiana. Capt. Lucas leased over six hundred acres from the Gladys City Oil Corporation, an outfit that Higgins had formed with members of the Baptist church in Beaumont, though over time, many of his investors had tired of Higgins and his boastful salesmanship and abandoned him.

Drilling began in June 1900 at the exact spot where Higgins had lit the match. The local farmers gave us only brief looks as they worked their fields and tended their cattle. We drilled all summer in the heat, but our drilling brought up only mud and sand. More investors began to drop out, and others took their place. And the drill sank further into the earth. Some people were worried that we would drill right into the devil's parlor and release his hellfire, but we continued downward, too curious about what was down there to stop. We would risk a meeting with the devil.

Much of the summer, it rained, and rained heavy. Everything—wagon wheels, shoes, hooves—everything took on barnacles of mud. At night, brilliant sparks of lightning and loud grumbles of thunder announced more rain. On days that it didn't rain, we dripped with sweat merely from rising in the morning. The mosquitoes were thick, buzzing in gray clouds and ringing in our ears at night, when things croaked and grunted in the blackness. The other men and I slept in a shack at the drill site, taking turns stoking the boiler to continue drilling. The far off bells of the churches in Beaumont rang in faint pastels in contrast to the huffing of the steam engines. And the drum of more rain.

Captain Lucas stayed in town at the Crosby Hotel with his wife and son, and kept an office at Meyer's dry good store. The captain would come down early every morning under an umbrella to examine the night's spoil, putting it under his nose and moustache to smell the secrets the earth had given up.

At almost 600 feet, the sand formations fouled our drill shaft and closed in on it, halting the bit. Our equipment couldn't keep up with it. We were frustrated and began to doubt ourselves. There was no oil, but there were more and more disgruntled investors. Capt. Lucas yielded to their pressure and hired a geologist from Austin to come down and doublecheck the site. The man, a Mr. Kennedy, confided in us that he thought that Higgins was an 'idle dreamer' and 'insane.' Everyone, he said, including John D. Rockefeller of Standard Oil, thought Higgins was a man of grandiose plans—yes, he was intelligent, ambitious, and self-confident—but he was also long-winded and downright crazy. He implied that because Capt. Lucas had gone in with Mr. Higgins, by association, he was just as crazy. Still, Higgins was convinced that there was oil there.

"Got to get down to it," he said, pushing his empty sleeve into the waist of his pants as he peered down the shaft.

Toward the end of the summer, Capt. Lucas was down to his last cent and could no longer pay me. But I stayed on, determined to see it through. By September, we were out of money completely and out of hope. We felt as if we could drill clear through to the other side of the earth and not find oil.

While we contemplated our next move, a hurricane rose out of the Gulf and hit the Texas coast, devastating Galveston and halting any thought of drilling at Beaumont. Out of a sense of duty, I went with a train of relief supplies to lend a hand to the sufferers on the coast. When I arrived at Galveston, I saw the outline of a crumbled city. We could smell the putrefaction of the unclaimed as we crossed the bay. A line of debris towered along one of the streets where the storm tide had pushed it. It brought back memories of the battlefields of my war years, except that the bloated dead on the beaches and under timbers and bricks weren't only young men, but women and children as well, many of them stripped of their clothes by wind and water. The little bodies of children were the worst. Rocking horses, stuffed animals, beloved pets, all equally lifeless in the debris and steamy air. And the quiet crash of the Gulf surf mocked all of it.

Buildings teetered. Second storeys of houses sat next to their first storeys which sat next to the pilings their builders and owners had thought would keep them out of harm's way. Families were separated, men from wives, wives from children, children from fathers. Over it all, a horrific smell that you never got used to. Identification of the dead was soon given up, and then burial was given up in favor of cremation. The night sky was filled with the light and smoke of the pyres. Somewhere in the dark, the sound of the blue-eyed ocean reminded everyone that it was both responsible and satisfied—for now.

There were no more survivors on Galveston Island, only the destitute and the hungry, and they were begin fed and housed and clothed. The dead were being buried or burned. The futility was catching up with me, and so when I received the message from Capt. Lucas requesting my presence in Beaumont, as our last investor was threatening to pull up stakes, I finally relented. I did not cry while I was on the island. It was of no use. But as soon as I stepped off the ferry at Bolivar Point, I wept like a small child. No one paid any notice. We were all doing it, suddenly breaking down under the weight of sequestered emotion.

On the train to Beaumont, two boys, one a little older than the other, were being escorted out of the city by a nun. I suspected they were orphans, and I overheard the nun quietly tell them that each was all the other had left and that with God's grace, that would surely be enough. I thought of my own brother, and I ached for the sense of family and brotherhood that these two boys now had, though it was all they had. The good sister said it would be plenty.

When I arrived at the Crosby Hotel in Beaumont, a carriage was parked out front with a driver patiently waiting in the buckboard, eating an apple with his arm resting across the backrest of the black-leather seat while he studied the sky. Inside, a meeting was taking place between an investor and his wife, and Mr. Higgins and Capt. Lucas.

As I entered the lobby, I heard a familiar voice haughtily saying that 'his man,' one of the foremost geologists in the country, said that they would find the devil in that hole before they found oil, and that he and his wife wanted their money back. He derisively told Lucas that he should go 'back to the salt mine' and that Higgins should 'stick with bricks.' When he chuckled sarcastically, I instantly recognized who it was.

I paused at the foot of the stairs and then quietly went up them one soft tread at a time. I had labored in the heat for more than a week without the benefit of a bath, and I was afraid my scent would announce my presence.

When I got to the landing that overlooked the lobby, I saw my brother and his wife. They, like the other investors, were demanding their money back.

Higgins said, "Now just you wait, Mr. Teague. I swear there's oil down yonder somewheres. We just ain't found it yet. Might be as much as a thousand feet down, but it's down there." And then he repeated his heavenly revelation. "I done prayed on it."

"Prayed on it!" my brother erupted with a fist pound on the table. "Then pray give me my money back, you one-armed scoundrel!" and then he yelled to Capt. Lucas, "And you! Dego swindler!"

I could see a flash in Higgins' face, the look of the younger man who had once shot and killed a deputy sheriff. But he subdued his fury, and the Sunday school teacher he had become calmly wrote my brother a check, though Higgins could not resist telling him, "Cash it at the bank here in Beaumont and then get the hell on your way, you faithless son-of-a-bitch!" Coarse words from a man who had found religion. I suppose he had misplaced it for a moment.

All other conversations in the parlor tumbled into a hush, then there was an angered scraping of chair legs on the floor of the lobby, and I quietly scampered to the window at the top of the landing. Through it, I saw my brother limp to his carriage, putting the check in his pocket before pulling himself up into his seat. The driver was in a daydream, but on seeing the two, he tossed the core of his apple away and got out to help Mrs. Teague. My former lover had become portly, and when she tried to climb into the carriage, it lurched in a sideways tilt. The driver kept her from falling out onto the muddy street. She smiled back to him as his hand inadvertently supported her backside.

When I went back downstairs, I found Mr. Higgins massaging his temples with his lone hand and Capt. Lucas with his jaw clinched. I told them, "We're all better off without them." And that, Father, was the truth. Still, we were left with no money and no oil and no prospects.

That was settled a few days later, when two men arrived in Beaumont, a Mr. Guffey and a Mr. Galey. They were experienced drillers from Pennsylvania who were, in turn, backed by the banker Andrew Mellon up in Pittsburgh. They drove a hard bargain, giving Capt. Lucas a small slice of the pie and Higgins, none. Higgins didn't seem to care. This was personal to him, more than money. It was a matter of honor and of faith. With the new infusion of cash, the project at Big Hill was brought to its feet again. That afternoon, Mr. Galey walked the grounds of Big Hill and smelled the air. Finally he plunged a stake into the dirt and said, "Gentlemen, right here."

His partner, Mr. Guffey, knew of some brothers named Hamill in Corsicana, Texas, who had the equipment and expertise to go further down into the ground. Using a rotary bit, they were contracted to go down to 1200 feet at a cost of $2 a foot. Within a few days, pipe arrived from Pittsburgh. Slush pits were dug to put the spoil from the drill shaft in. We drilled a little water well to flush out the drill shaft, but it hit a pocket of gas that blew out the water, and so we pumped water from a little creek a hundred yards off.

The Hamill brothers had never actually built a derrick. There were men in Corsicana with whom they had always subcontracted for that purpose. To make matters worse, the man they had hired for the Big Hill derrick, a Mr. McLeod, left suddenly and there was no one who had the expertise. And so I took up the task. We settled on a design that was twenty feet square at the bottom and five feet square at the top to stand sixty feet tall, a simple structure any cadet could draw. We bought lumber from the Beaumont Lumber Company and had it trundled to the drill site by a team of oxen. By October, the derrick reached into the sky and the drill bit reached down toward the center of the earth. We would stop at twelve hundred feet, oil, or the devil, whichever came first.

Eva

The 'one-armed scoundrel' Higgins and the 'dego-swindler' Lucas, as my husband referred to them, returned our money, though we never saw their partner, this man John Jones, who was described to us as tall and wearing an eyepatch. I suppose that my husband would have called him a 'lanky one-eyed son-of-a bitch.' I was certainly enthralled and, I must say, titillated by my husband's display of dominance, if not by his command of the English language. I found it rather arousing. Too bad his abilities could do nothing to quench me. I suppose it is the thought that counts, Mrs. Leonard. And I suppose I have always had other avenues for that. But let us not speak of it.

It was September, too late in the season to go to Europe with the money, so I pressed Mr. Teague to have Mount Teague razed and rebuilt in the new Victorian style. I was tired of this musty old house, filled with memories of former Mrs. Teagues. He was squarely against it, but I whined and pouted and sulked until at last we hired an architect, a Mr. Allen from Shreveport, who drew up plans for a castle-like affair with garrets and turrets and dormers and so forth. Demolition and construction would begin after the cane was brought in.

Junior returned from college in Mississippi and sided with his father, resorting to a display of nostalgia and melancholy. At last, we dismissed the contractor after only a day of work, in which he had taken down the old covered walkway that led out to where the ballroom once stood, the one that went up in flames with the prior Mrs. Teague. And so the old gal was spared the axe. The house, I mean.

My husband did consent to having Mount Teague furnished with electricity and indoor plumbing, and that new technological curiosity, the telephone. What a marvelous invention, Mrs. Leonard! Now I could use it to cast my spell and weave my web at treble the efficiency of before. Gossip didn't need to be restricted to the steps of church or chance encounters at Aucoin's store anymore. Why, now it could be introduced into the social circle with the lift of a receiver and a request to be connected!

Gossip has always been a favored method of mine. Though you may think of them as different as night and day, the principle difference between gossip and the Gospel is that people are more inclined to believe gossip. We may try and deny it, but it is a simple fact and one that has been the key to my advancement and reign over social matters here in St. Matthew Parish, always set in place with a simple, innocent preamble, something such as, 'well, it is none of my business, but—' or a well-placed pause and then a 'well, I don't know, it's just that I have heard—'

That winter, when grinding was complete and the improvements to our home installed, Mr. Teague decided that a portrait of himself in the central hallway was not enough and that he would like a bust of himself done also, with a fancy pedestal to put it on. I had long wanted a portrait of myself to go on the wall next to his, and we quarreled over which we would have done first, his bust or my portrait. With time, we had them both done, but, as you can see, Mrs. Leonard, we are missing both my portrait and his bust. But more about that later.

How I would dearly love to have the telephone back, madame! Financial strain has taken it from me, but I have every bit of faith possible in you to correct that reverse. Is there any chance we can hold the séance this evening?

Very well, when you are ready, Mrs. Leonard. If you will excuse me, it is time for my afternoon bath.

Ruthie? Ruthie! Draw me a bath!

Yes, Mrs. Leonard? If you need the telephone, Mr. Aucoin has one at his store, just up the Bayou Road. What in blazes would you need it for?

Yes, never mind then.

Faustina Templet

Bonjour-hello-St.Matthew-Telephone-exchange-mais-who-you wanta-talk?

Ma'am? Madame? Pardon, madame. You accent threw me off, yeah! Where you from, madame? England! Mais, I can understand you perfect, almost. Yes, this Faustina Templet. How you know my name? Yes, madame. I run the switchboard 'cause I can speak French and English just fine, me. Who you need to talk to?

You want to speak to me? Yes madame, but for just a little while. A call might come in the next fifteen minutes and I'm gonna have to put 'em true.

I see you callin' from the line at Mr. Aucoin's store. That's right, the telephone company had to switch off Miss Eva's telephone. I ain' suppose to say, no, but she weren't payin' the bill. She's broke, or *pas le sou,* we say.

My daddy used to work for Mr. Sam and Miss Eva. Me, I didn't know too much about Mr. Sam, *pauvre defan,* just he could get real *faché* on the telephone if things didn't go too good for him. Yes ma'am, mad is what I mean.

Hold on, Madame Leonard, I got a call.

Hello Mrs. McKnight. Mrs. Pugh? Yes ma'am, I'll put you true.

That was Dr. McKnight's wife, Miss Lillian. I was the one put the call true to Dr. McKnight when Mr. Sam—Mr. Sam Teague—got killed.

Hold on, madame—

Hello, bonjour Mrs. Waggenspack. Yes, ma'am, I'll ring Mrs. Singletary.

Madame Leonard? Yes, ma'am, I been get a lotta calls today from them high-up women of St. Matthew. They been lightin' up dis board, yeah! Now I ain' suppose to listen in, no, but sometimes a girl can't even help it.

Them women, Madame Pugh, the widow Anderson, all them women in that Altar Society and Garden Club and Whist Club and that Krewe de Jupitre, all them high-up women, they all *agiteé* about somethin'. Ain' none of em come out and say it, they only say, 'Did you get one? I got one! Came in the mail!' And things like that. They all shocked but won't none of 'em come out and say what they got in the mail. One of 'em said somethin' about one of them other high-up women but I had to take a call and I didn't hear who they was talkin' about. And it ain' right for me to listen in to other people's talk, no.

Yes, madame. Here come another call. Good to speak with you. I ain't never talked to nobody from England, and now I have! Me, Faustina Templet! Au revoir, madame.

Jack

Good morning, Father, and such a gray one, too. Let's see if the steward will bring us a coffee and a tea. I believe we were talking about my career in the 'oil patch' as some call it, weren't we?

Now that October 1900, we began drilling at Big Hill. The days remained hot, but the nights were cool, and then the days cooled and the nights were cold enough to drive away the mosquitoes. Geese and ducks returned from the north, and Al Hamill and I listened to them babble and squawk in the evenings against the sunset as we stoked the boilers that turned the drill.

I became fond of Al Hamill's frank company, and we traded stories as the drill shaft turned, though I mostly listened as I was reluctant to expound upon my past. Here is the thing about the oil field, Father. A man's past was never discussed, no matter how littered with debris, sins and sordidness and broken hearts. Only the present and the future were spoken of, for that was all that mattered. Things that had occurred previously were brought up only if they had a connection to what was necessary now. The only thing that Al would say is that he thought I was 'awful old' to be doing rough work like that at my age. I responded by trying to outwork him, and it was hard work, 'pitchin' hay' as he called it. Some of the men called me 'old timer' or 'gramps.' But it was Al who took one look at my eyepatch and gave me the nickname that stuck. Pirate.

We worked eighteen hour overlapping shifts, and I grew to enjoy the company of that easy-going Texan with a head full of common sense and a chest full of heart. Between lifting new sections of pipe and guiding them down, we talked of water wells and oil and the reelection of William McKinley. We were both William Jennings Bryan men, though we had not voted. We had been too busy. We often were so busy that we ate like soldiers or vagrants, with spoons from tin cans as the drill spun into the heart of the earth, down, down, down, slowly, slowly and we bailed out what the bit had digested and fed it more lengths of pipe.

At night, when we fed the boiler slabs of wood, the opening of its door flooded our faces with golden light. To the midnight crackle of the fire in its box and the hiss of its steam, Al said that once when they were drilling for a water well for a rancher outside of Waco, they hit a patch of oil. The man who had contracted them was incensed with the discovery. "My cattle can't drink oil," the old rancher had said, "nor can my thirsty family!" The man demanded that they plug the well and burn away the oil. Then he refused to pay them.

Al said there was a Mr. Cullinan who recognized the use for oil and built a refinery south of Corsicana to make the stuff into kerosene and then gasoline. He said there would be a great need for it, that one day locomotives and steam engines would run on it. Mr. Cullinan himself had come down to Big Hill earlier in the year and didn't think there would be enough oil there to make it worth anybody's while and that a man named Walter Sharp had drilled at Big Hill back in 1893 but could never get past 400 feet due to quicksand fouling the bit. Two brothers named Savage had tried, too, but without success.

Nor did we find success. A group of carpenters watched us as they built a barn across the field, surely thinking we were wasting our time like the ones before us. Beyond them, the trees took on the yellow, orange, and brown of autumn as our steam engine grunted among the rice fields and the pipe revolved and the bit plowed a half-a-foot wide circle deep into the earth. Captain Lucas came down frequently to examine the spoil for salt, sulfur, oil, water, anything to give a clue to success.

The days got cold as the earth tilted away from the sun and we pierced into the earth. One bright winter day, a hawk roosted at the top of our derrick, calmly surveying the adjacent rice fields and gauging the things to hunt and eat that might hide in them. He was regally concealed inside his feather coat and unconcerned with the slow revolution of the drill shaft below him. When the traveling block ascended to the top of the derrick with the next length of pipe, his wings stretched and gathered air and he lifted away into the intense blue of the cold sky.

I asked Al, "Do you think man'll ever fly?"

Al squinted up to the hawk and the sky, and then looked down to guide the new pipe onto the length within the well casing.

"Well, Pirate, I've heard it might happen." He engaged the clutch and the drill started turning again. "Reckon it will, someday." The new length of pipe turned with the others on their slow descent toward oil or the devil's parlor. I put my muddy glove to my brow and looked skyward. The hawk flew into the sun, and the intense light repelled my gaze.

By December 1900, we were at 900 feet, and Captain Lucas suggested we take a break for Christmas. We would resume after the holidays, but if we didn't find oil in the next three hundred feet, we would call it a dry hole. We would call it our best effort. But we would have to call it quits.

Being the only one of us without a family, I agreed to stay in our shack and watch over our operation. Al and Curt Hamill returned on the train to Corsicana, where Curt had a brood of four children and a loving wife who were waiting for their daddy and their Uncle Al. Captain Lucas and his wife and son departed to visit her people in Washington D.C. I watched them all happily board the train for home, to houses filled with the smells of cooking and the shouts of children and the welcomes of seldom-seen friends and relatives. And I envied them, I did. And that's a sin, isn't it, Father?

I stayed in the shack and celebrated Christmas alone, stoking the potbellied stove and cursing my brother, who celebrated the holiday with his blue-eyed wife and his children in his fine old home in Louisiana. I tried to rise above it, thinking of the suffering still taking place in Galveston where so many lost everyone and everything. But self-pity crept back in, no matter how I might try to drive it away. I was almost sixty and spending another Christmas alone.

I was glad when everyone returned after the holidays. On New Year's Day, the boiler was lit again and the steam engine gasped to life and the drill pushed its bit downward in a slow, insistent revolution. The iron pipe was especially cold, even though Capt. Lucas had presented each of us a new pair of woolen gloves. But my heart was warm to be among these men, part of what is now called the 'oil fraternity.'

At 1000 feet, the bit stuck in something, a crag in the rock almost a quarter mile under our feet. We retrieved the bit and then sent down another one, a new one that Jim Hamill had sent us from Corsicana. It stuck again, and we pulled it up again, dressing it with hammers at the blacksmith's forge we had set up by the boiler. Al inspected it, guided it to the shaft, and signaled up to Curt who was up in the derrick with the cable and traveling block. When the bit found the hole, Al lowered his arm.

More pipe went down, and suddenly it was as if we had hit the back of the earth's throat. At first the well casing rose up out of the ground, up through the derrick, past the cables that had been used to lower down the lengths of pipe. The surging pipe took the elevators and the travelling block and knocked the crown block off along with the smokestack of our boiler. Pipe went up through the derrick, breaking off in sections of three and four lengths at a time and falling over in a coarse metallic ringing. Then mud and rock vomited up through the shaft.

Curt feared our fires would ignite gas or oil, so he scrambled down from the derrick and put out the boilers. Just as he did, more pipe shot up through the derrick. It launched into the air and hit the ground with a resounding clang. Great iron lengths were raining down like matchsticks around us, singing loud metal notes as we scattered away from the drilling platform, our feet pulling furiously at the mud as we made our getaway. We crouched on the ground at a fence about a hundred yards away.

Another eruption shook the derrick, releasing the violence from under the earth into the sky. I flopped to the ground and covered my eye, afraid that I would lose it this time and be rendered completely blind. Rocks and dirt and mud were falling everywhere. I was sure the devil would crawl out of the shaft

331

and curse us all for disturbing him. We waited, and finally Al tapped my shoulder and said, "Alright, Pirate, better go see to it."

Mud was everywhere. We were terrified, but we approached the hole and looked down it. The situation had quieted, and so we grabbed shovels to begin removing the six inches or so of mud that caked the drill platform. No sooner than we had started than there was a loud, booming belch and a jet of blue gas. Oil began to gurgle out of the hole, in and out like respirations of the earth, until the geyser came in almost 200 ft in the air. Green-tinted black pudding tumbled down on us, but this time, rather than run, we shook hands and then we embraced. We were all oil-covered like we had been dipped in chocolate. Someone, either Al or Curt—I couldn't tell, for we all looked the same—yelled for Peck to run and fetch Capt. Lucas up in Beaumont. I recognized the voice as Al's, shouting above the spray.

"Tell Cap Lucas that Old Providence was with us!"

Peck took off up the road, and within an hour, a buggy appeared on the horizon at a full gallop, Captain Lucas driving it, holding the reins in one hand and his hat down with the other. He stopped at the gate and tied his horse to it. He yelled something to us we couldn't hear over the roaring spray, and then he ran to us. He was a pretty heavy man and was huffing and puffing when he got to the derrick. Al offered his hand in congratulations, but Capt. Lucas hugged him, and then he hugged all of us in turn, never mind the oil, saying, "Thank Got! Thank Got!"

By midafternoon, the whole town of Beaumont had come out on horseback and in buggies. The breeze gusted and sprayed them all, but it had the feeling of a county fair. The fountain of oil pushed nonstop and drifted on the breeze. That week every house in the town of Beaumont had to be repainted. The next day, just below a single sentence coldly announcing that bodies were still being found in Galveston, the *Houston Post* carried an equally terse declaration: "Petroleum in large volume has been found near Beaumont."

That announcement was in the Friday paper. By Saturday, however, word had spread around Texas and the world. Leases were bought and sold and traded, and derricks were built a jump-step apart and pipe brought in by train and trundled out to Big Hill, now called Spindletop, behind mules and oxen and the whips of muleskinners. Men came in from elsewhere, fields and farms and piney woods, and the town of Beaumont became the city of Beaumont. In a chorus of saws and hammers, buildings went up, everything from banks to bawdyhouses.

The pent up oil was released, pushing up out of the ground as fast as it could be sold, and then more oil was found and sold. Fortunes were made overnight, gambled away, and then made again the next day. Men who had never worn anything more than overalls and straw hats and boots walked the plank sidewalks in the rigid confines of new wool suits and felt hats and wingtip shoes. Beaumont and Texas and America were changed forever by this rocketing plume from the center of the earth, this sudden shift of fortune. There was enough money being made to provide for the rest of one's life, and his children's life, and his children's children. I knew that it would only be a matter of time before my brother and his wife would want back in.

Pinch

We dogs would never have spent so much time and effort on one hole in the ground. Whatever creature was under there, the men, including my master Jack who was now called Pirate Jones, kept at it for quite a while, enough time for the moon to cycle from full to broken in half to gone and then back, and several times. They huffed and sweated and stuck huge metal limbs into the hole to stir up whatever might be hidden down in its burrow. At night they lit lanterns as they kept digging, digging, digging, sometimes stopping to sniff the hole like we dogs might.

I was mildly interested, though I spent most of my time napping in the sun, unseen to them as they swapped more and more of the great sticks down into the ground. Occasionally they would whistle a few bars of a tune or one of them would tell a story and the others would laugh. And I relaxed with a tongue-curling yawn and waited to see if they could pry out whatever mole or rabbit they were after.

It was on a cold day that they finally did. The men wore heavy clothes to keep themselves warm against it. The iron limb in the ground rattled as it struck something, and I raised my head as I felt whatever it was deep in the earth begin to shake itself. Suddenly, the iron limbs rose out of the ground. I started barking as wildly as I could for the men to run, for whatever was under there was certainly something much bigger than they were and would have them as a meal.

The men must have heard me, for as the limbs lifted up in the air and rattled and crashed around them, they did run, as fast as they could, high-stepping through the mud that was falling from the sky. I barked and barked, run! run! run, run, run, run! and the men did run, holding onto their hats and at last falling at a fence. It was great fun, at last we would see what creature had been hidden in the den deep under the earth.

A black spout went up with the scent of sulfur to it. It was a skunk! They had alarmed it and it was spraying them from deep with the ground. *A skunk! A skunk! A skunk!* I shouted, running in a circle, but the men couldn't hear me, for I was a spirit, and even if I wasn't, it was too noisy to hear anything over the roar of the skunk's spray. It must have been enormous, as big as an elephant or bigger! If it came up, they would have to shoot it.

The men could never get the skunk out of the ground, but that didn't keep them from their happiness. They jumped up and down and shouted and did jigs with each other while the skunk's spray rained down on them. Later, they all cleaned up and went to town and celebrated with a meal and singing. And I was content, though unseen, under the table at the feet of my master Jack now called Pirate Jones.

If a dog pulls something from the ground, whether it is a bone or a mole or a rabbit, and another dog sees it and covets it, the second dog will challenge the first dog. He will nip at the thing and try to pull it away, even though the second dog did none of the work in uncovering it. It is a truth that applies to humans as well as dogs.

Eva

Yes, madame, as I was saying, it was a little after the grinding season that year. It had been neither a bad year nor a banner year, just average now that our old mystical oddball, that French recluse Monsieur Barber-whatever-his-name-was was gone and our impeccable timing with it. Mr. Teague was in his study downstairs, and I still abed reading the type of romance novel I have always favored, hidden within a copy of *Godey's Ladies' Book*. I was thinking how much I might like a Victrola to listen to on such slow days, when my husband shouted up to me from his study.

"Mrs. Teague, come and see this!"

"You come and show it to me," I answered back, as I had gotten to an especially sordid scene in my reading.

"Come here now!"

I was exasperated. I yelled down, "What?"

"They've struck oil in Beaumont. The swindler and that dego!"

Well, Mrs. Leonard, I put my finger to mark my place and ran down to my husband's study. There it was in the *New Orleans Times-Democrat*, the *Memphis Commercial Appeal*, and all the newspapers. That one-armed scoundrel Higgins and his partners, the dego-swindler Lucas and that one-eyed son-of-a-bitch Jones (of course, the newspapers didn't say it that way, those were my husband's names for them) had found oil and quite a lot of it. Higgins had gone from being an odd man and the butt of jokes to being hailed as a prophet. People with any sort of means were flocking to Beaumont and Big Hill, which was now being referred to as Spindletop.

Our error was suddenly and painfully exposed. I say our error, but really, it was my husband's, for he had allowed me to change his mind. If he had been a man in charge of his own affairs and followed his own course, we would have had more money than we could have spent in a hundred years. We sat and contemplated the error of our missed opportunity as the clock that that traveling tinker had fixed years ago clacked and then chimed as if mocking us in our misfortune. I quietly left the study to return upstairs to bed as my husband stewed over the blaring announcements. I was equally frustrated. I paused on the stairs, and before the clock could stop chiming the noon hour, I threw my book into the glass case of the clock and shattered it. We had to send for a man in New Orleans to come and fix it.

It took a day or two for me to cool off. I decided the best course would be to try to find our way back into their good graces somehow. I sent letters to Mr. Higgins and Capt. Lucas apologizing for my husband's hot head and theatrics and hoped that we might be allowed to reinvest at the old rate and conditions. The letters came back unopened a week later. The one from Lucas had an emphatic NO written on the back. He had guessed its message from the start.

There was nothing left to do but to go and seek an audience with this Mr. John Jones, the only one of the three my husband had not offended. Mr. Teague offered to go to Beaumont to help me, but as you might imagine, Mrs. Leonard, he would have been no help at all. This would take finesse, something he lacked more every day, which could also be said for his conjugal abilities. I told him to leave it to me, that I would get us back in good standing with my charm.

Jones was our only hope, the only one who might listen. And I thought he might listen best if we had our interview in person. In private. I did not tell my husband, but I would do whatever I must. I packed my finest in a trunk, including my most memorable of underclothes, and took the train to Beaumont. It was my hope to meet this man Jones and fill his remaining eye with sights that might entice him to admit me back into the fold and, of course, the money.

Oh, yes, of course, Mrs. Leonard. And admit Mr. Teague as well. Certainly.

Jack

Well, it appears the weather has turned on us, Father. The crew is left to manage in it out there on the deck. Just look at them out there in those yellow oil-cloth slickers and hats, their only protection from the gale and the waves. They're actually quite similar to what we began wearing that January in 1901 in Beaumont.

The oil came down for ten days. We had struck it big, but now we had to contain it. It seems that no one had thought of that. The whole town smelled like oil, bright, rich, aromatic, so much so that you didn't notice it until you went to another town that lacked the scent of oil.

The morning after the well came in, Mr. Cullinan showed up to breakfast at the Lucases' place. Mr. Cullinan was an acquaintance of the Hamill brothers from their Corsicana days. He bought adjacent leases from Mr. Guffey, and Pattillo Higgins bought himself back in also. Within a week, close to a dozen others had bought in with them.

The Burden of Cane

The well was going wild this whole time, the spray drifting with the wind. A lake of thick, black shimmering oil collected around the base, and throngs of sightseers and gawkers had collected around it. Capt. Lucas hired men to dig a levee to contain the oil and men with shotguns to hold back the people who had come down on excursion trains just to see the gusher. Railroad tracks ran adjacent to the well, and he was afraid, as were we all, that a spark from a passing train or a careless cigarette butt might blow the whole works to kingdom come. We had found our oil, all right. Now we just needed to figure out what to do with it.

Capt. Higgins took out an ad in the newspapers offering $10,000 to anyone who could cap the well. All sorts of offers came in, most of them implausible daydreams and unworkable schemes. The Hamill brothers finally came up with a plan and asked me what I thought about it. It was genius, an idea still used today from the design they sketched out on the back of an envelope in our shack across a field from a half-finished rice barn, both buildings dripping black.

The idea consisted of an iron valve, what they call today a Christmas tree because it sits up like one and is about the same size. We were fairly sure, but not dead sure, it would work. We sent to Corsicana to have the thing forged and a few days later, it arrived on the train in Beaumont. We examined the valve, and it was just like we had wanted it. Now we had to figure a way to attach it to the well casing that was sticking up out of the ground. It would mean taking off the top part of the pipe as it spewed oil, and then using a file to dress threads into the pipe so we could secure the valve to the stub. The process could raise sparks, which would be deadly if the oil or a gas flare ignited. The man at the shaft would be lost and nothing would ever be found of him.

Disappearing from the face of the earth is something I had done twice, so I volunteered to risk doing it again. This was met with protests from Peck Byrd and the Hamill brothers and Capt. Lucas. They said I was too old, that it would take the stamina of a younger man. I think also, Father, that they had begun to think of me as a kindly old uncle. At this point, Al Hamill stepped forward saying that since he was both young and single, he should do it. We agreed, though I did so reluctantly.

337

He put on an oil-cloth slicker, just like those sailors out there. Then he shook each of our hands and said that it had been good to know us and if 'Old Providence' deemed fit, he would signal for the valve to be brought down to the pipe. Then he waded out into the lake of oil to the stub of pipe and the plume it was ejecting. It was loud, and had been, but we had all gotten used to it. We held our breath.

Al used a diamond blade to cut off the end of the pipe and then a file to begin dressing threads onto the pipe. He was calm and methodical about it, like a man puttering in his workshop on a Sunday afternoon. One spark and the whole thing would have ignited, and Al wouldn't have had a chance, we'd never see him again. But he did it, under a relentless gale of thick, black rain as we watched and held our breath.

It took him most of the afternoon. When he was done with the file and the threads, he signaled for the valve to be driven down in a wagon. His face grimaced through the coating of oil as he hoisted it up over the metal stump, and I could see why they had urged me, at my age, to let a younger man do it, even though I was still fit. As the connection was made, oil spilled out of the joint onto his rubber boots and the derrick floor. When it was fastened, it began rushing sideways through the side valve of the iron tree. Men who were watching from that direction ran from the spray. Al began walking the valve around in a circle, onto the threads he had cut into the pipe as he screwed it down. The oil sprayed around like a merry-go-round, scattering onlookers as they evaded it. Finally, the valve was seated, and Al closed the side valve. The roar stopped and a cheer went up. After ten days, the gusher at Spindletop was contained.

And I tell you this, Father, that was the single most heroic thing I have ever seen, including my days in the army. Al marched back to us, stepping high and carefully through the lake of oil, file in hand, as nonchalant as if he had gone out to check on a stray cow in a muddy pasture. The crowd gathered around him, slapping him on the back and shaking his oily hand. The first thing he told me was, "Well, Pirate, believe I'll go into town for a bath."

Al got his bath, and then Capt. Lucas bought him a steak dinner at the Crosby House. After all, Al had saved him $10,000. Mr. Cullinan soon went to work constructing tanks for the oil and a pipeline to Port Arthur, founding an outfit that's now known as the Texas Company. Oil leases were sold and then resold as speculation in them took off like an oil well-fire. Oil had come to Beaumont, and ballyhoo was to come in right after it. I didn't know it then, but someone from my past would come in with the ballyhoo.

Well, it seems the wind and rain have picked up out there, Father. I believe we might retire to our cabins. I'll see you in the dining room for breakfast in the morning, then?

Eva

Well, Mrs. Leonard, the train ride to Beaumont began pleasantly enough. Spring was beginning to emerge from the cocoon of winter. I have always found early spring to be an especially erotic time of year, and I found myself contemplating how I might persuade Mr. Jones. Would I reason with him first and hold the idea of romance in reserve? Or would I apply feminine pressure from the outset and then innocently ask for readmittance while he was in the throes of ecstasy? The rhythm of the train lulled me into daydreams of passionate things.

At midday, we passed from sugarcane country and into rice country. My husband always considered rice farmers to be on a much lower scale than us. They stooped and tended an aquatic crop that grew in flooded fields and were one rung below cotton farmers, who were several rungs below us. We were sugarcane *planters*. They were cotton and rice *farmers*, the kind of people who went barefoot most of the year and wore overalls and Mother Hubbard dresses, people who kept goats for milk and fed chickens from the pocket of an apron. Yokels who went to town once a week in worn clothes, homemade and shapeless, and stared wide-eyed and slack-jawed at the sappy traveling theater productions that were presented for them.

We stopped to pick up travelers in one such outpost where a rice silo rose out of the horizon and loomed over a red brick town. The water tower that shared dominion over the town with the rice silo announced that the place was called Crowley. As the train eased up to the platform with a great release of steam, I saw that a crowd had gathered around something at the station. When we came to a stop, the people in our car rushed to the windows on the station side of the train. I confess I craned my neck to see as well, though I tried to avoid appearing overly enthralled with the spectacle.

It was an automobile, the first I had ever seen, with spoke wheels like a bicycle and a tiller to steer it rather than a wheel. A tall woman, and, I'll admit, a rather beautiful and well-dressed one, was helped from it and boarded the train. She had a sheer scarf tied over her bonnet and fastened under her chin. Her husband was equally handsome and well-dressed, as was their daughter, a girl of five or six. Though they were newcomers and strangers to the train, the other riders hailed them as celebrities or royalty. The man and woman waved through the window to the man in the automobile, who in turn waved back and blew kisses to the little girl. The little family settled into the seat right behind me.

The passengers in the front of the car turned around to see them, and it felt as though all of their eyes were upon me. Questions came from every corner of the train car. How fast could it go? Did it come with a cover for inclement weather? Could you get one in a color other than black? And the biggest question, did it run on kerosene or that new gasoline business?

"Gasoline," the man said. In fact, he said, they were going to Beaumont to handle some oil investment business, now that they had put in their rice crop. A refinery was being planned to distill the oil into this gasoline. 'Like oats for horses,' the man said, and the entire train car laughed, though I could only manage a pained smile.

Then I was treated to a hundred and fifty mile, six hour discussion of their newfound wealth, while their daughter kicked the back of my seat. I kindly asked the little girl to stop, several times. She finally did, but then she looked over my shoulder and asked me what I was reading.

"A book," I said.

"What's it about?" she asked. "Is it about princesses and dragons?"

Her mother leaned forward and looked over my shoulder. She read a little and frowned.

"That's not the kind of book that a proper young lady should read," she said to the girl.

I marked my place and put the book in my traveling bag and looked out the window at the rice fields racing by. As we headed west, we picked up more passengers at each stop. Everyone was going to Beaumont. Farm boys to cut lumber and drill the earth. Girls to cook and wash for them. And some, I'm sure, to entertain them. They looked out the windows of the train, rising in their seats to see the great Sabine, all the while the rice farmer behind me answered the other passengers' questions about the oil field.

When I stepped off the train in Beaumont with everyone else, it startled me how much everything had changed. The air itself smelled like oil. Some of the houses were splattered with it, and painters were hurrying to keep up with the job of making the town presentable. Also in the air was the smell of fresh-cut wood and the rapping of hammers and the rasping of handsaws. Sawmills snarled and screamed. Bricklayers buttered bricks with mortar for the walls of new buildings on both sides of every avenue. In the six months since we had last been there, Beaumont had doubled in size and then doubled again.

Teams of oxen and mules strained through the mud pulling wagonloads of pipe, often having to stop for each other at cross-streets. Off to the south of town, a forest of derricks rose against the sky, attended by tanks like enormous cisterns to hold all the riches. It was the sound and smell of money, and I was going to get us back in.

I arrived at the Crosby Hotel to find that there were no rooms, and boardinghouses were being filled as soon as they were built. Men slept in shifts, in cots in hallways and on porches, one getting up out of bed to work as another returning from work got in it. Everything was at capacity, and even the wood plank-sidewalks were full of men who had abandoned their cotton and rice fields to seek work in the oil field. Farm wages could not compete with oil wages.

I approached the desk and was told to kindly wait in line. I went to the end and waited as patiently as I could as people were turned away with a referral to a boardinghouse here or there that might have a room, 'though that's not likely,' the clerk added.

When it was my turn, I stepped forward and asked about the whereabouts of this Mr. John Jones, and the clerk said, "Old Pirate Jones? He's down with Al Hamill drillin' for Mr. Sharp. But the oil-patch ain't no place for a lady, no ma'am."

"I simply must see him," I said, annoyed at having this clerk do my bidding. "Is there any way you can send him a message? He is an old and very special friend of mine."

This, of course, Mrs. Leonard, was a lie—I had never seen this John Jones in my life and still couldn't tell you what he looks like. I narrowed my eyes and with another wink, I murmured to the clerk, "And I am just *aching* to see him again."

He cleared his throat and stammered, "Well, ma'am, um, Mr. Sharp put a telephone line down to their works, case they need somethin'. I'll put a call to him, see if'n he'll come up when they're done fer the day."

"Well, then do it," I snapped, but then I was able to recover and coo, "Tell him that Eva Teague from Louisiana has come to see him about an investment and other matters," I said, and with another wink to the clerk, I repeated, "*and other matters.*" His pencil paused in writing my instructions, and he looked up to me and my smile as I said it.

I waited on a divan in the lobby with my trunk while the clerk held the receiver to his ear and waited for Mr. Jones to answer. The clerk and I exchanged meaningless smiles from time to time, until at last I could see him speaking into the telephone. While the clerk talked on the telephone, casting a furtive glance to me from time to time, I began thinking about what this 'Pirate' Jones must be like. I will confess to you, Mrs. Leonard, that pirates have always populated my private *daydreams*, as I like to call them. Perhaps this is the result of the sort of romance novels I prefer. Nevertheless, I was entirely ready to henceforth populate the private *daydreams* of this man, this Pirate Jones.

Not only was I counting on securing a contract admitting me back into the bonanza—yes, madame, of course, and my husband also—but, owing to the sudden popularity of Beaumont hotel rooms and boardinghouses, I was counting on taking lodging for the night with Mr. Jones. I was wondering how he might have lost his eye, when the clerk replaced the receiver on the cradle and motioned for me to approach the desk.

"He said you'll have to speak to Mr. Guffey about it, ma'am. Mr. Guffey's got most of the leases now, he says."

I was directed to Mr. Guffey who was renting a house on Pearl Street. We talked business and got nowhere, so I subtly tried to steer him into a discussion of pleasure. He resolutely rejected my sly and delicate advancements, trumpeting that he was both a married man and a Christian man. And so, without a contract and without a room for the night, I had no choice but to return home on the evening train.

On the way back to the station, we passed the new businesses that oil had fertilized into existence, banks, ironworks, mechanic shops, saloons, gambling houses, and, of course, brothels. Night was falling, and the pretty-enough inhabitants of the assorted bawdyhouses were on the balcony in their nightgowns and drawers, calling out for the men to come and spend some time—and money—with them. I drifted into a memory of once being one of them, and my head turned and followed the girls on the porches and balconies as we passed. I watched them, and even turned to keep watching them, until one of the carriage wheels gouged a rut into the muddy street and I grabbed the edge of the seat to steady myself. The driver smacked a heaving flank with a crop, and the carriage jerked again as the horse pulled us out of it.

I looked up, and in the gathering evening shadows, I saw a mud-covered man on a horse that was a rich, shiny black, the color of oil. There was something familiar about the way he sat his horse, something regal and resolute, something that refused to believe in the idea of defeat. He was little more than a vague silhouette in the evening shadows. I tapped my driver on the shoulder to ask him to stop, and when I turned again to peer into the shadow, the rider turned his horse and disappeared deeper into it and was gone. We remained for a moment as my eyes searched the darkened lot, which was between a barbershop and a brothel.

"Never mind," I told my driver. We continued on and passed in front of the brothel. From the balcony, girls made eyes at the passing men and palmed themselves and called out to them, "One a you boys oughta come in here and see if you can figger me out! Betcha can't!" All the sorts of things we used to say thirty years before, though we didn't yell them from balconies, Mrs. Leonard. Shreveport was a respectable place—they had a city ordinance against it.

Below the balcony, on the front porch, a girl with a cigarette in her lips perched on the railing and rolled up her stockings as an older woman, likely the madame, lit the first of the night's lanterns. The girl blew out an open mouth of smoke into the pale light of the lantern and shook out the match.

Inside, the sound of a Victrola crooned a scratchy tune, a song sung by a nasally-voiced boy professing his love for a rather disinterested girl. As we moved on from the sound of saloons and conversation and laughter and the Victrola, I thought perhaps I might like one for Mount Teague. And as you can see, we have one, and I do enjoy it so. One of the few luxuries I haven't had the heart to sell. I trust that with your help, I won't have to.

Shall I put on a little music for us? Perhaps a little ragtime? And would you care for tea, Mrs. Leonard? I myself will have another cocktail.

Ruthie!

Jack

Yes, Father. Calm seas this morning. Have a seat and I'll have the waiter bring you some tea. When does spring usually roll around in Ireland and England? April? May? I'm looking forward to it, that, and a more clement summer. Spring has always been a favorite time of year for me.

It was the spring of 1901 when I saw her again, not even two months after we had struck oil at Spindletop. The cypresses and oaks and pines were lime green and the redbuds a reddish-purple, and the fields were sprouting rice and cotton and sugarcane. We had contained what was now being called the Lucas geyser, named after Captain Lucas, and the Hamill brothers and I had been retained by a Mr. Walter Sharp to drill a well on his lease adjacent to that one. But that lease wasn't the only one. There were dozens then, all probing the ground for oil. Beaumont had grown and was still growing. Along its mud-churned streets, a half dozen new businesses opened every day, and the adolescent town strained at its seams.

Our derrick was up, following the design of the first one, and we had drilled down a couple of hundred feet. Mr. Sharp had put in a drilling shack with a telephone in it, in case we had to order anything, casing, bits, tools, and so forth, or if a man got hurt, which was also becoming more frequent. We had an errand boy in there, what Al called a 'Fetch-it.'

Al and I were about to stab another length of pipe when our Fetch-it, a boy name Hobie, shouted that I had a call on the telephone. As soon as we were at a place I could stop, I came in to take the call. The boy put the receiver to my ear as my hands—and all of me, really—were covered with oily mud. It was Mr. Doughty, the desk clerk down at the Crosby Hotel.

"Jones?" he said, "Lady here name a Teague come over from Louisiana to see you. Asked for you by name."

I had an idea, but to be sure, I asked him what she looked like.

"Well, she's a looker, but a little hefty. Black hair—"

"—what color are her eyes, Doughty?" I interrupted. Behind me pipe clanked as Al engaged the clutch to turn the drill. Further in the distance, a sledgehammer rapped on a wooden peg a few derricks over from us.

"Blue as violets!" Doughty's small, crackly voice exclaimed through the receiver. "I'd say her best feature. That, and her skin's smooth and pale as a bucket of cream! Says she wants to see you about an investment—" Doughty wheezed a quiet chuckle like he knew a vulgar secret, "—and other matters."

And other matters.

Suddenly everything seemed so far away as my mind replayed those scenes from decades ago, scenes that were both cherished and unwanted. Every other sight around me became a distant shimmering, every other sound a murmur. The hammering of the sledgehammer on the peg was a mere tapping. On the platform just outside the door of the shack, the drill smoothly penetrated through the friction of the shaft, piercing the ground and driving down to the bottom. The engine huffed and grunted softly, the steam in the boiler whispered and sighed. Muleskinners exclaimed small shouts and smacked straining muscular flanks. Derricks rose wooden and erect into the spring-blue sky, a sky as blue as the eyes of a long ago lover, forgotten for a time and now remembered. It was all so far away, so dreamlike, the idyll of a spring day.

The voice in my ear said, *Jones? Jones? Pirate?*

I opened my eyes and took a deep breath and spoke into the hole in the box on the wall again.

"Tell Mrs. Teague from Louisiana that Mr. Guffey has the rights to the remaining leases. It's him she ought to see."

As soon as he hung up, I had our Fetch-it get the operator to ring Mr. Guffey.

"Why, hello, Jones," Mr. Guffey answered. "Have you run into any problems?"

"No sir," I said. "I'm calling to let you know of an issue that you might have coming your way." And then I warned him of the Teagues from St. Matthew Parish, using expressions like 'ten foot pole,' and 'avoid like the plague,' and 'nothing but trouble.' I told Mr. Guffey to warn Mr. Cullinan and everyone else, unless he had an enemy he wanted to get even with. To those people, Mr. Guffey might recommend the Teagues as partners and investors. And so I ruined the chances of my brother and his wife, and I confess to taking great glee in it, Father.

After another hour or so, the close of the day, I could no longer resist giving into my morbid curiosity. As the shadows lengthened east and the sun set west, I borrowed a horse from one of the men, a midnight black mare named Mariah, and I rode into town. I waited in the shadows near the train depot by one of the half-dozen new barbershops that had gone up in the last month.

Silhouettes of carriages paraded by against the sunset, and I looked into each one. And then, hers appeared, and she looked to me, and even in the fading twilight of early spring, I could see the same blue eyes. I was still covered in oily mud, a shadow among shadows. Our gazes locked for a brief second as she narrowed her eyes and tried to place me, tried to make sense of me. She touched her driver on the shoulder, and I turned my horse and descended into the night. That night after I saw her from the alley by the barbershop, I dreamed of her, and then I dreamed of her several times the next week, always waking in a cold sweat.

Mr. Guffey later told me that he had received Mrs. Teague and politely entertained her proposal but with no thought of accepting it. He said that he was quite sure that Mrs. Teague had tried to seduce him, coming in alone with a low cut dress, a good part of her bosom exposed. Mr. Guffey said that if he were not a happily married, God-fearing Christian, he would have succumbed to her charms, though he said she was 'a tad on the corpulent side.'

I knew that my brother would be persistent in trying to get back in to where the money was. They would send back attorneys who would battle the Guffeys and the Cullinans in the courts, and I might be called to testify. I was afraid that if I remained in Beaumont our paths would cross again.

Before I left Beaumont, I made sure of one thing. There was a list in those days, never written down but always consulted, of those who were to be shunned in the business of oil or, at the very least, admitted only at an exorbitant price. As a founding and trusted member of the oil fraternity, I saw to it that the names Sam and Eva Teague were always to be inscribed upon that unwritten list. And so my brother and his wife were left like the wicked banging on the hull of the ark while the rain fell and the water rose. The oil field had plenty of suitors when it came to opportunity and would have plenty more, but for now Mr. and Mrs. Sam Teague of St. Matthew Parish were pronounced unwelcome.

Eva

Good morning, Mrs. Leonard, or rather good afternoon. Sorry to keep you waiting. I seem to have overslept. Listen to the time! Two o'clock!

Ruthie! Bring me some toast and scramble me up an egg!

The old clock there once kept company with a bust of my husband which resided on that empty pedestal and my portrait in that blank space on the wall beside it. Both have departed Mount Teague, but perhaps if you look hard enough into the netherworld you might see where they are now. We were discussing our mistiming in the oilfield, weren't we?

I returned from Beaumont dejected and emptyhanded. It was a long night on the train, sleeping and waking to see my reflection in the night window. The shape of the glass must have been uneven, for it gave me a rather jowly appearance, so I would turn away from it. I hadn't the desire to read or even think, though I couldn't keep from wondering who the man in the shadows on horseback was. The more I thought upon it, the more I considered it was the traveling tinker turned failed sugarhouse engineer, the fixer of the clock there, my husband's brother.

I returned to Mount Teague around midday and found my husband poring over the day's news. His look questioned me as I appeared in the door of his study.

"It was no use. I fear a conspiracy against us," I told him as I went upstairs to sleep, leaving my trunk of seductive finery on the front steps waiting to be brought up by the servants.

Mr. Teague and I were left on the outside looking in. We retained an attorney, but he said that we had no case. So we dismissed him for incompetency and hired another who concurred with the first. We had clearly cashed out and had no claim. He told us we might wait for another time to reinvest, but he advised us to be careful about getting back in just yet, as boom certainly turns to bust. True to his warning, we would get in several years later, but at a premium and with little gain to show. And so in the meantime, we consoled ourselves with the enjoyment of spending what we had left.

To make matters worse, our daughter Missy was turning fifteen and discovering the opposite sex. She was taking on unacceptable playmates, far below her status as a Teague. We caught her sneaking out of her window one night, and rather than stop her, we woke Ruthie and had her follow our daughter to see what magnetism was attracting her. We found that she was consorting with some of the locals, laughing and dancing to 'fiddle-music' with the common French-speakers! Think of it, Mrs. Leonard! Some ordinary jabbering idiot with rough hands—they eat with their hands, of course, or that is the common perception. Never mind knowing which was a salad fork and which was a dinner fork! I wasn't about to submit the Teague name to such debasement! We had, and still have, our social standing to uphold, and the pinnacle of it at that! To risk it all for a boy with dirt under his fingernails? Unthinkable. She was naïve about social conventions and what was expected of her. It would have been a wreck to our standing for our daughter, a girl of the house of Teague, as it were, to become entangled, physically or socially, with such a character as one of the local French simpletons. It was ill-becoming a Teague to consort with members of that level of society, several rungs below us. I wasn't about to stand for it.

I felt that perhaps some time away was in order, so I arranged for us to summer together in New England, where perhaps she might meet a Cabot or a Lodge or a member of some other family of noble rank. She was an uncommonly pretty girl with a sweet face and my blue eyes. Her hair was the sandy color of her father's, when he was younger, but the rest of her features were mine. So luck was with her on that score. Looking so much like me, it was impossible that any male of any status wouldn't find himself enthralled with her.

The Burden of Cane

My husband, being a very vain man, had always wanted to have his bust sculpted in the manner of the ancient, learned men and modern heroes. He would often think upon it, quietly musing, "Why, even when I'm not here, I'll be here in marble, presiding over our affairs!" I would silently add to myself that the stony bust would have the same mental acuity as its model. But I didn't say so. I would save it as a barb for a later argument.

It just so happened that there was a man in New Hampshire named Saint-Gaudens who had done the likenesses of Lincoln and several of his generals and other important personages. Yes, madame, Augustus Saint-Gaudens, the preeminent sculptor of our era! We contacted Mr. Saint-Gaudens, and he agreed to sculpt the head and shoulders of Mr. Teague. And so we took the train to Boston and then New Hampshire.

The sitting was a tiresome affair for everyone except Mr. Teague. He sat for the bust, droning on to Mr. Saint-Gaudens about his political views and the unfortunate outcome of the late war, all the while grinning like a pirate, only to be told quietly by the artist to observe silence and keep still and please, do not smirk, sir. The sculptor dabbed clay on the mass that would become the preliminary model of my husband's head. Missy and I were expected to sit there and keep silent and still with him like a couple of nuns adoring an old relic.

It became unbearable, and at last I told Mr. Teague that his daughter and I would sail for home. He was so engrossed in his sitting that he clenched and unclenched his jaw from fatigue and said, "Certainly, certainly," to which Mr. Saint-Gaudens snapped, "Please, Mr. Teague, silence, sir. And do keep still." I believe my husband was so vacantly absorbed in what he felt was admiration of his noble head by the great sculptor that I could have told him we were going to the moon on a magic carpet and he would have murmured, "Bully!" like President Roosevelt.

I had been stewing there with a lovesick daughter watching my husband having himself immortalized. It was unfair to me that he should have both a portrait and a statue of himself in the central hallway at Mount Teague while I had neither. So Missy and I boarded a liner for Southampton, though I told her that we were going back to New Orleans and home. Otherwise, Mrs. Leonard, I would never have gotten her on board.

Underhanded, Mrs. Leonard? I believe that a very strong word. I was merely guiding the girl away from the sorrow she courted in associating with those below her caste. It was my hope that she might develop a little refinement and be cured of her lovesickness, which can be as debilitating as cholera. Perhaps she would forget whatever she found alluring about the boy. But, as they say, absence only makes the heart grow fonder.

After a week at sea, on a boat filled with English accents, she figured out that we weren't sailing for home and New Orleans and her mongrel love-interest. She kept to her cabin, moaning and complaining. Once, I caught her trying to have the ship's wireless operator send a message to Louisiana. Of course, I put my foot down, telling her that it was outrageously expensive and that her boy had certainly moved on to another girl, one more in keeping with his place in the world. She hit me in the chest with her fists and squalled, and the wireless operator had to pull her back.

For the rest of the crossing, she was absolutely pitiful, sitting in a downpour and looking out on the sea as the rain dimpled the surface of the water, or keeping to our cabin and weeping into her pillow at night. I began having to physically dress her and do her hair and insist that she come down to eat dinner. There might be young, well-off bachelors waiting as dining companions downstairs! She would do it, but then only pick at her meal. I was becoming afraid that she would grow gaunt and spare and become unappealing to appropriate members of the opposite sex. But her fork only pushed this way and that as her cheek rested in her palm. Once at dinner, a woman told her that she was quite lovely and would have her pick of suitors.

"That is exactly what I have told her, and that she should choose well, madame," I said.

"Yes," the woman said, "to marry well is very fortunate."

To this Missy burst into tears and ran out of the dining salon, disappearing up a set of stairs as a couple coming down them made way for her.

Of course, Mrs. Leonard, there was another reason for going to London, aside from trying to separate my daughter from her commonplace temptation. I greatly desired to have my portrait painted by Mr. Sargent. As I'm sure you are aware, he was the foremost portrait painter in the world at the time. I sent a cable to him on the ship's wireless that I would be in London for the month of August and that mornings were free for me, but not too early and that I would arrive promptly at eleven for my sittings. I was bringing a trunk of clothes and jewelry from which to select for my portrait, and we would negotiate his fee when I arrived and that money should be no great object as long as his offer was reasonable—

—*Ruthie! Didn't I tell you I wanted bacon? Come get this plate and don't bring it back unless there is bacon on it! Now!*

Now, then, madame, we were speaking of Mr. Sargent, weren't we?

As I'm sure you are aware, he was simply the best portraitist, painting the best people, the finest of Boston and New York and London and Paris society. To have one's portrait done by him would be the coup of a lifetime. Why, there were society women of New Orleans, even former Mardi Gras queens, who couldn't get a sitting with Sargent!

We arrived in London and took rooms at Claridge's, which had been completely redone a few years before and was simply magnificent. My daughter stayed sequestered there, and I left her and her droopy face and posture looking out over the housetops of London. On leaving the hotel, I told the man at the front desk that there were to be absolutely no cables to America from my room.

I took a hack to Mr. Sargent's place on Tite Street in Chelsea. I asked the cabbie if he was sure this was Mr. Sargent's dwelling, and he assured me that this was his residence, 31 Tite Street, and I paid him. He lingered for a moment, certainly waiting for a tip, but he soon gave up and put my trunk of potential portrait clothes on the sidewalk, rather roughly, before snapping his whip and trundling away.

I knocked on the door. There was no answer. I knocked again. No answer. I knocked and knocked. I had come halfway across the world for this, and I wasn't going to leave. At last, Mr. Sargent himself appeared at the door.

"Yes, madame?" he asked. He looked at me as if I had come to clean his house or sell flowers door to door. He wore a paint-smeared smock over shirtsleeves and pin-striped trousers.

"I am Eva Teague. I have come from America for my sitting" I said, extending my hand. He didn't take it, though I suppose it was due to the paint on his hands.

"I am afraid, madame, that I am already engaged," he said.

"Didn't you receive my telegram?" I snapped, and then I recovered my emotions and repeated more civilly, "didn't you receive my telegram, sir?"

"Yes, madame, but I had no way of returning it. I can accommodate you in the spring, perhaps, but after my current patron, I shall be off to winter in Naples."

We discussed his calendar and his fee, but in the end, he refused to clear out his schedule and paint me. And his fee was enormous.

The untipped cabbie had left without me, and none would stop to bring me back. And I was left to push and pull my trunk through the streets of London as the muddy scent of the Thames on the south breeze ushered me back to my hotel. After ten blocks, I finally managed to hail a cab. This one I offered a small tip in the form of a glance at my bosom when I leaned down to button my shoe.

My true errand thwarted, I was left with the company of my moping daughter. We visited all the sights, Hyde Park, Buckingham Palace, Big Ben. We picnicked by the Marble Arch and toured the halls of the National Gallery. Still, she pouted and sulked and pined away for her little frog prince. Her company was barely tolerable. At night, she moaned and cried into her pillow and wrote letters to this boy using as much French as she knew to keep the true meaning from me. It was all for naught, as I collected them from the front desk and threw them away before they could be posted.

We spent a week in London, crossed the Channel, and then spent a week in Paris. Each grand monument was met with nothing but pouting and huffing and eye-rolling, each new and unknown cuisine prodded suspiciously. So much like her father in that respect. We toured the Louvre and rode to the top of the Eiffel Tower, lunched in the finest restaurants where she insisted on using her French, *bonjour, monsieur, merci, s'il vous plait*, no doubt words picked up from her friends in St. Matthew. We ended our tour with a week in the mountain lake country of Switzerland and then a week in Venice, a rather smelly, fishy place that I did not at all find romantic, though the young gondoliers were rather exquisite.

At last we sailed home, landing in Boston. When we disembarked, my husband was there to greet us. He was in high spirits and had just gotten a haircut and smelled of sweet talcum. The bottom of the back of his neck was a fine, mottled pink from the razor.

"I have two bits of excellent news, Mrs. Teague!" he proclaimed.

The first of his good news was that the president had been shot and killed. Mr. Teague was never an admirer of Mr. McKinley. The second piece of excellent news was that Mr. Saint-Gaudens had completed his bust and was sending it to us in Boston. With this tidbit, my husband rubbed his hands together and then clapped them, almost like a child might.

It arrived in a crate with old newspapers and wood shavings as packing. He was instantly and insanely enamored with his graven image. I thought my husband's face, the one hewn in marble, looked rather concerned or perplexed. Constipated, perhaps.

"That's very nice, Mr. Teague," I said, which was about as charitable as I could manage, having been denied a chance to bring home my own graven image.

It rode home on the seat between us, stony-white and dense with a pompous look on its face. My husband kept his arm around the shoulders of his white marble other-self as if it were an old friend. It went everywhere on the train that we did. In fact, I'm surprised he didn't order it a meal in the dining car.

When we returned to Mount Teague, he placed it on the pedestal there, and we had a soiree inviting all of our acquaintances. At the appointed time, after cocktails and hors d'oeuvres, a velvet cloth was lifted from it and it was presented to our friends. Their looks were surprised and jealous, and then I realized it had all been worth it. The bust of my husband resided there on that mahogany pedestal until it departed Mount Teague a good ten years before my husband did. But that is another story.

Well, Mrs. Leonard, there is the half-hour. I can't keep my cocktail and cigarette waiting any longer. Tell Ruthie that I have decided not to have breakfast.

Jack

Good evening, Father. Pull up a deck chair and we'll have a steward bring you a blanket. Maybe a little hot toddy on a chilly night like this would be pleasant.

Pardon me, steward, sir, could you bring his holiness a blanket and the two of us something warm and bracing from the bar?

I believe we were speaking of the oilfield, weren't we?

Well, then. After the near-encounter with my brother and his wife, I took my leave of Capt. Lucas and Pattillo Higgins, and I moved on with Al Hamill to drill for another Texan, a man named Walter Sharp. But I kept the name John Jones. It was plain enough to bring with me in my disappearance. Our success at bringing in wells had given us a measure of fame and put us in demand, and it troubled me that my brother and his wife might come to town trying to pry themselves back in. Indeed, they had made a couple of inquiries, but the Teague name was still considered poison. I confess, Father, that I did all I could to keep it so. It was meanness, pure meanness. Perhaps a better man would have done differently.

The demand for oil and gas was rising as the world developed an appetite for it. The number of companies making automobiles grew weekly, and train engines were readied to run on oil rather than coal. Word was out plainly and loudly that there was money floating in black pools under the earth for men brave enough to go and get it. And come they did, amid the smell of mules and mud and woodsmoke and kerosene.

Men came from all around, from piney woods, farms, swamps, bayous. Almost overnight, the oil field contained a sea of men, many of them like me, men with murky pasts which were implicitly not spoken of. As long as you were open to hard work, no one said anything. If a man wanted to patronize the saloons and bawdy houses that followed the oil camps, no one judged him. If a man wanted to attend the camp revivals and listen to the preaching delivered from the backs of wagons, no one judged him. If a man wanted to do one of those one night and the other the next, no one judged him, as long as he was up for work the next day. The camps and hastily thrown-up towns were filled with the things that bored and lonely men pour themselves into, fancy-façaded saloons, gambling dens, and houses of assignation, and, occasionally, in a town here and there, a crudely constructed chapel.

We banded into teams and feverishly hunted the oil that slept deep under the ground. During the day, in the perilous work searching for it, men were maimed and gassed and crushed. At night, in resting from the work, men found card games, drinking binges, fistfights, knife fights, gunfights. Men would disappear after payday and be found floating in creeks and bayous days later, or never found.

But the work always continued on, in the heavy swelter of summer, the sharp edge of winter, and the in-between times, in weather fit for a church picnic. We tested the earth like a lover for her secrets, and when she answered in a heaving, emphatic yes, fortunes were made and bonuses were given. And then we moved elsewhere to probe her with gasping steam engines and hissing boilers, hoping she would divulge more of her secrets. Like bees exploring and penetrating a field of wildflowers.

In 1903, I turned sixty. I was working like a man half as young, but my body was beginning to whisper my age to me with each trip up a derrick and howl it to me with each trip down. The mirror constantly reminded me that my hair was no longer thick and sandy-brown, but grayed and thinned. There was even a little gray in my one eyebrow. My dreams at night were mostly things that had happened, not dreams of things to come, and often, I was visited in them by the young woman with blue eyes and, just as often, my father. Sometimes I dreamed I was flying, that the earth and its oil and its men and women could not hold me, and I would soar over it and see how small it really was. But sometimes my dream would turn nightmarish, and I would crash painlessly into a patch of cane, and my brother would appear in a parting of stalks and sneer, 'See, Jack? You'll no more fly than a pig.'

Well, that fall, we had just brought in a well for Mr. Sharp in Humble, Texas, and Al thought it would be a good idea to take a rest for a while, and in the spring we would move on to Caddo Parish in north Louisiana. Doc Morrical and the Savage Brothers were planning on drilling up there in what would become the Pine Island field. They had brought in the first well in Louisiana at Jennings for a man named Heywood, and hushed talk circulated that the next big field was to be up in Caddo. Money was good, and Al and I had taken rooms at the Rice Hotel in Houston.

That's exactly where I was when I first heard about it being done. It was a Sunday afternoon, and I was up in my room at the Rice reading the latest edition of *Scientific American*, an article about the Aurora Borealis, the northern lights. I would have much preferred reading down in the lobby in front of the fireplace. They had a Christmas tree set up down there, a real one, not an oil field one, and children and their parents were coming in on their way home from church to see it, all bundled up in their winter coats, held up by their mamas and daddies to see the ornaments at the top branches. I would have liked to have seen the looks of wonder in their eyes, but I couldn't run the risk of my brother and his wife, or an agent of theirs, suddenly making an appearance in town. So I tended to keep to my room as much as I could. Sometimes I felt myself a prisoner.

The bellman had just left with me a coffee service, a sterling silver pot with a fine china cup and saucer, when there was a knock on the door.

"Who is it?" I asked.

"Dang it, Pirate, who else would it be? It's me, Al."

I opened the door, and there was Al with the Sunday edition of the *Houston Post* folded open to an article. Al tapped it with the back of his fingers and showed it to me.

"Well, Pirate, they done done it," he said.

"Done what?" I asked trying to see the newspaper.

"Some Ohi-ya boys name a Wright flew their machine over in North Carolina."

I took the paper and focused my eye. And there it was. They *had* done it. Two brothers from Ohio, bicycle mechanics, had built and test-flown a flying machine on the dunes of the Outer Banks of North Carolina. The story was on page 37 of the Sunday *Houston Post*. The article seemed to approach the subject with skepticism, as if reports of the brothers' success were a hoax or an elaborate prank that could only be whispered, that men flying in machines was a tale almost too wild to tell.

So it was possible. I set down the article about the northern lights and read the article in the *Post*. They had flown four separate times from a place called Kill Devil Hill in a machine made like a box kite with canvas stretched over light wooden timbers with a rudder to guide it. It was propelled by a gasoline engine that turned two propellers. It might have only gone 120 feet, but these brothers named Wright had flown. They, mere men, had defeated gravity, if only for twelve short seconds. Al left me in the doorway to my room and went to the trainyard to see about our equipment. I read it again and again and put the paper among my things.

By the spring of 1904, we were in Caddo Parish in a little place called Ananias. It would later be renamed Oil City, but then it was just a former fishing camp stop on the railroad named after Ananias, the man in the Bible struck down with his wife for lying.   We were working with Doc Morrical and the Savage Brothers in the Pine Island field.   In our crew was a man named Alphonse Verret who everybody called Frenchy.

Frenchy was a squat and powerfully built man who came up from south Louisiana with his new wife Maude, whom he had met in Jennings where they had last worked. She was obviously in the family way, very likely a honeymoon baby. Maude Verret was a cheerful, handsome young lady with a round face and freckles. She cooked and did laundry for us, singing songs as she placed a hand lovingly on her belly as her other hand stirred a laundry or cooking pot. They were a happy couple waiting for their home to be expanded by 'two little feet' as the saying goes.

At the end of the day, she would have a meal for us and take our muddy clothes as we dressed in the ones she had just taken off the line outside. Then she would serve us, and we would talk over the day's events, which for us varied little, almost exclusively how much pipe we had put in and what sort of soil we had bailed out. Her brown eyes would meet the eyes of the speaker, and she would smile when we laughed and take our plates when we were done, scraping them out the back door for the pig that kept company with a milking cow. Then she would return and wipe down the table, pausing to put her arms around her young husband and kiss his cheek, and he would take her hand and smile. And we bachelors, young and old, would wish for such profound contentment.

One day Frenchy and I were at the top of our derrick guiding the traveling block over a string of pipe. We nudged it back and forth a little until it found the end of pipe halfway between us. He shouted down to Al who engaged the clutch and the chain-links spun it around. Frenchy paused and looked out onto the bayou and swamp and the distant shimmer of Caddo Lake off to the west. Before climbing down the ladder on the side of the derrick, I took a look over the scene and told Frenchy, "Not bad looking country."

"Reminds me so much of home," he said with another long look.

"Where's home?" I asked.

"St. Matthew Parish," he said. "Sout' Louisiana. You ever been there, Mr. Pirate?"

"I believe I might have passed through there, once or twice," I said, an understatement.

"Prettiest women, too. And I had one, me. Once. Before I met Maude."

"She must've been something then," I said.

"F'sure, Monsieur," he said, one of his favorite sayings. "Sandy brown hair, blue-blue eyes. Blue as the sky. Mais, she was somethin', her."

"What ever happened to her?"

"She was too high class. Her daddy was one of them high-up sugarcane men. I worked for him, drove his mules at grindin' time."

"What was her daddy's name?" I asked, though I was almost certain that I already knew.

"Samuel Teague. The daddy Sam Teague. They's a junior too. Ol' Sam Sr.'s a real *pas bon*. A no-good. Everybody hate that son-bitch," he said and he spat as if to get the taste of my brother's name out of his mouth. The spit drifted down, veering with the wind.

"I know him," I said, and then, "That is, I believe I've heard of him."

"Mais, you lucky if you ain't met him," Frenchy said, lightly pounding the cross-timber with his work-gloved hand in thought and looking up at the sky. "But that Teague girl was crazy for me and I was crazy for her. F'sure, Monsieur. We made up our minds that we was gonna run off, but she come down with that leopard-sy and her mama put her up in Carville."

His pause told me that it had once stung unbearably and still did and always would.

"But Maude, she's a good woman," Frenchy said. "She's real good to me. So I'm gonna be good to her." It had the air of a dutiful understanding, an arrangement that was by default.

He didn't say anything the rest of the day, the sure sign that something was eating him from the inside. Only at the end of the day did he say, "As blue as the sky up there." And I knew something of the emotion that must have complained within him.

Well, Father, I bid you goodnight. You've been a good sport sitting out here in the cold listening to the ramblings of an old man—

—Look there, Father. The northern lights glowing and wavering up in the night sky. I may stay out here on deck under this blanket for a while and watch them.

Eva

There you are, Mrs. Leonard. Would you like one? They're in that silver cigarette case with the T embossed in it. Very well, they're on the table there if you change your mind. Not the French ones I have always preferred, but I am in no position to afford anything else.

Have a seat. The weather is almost warm out here. A patch of sun and a place out of the wind serve nicely. Mr. Teague never knew I smoked. I had to go behind the old ice barn to do it. Now I can smoke wherever I please. We were speaking of his marble head, weren't we?

I believe the stone head of my husband's bust was equally as hard as his own. He kept scrambling trying to get back into the oil field, but it was a case of 'Johnny-come-lately' as far as that was concerned, and he was shut out. Many were the nights that I ascended the stairs leaving Mr. Teague in his study, looking over the newspapers at oil speculations. Meanwhile, his marble-headed other-self sat on its pedestal looking out into the shadows of the central hallway while the clock there ticked away patiently. That clock in the hallway—I have always wondered what became of the traveling tinker who once fixed it, my husband's brother. I'm sure he ended up leading some ruined life. It is regrettable, but it simply could not be helped.

My portrait once flanked my husband's, in that blank spot on the wall. His was done by some itinerant French nobody in New Orleans when he was married to the prior Mrs. Teague, Alice. She perished when the ballroom went up in flames. Tragic, yes, tragic, but if she had not died, then I would not have ascended to the throne of Mount Teague. So that is a silver lining. Everything always works out for the best!

It truly irked me, however that my husband had both a bust and a portrait and I had neither. His two-headed effigies scowled at me, and when I was alone with them, I scowled back. Why, once I pushed his bust off its pedestal hoping it would shatter, but it only made a hollow thud on the floor, and so I lifted it and put it back on its pedestal, though I scowled again and I spit in its blank, white face.

It was becoming the thing then among those who could afford it to have one's portrait done, and the one to do it, if you could arrange it, was Mr. Sargent in London. I believe I have told you that there were New Orleans Mardi Gras queens who tried to get a sitting with Mr. Sargent and failed and that I myself had tried and failed. But I was determined to have mine done, and I am not so easily thwarted, as I'm sure you now know.

In the spring of 1902 I sent a cable to Mr. Sargent requesting a sitting for later that summer, plenty of time for him to carve out a place for me on his schedule. After several days I received his reply, a terse, *AS YOU WISH MME.* I could almost hear the sigh in it, but for that, I did not care a fig. I had succeeded. Now the only thing left was to finance it. Certainly, Mr. Teague wouldn't have approved of such expense, let alone a transatlantic trip for such a large purchase.

I considered selling his bust and telling him that Ruthie had knocked it off its pedestal and that it had shattered into a million pieces. He would have been enraged at Ruthie but that would have been their affair. But I thought better of it—Ruthie might have cracked under his interrogation and rightfully put the blame on me. Then I struck upon another, easier plan.

First, I told Mr. Teague that Missy and I were headed to Europe again and I didn't want to bore him with the trip. As an enticement, I favored him with a trip to hunt bear with the famous Ben Lilly and his celebrated hounds in Morehouse Parish. Mr. Teague himself had long since become like an old mongrel hound to me. He wasn't much to look upon, he couldn't do many tricks, but I knew where he liked to be scratched, his pride, and I could make him fetch occasionally. And so I threw the stick, so to speak, to Mr. Lilly in Morehouse Parish, and Mr. Teague took his guns and shooting vests and merrily went to fetch it.

Now, in those days, Mr. Teague kept racehorses. He was quite proud of them, and I knew that they were worth something. So, as soon as he left for his bear hunt with Mr. Lilly, I sold one of them with the plan to tell him on his return that the horse had come up lame and had been put down. Actually, it ended up coming up first and winning regular purses at the Fairgrounds track in New Orleans and even went on to finish fourth at the Belmont, though under a different name, High Stakes or Big Shot or something like that. The change of name was one of the conditions of the sale.

The Burden of Cane

I now had enough money for my portrait, as long as the price had not gone up, and a ticket for a first class cabin on a transatlantic steamer. I didn't have enough money for two tickets, however. Something had to be done with Missy. I couldn't leave her in the care of the servants. I was certain that she would be beyond their control and that they were secretly sympathetic with the girl. But neither did I want to take her to Europe with me. I wanted to enjoy myself this time, not endure her sighing and eye-rolling. She would have been more lovesick than ever, pining away for her frog prince. She was about the age at which I had begun my amorous career.

I would return from town in my buggy to see them walking and holding hands. They would look over their shoulders and separate to opposite sides of the road. She was picking up words and phrases in that mongrel tongue. It was the worst possible news for someone of our position and privilege. And as she got older, it got no better. I thought a summer of contemplation of what it would be like to be a social outcast would serve her a good turn. I had a plan for that as well. It worked well, in fact, in the end, *too* well.

A leprosarium had been set up then in Carville, and once committed there, there was no getting out without a letter from a doctor. Of course, there was also no getting in without one either. I convinced my daughter that the teenage blemishes on her face were possibly signs of something more than acne and spun stories for her of girls in neighboring parishes who had found themselves in the same dilemma, a welp of red skin that had festered into a bulging mass that was diagnosed as leprosy. Perhaps Missy was surprised in my sudden interest in her welfare or perhaps she was worried about her good looks, being a teenager and being my daughter.

I took her to see our physician, Dr. McKnight, who was unwilling to diagnose her with it, he being unimpressed by her case and overly burdened with principles. I told Missy as we left that Dr. McKnight was good for some things such as sore throats and menstrual cramps, but that some conditions were far beyond his expertise. And so my daughter and I went into the city and made a day of it, enjoying a fine lunch at Antoine's and visiting some shops before consulting with a physician in the city, who, for the professional fee of ten dollars and a pint of gin, diagnosed her with it, a classic case of early leprosy. He signed the commitment letter with a flourish, ripping it from the pad and giving it to me as I handed over the bill and the bottle.

We took a steamer to Carville, as that was how one gains admittance to the sanitarium, from the river. I told her that the facility there had the best doctors and that they would surely cure it before it got out of hand and ruined her good looks and that I would be back for her when I returned from London. I didn't fail to add that she had likely contracted it by consorting with the lower classes, as they are widely known to harbor such diseases.

Honestly, it was my plan to retrieve her after she had learned her lesson. Yes, you might think that extreme, ma'am, but to be sequestered might do her some good, a chance to reflect on poor choices and the consequences they might bring. Nevertheless, unencumbered by both husband and daughter, I set off for England and a sitting with the finest portrait painter on the planet. It was simply thrilling to be a woman traveling alone.

Ma'am?

Scandalous? Yes, but aren't you also a woman traveling alone, Mrs. Leonard?

Immediately upon arriving in London I went directly to Tite Street for my sitting with Mr. Sargent. I found that he seemed to have changed his mind, but I refused to let the matter rest. I visited him day after day at his studio, until finally he agreed to paint my portrait. Perhaps it was the amount of money involved, though he was known to be a man of independent means. I suspect that he was worn down. And so I had won that one.

He agreed to begin the following day. We discussed dresses and poses and jewelry. He made a few sketches of me in different attitudes, looking straight on, or off to the side, a hand on the back of a chair or touching a strand of pearls around my neck. At last we decided on an off-the-shoulder gown of black satin with matching evening length gloves. He had me look away and lengthen my neck to expose the paleness, and, in the end, he had me hold the gloves in my hand. He sketched me thusly, and I became aware of his quiet appraisal. Let me say this, madame: being watched in that calm, unhurried manner made me become quite aroused. There, I have said it.

Day after day I came to sit for him, changing into the black dress behind a screen while he mixed paints. I made small talk with him and at the same time gravitated to the edge of the screen so that he might get a glimpse of my nakedness. But every time, I found him absorbed in his preparations, his palette knife kneading the paint into a new color. He was clearly uninterested, or perhaps playing the coy one, and playing it in spades. I couldn't tell just yet.

I dreamed of him throwing down the screen and ripping off his tie and waistcoat and all else and taking me and leaving paint splotches on my tits—sorry, madame, *breasts*—and feeling his beard on my neck and then my inner thighs. The long hours became agony until at last, I made a bold ploy by lowering my neckline to show a thin arc of pink.

He calmly dipped his brush to his palette and said with his monocled look, "Madame, that really won't be necessary. Unless you would like to sit for a nude portrait, which for a lady of your station would be absolutely scandalous and a blow to your reputation and place in society." He touched the canvas and added, "Really, madame, think upon it."

He had balked at the gate into the forbidden garden of a tryst. I was puzzled until later when I heard that it was widely known that he preferred the sexual congress of athletic young men. I do not fault him in that—it is what I myself have always preferred. And so our dealings became simply a matter of a portrait sitting.

Halfway through our sessions, as my image began to emerge, I remarked that he had painted me as rather rotund, with one chin too many. He ignored me and kept painting. I told him that he must fix it or I would not pay the balance of his fee, not one cent!

He shrugged his shoulders and sighed and paused and then portrayed me as younger and thinner, though perhaps not accurately. Over a period of two weeks, twelve sittings in all, he labored in silence. When he was finished, I had it crated and shipped back to Mount Teague with the promise that I would pay him the balance when I returned there. I believe he was glad to be done with me. Old goat. Old, bearded goat. I hear that it was just a short while later that, after a particularly difficult client, he stopped painting portraits altogether to concentrate on landscapes.

I toured the rest of the continent and enjoyed myself splendidly, drinking and flirting and wholly enjoying numerous *tête-à-têtes* across Europe. When I returned home several months later, the portrait was still in its crate in the hallway. I had several of the servants place it on the wall, and it was just as I had planned: my portrait was half a foot larger in both dimensions than my husband's! Ha!

This irked him constantly, provoking a snort whenever he passed by it. I, for one, could not look at it enough. He had captured my ivory skin and my delicate features. He had matched the blue of my eyes perfectly. He had also left off a chin or two, which also met with my approval.

Life was so much easier without Missy around. Her absence also proved to be a social coup. At the unveiling of my portrait, painted by *the* John Singer Sargent in London, I told my society friends that she had stayed in Europe where she had caught the eye of a nobleman and was studying at an elite school for girls on the continent. Actually, Mrs. Leonard, I was receiving letters from her at a rate of two a day, some saying she hated me, some saying she loved me, all of them begging me to come and release her. Her letters insisted that she felt and looked just fine. Then her letters stopped coming.

It was close to Christmas when I thought that perhaps I should go and fetch her, or at least visit her. The old doctor in New Orleans had succeeded in drinking himself to death, and so I brought Dr. McKnight up to Carville to examine her and pronounce her fit. By this time, her little frog prince had moved on to someone else. It was all for the best, for her own good, and, more importantly for the good of the Teague name. When I returned to retrieve her, with Dr. McKnight to vouch for her health, I discovered that she had escaped by jumping the iron fence. Good riddance, then. Little floozy.

Well, then, Mrs. Leonard, would you care for tea and music? Perhaps a cigarette? Very well, suit yourself.

Jack

Good morning to you, Father, after our rainy night. The rain was so much louder hitting the sea than on land, almost a crackling sound. Do have a seat in this salty breeze. I hope you slept well. I was just thinking about Frenchy and Maude's little baby. He must be about ten years old by now. I suppose, Father, that Catholic infants are still baptized as soon as possible? Am I correct in that?

He was born on a rainy night up in the Caddo oil field. Frenchy and Maude, being a married couple, had a cabin to themselves, and on that night we men sat outside of it on a crude wooden bench as the rain pounded on the roof and rolled off the eaves into a roaring curtain. We smoked nonstop, even those of us who didn't normally smoke, and we prayed, even those of us who didn't normally pray. We smoked and prayed and waited under the eaves to the drum of that deluge, listening to Maude becoming increasingly unsettled inside until Frenchy cracked the door and asked that we call the doctor. The drill shack had the telephone, and Al ran out in the deluge and called down to Mooringsport for Dr. Tillinghast.

The doctor came within the hour, vaulting down from his carriage and scurrying in under his coat which he held high over his head and his bag to shield himself against the downpour. He knocked hard on the door and announced himself, and Frenchy opened it, let him in, and shut it again. We men under the eaves strained to hear them inside under the roar of rain. Maude's voice rose in a furious cry, and we were silently grateful that we were men and not women. Then there was the sound of whimpering like the mewl of a kitten and Maude's crying stopped and we heard Frenchy crying in astonishment and relief and gratitude.

Toward sunrise, the rain slackened and we were ushered in. Maude held a small bundle and Frenchy was laid out asleep next to mother and baby. With the sound of the door, Frenchy's eyes snapped open. Dr. Tillinghast was rolling up his sleeves and putting instruments in his bag. He took one more look at the tiny face among the blankets and said, "Mrs. Verret, I wouldn't get real attached to the little fellow, I don't think he's going to live very long."

Maude stroked the little cheek among the blankets and said, "You wrong, *monsieur le docteur*. You wrong."

The doctor nodded as if he were allowing her to have a little useless hope, a hope that would not be denied nor shaken, for it wasn't merely hope but something stronger. Faith, perhaps.

Well, Father, the little fellow exceeded the good doctor's expectation, and he did live. A day. And then another day. And another. And another. He kept living one day after another like everyone else. So Maude, being a devout woman, and Frenchy, who was along for the ride with her when it came to her faith, took their new boy down to Shreveport so he could get baptized and avoid purgatory just in case Dr. Tillinghast was proved right. The well site was still too wet from the rain, and so we decided to halt drilling for a while. I took the chance to go to town with them.

When we stopped in Shreveport, the Verrets went directly to the priest at Holy Cross or Holy Name or something like that. While they did, I amused myself with a long walk around town. It was a Saturday, and the streets were packed with people in from the country for the day. As I passed by the Post Office, a notice in the window caught my eye. It was handwritten on a plain piece of paper and read, "Anyone who knows the whereabouts of Alphonse Verret, please contact B. Fenerty at her home on Crockett Street." I snatched the notice from the window and looked around before folding it up and putting it in my pocket. I ducked in the next alley and took it out and read it again. I walked the streets of town for an hour looking for similar messages in shop windows or on telegraph poles, but there were no others. The first person I asked knew exactly where *B. Fenerty* lived.

At the house on Crockett Street, I knocked on the door and was greeted by a woman with graying red hair and pale green eyes. I showed her the notice, and we introduced ourselves. She offered me a beatific smile and ushered me in.

"Mr. Jones," she said in a hush with a distinct Irish accent, "if ye would, sir, please keep yer voice down. My young houseguest just drifted off to sleep. Hasn't slept since she got here day before yesterday. Distraught and bedraggled, she is."

The old Irish woman put a finger across her lips that had curled into a pleasant smile, like an old painting of a kindly saint's benediction, and she ushered me into her parlor. I sat on her sofa while she went to the kitchen to put on tea. The house smelled softly of vanilla and the many years of things baked with it and the love they were baked with. Singing and laughter seemed to have seeped into the walls and were leeching out silently into the air again. In the kitchen, the kettle whistled and stopped, and she reappeared with tea and biscuits and jam.

"You caught me just in time," she said. "I was just about to walk down to the *Times* and put a notice in the newspaper."

Thank God, I thought.

She poured me a cup of tea and presented me with the handle end of the sugar spoon. "Poor dear," she whispered as she poured a little cream into her tea. "She appeared on the train from Houston, ragged and without a cent to her name. The stationmaster brought her over to me. I suppose I've a reputation for taking in strays." She laughed quietly to herself and to me. "The *garl's* hair was stringy and shiny from lack of washing, and her appearance was scruffy like a kitten brought in from the rain."

"What else do you know of her?" I asked. I had no appetite for tea or biscuits just then.

"Her name is Missy Teague—"

How odd to hear my own true last name. Like a glimpse of home from far away, a home to which I could never return.

"—her mother had put her away at the sanitarium in Carville under the false diagnosis of leprosy to keep her and this boy apart and make the boy move on, and he did, heading off into the oilfield. After months of being held with the lepers, she jumped the iron fence and came looking for him, her dear Alphonse."

She stirred cream into her tea.

"The girl's been to oil camps and sawmills, farmhouses, saloons, gambling dens, places a young lady shouldn't have to go, asking for this Alphonse. Now I tell you then, Mr. Jones, 'tis true love, and certainly that! Well, she was down to her last cent and heard that he might be here drilling for oil up at the lake. And so she appeared at the station day before yesterday. Scruffy, she was. Took some cleaning up."

She tapped her spoon on the ridge of her cup. Her tea was a light brown now. She turned her eyes to me. They were as green as absinthe.

"And so, Mr. Jones, I put the message in the Post Office window so it might be noticed, as so it was by you, sir. And so I ask you, would you know where her precious Alphonse might be, then?"

I was afraid I did, and I was about to tell her, when, from upstairs there was a shifting of bedsprings and the hollow sound of feet finding the floor and the brisk thump of them down the stairs. And then she was there.

Her eyes were just as blue as Frenchy had said, like violets, like the sky, like the ocean. Like her mother's. But her hair was sandy brown like the Teagues, like mine used to be. Mrs. Fenerty introduced me as Mr. John Jones and told the girl Missy that I had seen their notice at the Post Office. The girl's face lit up, and my heart shrank. She came and sat on the sofa next to me and took my hand like a beggar asking for alms.

"Excuse me, sir, I'm looking for Alphonse Verret? Do you know him?"

Father, there are times when the truth is so ponderous and painful that it cannot be shouldered. I thought of that happy little family, those gleaming proud faces gathered around the baptismal font on the other side of town. The new father with big, rough hands holding his son and the priest genuflecting over him, the exhausted but proud mother whose faith had endured through hardship. And so I again violated the Honor Code. I lied to that poor, blue-eyed girl. I snuffed out the truth she craved, a stunted hope that would not live long, a hope she should not get attached to. And I did it with a lie. I told her the thing which by sheer necessity had to be told as a truth, for her sake and for that new family. I told her that her beloved Alphonse, whom she had pursued so tirelessly those many months, was dead.

She sat looking at me in disbelief. In the thin, crushing ether before there can be any reckoning or grief, she told me she wanted to visit his grave, as if that would prove the truth to her. Then I told a puny, stunted truth and said he didn't have a grave. My lie took root and flourished. It sent out shoots and leaves as I told this poor, pretty girl that her love had been consumed in a blowout and fire at Sour Lake and there was nothing left to bury. And as soon as I had uttered that compassionate falsehood, I wished that I had told the hard truth instead, but the lie had already surrounded me and cut off my retreat. But one shattered life was enough. I couldn't endanger the happiness of the other three lives involved.

Her face collapsed in agony, and she put her head to my chest, and I cradled her as if she were my own child. She began crying, an intense, feral cry, sobbing so that my shirtfront became wet. Her hair smelled of lilac soap, so much like her mother's, and I felt as though I might cry with her. She heaved and shuddered as I held that poor girl next to me. But my lie could not be budged now. I felt it would suffocate me.

Her grief became exhausted, and she was able to ask me, "Excuse me, sir—Mr. Jones, did you say?—did he leave any effects? Letters, a locket? I once gave him a locket."

"I'm afraid not," I said.

She began crying again, and this time, Mrs. Fenerty came and sat next to her and consoled her with an arm around her, kissing her forehead and stroking her sandy-brown hair.

"I've always felt myself an orphan and Alphonse my only family," the girl whimpered into her lap.

"Maybe you should return home," I said, but when I did, it was as if the idea put a bad taste in my mouth. It was like asking Daniel to crawl back into the lions' den.

"Mr. Jones, I don't want to go home. I can't go home."

She was terrified at the prospect of going back to St. Matthew Parish. You can very well understand why, Father. She leaned back on the sofa and looked up to the ceiling, and she was seized by a fit of grief for the boy she thought dead. Her mouth curled and her blue eyes, tinged red, shut against the world and she shook again. Inside, I shook also. I reached over and put my hand on her shoulder in an awkward show of sympathy. When I realized it was I who was the cause of it all, I withdrew it.

Mrs. Fenerty gave her tea with a pinch of laudanum in it and the girl sipped it absently. When she became drowsy, the Irish woman put her to bed, and while she slept we discussed her fate. Mrs. Fenerty said that she kept the house for a family that was away in Arkansas visiting relatives and that it wasn't her place to accept boarders. We agreed that the girl should continue her education so she could get on with her life.

There was a convent and school for girls there in Shreveport that accepted boarders, St. Vincent's Academy. Mrs. Fenerty said that she would take her there when she awoke and turn her over to the Daughters of the Cross. I agreed to pay the girl's way and left a note urging her to seek knowledge, for that is the thing that cannot be taken from us and it would surely serve her a turn in her life.

I thanked Mrs. Fenerty for the tea and the company as I rose to leave. I complemented her on her comfortable and cozy home and wished her good health. As I stood on the porch, the woman asked me, "Mr. Jones? Are you a relation of the girl? When you were seated together, I could see a striking resemblance."

Another lie dribbled out of me.

"No," I said, "I suppose it's mere coincidence."

"Surely," she said as she thought, though I could tell she wasn't sure at all. In fact, the more I've considered it, the more I'm convinced that she knew of our connection.

"Well, why are you doing this, then?" she asked.

"It's the honorable thing to do. The Christian thing." I didn't say that it was because she was my niece. I couldn't risk being found out as Jack Teague and taken into custody on a twenty-year-old arrest warrant. And so, I turned and left.

At the train station I met Frenchy and Maude and the baby. They had named the baby Joseph Edmond Verret after their fathers. The church had given the little fellow a white gown for the ceremony, and there was still a little sheen of clear ceremonial oil on his forehead. He seemed a little more robust every time I saw him now. His color glowed, and he smiled at the angels in the sleep.

With a rush of steam and the slow turn of big iron wheels, the train back to the oil patch approached the platform. Maude and the baby stepped up first, assisted by the conductor, and then Frenchy, and then I did. The folded flier asking for his whereabouts poked its corner out of the pocket of my trousers, and I pushed it down into the darkness. And together we rode the evening train back to Ananias, the town named after the biblical liar.

Eva

Those are collard greens you smell, Mrs. Leonard, collards and cornbread, not exactly a meal fit for the banquet hall of Buckingham Palace or the Court at Windsor. Sunday dinners were once lavish affairs here at Mount Teague. Three kinds of meat, champagne, chocolates brought in from the city, sweets of all sorts, with port and dessert wine after dinner. And so now it is collards and cornbread for Sunday dinner. A little salt improves their flavor.

Ruthie? Ruthie! Bring us some salt! Now. We're waiting!

We once had a little silver table bell to summon our servants, but now shouting must do. Dear Ruthie. She is the last, loyal subject here in my sad kingdom. When our fortunes improve, which they surely will with your good help, Mrs. Leonard, I might release her from her debt, though then I'm afraid she would scurry off, and I would be forced to start over with new servants.

The Burden of Cane

Please, no need to say grace. That is only a tiresome recitation done for show. We haven't said grace before a meal in this house since I don't know when, though I never miss Sunday morning services. Now that I am without a telephone, two of the last places that I can hear and spin news is over the backs of pews beforehand and the steps of church afterward. And, of course, one must always project a façade of piety, madam.

This morning there were quite a few quick glances and smug grins behind fans and under bonnets. I wonder if they might have a secret on me. Oh well, I will simply launch a counter secret when I get wind of theirs. I say let the hens in the St. Matthew henhouse cluck all they wish, Mrs. Leonard, let them cluck until they lay an egg. They only wish they had my position, heiress of the Teague fortune, perhaps not presently, but it will surely come around again! Not to mention my looks, even here, at fifty—forgive my impatience, but when do you think we might contact my husband? This evening, perhaps? I admit to growing weary at the delay. Very well, Mrs. Leonard, but any time now will do.

Ruthie! Bring me a cocktail! A gimlet and a—anything for you, madame? A gin and tonic, perhaps? *Just a gimlet, Ruthie.*

I don't believe I've explained what became of my husband's bust and my portrait on the wall there in the central hallway.

Please pass the salt, would you?

Bust and portrait, gone away! The pedestal is beheaded, and the blank wall yawns. I suppose it is rather noticeable, isn't it? I would put a crystal vase of flowers on the pedestal. If I had a crystal vase.

Well, then, in those days, several of the families of rank in the parish had gotten automobiles, even though they frequently became stuck in our muddy roads. Sam got it in his head that he wanted an automobile also, and he got one, though he was a horrible driver and we had to hire a man to do it. Eventually, the man was let go, owing to our reverses, and Junior drove until we had to sell the contraption to meet a mortgage payment. We ended up buying a secondhand Model T, but that has also been sold.

It was the year Junior had finished up at Oxford and was courting a girl from one of the finest families in Mississippi. I'm sure it appeared to Sam Jr. that their meeting was all by chance. Actually, it was carefully orchestrated with a flurry of polite correspondence with the girl's parents in Bolivar County.

C. H. Lawler

I have always been a believer in arranged marriages. Why, I even arranged my own! Children are much too young to have any idea about these things. Matters of the heart? Ha! More like matters of the genitals, if we are to speak plainly about it! My daughter is an example of that, she and her French-babbling paramour.

I had gone up to Bolivar County in Mississippi for an engagement party. My husband begged off, saying that he had a matter to attend to. After a few days of pasted smiles and tiresome conversation, relieved only by surreptitious flirtation with the men of that fine old family, I returned home to find our new automobile. It was an Oldsmobile Brougham, shining like a jewel under the oaks. It really was quite exquisite, with tufted seats and a canopy and headlights for driving at night. I was very excited at his purchase, as we were quite behind the crowd when it came to having one.

I was thinking of driving to church in it as I ascended the steps to go in the house. When I took off my gloves and set them on the sideboard in the hallway, I noticed it. Or, rather, noticed it gone. My portrait.

My first thought, of course, was that one of the servants had stolen it. That is always the first thought around here, madame. It is just our way. I rounded them up, but none of them would speak of it. They would only gaze at the floor as I ranted. I was about to call the sheriff when, at last, my husband returned from the fields.

"Mr. Teague, someone has taken my portrait!" I exclaimed, looking at the line of dark faces, sure that he would join me in their interrogation.

"I did," he said, as he nonchalantly hung up his coat. "In trade for our new auto. A painting just sits there and stares at you, but an auto, well, an auto will take you places!"

He completely failed to see his offense. Then he calmly told me that he had sold the painting to a New York collector who was on business in New Orleans and that the New York man had a buyer in Milan.

Can you believe it, Mrs. Leonard? He had sold my portrait rather than his! And he justified it by saying that mine was by the renowned portraitist John Singer Sargent, and his was by some anonymous itinerant French nobody. I felt robbed. It was a bit like having one's soul taken from them. But, really, what use is a soul to someone like me? It is nothing more than an encumbrance, a useless encumbrance. Nevertheless, if you and those powers of yours can locate my portrait, I would certainly like it back.

I made sure that my husband felt my wrath. I beat him with my fists, pounding his chest and slapping his scarred face as the servants looked up from the floor and to each other and then the door, through which they gingerly evaporated. Mr. Teague serenely held my wrists and dismissed my tantrum, asking me if I wanted to go for a ride in our new Oldsmobile. I told him he might as well get in it and take the road to hell.

He shrugged his shoulders and limped out the front door. I watched him through the window as he spent half an hour trying to figure out how to start it, then another half an hour trying to convince it to go forward. Finally, it lurched ahead, swerving and narrowly missing one of our large oaks. He made a rather hasty turn onto the Bayou Road, almost upsetting the contraption.

When he came back after nightfall, I had cooled off only a little. The blank space on the wall taunted me with its emptiness, as did his sneering white-marble noggin on the pedestal. I still had anger enough to pound him with my words. He again said that my portrait was the only one worth something. To this, I sniveled and pouted. "You only wanted to keep yours because in it you are still young and handsome, not old and dilapidated like you are now!"

Of course it was a hateful, dreadful, spiteful thing to say, Mrs. Leonard. That is why I said it! And so you ask about the empty pedestal? I sold his bust to a second-hand man on Magazine Street in the city, one step up from a junk dealer, just to see how Mr. Teague liked it. Then I had second thoughts about it, so I told him that Ruthie had knocked it over in cleaning and it had shattered into a million pieces. Perhaps that is why she has stayed on, trying to pay off the steep price of a marble bust by Saint-Gaudens. Of course, she could not do it in two lifetimes.

Anyway, thus the blank space on the wall next to my husband's portrait. I am hoping you will also be able to help me find it, wherever in the world it might be. No, Mrs. Leonard, I have no interest in my husband's bust.

I thought also of leaving him then, or taking out a large life insurance policy. I did neither, though if I had taken out the policy, I would not have had to send for you, madam. I did, however, come very close to leaving him. For weeks I remained as mad as a hornet. I even went in to New Orleans to discuss the matter of divorce with an attorney there. My mind was changed by a story that ran in the *Compass*.

It was spring time, and the newspaper ran a story about a local sugarcane planter who had stumbled upon an object near the base of an oak tree. Upon unearthing it, he found it to be a moldering old wooden chest filled with all sorts of treasure. I asked Mr. Teague about this, and he only grinned as if he knew all about the chest. I couldn't be sure, but I thought it best to reconcile with him, lest it be true and I found myself divorced, literally, from this sudden change of fortune.

Mr. Teague was happy to have me back, his own 'crown jewel,' as he said, certainly in reference to the treasure he had laid up somewhere. To appease me further, he threw a large gala upon our reconciliation. It was an ostentatious display, and a certain sign to me that he had of course found the old pirate's treasure and was willing to spend it on me. And so—

Yes, I can have the carriage harnessed up for a trip for you into Napoleonville, if you don't mind being pulled by a mule. Do whatever you must if it will hasten our conversation with my husband.

Editor Lucien Braud

Well, Mrs. Leonard, how nice to see you again. Just getting the Monday edition set. Forgive me for not shaking your hand. Ink, you see. Part of a newspaperman's lot, inky hands and working on the Sabbath.

You ask me about Laffite's treasure. It's always been a legend around here that the pirate Laffite buried his treasure in St. Matthew and quietly became a farmer. We ran a story about it, oh, five or ten years ago. Let me see if I can find it here.

Yes, here it is.

A Local Legend Unearthed

The *Compass* has it on good word that a local man, a pillar of St. Matthew Parish, has indeed found Laffite's treasure buried under an ancient oak on his place outside of Napoleonville on the Bayou Road. He and a hired man dug it up and opened the chest which was well on its way to becoming rotted wood and corrupted iron hinges. In it was a veritable pirate's booty, diamonds, sapphires, and other precious stones, as well as Spanish doubloons. He has taken the prize and hidden it away in a safe in one of his outbuildings. And so the rich get richer.

Well, most people took it for what it was, but Miss Eva began coming around asking about details. I told her that I wasn't at liberty to divulge the identity of the lucky man. She threatened me, and, in the end, I'm fairly certain that she tried to seduce me, which ten years earlier would have been a temptation but at the time and her state of, well, personal dilapidation, was laughable and pathetic. I brushed it off as painlessly as I could. She's as desperate as a cornered moccasin, still able to inflict a fatal bite to a man or woman's reputation. It's a whispered secret how deeply in debt she is to the bank and every merchant in St. Matthew Parish. No one may speak openly of it, though, and I ask you not to tell anyone that I mentioned it.

I once made the mistake of including them on the published list of those delinquent on their taxes, something which is required by state law. A few days after it appeared, my wife found herself excluded from Garden Club. She was in tears and said that she suspected Mrs. Teague was behind it. I met with the Teagues and printed a front page retraction. A few days after the retraction was printed, my wife was reinstated.

Mrs. Teague remains convinced to this day that her late husband has Laffite's treasure squirreled away someplace, and no one can persuade her otherwise. Of course, no one wants to. I don't think she ever noticed that the story ran on April 1, April Fool's Day here in America, a day set aside for tall tales and practical jokes.

Jack

Yes, Father, about the girl.

I began visiting on Sundays, and on the Sundays I couldn't get down to Shreveport, I would send a letter with money and a note for her to go down to Hearne's and get herself a new dress or a hat or a bow or to go to Mr. Bath's and get new stationery or such.

On March 28th of that year, 1905, oil came in at 1556 feet. I say oil, it was mostly gas, but it was enough to spur a boom to drill more wells. Before long a rash of derricks bristled above the pines and cypresses of Caddo Parish and more men came in with the same attendants, barkeepers, gamblers, and prostitutes that we had seen in Beaumont. One of the men brought in a copy of the St. Matthew Parish *Compass*, and I began subscribing to it again. Each week it arrived at the Ananias Post Office, care of the postmaster.

The oil field wasn't the only thing growing. Maude was quickly pregnant again, and she was just as industrious with her housekeeping as she was with filling it with children. She kept a garden. She kept beehives for honey. She shot squirrels and rabbits and dressed and prepared them. Her hands were rough and strong and loving. Her smile was an unspoken blessing. She cared for her family and for all of us rough-hewn oilfield men, for she saw us all as her family. I had left that little family intact, and for that, I was happy. It had been the right thing to do.

The Burden of Cane

In the oil patch, Sundays were a day of rest for some and a day of recuperation from Saturday nights for others. I had never been one to spend long nights out, and I certainly was too old now to chase skirts and play cards and drink to excess and other such tomfoolery. I myself spent Saturday nights reading by lantern light, *Scientific American* or *Popular Mechanics*. There had been no news of the Wright Brothers since the initial word of their success at the end of 1903, and then only a newspaper article that carried a headline about them, *Flyers or Liars?* I along with the rest of the world had given up on the idea of man flying.

I turned my attention to the center of the earth. I had an idea for a drill bit that could chew through the layers of rock deep in the ground. I made drawings of what it might look like and imagined how it might perform, twisting deep into the hidden secrets of the earth. I spent nights at our forge while the rest of the camp yowled and prowled in the saloons and gambling houses set up for them and their paychecks. Frenchy, being a married man, would keep me company, our faces golden in the light of the forge while I beat the red-hot glow into a desired shape and sealed it in the water bath to a spray of steam. We would work into the night on Saturdays, at last turning in to leave the rest of the camp still working on the next morning's hangovers.

But on Sunday mornings I would rise early and bathe twice to get the mud and oil and brine off me. Maude and Frenchy would be on the bench in front of their cabin as I walked to the Ananias station to catch the train into town. Frenchy would wink at me and say, "Sound like ol' Pirate got hisself a *belle-amie*." Maude would shush him and smile with little Eddie drifting off to sleep at her breast and then gingerly wave to me so as not to wake him.

In Shreveport, I would meet Missy for a picnic on the grounds of St. Vincent's when she was released from the Catholic Mass. When the doors of the church were thrown open and the priest and his attendants waited for the congregation to file out, she appeared with her hand against the sudden sun looking for me. And when she saw me, her hand rose into the air in a wave, and she ran across the churchyard to see me. The girl was slowly coming to grips with her new life in the care of the Daughters of the Cross, and, though she never spoke of her dear Alphonse, I'm quite certain she continued to think of him. Just as I have always thought of her mother.

I gave the girl murky explanations on what I did the rest of the week, and she never pressed me on it. Nor did she press me on what had become of my eye. She asked only once, and I answered her with the unconnected truth that I was in the war. Then, on a bench on the school grounds, I would tutor her in mathematics and science or quiz her on her history.

I gave her presents on her birthday in May and at Christmas and times in between, usually something practical like a pocketknife or new pencils and a pen and a diary or a book on the solar system or how electricity works. Sometimes I would bring her flowers. She seemed to like those the best, dipping her nose into them and smiling broadly with a blush and a press of her cheek into my chest.

Bridget Fenerty sometimes joined us on those picnics and rides around town. I found that Mrs. Fenerty was actually *Miss* Fenerty, but in contrast to Frenchy's assertions, I was much too old for anything like courting and lady-friends, and I'm sure she felt the same. An old one-eyed, gray-haired, oil-patch roustabout like me? I also knew that I could never get close to anyone and keep my true identity, Jack Teague, safe. It was better to keep a safe distance as John A. Jones.

We talked about flight, though there had been no new word about the Wright Brothers or anyone else having done it, and we talked about Madame Curie winning the Nobel Prize for physics with her husband Pierre. We never talked about Missy's mama or her daddy, save once.

It was on one such Sunday afternoon in March, and the three of us were enjoying a picnic on the convent grounds. It was a blissful day, the perfect temperature, watching the bright green trees sway in the wind, brushing across the spring sky. My coat was rolled up behind my head and I was studying the uninhabited skies, as blue as a pretty girl's eyes. The tranquility murmured to me, and I was fighting sleep and losing and about to give in to a nap. The three of us had been talking about the level called the stratosphere, newly discovered by a French scientist. Missy wondered if God was just above it or within it and merely unseen. A lull drifted into the conversation and the distant sounds of playful shouting of the younger girls filled it, and then she said, out of that same clear blue, "Mr. Jones, you seem like my daddy except so much kinder, friendlier, nicer."

I smiled, though being kinder, friendlier, and nicer than my brother was no great feat. Almost anyone could have done it. Then she added, "Mr. Jones, why have you done all this for me?"

She was clean and calm and beginning to glow with hope, her sandy brown hair pulled up in a big bow. And her eyes were as blue as her mother's, with the same haunting shape. She was truly lovely in manner and appearance.

"It's the Christian thing to do, I guess," I replied, as good an answer as any.

Just then, she recognized a friend and took off to speak to her, her bow bouncing with her steps as she ran and brushed off her skirts at the same time.

"Just look at her, then," Miss Fenerty said, "still so much a girl, even though she's to turn twenty in May." Her tone became one of gentle frankness. "Why *do* you do all this for the girl?" The old woman was taking things out of the picnic basket and placing them on the blanket. She looked up to me with brutal sincerity and asked, "Tell me something, Mr. Jones, and forgive my bluntness if it offends you. Are you this girl's father?"

"No," I said. "Just someone, an old bachelor, who wishes her well."

She turned her attention to the basket again. "Yes. Yes, and forgive me, then. Would you like some apple pie? I've packed us some, with forks and napkins."

I had never considered it until then. I did the arithmetic. I had last been with Eva the summer before the sugarhouse explosion, in 1885. It was certainly possible.

Missy came running back, clutching the bow in her hair. She was as pretty as a Gibson girl, and I told her so. She smiled and blushed, and we ate and I watched her and the more I did, the more I saw my own mannerisms displayed, but in a lovely, feminine form. Miss Fenerty didn't mention it again, but I am sure she knew.

Evening came early, and I had a train to catch, so as our shadows crept away from us, we bid Missy adieu and she went to her quarters in the boardinghouse on the high floor with the older girls. It turned out to be the last time I saw her.

Well, there's the bell for supper. While I go up to get my dinner jacket, could you get us a table in the dining room, Father?

Junior

Why, hello, Mrs. Leonard. I was hoping to see you so that I could tell you that I won't be making the séance. Mama thinks it would be too upsetting for me.

Please have a seat. I suppose daddy's study is mine now. So many a day and night I would see him in here, reading, napping, looking out the window over the fields. I was just going through these ledgers now that he's passed on. My responsibility now. For the life of me, ma'am, I just cannot begin to tell you where all the money's gone. I'm afraid I'll have to go see my wife's parents in Mississippi and ask my father-in-law for another loan, though it won't be the first time. He pretends that it doesn't bother him, and perhaps it doesn't, but it certainly bothers me.

I met his daughter at Ole Miss. Our paths were always crossing, she always seemed to be where I was going. Some things are just meant to be, I guess. We courted, but it always seemed like it was all proceeding against our will, as if we were caught in a current together, holding hands not out of affection, but to keep from drowning. We had a lavish wedding in the manner of big Mississippi weddings, white gloves and table cloths and silver chafing dishes under green oaks, a receiving line that was a blur of people, studded with senators and congressmen and cotton factors and bankers and their wives.

My sister didn't make it to our wedding, nor did she make it to Daddy's funeral. She's been locked up in Carville for years. Leprosy. Mama says that it's progressed so that she can't have visitors or even correspond with us anymore. Too risky to spread the disease. I haven't seen her since I briefly spoke to her through the iron bars of the fence. She looked all right to me, but I don't know about things like that. Maybe she has it in some delicate part of her, hidden under her clothing. Regardless, we didn't talk long. The nuns came and shooed us away from the fence.

The last time I really got to talk to her was when I was in from college, in the days before she went to Carville. She met me at the door and was almost in tears. I set my things down and we took a long carriage ride so we could talk. She told me she was in love with a boy but that our mother didn't approve, but Missy didn't care, that love was that away. I told her to be careful of what might come of it because once, when I had gone to Puerto Rico to study sugarcane cultivation methods, I met a lovely girl who was the daughter of a planter there. I thought it was a fine match, but Mama put her foot down, objecting to my marrying and fathering children by a 'cigar-skinned mongrel.' She even threatened to have Daddy disinherit me. That was the end of that. Soon after I returned to Oxford I met the girl who was to be my wife. Yes ma'am, Oxford. The one in Mississippi.

Missy and I rode around for a while and returned to find Mama waiting for us. We had a chilly meal, the four of us, Mama, Daddy, Missy, and me. When the break was over, I returned to finish out school. When I came home at the end of the semester, I found that my sister had been put away for that terrible disease.

The last time I heard from her was in a letter in early 1906. She didn't use her name in fear of Mama, I guess, or maybe the inmates at Carville are encouraged to take on new names, but it was addressed to Dear J-B from your M-S. Those were our pet names for each other, Junior-Bug and Missy-Sissy. The strange thing was that the letter was postmarked from Shreveport, but I'm no more an authority on the post office than I am on leprosy. She said she was well and had met a man named Jones who wore an eyepatch and was so much like Daddy except a lot kinder and gentler. I guess her friend there, this Mr. Jones, was missing an eye from the disease. So many there are disfigured like that.

There's Mama coming in from her cigarette. I'll look at these ledgers later. Don't let her know that I was looking at them.

Jack

Well, there you are, Father. So I was telling you about the girl Missy Teague.

My trips to Shreveport were becoming frequent enough that I began letting Frenchy believe that I did indeed have a lady-friend, but to discourage him from coming to see her or know more about her, I told her she was very shy. He spent his Sundays fishing with his family or catching up on chores or napping when it rained. I'm sure that if there had been a priest nearby, Maude would have had them all at Mass. She made do by praying the Rosary on Sunday mornings. About once a month the priest would come up on Sunday afternoon to give communion.

That picnic I was telling you about had been so restful that I couldn't wait to return the next Sunday. I rose early again and stepped off the train at the station in Shreveport, picking up a newspaper and the new copy of *Scientific American*. The market had some nice strawberries, the first of the season, so I bought some, for I knew they were Missy's favorite. The sweet fragrance of them rose from my lap as I rode the trolley down Line Avenue past the fine new homes being built. At Stephenson Street, I got off to make the short walk to St. Vincent's. It was noon, and I checked my watch, finding it odd that the church bells weren't ringing. I looked for the bell tower of St. Vincent's through the treetops but didn't see it. When I arrived on Fairfield Avenue, it all became clear to me.

Where the church, the school, the boardinghouse, and the convent had been the week before was an immense pile of charred timbers. I stood there in disbelief as smoke meandered out of the seared wreckage. Just then, a man was passing down Fairfield in a gig pulled by a dappled mare. I asked him what happened, and he pulled the reins and stopped.

"Haven't you heard, sir? Burned down on Friday. It was in the paper."

I gave him the box of strawberries and pulled the newspaper from under my arm, and there was the headline. A fire had consumed the convent two days before, on Friday afternoon, the day before St. Patrick's Day. Chief O'Brien's crew didn't have enough hoses for the half mile to the nearest hydrant, and so they watched it burn, the church and the dormitory and all the pianos and books and the girls' belongings. The nuns had acted heroically to save everyone, and the girls were taken into the homes of the citizens of Shreveport. The nuns themselves had been taken in at St. Mary's downtown.

The man offered me a ride back downtown, and so I climbed in, and he flicked his crop with a snap and the horse pulled us away. I looked back as we departed. One of the workmen clearing the wreckage pulled at a blackened timber and quickly released it. It was still too hot.

The man and I rode, though I was too dumbfounded to say anything. He asked if he might have a strawberry and I silently displayed the box to him and nodded, and he took one in a delicate pinch. After several more strawberries, we arrived at the house on Crockett Street. I took my newspaper and my *Scientific American* and my strawberries and walked up to the porch. Inside was the sound of a multitude of children playing, the sound of cheerful chaos. Someone was rendering a hesitant tune on the piano, and small feet were drumming up and down the stairs. The smell of Sunday dinner, something rich and nourishing, seeped through the door and onto the porch.

I knocked, and the door opened and there was no one there for a moment. I looked down to see a barefoot child in Sunday clothes which he had partially loosened from his small body. From the back of the house, Miss Fenerty came quickly, pausing to lightly touch the shoulder of a little girl at the piano and say, *why, 'tis lovely, me garl, surely, but could ye rest for a minute, then, as I talk to this gentleman.* The girl dutifully stopped and put her hands in the lap of her Sunday dress as Miss Fenerty approached the door with a look of worry on her face.

"Mr. Jones," she said as she wiped her hands on her apron. Her concerned face said everything we both felt.

"Missy," I said. "Is she here?"

"Well, I was hoping she was with you."

The little barefoot boy returned and came to Miss Fenerty's side and held her leg, and she put her hand on the little boy's head. "Your grandchild?" I asked.

"No," she said, "just one of the children of the people I keep house for here."

I left the strawberries there for the children and spent the afternoon searching the town, knocking on every door, even the brothels, but no one had seen her. I caught the last train back out to Ananias. Frenchy commented with a wink that I must have had some visit with Madame, as he called my mysterious, and non-existent, paramour. I'm afraid I may have snapped at him.

I put ads in the newspapers, first in Shreveport, then later that week in Jefferson and Marshall and Texarkana, Monroe and Alexandria. I was afraid that the name Missy Teague would attract the attention of Frenchy or her parents in St. Matthew, so I only asked about a student named Missy who had not been seen after the convent fire of March 16, 1906. I received a few messages, vague reports of a girl about her age being seen, but the town had been flooded with girls as the boardinghouse occupants were dispersed into the homes of the city. It was like a trying to find a face in an immense crowd of girls, a needle in a haystack.

In the weeks that came, there were no more responses to my pleas. I never saw her again, and I have always wondered if she perished in the schoolhouse fire, or if the crisis forced a reconciliation with her parents in St. Matthew and she left for home. I think about her often, that sandy-haired, blue-eyed, bow-headed girl with the smile which was beginning to emerge from her personal winter. I don't pray as often as I should, Father, but when I do, it begins with a plea for her.

The church and school and convent and boardinghouse were quickly rebuilt after a fund was set up for it. Most of the town contributed something to it, but the biggest contributor was a mysterious 'anonymous benefactor' who refused to be identified. It was a source of much speculation as to who this was, most of it pinned on the usual nominees when anonymous, charitable things were done, all of whom blushed and denied it was them in such a way that humility was also added to their attributes.

It took most of my savings, Father, but it was my only hope, that if she were still alive and the school were rebuilt, she might come back to resume her studies and I would see her again. But despite the exhausting of my funds, she didn't.

I stopped going to Shreveport as much, and Frenchy never said anything about it. He likely believed that my romance had gone sour. In reality, Miss Fenerty had a family with a houseful of children to care for. But the real reason is that she and I had lost the one thing we had in common.

The years moved on without anyone's consent, and there has never been any word of Missy, the girl who might have been my daughter. I am now convinced she was consumed by the fire, just as I had told her that Frenchy had been. My lie to her about Frenchy's demise has been repaid to me in flames. And so I have accepted it, and I have mourned alone.

But life pressed on, and so did drilling into the earth. We drilled for a man named Walter Sharp, a tall redheaded Texan with a genial disposition who had an easy smile and laugh. He was a favorite of little Eddie Verret and the other children of the camp, always bringing sweets and chewing gum and so forth, exchanged in the palm of a Texas-sized handshake and followed by a tousling of hair.

Little Eddie Verret grew from a toddler to a little boy. From atop the derrick, I would see his small form playing in the yard while his mother tended the garden in a *garde-soleil* bonnet, her hands moving in and out of the green leaves of the beans and okra and to her apron and back again. While she worked, the little fellow would move among the stacks of drill pipe as his mother's voice, small and softened by the height and distance, warned him to watch for snakes. He would watch us up in the sky and then take a stick and place it on end and roll it with his hands into the dirt in a drilling motion. Once he climbed a fence and was about to transfer himself onto the back of a mule when his mother came running, gently scolding him to *garde-toi*, watch out. But his favorite thing was for me to make paper gliders out of folded up newspaper and release them from the tops of the derricks for him to chase as they leisurely floated to the ground in sweeping arcs and graceful curves.

"Pirate Jones! Ain' payin' you to make paper gliders!" Mr. Sharp would shout up with a Texas grin. And then Mr. Sharp would pick them up and sail them for the boy.

I was still working on a new and improved drill bit, sketching late into the night and sometimes walking out to light the forge as crickets rang and bullfrogs grunted. I shared my plans with Mr. Sharp, and he made suggestions, and we changed the design. On the day we tested it, we drilled double the daily depth we had ever done.

Through Mr. Sharp I met a man named Hughes, who had come to town and through the sheer force of his personality become sheriff of Ananias. He had the foresight to propose that the place be renamed Oil City to give it an air of respectability. He correctly understood that no honest man would want to invest in a town named after a biblical liar.

He took our idea for a new drill bit and he gave it an audience, he gave it investors, he gave it wings. Mr. Hughes knew the language of business, a language which I neither spoke nor understood. I was a science and engineering and mathematics man, as simple as that. But I was fortunate to have met Mr. Hughes, a man who spoke business-language fluently and translated for me. In December 1908, we received a patent for the Sharp-Hughes rotary drill bit. I requested to be filed as a silent partner, identified only as 'an equal third party.' It was Mr. Hughes' idea to lease the bits rather than sell them.

Suddenly, I had more money than I could ever spend. But I kept on in the oil field. A man needs friends and a man needs a purpose, even more, much more, than he needs money. Wells were coming in one after the other, though at greater depths than at Spindletop or Jennings, but in suitable quantities to make men rich as demand for the gasoline begot from it increased. It could not be got out of the ground and sold fast enough. I had figured out how to do it, and Mr. Hughes had marketed it. I had become a man of means again, though my true name was forever ruined. I would have gladly traded it all back for my name, the name my father had given me, Jack Teague. But John Jones would have to do.

In the summer of 1909, word got out that pearls had been discovered in the mussels of Caddo Lake and there was a Japanese man named George Murata who had found one worth $1500 and then another of equal price after that. Crowds flocked to the shoreline, wading in overalls and plain summer dresses, pulling up shells with the grip of bare feet or with hoes. Frenchy, Maude, and I would see them as we taught Eddie to swim in the lake's sandy shallows.

Mr. Murata was like an old time preacher leading his flock into the water for baptism. It was always a lighthearted affair akin to a picnic, with people crowding around and congratulating anyone who had found one, especially if it was a youngster. For a farmer who might make $500 a year if his land and the weather were kind to him, finding a pearl was a boon. But, nevertheless, the excitement was shared, even by those who had not found a pearl.

As the evening shadows lengthened, he would fry fish for us and we would gather around him, dozens of us, and he would tell stories, his Japanese accent tinted ever so slightly by his years in the South. He told stories of his youth in Japan and leaving there as a young man to become a steward for an American admiral, and how grateful he was to be an American himself now, among good people and the bounty of the lake.

Then one of the young people would ask for ghost stories, and he would tell the hushed, golden faces gathered around the fire the classic ghost tales from his youth in Japan and end with the story of the *Mittie Stephens* which had burned out there across the lake many, many years ago with a great number of people perishing. He said that on moonlight nights when the wind was still, he would hear a distant tapping that grew louder, loud enough to rouse him out of bed. A wind would push up from the still of the night from the south, *always south*, he would say with a finger extended, blowing across the lake. He said that from the dock of his camp, he would hear the drone of a steamboat whistle. Then Murata's folded upper eyelids would sink over his eyes and he would turn his face up into the darkness as the embers floated up, and he moaned the plaintive notes.

Small children would crawl into their mother's laps, including little Eddie. As the fire burned down to coals on those Sunday evenings, the crowds went back to rest up for a week in their fields and, for us, a week in the oil patch. Children slept wedged between their parents on wagon buckboards and Model T seats.

Monday mornings always found me manning the drilling platform or ascending the ladder of the derrick and nudging a traveling block into place over a segment of pipe listening to the gasping of the steam engine and the other men's short-whistled bursts of message or mere song. The oil patch was all I knew now. I also knew that I didn't want to die in the oil patch. But inertia has a way of holding us to what we know and keeping us from what we would like to know.

At the top of every derrick, I would look up to see the birds flying below me. I still dreamed of soaring with them one day. In August of 1908, almost five years from that day at Kitty Hawk, the Wrights were finally believed when they demonstrated flight in front of hundreds of thousands of Parisians. That same summer, an American named Glenn Curtiss flew close to a mile to win the *Scientific American* trophy. Soon others were duplicating their results. The following summer, 1909, the first summer of the Caddo Lake pearl rush, a Frenchman named Bleriot became the first to fly across the English Channel. A Brazilian named Santos-Dumont was designing aeroplanes and flying them over his adopted home, France. The empty, waiting pages of my scrapbook began to fill up. And then came the day I saw it for myself.

It appeared on an autumn day in 1910. We heard it before we saw it. At first we thought it was the growl of a bobcat or the snarl of one of the engines across the oil field, but it continued on, low and guttural, increasing in pitch and clarity. Everyone stopped what they were doing and looked up, all of us with our hands to our brow. Clutches were disengaged and drill pipe stopped turning. Maude came out of the cabin and looked up, holding their second child, Monique, on her hip. We recognized that it was the sputter and whine of an engine like an automobile. And then it appeared from over the tops of the cypresses. It was an airplane, droning a single monotonous note high above the mechanical sonnet of the oil field.

"Garde donc ça," Frenchy said under his breath, and I replied with the English version of it under my breath, "Look over there." We had all picked up snippets of each other's lexicon, exclamations, musings, curse words. The pilot wore goggles, but waved to us and gave us a thumbs up and dipped a wing. He circled our outcropping several times. It was a two-winged thing, simply a framework of struts and wires. We shouted and cheered and waved our hats in the air at the pilot, who flew on, no longer concerned with us. He became a distant, droning speck away out over the tree line, and then he was gone, leaving me behind, a prisoner of the earth again.

From then on, Eddie began playing with an airplane made from two crossed sticks which also functioned as a sword depending on how he held it. Frenchy erected the boy a swing, a simple plank held up by a tree limb with old drilling cable, and now the boy held his arms out as he swung up and out and back, his lips making the noise of an engine. He kept his eyes to the sky, just like I did.

That winter, the end of 1910, we were given the week off for the holidays, and I went to New Orleans. There was to be an aviation tournament there to run until January 2nd, with racing and a reported $10,000 in prizes. I was as anxious as a child waiting on Santa Claus. I arrived in town on the train a few days before Christmas and took a nice room at the St. Charles Hotel and ate chateaubriand at Arnaud's. I could afford it now.

From the moment the aeroplanes began to arrive—by train—the city newspapers could write of nothing else, particularly an American of French Canadian descent named John Moisant. His name and fluent French captured the affection of the city, as did his habit of flying with a kitten named Mademoiselle Fifi, or sometimes, Paris-Londres, named after his flight from Paris to London. Putting himself further into the hearts and starry eyes of New Orleanians, on arriving he made an unscheduled flight of over forty-five minutes, breaking the world's record for longest flight over a city.

The Burden of Cane

That week, the last of 1910, hordes of people, and I among them, took the streetcars out to City Park to watch what the papers called 'birdmen' race their aeroplanes against automobiles and perform stunts and break records for altitude and duration. There was talk of allowing those lucky enough to be selected to go up for rides with the aviators at the conclusion of the show on January 2nd. I hoped and prayed it would be me, a man of almost seventy behaving like a boy in knee-pants a fraction of that age. At night, I couldn't resist putting my head out of the window of my hotel room and watching the moon drift among the clouds, glowing white in the night sky.

The tournament came to an abrupt and tragic end on New Year's Eve when the city's darling, John Moisant, crashed just outside of the city in Harahan trying to break the record for longest continuous flight. He had made a hard landing and been ejected from his plane. They scooped him up and rushed him into town to the Charity Hospital, but he was dead when he got there. The papers said it was a broken neck.

The city of New Orleans developed a broken heart. Everything was cancelled, and everyone went home with the very real sense that Gravity does not give up so easily to men and that she will eventually claim us for her own. I returned to Oil City with my scrapbook filled. On the last page was the obituary of John B. Moisant, with a picture of Mademoiselle Fifi on his shoulder.

I returned to the humdrum and the commonplace. On a cold, gray, north Louisiana day, we were drilling on the No. 6 well for Producers, which was Mr. Sharp's company. We had just put on another length of pipe and set it turning and twisting slowly down into the earth. I was looking up into the sky, thinking of what it must be like to pierce a cloud.

"Well, Pirate," Frenchy said, "You never guess who I saw down at Peggy's over Reno Hill."

"Who's that?" I said with little interest as I tried to imagine how dense a cloud might be.

"That Ol' pas-bon."

"Who's that?" I asked as I looked down to find a rung on the ladder with my boot. My head was still someplace in the clouds.

"That sumbitch Sam Teague."

I paused halfway down the ladder.

"Don't say."

"F'sure, Monsieur," he said as he put his foot on the top of the ladder and waited for me to move down.

I realized what he was saying. My brother had found me, here in an oil patch in the middle of nowhere two hundred miles away. I gathered myself. He had come for me, and if he could find me here, he could find me anywhere. But I tried not to show concern to Frenchy.

"He have much to say?" I asked as I waited for him on the ground.

"Mais, nothin'. Nothin' at all. Just sat there with that same ol' *canaille grimace* on his face."

"You think he's still there?" I asked.

"Oh, I don't think he's goin' nowhere, no."

After supper and then a shot of whiskey, both of which I assumed might be my last, I looked through my satchel and found my revolver. I would not run again, I didn't care if it meant a jail cell or a bullet or a noose. Time for running was over. I waited until nightfall.

Well, here is our claret, Father. Cheers.

Eva

Good morning, Mrs. Leonard. It is still morning, isn't it? Yes, ten o'clock. I rarely rise so early.

I was thinking of going into Thibodaux to see the matinee of the new Mary Pickford feature, "Rags," it's called. The ones with Mary Pickford are my favorite, the plucky young heroine much like me in my younger years, both beautiful and intrepid, forced to weather difficult circumstances. The price is only a nickel in the afternoon, a novelty that is well within my reach. I have always loved the picture show, especially matinees, though I prefer to attend in New Orleans where I might be anonymous. Alas, madame, I can no longer afford the train-fare into the city and must take whatever the local theaters offer.

Aside from the feature, a movie theater is an excellent place to engage in good old fashioned schoolgirl flirting. Something about being in the dark seated near an anonymous gentleman, I suppose, and the silent intimacy. A good place for an exchanged glance and a sly smile or the quick pursed lips of a telegraphed kiss in the dim light and then a return of one's gaze to the screen.

I see that my son has been looking through the ledgers in his late father's study. Did he say if he found anything of interest? I ought to burn them before he does.

Ruthie? Ruthie! Gather some old boxes. We'll have to go through Marse Sam's study later.

My son is a bright enough boy, always keen on science and so forth. I have told him more than once that it's time he put away those boyish notions of automobiles and aviation and concentrate on the business of agriculture. Since we have been shunned by the oil industry, sugarcane is where our future income lies. As it always has, madame, as it always has.

Even though Sam Jr. is a father now, I refuse to be called grandmother or any permutation of it. His son, Sam the third, who is called Trey—*not my grandson, mind you, but my son's son*—was instructed since his first quizzical syllables to call me Mrs. Teague. Of course, he promptly corrupted it into Middie Tee, or just Tee, the local French term for 'little' or 'dear.' 'Dear' I have never been, 'little' is what I once was. I suppose I will have to bear it. Little Trey and my daughter-in-law are in Mississippi at her mother's. Junior's wife and I have never gotten along, and she keeps to their room when she's here. As for little Trey, I'm afraid I have as much natural affection for grandchildren as I had for my own, which is to say, not much. You asked for the truth and there you have it, madame.

When he's here, the little fellow plays by himself a lot, as his father, my son, spends a lot of time riding horses and automobiles. I suspect my son is financed by an overindulgent father-in-law. But I don't say it in the way of a complaint. Mr. Wilkerson has come to our rescue here more than once, enough to keep me from biting the hand that feeds us on occasion.

I'm sure little Trey will come to have the same fascination with the old ice barn that his father always had when he was a boy, always playing around it and poking through its ruins as if it were a relic of an ancient city. I have a strong suspicion that the ice barn is hiding something, and I've been through it several times but there is no safe or any other repository for a pirate's treasure. My husband did, however, give me this sapphire pendant which I am quite sure is part of Monsieur Laffite's haul, which Mr. Teague most assuredly has hidden away somewhere.

I say this because Mr. Teague once found me snooping around it, and he shooed me away. After that, he had the ice barn closed off with boards. I threatened to leave him if he didn't tell me where the treasure was, and he merely laughed at me and said that, 'well, then, maybe the next Mrs. Teague will get the use of the treasure.' Then he limped to the house, leaning on the cane he had begun using. The smug bastard.

There was a time when I thought that if I plied him with favors, I might persuade him to tell me. Such was the case in 1908, the year we sold the Oldsmobile and bought a second hand Model T. That year I surprised Mr. Teague with another hunt with Ben Lilly. Of course, when he returned, he was just as surprised or more so with the second mortgage I had taken out on Mount Teague in his absence. And, of course, his absence had also given me a chance to scour the grounds looking for where he had hidden the old pirate's treasure. But, unfortunately, Mr. Teague returned from north Louisiana early without so much as a bearskin rug, to find me directing some of the hands in prying back planks in the old dairy barn. And in that endeavor, Mrs. Leonard, we found only shit. Pardon me, madame, *manure*.

Mr. Teague had gone hunting with Mr. Lilly to find that Mr. Roosevelt was also present. Yes, the President of the United States, Mrs. Leonard. Teddy Roosevelt. Well, Mr. Teague asked Mr. President if he remembered our son Sam Jr. charging up San Juan Hill with him, but Mr. Roosevelt claimed not to know him, nor had he seen him at any of the reunions of what he called 'my Cuba boys.' My husband accused Mr. Roosevelt of lying and they argued, and Mr. Teague returned home early, compliments of the President's bodyguards. I confronted Junior with this incongruency, but he hemmed and hawed and questioned Mr. Roosevelt's memory, saying that a president has a lot on his mind and can't possibly be expected to remember someone from years before. Then Junior quickly left for his in-laws in Bolivar. It is well that he will miss our séance. He ought not be privy to the information I seek. He might feel entitled to it.

Do you think we might have our meeting with my husband soon? I grow weary of the delay.

Very well, let me put it to you plainly, Mrs. Leonard. I give you three days or else you may be on your way, madame.

If you will excuse me, I must go and make my morning *toilette,* while it is still morning.

Jack

To your health, Father.

Yes, so about my brother being in Peggy's in Oil City in 1911.

I patiently filled every cylinder of the revolver with bullets like a farmer planting seeds and calculating the harvest. It was January, and it was cold, and my feet crunched over the frosty ground and my breath steamed out into the brittle air. The sky was going from bright blue to deep, glossy indigo. In the black outline below it, the rectangular lights of Peggy's windows got larger as I approached, and the shouts and singing and the tinkle of the piano and the click of billiard balls got louder. My heart beat quick and hard, my hands were jammed into my pockets, my finger running over the outer part of the trigger guard. I was tired of running from my brother. I had contemplated ending him before but had failed to go through with it. I resolved that this time would be different.

At Peggy's door, I pulled the gun from my pocket. The checkered pattern carved into the grip pressed into my palm. I took a deep breath, perhaps my last breath as a free man, or perhaps my last breath of any sort. A chorus of laughter erupted, and then a cheer, and then another round of laughter. I pushed open the doors to the dim light. And there he was, stony and marble-white. The patrons of the bar had no idea of his real name or his past or his true nature, but they were heartily enjoying his company. I put the revolver in my pocket.

Peggy had named the marble bust Uncle Pucker because of the facial expression my brother's statue made, and I soon found out that there were a variety of drinking songs made up that rhymed with Pucker, which I will spare you, Father. It was also called Pucker because if the saloon girls were tipped appropriately, they would lewdly kiss it, and the higher the tip, the more so.

Patrons who tipped could put their hat on it for a moment and the barmaid would kiss it. For a better tip came a lewder kiss, and for the best tips, generally later in the night, a barmaid would get up on the bar and lift her skirts over Uncle Pucker. Patrons who tried to see past the tops of their stockings were given a sly smile and a tapping slap. Then the girl would pretend to be aroused and then passionately enthralled with the statue, lowering her head and then raising her face to the ceiling with squinted eyes while slapping the top of the bar with her palms or kneading the edge of it as she pantomimed the ecstasy that she pretended was happening under her skirts. The bar howled and roared, beating the tables in hilarity. And I howled with them. I could not help it. I was relieved. Only moments earlier, I thought I might be walked out in handcuffs or carried out in a pine box.

I was among the last people to leave Peggy's that night. My brother and I had round after round together, and he wore my hat many times, and, once or twice, on my account, he disappeared under a barmaid's skirt and while she pretended he was pleasing her. The night wore on, until Peggy went to bed and told us to lock up after ourselves. It was just me, my brother, and a roustabout who had passed out on the floor under a mirror that ran the length of the wall.

My brother and I looked at each other. His smirking pucker taunted me, and I slapped his marble-white face for it. I shook the pain from my hand, and I went behind the bar and found a nine pound hammer. I raised it, intending not to come down on his hard head, but I found the retribution was too delicious to pass up. I struck it, and a crack developed in his crown. I struck it again. And again. Again. Again. A blow for Homer Prentiss, a blow for John A. Jones. A blow for Jack Teague. A blow for my father. Another blow for Jack Teague. And another. Over and over again, into a shower of tinkling white shards.

My drunkenness faded suddenly, and I saw myself in the mirror with the hammer in my hand. My arm was slack and my chest was rising and falling. I threw down the hammer, and it landed with a thud on the floor. The roustabout woke up and scratched his head. He squinted at the marble ruins of the statue of Uncle Pucker and declared, "Miss Peggy's gonna be madder'n a hornet, Pirate. She paid fifty dollars for ol' Pucker down in New Orleans."

"He crossed me," I replied. The roustabout laughed but quickly put a hand to his head to hold in the ache. He attempted another laugh and held his head as if it might explode with any sort of exertion. Then he rolled over on the dusty floor and went back to sleep.

I took a shovel and a bucket and scooped up my brother's marble remains and dumped them in a pile behind the privy. I swept up the white dust into a dustpan and shook it out the backdoor. Then I left a fifty dollar bill on the counter where my brother's statue had been.

The next day was the first day of work I had missed in over thirty years, since the day that Pinch had died and I had gotten drunk. The next day was also my last day of work. My old body was no longer fit for the oil patch. It was not so much my safety that made me worried, but rather the men I worked with, Frenchy and Al and the rest. If I made a mistake, and, in the oil field, there was always an opportunity for one, they might be maimed or killed.

I went to Mr. Sharp's office and told him I would be moving on. He stood up from his charts and ledgers and papers and shook my hand. We sat in front of the potbellied stove, and he asked me where I was headed. I told him I didn't know just where yet, but I'd let him know where to wire the money from our drill bit leases. I said goodbye to Frenchy and Maude and little Eddie, and the crew. I packed my things, the revolver, my scrapbook, a card Missy had sent me once, and two changes of clothes. I left my oil-and-mud soaked overalls on a peg behind the door in my cabin.

On my way to the train station, I stopped at Peggy's. She was picking up shards of marble that I had missed the night before. She looked up as I came in.

"Somebody had it out with Ol' Uncle Pucker last night," she said as she looked down her cigarette and lit it with a couple of popping gasps. "Fatal," she added, squinting and shaking out the match.

"I suppose it was me," I confessed. "I do apologize, Miss Peggy."

She went behind the bar and brought around a mop and a bucket.

"No need, Pirate. Bought the weasely bastard on impulse from a shop on Magazine Street in New Orleans." She wrung out the mop and slapped it onto the floor, darkening the white powder. "Motherfucker always gave me the creeps anyhow. Made me squirm, and not in a good way, not like he did the girls," she chuckled as her cigarette bounced in her mouth and she slapped the damp mop onto the plank floor again.

Pardon my language, Father, but those were her exact words. The claret has loosened my tongue enough to repeat them.

I gave her a little more money, in appreciation for her good humor, and she slid it into her brassiere where the pale-white mounds of sunburned-pink flesh heaved a little and reminded me of the rumps of two scurrying pigs. I left Peggy's to the slap-and-slide of her mop, and I left Oil City and the roustabouts and roughnecks and drillers and muleskinners and tool dressers. I got on the train and I left all of them. They had taken me in when I was a stranger, and they had let me remain one to the degree that I needed to be.

I moved to New Orleans where I was one of ten John Joneses in the city directory, and I gave my occupation as 'retired harness maker,' just to cast doubt on my past. And I was lucky to have bought the house on Prytania Street next to Mr. Carriere the monument maker. They were good days, good enough to have been my last, if I had been able to leave well-enough alone.

Eva

There you are, Mrs. Leonard. Certainly, you haven't been avoiding me, have you? Let us repair to the Ladies' Drawing room, or *le salon*, as I like to call it. Do ignore the peeling wallpaper. This room was once the talk of St. Matthew Parish, and an invitation to appear in it was a coveted one indeed. As it will be again, I assure you.

I see you've noticed my sapphire pendant. I'll admit, a bit ostentatious for a Sunday afternoon, but it's the only piece of jewelry I have left. Unless, of course, you count the jewelry of a pirate hidden away in a safe somewhere in one of the sagging outbuildings here at Mount Teague. But that is why *you're* here.

Several years ago I had hoped to add to my jewelry collection, fresh from the shell. It was a Sunday and as usual, my husband and I were attending church. Out of sheer boredom, I was actually listening to the Gospel, a thing I rarely do. The reading was from Matthew, something about a pearl of great price. I idly thought that it would be something nice to have, a string of them to adorn myself or to sell for this reported 'great price.'

That very afternoon I came across an article in the *Compass*, wedged between an ad for Hofstetter's Bitters and the society column, *On Dit*. Incidentally, madame, for a short time I wrote the column under the *nom de plume*, Miss Honeysuckle Breedlove, but my insinuations became too intimate and too uncomfortable for some. So, facing possible allegations of libel and a potential investigation for violation of the Comstock Laws for lewdness, Mr. Braud the editor took it over himself under the pseudonym Merry Chatsworth. It returned to mere mush, wedding announcements and mindless reports of arrivals and departures of visiting friends and relatives.

Well, as I say, there in the *Compass* was an article about the 'Great Pearl Rush' in Caddo Parish near a town called Oil City, a place which didn't exist when I was growing up there decades earlier. It said that a man named Sachihiko 'George' Murata had found pearls a summer or two before and sold them to Tiffany's in New York for $1500 apiece and that the local populace was still finding them. Mr. Teague listened and puffed on his cigar as I read to him.

"Murata," he said in a mumbled snort, "Must be some kind of dego or chinaman."

Well, chinaman or not, we took it as a sign, a heavenly divination, as its inspiration had come directly from the Bible. We made plans at once to travel there and gather as many of these 'pearls of great price' as we could. The gold of the Yukon and the silver of Nevada were too far away and frankly too much trouble, and we had been excluded from the oil field, as I am convinced to this day. But these pearls of great price were just a day's train ride away. We brought suitable clothes in case there was to be any dickering over pearl leases, if there were such things. We may have been new to the pearl business, but we were certainly not going to appear to be a couple of out-of-town 'greenhorns' ripe for the picking.

It was also an excellent excuse to leave Mount Teague for a while. We were sharing the house with Junior and his wife and their new baby. My son's son—I refuse to use the term grandson—was a year old, a tot who shrieked and whined and cried incessantly, taking no regard of others and their need for sleep, and who was a veritable fountain of runny phlegm. I could scarcely be in the same room with him, let alone be expected to pick him up. And, of course, it is a well-known fact that children carry all sorts of diseases.

We no longer had nursemaids or wet nurses as we did in the good old days. I had mentioned that perhaps my daughter-in-law and the baby might spend a few nights in one of the old cabins that once housed our field hands. Each year more and more of them have drifted away to the city and to the north, leaving their former habitations empty. She laughed, but when she realized that I was serious about this proposition, she was aghast and for almost a year, she spoke to me even less than before.

And so, Mr. Teague and I packed two trunks apiece of nice things, for one never knew what sort of opportunities might be missed if underdressed. Presentation is everything, Mrs. Leonard. We left word with the *Compass* that we would be summering in Europe once again. That sounded far better than this Oil City whistle-stop. When someone asked if we were going to visit our daughter who had married a viscount or some-such, I had to think for a moment before I remembered the concocted tale and said, "Oh. Oh, yes, of course!" And then I added, "At their estate in the countryside this time of year."

We arrived in Shreveport on the train and took the cheapest rooms at the Phoenix Hotel, two singles with a shared bath down the hall, one for men and one for women. The city had certainly changed. The streets were paved, and well-dressed people drove new automobiles down them to nice restaurants and ornate theaters. Downtown, new buildings were creeping into the sky, and fine homes were being built down a thoroughfare called Fairfield Avenue. The smell of newly made fortunes was everywhere. Oh to be young and single again, enjoying the society of the young stallions the city had attracted. Instead, I had thrown my saddle over an old, limping, cantankerous ass of a man. But, barring an appearance before a judge, either in divorce proceedings or as a defendant in a murder trial, he would have to do.

I left Mr. Teague snoring in an afternoon nap that could be heard through his door, and I toured the sights from my youth. The apartment overlooking Texas Street I had shared with my grandparents appeared uninhabited and a repository for boxes. The Presbyterian Church was still there, the marquee outside announcing the topic of what were surely the same sermons I had heard as a girl. The Grand Opera House was still there and accompanied by several other theaters. The Methodist Church had moved to the head of Texas Street, but the courthouse was still at its corner of Marshall and Texas, halfway down to the river, and the post office just down from it. Trolleys fed by electricity crisscrossed the city which had sent out tendrils like a flowering vine, west to an expanse called the fairgrounds and south to a convent and boarding school for girls called St. Vincent's, the latter recently rebuilt after a fire some years before.

The bawdyhouse of my youth, on Commerce Street, stood empty. Kudzu raced up the downspouts and down the gutters and was devouring the roof. The porch where so many men had come with their paychecks and their straining flesh drooped at one corner, and the windows had only cracked and missing panes of glass. I looked in a window and up the stairs which I had been carried up to be deflowered, and the room where my patron Mr. Standproud had died in my arms, in a most unromantic way, of course, and I had wriggled out from under him, composed myself, and stashed away his money. My mind wandered over those days, and I saw us girls in our fancy drawers and nightgowns and heard the sounds of our giggles and moans and the piano downstairs. As I reminisced, a pair of rats scurried down the hallway, and I shrieked as the place was again just a long-vacant house of assignation.

I found Texas Street and followed the crowd down its paved sidewalks. At the head of Texas near the Methodist Church, the crowd became more and more male, both young and old. I followed them across Common Street, listening to their conversations. One young man remarked to another that Miss McCune's place had the finest girls in the city, and they were headed there. I felt oddly proud to have been a graduate of her dear institution.

I followed them to my alma mater and found it had been transplanted from Commerce Street to a fine two story home on Fannin Street, where it had been joined by dozens more, the girls in them no different, I'm sure, than we had been, nor any more different than the ones in Beaumont or anywhere else, pretty-enough girls who were selling their bodies and their youths. Selling them until they were no longer pretty-enough. And young men were still coming to pay them for their youths and their bodies with scarcely a thought in their heads other than carnal excitement. 'Is, was, and ever shall be,' Mrs. Leonard.

I let the boys go and have their fun, and I turned to go back to the Phoenix Hotel. Passing the City Market, from afar I saw old Miss Fenerty there, her mannerisms friendly with everyone. Smiles were being given and received so that what might have been a fifteen minute errand was stretched into an hour or more by the meeting and greeting and conversing with those she held as friends. How differently would my life have turned out if I had been taken in by her on the death of my grandparents rather than by Miss McCune? How close had I come to some other outcome?

I was thinking thusly when someone asked, "Eva? Is that you?"

I turned to see another face from my past, the upturned Pekingese nose set in the round, doughy face of Polly Calhoun.

"Yes," I said. "Polly Calhoun?"

"Polly Calhoun Simmons, now," she said. "Why Eva, what are you doing returning from the sporting district?"

The clever meanness of girlhood had been translated into the subtle meanness of a society woman. I no longer felt it necessary to hold my tongue and endure her needling.

"Why, Polly, I've heard it all over town that you and Gwendolyn Mosey were working down there, trying to improve your stations in life by entertaining river wharf stevedores and oilfield roustabouts. I meant to pay a call on you so we could catch up on old times. Perhaps you could share the secrets of some of your love-tricks."

Her mouth opened and closed as words failed her. She turned and stormed down Texas Street, blustering and too angry to speak. Ha! So I ask you Mrs. Leonard, who won that one?

I thought of one last visit I should make and turned back toward the west end of downtown. Overseen by two deputies, a group of convicts in stripes were weeding the graves in the Oakland Cemetery. I poked through the headstones, recognizing some names but not others, until I came to an area called the Yellow Fever Mound, wherein were buried my grandparents and my childhood friend Willie Bissinger, and very nearly, me. I sat for a time and thought of those days. What if he had lived? Would I be Eva Bissinger, the saddlemaker's wife? Would we have a house on Fairfield Avenue, full of little blonde heads and blue eyes? Would I have learned to cook and clean? Joined the Catholic Church? Would we have enjoyed the marital rite as part of a loving marriage? What was love, anyway, apart from some physical struggle, a jousting between sheets?

But sentimentality is a useless exercise and a fool's indulgence, and so I rose and returned to the Ladies' lounge at the Phoenix to dissolve it with a series of cocktails, even though Shreveport had outlawed liquor. Nature finds a way, Mrs. Leonard. As they say, you can make liquor and prostitution illegal, but you can't make them unpopular.

My husband arranged for us to take the train to Oil City the next day, a trip of scarcely an hour. We detrained there in the afternoon. It was hot, so I wore a light summer day dress with a wide brimmed bonnet and carried a toile handbag and parasol in case the sun became too accosting while we toured the pearl fields looking for our lease. Similarly, Mr. Teague wore a white linen suit with a Panama hat. His trousers were carefully starched, and we felt confident that no one would notice Ruthie's discreet patching.

We found the place studded with derricks, and when we asked where the lake was, a man offered to drive us out to it. Pumps rocked up and down as if making love to the earth, drawing out its essence. Then the lake opened up on the hillside, dotted with the wooden towers of that fickle business, the oil field.

A crowd was gathered at the water's edge. Many had boats they pulled alongside them as they waded in. On the bank, women were setting away dishes after what appeared to have been a big, communal barbecue supper. Men were relaxing in the shade before wading in after pearls. It looked less like a boom camp and more like a Sunday afternoon picnic, which I suppose it was. One of the men approached Mr. Teague and gave him a long, sideways look.

"Say, Mister, you got a brother? You look like a feller used to be up here name a Pirate Jones."

Another said, "Naw, naw, that ain't it. I think he looks like old Uncle Pucker used to hang out down at Peggy's. Remember him?"

"Why it's old Uncle Pucker. Look here, boys! It's old Uncle Pucker!"

Some of them, the ones who had drank a few more beers than the rest, began singing a bawdy song about my husband's sexual prowess, of which they obviously knew nothing. After all, I had been married to the man for thirty years and he couldn't do a tenth of the things they purported in their off-key ditty. My oblivious husband politely smiled and lightly clapped his hands and tapped his foot to the tune until the women present put their hands over their children's ears and scolded the men to stop.

The men finished their beers, and then it was the women's turn to rest in the shade. Men and boys waded into the water with boats at their sides. The boys would feel with their feet for the shells and then dive down to dig them out with their hands and deposit them in the boats. The men dug at the bottom with hoes or special devices called tongs which they pronounced 'tawngs.' I was about to go and sit in the shade with the women while Mr. Teague joined the men in the water. But I was mistaken about our roles in the process.

"Well, Mrs. Teague," my husband said, "Run in and get yourself a pearl."

"What?" I asked in disbelief. I wasn't about to go in that water.

"Go ahead," he insisted. "Wade on in."

I told my husband at the water's edge that this would all be easier if he would just tell me where the old pirate's booty was so we might sustain ourselves from it, and he only laughed and said that was his affair and not mine. I do believe he was quite enjoying himself at my expense. I demanded that he go in after a pearl for me, but he stubbornly lit a cigar and threw the match in the lake. I knew he would never budge on the matter, so I took off my shoes and, in exasperation, threw them at him, and he ducked one and then the other and laughed. His lips pulled and popped on his cigar, and he leaned on his cane which was becoming necessary for him to get around.

I joined the rarely-washed country people in their overalls and slouch hats. The lake was not at all unpleasant, with a sandy bottom that sloped gently into the lake. I waded in with the men in their search, which delighted them, and they said to each other, "Look here, boys! Gal's got spunk!"

We fanned out into the lake, the rush of water pulling to the surface when something was found and the clink of mussels shells as they filled up the boats. We neared a cypress tree in the water, and I saw that an old strip of rubber had become lodged in its branches. As I got closer, I discovered that it was something else.

"Sir," I said to the man nearest me, "there's a snake in that tree."

"Oh, don't give him no mind, ma'am. Leave him alone and he'll leave you alone, is how it works." The man continued raking along the bottom with a pair of 'tawngs' as a small child rode on his shoulders, also unconcerned with the snake.

Beneath my feet, things began to slither. The sandy bottom had turned to a slick mud which gushed between my toes. The snake was a good ten or twelve feet away, but I felt his yellow eyes and slitted pupils on me. I was becoming ill. Then, my foot brushed something hard.

I whooped and said, "Something. Under my foot. Hard."

"Probably a mussel," the man said. "Git it. Pry him out with yer toes."

With one eye on the snake, I worked whatever it was out of the bottom and trapped it against my leg and moved it up to my hand. Just as I did, the man added, "Unless it's a snappin' turtle."

I hastily pulled it to the surface, expecting to see the pointed snub-nose of a 'snappin'' turtle, but it was the yellowed shell of a mussel. Its curved surface just filled the palm of my hand, like the small breast of a woman. Don't ask me how I know this, Mrs. Leonard. I was once a working girl, asked by gentlemen to do certain things. I will leave the rest to your imagination.

Well, so, "I've got one! I've got one!" I cried, but the men continued working out in a line with their boats trailing by their sides.

"You can put it in our boat yonder," the man next to me said. His child had his hands laced over the top of his father's head and his feet dangled over the straps of his father's overalls and into the water.

"Not on your life!" I said. "This is mine."

"Suit yourself," he said as he pulled up his 'tawngs' again with a rush of muddy water.

I was in water to my shoulders, but I had my mussel and my pearl of great price, and so I turned to bring it back to the shore to open it. I emerged from the water with my dress clinging to me, and I will admit to enjoying the sidelong glances and the outright stares and the play of eyes over my figure, no matter how overly ample it may have become.

The chinaman Mr. Murata was on the bank, helping people open their catch and examining them for pearls. Whenever someone brought him a pearl, no matter how small, he flipped his glasses down from the top of his head to the tip of his nose and quietly praised it and gave it back to the person. I pressed forward and cut in front of the crowd that was waiting for his help, and he looked at me.

"Well, open it," I said as I shook my mussel before him.

He pried it open as I waited for the cloudy glint of a white sphere. He put his glasses down on the tip of his nose again and looked down through them. His lips pursed, and he handed the empty shell back to me. My mussel did not have a pearl in it. I was done with pearl hunting, and so I went to join my husband in the shade.

The people were bringing in their mussels while Mr. Murata cleaned fish and oil in a kettle boiled over an open fire. He would take time to look down through his glasses at each offering and say, "That a good one."

A boy of about ten found the largest pearl of the day. Someone looked at it and said, "that'n there'd go fer bout a hunnert dollars or more! What you think, George?"

"Aw, that a good one! Maybe two hundred." And he returned to the business of cutting up fish to fry.

The boy with the celebrated pearl worked the crowd, proud of his find. He made his way to us, and Sam asked to see it. The boy grinned so that his head might pop in two and innocently gave the pearl to my husband. Sam scowled and said he doubted it would be worth a fraction of that, and he put it in his pocket, telling the boy that he should go try again. The boy didn't cry, but he came close to it, as his blind trust in the decency of grownups was suddenly blown apart. He pleaded with Sam, who told him again to run on and find another pearl. The boy left with a quivering lip.

A circle formed around us, and at first I thought the men had come to look at me and my clinging wet dress. But they did not meet my coy smile, and I realized that they were instead angry at my husband. The boy returned with his father who pushed his way past the shoulders in the circle of men. The boy's father was a powerfully built man with a sunburned neck and copper hair that was still slick with lake water. He stepped forward and said, "My boy found that pearl yonder in your pocket. Kindly give it back, sir."

"I don't know what you're talking about," my husband said, and he reclined back onto the trunk of our shade tree. But the circle of men stayed put. There was a murmur through the crowd as the boy's father turned and disappeared with a look of indignation. Moments later he returned with a shotgun. Mr. Teague stood up when he saw the gun, but the man already had it under my husband's chin.

"Give my boy that pearl back, or I give you a load of little lead pearls. You choose, mister."

It was a tense moment to say the least. After what seemed to be an hour but was really a minute or two, the chinaman Mr. Murata approached with his bloody fish knife. He stood beside the man and, with a few soft words, pushed the muzzle of the shotgun away from my husband's gullet and retrieved the pearl from Mr. Teague's shaking hand.

"Perhaps, perhaps you and lovely wife go, sir. The train back into town leave in next half hour," he said with a look of kindness. I will admit that it is a look that I have never found appealing. It reeks of weakness.

We walked back to the station at Oil City, me in my wet dress and barefooted and my husband in his white linen suit, though it was no longer completely white. I will say only that on the way back to Shreveport, no one wanted to ride in the same train car with him, nor did I. We skipped the bill at the Phoenix Hotel, leaving them to seek the nonexistent man under whose name we had checked in, and we returned to St. Matthew with the report that we were returning early because we had seen everything in Europe there was to see and had become bored with it.

It was when we returned that Mount Teague began to sink like an overburdened balloon. We threw everything over to keep it afloat. We sold my husband's remaining racehorses and then our carriage and its horses, the white geldings. Some of the washroom fixtures and silverware. What I did not give up, and will never give up, is my grip over social matters here in St. Matthew Parish. Instead, I tightened it. It was all that was left to us.

The Krewe of Jupitre was still a coveted invitation, and the annual Planters and Harvest balls were still circled days on the entertainment calendars. To finance our fancy gatherings, we borrowed from the bank, and when the banker balked at loaning us more money, he found himself excluded from the Krewe that year. When he agreed to a second mortgage, he was readmitted.

Mr. Teague and I would travel into the city, leaving word that we would be staying in the St. Charles and dining at Arnaud's, though in reality, we would dine in our room at a cheap flophouse, sharing a sandwich of the type called a 'po-boy' and arguing over who would get the bigger half. Then, if there were money left over, we would go to the nickel matinees at the movie-houses. When we returned to St. Matthew, we told tales of the opera and the theater.

We had long since sold our fancy Oldsmobile and bought a simple model T Ford. But Junior, who had a reputation of being a reckless driver, ran it into a tree on the Bayou Road. We had the Mount Teague blacksmith bang it back into shape as best he could. Then, with time, it too was sold.

A good harvest came every few years to satisfy our creditors, but my husband and I still waited for admittance into the oil field, which was expanding into Louisiana from Texas. Though we might scrape up enough money and be on the verge of being allowed to invest, upon drawing up the papers, when the name Samuel Teague was typed, the paper was ripped from the typewriter and we were politely sent away. We were being blackballed, certainly we were, for I have done it many times to the people of St. Matthew. I could not be sure, but I believe Lucas and Higgins were behind it, that 'dego-swindler' and that 'one-armed scoundrel.' Those are my husband's words, Mrs. Leonard, not mine.

All the while, my husband denied that there was any treasure or safe. He taunted me with the idea of it, and we quarreled constantly about it. Sam thought of searching for his brother Jack so that he might ask for a loan, but that man had long since disappeared. I might have offered him my garden of earthly delights again. A shame, really. I would have enjoyed his company.

Junior once again borrowed money from his father-in-law, and I borrowed it from Junior with the intention of taking out a life insurance policy on my husband.

About all that is left of any value at Mount Teague is this sapphire. It is certainly exquisite, isn't it? Here, see how it reflects the light? I shall not part with it. Mark my words, madame. I will give up Mount Teague before I give up this sapphire pendant.

Jack

It seems the gulls have come out to greet us, Father. That means land can't be far. Watch them, how they hover without so much as a flap of their wings. Some dreamers speculate that one day a man will be able to fly across the Atlantic just as Bleriot and then Moisant flew across the English Channel. An entire ocean would be a great distance indeed, and I myself doubt it will ever be done. We have, however, successfully put bombs and guns on airplanes, barely ten years after the Wright brothers' first flight. Now we can rain fire down on one another from the sky. What does that say about us, Father?

Well, it's too nice a day for such talk. I believe I was telling you about my move to New Orleans, wasn't I?

I had more money than an old bachelor would ever need, more than a rest home of old bachelors would ever need, and so I bought a nice house with gas and electricity and a telephone, and I listed myself in the New Orleans city directory as *John Jones, harness maker, retired, Prytania Street*. By some happy accident, my house was next door to another old veteran named Carriere and his family. He was a monument maker, a sculptor, though he was missing a finger from a childhood mishap. We got on well from the beginning, perhaps because we had both lost parts of ourselves.

He was a thoughtful man, and many a night I would listen to the rap of his mallet on a chisel as man and instrument pared away marble with a clink-clink-clink, chipping away what was false to get to the inner truth contained within the stony white block. As I got to know him, he invited me to keep him company, and I would join him and watch him work. In the dim electric light, an angel or a saint would emerge from the marble or granite, something beautiful and immortal perfected from a simple square monolith harvested from a quarry somewhere in the earth. Sometimes we would talk, and sometimes we wouldn't. From inside his house would float the sounds of his wife and family, she putting to bed their grandchildren who would frequently stay with them, as Papere and Maman's house was a blessed wonderland to them. As it became to me.

Through Mr. Carriere I met Mr. Leitz, the undertaker. Through him, I met Mr. Davis the director of music at the Methodist Church. Through him, I met Isaac Cline, the forecaster with the U. S. Weather Bureau and Ellsworth Woodward, a professor at Tulane, and through them, Dr. Albert Dinwiddie, professor of math and astronomy at Newcombe College, and through him, Professor Jacquet, a professor of the classics at Newcombe. She was a lively spinster who shared a house with her close friend and lifelong companion who

C. H. Lawler

was also a spinster. One introduction led to another and soon there were a dozen or so of us who gathered to discuss art, science, politics, and history.

We would talk over the events of the day, or we might read to each other from the newspapers or from some work of literature. They were as good a group of friends as a man could ask for. We met once or twice a week to discuss these things late into the night over cigars for some and port for others amid the scurrying of Carriere's grandchildren. One of them, a little girl named Delphine, was particularly taken with me and called me Monsieur Laffite after the pirate, even though the old pirate by all accounts had both of his eyes. They were good days, surrounded by these friends, these people of different backgrounds freely discussing things, all of us knowing implicitly that we didn't have and would never have all the answers and so it was important to listen as well as to speak.

The winter of 1911, on the one year anniversary of Moisant's death in the fields of Harahan outside the city, a man named Robert G. Fowler landed at City Park on his way to becoming the first aviator to cross the country from west to east. He had begun his journey in Los Angeles in October and I had followed his trip in the newspaper, keeping clippings in my scrapbook as I anticipated his arrival in New Orleans. Along the way, Mr. Fowler had made the first air delivery of medicine, between Evangeline and Jennings. His airplane had been the first to be launched from a railroad handcar, and in Beaumont he had taken up a passenger named Shaw who had made the first motion pictures from the air. The film Shaw had taken had preceded Mr. Fowler on the train and was shown as a newsreel before the feature at the picture show at the Greenwall Theatre on Dauphine. In the darkened theater, we the moviegoers were entranced with the scenes taken from high above the oil fields around Beaumont, the view that had always looked back at me when I scanned the skies during my days there.

When he landed at the racetrack at City Park, I was among those waiting for Mr. Fowler. His airplane carried a lucky rabbit's foot and a squirrel tail mounted behind the engine and an American flag behind the tailfin. He shook hands all around and waved to the crowd before being taken to stay at Mayor Behrman's house. When Fowler left, I cautiously approached the plane and looked inside at the levers and pedals. I would have given everything but my remaining eye just to get in and sit there for a moment, but one of the New

Orleans policemen hired to watch the airplane politely told me, 'Step away, sir. Thank you.'

The next day, Fowler gave a flying exhibition which included several figure eights over the lake. There was talk of him taking someone up, and it was my hope that it would be me. But I was one of dozens of people who wanted to go. I crowded around the schoolboys in winter hats and coats, and I was as wild as they were to be chosen to go up. After half an hour of giddy anticipation, some kind of fancy touring car drove up, and out stepped a well-dressed man in a felt duster coat with a bruise along his cheekbone.

"That's Battling Nelson, the boxer!" one of the boys said.

Battling Nelson strode across the wet ground with the light step of a prizefighter, as if he were floating. The boys and I watched as he was helped into the airplane. Mr. Fowler had been shaking hands and answering questions, but when his passenger arrived, he looked at us, and his eyes caught mine. As he turned away and began stepping lightly across the soggy ground toward his airplane, he said, "Sorry, Pops."

Fowler vaulted into the cockpit and fastened his leather flying cap under his chin, and a man pulled the propeller and the engine coughed once and then growled smoothly to life. It trundled over the ground where canvas tent-cloth had been laid down as a runway over the wet lawn of City Park. The engine raced louder and the propeller revolved into a blur, and the water in the puddles rippled and the winter grass vibrated. The airplane began to race down the canvas spread out for it, and the attendants ran out of its path as it lifted up into the sky. The wind gently pushed it sideways and the airplane pushed back against it and climbed. The boys ran after it, and we all watched it sail up over the city behind the round haze of propeller, with a rabbit's foot, a squirrel tail, and an American flag. And the boxer Battling Nelson.

I turned and made for home before the pilot and the boxer returned to earth. Behind me the crowd cheered as Fowler made figure eight after figure eight.

There was some hope that there might be others chosen to go up, but the next day, Robert G. Fowler took off for Pascagoula and points east, Mobile and Birmingham. The *Times-Democrat* said that the aviator soared into the blue eastern sky to the cheers and waving of hats of those gathered earthbound at

City Park, and then he faded to a pinpoint and vanished. Just like my hopes for flight.

Sorry, Pops.

You'll no more fly than a pig.

I resolved that I would be earthbound forever. I would no longer thrash against it. And so I threw away my scrapbook.

In the spring of 1912 the Mississippi River flooded and threatened the city. A member of our group, Isaac Cline, who was the head of the Weather Bureau, reassured us that the waters would pass us by, which they did. He held the same passion for weather that I had had for flying, and he spoke reverently of what the weather would do and why it would do it. He studied the weather in the way that a big game hunter studied the habits of his prey. It was only after I had known Mr. Cline for some time that I learned that he had lost his wife and unborn child in the Galveston hurricane of 1900.

He said that at the heart of it all, weather depended on the weight and temperature of air, which created currents in it. Currents in the air affected the movement of water, and then the weight of water moved against the weight of the earth and the things men had put upon it. All of it deriving from the weight of something thought to have no weight at all, air.

Our discussions would sometimes turn philosophical, and in this case it turned from the weight and power of air and water to the power of human emotions, weightless and unseen but powerful enough to move armies with the same destructive forces of an angry ocean. Envy, anger, bitterness, the lust for retribution, all fueled by the weightlessness of grudges and enmity. Someone offered the opinion that societies wither and collapse not from lack of money or military might, but rather from lack of empathy. And the weight of grudges and enmity. I sipped my port and thought again of my brother and the promise I had made to my father on his deathbed.

The nights on Prytania were passed thusly, with cigars and port and companionship, laughter, and conversation. But the days were long. I no longer had a class to teach or a well to drill or a mill to design. I spent them waiting for nothing to happen. Excess leisure time was strangling me.

In November of 1912, I received a telegram from Mr. Hughes saying that our partner in the drill bit leasing business, Walter Sharp, had died in Chicago, and the body was en route to his home in Houston for funeral services. I took the train to Houston to pay my respects to him and his widow Estelle and their children. My dealings with them had always been very fair and pleasant. It was hard to comprehend that he was gone. So I went to Houston.

The train moved arrow-straight through the Louisiana and Texas countryside. It whistled at each new town and hooted at the frenzied clusters of derricks and drilling sheds and pump jacks of oil field after oil field. Both towns and fields held the licorice smell of petroleum in their air, and there were as many automobiles as buggies on their streets and roads. Derricks stood watch over the prairies and rice fields. Deep in the ground below them, Sharp-Hughes drill bits, *our* drill bits, probed the earth like hounds feverishly nosing for a rabbit. Ten years before these fields had raised rice and cattle. Now the farmers and ranchers could afford to drive automobiles fueled with the liquid under their feet rather than horse-pulled carriages.

In the towns, each hoping to become a city before the others, those automobiles scurried along streets that were newly paved and released nicely dressed men and women in front of churches and stores and theaters and movie houses. Town by town slipped away, and the train moaned and jostled and moved on to see more. When we stopped in one of the bigger towns, I was surprised to find that it was Beaumont. I would not have recognized it were it not for the name over the platform. It had easily quadrupled in size.

At the house on Main Street in Houston, we lined up to say our last goodbye to Mr. Sharp. We mourners were men who had gone from overalls and work boots to nice suits and wingtip shoes and were now equally comfortable with either. Talk in the line to offer condolences to Mrs. Sharp revolved around the events of his death: putting out an oil well fire in the Caddo Field, an injury, a trip to see the famous Dr. John B. Murphy in Chicago, and treatment that was in vain.

At last, the line advanced, and I spoke with Mrs. Sharp and her children. Though her eyes were red, she managed a smile through the black lace veil.

"Dear Mr. Jones," she said as she grasped my hands in hers, "Walter always admired your wise counsel and honesty."

I wonder if she could see my sympathetic smile fade as I thought that Walter had never known my real name and that my very identity there in her parlor was a sham.

It was odd to see him laid out. I had never seen him doing anything but working, and he looked bored. It made me think of my own end. So many things undone. We may take what we please from the earth, but one day the earth will take us. After the rites were conducted, the half-open casket was closed completely and a man disappeared forever like some kind of macabre magician's trick. And so the earth took back Walter Sharp through a rectangular hole in the Glenwood Cemetery in Houston. He had barely made forty.

At the gravesite, the Episcopalian priest raised his hand over the casket and said one last prayer. Mrs. Sharp and his children stood, and she draped herself over the casket and put her cheek to it while her children cried and put their arms around their mother. We all turned away to leave them with this most private of moments. Then, out of the corner of my eye, I saw a man make the sign of the cross. I looked closer and saw that it was Frenchy Verret. I had never seen him in a suit and had failed to recognize him. We exchanged a hearty handshake and rode back to the Sharp's house together in one of Mr. Sharp's autos driven by one of his hired men. The car smelled like new leather and polished woodwork. We were nicely dressed in suits and shirts with starched white collars and waistcoats with pocket watches. We were what oil men were beginning to look like.

Mr. Cullinan and Mr. Guffey rode with us. On the way, Mr. Cullinan told me that that Teague feller in Louisiana had been trying to get back into the business like a stray cat scratching at a screen door, but as far as he or anyone else in the oil patch was concerned, the name Sam Teague was mud and to be treated like poison. Mr. Cullinan asked me if I still thought that was the case, for Mr. Teague and his blue-eyed wife were single-minded when they wanted something. I said that everyone would be better off if the Teagues were kept out. Mr. Guffey said, "It's agreed then. I'll let the other men know."

We got out of the car and went back into the Sharp's house. Servants were straightening the parlor, putting up chairs and putting out food. We oil men and the wives who had come visited while trays of things to eat and drink circulated the room. Pattillo Higgins and Al Hamill were there, and we rehashed our adventure at Spindletop, laughing about the falling lengths of iron pipe that could have crushed us or the well fires that could have consumed us or the gas blowouts that could have suffocated us. Frenchy listened and laughed as well, but my laughter fell short as I thought of how I had lied about his fate, and how I withheld the truth from him about his first love, the girl who had perished from the same lie I had spun about him. If I had told her where he was and that he was alive, perhaps *she* would still be alive.

Talk was also of oil under the ground in places as disparate as Arkansas and Mexico. It was impossible for any oil man to walk over a parcel of ground without thinking of the oil that might be simmering below it, a hundred feet or a quarter mile. Capt. Lucas himself was in Mexico just then, though he had sent an immense spray of flowers. He was perhaps the only oil man of any rank who was not in the Sharps' parlor that afternoon in early December 1912.

Mr. Hughes was there, too, of course, with his wife and with Howard Jr. After the services, he took me aside to discuss the future of the Sharp-Hughes Tool Company now that Mr. Sharp was gone. Mrs. Sharp had asked to be bought out, and Hughes wanted to know if I did also.

I had always had a nagging worry that one day someone would connect the dots between John Jones, Homer Prentiss, and Jack Teague. So when Mr. Hughes offered me a generous sum, I took him up on it. I was officially out of the oil business. I did leave a final admonition about my brother and his wife, however. He said for me not to worry, that Teague and his wife would never be 'allowed in.'

About this time, Mrs. Sharp and her children arrived from the graveside. We visited a while, but eventually the time came that the family had to be left to grapple with the emptiness of grief, to begin filling the vacancy with something. I left the new widow with the sense that I should have died before her husband, this much younger man, did. Death is not fair. It is only insistent. In the end, it always gets its way.

Frenchy and I rode home on the train together. He had been working in the Jennings field, and Maude was there with the children. They were planning a move to Baton Rouge where Frenchy was beginning a job with the Standard Oil refinery. He had finally quit the oil field. He wanted his children, now four of them, to have a better education and lifestyle than the itinerant oil patch life could give them. Besides that, the oil field was a dangerous place. Mr. Sharp, dressed up, laid out, and given back to the earth, was testimony to that.

He said that they left Caddo just after I did and had been in the Jennings Field for about a year, trying to find some sort of better life for the children.

Just after they arrived, the aviator Robert G. Fowler had been through on his cross country flight, taking medicine from Jennings to Evangeline. Frenchy said that he bet I would've liked to have seen him.

"Yes, that's what I heard," I said in an offhand way.

Frenchy asked if I had gotten to fly, but I said that I had given up on that. "Put away childish things," is the way I put it, echoing the Apostle Paul. To change the subject, I asked him if he had any news from home, St. Matthew Parish.

He spoke of his many relations still there, those who had married, had children, had passed. Then Frenchy said in a low voice, "Mr. Pirate, mais, you never guess who showed up down at Caddo Lake summer before last. That ol' coullion Teague. Almost got his *cal-basse* shot off." Frenchy drew a finger gingerly across his throat. "*Guelette-fouetté*. My cousin Faustina is the operator for the St. Matthew Telephone Exchange. She say he and Miss Eva, they on hard times but don't nobody talk about it, no."

The news cheered me, but I tried not to laugh out loud or even smile. Instead, I asked him about his family, and we talked about his children, Eddie, Monique, Walter, and John. Walter was named after Mr. Sharp, and John was named after me. Frenchy said they were buying a new house on Chippewa Street in Baton Rouge with a front porch and a sunny back yard for Maude's garden spot, with a shade tree in the corner for a swing for the children. The schools there were real schools, and little Eddie was looking forward to watching the boats on the river and playing baseball with boys his age.

We got to Jennings much sooner than we would have liked. When Frenchy got off the train, his family was there to greet him. I saw him off at the steps, and Maude came up and hugged my neck as the conductor smiled at us and looked down to check his pocket watch. She was wearing a nice new dress and stylish bonnet, and the children were also dressed nicely. The oil field had been good to that little family. Eddie was directed to shake my hand, and he did, but he did it like he was working a pump handle. As that waving family and the sign announcing Jennings faded behind me, I thought perhaps I might take the train up to Baton Rouge to visit sometime. But in the end, I never did.

I looked out the window as the fading light moved across the green velvet of the seats. My brother's situation was no news to me. I had been reading the *St. Matthew Compass* for years now, and it wasn't uncommon to see ads selling the goods of Mount Teague 'for best offer.' A carriage and the white horses that had pulled it. *Magnificent white geldings*, the article had said, *apply S. Teague Bayou Road, Napoleonville, serious offers only*. Then an Oldsmobile, *some damage to upholstery work*. And then, *Ford Model T, some structural defects owing to minor collision, engine works splendidly*. The ruination of my brother and his wife was a source of great entertainment for me. May God forgive me, Father, but it was.

There had also been a notice in the *Compass* that Samuel M. Teague, Bayou Road, St. Matthew, was delinquent on his taxes. Then, a week later, the newspaper printed a front page retraction that it had been an error and that Mr. Teague was and always had been in good standing with the Assessor's office and that the *Compass* sincerely regrets the error at the expense of one of St. Matthew's oldest and most venerable citizens. Just about anyone who had read both articles a week apart could see that pressure had been applied to someone somewhere.

The train pulled into New Orleans after midnight, and I went home to my empty house on Prytania Street.

Faustina Templet

Bonjour hello, St. Matthew operator. Mais-who you wanna talk wit?

Well hello Miss Gladys! Mais, I knew it was you right away. By the funny way you talk, yeah.

This switchboard! Them high-up women havin' a time. I ain' been listenin', cause I ain' suppose to, no, but it got somethin' to do with *la veuve Teague*, I mean, the widow Teague. But I ain' been listenin' and even if I had, I can't talk about it, no.

Yes ma'am, *mon cousin* Alphonse was in love with they daughter Missy before she come down wit that leopard-sy. She was real nice and we all liked her. Yes ma'am, she was so nice we always thought she might be adopted, but she had them blue-blue eyes like her mama. So I guess she wadn't, no.

Yes ma'am. Alphonse and his wife Maude, they live up in Baton Rouge now. He works at the refinery up there, that Standard-All.

Yes ma'am, who you need to talk wit? Mr. Landry down the *Compass*. Oui, madame. Then Dr. McKnight. Yes ma'am. Then Rev. Gladney at the 'Piscopal church vic'rage. Yes ma'am, I made a note all t'ree. Sound like y'all gonna have a party over Mount Teague. What kind of party y'all gonna have? You need me to call any them high-up women? Never mind, that ain't my business, no.

Let me connect you with Monsieur Le Docteur McKnight firs'.

Jack

I returned home to New Orleans and my circle of friends. One and then two years passed. Wilson was sworn in as president, the first southerner since the late war. There was more talk about a war in Europe every day, but no one in America wanted any part of it. In the meantime, people were flying longer and over vaster parcels of earth every day. In May, a Cuban aviator flew across the Florida Strait from Key West to Havana, and Robert G. Fowler, who had left me on the ground in New Orleans, flew across the isthmus of Panama, from sea to sea, though it was only fifty miles. I tried not to pay any attention to it.

That summer, 1913, I turned seventy. Seventy, Father. Suddenly, seventy didn't seem that old. My friends gathered for a birthday party. There were seven candles on my cake, one for each decade of my time on earth. As the candles of my cake burned in the dim room and illuminated the smiling faces of my friends as they sang happy birthday, I pondered my life. So much had happened, so much had been left undone. With old age I was developing a debilitating timidity. Daring things like flying were for the young. Daring things were for fearless men, and for some women also, for whom death was a long way off. They could afford to toy with it, but I had no desire to taunt death. I was closer to it than they were. It could take me any time it wanted and with little provocation. Mr. Fowler had implied it in two simple words, *sorry, Pops.*

I now understood that I would fly only if I were to die and be permitted angelhood, if there were such a thing. But I am afraid that my angelhood is doubtful. As my circle sang happy birthday, I looked at the seven candles trailing hot wax down their stems. I took a deep draught of air and thought of the biblical admonition to forgive your brother seventy times seven, and I realized that I couldn't even do it once. And so I blew out the candles. It took four tries.

At the next meeting of our circle next door at Mr. Carriere's house, we fell into a discussion of happiness and whether money could buy it. Mr. Leitz said that if it could be bought, it would come at a great price. Mr. Carriere said that he believed that happiness could not be bought at all but rather only given or received as a gift. Professor Jacquet said that she thought happiness could be neither bought nor given but, rather, grown from the inside. We agreed that was probably the case, and we toasted to it.

We spoke of what would make us most happy. There were a variety of answers. Everyone had something different. Long life for them and for those they loved. War to be averted in Europe. Harmony among men. One of the more devout among us said for everyone to turn to Jesus. Eyes turned to me when it was my turn. My wish for happiness was less altruistic. My secret happiness was something I had never told them before. I said that I had always wanted to fly, but I was now too old for it and that such daring exploits belong to younger men. And women, I added to Professor Jacquet.

It seemed to take the air out of the discussion. Luckily, at that point, Carriere's beautiful wife, gray-haired, green-eyed, beige-skinned Mathilde appeared and announced that dinner was ready. We were seated, and as we ate, the conversation turned to weightier matters like the war that was developing in Europe. The Archduke in Serbia had been shot just a few weeks before, and there was fear that the situation would escalate, which it has, into trenches and bayonets and U-boats and tanks and hellfire dropped from the heavens. Someone proposed a toast to the war's quick demise.

That night, I dreamed of my father. In fact, I awoke to the buzz of the electric fan beating at the summer swelter to imagine he was sitting in a chair at my bedside, like he would sometimes do when I was a boy in Mississippi. He smiled at me and looked up and out my window at the summer moon and stars. A breeze nudged the curtains, and a dog barked somewhere out in the night. Wispy white clouds moved over the moon in shapes that I couldn't see clearly. When I rubbed my eye and reached for the eyepatch on my bedside table for the other, the chair was empty. I could not find sleep again, so I rose and made coffee and went to my study to read.

The next day there was to be a flying exposition at City Park. I resolved that I might attend it but stay up under the boughs of the oaks and remain disinterested. But by morning, as I prepared to leave the house, a rain began to fall and those plans were cancelled. Instead, I went next door to my friend Carriere's workshop. I shook out my umbrella and sat in my usual spot, and we chatted while he chipped away at a monument. The chips reminded me of my brother's shattered image, Old Uncle Pucker, reduced to rubble.

"You look a little disappointed," Carriere said as he watched his chisel do its work.

"I thought I might go and see the young folks fly, but the rain's cancelled those plans."

"Weeping endures for a night, Jones," he quoted the Psalm between taps of his mallet, "but joy cometh in the morning." He smiled to his chisel as the mallet rapped away at it and chips of marble fell at his feet. The rain paused for a few minutes, and there was a lull, a small oasis of quiet. I could hear acutely in it. The chipping tink-tink of stone. The ding of the streetcar bell a few streets away on St. Charles. Somewhere in the house, Carriere's wife Mathilde speaking tenderly to their dog Zipper and then singing the grandchildren to their afternoon naps with soft French lullabies.

Perhaps I could have had a life such as that with Fanny Sloss. But like dull and hungry Esau, I had traded it all away for a bowl of soup. And a pair of sapphire-blue eyes, as worthless as blue glass. The stone chards fell in a slow metered cascade to the workshop floor, not the shattering crescendo of a man's bust in an oil field saloon.

I took leave of Carriere and went to the picture show. I was in the habit of going, not for the feature, really, but for the newsreel that preceded it. I also liked the Little Nemo cartoons, if I'm to be honest. The rain began again, and I huddled under my umbrella, avoiding puddles.

It was coming down hard again as I slipped in under the shelter of the marquee. The feature starred Mary Pickford, and because of the pull of her popularity and the push of the rain, the matinee crowd strained in to get a ticket. There was some sort of disturbance behind me as people moved in to take shelter from the deluge. Someone said, 'I'll thank you not to push, sir.'

I got my ticket and went in and took a seat. The newsreel offered information about the events in Europe, hopeful, like in all wars that it would be resolved in a matter of months. A few minutes into the Little Nemo cartoon, as the pianist plunked along in accompaniment, the light from the lobby pierced the darkness and then shut again. About the only seats together that were unoccupied were next to me, and a couple came in and took them. The woman, who was somewhat plump, sat next to me, while her husband followed, disturbing the moviegoers and grumbling, *move it, sir* under his breath. The silhouettes of the patrons in front of us tilted to see what was going on behind them and then pivoted back to the screen.

The woman nestled in next to me like a hen setting on a nest. She smelled like cigarettes, some brand that was bittersweet and cheap. The light from the screen illuminated her, and I recognized her profile almost immediately, though she had grown a chin or two since I last saw her over twenty years before. I turned my collar up and took my hat from my lap and put it on, tilting the brim down over my face, even though I was raised that a gentleman doesn't wear a hat indoors.

Eva kept a watch on the screen, and I stole a glance at her now and again. I wanted desperately to leave, but I was afraid that if I did, she and my brother would get a good look at me. The piano jauntily carried the drama on the screen as the intertitles flashed and Miss Pickford put the back of her hand to her forehead and blushed and batted her eyes, at which the piano clanged in low, dramatic notes.

My sister-in-law read the intertitles to her husband, which provoked more shushes from our neighbors. Finally, Sam announced loudly that he had 'had enough of this tripe' and was going outside to smoke a cigar, which was answered with more shushes in the darkened theater.

'Suit yourself,' Eva hissed, and my brother rose and made his way out, this time in front of me. He tapped my foot with his cane and snarled, *move it, sir*. His arm brushed my hat and I straightened it back over my face. He moved down the row toward the aisle, stepping on some toes and planting a cane on others without so much as an apology. He limped up the aisle, and the light from the lobby lengthened and extinguished with the opening and closing of the door.

As Miss Pickford faced a dilemma on the screen, I could tell that Eva was paying less and less attention to the picture show and more to me, her unknown seatmate. First, her knee brushed mine, and I withdrew it. She shifted in her seat so that our shoulders touched, and I shifted away. She whispered something about being wet, leaning into my ear to add with a light, girlish giggle, *from the rain, I mean.* Her breath brushed my ear, and then her hand brushed my knee, and I took a deep breath. It slithered to my inner thigh, but I was not aroused at all by her aggressive flirtation, rather, I was repulsed, for I knew where all this would lead, straight to a nightmarish world of profound misery and torment.

I picked up her arm by its sleeve and dropped it in her lap, and I rose and followed the path blazed by my brother as the intertitles continued to flash and plucky little Miss Pickford gave the villain a scolding and the crowd laughed and the pianist gaily tinkled the story along. Under my hat and umbrella and behind my collar, I walked out into the rain through the haze of my brother's cigar. I went down the alleyway and took a circuitous route home. I am sure that my brother didn't recognize me, nor did my sister-in-law. To her, I had been an anonymous afternoon plaything to tease and torment, like a child pulling a cat's tail.

I felt emasculated by both my brother and his wife, like the worthless bits of uneaten offal left in the corner of a cage by a lion, something of lesser value and purpose. And I have not been to the picture show since. But the next day, something would happen which was magnificent and worth just about any trouble I had ever had in life.

Eva

It's no use. We'll try later, Ruthie. Leave our guest and me to ourselves. That will be all for now.

Corsets. *McCall's* says they may go out of fashion in the next few years, but how else is one to continue fitting in dresses that have failed to keep up with one's girth and can't be readily exchanged for new ones? Fashion will have no say in the matter. They are a necessity and more so every day. Either corsets or bigger dresses. Do forgive my state of undress. You needn't look away, madame. Certainly you've seen a naked woman before.

Well, don't just stand there, please have a seat, Gladys. Yes, of course, *Mrs. Leonard.* Would you care for a cigarette? Very well, I myself will have one. Hand me that ashtray, will you? There by that matchbook.

So I understand that you insist on having others present at our little soiree. Is there no other way, madame? The information I seek is personal, and the fewer ears present the better. Very well, then. As long as you are successful in contacting my husband.

I've gotten out of the habit of having guests here at Mount Teague. We've not had a gathering of any size here since Mr. Teague's funeral in October. Most of my time since then has been spent searching for the treasure he hid from me. I've looked high and low for the safe and the fortune it contains. Every nook and cranny, every shed, cabin, barn, everywhere in pursuit of the safe or chest or whatever receptacle that might be hiding it. But in that I have been unsuccessful. So far, that is. It was only then that I sent for you. And so I trust our séance won't be long in taking place.

I will be frank with you—I've grown tired of the delay. You have twenty-four hours, Mrs. Leonard, and then you might as well be on your way.

Pardon me, then. I must dress.

Jack

I haven't been to the theater since that rainy summer afternoon. That evening as the steam boiled up from the rain-cooled streets, I kept to my house and missed dinner at Carriere's house, still agitated by my encounter with my brother and his temptress wife. It was a hot and muggy summer night filled with unsettling thoughts.

The next day, I was in my back yard cutting roses for Carriere's wife Mathilde and his granddaughter Delphine. I grew the roses more for them than for me and at least once a week I brought over the best of the new buds in a vase. I always tried to time my gift when Delphine was there visiting her grandparents, for she would give me a big hug around my neck and kiss my cheek and say, "Merci, merci, *c'est jolie*, Monsieur Laffite."

The rain from the day before had done a world of good for the roses, and I cut stem after stem, enough for two vases. Butterflies and bees flitted and buzzed in the morning heat, while next door Carriere chipped away at a monument. I had thought before of having him do my gravestone. He would be the one I would want to do it, but I thought that to ask him would be uncomfortable for him and, frankly, a little macabre. As I worked in the rose beds, pulling away weeds from the wet ground, I noticed that the tapping from his workshop had stopped. It was close to noon time and I figured he had gone in to have lunch. I went inside and put the flowers in vases, and then I went next door with them to give to Mathilde and Delphine. When the door opened, I found not only Carriere, but also Mr. Leitz and Professor Jacquet.

"Come with us, Jones," they said. "We have something you might like to see. A surprise. But you should bring a jacket."

This didn't make sense. Mr. Cline predicted that it would rise into the low nineties that day. And they weren't bringing their jackets.

"A surprise?" I asked.

"Yes, well," Professor Jacquet said evasively. "The Delgado Museum in City Park has just launched another exhibition."

I thought that perhaps Mr. Carriere had placed a work of art there, as he had spoken of his plans to make a sculpture of a triumphant winged angel as a gift to the city, a copy of the Greek "Winged Victory of Samothrace" which resides in the Louvre. Carriere had never seen it in person but had been looking over pictures of the statue and had even done a miniature study of it in clay. He called his version, "Winged Triumph."

"Is it to see the 'Winged Triumph?'" I asked as they pushed me out the door.

"Something like that," Mr. Leitz said.

I got my coat, and we set off for the trolley stop on St. Charles. We boarded, and after a few stops, Professor Jacquet had me put my hand over my eye. When I felt us make the turn from St. Charles onto Canal Street, I peeked, and she took her handkerchief and blindfolded me with it. It smelled sweet like gardenia soap. The sights of the world went dark, and the sounds emerged.

I tried to gauge where we were. I heard the voices of young men and the distant sounds of pianos and laughter, and I knew we must be passing the saloons and brothels of Storyville. I heard the clop of carriages, the sputter of autos, the greetings in French and English and Italian. I heard the city of New Orleans. At last the conductor announced, *City Park!* We got down, and they led me as we wandered under the oaks. At last they removed the handkerchief from my eyes.

There sat an airplane, a two-seater Bleriot XI, and next to it stood its pilot. He wore a leather helmet and goggles and was smoking a cigarette. When he saw me, he threw it down, mashed the butt with his heel, and raised a hand in a quick wave. I still didn't fully understand.

Professor Jacquet said, "The triumphant one with wings is you, Jones."

If I had contemplated what my friends had done for me, I would have been in tears. But I didn't just yet. The pilot bowed and motioned to a step ladder at the rear seat. I looked to my friends.

"Go on," they said.

I wandered up to it, waiting for someone to stop me or speak against me going. Carriere and Leitz helped me up. I threaded my old bones up into the seat. The pilot had the lithe, athletic mannerisms of a younger man and vaulted up into the front seat effortlessly and without a step ladder. I was still in a state of disbelief.

Another man pulled the propeller once, and then again, and then on the third try it sputtered and buzzed into a blur. The pilot reached at his feet and put on a fur hat, made out of some sort of animal. Then he turned to me and offered his hand. I didn't catch his name at first over the roar of the engines. But he shouted it again: HENRY. TURNER. Then he pointed to his head and yelled a joke that the beaver pelt hat kept his ears and his brain warm. How odd, I thought. My father used to say that, some sixty years before.

"GETS COLD." Turner pointed a finger up and yelled over the engine, "UP IN THE SKY."

He gave a thumbs up signal to his man on the ground. Embossed into the leather of his gloves at the base of his thumb were his initials HT. The man who had turned the propeller to life withdrew the chocks from under the wheels and ran off quickly to join my friends under the shade of an oak.

The airplane was noisy. I had never been so close to one to comprehend how loud they were. With the slightest bump, we began to move. My friends waved as we slowly passed them, and I raised a hand to them. I still could not believe it was happening. An hour before I had been cutting roses.

We began to pick up speed as the oaks of City Park raced by and the people picnicking under them waved to us and the children stood up from the blankets spread out and brushed off their backsides and began running down the field with us. The bumping of wheels over the uneven ground suddenly surrendered to the smoothness of air, smoother than I had ever imagined. Our seats seemed to be lifting us, urging us into the sky. My heart beat wildly in my chest. My hair strained the air like a sieve.

We flew over men in jackets and caps and women in dresses with puffed sleeves and bonnets playing golf on the course laid out in City Park. One of them paused in addressing his shot, and all four of them and their caddies waved as we flew right over the trees. They were gone in an instant. Bayou St. John below us became a mere narrow ribbon and then we left it behind. Pelicans and ducks on the lakes of the park were specks, like discarded handkerchiefs.

We turned gracefully and flew over the city, over the oval of the race track where horses were being put through their paces, over the small fish-scale cobblestones of the Old French Market, and then the straight line of the Basin Canal. We flew over Metairie, and Mr. Turner pointed off and down. I followed his finger and saw a church and a row of girls in white dresses lined up outside. "FIRST. COMMUNION." He shouted. "SEE IT ALL UP HERE." I watched the angelic figures waiting with bouquets in their white-gloved hands, and then we left them and the city behind.

We flew over a farm at the edge of the city, and two boys with sticks looked up at us and waved and ran as far as they could before we left them behind. At the far reach of the field was a pen. The animals in it scattered as we passed overhead, taking shelter in the lee of the fencing, huddled in a mass together at the commotion passing in the sky. When we were directly over them, I looked closer. They were pigs.

We rose, higher and higher, cleaving the air like a swimmer through water, as if we were both supported and propelled by it. Below us stretching out in the glint of the morning sun were the mirror smooth and closely placed twin circles of Lakes Maurepas and Ponchartrain. Following us projected on the surface of the water was the only thing about us still earthbound. Our shadow.

We flew away from the sun, across the broad river where boats blew throaty blasts at us and Mr. Turner dipped his wings in counter salute. The air up there was indeed cooler and I understood why I was instructed to bring my coat. Down below, the grids of towns hugged the river and the thin line of the railroad right-of-way connected the grids. We followed the river for a while and then found a smaller, weaving ribbon lined with the cloudy dark green of tree tops. I tapped Mr. Turner on the shoulder and shouted WHAT'S THAT?

He tapped a jabbing finger at it and shouted back over his shoulder BAYOU LAFOURCHE. I pointed down it, and he nodded. The wings tilted, one up and one down, and we turned, following the bayou, threading its way like a serpent through the green corduroy of the fields. Hands in the fields looked up and waved, and I waved back, though I don't think they could see me from that height.

And then there it was, the water tower with MT painted on it. From so high up, everything was made small, the great house, the outbuildings, the water tower. And the fifty year old feud between brothers. I began to think that I should grant my father's wish and reconcile with my brother. But not today. With time, but not today.

We flew back into the city, our shadow chasing on the ground behind us. The houses in town became closer together, the river crowded with ships. Across the levee from them, the tracks were thick with boxcars. We flew over Audubon Park, over the expansive glass roof of the Horticultural Hall where the serpent had beguiled me, and I did eat. We flew over Prytania Street and Carriere's workshop and my house and my rose garden. Up ahead I saw the bell tower of St. Patrick and, further on, the spires of St. Louis and Jackson Square and the statue of my namesake doffing his hat as his horse reared. Our wings banked and we flew up the length of Canal Street as the cross of our shadow slid over pedestrians on the banquette and they put their palms to their foreheads and looked up to us.

The oaks of City Park grew larger, and then the picnic blankets and the people. Some of them came out from the shade of the oaks, and I saw that they were my friends. The ground approached us, and I felt that if I were to die now everything would have been worth it. I had flown. By God, I had flown.

The ground welcomed us back with a gentle jolt. The engine sputtered to a halt. I wanted to go up again immediately.

My friends rushed the plane as soon as the propeller stopped. My legs felt weak, but they helped me out. They held me up and stood proudly as they shook my hand one after the other. A man with the *Times-Democrat* came forth and pulled me aside to get my name for the paper. I looked at the newspaperman, and then I responded clearly and calmly.

"Teague. Jack Teague," I said, and I did not regret it, though later I wondered if my brother would read it and recognize my name, the name we shared. In some ways, I wished he would.

Back on Prytania, our circle had prepared a luncheon in honor of me, the first of us to fly. Mathilde had made a cake in the shape of wings. There it was on the white lace table cloth with two vases of fresh-cut roses.

"Monsieur Laffite, Papere said you flew!" Delphine said. "Are your arms tired?"

I laughed at her simple concept of it all and swept her up into my arms, and she kissed my cheek firmly. We had cake and punch and champagne and I gave an account of it, over and over again, and no one let on that they were tired of my recitation of the events of the day. That night I could barely sleep. But when I did, I dreamed I was flying.

The next day the *Times-Democrat* carried the announcement on page 4.

Old Man Flies

72 Year-Old Aviator Thought to be Oldest Man to Ever Fly in City, Perhaps Country

I could have taken umbrage at the headline. I was only seventy-one at the time. But I let it stand in case I had indeed broken some kind of record. My friends laughed wryly at the newspapers having gotten my name wrong, and I laughed with them. Mr. Leitz offered to call the *Times-Democrat* and have them print a correction, but I told him that it didn't trouble me in the slightest. Truthfully, Father, I was delighted that the feat had been registered under my own true name.

From that day forward, I flew every time that the weather permitted. I would arrive every morning at half past eight at an old barn at the edge of City Park, one that once housed mules in the days when they were used to pull streetcars, before electricity. Henry Turner would have the airplane outside and be leaning against it, smoking and studying the sky. When he saw me approaching, he would hastily throw down his cigarette and smile and ask me, "Where to today, Jones?"

He would already have his goggles and flying cap on, and I never got a good look at his face. Not once. I knew so little about him. He said that he had worked as a machinist and mechanic at one of the automobile dealerships in town, but that's as much as I knew, that and the fact that he loved to fly as much as I did. I paid for the upkeep and gasoline for his airplane and gave him a generous salary so he could fly full-time. He kept the Bleriot running smoothly, meticulously checking our airplane before and after each flight. If I had had two good eyes, I would have contemplated learning to fly myself, but I knew that my vision wasn't suitable for managing an airplane.

I bought a leather flying cap and goggles also, though behind one of the lenses there was only the black of my eyepatch. Our shadow trailed us as we flew toward the sun and went before us as we flew away from it. We pierced cloud banks. We flew with the geese as they arrived from the north in the fall and when they departed in the spring, their honking obscured by the drone of our engine. The world was so simple when seen from up there, as simple as it was intended to be, as if I were seeing it with the eyes of God himself.

That winter, 1914-1915, we bundled up in several layers of clothing and heavy winter coats and flew over the bare, sleeping fields. Once I dressed as Santa Claus and landed at the parade grounds of the campus in Baton Rouge to deliver Christmas presents to Frenchy and Maude and their children in Baton Rouge. Frenchy's youngest asked innocently, "Papa, why Santy Claus got one eye?" Maude told him it was a reindeer accident.

The weather warmed and the fields went from gray to brown to green, and we kept flying. We flew down to where the river spread its fingers into the Gulf, and people lived in shacks built up on stilts in the marsh, unaware of what would rise out of the sea later in the year. We flew across the twin circles of the lakes and then to the north shore, where down below us, workers dotted the green rows and the trucks at the end of the tree lines held the big, red squares of picked strawberries. The weather warmed yet again and turned hot, and we flew over the bathers in Lake Ponchartrain and the people gathered at Spanish Fort. I wondered at the small dramas being played out down there, people taking on friendships and falling in love and dreaming dreams and making plans.

We flew over laundry wagons on Carrollton and the white Roman candy vendors and the rows of houses nestled under oak boughs. At the church on the Metairie Road, we saw a bride and groom step out to the blessing of a priest and run cowering under a shower of rice thrown by well-wishers. I turned and watched them get in an automobile with cans tied to the bumper. I had been present with them for the first five seconds of their married lives. They became smaller and disappeared to live the remaining decades of it.

At the edge of the city, we flew over herds of cattle that loped off together to the shelter of shade trees as our engine and our shadow scared them away. We flew over the thin strips of the barrier islands, rimmed in white sand and parallel edges of surf in water that faded from green to deep blue. The only days we didn't fly were days that the weather kept us on the ground.

On a day a few months ago, we took off from City Park and flew over Straight College on Canal Street. It was a Saturday and down below a football game was being played. The field was ringed with men in long coats and bowler hats who watched the young men go at it. The players were lined up and completely still, and then they swarmed suddenly as the play unfolded. The dark faces craned up to see us from the sidelines and the huddles, and we moved on.

Smoke crawled from chimneys over the city into the crystal blue air, and then from boats on the river. We crossed the river and Algiers, and then over fishermen in the swamps and cane-cutters in the fields and men driving cattle and boys tending pigs.

Pigs much like the one I carried in my lap. His cloven feet had struggled at first as we bumped down the field between the oaks of City Park, but once we gained the smoothness of air, his eyes looked out as if genuinely interested, and his flat, pink snout wriggled in the air that only held the smell of the oil and gas from the engine that propelled us. The wind lifted his ears and the white bristly hairs around them, and he squinted against it as we flew higher.

We followed the river as before and found Donaldsonville and then at its side, Bayou Lafourche. The twisting bayou wove south among fields that were being shorn of their cane. I knew every curve of it by heart now. There was Paincourtville and Napoleonville, down further was Labadieville, and then, a small outline of chimney smoke on the horizon, Thibodaux. We found the house and the water tower with MT on it and circled around them. At the outer edge of my brother's property, Mr. Turner set us down in a fallow field where a group of hands rested in the shade of an oak.

One of the hands put out his cigarette on the trunk and approached with his cane knife held at his thigh. I handed the pig up to Mr. Turner while I extricated myself from my seat. When I was on the ground, I took the pig from Mr. Turner who stayed in the airplane and lit a cigarette.

"You work for Mr. Teague?" I asked the field hand.

"Yessuh, Marse Sam Teague."

I gave the pig to the man and said, "Could you see to it that he gets this pig and reads the note around its neck? The note is important."

"Yessuh," he said, though his eyes narrowed as he wondered why a man would fly in an airplane just to deliver a pig. He whistled over his shoulder. From among the men in the shade, a boy who could not have been more than twelve or thirteen came forth in overalls that were both old and too big for him. He was at that point in a boy's life, on the verge of such growth, that I couldn't help but wonder if before grinding season was over, the overalls would fit him.

"Take this pig here up yonder to Marse Sam. Tell him they's a note around his neck. Now git on."

The boy took up the squirming pig but managed to put the silver dollar I gave him in the pocket of his voluminous overalls. Then he took off with his freight wiggling against its abduction. I visited with the men in the shade for a moment, giving each of them a silver dollar, about as much as my brother would give them for their day's labor. In my goggles and my leather flying cap, I must have seemed like a man from Mars to them.

They stood and watched as Mr. Turner and I took off across the bumpy field. The distant tree line grew tall, and we vaulted up and over it. Our engine growled into a silky purr. Everything on the ground became smaller, the field hands and the cane and a boy running with a pig toward the great house next to the water tower with MT on it. How I would have liked to have been there when my brother read the note tied around the pig's neck:

Dear brother,

This pig has flown and so have I.

Your brother Jack

The early shadows of a day that had been shorter than the one before it met us on our return to City Park. Mr. Turner taxied us between the oaks, and we shook hands and talked about where we might go the next day, perhaps a flight over the Rigolets and Ship Island on the Mississippi coast. As I walked toward the streetcar stop on Canal, I heard the cricket noise of my youth. I made the sound back, though my aging lips were not as limber as they used to be.

From under the oaks came my old friend, my first friend, Neely Moses. He was gray-headed and had a thin cloudy rim of age around his pupils. Beside him were grown men who said they were his sons, and two teenage boys who said they were his grandsons. One of them wore the crimson uniform of a Straight College football player and held a leather helmet in his hand. I couldn't believe they were that old. Neely stepped forward, and we just looked at each other with stares that couldn't believe we were there and that we were both old men.

"Well, Jack, you did it. I always knew you would. I always knew it. You flew, Jack Teague, you flew."

We grasped hands and shoulders and smiled greatly and genuinely.

"What are you doing in New Orleans? I asked him.

"Oh, I live here in New Orleans. I teach at Straight. I was recruited to come down from Tougaloo."

"Since when?" I asked.

"Since '02."

"I wish I had known."

"I wish I had, too. I read about the flyer Jack Teague in the newspaper a few months ago. But I checked, and there's no Jack Teague in the City Directory, nor a Homer Prentiss. So when I saw you go overhead this afternoon at the football game, I reckoned I better get over here to see about who this Jack Teague was before he flies away for good."

His grandsons looked into the cockpit as Mr. Turner explained the levers and pedals. The boys looked back and forth as each manipulation in the cockpit turned a rudder or a flap. They helped Mr. Turner push the airplane to its barn hanger beyond the lane of oaks, still asking him questions, and Mr. Turner answered them, complete with hand gestures that banked and soared like a bird riding air currents.

We rode in Neely's son's auto to their home, a two story-house with square columns and upper and lower galleries that faced the campus of Straight College. Inside the house were shelves full of books and walls full of art and a china cabinet with china and musical instruments arranged around a parlor with tufted settees and wingback chairs. It was the house of a cultured man, a far cry from the house he had grown up in, if that could be called a house at all.

I thought of that dwelling place, a shack, really, and the ones like it, and the night my brother had taken me there for a little recreation at the expense of someone who could not give no for an answer. Whatever happened to that poor woman, I wondered, the one for whom I had bought the nice new Bible in Memphis? Had she gotten to live in a nice house like this one? Did she bear a child with the gray eyes of the Teagues? Where was she now? What was her name? I think it might have been Sara, but I couldn't remember.

"Jack," Neely said, "dinner is prepared." The men and boys wore jackets and neckties, the women and girls wore dresses with high collars and had their hair put up. I was the only one underdressed, but no word was said of it. I was a rare bird who had come down from the sky and landed at their dinner table, and I suppose my appearance was excused on account of it. We sat around a table set with smothered chicken in a dish and corn macque-choux in terrines and rice dressing and several other dishes. The youngest child read a verse from the Old and then the New Testaments, which was the habit of the Moses family. The Old Testament verse was from Ruth, the one about 'where you will go, I will go, and your people will be my people.' The New Testament verse was from Matthew's gospel, 'even as you have done to the least of these my brethren, you have done it unto me.' Neely himself then said the blessing, thanking God for the reunion of old friends, as Jesus smiled down from the picture on the wall, a picture in which he cradled a lamb to his chest.

Halfway through dinner, the grandson who had played in the game against Tuskegee came in. His place was waiting for him, but Neely adjusted his own tie as a reminder for his grandson to go up and put his on. The young man went upstairs and came down in jacket and tie.

After dinner, one of Neely's older grandsons read to us from Lord Byron and the *Iliad*, and then a granddaughter played a piece by Chopin on the piano and then one by Gottschalk, and then her cousin joined her on his trombone to play a little ragtime number. Neely frowned and called it bawdyhouse music and asked for 'Nearer God to Thee,' which they played but with a jaunty ragtime air to it. Neely sighed and chuckled and called them uncultured heathens.

During the reading, the telephone rang with a call for Dr. Moses. Neely's son excused himself to go and make a house call on a patient and offered to drop me off at my house. I took him up on it. He gathered his black bag and his overcoat.

At his door in the chilly autumn darkness, Neely and I shook hands, and then we embraced as brothers would because, without saying so, we knew that we were. He was more of a brother than my own, real brother was.

"I'm sorry I haven't kept up with you," I said. "Think of all the years—"

"—you had to keep a low profile, Jack. We can only look ahead, to better days, as old men."

On the drive home under the light of one streetlight fading into another, Neely's son spoke of how this was the time of year when the old folks take sick and to remember to dress warmly, Mr. Jack. When we arrived at my house, I got out and shut the door. Through the window, to the quiet chuckle of the auto's engine, the young doctor said, "It was an honor to finally meet you, Mr. Jack. We've grown up hearing the stories about you. Our family owes so much to you. Daddy has always said you went out on a limb to teach him to read, and that's been the key that's opened every door since."

"I suppose he didn't tell you how he saved my life. By feeding me and clothing me when I was in prison."

"Prison? You? No sir. He's never mentioned that."

"Your father is a modest man. I'll tell you about it sometime, doctor," I said, and I stepped away from his Ford, and he trundled away into the night to some sufferer who had called out to him.

Neely Moses became part of our circle, though when I introduced him, I said he was an old family friend and that we had been in the late war. I didn't tell them that my family once owned him and that he had picked our cotton. I was ashamed of it. Neely never said a word about it.

Henry Turner and I continued to fly, and at least once a week, we flew over Mount Teague. Flying was becoming such a commonplace that it no longer interested the newspapers, and so I was comfortable that I had remained anonymous to my brother. Besides, from what I gleaned from the *St. Matthew Parish Compass*, he no longer had the means to hire someone to find me.

Sometimes in flying over Mount Teague, I would see a certain black-haired woman smoking behind one of the outbuildings. When we passed, she would blow out a small tuft of smoke and put her hand to her eyes to look up at us. Mr. Turner would bank into a turn around the water tower close enough for me to see the black and white spots the birds had left on the M and the T.

Each week we made our pilgrimage to the sky over Mount Teague. On our last such visit, summer was pouring out the last of its heat on the earth and the cane. It was feathery green, like velvet when viewed from the sky, and was about ready for harvest. Down in the fields it was hot, but the wind aloft was refreshing. The fields were speckled with workers, wagons, and mules. Boys fishing in the bayou waved up to us, even those with fish on the line. And on we flew. Telephone poles marched over the cane fields in a line of crosses, the scene on Calvary repeated over and over into the distance.

There was the familiar bend in the bayou. And there was Mount Teague. We flew over, and I saw him, my brother. He was leaning like a burden on the cane that supported him. He put his hand to his eyes to block out the sun. I looked up into the front seat at Mr. Turner. His hat, a fur thing, looked so much like my father's beaver pelt hat that I was sure that if he turned his head in the wind, I would see my father's face, that if he gestured to something on the ground far below us, I would see the HT imprinted in pink scar at the base of his thumb, Horse Thief. I felt a strong desire to land and reconcile with my brother, but the wind was too heavy, and so we turned back to New Orleans.

A man grows tired of running from his past, Father. He begins to slow down, thinking in some small way that he might let it catch him. He can hear its footsteps in the leaves on the trail behind him, feel the breath of it on his shoulders and neck. He wants to turn and face it and say, 'so, where have you been? I've been waiting. I knew you would come for me.'

Thirty years had passed. I resolved that I must go and see my brother. He was old; I was old. I would say my peace and he could say his, and somewhere in the middle ground, we might find enough common peace to assume a grudging truce. It wouldn't have to be a long meeting, just enough for me to satisfy the debt to my father.

What harm could come of it?

Eva

Yes, Mrs. Leonard. I was just checking the sky. There's an airplane with two men who fly overhead once a week or so, though I haven't seen it in several months, since before my husband met his end. The man in the back seat of the thing waves sometimes. He wears a leather flying cap and goggles and is too far up for me to see who it is. It's a great curiosity to everyone here in St. Matthew, and when it passes overhead, very little work is done. Junior and Trey are always thrilled to see him. Junior always pulls over on the side of the road to see him pass overhead.

These airplanes. I hear that they are waging war with them in the skies over France. But that is only what I've overheard from the men who sit on the front steps of Aucoin's. I hear very little news of the outside world these days. We haven't taken the newspaper regularly in years now. But about that little war your country has so foolishly gotten itself into. Like stepping in something a dog has left, and now it will take years to get it off your shoes. On the other hand, so many young men in one place. I could've made a fortune in my heyday.

I understand you went into town again this afternoon. And so what news do you bring this morning, Mrs. Leonard? Did you notice the smirking faces of the women of St. Matthew? It's been that way the last few Sundays in church. Smiles that look away during the hymns, whispering behind fans and under bonnets after they catch a delicious glimpse of me. They try to conceal something, perhaps a secret glee that Mount Teague is on hard times and that I am now a widow and must face them alone. Well, by God, I shall do it, even if it takes marrying another rich husband. Why, I might just take one of their husbands if they aren't careful. Certainly, the women of St. Matthew Parish wish they were me and the men wish they were with me, both publicly and privately. Those clucking hens grin tightly and bat the air with their fans. They look at me and judge me as if they have a secret on me. Well, I say let them smirk and feel their superiority. They may still have their rich husbands, but I still have my dignity. My beauty may have faded however so slightly and my fortune lost, but my dignity is still my own and ever shall be! Mark my words! These cackling biddies in the Garden Club and the Altar Society will never take it from me. Mark my words and write them down, madame!

So when, then? When will we contact Mr. Teague? My patience is as exhausted as my bank account and my credit.

Finally! Let me have Ruthie prepare the room to use. Shall it be in the dining room or the parlor?

Oh yes, certainly. Certainly, we must wait until nightfall.

Are you quite sure that it can't be just the two of us at the séance? If it's what must be done, then invite whomever you must and no more. I am not at all in favor of it, but if you insist it is the proper form for séances, very well, but they must be sworn to secrecy.

Jack

Good morning, Father.

Did you hear the ship's boatswain chastise those boys this morning at lifeboat drills? I believe his Irish accent was thicker than yours. *'No horsing around, no joking, everyone all ears. These are the same waters where the Lusitania went down last May, and bodies washed up all summer.'* That got the boys' attention. They're too young to know it yet, but it's important to know whose lifeboat you would get in and whose you wouldn't.

I believe I was telling you of flying and seeing my brother and reflecting on our feud, wasn't I? As it turned out, that was the last time I ever flew. September 27, 1915. A Monday. It had been a hot day, still hot enough to appreciate the coolness up in the sky. When we landed at City Park, Mr. Turner said he would have some work to do on our engine the next day, Tuesday, so we planned to fly down to St. Matthew Parish on Wednesday, the 29th.

That Tuesday night, we gathered at Carriere's. As a matter of fact, we were speaking of the sinking of the *Lusitania* and the prospect of war. There had been Americans among the dead, and the wound was still fresh. Talk in the newspapers and on the streets was becoming more and more war-like, as it still is.

Sometime during our discussion, Mr. Cline arrived from the weather office saying that he feared there would be a storm. Monday evening's sunset had had a red glow like brick dust, and Tuesday morning there were high cirrus clouds, just like there had been before the Galveston storm fifteen years before. He said that weather stations in both Cuba and Mexico had reported that a storm had passed between them, and he was afraid that we in New Orleans were in danger of being hit. That was hard for us to imagine, as Tuesday had been a breezy day, nothing more.

That evening as we enjoyed the 3 C's, cocktails, cigars, and conversation, Mr. Cline kept getting up from our discussion to telephone the Weather Bureau. Each time he returned to the parlor, he brought news that ships offshore were reporting high seas and winds and falling barometers. By the time we bid one another adieu on Carriere's front porch, the winds had picked up, prodding the oaks and palms in the yellow glow of the street lamps.

Just before dawn, Mr. Turner telephoned to say that it was far too windy to fly. We agreed to wait until whatever storm was coming to pass over us. By mid-morning, winds were gusting up to forty miles an hour in the city. They picked up in frequency and intensity during the day, and the storm began firing squalls and hard, battering rain showers which let up from time to time as if taking a deep breath before the next one.

Later in the afternoon, the wind picked up even more, making the trees dance to its tune. Electric lines sparked as the poles were pushed, and when they finally fell to the ground, we fell into darkness, just as I was talking to Neely on the telephone. I was lighting a candle and preparing to search for the kerosene lamps when Carriere knocked on the door. He said that Mathilde had 'an authentic old-time supper, cooked with love over a coal stove,' if I cared to come over. I was glad for the invitation, as I had sent my cook and housekeeper home that morning. It was a good thing, too. The city had sent the streetcars back to their barn shortly after.

Next door, Carriere had gotten out his set of old kerosene lamps, pulled down from the attic and from closets, and we ate by their dim, friendly glow. Tree limbs rose and fell over the same amber light that filled every window on our block and every block on Prytania and I'm sure every other street in the city.

After supper and coffee, I returned home. My walls creaked with each new gust, one coming right at the heels of the previous one. My front door slapped open upon turning the doorknob and required a generous push to close it. The winds pushed and pulled at the trees, brushing through branches and scrubbing off leaves and then limbs. Shingles lifted and scattered off in a straight line with the force of the wind, and upstairs in one of the spare bedrooms, rain dripped where the shingles had been. I gathered pots and pans from the kitchen to collect the rivulets that fell through the seams. I bailed them every hour and then half hour and then on the quarter hour. Finally, I put down a big No. 2 washtub and nudged it under the leak. Through the window across the way, I could see Mathilde kneeling at the prie-dieu, no doubt saying a prayer for the invocation of St. Medard, the saint she always called upon during bad weather. I went to bed around ten to the insistent song of the gale and the crash of things it was bringing down.

The next morning, the winds and rain had let up and become simple breezes. Outside my window, Prytania was carpeted with green-leaves from limbs and boughs that had been brought down. The tombs across the wall in Lafayette Cemetery had leaves and limbs on them as well, though, of course, the residents of the cemetery had slept through it all and were sleeping yet.

The washtub under the leak was up to its rim. I was bailing it out when I heard the muffled clop of hooves and then someone knocking on Carriere's door across the way. It was Carriere's son Simon and Mathilde's brother Etienne Savoie and their sons. Etienne's sons were almost as dark and big as their father. Carriere opened the door and shook his brother-in-law's big, black hand and they exchanged a kiss on both cheeks and disappeared inside. The younger men, light and dark, walked around the house sidestepping limbs or reaching down to toss them aside, all the while looking up to the roof of Carriere's house. They made one loop around the house before removing ladders and stacks of shingles from the wagon. Within fifteen minutes hammers were rapping and within an hour, they were done.

One of the Carriere grandchildren, Nicolette, came by and said that her Mamere had coffee on her 'old-timey' stove and that her Nonc Etienne was drinking some with her Papere and that they wanted to know if I wanted some. The child took my hand and led me next door. I found the older men in Mathilde's kitchen where she was making pain perdu. Etienne and Carriere switched from French to English when I came in.

Etienne had ridden in from Mid-city with news that the streets were a mess, with limbs crushing automobiles and telephone poles. Lines were down, though it didn't matter because the electrical plant was down also. The St. Louis Hotel had been destroyed. The cupola of the Presbytère in Jackson Square had come down, the Presbyterian Church on Lafayette Square had fallen onto a boardinghouse next door. The clock on the St. Louis Cathedral next to the Presbytère had stopped at ten minutes to six. There was talk that half the rides at the amusement park at Spanish Fort were destroyed.

"Them kids gone be some disappointed," Mathilde said as her busy hands cleaned.

Etienne said that when the electrical plant went down, the pumps had failed and that some streets were flooded. I wondered about Neely and his family. Outside, hammers began rapping again.

But the worst news that Etienne had was from St. Bernard Parish. The levees downriver had been breached, and there were reports of great loss of life there, though no one could be certain. Mathilde and Carriere genuflected.

The hammering had stopped again just as we finished our second cup of coffee and our pain perdu. Outside on the street, the Savoie and Carriere men were putting ladders and unused bundles of shingles on the back of the wagon as the horse stared from behind her blinders and swished her tail. I looked up to my roof. It had been repaired while I had sat inside and drank coffee.

The shingles were mismatched, which the Carriere and Savoie men apologized for, and I assured them it was certainly worth it to have a dry house and that I was grateful. I said I would see to the water stains and the curtains later. They refused payment and were emptying the washtub of rainwater out the window when Neely's son Dr. Moses drove up in his Ford. I went downstairs and met him on the front porch. In the street, his auto quietly murmured. We got in, and he took us up St. Charles.

"Mr. Jack," he said, "Our house is wrecked but Papa won't leave it. I'm afraid it might fall down on him. We have to go down to Carrolton and then go up that way. Some of the streets are still flooded. I was out on a call, or the Ford would have taken water, too."

We crept over the green carpet of St. Charles, around fallen limbs and over electrical cables. At Audubon Park, I looked over to see the Horticultural Hall, where I had met Eva Teague the second time at the Cotton Exposition. The magnificent building, once the largest in the world, had been reduced to twisted metal and acres of broken glass. Up Carrolton, house after unroofed house sat beheaded as families gathered things from inside and began to inventory them on soggy front lawns.

The scene was no different at the home of Neely Moses on Gasquet Street. It was also partially unroofed with sagging walls and puddles of rainwater, a study in skewed lines. Nothing about the house was parallel or perpendicular, and it looked like it would only take a heavy sigh to bring it down. Things were scattered around the floor where the wind and water had rearranged them. Inside, Neely sat in a wooden dining room chair with his arms clutching himself and a resolute look on his face. I walked in through a door that had been plowed open and left that way, and I gingerly took a chair and sat beside him. For what seemed like an eternity, we said nothing. I was scared that with any sort of talk, the house would suddenly give up and come crashing down on us.

Finally, I said, "You can't stay here, Neely. Not right now. Come stay with me until we can get your house right again."

That was somewhere between blind optimism and a lie. This house would not survive. And it didn't take an engineer to tell it.

"This is my house, Jack. I'm not leaving it."

Neely looked around, perhaps seeing his home, his castle, reduced to the shack he had grown up in and then fled. Shafts of sunlight pierced it. The breeze whistled through it and made it creak.

"Come on, Papa," his son said from the doorway. "Let's go stay with Mr. Jack for a little while."

"I'm not going. This is my house. I want to stay in my own house." He jabbed his thumbs toward the floor. "My own. House."

"All right," I said, nodding. "All right. We'll come and get you if it rains. You'll sure get wet without a roof."

We left him there as the rest of the Moses family went through the things collected during their lifetimes. Musical instruments, books, clothes, kitchenware. All scattered and being sorted on the front lawn. I asked Dr. Moses if he would drive me up to City Park. He took one more look at the house and shook his head as we got in his Ford.

"I think it hurts Papa more that we might become scattered," he said over the steering wheel and into the windshield. We snaked our way through side streets I never knew existed, though Dr. Moses had been in almost half of the houses on them, both in daylight and in dark. His black bag rode between us, *Paul Moses, MD* embossed in gold in the leather.

City Park was also blanketed with limbs and leaves as far as the eye could see. The barn was still intact, and I saw that that Mr. Turner had the airplane out on the grass in front of it. Dr. Moses let me out, and I walked through puddles to where Mr. Turner was removing limbs to clear a path between the oaks for takeoff.

"Levees broken downriver," he said after barely looking up. "Wireless from St. Bernard says that there are people trapped down there. I'm going down to spot them and then come back to direct the rescue boats."

As he hastily threw debris left and right, I offered to go with him. He stopped what he was doing and said, "Jones, what I really think you should do is go down to St. Matthew and check on that fellow with the water tower, the one's got MT on it. I see you watching that place, and I know there's a reason you have me fly over at least once a week." He resumed clearing a lane and said, "Take the train. Probably too wet to set down there anyhow."

My silence agreed with Mr. Turner. He climbed into our airplane, and I pulled the propeller for him. The engine turned and coughed and started on the first try. I pulled out the chocks from under the wheels and retreated under the oaks. He turned into the lane, and after a thumbs up and a wave, he shouted, "Send my regards to MT." With that, his engine roared, and the airplane splashed through puddles and then rose and cleared the tops of the oaks and careened a little. He dipped his wings and I waved, and then he banked from due east to due south.

Dr. Moses and I stopped again on Gasquet. Some of the family got in with us, each carrying something cherished from a former life, a book, a hair bow, a trumpet, the cat. Neely's granddaughter Clara lingered on the porch, pressing keys on the piano that they couldn't bring. Each key had either no sound or a dull, dissonant tap. They had managed to move it out on the front porch, but the case of it was bashed into a V. It was no use. She wiped her eyes and came and got in the car next to me. Dr. Moses put his head in the doorway and said something, and I heard his father's resolute voice again, *I'm not going.*

We packed into the auto and retraced our circuitous route via Carrolton and down St. Charles with all but one of the Moses family. Evening was falling. Cool weather was beginning to stir, and we kept the windows open. I settled them into bedrooms that had not once been occupied since I bought the house. Each of those handsome brown faces thanked me but retained a blankness, the hopeless stare of someone who had been wronged by nature but could do nothing about it. I told them that my home was their home, but I knew for them, it wasn't. Their home was a wilting mass of splintered lumber, sagging down around their patriarch.

Dr. Moses asked if he might have the hospital ring my number when the telephones came back up. Certainly, I said, and I asked if he might drop me off at the train station. I said I had to check on an old acquaintance who lived down in St. Matthew. As he dropped me off, I gave him my house key and again told him to make himself at home. He thanked me profusely and said he was going by one more time to try and get his father to come.

"Remind your father that I owe him a favor, that he helped me out and took me in when I was in a tight spot," I said.

"Hard head," his son said.

"And an aching heart," I replied.

He pulled out onto Canal Street. Crews were getting it cleared of wires and toppled palms, and he weaved between them. I turned to see that Werlein's was open. I told Dr. Moses to drop me off there, that I had an errand to run.

Inside, a man was taking inventory of what the storm had done. There was no damage that I could see, but the man was checking each piano like a worried hen looking over her eggs. I went in and bought a piano and had it shipped to my home on Prytania. I put 'for Miss Clara Moses' on the delivery instructions.

The agent at the train station said that no trains were running and probably wouldn't be for several days, so I walked down to the foot of Iberville Street and booked passage on an upriver steamer for first thing in the morning, October 1st. I thought of walking back home, but instead I took a room for the night at the Monteleone on Royal.

Night fell quickly on the exhausted city. I turned in early, but I couldn't sleep. My mind raced, worried about Neely sitting in his ruined house, like a mouse sitting in an un-sprung trap. Every time a wind came up and nudged my curtains, I feared that some small beam or brace in his house might shift and the whole thing would come down on top of him. But that wasn't all that kept my eyes open.

I was also worried about my brother. I wondered if he had survived the storm. There had been no word from St. Matthew. Yes, Father, I was worried, but I admit it was not entirely for his well-being. I was worried that if he had died, my promise to our father would go unmet. Such a horrible thing to say, but it was the truth.

After a restless night, I was checking out in the lobby. A boy of about five or so was looking at the grandly ornate clock in the lobby. I paused and looked at it with him.

"That's a real nice clock isn't it?" I said. "Can you tell time yet?"

"No sir," the lad said. He had on a sailor collar and knee pants. It was the kind of outfit that would make him a mark for other boys if he wore it much longer.

"Well," I said, "the little hand there is the hour. It's pointing to eight, and the big hand points out the minutes. So it's eight-oh-five."

He seemed starved for company, like a hothouse flower suddenly seeing the sun. We talked for a few moments. A man was having a mild argument with the desk clerk, something about what was available to eat. He had been standing right behind me as I checked out and smelled like bay-rum aftershave. When he was done, he came folding a piece of paper and putting it in his coat pocket. He looked up to me, and I saw him clearly for the first time. That is, the first time in over twenty years. A look of wonder came over his face.

"Professor Prentiss?" he asked.

The Honor Code that I had once carried so proudly had been beaten faceless and no longer mattered.

"No," I said as I extended my hand, "John Jones."

"Samuel Teague, Jr.," he replied. "I have to say, Mr. Jones, you look just like a professor I had when I was in school at Sewanee, a man named Professor Homer Prentiss. Even down to the eyepatch. Of course, that's been some twenty years ago."

"I've heard that once before," I said with an affected English accent. "I should like to meet this Harry Prentiss fellow sometime."

"Homer Prentiss. Homer," Junior Teague corrected me.

"Yes, yes, Homer," I said. "Well, Mr. Teague, I must be going. Boat to catch."

"Yes, us too, eventually. Going to Havana. Vacation before grinding season begins. We've been delayed by the storm."

"Yes, very well, safe trip, then," I said.

The doorman opened the door, and in the glass I saw the reflection of the man and his son watching me go. I walked hurriedly down Royal Street and into the first alley I came to. When the man and the boy passed by, looking around and heading for Bienville Street, I slipped out and went down Iberville. I boarded the steamer and went below deck. As we pushed away from the dock, I saw the man and the boy looking across the water from the wharf. I ducked back down below until we were well upriver.

And so I went to St. Matthew. I had no plans of staying and took no change of clothes or anything else. Maybe my brother would offer for us to have a toddy in his parlor. Should I accept? It would mean being under the same roof as Eva, she who had maddened me with the gift of her body. I would ignore her. Yes, I thought, I would ignore her and focus my attention on my brother. The sin I committed with her had been thirty years ago. Certainly time had run out on it. Certainly it was cancelled. I would ignore her, declare a truce with my brother, and satisfy my promise to my father. Then I would return home, and my burden would be lifted.

As I sat and watched the riverbank scroll by, cold air began to push at the river. The surface of the water slid sideways with the insistence of the north wind.

Pinch

When he got on the boat, I got on with him and stood at his feet. He looked back to the land and then I looked. The man and the boy were coming. They wanted to see Jack. But Jack didn't want them to see him. I was certain of that, for Jack went down below the floor into the boat. I barked a silent shout, and then I went down with him.

Once the city had gone away, he returned and sat outside. He was thinking. When he thinks, he rubs his forehead and squints his eye. He might have been thinking of the man and the boy, but I didn't know for sure. Even we spirits do not know everything.

The wind pushed the gray and white sky, and it rolled over us and headed south, where we were headed. There were faces in the wind, faces that were blowing in without form. They curled out of the gray sky and uncurled in tendrils like cold smoke. Eyes, noses, mouths appeared and disappeared. I watched and lifted my ears and tilted my head as the cold pushed in around those faces that came from the clouds. They pushed past us, howling and whispering, though only I, a dog and a spirit, could hear them. If he had seen or heard the figures, Jack would have been frightened of them.

But he didn't see them and he didn't hear them. I lay at the feet of my master while he hugged himself against the cold. It became too uncomfortable for him and he went inside and I went inside. Something was going to happen. It would be good and it would be bad.

Jack

In Donaldsonville, I rented a horse and took the Bayou Road south. It was paved with shells, and so, despite the soggy ground, the footing was good. Telephone poles had fallen across the road, and downed limbs had cracked open houses. In the fields, cane lay like fallen soldiers, great matted weaves of it all the way from the road to the tree lines. Neighbors fixed neighbors' houses and fences. Saws rasped and hammers drummed against boards that slapped over other boards. Elsewhere a family had gathered to butcher a pig, whose carcass hung from a limb while a pot boiled in the yard and a dog circulated and barked among the crowd. The dog made me think of old Pinch. I had buried him somewhere around there.

I followed the bayou and the road that bore its name. Brown water was pouring out in its route to the Gulf. The cold wind nudged at my back as I followed the white shell path. Two men were righting a Ford Model A with a mule. I asked them how Mount Teague had fared. One of them spit on the ground at the mention of the name Teague, but neither answered. I continued on.

I scanned the horizon for the water tower, MT, but I couldn't see it. I was afraid that I had passed it or that the house had been wiped out, until I came across a sign that was blown down that said, *Now Entering Property of S. M. Teague, Mount Teague Plantation.*

About half a mile down, I recognized the lane of oaks, and I paused at the end of them. The mailbox lying on its side simply said, TEAGUE. I rode down the white shell lane, recalling the day that I first arrived, heavy-hearted from having buried Pinch. I could almost feel his presence, his merry trot, his happy bark. To the side of the house, the water tower with the great MT written on its side had been pushed over, the tank burst like an overripe melon. It had barely missed the rear gallery of the house. The house still stood, though there were bare patches where entire sections of shingles had been taken by the wind.

No servant came to greet me and take my horse, and the railing was missing from the front steps, not blown down but worn out and removed well before the storm. I tied my horse to a limb, took a deep breath, and ascended the steps. After another deep breath, I knocked on the door. A servant opened it and greeted me.

"Ma'am—" I said.

"Miss Eva," she called out behind her. A voice answered from the darkness of the house.

Who is it, Ruthie? Is it the curtain man?

"You the curtain man?" Ruthie asked as if I hadn't heard her mistress.

"No ma'am," I said. "I've come to speak with Mr. Teague."

Eva emerged from the darkness of the house and came to the door. She peered at me with the baffled squint of a mid-afternoon drunk. Her hair was disheveled, her face was jowly. She put her hand up to shield her aching eyes from the light, though it was an overcast day. She wore a thin nightdress, so thin that her nakedness under it required little imagination. Her breasts sagged dejectedly down to nipples that looked in sorrow at the potbelly that had developed, an overturned kettle of doughy flesh. But her blue eyes were the same, almost mesmerizing enough to make up for all her other deficits. I kept my eyes on Ruthie's brown ones.

With a dried, raspy voice, Eva asked me again if I were the curtain man come up from Thibodaux, as she had guests coming later in the week for some sort of meeting and they would recognize the curtains from the last meeting there. She braced herself with one hand against the door frame. Her breasts lounged over her stomach. I don't think she remembered who I was. Perhaps she was too drunk. Or perhaps her catalog of lovers and conquests was too great to recognize a few entries from long ago. But she stared at me as her bloodshot blue eyes strained to both see and avoid harassment by the light.

"Who're you? Wazzure your bidness here?" she slurred. It seemed to hurt her head to talk or look into the light or both, or maybe her head hurt no matter what she did.

"I've come to see your husband."

"That eyepatch," she said, and she gave a drunken gesture of grandeur and put one hand over her eye. "Er yoo the pirate Jean Laffite?"

I made no reply to her mockery of me, and then she said, "Where's your Got-damned treasure, Mizzure Laffite?"

She stifled a watery belch with the back of her hand. Her other hand motioned with a flicking gesture out where I might find her husband, my brother. Ruthie answered for her mistress.

"Marse Sam out in them Barbagree Fields. You know where they at, sir?"

"Yes, I believe I do."

I remembered clearly where the Barbagree Fields were. They were the ones with the abandoned shack in the middle of them. I had seen them coming in. I turned from the two women and returned to my horse, who was patiently clipping grass. I pulled myself up into the saddle and began riding down the lane of oaks.

"Wait," Eva called out. I turned my horse. "Wait!" She shouted again, and I could feel my own head bulge in sympathy with what hers must have felt like. "Who're you? Wazzure name? Got-damn it, wazzure name, sir?"

I turned my horse away from the house. Behind me, there was a retching and a splatter and the servant said, *Miss Eva, you go on lay down. I clean it up.* Halfway down the lane I looked back to see the servant Ruthie with a rag over her shoulder bringing a bucket and a scrub brush.

I found my brother in his fields. He looked so much older than I had imagined, but I suppose, so did I. Fallen cane lay like the weave of a basket as far as the eye could see. A gang of Negroes was lifting the stalks and hacking at the bases. Even in good weather it was difficult work, but the sodden stalks were heavy with moisture and in danger of rotting if they remained in the field much longer. All of the men wore jackets and coats recently taken down from pegs for the return of cold weather.

My brother was smoking a cigar, his hands pressing into the top of the crook of his cane, pausing only to harangue them as they chopped. At his back was a cane wagon, loaded impossibly high with stalks. And yet he had them piling on more. I came from around the wagon, and when I did, my brother followed the eyes of his field hands to me.

"What is your business here?" he growled, "I have cane to get in."

I wanted to recount happy events from our boyhood, holiday meals, secret shared jokes, hunts and fishing trips, but I couldn't think of any. A slurry of words spilled out of me.

"Brother," I said, "We're old men now. Come, let us make amends so that we might spend a few happy years and then die as friends and so make our father proud."

"Ha! That old horse-thief?" Then it dawned on him that I was no ordinary stranger. "My brother? Jack? Why, there's a thirty-year-old warrant for your arrest!" He pulled a long inhalation through his cigar and then let it out as he spoke over his shoulder.

"One of you niggers take a mule into Napoleonville for the sheriff." The field hands paused in their exertions and looked at one another. We appeared to be two old men on the verge of a fistfight. Our chests were puffed out, our eyes were locked. Finally my brother looked over his shoulder and said, "You, Curtis. Run and fetch the sheriff."

Curtis dropped his cane knife and struggled through the muddy earth toward one of the mules hitched in the traces of the wagon. I turned and walked away. I could see the rest of my life shortened by the noose or lengthened by life in prison, deprived of the friendships I had made in the city with Mr. Carriere and Mr. Leitz and Neely and the rest of my circle. I was gripped by a remorse that I had come at all, a remorse so heavy that it seemed to pull my shoes into the black mud like the weight of sin. I left my brother with his chest puffed out, and I stumbled away and stopped on the other side of the wagon and braced against it. I could hear him laughing derisively on the other side. In my anguish, I leaned into the cane wagon, fighting the urge to weep, my face pressed into the dense, heaping mass of heavy, sweet stalks. The wind piled in from the north and nudged the pale cane at the top of the wagon. It twitched and rustled in the cold air. And then it all gave way in a sudden, swinging, downward curve.

The two wheels of the wagon opposite me and closest to my brother sank into the ground, giving way into the mud. The wagon dipped toward the earth and the gray sky emerged above it. I could feel the sudden change of angle, the sweep of an arc as mass became energy. The cane wagon tipped over, slowly at first and then in a rustling plummet into the black mud on top of my brother. The transfer of forces, mass becoming energy through acceleration, a formula written by a cadet on a sheet of paper. The mules that were still in the traces hawed and struggled in the mire, and several of the men unhitched them. The mules flopped to a standing position and trotted several dozen yards away and stood and eyed us indifferently with flattened ears.

"Let's get this off of him," I said, and I pulled at the edge of the wagon. I could not move it. Ten men might have had a chance.

"Let's empty the wagon, so we can right it. This man's life is at stake!" I yelled.

"Hold on, now, suh," one of the men said calmly. "Marse say he want them wagons stacked high-high, full-full. Boo-coo full, suh."

They began laughing, all of them laughing through the cigarettes they had lit and were smoking leisurely. Laughing like a tree full of starlings.

I waited on the men to act on the wagon, but they made no move to right it. Instead, they slowly enjoyed their cigarettes and leaned against it. By and by, the muffled supplications of my brother from under the great burden of cane stopped, and the hands began singing. Not one of them had made a move to raise the wagon. In fact, while I waited, they did not so much as stoop and swing a cane knife. A pale hand was all that protruded from under the heavy cane wagon. An older field hand, gray-headed with skin so black and a beard so white that he looked like the photographic negative of a man, came and nudged the arm with his boot.

"Marse Sam show nuff dead."

"Praise Gawd," one of them said as he stared at the cigarette he was lighting.

"Should we run fetch somebody? Doc McKnight?" someone asked.

"By and by, child, by and by. He ain' gone get nary a bit less dead from here on."

Someone snorted, and then they all laughed again, bending forward, some dropping their cane knives. A couple of them crawled onto the overturned wagon, and they sat and smoked and sang. And they paid no heed to me as I walked away and took the reins of my horse from an oak limb. I had done the best that I could, but I had failed.

I had failed my father. And I had failed him miserably.

Eva

Yes, Mrs. Leonard, about my late husband and the events of his demise. It was just after the hurricane had passed. He had been out supervising our remaining hands in gathering up what we could of our storm-flattened cane. He was supposed to come in for his noon meal and nap but had not arrived. I was not feeling well and had laid down for a nap. During it, I had the oddest dream that the traveling tinker, my husband's brother and our sugarhouse engineer, had paid us a call. But he had been ruined into the dust by his failure, and I'm sure he would never show his face here again.

A little after one in the afternoon, one of our field hands, Curtis Favorite, came running up with word that something dreadful had befallen Mr. Teague and that another of the hands had gone off to Napoleonville for Dr. McKnight. I contented myself with my Victrola and a romance novel as I waited for word.

Dr. McKnight came to the house later that afternoon and confirmed that my husband had indeed met his end. I sent word to the *Compass* immediately that Mr. Teague had passed, including the obituary that had been prepared anticipating just such an event. Such things simply cannot be left to chance, madame. It extolled his life as one of St. Matthew Parish's earliest and most prominent citizens and was carried on the front page, as the society column of 'Merry Chatsworth' could not have held its length nor its importance.

Rather than announce that just anyone from the public could attend his funeral, invitations were sent, and we held it in this very parlor. All the best people of this Parish and surrounding Parishes attended. I had proposed a seven-course dinner, but Rev. Gladney advised against it, and only hors d'oeuvres were served.

The funeral was delayed, however. My mourning dress being made by a seamstress in Donaldsonville was held up in a dispute relating to my credit, and so the invitations had to be recalled and then resent. The dress, however, was simply divine! Why, President McKinley's wife had no finer attire for her mourning. It was a black silk dress in the Henrietta style with a long veil and bonnet, all crape-trimmed with a matching silk parasol, kid gloves, and cambric handkerchiefs, ivory with a black border. Simply exquisite, Mrs. Leonard, simply exquisite. All the perfect backdrop for a sapphire pendant and blue eyes, as I'm sure you can imagine.

But not a word of it in Merry Chatsworth's society column! Imagine! The seamstress in Donaldsonville continues to demand payment for my mourning ensemble. And me, a poor widow. Everything else for the service had been donated, the flowers, casket, and so forth, and I suppose I should be grateful, and I would be if I were in the habit of that pernicious emotion. But gratitude is nothing if not an invitation to weakness.

Junior was more affected by Mr. Teague's death than I was, muttering to the casket with dripping eyes, 'Were you proud? Am I a credit to you and the name Teague?' Such sniveling was unbecoming a Teague, so I quietly admonished him to dry it up immediately, that his father could not hear his crying now nor would he have heard of it before he departed. *Buck up and be a man*, I murmured to my son under my breath as we stood side by side with the rest of the invited behind us. He wiped his eyes with the back of his wrist and nodded. As we sat down, he asked again in a sniveling whisper if his sister might not be removed from Carville in time for the internment and given a chance to come and grieve for her father, separate, of course, from other mourners owing to her condition. I told him it was out of the question, that such lapses are how diseases like leprosy spread. Why, we would all come down with it! And then what!

We stowed my late husband away, casket and all, in the ice parlor for safekeeping while I had a man come down and prepare a fine mausoleum. I asked the sculptor, a Mr. Carter or something like that, if he could do it on credit, and he replied that he had had dealings with my husband years before and that it would be his pleasure to prepare a final resting place fitting for Mr. Teague.

Is there anything else you wish to know, Mrs. Leonard?

Very well, I must take leave to ready myself since we will have guests arriving shortly. You have a very important task ahead of you. Contacting my husband. Do not fail me.

C. H. Lawler

Curtis Favorite

Yes ma'am, Miss Gladys. Ruthie say you wanted to see me. Yes ma'am. This time of year we layin' down seed cane, bustin' stubble on the rest. Yes ma'am.

I'll tell you 'bout that day, that day Marse Sam passed, but you can't tell no body, not a soul, no ma'am.

It was a cold, cold day, first one of the year. We out in ol' Barbagree's Fields, what we call 'em, where he used to stay, house out yonder. A man come up on a horse, got one eye and a patch on the other. Well, he come down and Marse Sam out there d'rectin' us to get that cane in, and it's hard-hard work that, cause all that cane wet down on the ground. Heavy, heavy, boo-coo heavy.

This man got a patch come round the side of that cane wagon, loaded high and Marse Sam still want it higher, so he can get it in faster. Cause if'n it stay out yonder much mo' it gonna be rot and Marse ain' get paid no way for it.

Yes ma'am, well this man come and he say he Marse Sam's brother and he want to make up and make they daddy proud.

Marse Sam say for me to unhitch a mule and git on up to Napoyun-ville and fetch the sheriff cause Marse Sam's brother got a warrant for his arrest. Well, the man with the patch, Marse Sam's brother, he turns to leave and bout that time the wheels on that cane wagon start sinkin in the ground like dis.

Well, ma'am, on a cloudy day don't nobody or nothin' throw no shadow. No man, no mule, no ma'am. And f'show no cane wagon. So Marse Sam ain' seen it. But down it come, straight on top he head. That other man with that half a mask on he face come round t'other side and he say you men help me get this here offa dis man. Ol' Jeff say, suh, I believe dis here man done fo. This prolly close to a ton a cane, yassuh.

But Marse Sam ain' dead yet. He still groanin' up under there and his arm the onliest thang out from under there and it jussa twitchin' like dis. Marse Sam's brother the man wit dat mask on his eye, he struggle and struggle but he see it ain' no use, and he beg us to help but ain' nobody want to help. So he

452

just up and leave and head back to Napoyun-ville and that's the last I see that man.

By and by, Ol' Jeff he come up and nudge Marse Sam's arm wit his boot and he say I show believe he dead now, 'bout as dead as he gone get.

God help me for laughin' Miss Gladys, but I can't hep it. I can't hep it no more than I can hep breathin'.

Yes ma'am. Nary a word is your promise, and your promise your bond.

Pinch

While we are living, we dogs can see spirits, and when we are spirits ourselves, it is no different. On that day that the wagon fell on the man who was the littermate of my master, the souls of many came up in a sudden wind that could be felt by both the living and the dead.

They assembled, and I could see that they were the spirits of those who had been harmed by the man who smoked the cigar on the other side of the wagon from my master Jack. The spirits gave their shoulders to the wagon and it sank away from them and it fell. I found myself barking wildly, prancing and pacing up and down the line of men and women, all shades and sizes and ages, people who had been wronged by this cigar-smoking man. Their spirits gave their shoulders and hands and backs into the wagon that was loaded with the big, sweet grass, taller than a house.

It fell and crushed the man and then in an instant they were all gone, and there was only my master Jack. He seemed confused that he could have pushed over the wagon for he had not tried to and he did not see the others and could not see me, though I sat next to him at his feet and looked up to him and then the overturned wagon. The spirits were gone. Their work was done. The last of them had a beard as gray as moss. He was the man that in life had been called Barbagree.

Dr. George McKnight

Yes, Mrs. Leonard. I'd be happy to visit for a moment before we begin the ceremony, if that is what it's called.

So on October 1st, 1915, the first truly cold day of the year, I was called to the deserted shack once occupied by the old man Barbagree. I had my gig readied and proceeded there on the double-quick. There I found the subject placed on a cypress plank, one end resting on a windowsill and the other on an old chair. The body was encased in mud and bore the striations or I should say imprints of the cane wagon that had toppled over and upon him. I examined the deceased and identified him by the scar on his face and on his hip, two old wounds which all knew him by, though none would be so bold as to speak of them. I verified that it was the body of my friend, and I say friend because having him as your friend was still better than having him as your enemy, though only marginally so.

It was clear what had happened. There were striations upon his body from the ribs of the cane wagon and the stalks of the cane itself. Forgive me for putting it bluntly, ma'am, but he had been flattened. The hands said that he had been pressed a foot or two into the earth, and they had dug him out as quickly as they could.

I fixed the cause of death as heart failure secondary to asphyxiation secondary to an agricultural accident. I could have also included moral failure as a cause, but that is not fatal, and, in fact, many people walk around with it daily. It is only the people who come in contact with them who suffer from it.

Is there anything else you wish to know?

Yes, I will be there momentarily.

Jack

I left St. Matthew Parish, but I didn't return to New Orleans right away. Instead I took a room in Donaldsonville and waited, guilt-ridden over having killed my brother. I took my meals in my room. The cold wind diminished, and the warm wind of an Indian summer blew in from the south. I wanted to go and pay my respects to my brother, but I knew there was no way I could do that without taking the risk of being arrested. And so I waited, unable to stay or go.

The *St. Matthew Parish Compass* settled the matter for me. The following day, it carried a special edition with a full front page story of my brother's demise, replete with scriptural references to the wise kings of Israel. There was no mention of Pharaohs or Pharisees as, perhaps, there should have been. The article said that 'a jewel, an irreplaceable jewel, had been plucked from the crown of Mount Teague.' A special invitation was required to attend the funeral to be held at the residence of the deceased. Of course, I knew that I would not be included on the guest list. I headed back to New Orleans.

When I stepped off the landing at the Iberville Street wharf, I saw that the streetcars were running again and the streets had been cleared of debris. I took the Canal Street car to City Park to see if Mr. Turner might fly us over St. Matthew for the funeral, as I was not going to be among those whom the *Compass* said would be receiving a 'coveted invitation.'

There was no sign of activity at the barn. I unlocked the padlock and swung the doors out over the twin ruts made by our coming and going. The airplane was not in there, nor was Mr. Turner in the small office he had made for himself in what used to be the tack room. A policeman patrolling the park looked in on me and said that Mr. Turner had failed to return. There were reports of an airplane flying out over the Breton Sound, continuing on as a speck and then disappearing, the drone of the engine becoming like the hum of a mosquito. After a week, Henry Turner was officially listed as lost at sea, the last recorded fatality of the hurricane of 1915.

I thought he must have family somewhere who should be told of his disappearance and presumed death. None of my circle seemed to know any more about him than the fact that he flew airplanes. Professor Jacquet had met him only by chance when he was flying in City Park.

I returned to search his small room in the barn at City Park. It smelled of grease and aromatic dust amid the faint, forgotten aroma of mules and horses. On his workbench were wrenches, an oil can, a fifteen gallon gasoline can, a piston that he had changed out, his wireless set. Pinned to the wall were a

1915 calendar with a pretty girl on it, put out by the Prudential Insurance Company, and a receipt for gasoline from the Texas Company, Mr. Cullinan's outfit. In the desk drawer of the workbench were a pack of Pirate brand cigarettes, a box of Old Man River matches, and a fifth of Old Monongahela brand rye whiskey. I had not seen a bottle of Old Monongahela since I was a boy. My daddy drank a jigger of it every evening after dinner, for good digestion, he said.

That was all that was left in Mr. Turner's makeshift office. There were no letters from home, no Christmas cards or cards delivering birthday wishes, no deeds to anything, no bank account receipts, or anything else of the sort. It was as if Henry Turner had only existed to take me flying. I walked away from the barn and toward home. A week later, the city condemned the old barn and had it razed.

It wasn't the only building that would come down. On Gasquet Street, the Moses house had finally given up. I would not have recognized it if not for the piano which was barely visible on what used to be the front porch. I peered into the wreckage, the ruins of a man's beloved castle, the jumble of a former life. A cabinet with cracked white shards of china. Books whose pages had been bloated with water and now were dried and bulging. Splintered limbs of furniture.

I turned and walked down the street toward home. Along the way, people swept and loaded. Crews were replacing poles and stringing wire. Men in aprons swept shops and greeted rival shopkeepers across the streets, subtle animosities set aside for a while.

I half-expected to find Neely laid out in my parlor like my brother was laid out in his. I arrived home in the fading light of a shortened day and found Neely very much alive, reading Chaucer under a kerosene lamp while Clara played the new piano that had arrived for her. Her hair was fixed in a bow, and all the other members of the Moses household were as well-dressed as circumstances would allow. Something in the kitchen smelled good.

"Jack, you're just in time for dinner," Neely said as he tucked a marker into the book and shut it.

We prayed and then ate and talked amid silverware clicking on china. After dinner, we listened to music and the children read to the adults. Neely and I stayed up until the young retired to bed, no small feat for gentlemen of our age. The Moses family had been transplanted from Gasquet Street and was putting down roots into the soil of Prytania Street. As they went up to get dressed for bed, they came and shook my hand and quietly embraced me. When the last ascended the stairs, Neely said, "I saw in the paper that your brother died down in St. Matthew."

"I had heard that, too."

"You're not going to the funeral," he said.

"Afraid not. Don't think I'd be welcome."

Neely nodded thoughtfully but didn't say anything for a minute.

"Sometimes reconciliation never happens, Jack, never can happen. It's as foolish and fruitless as planting stones instead of seeds and expecting a harvest."

Upstairs, the sound of bedtime stories and then the murmur of the young reciting prayers under the supervision of the old scented my house with warmth.

"Jack," Neely said, "As far as I'm concerned, any debts we might have had one against the other are hereby satisfied."

We clasped hands in agreement, and then he went upstairs, peering up into the darkness at the top of the steps amid the satisfying quiet of a dry, safe household. I was left in my parlor in the gentle wake of happiness finding another way. In the silence, I heard the faint chink-chink coming from Carriere's shop next door. I went to bed myself listening to him working into the night, preparing a marker to commemorate a life.

In the coming days and weeks, I struggled with the company of others. Obeying the vulnerable instinct of the guilty and yet undiscovered, I stayed inside, afraid of the outside world and the judgment it might render against me. I was convinced I would be hunted down, so I kept to my house that was now animated by the sounds of a loving family. A week passed, then a month. I waited, both patient and hopeless, sure of the incipient calamity that I was convinced would follow. I suppose the Proverb is correct, Father, *'A wicked man flees when none pursue, but the righteous are as bold as a lion.'*

October fled, then November. The *Compass* reported that my sister-in-law had welcomed an English spiritualist, and I wondered if it was an attempt to see if my brother had money hidden away, either at Mount Teague or in a bank somewhere. On a cold night in early December, I heard the sound of

Mr. Carriere working in his shop. It was freezing, but I wanted to go and visit. My circle had begun to notice my absence.

"Well, the hermit of Prytania Street," Carriere smiled over his glasses. I also found Mr. Leitz the undertaker there, visiting with Carriere as he chipped away at a block of marble. It was a monument for a child, a cherub holding a lamb. The face of the cherub was soft and reassuring, solace emerging from hard, white stone.

Under the electric lights, now long since turned back on after the hurricane of September, Mr. Leitz produced a shoebox. In it were items sometimes referred to as 'French postcards.' They had been given to Mr. Leitz by the family of a recently deceased man on Napoleon Avenue. Mr. Leitz will, from time to time, receive things like them in the effects of some old bachelor or widower from his flustered survivors, titillating nudes that the deceased might have had hidden away for private study. Mr. Leitz wanted Carriere to see them, to see if he could use them as nude studies, as Mathilde would frown upon a man of her husband's age using living nude models. Carriere paused from his chipping and tapping and looked over his glasses.

"Well, what a coincidence," Carriere said. "I believe the woman in those could well be the widow for whom I prepared that red marble tomb. Those eyes." He smiled again and resumed his tapping, the musical notes like the highest keys of a piano. Mr. Leitz passed them to me.

The pictures were almost forty years old, marked by a photographer in Shreveport and taken in the year 1877. In them was a certain dark-haired girl, naked except for stockings and a bow in her hair, on horseback in one, with another girl in a rather intimate pose in another, brandishing a whip and a chair as if taming a lion in yet another. The shape of her body, her breasts, her thighs and the dark shield of hair, her coy smile. And her blue eyes a pale shade of gray in the monochrome. They pierced me again. She was certainly beautiful, and, in fact, she was so striking that anyone who ever knew her would be able to recognize her immediately, even if she were much older and heavier. The back of them said only, '*Sometimes haughty, always naughty, on Commerce Street, ask for Lottie.*'

Mr. Carriere had recognized her at once. He said that the subject of the photographs was almost certainly the widow who had commissioned a fine mausoleum for her husband. The man was a sugar planter who had been crushed by a great burden of sugarcane in a sudden and unfortunate accident. It had taken Carriere several weeks to complete it, all the while being pestered by the defunct occupant's widow, this blue-eyed woman who so resembled the woman in the French postcards. She and her husband had once been powerfully wealthy, but in recent years, they had fallen on hard times. Mr. Carriere doubted he would ever get paid for his work. It is Mr. Carriere's way, however, to perform acts of charity and kindness.

Carriere declined the postcards, and Mr. Leitz was about to throw them in the fire of the stove, but I stopped him and asked that he let me have them. He raised his eyebrows and gave them over. He has known me for a number of years and knows that I am not in the habit of keeping such bawdy items.

"Those eyes. Such beauty," I said.

"Are you sure it's just the eyes, Jones?" He laughed, and he gave the box to me.

Later, I looked at them, not titillated in the least. I am too old for that. It was more like mourning. I reviewed the bad bargain I had made, selling my future and everything else for temporary pleasure. I had gone on a fool's errand and come back emptyhanded.

But I didn't keep the pictures long. The next morning, and may God forgive me, I mailed them to the wives of the best people in St. Matthew, 'them high-up people' as Frenchy always called them, one or two apiece. I mailed them to the wives because I knew the husbands would keep them hidden to look at in moments of leisure. But as much as the husbands might have enjoyed them, I knew that their wives would enjoy them more. They would find them the source of delicious gossip, at the expense of the woman in them.

And then I made preparations to leave New Orleans and America for good, in case charges were brought against me for murder, manslaughter, or violation of the Comstock Laws against sending lewd materials through the mail.

I packed a suitcase, and I left the Moses family with the house, saying I was going on a trip for a while and for his family to make themselves at home until I returned. I didn't tell him I wasn't coming back. I bought a ticket to New York and, from there, England.

And so I now flee east like Cain, while I am still able.

Editor Lucien Braud

On the last night of her stay in St. Matthew, a séance was held (or perhaps, performed, I'm not sure which term is more correct) by the English spiritual medium Mrs. Gladys Osborne Leonard at Mount Teague. She has served as the spiritualist for such notables as Sir Arthur Conan Doyle and the renowned physicist Sir Oliver Lodge. In attendance were myself, Lucien Braud, Dr. George McKnight, Mrs. Teague, and the Rev. Orville Gladney of St. Margaret's Church in St. Matthew Parish. Samuel Teague Jr., the son of the departed, the late Samuel Teague, Sr., was not in attendance.

The gaslights were dimmed and candles were lit as we gathered around the table. Rev. Gladney insisted upon a prayer to avoid the illusion of this being a sinister and unholy proceeding, and Mrs. Leonard allowed it. After a great and lengthy supplication by Rev. Gladney, brought to a hasty end by the clearing of a throat (Mrs. Teague's, I believe), we were instructed to close our eyes and be still.

Mrs. Leonard asked the darkness to summon the spirit of Samuel Teague, quite like an operator asking someone to come to the telephone. There was a distinct chill to the air and the slightest of breezes, which caused the candle flames to tilt and bob and shimmy. We held our breath as the medium Mrs. Leonard raised her chin and spoke to the darkness that hovered over the candles.

"Are you the spirit of Samuel Teague?" she asked in a flat monotone.

"Yes," her voice said, to which we opened our eyes and exchanged excited glances to one another, none more so than Mrs. Teague.

"Ask him!" she demanded, "Ask him!"

"Silence!" Mrs. Leonard warned.

Mrs. Teague paid her no mind.

"Sam!" she said, fairly breathless. She seemed to be trying to keep herself in a fair countenance. "Sam, darling. Where is the safe? And the keys to it? Tell me. You'll tell me, won't you? Sugarplum? Honey-pie?"

Like two schoolboys, Dr. McKnight and I stifled giggles and exchanged amused glances in the candlelight.

"Silence!" Mrs. Leonard exclaimed again. "Samuel Teague." The air hummed in the amber candlelight, "Tell us from whence you speak."

There was a silence that seemed to trail into a vacuum, and we could easily feel our own hearts beating and could almost hear the rhythm of each other's hearts. Mrs. Leonard's voice spoke again, this time in a southern drawl, sounding so much like Sam Teague's.

"*Gawd...*" she (or he) said.

"He's in the presence of the Almighty!" Rev. Gladney exclaimed, exchanging a congratulatory glance with each of us, as if a lifetime of nagging doubt on the existence of God had just been erased and, in the end, blind faith had been rewarded. "Tell us, Sam, what does He look like? Are there angels?"

The curtains tapped against the window sill with the breeze that stirred them. Mrs. Leonard's face was slack and flat, her eyes closed and relaxed.

"*Gawd...*" Mrs. Leonard's voice said again.

"God what, Sam?" Mrs. Teague asked as she slapped her palms on the table, so hard that the candle flames danced a violent, confused dance and almost went out. She yelled to the ceiling, "Oh, where is the God-damned key and the God-damned safe? Where Sam, where?"

Rev. Gladney squeezed Miss Eva's hand to quiet her. Mrs. Leonard's eyes rolled around in their sockets behind heavy lids. Her jaw trembled. Then the voice that emanated from her was clear and unequivocal.

"*Gawd...*" Mrs. Leonard leaned backward and launched her voice to the ceiling in a tone that was plaintive and anguished as she shouted, "...*dammit!*"

A sudden draft of cold air lifted the curtains and extinguished the candles, all at the same time. We were plunged into darkness, though Dr. McKnight and I could not help but to snicker to ourselves. We could faintly hear each other, but we managed to suppress our whimpering laughter and regain our expressions when the gaslights were turned up.

Then the evening came to an abrupt end as Mrs. Teague ushered us out like we had snuck in through the back door rather than been invited guests.

Eva

Here are your bags, Mrs. *Gladys-Osborne-Leonard*, you fraud! And so what of your fee? You may as well go to hell for it! You have been as useless as teats on a boar hog! As socks on a rooster! Take your things and find your own way back to England, you-you-you whoring fraud! You and your fox-fur stole and your English way of speaking! You think yourself so important. I may be broke, but I am still a woman of prominence and social importance. And dignity. Remember that! Dignity, Mrs. Leonard! Dignity! I am feared and admired in St. Matthew Parish, and I will continue to be so, despite the sneers and whispers under bonnets and behind kid gloves. They are merely stricken by jealousy, Cain's burden and undoing.

And you, *Gladys, Gladys, Gladys, Gladys!* You might aspire to be one of them! Why, you are no better than these small women who feel greatness here, these Lilliputians. You and your so-called abilities aren't worth a pinch of snuff! Say what you will about me, but you are the one extorting a poor, impoverished widow for services which you did not render. Now get on from here, and take your lies with you!

Mark my words, madam, I shall not live in poverty, not for long.

Ruthie

Mr. Braud, don't put none a this in your newspaper, but I tell you straight and I tell you the truth like I tell God hisself. Miss Eva up and throw that woman out this house! Show did! She take that woman bags and toss 'cm out over the rail and them 'zalea bushes into the front yard. She say, 'Now you git on way from here, you a fraud! Yes you is! Don't even think I'm gone pay you cause you ain't tol' me nothin'! You worthless as that woman I brought down Boston." And she shake her head like this and she say, "Git on, Miz-riz Glad-dis Oz-bun Lennid, git on!"

Then Miss Eva she came back inside and slammed the do'. Swearda Gawd she did, yes, Lawd. Put on that Victrola and sat right there that settee and listen to that ol' ragtime music.

Father Michael Connelly

'And now I flee to the east like Cain, while I am still able.'

I smiled at his pun but he didn't, and I realized it was unintended. Out in the darkness, a bell on a buoy at the entrance to the Queenstown harbor clanged irregularly as the waves pushed it up and down and tilted it sideways. The last of the day's lights had long since fallen, and the small specks of lanterns were shining on the coast. The pianist was playing quietly for the remainder of us scattered about in the saloon.

"And so what of the future?" I asked him. "Now that you are leaving America for the first and last time?"

He rubbed under the eyepatch where the eyebrow had once been. I tried not to strain to see what was under it, but I couldn't help it, and I glimpsed the sunken emptiness. He paused and looked to me, and I looked out on the sea and the lights of Ireland.

"My friend Mr. Carriere, when he went down to St. Matthew to speak to my brother's widow about his mausoleum, found the address of my brother's oldest child, Jenny, from his first marriage. The flowers and the card had been tossed out by Eva. Maybe she feared that the daughters of his first marriage might make a play for his estate. Regardless, before returning to New Orleans, Mr. Carriere gathered the flowers and the card and returned to the city with them. He put the flowers on the graves in the Lafayette Cemetery across Prytania Street from us, but he kept the card with the address, *Jenny Teague Wheeler, Basingstoke, England.*"

"So Basingstoke, then?" I asked to the last of the whiskey in my glass. I was relieved that he had made plans, that he still had hope for something. I confess that there had been times during the voyage that I thought he might throw himself in the ocean.

"Yes, Father, Basingstoke. I'm going to visit my niece and her family. When I was in the army, she and I would exchange letters, though I have not heard from her since I was captured and sent to prison, fifty years ago."

The waiter came and asked if we wanted another round. We both declined, and so he returned to the bar and began wiping it down, humming to the tune the piano played to the near-empty room.

"And so what of your hopes for the future? Will you keep the name Jones?" I asked.

He smiled and shook his head.

"I believe I'll take up Jack Teague again, now that I have an ocean between me and my past. Maybe this will be a chance for me to enjoy the society of my niece and her family as an old uncle, to feel beloved and to belong. Perhaps there's still a chance for me to enjoy that. I returned to St. Matthew looking for reconciliation, Father, but I left with retribution. And so I no longer ask for justice. I can only plead for mercy. It will have to be enough."

"I pray it will, then," I said. He picked up his glass and looked at it in the dim light. I got the sense that even if he had still had his left eye, he would have squinted it. The amber glimmered like a gemstone.

"There is something in human nature which confounds us, Father," he said, "We are all born with desires, as indelible as the mark placed by God on the faces of the refugees banished from Eden. The desire for pleasure, the desire for peace, the desire for position, the desire to be revered by one's peers, for honor and praise, to be set above others. All these are fueled by desire, desire and an appalling lack of humility. And a lust for retribution, the true burden of Cain."

He brought the glass to his lips and finished it.

"I cannot bless God nor give him glory," he said setting down the empty glass. "I am neither worthy nor capable of blessing anyone, let alone God, and I have no glory to give. And so I wander forward, still feeling the black mud of St. Matthew clinging to my boots like sin, like on that day I killed my brother. My hunger for retribution has been satisfied but replaced by a weight like a millstone and a bitterness as hard to swallow as a peach pit. I have killed my brother and ruined the reputation of my sister-in-law, my former lover. Perhaps I should have thrown the postcards into the fire. But what's done is done."

The Burden of Cane

"Well, Jack Teague," I said, "I believe we are all imperfect men, making our way through an imperfect world. The best of us try to repair it with tools that are flawed and inadequate. The rest of us stagger on under the weight of our imperfections. I dearly hope that God will recognize this when He sees us gain. Perhaps our imperfections are what He cherishes most about us. Perhaps they are proof that we still need Him."

The pianist began the song that signaled that the saloon was closing for the night, Brahms's Lullaby, and I raised what was left in my glass and finished it. We looked out the window at the black Atlantic flashing under a pale-bright moon and the lights of the Irish coast twinkling in the blackness. A small group of Canadian officers rose from their table and put on their caps and left, as the piano played to the clatter of busboys clearing tables and the drone of the ship's engines down below us and the bells on the buoys at the entrance to the Queenstown harbor.

"Father," he said, "if it had come down to it, would you have gotten in my lifeboat?"

"Yes," I said, "Yes, I would have. You have a good heart, a concern for others."

He would not look at me, but instead kept looking out the window. His reflection in the blackness looked back to him, two men with one set of eyes. There was a sparkle in the reflection, and when I looked back at the man, I noticed that a tear had trickled from his eye.

"If there is a God, Father, then surely you have done His work these last few days," he said.

"My son, actually 'tis the other way around," I replied. "If we do His work, then surely 'tis proof that there is a God."

I granted him absolution on the condition that he would pay off the debts of his sister-in-law, his lover, if he had he means to do so. He said that he did have the means, but he would have to think upon it. I told him that I understood and that God will understand and remember how he made us and if there is a balance due in St. Peter's ledger, then fear not, for Christ has already paid it. I told him he could keep my handkerchief, and he thanked me for it and sent along his regards to my mother in Cork. He said to tell her that she has a son to surely be proud of. Then, we shook hands. And that was the last time we spoke.

The next morning, I disembarked at Queenstown. As the ship's horn moaned the signal that she was pulling away from the dock and those on both land and sea waved our hats and handkerchiefs one group to the other, I saw him standing along the rail by himself. He was looking up, watching the gulls gliding over the sea breezes, and I could almost see him doing it as a boy. And then I thought I saw the shadow of a dog at his feet. A porter passed between us with a baggage cart, and when I looked again to the railing, there was only the man Jack Teague there. And that was the last time I saw him, though it is certainly not the last time I have thought of him. I think of him regularly, especially when someone enters the confessional with a heavy conscience. Every time. Every single time.

Pinch

After the man in the black suit with the square of white at his throat departed for land, we spent another night on the great iron boat. My master, the man now called Jack again, sat and looked out at the sea and I sat at his feet. I knew it was cold only because he had a blanket brought out and wrapped himself up in it.

The next day brought us to land again, and we departed the boat and boarded a train. Unseen, I was allowed to ride, which is an advantage to a dog in the spirit world—we are granted admission to places forbidden to us in life. He was on the verge of a nap and so was I when a woman with a fox-fur stole spoke to him, fetching him from sleep.

"Sir, the next stop is yours, isn't it? Basingstoke?"

"Yes," my master said, and I heard a tinge of a question in it, of him not knowing how she knew he was going to Basingstoke.

"You're American," the woman said, her gloved hands carefully arranged in her lap.

"Yes," he said, "I suppose you can tell from my accent."

"Yes," she said, "I have just returned from a visit there, though I'm afraid it was a fruitless one, and my client was greatly displeased."

"I'm sorry to hear that, then," he said.

"And you have come to England to visit a girl grown into a woman, a daughter, or a niece, perhaps?"

"Ma'am, you seem to have read my mind, though I'm sure this train is full of men come to see their families. That can be nothing out of the ordinary."

"Certainly," she said and her look became one of frankness and sincerity, as when one is telling a secret, whether it be bitter or sweet. "He is with you."

"Who is with me?"

"Your dog."

"Excuse me? My dog, do you say?"

"Yes, your dog. Patch or Punch or something like that. A red stray, very friendly, and very attentive to you."

"Pinch. His name was Pinch. Where is he?"

"At your feet."

He looked down on the floor, though not exactly to the spot where I was, and I wagged my tail and it thumped on the floorboards of the train, but of course he could not hear it. He pulled his coat around his shoulders and scoffed, "Lots of men have had dogs they have outlived."

"Yes, certainly, but this one has a white patch on his forehead. The shape of an hourglass," the woman said, and my master's facial expression changed completely. "He has followed you here. After your brother died."

"How did you know that?" he asked quietly.

She did not offer her paw or an introduction.

"I have a gift, I am a spiritualist. I am able to communicate with spirits. The dog wishes you to know that he has followed you through everything. Like the words from the book you would read to him when he was alive. The Twenty-third Psalm. He has followed you like goodness and mercy."

My tail wagged despite myself, and my master the man called Jack wiped his eye with the handkerchief given to him by the man in black on the ship, the one with the white square on his throat. He could not see me curl up again at his feet, but even if he had been clear-eyed, he could not have seen me.

"It was not your fault," she said softly, just above the muttering of the train.

"My fault?"

"It was not your fault that your brother died. There were others behind that greatly loaded wagon, that burden of something. Some sort of vegetation, sugarcane, wasn't it? You could not see them, as they were spirits. But you did not push it over on your brother. It was an accident."

My master sat speechless as he looked into the face of the woman who could see spirits. The train slowed and there was a great groan and exhalation of brakes and the conductor called out *Basingstoke!* My master stood to get his belongings. She offered her paw, and he took it, like when he taught me to shake. I stood and yawned and shook myself in a flurry of half-barrel rolls.

"Your father has something to say as well," the woman said, "He says that he releases you from your promise. The promise to reconcile with your brother. He says he appreciates your diligence, but he had no idea how hard it would be."

I looked around to see the man in the beaver pelt hat evaporate with a smile that evaporated with him. She leaned in, her voice very soft, barely above a whisper.

"There is a telegraph office in Basingstoke. In case you need to wire money to America. I would send it directly to your son, in Louisiana, and warn him to watch his mother's spending from now on. Tell him you are proud of him. That part is very important. Tell him. Make sure of it."

"What about my—"

"—yes, your daughter." She paused as she thought, staring at the floor as if she were looking into a body of water to see what was under the surface. At last she looked up and smiled, "She is alive. And she is surrounded by children."

"Children? How many?"

"I don't know. Several dozen."

The conductor said again, "Basingstoke. Are you getting off, sir?"

"Yes," my master paused. "Yes."

As he stood, he turned again to the woman who can see things that others cannot.

"And what of my brother, his soul?"

The lady who could see us took a deep breath and looked away. My master touched her shoulder, and she looked back to him briefly and then down at her hands as she weighed her words, the ones she did not want to say.

"It is—" She looked up to him and narrowed her eyebrows sorrowfully and said in a frank tone, "—it is not well for him."

The Burden of Cane

The very old man in the beaver pelt hat was gone now, having said what he needed to say, and my master the man called Jack fought the tears from his eye as the conductor helped him with his valise. Together they watched his old steps off the train. And I followed him, unseen, jumping from step to step and onto the station platform of Basingstoke.

A woman emerged from the crowd of people at the platform. She waved to my master Jack and called to him in a question, *Uncle Jack? Uncle Jack? Is it really you?*

He offered his paw and instead he received an embrace from this niece he has never met. Her husband did not embrace, but instead they clasped paws and shook. The niece is a grown woman on the verge of gray, but she talked on and on like she was a girl. She was so excited that she could not stop talking.

She told her uncle that her sisters, his two other nieces, will visit with their children and grandchildren when the war is over. She told him now nice it was to hear the southern accent again and she hoped she had not lost all of hers. She told him that she still has the letters he wrote her when he was a soldier and she was just a girl. She told him that she has always dreamed of meeting him and now that she has, it's like a dream come true. She told him that he can stay as long as he likes, that they have a room for him. She told him that she hopes he likes dogs, for they have three, spaniels, and she embraced him again, and there was no use in him fighting his tears this time.

When we arrive at their house in the country, his niece, called Jenny, will show him the letters he sent her fifty years before when she was a girl and he was a soldier. She will ask where he has been all these years, and he will say it is a very long story. The children of the house will ask about his eyepatch, and my master Jack will tell his great nieces and great nephews that he wears it because he was once a pirate, but he has long given up the sea and pillaging. The children will ask about the scars on his face, and the adults will scold them, but he will say that they are from a fall from a horseapple tree when he was their age. And even if I were alive and human and could speak, I would not contradict him.

A breeze stirs the clothes of this woman and her husband and frees the scent of their home. It is the scent of the countryside, of foxes and rabbits and dogs. The dogs will be able to see me, the red cur with the hour glass shape of white on my forehead because they are dogs and can see things that people don't. They will bark and bark, and the niece will say that they are quite taken with her Uncle Jack. In time, I will become a commonplace to the spaniels, and we will nap together in patches of afternoon sunlight at the feet of my master the man now called Uncle Jack, who will nap with his great nephews and great nieces in his lap. But today the spaniels and the nephews and nieces wait at home, waiting for a visitor, their great-uncle from America.

At the station, Jenny's husband opens the door of their automobile, and no one sees me jump in before my master. In the window of the train, the woman who can see all is looking straight ahead with her hands in her lap. She hopes she has not said too much. Steam boils from the engine at the head of the train, and the cars are pulled forward and disappear into it.

Acknowledgement & Gratitude

It takes a village to raise a child. The same is true for a book.

Thank you to my first readers who read and helped refine *The Burden of Cane* and hopefully made it a more pleasant experience for you, the reader: Steve Feigley, Gloria Landry, Flavia Lancon, Gina LoBue, Dawn Jelks, Nan Murtagh, MaryBeth Sherwood Garic, Liz Parker, and Emily Aucoin, and, of course, Katie Schellack, my editor at Walrus Books, who helped me get some of the weight off the story. All of you have my appreciation. I'm glad I trusted you with my child.

There are so many characters in this story who were real people. The rest I tried to breathe life into their crude forms of paper and ink. I invite the reader to search the names to see who was real and who was not. But, of course, like every other writer of fiction, my goal was to make them all real.

If you would like to sample some of the things I read in preparing for *The Burden of Cane*, let me recommend Stephen Ambrose's book about the building of the transcontinental railroad, *Nothing Like it in the World;* for a behind-the-scenes look at the life of a prostitute, although in the twentieth century, *The Mayflower Madam* by Sidney Biddle Barrow; for a description of the prisoner of war camp at Point Lookout, *Hell Comes to Southern Maryland: The Story of Point Lookout Prison and Hammond General Hospital*, by Bradley and Linda Gottfried; and for a glimpse into the rules of polite society in the nineteenth century, *The Ladies' Book of Etiquette, and Manual of Politeness: A Complete Hand Book for the Use of the Lady in Polite Society* by Florence Hartley. Most of the quotes that Eva uses in this book are verbatim from Miss Hartley's.

If you enjoyed *The Burden of Cane*, you are cordially invited to spread the word via Facebook, Goodreads, and Amazon. Reviews, good or bad, are the lifeblood of independent authors.

Also by C. H. Lawler

The Saints of Lost Things
The Memory of Time
Living Among the Dead
What Passes for Wisdom

Made in the USA
Coppell, TX
27 October 2023

23468104R00262